VIKTORIA

The Hotel Quadriga Trilogy
Book Two

Jenny Glanfield

SAPERE
BOOKS

To Dad and Mum
with love and thanks for everything

PROLOGUE

28 April 1915

In the centre of Berlin, a short way down Unt
Brandenburg Gate, a long colonnaded
pavement. A stately flight of white marble
revolving doors. Beside them, two imposing
rigidly to attention, immaculately uniformed
coats and top hats, ornately decorated with go
brass buttons and wearing spotless white glo
boots. They were on guard before the entrar
exclusive hotel.

No garish sign advertised its identity, be
historians, a small, highly polished brass plaque
inscribed in Gothic script, discreetly annou.
Opened by His Majesty Kaiser Wilhelm II. 15 June 18

On that very day Viktoria Jochum-Kraus had
Now, just over twenty years later, in the same
she had given birth to her own child.

Her blonde hair lay damply on the pillows an
by a great weariness, but this was her moment o
nine months of mental anguish, of remorse a
deception. She held the wrinkled bundle that was
against her breast and vowed, 'You're mine and r
you away.'

She was overwhelmed by a greater sense of loy
experienced before. 'I love you, oh Stefi, I love y
you before you were born, but now you're here,
my whole life proving how much I love you.'

The nurse ushered in Viktoria's husband. 'Co
Kraus, a fine baby boy.'

Benno crossed the room and knelt down besid
expression on his face. Tentatively, he reache

:d the child's head, then he kissed his wife gently. 'How do you
ιy darling?'
:d, but very happy. So very happy. Benno, don't you think he's
ful?'
no nodded wonderingly. 'He's so small, it doesn't seem
le that he will one day grow up to be a man. Somehow he
me feel humble...'
Blattner coughed discreetly. 'Herr Kraus, I'm sorry, but your
nust get some rest...'
se Bauer took Stefan from Viktoria's arms. Benno kissed his
gain and anxiously followed the nurse into the nursery. 'Will he
right? After all, he wasn't expected until June.'
course he'll be all right, Herr Kraus. Look at him, the little
g. He's perfection itself.'
, Benno thought, gazing down at Stefan. He was so perfectly
:d, it did not seem possible that he was premature. Gently, he
the tiny hands with their minute fingernails, then smiled as they
ned into a fist around his finger. He looked at the soft, brown
on Stefan's head, the button nose, the tightly closed eyes and
recurrence of his old fear. Was this his son? Or was the father
his cousin, Lieutenant Count Peter von Biederstein?
fan opened his eyes and stared back at him, more like a very
old man than a helpless infant. They looked at each other for a
time and suddenly Benno had the sensation that the child was
g to tell him something. He was gazing at him intently, as if he
ed to get to know Benno as much as Benno wanted to know
Then he yawned, as if to say, 'You'll do.'
ello, son,' Benno said.
fan started to cry. 'Bless his little heart,' Nurse Bauer exclaimed,
telling us he's hungry.'
t Benno knew differently. Stefan had just assured him that,
ever the truth, he considered him his father.

ιe months that followed, the nurse and Viktoria found it almost
ssible to keep Benno out of the nursery. 'It's amazing!' he said.
n his hair and eyes are like mine. And look at the way he curls his

fingers. Just like I do. But, of course, it's natural that he should resemble his father. Stefi, say hello to Papa.'

The baby gurgled and Benno cried, 'Did you hear that? He said Papa.'

It was then Viktoria finally decided never to reveal to Benno that he was not Stefan's natural father. The most important thing was that he and Stefan believed they were father and son. But deep in her heart she knew she was doing them all a wrong, because, for the rest of their lives, they would be living a lie and one day that lie would find them out.

CHAPTER ONE

Under the Brandenburg Gate they marched that wintry Monday evening of 30 January 1933, rank upon serried rank of brown-uniformed SA and black-uniformed SS men, the black insignia of the swastika within a white circle upon their blood-red armbands and the gigantic standards borne before them, triumphantly celebrating Adolf Hitler's appointment as Chancellor of Germany.

Drums rolled, trumpets blared and blazing torches were brandished in the air. In steady tempo, burnished black boots goose-stepped over the cobbled roadway, thousands of them, hour after hour after hour, while the crowds that packed the pavements raised their arms high in the Nazi salute, roaring deliriously, '*Sieg Heil! Sieg Heil! Sieg Heil!*'

On the balcony of the Hotel Quadriga, Viktoria Jochum-Kraus turned up the collar of her sable coat against the bitter night air so that it framed her pale face, crowned with a coronet of golden braids, a face too square for conventional beauty, but with a perfection entirely of its own, with its blue eyes, long, straight nose, determined jaw and wide mouth.

Apprehensively, she stared down at the flaming torches moving like a river of fire over streets of molten snow. The voices of the stormtroopers were raised in the 'Horst Wessel Song':

'Raise high the flags! Stand rank on rank together.

Stormtroopers march with steady, quiet tread...'

'That's what they sang the night they broke up Emmy's last concert at Café Jochum,' Luise muttered. 'For as long as I live I shall hate that song.' She clutched Viktoria's arm. 'How many of them are there?'

Viktoria glanced sympathetically at her sister. Six years her junior, Luise was tall and slim like herself, but with a mass of auburn hair and huge green eyes in a white, heart-shaped face. However, before she could say anything her father-in-law announced portentously, 'I would estimate that there are well over two million stormtroopers in the whole of Germany.'

Viktoria cast him a malevolent look. One of Germany's wealthiest industrialists, Baron Heinrich von Kraus zu Essen was a giant of a man weighing at least twenty stone, with a florid face and small eyes behind gold-rimmed spectacles. Leaning on a stick, he threw the butt of his cigar contemptuously into the crowd. 'Bolsheviks like your cousin Olga Meyer don't stand a chance against them.'

'And us?' Luise whispered. 'What sort of chance do we stand?'

Viktoria squeezed her hand comfortingly.

'Doesn't it make you feel proud to be a German?' Benno asked. Of slim build, with waving brown hair and brown eyes, Benno was more Biederstein than Kraus in appearance, but although he bore scant physical resemblance to his father, his mind still worked in the Kraus pattern. Viktoria could almost read his thoughts. This display of military strength conclusively proved that Germany need no longer bow her head in shame for having lost the war and need suffer no more under the humiliations of the Versailles Treaty. She might still have only a one hundred thousand-man army, but the legions of Hitler's stormtroopers who proudly strode before them made a mockery of that myth. Germany was strong again! Germany was, once again, a force to contend with!

Their twelve-year-old daughter, Monika, frenziedly waved her swastika flag, her grey eyes shining and her voice hoarse with excitement. 'I wish I were a man,' she sighed wistfully, 'then I could join them.' She turned to Stefan. 'Stefi, wouldn't you like to be a soldier?'

Stefan tugged her thick, blonde pigtails affectionately and, not for the first time, Viktoria wondered how her two children could be so different.

Stefan was seventeen now and looked very much as Benno and Peter von Biederstein had done at that age, brown-haired, dark-eyed, but with a serious intensity all of his own. 'Not really,' he replied, 'and I certainly don't want to belong to the SA.'

'Victoriously, we shall defeat France...' The voices of the stormtroopers passing beneath them roared the old battle song, dating back to the Napoleonic wars. In a fever of excitement, the crowds joined in, lifting their voices in a triumphant crescendo. '*Sieg Heil! Sieg Heil! Sieg Heil!*'

'That slogan, "Hail Victory!" and these crowds, don't they seem menacing to you?' Stefan asked.

It was his grandmother who replied. Ricarda Jochum was an elegant lady of sixty-five. Her once auburn hair was now white and beautifully set in a chignon. She was dressed, as she had been ever since her husband Karl's death, in a black costume offset by fichus of ivory lace, a fur coat draped gracefully around her shoulders.

'Stefi, you're a Berliner, born and bred, and you should understand the Berliners. In the past, we lined the streets in our thousands to catch sight of our Kaiser, to watch wedding processions and funeral cortèges. Yesterday, it was to see the communists. Tonight, it is to celebrate Hitler's appointment. But the wonderful thing about us Berliners, as I realized a long time ago, is that deep down inside we always retain a native scepticism. None of us like the stormtroopers, but we'll put up with them for a bit longer while we give Hitler a chance.'

Viktoria experienced a sudden, overwhelming sense of gratitude at her mother's serene level-headedness. 'I'm sure your grandmother's right,' she assured Stefan, but there was still an edge of uncertainty in her voice. 'And after all, darling, if we don't like what Hitler does, we can always vote him out of power.'

Her words were almost drowned by a roll of drums in the street below, followed by a powerful rendition, by percussion and voice, of Germany's national anthem. '*Deutschland, Deutschland über alles…*'

Viktoria's eyes travelled up Unter den Linden, past the leafless linden trees which gave the wide avenue its name, to the twelve doric columns of the Brandenburg Gate. Through the falling sleet, she could dimly make out the bronze statue of the Quadriga, a four-wheeled chariot driven by four prancing horses. It was after this statue that her parents had called their hotel.

But it was at the figure driving the chariot that Viktoria was gazing. Cloaked with a caparison of snow, Viktoria, Goddess of Victory, held her arm valiantly raised, as she kept vigil over the streets of Berlin.

The day following Hitler's appointment and the torchlight procession marked a sad anniversary in the life of the Hotel Quadriga, for it was exactly fourteen years since the burial of Karl Jochum, a day which newspaper headlines in 1919 had described as 'The true end of the Wilhelmine era'.

Benno rose early and took his habitual solitary breakfast in his office with the morning newspapers. Ricarda and Luise ate in their rooms and Viktoria breakfasted in the family's first floor apartment with Stefan and Monika. Stefan was unusually quiet but Monika still bubbled with excitement about the parade, a subject upon which Viktoria preferred not to dwell. As soon as possible, she saw them into their outdoor clothes and off to school.

Then came a precious quarter of an hour, when Viktoria sat alone over a second cup of coffee before going downstairs to her office. That morning, however, she was just lighting her first cigarette of the day when the dining room door opened and her mother entered. Ricarda kissed Viktoria on the cheek and sat down across the table. 'It doesn't seem possible that your father has been dead fourteen years, does it? After all this time there are still moments when I think, "I must tell Karl this" or "I must ask Karl that". Last night, when I went to bed, I thought, "I wonder if Karl enjoyed the procession." Do you remember how he loved military parades, Vicki?'

Unwilling to spoil her mother's memories, Viktoria said nothing about stormtroopers but laughed, 'Particularly if the First Brandenburg Guards were marching.'

Ricarda poured herself a cup of coffee and sighed nostalgically. 'Dear Karli, to listen to him talk one would never have known he had only been a private during his military service. He always spoke as if he had been a commanding general. And if he had come from a different background, he could have been one. He had tremendous organizational ability and inspired great loyalty in his staff. In a way, he ran the Quadriga as though it were a Guards regiment.

'I shall always remember the way he lined up the page boys in descending order of height in preparation for the Kaiser's visit. I can hear him now, telling them, "Don't forget, His Majesty is a Colonel in the Death's Head Hussars. You will stand strictly to attention and only move when you are ordered." And the Kaiser inspected them, just as though they were real troops. Karl was so proud. But then Karl worshipped the Kaiser. It was the greatest moment in his life when His Majesty opened the Quadriga.'

Ricarda paused. 'Of course, you had just been born, Vicki. I was so annoyed. We had worked so hard to get the hotel ready in time and then I missed the great moment.'

Viktoria smiled fondly. She had heard the story so often that she felt she had been personally present as her father conducted the Emperor, the Empress and their retinue through his new hotel. 'I should love to have been there when the Kaiser insisted on testing the hot water taps!'

'Ours was the first hotel in Berlin to have private bathrooms attached to every suite and certainly the first to have constant running hot water and gold-plated taps. But it must have been even more amusing when the Kaiser drove the lift. He'd never been in an electric elevator before. He made three trips up and down from the fourth floor to the cellar before the Empress complained. But when he saw Karl's wine cellars, he forgot all about the lift.' Ricarda chuckled. 'Karl and his wine... He had the cellars specially extended out under Unter den Linden so that he had room to store a million bottles. Apparently, the Kaiser asked him if he were preparing for a siege!'

Viktoria bit her lip in a characteristic Jochum gesture. The wine evoked quite different memories in her mind. She remembered how her father and Benno had barricaded the cellar doors during the Spartacist revolution at the end of the war to prevent the communist soldiers finding it, and her father's words afterwards: 'I'd rather have died than let those reds have my wine. Yes, I'd rather have given my life.'

Revolution on top of defeat — that had been too much for Karl Jochum. Unlike Ricarda, who had ceased to play any active role in the running of the hotel after her two daughters were born, Viktoria had worked closely with her father during the war years. After many of the hotel personnel had been called up in 1914, she had begun helping him with the administration and, despite Stefan's birth, she had slowly taken over many of his duties, so that, by 1918, she was virtually running the Quadriga.

More clearly than anyone else, she had seen her father's baffled incomprehension as it became clear that Germany was going to lose the war. When the Kaiser had abdicated and the armistice was signed, her father had suffered a near-mortal blow.

A scant two months later, he had been killed standing under the central arch of the Brandenburg Gate, a solitary figure in the middle of an urban battleground, as a rain of bullets crashed around him and vehicles from a Free Corps brigade hurtled through the archway once reserved for the use of the Kaiser alone, one of them tossing him high in the air and into the path of an armed truck. Briefly, Viktoria relived those dreadful moments, as she, her mother and Benno had rushed to him. Ricarda had cradled his battered body in her arms, and Karl had muttered, 'Save the Quadriga.' They had been his last words.

Viktoria shook her head to rid it of such gloomy thoughts. It was much better to be like her mother and remember the happy days.

Laying her hand on Viktoria's, Ricarda went on, 'I have been very fortunate. Karl and I had thirty happy years together. And I was lucky with my children. Not many daughters would have coped as well as you during those difficult days after Karl died.'

'I couldn't have done it on my own,' Viktoria admitted honestly. 'If Benno hadn't resigned from Kraus Industries when he did and taken over the financial side, I shouldn't have been able to manage the Quadriga.'

'Yes, Benno has been wonderful and he is undoubtedly a very shrewd businessman — like Karl and his own father. But don't underestimate yourself, Vicki. I may have very little to do with the hotel, but I am not unaware of what goes on. The Quadriga's reputation is based on much more than business expertise. It's your natural flair for dealing with people which ensures that our guests return and our staff remain loyal. Looking after three hundred guests and supervising two hundred and fifty full-time staff is no mean achievement for a woman.'

'Thank you, Mama,' Viktoria said, deeply touched by these unexpected words of praise. Then she looked at her watch. 'Good heavens, it's nine o'clock already! Much as I'd like to stay here with you, talking isn't going to keep the wheels of the Quadriga rolling!'

'Nine o'clock!' Ricarda jumped up. 'I'm due at my charity meeting at ten.'

Viktoria took her in a quick embrace. 'I am fortunate, too, to have such a wonderful — and sensible — mother.'

A few moments later, she was making her way down the magnificent sweeping staircase into the foyer which, to her dismay, was still festooned with swastika banners. Over the reception desk hung a portrait of Hitler. Viktoria pursed her lips, then recollected herself.

The foyer was crowded with departing guests, many of whom had made a special journey to Berlin to watch the previous evening's procession. The Reception Manager, Hubert Fromm, and his bevy of clerks were dealing efficiently with the checking-out formalities, while, under the eagle eye of the Hall Porter, page boys carried the guests' luggage out to limousines and taxis waiting on Unter den Linden.

Greeting her guests courteously, smilingly wishing them a good journey and expressing the hope that she would see them again soon, Viktoria went behind the reception desk to the small ante-room where her secretary was already hard at work. 'Good morning, Helga.'

The young woman jumped to her feet. 'Good morning, Frau Viktoria. I have put the post on your desk.'

'Thank you. Tell the maintenance men to remove the swastika flags, both from the foyer and the hotel portico, immediately.'

'Certainly, Frau Viktoria.'

Viktoria entered the office that had once been her father's and was now hers, sat down behind the large, leather-covered, dark oak desk and went quickly through her correspondence, jotting down notes for Helga Ruh to type replies and putting others on one side for discussion with the General Manager at their morning meeting.

Nearly forty years after its opening, the Hotel Quadriga was still run along military lines according to Karl Jochum's original precept and, just as the Kaiser's Army had once been the greatest in the world, so the Quadriga functioned with a precise efficiency of which any general would be proud.

But whereas in Karl's day there had been one Supreme Commander, now Viktoria and Benno shared the position. On the whole, the system worked very smoothly. The hotel was divided into eight departments, each with its own manager answerable to the General Manager, Fritz Brandt, who in turn reported to either Viktoria or Benno.

While Benno concerned himself with each department's profitability, buying, pricing, stock control, wages, guests' accounts and other financial matters, Viktoria's responsibilities were primarily on the social and domestic levels. Like the army, the hotel staff could be divided into two broad categories — front line and rearward — those who had contact with the guests and those who operated behind the scenes. Viktoria was usually concerned with the front staff, for it was they who saw to the guests.

She herself kept a meticulously maintained card index in which she recorded pertinent details about every guest: rank or title; Christian names of his children and their birthdays if known; breed and name of dog, if any; personal likes, dislikes and idiosyncrasies; his preferred newspaper; the flowers and fruit he liked in his room; his eating and drinking habits; and other such details as would be kept by any normal hostess.

From the moment a guest placed a reservation, she made it her business to check that all arrangements for his stay were perfect. The card index was consulted and the hall porter, housekeeper, restaurant and bar managers were advised. The hall porter would be ready to greet the guest by name. Newspapers would be waiting in his room, the correct number of pillows on the bed, his whims regarding food could be observed and his favourite tipple would be available in the bar.

This was by no means the full extent of Viktoria's duties. Among her other vitally important tasks was the final approval of arrangements for all social functions. The hotel had the capacity to accommodate five banquets simultaneously with well over a thousand visitors present and requiring an extra complement of several hundred staff. Under such circumstances mistakes could occur and it was Viktoria's job to make sure they did not.

That evening, two dinners were taking place — one in the Jubilee Room, one in a private banqueting room. Viktoria was just casting a practised eye over menus, seating plans and staffing arrangements, when her office door burst open and Benno entered, elegant as always in black morning jacket and pinstriped trousers. He shut the door behind him and demanded, tight-lipped, 'Who gave orders for the banners to be taken down?'

'I did. Yesterday's celebrations are over. This is an hotel, not a Nazi Party rally ground or a stormtroopers' barracks.'

Benno sighed impatiently, pointedly fingering the Nazi Party badge in his lapel. 'Vicki, when are you going to be realistic? Hitler is the new Chancellor. We have to show due respect.'

She glared at him icily. Benno's support of the Nazis had been the only major issue to mar the seventeen and a half years of their marriage. When the first Nazi deputies had been elected to the Reichstag in 1929, Baron Heinrich had cultivated the acquaintance of Hermann Göring and, in due course, become a Party member, encouraging Benno to follow suit. However, Viktoria did not object so much to Hitler, Göring and their policies, as to their private armies, knowing from bitter experience the terror they could strike into the hearts and lives of innocent civilians.

'I think we have done our duty,' she said coldly. 'Once Christmas is over, we take down the decorations. The same presumably applies to political festivals?'

Benno shrugged. 'Have it your own way, my dear, but mark my words, Hitler is going to last very much longer than any Christmas.'

'That doesn't mean *my* hotel has to be turned into a Nazi shrine.'

Her emphasis on the word 'my' was not lost on Benno. With a strange, almost sad little smile, he turned and quietly left the office.

A few moments later, Helga ushered in Herr Brandt and, putting Benno and Hitler to the back of her mind, Viktoria concentrated on the day's activities. As always, they started with guest lists and room allocations, then they progressed to the kitchens and Maître Chef Vittorio Mazzoni's proposed menus and catering requirements. 'The two functions this evening — are they political?' Viktoria asked.

'One is a trade guild, the other Freemasons,' Herr Brandt replied.

Relieved, Viktoria nodded. 'Two hundred places in all. Is Herr Krosyk taking on more restaurant staff?' As well as its contingent of two hundred and fifty permanent staff, the hotel had a register of several hundred temporary staff.

'He doesn't consider it necessary.'

'Good. Is there anything else, Herr Brandt?'

'I don't think so, Frau Viktoria, except that the Nazi banners have been removed, as you ordered.'

She nodded impassively. 'That is all, Herr Brandt.'

When she eventually entered the foyer again, she found it restored to its original pristine state. Only Hitler's portrait remained.

A few days later, Mortimer Sydney Allen received a summons from his chief, Bill Wallace, the European editor of the *New York News*. His fedora pulled down over his forehead and a damp cigarette clamped between his lips, he came in from the driving sleet of London's Fleet Street and toiled up three flights of dimly lit, uncarpeted stairs. At the top, he was confronted by an opaque glass door bearing the legend *New York News* and, as always, he thought sardonically, *So much for the London office of America's most prestigious newspaper!*

He pushed open the door and a cloud of stale cigar and cigarette smoke gusted out at him. A frumpy, middle-aged woman looked up from her typewriter, her face creasing in an unexpected smile. 'Mr Allen, there you are! Mr Wallace wants to see you immediately.'

Mortimer took off his hat and launched it at the coat stand. As usual, it missed and Miss Thoroughgood tittered. 'Oh, Mr Allen, you are a one.' Mortimer was her favourite among the American journalists. Her only regret was that she didn't see more of him, because he spent much of his time on foreign assignments.

Forty that year, Mortimer Allen was six feet tall, with a broad, muscular body, through which flowed Irish and Scottish blood from his father's ancestors and German from his mother's. His looks were an unusual mixture of both parents. He had his father's clear, blue-grey eyes, fringed by dark lashes, and his mother's thick, light-brown hair and generous mouth.

He grinned at Miss Thoroughgood and entered the main office, an untidy clutter of ancient desks and dusty papers, echoing to a clatter of typewriters, a ringing of unanswered telephones and a hubbub of excited, mainly American voices. Bill Wallace's office was a glass cubbyhole on the far side, with dirty windows overlooking Fleet Street. Mortimer walked in unceremoniously, pushed aside an overflowing in-tray and perched himself on the edge of the desk.

Big and balding, his tie unknotted, his gut hanging over his trousers, Bill slammed down the telephone. 'Hi, Mort. This guy Hitler has called an election for 5 March. That's the fifth election in Germany in a year. What do you reckon? Is it worth covering?'

'If I know anything about Hitler, it will be.'

'The last Chancellor, General Schleicher, lasted fifty-seven days. Do you think Hitler will hold out any longer?'

'Provided he can get a parliamentary majority, I guess so.'

Bill Wallace looked dubious. 'The Nazis hold only three of the eleven cabinet posts and the Social Democrats still hold most seats in the Reichstag. There have been coalition governments in Germany since the war.'

Mortimer stubbed out his cigarette and lit a new one. 'You know the situation as well as I do, Bill. Germany's suffering badly from the effects of the Depression. Her economy is in a parlous state and she has over six million unemployed, many of whom are virtually starving under a totally inadequate unemployment relief system. In my opinion, if they don't put a strong man in charge, there is a very real danger that the communists will take over.'

'Do you think Hitler is the strong man they need?'

Mortimer shrugged. 'I guess if I were a German, I should vote for him.' To an outsider, Hitler's rise to power seemed almost miraculous. To anybody who had experienced Germany in recent years, it was more understandable. It stemmed back to 1919 and the terms of the Treaty of Versailles, which had laid impossible peace conditions upon Germany, demanding war reparations which the country could not pay, denying her the right to build any military equipment and limiting her Army to a hundred thousand men.

Hitler's success hinged upon his determination to make Germany once again the great power she had been under the Kaiser. He wanted the abolition of the Communist Party and the trade unions; he intended to lessen the financial power of the Jews; and, most importantly, in defiance of Versailles, he wanted to rearm Germany, increase the size of the Reichswehr — the armed forces — and create an air force and a navy.

'Some of his policies are a bit extreme, aren't they?' Bill persisted.

'To me, certainly. But I guess if I were a German, I'd see them as patriotic. And faced with the choice of communism or national socialism, which would you prefer, Bill?'

Bill grunted. 'OK. Tell Thoroughgood to book you a train ticket and a hotel room.' A hint of a smile flickered across his face. 'I suppose it will have to be the Quadriga?'

'Of course. However, you can console yourself with the thought that they'll probably give me a favourable rate.'

'They'd damn well better after the publicity you've given them!' The telephone jangled. Bill picked up the receiver. 'OK, Mort. Get your ass out of here.' Mortimer grinned and slid off the desk. Bill bellowed down the phone, 'Yeah, Wallace speaking…'

Back in Miss Thoroughgood's reception, Mortimer said, 'Will you book me a train ticket to Berlin and a room at the Hotel Quadriga? I'll pick the ticket up tomorrow.'

'How long will you be gone this time, Mr Allen?'

'About a month, I should think.'

'You like Berlin, don't you?'

'Yes,' Mortimer admitted, 'Berlin's my spiritual home.'

As he made his way back down the dilapidated staircase, he reflected how true this was. He had grown up speaking German as his second language and, on his very first visit to Europe twenty years earlier, he had confirmed what he had always suspected — that he was more European than American. In Berlin, with its cafés, cabarets, theatres, concert halls and operas, and its vibrant, cosmopolitan atmosphere, he had found his spiritual home.

It was where his mother's family had come from before emigrating to America in the late 1800s, but there was more to it than that. Mortimer identified with Berlin because, like him, the city had been formed from a hotchpotch of nationalities. In origin, the people of Berlin were Huguenots, Jews, Silesians, Pomeranians and Austrians. By an accident of birth he was an American. Through his marriage to an Englishwoman, he had become a British resident. But at heart, he was a Berliner.

That evening, at his home on the outskirts of Oxford, while Joyce was packing his case, he took out the article *Harpers* had commissioned him to write in 1930 on the Hotel Quadriga and its sister establishment, Café Jochum on the Kurfürstendamm.

Amply illustrated with glossy photographs, the article was in a more flowery style than Mortimer's normal terse journalistic prose, but it conveyed very accurately the atmosphere of both hotel and café. Mortimer's eyes scanned the page. 'To enter the Quadriga is to experience the very essence of the gracious, elegant days of the Imperial Era. Beyond the revolving glass doors stretches the foyer, laid with white Tuscan marble, spread with blue Savonnerie carpet, into which is woven the symbol of a prancing horse…

'The rest of the ground floor is taken up by elegant public rooms: restaurants celebrated for the excellence of their cuisine … the famous Quadriga bar, with its deep, comfortable, leather armchairs and settees … the Jubilee Room, silver and blue, opened to commemorate the hotel's twenty-fifth anniversary in 1919 … the massive ballroom … the Palm Garden Room…

'Nowhere in all the hotels in which it has been my pleasure or misfortune to stay, have I encountered service as excellent, unobtrusive, deferential, but never obsequious, as at the Quadriga… Frau Viktoria and her staff do their utmost to satisfy the greatest or humblest wishes of all their guests… At the Quadriga the motto is: "The guest is always right."'

Mortimer glanced at the photograph of Viktoria, vividly recalling his interview with her and looking forward to meeting her again. Then he passed on to the next section of his article, which dealt with Café Jochum.

'No two establishments could be more different than the Hotel Quadriga and Café Jochum. While one is steeped in the tradition of Wilhelmine Germany, the other is the hub of Berlin's cultural society. Café Jochum is a vast, avant-garde, concrete edifice, designed by the Bauhaus architect, Erich Mendelsohn. Giant neon letters on its roof proclaim its identity, rivers of orange light flowing over its rounded balconies. Its upper floors are leased out as offices, but the entire ground floor is dedicated to the glassed-in, terraced café, which can seat a thousand customers.

'The most celebrated features of Café Jochum are its black leather and chrome furnishings and a huge mural by Otto Dix which occupies the entire length of one interior wall, depicting, with savage realism, the amusements of bourgeois Berlin in the 1920s.

'Against this backdrop, playwrights and poets rub shoulders with artists and actors, musicians and film stars. And, in their midst, moves the vibrant figure of Luise Jochum. Like her sister at the Hotel Quadriga, Luise knows them all by name, is aware of their latest oeuvre, their dreams and aspirations, their successes and their failures.

'Luise Jochum is a success story in her own right. It was she who discovered the incomparable talents of the jazz musician, Georg Jankowski, and the singer, Emmy Anders. It is due to Luise Jochum that Jankowski and Anders have sprung to world-wide fame and that they and Café Jochum have just been immortalized in Germany's first talking film, *Café Berlin*...'

Mortimer let the magazine fall. The article had been written three years ago and a lot had happened in the meantime. Nazi stormtroopers had frightened many intellectuals away from Berlin, particularly if they had left-wing sympathies or were of Jewish blood. Georg Jankowski, for instance, was now living in California. Emmy Anders was in Paris. Mortimer knew he was about to return to a very changed Berlin.

Situated at the heart of Berlin's diplomatic, commercial and political centre, close to the Chancellery in the Wilhelmstrasse and neighbouring the most important ministries, the Hotel Quadriga had long been a base for journalists of all nationalities. Immediately the election was announced, Viktoria prepared for an influx of foreign correspondents and was delighted when she saw the name Mortimer Allen on the guest list Herr Fromm submitted for her approval. Reference to the card index revealed:

ALLEN, Mortimer Sydney. (Article *Harpers Bazaar* May 1930.) Now with *New York News*. Reads selection of German newspapers. Types in room. Drinks Jack Daniels Whiskey. Chain-smoker.

Compared to the amount of information he had gleaned about the Jochums and the Quadriga, it was very little, but sufficient for the hotel to prepare for his arrival. 'I propose to give Herr Allen room 401,' Herr Fromm said.

Viktoria agreed. On the fourth floor, overlooking Unter den Linden, it was an end room, so that even if the reporter typed all night, he would disturb nobody. 'Make sure his desk is equipped: several quires of paper, carbon paper, an eraser, a spiral-bound notebook and some pencils.'

'Certainly, Frau Viktoria.' Herr Fromm made the appropriate notes.

'Several large ashtrays — and a metal wastebin.' The risk of fire was a constant hazard, particularly with chain-smoking writers, who emptied ashtrays into wastebins overflowing with screwed-up paper.

In the course of her busy day, Viktoria alerted, Johann, the Hall Porter, to Mortimer Allen's arrival, then went to see Hasso Annuschek, who had overall charge of the Quadriga bars. A well-built man in his late forties, going slightly bald, with an open, good-humoured face, Hasso had been at the Quadriga since 1919.

As it transpired, she did not need to remind Hasso about Mortimer Allen. 'Ach, the German-speaking American! A serious drinker, Frau Viktoria. Jack Daniels, as I recall. Never takes cocktails, never mixes his drinks and knows how to hold his liquor. My favourite sort of customer.'

Viktoria smiled. Hasso was her favourite sort of employee — a true professional and a worthy successor to the legendary Arno Halbe , who, after running the bar since the Quadriga's opening, had recently retired. Of all front staff, the positions of barman and hall porter were probably the most important. They were the only staff with whom guests were likely to be upon Christian name terms and they were frequently the recipients of intimate confidences. It was essential then that they were utterly trustworthy and discreet.

When Mortimer Allen arrived the following afternoon, it was to a warm welcome. The two commissionaires, in cobalt-blue and gold braid, bowed him through the revolving doors and page boys hurried to convey his luggage from his taxi up to room 401, one reverently carrying his portable Remington typewriter as though it were the crown jewels. Johann emerged from his porter's lodge and bowed deferentially. 'Good day, Herr Allen. How good to see you at the Quadriga again.'

Herr Fromm inclined his head. 'Good day, Herr Allen. I trust you had a pleasant journey. If you would kindly complete the registration card…'

A clerk slipped from behind the desk and told Helga Ruh, 'Herr Allen has arrived. Will you inform Frau Viktoria?'

Dressed in a severely cut navy-blue costume with a crisp white blouse, Viktoria came out of her office, her hand outstretched in greeting. 'Herr Allen, it gives me great pleasure to welcome you once more to the Quadriga.'

He took her hand in his, bowed low over it, so that his lips brushed her skin, and said, 'Frau Jochum-Kraus, how delightful to see you again.'

'I hope you will find your room to your satisfaction. We have put you on the fourth floor, overlooking the Linden.'

He let go her hand and grinned, that disarmingly mischievous smile that she had forgotten. 'Simply to be back in Berlin is happiness enough. To stay at the Quadriga is to have a foretaste of heaven.'

'You are too kind… Herr Allen, our family normally gathers for aperitifs in the bar at seven. Would you do us the honour of joining us this evening?'

'I should be enchanted.'

Viktoria returned to her office and Mortimer followed a page boy into one of the electric lifts and to his room on the fourth floor. He looked around him admiringly. Kaisers and Chancellors might come and go, but the Hotel Quadriga was unchanged, its rooms as tastefully immaculate as ever, its standards as impeccably high as on that very first day when Karl Jochum had welcomed Wilhelm II of Prussia as his first guest.

Although they all lived under the same roof, dinner was the only occasion of the day when the entire family was brought together. By seven, Viktoria and Benno had dealt with most of their daily problems; Stefan and Monika had completed their homework; Ricarda had finished with the various charitable committees and functions which, along with her hobbies of watercolour painting and embroidery, occupied her day; and Luise had returned from Café Jochum. They were usually joined by Baron Heinrich, who was currently residing in the Kraus suite on the first floor while his newly acquired villa in Grunewald was being refurbished.

That evening, elegant in an ice-blue evening dress, with an ermine stole round her shoulders, Viktoria arrived in the bar to find the rest of her family already gathered at their corner *Stammtisch*, with Mortimer Allen ensconced in their midst. Benno, Stefan and Mortimer stood up politely and the Baron made a tenuous effort to move his bulk, as Hasso held her chair. She motioned them to be seated, asked Hasso for a martini cocktail, then turned to the journalist. 'I trust you find your room comfortable, Herr Allen?'

'Excellent, Frau Jochum-Kraus.'

'How long are you intending to stay, Herr Allen?' Ricarda asked.

He shrugged. 'Long enough to cover the election on 5 March. After that, it will depend on Hitler.'

'Yes, of course.' Ricarda gave a little frown. 'Yours must be a strange and rather nomadic existence. Your wife must be a very understanding person to put up with your protracted absences.'

'Joyce could accompany me, but she prefers not to. For one thing, she has a career of her own, as a landscape artist. For another, there's our daughter, Libby, to consider. We don't fancy the idea of sending her to a boarding school and it would be unfair to drag her from country to country, just because of my uncertain life.'

'How old is your daughter?' Monika demanded.

'A bit younger than you, I should think. She's just ten.'

Monika sniffed disdainfully.

'Where do you live in England?' Benno asked politely.

Mortimer smiled. 'In Oxford. I went there as a student twenty years ago, met my wife and have stayed ever since.'

'Oxford!' Stefan exclaimed, his eyes shining. 'My governess used to describe it as the most beautiful city on earth.'

'"… whispering from her towers the last enchantments of the Middle Age",' Mortimer quoted in English.

Triumphantly, Stefan completed the quotation, also in English, '"Home of lost causes and forsaken beliefs, and unpopular names, and impossible loyalties!" That's Matthew Arnold!'

Mortimer nodded in surprise. 'You speak English very well. Are you thinking of going to Oxford?'

'I was brought up in England,' Ricarda interrupted. 'My father was a commercial attaché at the German Embassy in London. I have always thought it would be excellent experience for Stefan to study abroad.'

Benno added, 'Stefan is not only top of his school class, he is also very good at outdoor sports. He is assured of a place here at the Friedrich-Wilhelms University this autumn. However, I am prepared to consider an English university if that is the best thing for him.'

Viktoria's heart sank. Oxford! A little seed sown long ago had taken root in Stefan's mind, nurtured by Ricarda and Benno. Year after year, she had hoped he would forget the idea but instead it had grown to become almost an obsession. Didn't he realize that, if he left her, he would break her heart? 'I can't see that England offers anything superior in the way of education,' she said hotly. 'Stefi, why are you so set on going to Oxford when we have a perfectly good university here?'

'Be the making of the boy to get away from home,' the Baron grunted. 'You mollycoddle him, Viktoria.'

Mortimer studied Stefan thoughtfully. 'If you really are all that your father claims, perhaps you should seek election as a Rhodes Scholar. My scholarship certainly had a tremendous influence upon my life.'

'Stefan is not an American,' Viktoria said sharply.

'Rhodes Scholarships are also available to German students.'

At that moment, half a dozen stormtroopers swaggered off Unter den Linden into the bar, loudly demanding beers. There was a hush in the room and people looked anxiously at each other. Luise's face paled and she reached shakenly for a cigarette. Stefan glared angrily at the intruders, while Viktoria exchanged glances with Benno, who half rose to his feet. 'I'm sorry,' Hasso's voice echoed smoothly across the room, 'we don't serve draught beer.'

The stormtroopers stared around them in disgust. 'What a dung heap!' one exclaimed, grinding out his cigarette on the carpet.

Everyone in the room held their breath.

'If I might suggest it, Sturmführer,' the barman continued, 'the Kaiserhof is renowned for its beer. I often drink there myself,' he added confidentially. His ploy worked. The stormtroopers, muttering coarse invectives, took their departure.

'Why don't we serve draught beer?' Monika asked.

Mortimer pursed his lips and ran his finger through his forelock. Then, in a perfect Berlin accent, he asked, 'Do you know why stormtroopers wear brown shirts?' Grinning, he supplied the answer to the riddle. 'It's so that they don't need to be laundered too often.'

The atmosphere relaxed. Although Monika scowled and Luise just puffed nervously on her cigarette, Benno, his father and Stefan smiled wryly, while Ricarda did not attempt to suppress her amusement. 'Herr Allen, you not only speak the Berlin dialect but you know how fond we are of riddles. You must have Berlin blood in you!'

'My mother's family came from Berlin.'

Baron Heinrich slapped his thigh and snorted, 'Splendid! That makes you one of us, boy! Join us for dinner!'

Mortimer glanced at Viktoria, who inclined her head. 'You would be most welcome.' She signalled to Hasso. 'Tell Herr Krosyk that Herr Allen will be dining with us.'

A few moments later, they were making their way into the ornate, high-ceilinged restaurant, from which ponderous chandeliers were suspended, glittering like huge sapphires. The large room was laid with cobalt-blue carpets and hung with gold-flecked blue paper, against which the white damask table linen stood out crisply and silver cutlery gleamed invitingly. Although it was quite early in the evening, about three-quarters of the tables were already occupied, the gentlemen mostly in dinner jackets and the occasional military uniform, the ladies all in evening gowns.

Philip Krosyk, the Restaurant Manager, bowed them in and, followed by a phalanx of waiters in black frock coats and white gloves, escorted them to a long table. The Baron took his seat at the head in a massive, carved oak, winged chair, with Ricarda on his right and Viktoria on his left. Ricarda indicated the place next to her. 'Herr Allen, will you sit here?' Luise was on his other side, Benno at the foot of the table, then Monika and Stefan beside Viktoria.

Herr Krosyk dispensed menus, heavy leather folders containing details of the table d'hôte and à la carte dishes, superbly inscribed by hand. As always, Baron Heinrich chose the seven-course table d'hôte: Soup *à la Parisienne*, sweetbreads with truffles, turbot with caviar sauce, artichoke hearts stuffed with peas and asparagus tips, saddle of wild boar with potato purée and salad, followed by pineapple ice cream and cheese.

The others made more modest selections. Viktoria, always careful of her figure, decided to commence with a bouillon, followed by guinea-fowl. Mortimer followed her example. When they had all made their choices and Benno had ordered the wine from a list that resembled a Russian novel in length, the Baron turned to Mortimer. 'So you're here to cover the election, boy. Well, you're staying at the right place. If you want opinions, you'll find them here.' He waved an arm expansively round the restaurant. 'Businessmen, politicians, army officers — this is where they stay.'

Viktoria stifled a feeling of annoyance at the manner in which the Baron seemed to include the Quadriga within his own industrial empire.

Ricarda smiled. 'Herr Allen, I am sure you recognize one very great difference between us Germans and the English and Americans. Possibly because of our circumstances, we are a very politically aware nation. In England, the weather provides a staple topic of conversation, but whenever two or more Germans are gathered together, it will be politics they discuss. This is particularly true in Berlin, where feelings tend to run very high.'

Luise spoke for the first time. 'Leave me out of that statement, Mama. You know I have always found politics extremely boring.'

'However, they still affect all our lives, Aunt Luise,' Stefan said, seriously. 'Therefore, they are important.'

'How do you feel about Hitler and the Nazi Party?' Mortimer asked.

'I'll tell you now that Hitler promises to be the best thing for Germany since the Kaiser,' the Baron stated. 'During the next few weeks, you'll hear a lot of nonsense about socialists, but I can tell you, it's the socialist-dominated Weimar Republic that has got the country into the mess it's in now.'

'Not just socialists,' Benno added. 'Have you heard about the demonstration the other Sunday? One hundred thousand workers marching through the city centre, threatening to strike? That's what we have to defend ourselves against, Herr Allen. Bolsheviks like Olga Meyer were responsible for the Spartacist uprising fourteen years ago. So long as they are around, the danger of a communist revolution remains very real.'

'Olga Meyer's been a confounded nuisance for years,' the Baron snorted. 'Now she takes her brat round with her, vowing that one day her husband's dream will come true and the Communist Party will rule in Berlin. Not while I'm alive, it won't!'

Mortimer glanced at Viktoria. 'I believe Olga Meyer is related to you?'

Viktoria nodded slowly. Although she preferred to forget the relationship, it would be foolish to deny it. 'She's my cousin. My father's sister and her husband were both Social Democrats and Olga grew up a fervent Communist.'

'Wasn't she married to the journalist Reinhardt Meyer, who was killed during the Spartacist Revolution by one of the Free Corps brigades?' Mortimer asked.

Viktoria remembered again that fateful January of 1919. 'That's right. When it appeared that the Spartacist Revolution might succeed, the government called in mercenary troops — so-called Free Corps Brigades — to put it down. Reinhardt was one of the first to be killed.'

'But Olga escaped?'

'She had nowhere else to go, so she came to the Quadriga,' Ricarda explained. 'Vicki and Benno took her to our country cottage at Heiligensee.'

The journalist cast Benno a curious look and Benno shrugged ruefully. 'We couldn't let her be killed and we didn't know what was going to happen next.'

Mortimer frowned. 'It's all coming back to me now. Wasn't Reinhardt Meyer killed by Otto Tobisch, the captain of the Tobisch Brigade?'

'Yes, he was in charge of the witch hunt,' Viktoria said bitterly. 'He and his men stormed through the hotel looking for Olga, but of course they did not find her.' Her voice faltered, as she remembered how, after Otto's departure, Karl, in an apoplectic fury, had rushed out into the street, to meet his own death only minutes later...

Ignorant of the painful memories he was reviving, the journalist snapped his fingers. 'Didn't Tobisch once work at the Quadriga?'

'He was the son of our first General Manager and when he was old enough, my father employed him as a page boy.' Viktoria shuddered.

'Otto had an unfortunate background,' Ricarda broke in. 'His father was a compulsive gambler, who committed suicide when his debts got too high. Later, we learned that Otto's mother was an alcoholic.'

'Mama, don't make excuses for Otto!' Viktoria exclaimed angrily. 'He was always a nasty piece of work. I'll never forget the time I found him urinating into a plant pot in the Palm Garden Room. When I threatened to tell Papa, he tried to strangle me.'

Her mother stared at her, appalled. 'Vicki, I didn't know that!'

'I was only about five at the time. I was so frightened I didn't tell you. Then, on another occasion, he caught me alone on the fourth floor and tried to molest me. I didn't say anything about that, either.'

'Vicki, darling, I had no idea…'

Benno, too, was gazing at her in horror. 'Vicki, why on earth didn't you tell me this before? No wonder you hate Tobisch so much! If I'd known…'

'Benno, it happened a long time before you came to Berlin. Otto was already in the army by then.' And he had also made his parting shot, words which she would never forget: *One day, I'll be the one who gives the orders in this hotel! I'll get even with you yet!*

Mortimer scratched his head thoughtfully. 'Didn't he take part in the Kapp Putsch, as well?'

This time, it was Monika who replied. 'I was born in March 1920 during the Kapp Putsch. When it failed and the Free Corps soldiers left Berlin, Otto Tobisch fired his machine gun at our hotel.' She turned to her mother. 'That's right, isn't it?'

'Yes.' It was unfortunate, but Viktoria would always associate Monika's birth with Otto. Even now, she sometimes wondered if her daughter's present fascination for the stormtroopers was due to the turbulent events taking place when she was born.

'What happened to Tobisch after that?'

'Bah!' The Baron growled irascibly. 'Don't let these women mislead you, Allen. Tobisch was simply a soldier, typical of many. When the Versailles Treaty reduced the size of the Army, he became a mercenary. After the Free Corps were abolished, he went to Munich and joined Hitler's private army. Following Hitler's abortive *coup d'état* in 1923 — the so-called Beer Hall Putsch — he was forced to flee to avoid arrest. Now he's back in Berlin again, an officer in the SS.'

Stefan's face darkened. 'I once saw him kick in a man's head. From that day, I have hated the Nazis…'

Luise tossed her head of auburn curls angrily. 'All our troubles during the last few years have been caused by the stormtroopers. Take Café Jochum…'

Benno sighed in exasperation. 'Luise, when will you understand that your friends are exactly the kind of people who have made Berlin into the sink of corruption and the hotbed of revolution it is today?'

'My friends are artists, not revolutionaries,' Luise retorted furiously. 'For God's sake don't confuse them with people like Olga!'

'Luise,' Ricarda murmured, 'don't get so excited, darling.'

'That still doesn't explain the power invested in Göring and the political police, or that given to the SA and the SS, to men like Otto,' Viktoria added bitterly. 'So long as Otto is at large, I too shall never trust the Nazis.'

Monika said, 'I think the stormtroopers are exciting. The other night, at the torchlight procession…'

Viktoria gave an impatient sigh. 'Monika, you are only twelve. You understand nothing about politics.'

'I know more than you think. In fact, I probably know more about Hitler than you do,' her daughter retorted triumphantly. 'Our form teacher reads us excerpts from his autobiography, *Mein Kampf*, every morning before lessons. It's very interesting.'

Viktoria took a deep breath. 'It's a pity you don't take as great an interest in mathematics and English.'

Benno patted his daughter affectionately on the hand. 'I'm glad you're taking an interest in current affairs.'

Waiters cleared their dishes and there was silence for a while. When the next course had been served, Viktoria cleverly directed the conversation onto another topic, by asking Mortimer about his wife's paintings, and the rest of the meal passed more harmoniously.

They took coffee in the Palm Garden Room, after which Mortimer excused himself, thanking them for their hospitality and explaining that he felt rather tired from his long journey.

'Allen is a good journalist,' the Baron commented, after he had gone. 'Has a fair understanding of German politics, although I don't agree for one moment with everything he writes.'

'He speaks excellent German, which puts him above most other American correspondents,' Benno pointed out.

'Such a charming man,' Ricarda murmured.

'At least he doesn't appear to like the brownshirts any more than we do,' Luise said acidly.

'I don't like him,' Monika announced. 'I don't think he's a journalist at all. I think he's a Bolshevik spy — or perhaps a Jew.'

'Don't be ridiculous! You're only cross because we weren't talking about you,' Stefan told her dispassionately.

Viktoria said nothing. She did not know why, but she found Mortimer Allen a strangely attractive and rather disturbing man.

Up in his room, Mortimer was thinking about Viktoria. He had watched the changing contours of her face during their conversation: the flicker of possessive jealousy when they had talked about Stefan going to Oxford; misgiving at the mention of Olga Meyer; hatred when he had brought up the subject of Otto Tobisch. A strong woman, he thought, a coper and a fighter, a good friend and a pitiless enemy. It promised to be extremely interesting getting to know her better.

A satirical journalist had once written that when Baron Heinrich von Kraus zu Essen died, St Peter would lock the gates of heaven in case he tried to take it over. The Baron had kept the cutting, not only because it amused him, but because he had no intention of dying. There was still a lot of the world to take over before he turned his sights on heaven.

Known throughout the world as 'The Steel King', he was one of the richest men in Germany. An only son, he had inherited from his father a steel works in Silesia, gun shops in Essen and 'Kraus Village', a chemical plant in Berlin-Wedding. Now, in addition to these, his empire comprised a shipbuilding yard at Kraushaven on the mouth of the River Weser, a shipping line, an aviation company, and some four hundred subsidiary companies, that he had acquired during the Inflation and the Depression, as well as many foreign interests.

He owed his success to two factors. One was his connection with the von Biederstein family. His marriage to Countess Julia von Biederstein had opened many doors which would otherwise have remained closed to him and was indirectly responsible for the life peerage conferred upon him by the Kaiser. To strengthen the tie between the two families, the Baron had married his oldest son, Ernst, to his cousin, Trudi. Ernst was now running the Kraus-Amerika office in New York, while Trudi and her two sons lived in the Ruhr with Julia.

The main reason for the Baron's success, however, was his own political, commercial and financial astuteness. The Versailles Treaty, which had forbidden the construction of all military equipment, had affected Kraus Industries less than many of its competitors for, as early as the middle of the war, Baron Heinrich had accurately gauged the way the wind was blowing and made his plans accordingly.

Licensing deals for the manufacture of Kraus armaments and equipment had been set up in many foreign countries. He had made arrangements with the shipbuilding firm of van der Jong in Rotterdam to continue the manufacture of submarines and naval vessels. And, secretly, in collusion with the Reichswehr, research and development into the building of modern guns and tanks had been continuing in his factories in the Ruhr, whilst at his laboratories in Wedding explosives, synthetic oil and petrol were being investigated. His aviation factories, while ostensibly producing parts for civil aircraft, were actually working on prototypes for fighter planes.

So long as the socialist-dominated Weimar government was in control, there had been little probability of any of his plans coming to fruition. The Nazis, however, were a different matter. If ever a party programme was tailor-made for Kraus, it was Hitler's.

The Baron had been quick to recognize this. Although he had never personally met Hitler, he had cultivated the friendship of Hermann Göring and helped the Party through several financial disasters. He was already starting to reap the profits. As a result of the terrorization of the Jews, he had, the previous autumn, acquired the Jewish-owned Arendt Bank on the Behrenstrasse, renaming it the Liegnitzer Bank to rid it of its Jewish connotations and, as part of the deal, bought Theo Arendt's impressive mansion in Grunewald.

On 20 February, Baron Heinrich attended a meeting of industrialists at Göring's official residence, the Reichstag President's Palace. Göring was now a very important person — the Speaker in the Reichstag, the lower house of parliament; Minister of the Interior of Prussia; and Minister of Aviation.

The doors swung open and three men entered the room. Dr Schacht, a former President of the Reichsbank and an old friend of the Baron, greeted them gravely, peering over his spectacles, resembling the conventional image of a middle-aged university professor. In contrast, Göring, his round face beaming jovially, his figure more obese than ever in a pale blue, pinstriped lounge suit, appeared rather like an overgrown schoolboy.

But Baron Heinrich paid scant attention to either of them, because, for the first time, he was face to face with Adolf Hitler. Dressed in the brown uniform of his stormtroopers, his Iron Cross prominently displayed around his neck, Hitler looked exactly like his photographs with his small moustache and distinctive dark forelock of hair. But his complexion was paler than the Baron had imagined, pink-tinged like a girl's, and his blue eyes were strangely protruding.

After Dr Schacht had introduced the meeting, Hitler began his speech. His words were persuasive, his hoarse voice convincing, as he assured them that he believed free enterprise and competition to be absolutely essential for the highest possible production. The Baron relaxed. Hitler had no intention of nationalizing industry.

Next, Hitler fulminated at length against the trade unions and the communists, promising his audience that all Marxists would soon be eliminated and all trade unions banned. Baron Heinrich smiled inwardly. This was what he had come to hear.

And there was more. The armed forces were to be reinstated, an air force would be created, Germany would rearm and there would be a massive munitions drive. Baron Heinrich looked around him in satisfaction, noting the barely concealed smiles on the faces of his fellow industrialists. Their investment was to be repaid in the continuation of private enterprise, large government contracts, the abolition of trade unions and, most important of all, rearmament.

Hitler reached his finale. 'Now we stand before the last election,' he declaimed. 'Regardless of the outcome, there will be no retreat. If I do not win, I shall stay in power by other means and by use of other weapons.' Nobody in the room required a more detailed explanation. If the voters did not elect Hitler to power, he would use his brown armies to seize power by force. Amidst fervent applause, he took his seat.

Göring stood up. Bland and conciliatory, he pointed out that elections were costly, requiring financial sacrifices from their supporters. 'But these will surely be much easier for industry to bear, if you realize that the election of 5 March will certainly be the last one for the next ten years, probably even for the next hundred years.'

When the meeting was over, Baron Heinrich heaved his massive bulk out of his seat and waddled towards Göring. He often thought Göring was the son he should have had — an opportunist like himself, ruthless towards his enemies, though sometimes coarse, often obscene, vain and egocentric, but a man of sound political sense although not, the Baron suspected, with much commercial acumen.

He reached in his pocket for his chequebook and wrote out a cheque for half a million marks. 'My small contribution towards the election…'

Göring's eyes lit up. 'Thank you, Herr Baron, most kind.'

There was nothing philanthropic in the Baron's donation. He was a businessman and he was convinced that his investment would pay immense dividends in years to come. He had long ago discovered that it was not the politicians, but whoever held the purse strings, who had the controlling hand in a country's destiny.

Two days later, in his capacity as Minister of the Interior of Prussia, Göring established an armed, auxiliary police force of fifty thousand men, drawn mainly from the ranks of the SS and SA, whose orders were to show no mercy to anyone hostile to the State. Most importantly, they were ordered to break up all Communist, Social Democrat and trade union meetings. One of the first to be arrested was Joachim Richter, a particularly troublesome shop steward from Kraus Chemie in Wedding.

It was fairly early in the evening and the bar was comparatively empty when Mortimer sauntered in and settled himself on a stool. 'Good evening, Hasso. My usual Jack Daniels, please, and have something yourself.'

'Thank you, Herr Allen.' Hasso handed Mortimer his whiskey and poured himself a beer, gazing appreciatively at the foaming brown liquid. 'Schultheiss-Patzenhofer, the best lager beer in the world. And, did you know, the biggest brewery in the world? My father used to work there before he died.'

Mortimer looked at him with interest. 'You come from Berlin?'

'Certainly! I was born in Wedding.'

Mortimer's interest sharpened. 'Red' Wedding was where Olga Meyer lived. 'You still have family there?'

'My sister, Rosa, lives in the Max-Strasse. Her husband works for Kraus Chemie.' Hasso frowned. 'In fact, I learned something this afternoon that might interest you, Herr Allen. Last night, when one of the Kraus shop stewards — Joachim Richter — and some of his colleagues were returning from a union meeting, they were ambushed by stormtroopers armed with cudgels. While they were trying to defend themselves, the police arrived, charged Richter with assault and arrested him.

'There was a meeting this morning to discuss what action should be taken to obtain his release and that was also broken up by brownshirts. Now, by State decree, trade union and Communist Party meetings have been forbidden.'

Mortimer pursed his lips. 'Herr Kraus seems to believe there is a very real danger of another communist revolution. Do you think that's likely?'

Hasso shook his head. 'Olga Meyer is trying to persuade the workers to strike against the Nazis, but unemployed men can't strike, Herr Allen. No, there's no revolution being planned. All the workers want are their rights — and some money in their pockets.'

Later on, Mortimer encountered Baron Heinrich. 'Herr Baron, I've heard that one of your shop stewards has been arrested for holding a trade union meeting.'

Baron Heinrich retorted impatiently, 'Rubbish! Richter and his louts attacked a group of stormtroopers, injuring one of them quite badly. That's why he's been arrested. For assault!'

That same evening, in a drab classroom at the Wiesenstrasse Secondary School in Wedding, Olga Meyer was attending a parent-teacher meeting. A small, almost insignificant-looking woman of forty-one, her grey hair pulled back in a bun and her face lined beyond her years, she had devoted her life to the communist cause. Yet suddenly, she had the feeling that her work had been in vain.

'I want you to realize that nothing is going to change in this school, because Hitler has been elected Chancellor,' the headmaster, Dr Paul Lukas, was assuring the assembled parents and teachers.

The minute he stopped speaking, Olga jumped to her feet. 'Comrades, I don't believe you understand the extreme gravity of our situation. Have you not heard Hitler say, time and time again, that his intention is to train our children in the service of his "new national state"?' Her voice was shrill. 'Look at the number of students joining the Hitler Youth. We must take action now. We must strike for our educational freedom!'

An excited hubbub broke out, the small group rapidly dividing into two factions. 'I agree with Frau Meyer,' Hans Zitzlaff declared. 'We must strike.'

'I don't trust Hitler,' another teacher argued, 'but I think we should give him a chance.'

'Hitler won't put up with any opposition, certainly not from elderly schoolmasters,' a father shouted. 'Look at what's already happening at Kraus! All union meetings banned. We must act swiftly.'

'Nobody's yet asked us to do anything against our principles…'

'But they will! I've been a member of the Communist Party since 1919. I fought the Free Corps…'

'Dr Lukas is right. Our job is to teach, not get involved in politics. Our duty is to our pupils.'

Olga used her final weapon. 'What about Herr Schmidt?' she demanded. There was a momentary silence, as they thought about the deputy headmaster, Bernd Schmidt, a man who had never made any secret of his dislike of Dr Lukas, always trying slyly to undermine his authority. Herr Schmidt who, alone among the school's staff, wore a Nazi Party badge in his lapel. Herr Schmidt, whose son was one of the few members of the Hitler Youth in Wedding. 'Are you going to allow the Schmidts of this world to dictate the future of your children?'

'Frau Meyer, you seem to forget that I am still headmaster,' Dr Lukas said quietly.

As the argument continued to rage, Olga stood up and made her way to the door. She was wasting her time. At the end of this, as at the end of so many other meetings, nothing would be achieved. Ultimately, these people were all like sheep. They would take the easiest way out. Too late, they would discover they had been led astray.

At that moment, the door was wrenched open, knocking Olga back against the wall. Flanked by some half dozen stormtroopers, a policeman moved slowly into the room. His eyes surveyed the small, agitated group but did not notice Olga. 'As we were informed, quite an elite gathering… However, according to the latest decrees, communist meetings are strictly forbidden. I have no alternative but to arrest you.'

'This is only a parent-teacher meeting…' Dr Lukas stuttered.

Olga had heard enough. Drawing the collar of her coat around her ears, she slipped behind the stormtroopers, sped swiftly down the school's empty corridors and through the gates. Outside were two SS men, sitting astride motorcycles, in front of a black police car. As Olga approached them, one called something to the other, the flame from a match flickered in the dark. They bent their heads towards it. Silently, Olga slid past them into the dark streets of Wedding. Provided nobody mentioned her name, provided Schmidt never discovered she was at the meeting, she was safe. But for how long?

At the entrance to her block of flats, she stopped, hiding in the shadows. From the direction of the school came the sound of indignant voices, the slamming of car doors, the revving of motorcycle engines. The cavalcade roared past her. In the rear seat of the police car, wedged between two stormtroopers, she glimpsed the white face of Dr Lukas. First Joachim Richter. Now Paul Lukas. If they were not careful, there would be no communists left in Wedding. Inexorably, the net was closing in.

Next morning, an eerie hush, as intangible as the thin pall of smoke from the chimneys of Kraus Chemie, lay over the sooty tenement blocks of Wedding. No swastika flags emblazoned in red, white and black festooned the dark, dank streets. Patched, grey linen hung stiffly in the frosty air, these lines of frozen laundry the only banners. Tall, black dustbins, rimed with snow, stood sentinel in back yards where the sunlight never penetrated. Among them, small children played, strangely quiet, their bare fingers red and swollen, their lips blue, their noses dripping from perpetual colds. So palpable was the sense of tragedy, it was as if all Wedding was in mourning.

The same atmosphere prevailed in the school, teachers and pupils looking at each other fearfully. History was Basilius Meyer's favourite subject, but as Herr Zitzlaff's voice droned on, the boy stared out of the window, his textbooks unopened, his pencil untouched, the sheet of his exercise book void of notes, as he thought about his mother's news that morning.

What had happened to Dr Lukas? Where was he now? Basili felt a lump rise in his throat and he put his fingers to his mouth, chewing at nails already bitten to the quick. He was thirteen, short for his age, and with serious grey eyes like his mother's, hidden behind steel-rimmed spectacles. He loved Dr Lukas. For one thing, he was one of the few people who had known his father. Basili never tired of hearing his stories about the tall, untidy journalist, who had been shot a few months before his birth. He imagined his father as being very like Paul Lukas, gentle, scholarly and idealistic.

In many ways, Dr Lukas had been like a father to him. When he was small, Olga had left him with the schoolmaster and his wife, while she addressed political meetings, held rallies and led demonstrations. He had grown to believe that his father had shared Dr Lukas's concept of the ideal communist state, where all people were equal and those who had gave to those who were in need.

In recent months, Dr Lukas had often said, 'If only people would realize that, just because a man holds different political views, he is not their personal enemy. If our leaders could hold hands in brotherhood and try to resolve their problems to the common good, all our troubles would end.'

Basili tried vainly to reconcile Dr Lukas's views with his own experiences. Although he was sure the teacher was right, when he tried to imagine Stalin and Hitler, Ernst Torgler and Hermann Göring, Olga Meyer and Otto Tobisch clasping hands in friendship, he feared Dr Lukas's dreams could never be realized. Still, there had been no harm in those fantasies. They had threatened nobody. In all his life, Dr Lukas had never hurt anyone. So who could possibly hate him sufficiently to betray him to the political police?

The door flew open and Herr Schmidt entered the room. At a signal from Herr Zitzlaff, the class rose to its feet. Herr Schmidt stared at them coldly, then he announced, 'In the absence of Dr Lukas, the authorities have asked me to take over his duties as headmaster.' The atmosphere in the classroom grew even more chill.

'Today sees the beginning of many changes in this school,' Herr Schmidt continued, 'the first of which is the manner in which we shall greet each other. From now on, this is how it will be done.' He swung his arm stiffly in the Nazi salute. 'Heil Hitler!' There was a stunned silence. 'Heil Hitler!' Herr Schmidt repeated, glaring at them. As the history teacher, with obvious reluctance, followed his example, one or two hands tentatively stretched out. A few voices muttered unintelligible words. 'All of you!' Herr Schmidt roared. Only Basili's hand remained at his side.

Herr Schmidt stared at him with undisguised hostility. 'Very well, Meyer. Come with me to my office. Class, sit.'

They shuffled to their seats as Basili left the room, his hands in his pockets to conceal their trembling. The new headmaster led him down echoing corridors to his office, closed the door, then leaned back against the desk. 'Meyer, you are behaving extremely foolishly, but I shall give you an opportunity to redeem yourself. It is quite simple. All you have to do is tell me whether your mother was present at the meeting yesterday evening.'

Already, all evidence of Dr Lukas had been removed from the small room. The precious books, through which Basili had been allowed to browse, had disappeared. The print of Leistikow's painting, 'The Lake at Grunewald', no longer hung over the desk. In its place was a black and white photograph of Hitler. Stonily, Basili stared at it. He knew now who had informed on Dr Lukas.

'Very well, Meyer.' Herr Schmidt picked up a cane. 'Take down your trousers and lean over this chair.'

Basili silently obeyed, closing his eyes and tensing himself as the switch whipped through the air, biting deeply into his skin. Tears of agony started to his eyes and he clenched his teeth to hold back a scream. Down came the stick again, slashing into the cut made by the previous blow. A wave of nausea flooded over him. 'Little Bolshevik bastard,' Schmidt growled. The room spun round. Down came the cane, again and again and again. Basili could hear it sucking at the open weals on his buttocks. Then he fainted.

When he regained consciousness, he was lying on the floor. As from a great distance, he could hear Herr Schmidt shrieking, in near hysteria, 'Get up, you foul little pig. Get out of here! Get out of here!' He tried to move but an excruciating pain seared through him. He felt as though every bone in his body were broken.

The school bell rang and there was a knock on the office door. 'Herr Schmidt?' Basili recognized Herr Zitzlaff's voice.

Breathing heavily, Herr Schmidt started to push at his legs. 'Damn you, Meyer. Pull your trousers up.' Basili remembered what had happened. With a supreme effort, he moved and Herr Schmidt pulled the rough material of the trousers over the lacerations.

'Herr Schmidt?' The door opened. There was an intake of breath. 'What the devil…?'

'The boy is a coward, Zitzlaff,' Herr Schmidt snarled. 'I caned him for his disobedience and he fainted. Get him out of my sight.' He marched out of the room.

'Basili,' the history teacher asked gently, 'are you all right? Can you stand up?' It took a long time, but eventually he succeeded in getting Basili to his feet. 'Oh, why couldn't you have lifted your hand and just muttered something like the rest of us? It would have saved you all this.'

Still weak and giddy, Basili shook his head. 'No, it's wrong.'

Herr Zitzlaff sighed. 'It will be safer if you don't come to school for a few days. I'll get you some ointment, then I'll take you home and explain to your mother what happened.'

Basili staggered to the door, every step an agony but one that he was determined to overcome. 'Thank you, Herr Zitzlaff, but I shall be all right.'

He was almost home when the silence of Wedding was broken, as a column of brownshirts surged through, jeering and shouting, pasting Nazi posters on ground-floor windows, daubing walls with the hated swastika emblem. The children stopped their games and Basili drew into a doorway. When the stormtroopers eventually went, the people came out onto the streets, men and women wrapped in old, grey coats, grey caps and shawls protecting pinched, grey faces, lined beyond their years. Patiently, they started to scrape the windows and scrub the walls.

For a long time, Basili watched them, inspired by their silent act of defiance and, suddenly, he knew that their spirits — like his — would never be broken. At that moment, Basili was filled with a burning conviction that it was his mission in life to fight to save the people of Berlin from destruction, to free them from the thraldom of capitalism and the miseries of poverty and hunger. To ensure that no swastikas befouled their walls, but that they lived under the proud symbol of the hammer and sickle. One day, he would make his father's dream come true. One day, Berlin would belong to its people!

His mother was too immersed in her own problems to notice his physical discomfort and Basili managed to conceal from her the events of the day. This was his battle and he was resolved to see it through. Next morning, he went to school as if nothing had happened. There were startled looks as he entered the classroom and Herr Schmidt visibly paled when he saw him at his desk. The rest of the class made the Hitler greeting, but Basili's arm remained at his side, his mouth firmly shut. To his supreme gratification, Herr Schmidt ignored him.

Every moment of the next few days was filled with pain greater than any Basili had ever experienced but, gradually, as the wounds began to heal, he became increasingly confident that his tactics were correct. Herr Zitzlaff had been wrong. One did not raise one's arm and mutter something unintelligible. And Dr Lukas had been wrong. One did not hold out one's hand in friendship to one's enemy. One fought him. But not as his mother did, with angry words, or as Herr Schmidt had done, with blows to the body. No, this was a battle of wills — and, in it, Basili had won the first victory.

There was a quiet knock on Viktoria's office door and Mortimer Allen entered. 'I hope I'm not intruding?'

'No, of course not, Herr Allen .'

'Thank you.' Mortimer leaned against the wall, his face grave. 'I've just come from a press conference at Dr Goebbels' offices. Göring's police have raided the Communist Party headquarters and, although the building was deserted, a store of propaganda literature and other documents were discovered, which apparently prove that the communists are about to launch a revolution.'

'It won't be the first time…'

Mortimer shook his head. 'On this occasion, I don't believe it. I think it's another fantasy woven by Goebbels' propaganda machine, with the aim of discrediting the Communist Party. However, Olga Meyer's name was specifically mentioned along with other communist leaders. Since you helped her once before when she was in trouble, I thought you might want to help her now.'

Viktoria bit her lip. The other evening, when she had told the story of Olga's escape, it had not occurred to her that history might be about to repeat itself. 'Herr Allen, you don't understand. Olga and I were friends once, a long time ago, but since then, many things have changed.'

'She's still your cousin — and she's in great danger…'

She glanced down at the papers littering her desk. 'Herr Allen, please don't think me unkind, but Olga has caused a lot of heartache in my family.'

'Because of her communist sympathies?'

'Certainly none of us agree with her political aims, but there is more to it than that.' Mortimer Allen was a stranger, to whom she

45

owed no explanation, and yet she did not want to appear callous. She looked up. 'If Olga had not sought refuge here in January 1919, Otto Tobisch would never have come looking for her — and my father might not have died. That was the final straw so far as Papa was concerned. He was so upset that he stormed out of the hotel — and was killed. I have never said anything to Mama, but to this day, I am positive that Otto Tobisch was in the car that ran Papa down.'

There was genuine sympathy in Mortimer's eyes. 'I had no idea... But, even so, you can't hold Olga responsible for your father's death?'

'I probably wouldn't if she had shown any remorse, but she said something to the effect that nobody's life was important compared to the communist cause — that it did not matter how many people died provided her revolution succeeded.'

Quietly, Mortimer said, 'Thank you for being so honest with me.' Without another word, he let himself out of her office.

For a long time after he had gone, Viktoria stared into space. She had told him most but not all of the truth. Only she knew that Olga was the one person in the world who was aware that Stefan was not Benno's son. And during their last fateful meeting fourteen years ago, Olga had said, 'I shall bring up my child as a true communist, to take the place that Reinhardt should have occupied. The future of Germany depends upon children like the one I am bearing, for they will be the children of the Revolution.'

'Then I feel sorry for your child,' Viktoria had retorted angrily.

'And I am sorry for yours,' Olga had stated coldly, 'for he is growing up under a lie. One day, your son and mine will meet and then we'll see which of them has turned out best.'

Viktoria shivered. She could still see the implacable hatred in Olga's face and did not know which she feared most — Olga Meyer's fanaticism or Otto Tobisch's vindictive thirst for revenge.

A couple of evenings later, the family was having dinner, when the doors to the restaurant burst open and the Hall Porter hurried excitedly across towards their table. 'Herr Baron! Frau Viktoria! Herr Benno! The Reichstag is on fire!' Through the open doors, a stampede appeared to be taking place in the foyer. People were milling round wildly, hurriedly throwing on coats and hats, rushing out onto Unter den Linden.

The entire restaurant was on its feet now, but, with unusual agility, the Baron pushed through the diners, Benno at his side. Viktoria stopped only to tell Stefan and Monika to remain with their grandmother, then hurried after them. By the time she reached the hotel entrance, Benno and his father were getting into the chauffeur-driven hotel limousine waiting in front of the hotel portico. She jumped in with them and, almost before a commissionaire had shut the door on her, they were speeding towards the Platz der Republik. From the direction of the Reichstag, the sky was red.

Within minutes, they arrived. Crowds of people were standing outside the massive parliament building, staring, transfixed in horror, at the billows of smoke pouring from its windows and doors and the livid glow of its glass cupola against the sky. Fire engines were already in place, firemen directing ineffectual hoses on the mighty conflagration.

'Where the devil's Göring?' the Baron muttered, forcing his way through the spectators, waving his stick threateningly in front of him. Grabbing Viktoria's hand, Benno followed in his wake. The crowds parted. They approached nearer and nearer to the burning building, which groaned and screamed as the furnace took hold. Like bursts of rifle fire, panes of glass exploded, charred pieces of debris were tossed from windows in the draught of the flames, blackened doorframes tottered and tumbled inwards.

Police barred their way but, at a word from the Baron, allowed them through to where Göring's distinctive silhouette could now be seen waving his arms grotesquely and shouting, 'This is a Communist crime! This is the beginning of the Communist Revolution!' A crowd of newspaper reporters was huddled round him, scribbling feverishly.

Benno let go Viktoria's hand. 'Stay here. Don't move.'

So intense was the heat, she shielded her cheeks with her hands, but her mesmerized gaze remained fixed on the blaze. Nothing could shut out the din of the fire or Göring's crazy ranting. 'This is a signal for arson, looting, murder, mass poisoning! We must show no mercy!

Find the communist traitor who has committed this crime against the State!' Sweat was pouring down his face, over the flabby folds of his neck, glistening in the scarlet light.

'We must not waste a minute.' His excitement was almost obscene. 'Every communist official must be shot on the spot! Every communist deputy must be strung up this very night!'

Pitiful sprays of water from the firemen's hoses battled impotently against the inferno. The glass in the dome shattered, the steel framework supporting it buckled and clouds of black smoke belched through this vast, gaping chimney. Giant fingers of flame leaped high into the night.

Fighting against a sudden, rising nausea, her eyes watering from the smoke, sick with the bile in her mouth, Viktoria pushed her way blindly past the policemen. She stumbled through the gesticulating crowd, their faces glowing eerily in the flames which illuminated the square, towards the embankment along the River Spree and lurched up against a wall of the Reichstag President's Palace.

'Are you all right?' Mortimer Allen stood in front of her, his thin face pale under its shock of hair.

She nodded, incapable of finding words to describe the mixed emotions that were raging through her — an irrational fear of the fire itself, the noise and the heat and the destruction, the senseless joy she had seen reflected on Göring's face and, more than anything, a chill sense of dread.

'Göring must have had an amazing view of the fire from his Palace,' Mortimer continued thoughtfully.

'Do you think they'll find out what caused it?'

'They've already arrested a Dutch lad called van der Lubbe. The police caught him running away from the Session Chamber.'

'Is he a communist?'

He swung her round to face him, his clasp on her arm so tight, she all but cried aloud in pain. 'I don't know whether van der Lubbe is a communist or not, but by the time Göring's police have finished with him, he will be. And I have no idea if he set fire to the Reichstag this evening, but I assure you, he will carry the blame.'

Viktoria shivered, though whether it was from the bitter night air or from shock, she did not know. 'You mean…?'

He relaxed his grip. 'What you have just seen is not only the end of a building or even the end of a parliament. No, tonight, you have witnessed democracy and freedom go up in flames.' He paused. 'And there wasn't actually a damn thing you could do to stop them.'

Even in Wedding, the Reichstag fire was clearly visible. All night long, an orange pall hung over the sky, as the gutted remains of the building continued to smoulder, flaring up occasionally like a beacon, becoming obscured in a screen of black smoke, but never quite extinguished. From the window of her flat, Olga watched the fire, trying to come to terms with its significance, trying to decide what to do. In the early hours of the morning, Basili joined her. Together, they sat in the eerily lit room, as dawn came up and a few people nervously set out to go about their business. During the morning, motorcycles driven by black uniformed SS men roared by and truckloads of stormtroopers thundered over the cobbled streets. In an agony of tension, Olga and Basilius watched them pass.

At the Chancellery, Mortimer Allen and his fellow journalists were handed details of a new law, the implications of which stunned Mortimer. Called *The Decree for the Protection of the People and the State*, it purported to be a defensive measure against communist acts of violence endangering the State, but it effectively took away all individual and civil liberties, as well as imposing the death sentence for a number of crimes.

As a result of this Act, the government could now dictate what the press said. The police could open anybody's post and listen in on their telephone conversations. They could search private houses. And they could kill anyone whom they believed to be an enemy of the State.

After hammering out a furious report for the *New York News* on his portable Remington and posting it to London, Mortimer went into the bar. 'Hasso, a double Jack Daniels.' Then, in a low voice, he added, 'As a result of this new law, your friend Olga Meyer is in mortal danger. Can you get word to her? Tell her to get out of Berlin?'

'One Jack Daniels!' Hasso looked cautiously around. 'Yes, I can get word to Wedding. Thank you, Herr Allen.'

At last, dusk settled over Wedding. There was a quiet knock on the door of Olga's flat. 'It's Anton.' Olga breathed a sigh of relief. Anton and Ruth Stein were old friends. He thrust a newspaper into Olga's hands. 'Olga, the Nazis are blaming the communists for the Reichstag fire. A new law has been passed. There is a train that leaves for Prague at eight. You should try to catch it. Now I must go to warn the other comrades.'

'And you and Ruth?'

'We are also leaving Berlin. *Auf Wiedersehen*, Olga.'

Olga spread the paper on the table. 'Documents have been found proving government buildings, museums, mansions and essential plants were to be burned down...' she muttered. 'Basili, there never were any papers. There has never been any such plan.'

'And this new law?' he asked fearfully.

Her forehead creased in concentration, she waded through the legal terminology of the decree, but however many times she read it, its message remained the same. Wearily, she pushed the paper to one side. The last time she had been in danger she had sought refuge at the Quadriga, but there would be no sanctuary there this time. 'Anton is right. We must leave Berlin.'

'You mean, you're going to give up now?' Basilius asked incredulously. 'You won't stay and fight?'

In a rare gesture of affection, Olga drew him to her. 'Basili, we shall continue our fight elsewhere. Prague will only be the first step of our journey. Then we shall go to Moscow!'

It took them only a few minutes to pack their meagre luggage. Then they left the flat in Wedding. They were but a short way down the road, when blazing headlights pierced the dark. Instinctively, they drew into a shop doorway and a car, followed by two lorries, roared past them. The cavalcade drew up outside their apartment block. Stormtroopers surged out of the back of the lorries and burst into the building they had just vacated.

At the end of the road, they caught a bus, thankfully bundling themselves and their battered suitcases into it. As they entered the vast, glass-roofed Anhalter Station, it became apparent they were not the only ones leaving Berlin that evening, for the concourse was milling with travellers. There were also a lot of armed guards. Olga pulled a scarf over her head, took Basili's glasses from his nose and put them on.

'Mother, I can't see.'

'Hold my hand tight. You can have your glasses back when we're out of Berlin.'

The guards scrutinized their tickets but showed no more interest in them than the hundreds of other refugees boarding the train. Half an hour later, they were on their way. They had begun the first stage of their long journey.

His peaked cap on the seat beside him, SS-Sturmbannführer Otto Tobisch waited in the car outside the tenement block in Wedding, convinced he had finally caught his old enemy, Olga Meyer. Ever since the Spartacist revolution, she had eluded him, but this time, Otto was certain she could not have escaped.

It had been to put paid to her and her kind that SS-Reichsführer Heinrich Himmler had, in 1930, summoned Otto to the Brown House in Munich and ended his seven years of exile. Those years following Hitler's abortive coup in 1923 had been highly frustrating. Otto had found refuge on a farm overlooking the Traunsee in the Austrian Salzkammergut, married the farmer's daughter — a buxom young woman called Anna — and tried to settle down to country life, but he had hated it. When Himmler had offered him a position within the new *Schutzstaffel*, he had accepted with alacrity.

Any drunkard, thug or convicted murderer could join the brownshirted SA, but to belong to the SS, a man had to conform to Himmler's very high physical and racial standards. Just as there had been an elite guard in the Kaiser's Army, so there was now an elite corps in Hitler's private army and one to which Otto Tobisch was proud to belong.

Leaving Anna behind on the farm, Otto had gone to Berlin, his task to rout out enemies of the Reich — all Jews, communists and other anti-socials. It was a task for which he was ideally suited. Although he had been born in Berlin, he hated both the city and the Berliners. He loathed their cynical approach to life, biting wit, lack of nationalist feeling and, above all, their arrogance. Nothing would have afforded him greater pleasure than to see them all banished from the face of the earth.

There came the sound of running footsteps. A voice called, 'Herr Sturmbannführer, the flat is empty!'

Otto struck his hand on the seat. So the birds had flown! Where had Meyer and her son gone? Were they still in Berlin? And if so, who would give them shelter?

He knew only one person — the same woman who had protected them back in 1919 — Olga's cousin and another of Otto's sworn enemies, Viktoria Jochum-Kraus. He ordered his driver, 'The Hotel Quadriga!'

Viktoria was in the Jubilee Room with Benno, supervising last-minute preparations for a banquet, when she suddenly became aware of a change in the atmosphere. The babble of conversation in the foyer died away. There was a scurrying of feet, a scuffling of chairs, a muted, rather hostile muttering. In the ensuing silence, she heard the harsh and unmistakable voice of Otto Tobisch. 'Out of my way, fool! Where's the Hotel Director?'

She stood rooted to the spot. This was the nightmare that had haunted her ever since she was a little girl. She stared in horror at Benno and, as she watched, the colour drained from his cheeks.

Distinctly, she heard Herr Fromm reply, 'In the Jubilee Room, Herr Sturmbannführer.' It was so quiet, she could almost hear her heart pounding. Then came the sound of steel-tipped boots marching over the marble floor and, flanked by a group of stormtroopers, Otto appeared in the doorway, his blue eyes staring at them bleakly from beneath his SS officer's cap, a triumphant sneer on his thin lips. 'We believe you are sheltering Olga Meyer and her son.'

'Olga Meyer?' Benno exclaimed in bewilderment.

Otto took no notice of him. 'Search the place from top to bottom!' he shouted to the blackshirts behind him.

Months and years of pent-up tension exploded within Viktoria. 'Get out of here, Otto Tobisch!' she screamed. 'You know damn well that Olga isn't in the hotel and, even if she were, that's our business, not yours. You have no right to search it! Get out!'

With a strength she had not known she possessed, she hurled herself at him, flailing at his face with her fists, her fingers clawing at his eyes. For a few seconds, she had the advantage, because her attack took him totally by surprise. With immense satisfaction, she felt her long fingernails score deeply across his forehead and draw blood. He let out a roar of fury, seizing hold of her wrists so tightly that she thought her bones would crush, and began to shake her.

The almost electric silence in the room was shattered by Benno's voice. 'Stop that immediately! Take your hands off her, you bastard! That is my wife!'

Otto stopped, although he did not release his grasp, moving his head, as if to clear the blood from his brain. Benno ran towards them, but Otto ignored him. Pulling Viktoria close, so that his face was against hers, his rancid breath in her nostrils, he hissed, 'You little bitch, don't you understand yet that I have every right to do whatever I want in this hotel, because we are now the masters of this country. Now, we give the orders!' Savagely he flung her towards Benno. 'Keep your slut under control or you'll find yourself in serious trouble.'

A sea of anxious faces was peering through the doorway now, hotel guests and personnel alarmed by their raised voices. Accompanied by his two henchmen, Otto stormed through them into the foyer.

Benno put his arm round Viktoria's shoulders. 'Darling, are you all right?'

'Of course I'm all right,' she muttered between clenched teeth. 'Benno, get that man out of here, before I kill him!'

'I've telephoned the police,' Herr Fromm said nervously.

'Those are the police,' Mortimer Allen told him sombrely, 'and thanks to the new decree, their powers are now virtually unlimited. If they think Olga Meyer is hidden here, they can tear the place apart until they find her.'

There was a stunned silence as the implications of his words sank in. Staring at each other helplessly, they listened to the slamming of doors on the upper floors of the hotel, shouted comments from the stormtroopers, Otto's voice barking orders.

'But Olga isn't here!' Viktoria said, angrily.

The journalist looked at her thoughtfully. 'Yes, I happen to know that she and her son left Berlin for Prague this evening. And if I know that, I'm sure the police do, too.'

The sound of boots was heard descending the staircase. Through the open door of the Jubilee Room, they saw the blackshirts reassemble. For a moment, Otto stared into the room, the blood from the gash on his forehead dripping onto the carpet. Then, without a word, he marched his troops out of the hotel.

For a long time, nobody moved, then the silent tension in the room was broken as a telephone rang at the reception desk. Guests and staff drifted away from the doorway, back to their rooms and offices. Benno took a deep breath and said shakily, 'I'd better see what damage has been done. Viktoria, my dear, will you go up to the apartment and make sure the others are all right?'

Aghast, Viktoria realized she had forgotten the rest of her family. Hurriedly, she crossed the foyer which was once again a hubbub of activity. At the bottom of the stairs, she met Stefan, his face white as a sheet. 'Mama, that was Otto Tobisch! He searched our rooms.'

Ricarda was close behind him, holding Monika by the hand. 'He said he was looking for Olga.'

'He'd hurt his face,' Monika added. 'Blood kept getting in his eyes.'

For a split second, Viktoria's eyes met Mortimer's. To her surprise, they contained a look of profound admiration.

CHAPTER TWO

A slim figure with a mop of unruly auburn curls, the fur collar of her coat hunched high around her ears, Luise made her way through the snow-covered Tiergarten towards the Kurfürstendamm. She still went to Café Jochum every day, but it was with lagging feet and a heavy heart for, immediately after the Reichstag fire, the remaining artists, actors, authors and musicians, who had constituted the clientele of her café, all fled. Hitler's Berlin was an unhealthy place for the cultural revolutionaries of the Weimar Republic. Café society, as depicted in the film *Café Berlin*, was no longer fashionable.

Sometimes, it seemed to Luise that everything she touched went wrong. The men she had loved had all left her. Sepp Nowak, the fighter pilot, who had proposed marriage to her shortly after the war, had left Berlin when she had turned him down. Georg Jankowski, the Jewish jazz musician whom she had loved so passionately, had gone to Hollywood. Even Lothar Lorenz, the Swiss arts sponsor, had returned to Switzerland in the face of stormtrooper violence in Berlin. Now, all she had left was Café Jochum...

'Do you mind if I walk with you?' a voice asked and she turned to find Mortimer Allen beside her.

'Of course not, Herr Allen, but I don't promise to be very good company, I'm afraid.'

'I have fond memories of Café Jochum,' Mortimer said. 'I remember seeing Emmy Anders sing there, back in 1931.'

Luise bit her lip. If she spoke, she would burst into tears.

The Kurfürstendamm, when they entered it, was a mass of swastika flags, the pavement swarming with brown uniforms. A short way down, a concrete, four-storey building rose before them, giant neon letters on its roof proclaiming its identity as CAFÉ JOCHUM. 'You helped design this, I believe?' Mortimer asked.

Luise nodded. 'It was the most controversial building in Berlin at the time.' She stared into its interior. The café was almost empty. No more than half a dozen people sat desultorily on the distinctive black leather and chrome chairs, among them not a single face she recognized. At a far table, the waiters were playing cards.

Oskar Braun hurried forward to meet them, his elderly face pale and dark bags under his eyes. 'Fräulein Luise, I didn't think you'd get my message so quickly.'

'Message? Oskar, is something wrong?'

He pointed towards the Otto Dix mural on the far wall. Painted across it was a huge, black swastika. With a little cry, Luise sank down on a chair, burying her head in her hands.

'Early this morning, an SS officer came here with a bunch of thugs,' Oskar explained. 'He claimed Café Jochum was a meeting place for a group of Communist-Jewish conspirators. He threatened me. Then one of his hooligans did that. I think an expert could probably clean it up, but as I told Herr Benno on the telephone just now, I can't cope with this sort of thing. I've handed in my resignation.'

Luise's vision blurred. Café Jochum without any customers was bad enough, but Café Jochum without Oskar Braun would not be Café Jochum at all. 'No, Oskar, you can't leave,' she whispered.

'Fräulein Luise, I'm an old man and the world has changed too quickly. I've got a son in Brussels. I've decided to move there and join him.'

'And Café Jochum…?'

'Fräulein Luise, Berlin has changed. It's not our Berlin anymore. And the same goes for Café Jochum…'

She lifted her head and stared at the mural through a haze of tears, then she turned to Mortimer Allen in anguish. 'Oh, I wish you didn't have to see it like this.'

He put his arm round her shoulder. 'It was a remarkable café in its time.'

Tears streamed down her cheeks. 'I'm sorry, I'm being very silly, but you must understand, Café Jochum was all I had left.'

Mortimer looked up. 'Herr Braun, can you call a taxi, please? I'll take her back to the Quadriga.'

As he helped her into the cab, she heard Oskar Braun say, 'Poor child, poor, poor child.'

She wished she were a child again. Little children did not hurt the way she did. Mortimer's arm was still around her and, helplessly, she buried her head in his chest. 'Oh, what am I going to do? If Café Jochum goes, I've nothing left to live for.'

When they reached the hotel, he took her straight up to the Jochum apartment. Luise threw herself into her mother's arms and burst afresh into uncontrollable tears.

'There's been trouble at Café Jochum,' Mortimer explained.

Ricarda's calm, green eyes met his above Luise's auburn head. They were full of infinite wisdom, born of long experience. 'Thank you, Herr Allen. I'll take care of her now. Come, Luischen.'

'Oh, Mama, why couldn't they have left Café Jochum alone?' Luise sobbed. 'Why do people always destroy the beautiful things? Why must ugliness and wickedness always win?'

Later that day, Dr Blattner called to see Luise. When he had finished his examination, he told Ricarda and Viktoria soberly, 'She's very run down and under considerable mental strain.'

'Is there anything we can do?' Viktoria asked in dismay.

The doctor shrugged. 'I'm prescribing her a tonic and all I can suggest is that you keep her comfortable and worry her as little as possible.'

'I'm sure her depression is caused by loneliness,' Ricarda said after he had left. 'If only she had married. But I suppose it's too late now. After all, she's thirty-two. There aren't very many single men around when you reach that age.'

Viktoria sighed. Even if she and Benno didn't always see eye to eye, she always had her husband, but Luise had no partner to lean on.

Before the week was out, Viktoria wondered how much better off she actually was than Luise, because Oskar Braun left Berlin and, without consulting Viktoria, Benno appointed a new manager for Café Jochum, a former publican with a beer belly and a boxer's nose, called Fredi Forster, who was a Hitler Youth group leader in his spare time.

In the belief that Luise's responsibilities would automatically devolve onto her shoulders while her sister was ill, Viktoria decided she should pay daily visits to Café Jochum to ensure that everything was running smoothly. She arrived in time to find Fredi Forster taking down the defaced Otto Dix mural. When she asked what he thought he was doing, he licked his lips and replied, 'That's filth, that is. Look at those women, they've hardly got any clothes on.'

Viktoria fought back angry words and left the café, but the memory haunted her all day. When Mortimer Allen knocked on her office door to enquire after Luise, she found herself unburdening her heart to him. 'I admit the mural always made me feel uncomfortable, but I'm sad to see it go. I'm so thankful Luise can't see the changes that dreadful man is making to her beloved café.'

The journalist smiled sympathetically. 'I've had a look at Forster. Not exactly my cup of tea, I confess. Poor Luise.'

When he had gone, Viktoria reflected how strange it was that Mortimer could condole with her and Luise's loss, while Benno seemed immune to their suffering.

The colour panorama of the Bavarian Alps Forster put up in place of the Dix mural totally changed the atmosphere of Café Jochum. So, too, did the new clientele. Gone was the cream of intellectual society. On the podium where Georg Jankowski and Emmy Anders had once mesmerized the world, a zither player now entertained his audience of dowdily dressed, middle-class housewives with sentimental tunes, as they gossiped over coffee and cream cakes. At the back of the room, groups of stormtroopers swilled beer, their boots on the table.

Café Jochum had entered a new era.

Viktoria had little time to worry about Café Jochum, for the hotel was keeping her fully occupied. As the election campaign reached a pitch of nightmarish intensity, every room in the Quadriga was occupied, its banqueting facilities the venue for dinners at which prominent political figures were the guests of honour.

It was impossible to turn on the radio without hearing the voices of Hitler, Göring or Goebbels. The streets outside echoed with the tread of stormtroopers' boots. From every street lamp and tree, from every archway and portal, across every wall and balcony, hung swastika flags and Nazi posters.

'They've got to win an overwhelming majority,' Viktoria heard Chuck Harris, another American correspondent, tell Mortimer Allen, as she passed them in the bar on the eve of the election.

Involuntarily, Viktoria stiffened. Mortimer glanced at her. 'Are you going to vote for the Nazis tomorrow, Frau Jochum-Kraus?'

'No,' she replied firmly.

'So who will you vote for?' Chuck Harris asked.

Viktoria hesitated for a moment, then decided to speak her mind. 'I'm going to place my vote for Brüning's Centre Party.'

An arm rested lightly on her shoulders and she turned to find Benno beside her. 'Brüning hardly made a great success of being Chancellor, my dear. In fact, I'd even go so far as to say that his ineptitudes paved the way for Hitler.'

'Hitler's calling this his "Revolution",' Chuck Harris mused, offering round a packet of cigarettes, 'and I suppose, as revolutions go, it's been reasonably bloodless, so far, apart from the violence of the stormtroopers.'

'A number of people have been arrested for no other reason than that they oppose Hitler's ideas,' Mortimer pointed out drily.

Benno looked soberly at the two journalists. 'The stormtroopers have got out of hand and something has to be done very soon to control them, but I'm sure Hitler will take the appropriate action once the election is over.'

Mortimer narrowed his eyes. 'And the Jews?' he asked. 'Do you agree with the anti-Semitism of the Nazis?'

Benno shrugged. 'Personally, I've got nothing against the Jews. Indeed, probably half our guests are Jewish. But I think Hitler is right to a certain extent. We do have a Jewish problem. The Jews have never assimilated themselves into our society and are now taking jobs that rightfully belong to our own people. Our first obligation is to find jobs for our own countrymen. Germans must come first.

'I also think there is a certain amount of hysteria concerning the Jewish question. Ever since Kurt Eisner and Rosa Luxemburg, many of our leading communists have been Jews. It is not so much to their religion, but to their political influence which Hitler objects.'

Mortimer Allen looked sceptical, but Chuck Harris commented, 'You plead a pretty potent case for Hitler, Herr Kraus.'

'That's because I believe him to be one of the greatest leaders Germany has ever known — or ever will know,' Benno replied simply.

It was the first time Viktoria had ever heard him express his views so clearly and, for a moment, she wondered if her distrust of the Nazis was irrational and unfounded. Then instinct prevailed. 'I shall still not vote for him,' she announced.

The next morning, when they went to vote, Unter den Linden seemed strangely quiet after the excitement of the previous days. The Baron drove to the polling station, but the rest of the family preferred to walk. The bells from the cathedral called the faithful to morning service. It appeared a Sunday like any other.

Luise was still very shaky and, when Benno suggested they extend their promenade to wander round the Monbijou Palace, she begged to be excused. Concerned by her pallor, Viktoria took her back to the hotel. As soon as they entered the apartment, her sister burst into tears. Viktoria tried to comfort her. 'Oh, darling, what's the matter?'

'I don't know,' Luise sobbed, burying her face into the cushions on the settee. 'I know it's stupid, but I keep feeling as if the world is coming to an end. Oh, Vicki, what am I going to do?'

With a sense of inadequacy, Viktoria took her hand. 'Why don't you go back to bed and rest?' she suggested gently. 'I think the election has probably got on your nerves, as it has on mine. Everything will be better tomorrow, when the commotion dies down.'

After Viktoria had helped her into bed, Luise lifted a woebegone face. 'Vicki, you didn't vote for the Nazis, did you?'

'Of course not, darling. Now stop worrying and try to sleep.'

Luise closed her eyes and was soon asleep. For a long time, Viktoria sat beside her. As she was only too well aware, not everyone was like them. She had a dreadful feeling she and Luise were in the minority.

But she was wrong. Although over seventeen million people voted for the Nazis, fifty-six per cent of voters pledged their support for other parties. The Nazis were still far short of a clear majority.

Luise received the news apathetically. 'It's seventeen million too many,' was all she said.

Viktoria could not help feeling a grim satisfaction. When she encountered Mortimer Allen the next day, she said, 'You see, we Germans are not as easily intimidated as you feared. You must admit that we have made our feelings about the Nazis very clear.'

'Yes, and I wonder what Hitler's going to do about it,' he muttered darkly. He had believed his assignment in Berlin would last a month. Now he had the feeling he was going to be there for very much longer.

The ceremonial opening of the new parliament took place on 21 March, not in the gutted Reichstag building, but in the Garrison Church at Potsdam. The significance of both the date and the place was not lost on Mortimer. The first Reichstag of the Second German Empire had been opened there on 21 March 1871. Now, in a masterly piece of stage management, the newly appointed Minister of Propaganda, Dr Goebbels, created the setting for the first parliament of the Third Reich.

The small gallery near the altar reserved for the press, film crews and radio reporters broadcasting the ceremony live to the nation, gave an excellent view of the interior of the church. Led by the former Crown Prince and Field Marshal von Mackensen, dressed in the uniform of Kaiser Wilhelm II's own regiment, the Death's Head Hussars, the procession moved slowly down the aisle.

The next two figures seemed highly incongruous. Looking extremely ill-at-ease in a formal morning coat, Hitler approached at the side of President Hindenburg. The ancient Field Marshal was wearing field grey with a grand cordon of the Black Eagle, carrying a spiked helmet in one hand and his field marshal's baton in the other. As he passed the imperial gallery, the old soldier stopped and saluted the empty seat belonging to the Kaiser.

Even to Mortimer, there was something moving, even tragic, in the gesture. He stared across the church at the pews gradually filling with field marshals, generals and admirals all in the resplendent full dress uniforms of their regiments. There was not a man among them, he guessed, who was not unaware of that empty seat, who did not feel anger that the Kaiser was living in exile in Holland and could not take his rightful place among them. Yet for all that, the spirit of the Kaiser seemed to move among them, mingling with the ghosts of Frederick the Great and Otto von Bismarck, the heroes of Prussian history, the men who had made Germany great.

Then his eyes hardened. Behind the military elite and aristocracy, with their dazzling accoutrements, their ribbons and their medals, the officers of Germany's other army were marching to their seats. The dull brown of the SA and the stark black of the SS uniforms seemed to introduce a sinister note to the proceedings.

Chuck Harris nudged him and Mortimer dragged his attention away from the ranks of the stormtroopers towards the altar, where President Hindenburg was beginning a brief speech. Automatically, Mortimer's pencil recorded the words in his notebook:

'May the old spirit of this celebrated shrine permeate the generation of today, may it liberate us from selfishness and party strife and bring us together in national self-consciousness to bless a proud and free Germany, united in herself.'

When Hindenburg had finished and taken his seat, Hitler stood and began to speak about the crippling conditions laid on Germany at the end of the war in 1918, the iniquities of the Versailles Peace Treaty and the suffering it had caused the German people. For the first time, Mortimer personally witnessed the Nazi leader's gift for oratory — the spell his words could cast over an audience even as august as this. Hitler might appear ridiculous in his unaccustomed morning dress, his moustache and dark forelock might give him the air of a cartoon character, but his powerful eloquence lent him a stature that paled into insignificance the splendour of the old President and the imposing ranks of the Old Order.

His words were those of conciliation. 'Neither the Kaiser, nor the government, nor the nation wanted the war,' he declared. Even his hoarse voice held a magnetic attraction. 'It was only the collapse of the nation which compelled a weakened race to take upon itself, against its most sacred convictions, the guilt for this war.'

Then Hitler addressed Hindenburg. 'By a unique upheaval in the last few weeks our national honour has been restored and, thanks to your understanding, Herr Generalfeldmarschall, the union between the symbols of the old greatness and the new strength has been celebrated. We pay you our homage. A protective providence places you over the new forces of our nation.' He stepped down so that he was directly in front of Hindenburg, bowed deeply and grasped the President's hand.

The church was charged with emotion. Film cameras whirred, press photographers rushed forward to capture the scene, while a German radio reporter near Mortimer cried excitedly into his microphone, 'We are witnessing a unique moment in history. In a solemn handclasp, the old Germany is united with the new!'

Two days later, the new parliament convened for the first time, not in the Reichstag, but in the Kroll Opera House. As he waited in its ornate foyer with other reporters for an official communiqué on the day's business, Mortimer recalled, in a sudden access of nostalgia, performances he had attended in bygone days of works by Janáček and Hindemith, directed by that most talented of conductors, Otto Klemperer. What, he wondered, would Klemperer think of today's programme? Where, for that matter, was Klemperer?

His reflections were rudely interrupted by frenzied shouting and cheering from inside the opera house followed by an outburst of song. It was not, however, the kind of song to which audiences at the Kroll were accustomed, not a work of which Klemperer would approve, but it was one with which Mortimer was becoming very familiar: the 'Horst Wessel Song'.

'Raise high the flags. Stand rank on rank together…'

The doors burst open and an official hurried out, to be surrounded by reporters hurling questions at him. Before the doors closed again, Mortimer caught a glimpse of the packed auditorium. From the stage, Hitler was smiling triumphantly at the exultant Nazi deputies and the jubilant stormtroopers lining the aisles, their arms outstretched in the Nazi salute. With difficulty, Mortimer managed to pick out a few seated figures with drawn, grey faces — all of them Social Democrats.

A little later, the press were given written details of the Enabling Act for which four hundred and forty-one Reichstag deputies had just voted. It was called the Law for Removing the Distress of the People and the Reich and was brief — only five paragraphs long — but very much to the point. It removed constitutional power from parliament for a period of four years. From that day on, all powers of legislation, budget control, approvals of treaties with foreign nations and constitutional amendments were conferred exclusively into the hands of Hitler and his Reich cabinet.

There followed a summary of Hitler's speech to the deputies. 'The government will only make use of these powers to carry out vitally important measures... The existence of the Reichstag is not threatened... The position of the President remains unaltered... The separate existence of the federal states will not be done away with... The rights of the churches will not be diminished...'

Mortimer was sure this speech was meant to appease but he personally was not convinced by Hitler's words. The Social Democrats had obviously been forced, presumably by threats and intimidation, to agree to the Enabling Act. *So this was how Hitler intended to rule*, Mortimer thought grimly. He stared bleakly across the heads of the stormtroopers towards the blackened ruins of the Reichstag. In solemn mood, he made his way back to the hotel to cable his report to Bill Wallace in London.

His mood was still subdued when he took his usual place in the bar that evening. He lit a cigarette and listened morosely to the gabble of conversation. Nobody would believe anything out of the ordinary had occurred that day. Nobody seemed concerned that within less than two months, Adolf Hitler had become dictator of Germany.

Hasso Annuschek handed him his customary whiskey. 'Don't look so worried, Herr Allen. Hitler is our problem, not yours.' He leaned confidentially over the bar. 'Have you heard the latest one about Göring and matches? They say he was sent to Rome to see the Pope and cabled back to Hitler: "Mission accomplished. Vatican burning. Pope imprisoned. Tiara fits me perfectly." And he signed himself: "Your Holy Father". Isn't that wonderful?'

It was the kind of story Mortimer would normally have enjoyed, but that evening he was in no mood for jokes.

Shortly after the ceremony in the Potsdam Garrison Church, Otto Tobisch received orders to report to Reichsführer-SS Heinrich Himmler at Nazi Party Headquarters in Munich. With a feeling of smug satisfaction, he caught the night train.

If they had not understood before, the people of Berlin could not now be in any doubt as to their fate should they continue to oppose the Führer's will. And that included Viktoria Jochum-Kraus. His fingers touched the scar on his forehead and he spat on the compartment floor. As yet, she had only had a taste of the punishment *he* could inflict. But let her put one foot out of line and she would learn what happened to enemies of the German Reich. Like all other troublemakers, she would end up in an overcrowded, verminous prison. His signet ring would gash her face as her nails had torn his. The thongs of his whip would cut open the white flesh of her back and she would scream for mercy... At the mere thought, Otto started to get an erection.

He put his feet up on the opposite seat and closed his eyes. Nobody, not even the ticket inspector, disturbed his rest. The skull and crossbones beneath the eagle on his cap, the pips and SS runes on his collar, the gold ring, but, above all, the glowering features of the sleeping SS officer, were sufficient to deter even the most intrepid traveller.

Early next morning, Otto reported at the Brown House, newly redecorated and considerably more palatial than it had been at the time of his last visit three years earlier. An armed guard escorted him through echoing passageways to a door outside which two SS sentries were standing.

Otto clicked his heels and flung out his arm in the Nazi salute. 'Heil Hitler! Sturmbannführer Tobisch reporting to the Reichsführer-SS!'

He was left in the corridor under the eagle eye of one sentry, while the other knocked and entered the office. A few moments later, he returned. 'Reichsführer Himmler is expecting you.'

Otto stepped through the open door into an ante-room, where a uniformed aide got up from behind a desk. 'Sturmbannführer, follow me.' He led him into an adjoining office, at the far end of which Himmler was working, dwarfed behind a huge desk. He announced Otto's presence and withdrew from the room.

After advancing across what seemed like an acre of carpet, Otto again clicked his heels and flung out his arm. 'Heil Hitler, Herr Reichsführer!'

Himmler looked up, strangely like a schoolteacher in appearance, with a pince-nez, trimmed moustache, receding chin and pale, almost bloodless features, then he returned his salute. 'Sturmbannführer Tobisch, you have done well in Berlin. I congratulate you.'

Another man stepped forward from a corner of the room, whom Otto had never met before, but instantly recognized as Reinhard Heydrich, Himmler's right-hand man. Heydrich was head of the SD, the SS Security Service, his responsibility to identify all opponents of the Nazi Party, as well as any spies within the Party organization. It was through acting upon his expert information that Otto and his men had succeeded in surprising so many of their victims in their homes.

'Yes, an excellent job,' Heydrich said. The Blond Beast, as Otto had once heard Heydrich described, was about thirty, younger than himself by some ten years, but otherwise not dissimilar in appearance — the living embodiment of Himmler's ideal Aryan man.

'Thank you, Standartenführer.'

Himmler picked up a file and leafed through the pages. Otto found himself gazing at his hands in fearful fascination. If one touched them, Otto was sure they would feel quite cold, like a dead fowl from the chicken farm Himmler had once owned.

In a mild, almost puzzled voice, as if he were the victim of a tragic misunderstanding, Himmler said, 'We have so many enemies who do not want the Führer to succeed in making Germany great again. The prisons and SA barracks are already overflowing and we are having to erect detention camps in which to house the prisoners. They are very crude — but effective. Perhaps you know of the camp at Dachau, not far from here?'

Otto nodded. Dachau had been opened a few days earlier.

'It is hard to find officers of the right calibre to run such camps. However, the Standartenführer and I are agreed that you have both the knowledge and experience necessary. Another camp is being set up at Grubenmünde, to the north of Berlin. I am transferring you there — not, initially, as Commandant. That post has been given to SS-Oberführer Zumstein. You will be Chief Security Officer.'

Otto frowned. He was a fighting man, not a prison warder.

'You will, of course, be promoted for taking on these new responsibilities. The rank of Obersturmbannführer seems fitting.'

Otto felt slightly appeased.

'Grubenmünde camp will house political prisoners, mainly socialists and communists, but also monarchists, Freemasons, Jews and other anti-socials,' Heydrich said. 'Our purpose is to re-educate them and release them as law-abiding citizens. Sometimes, however, that is not possible.' Heydrich stared meaningfully at Otto. 'In such cases, special treatment has to be meted out. We believe you possess qualities that make you eminently suitable for such a task.'

'If you do well, you will be given command of your own camp,' Himmler added.

Otto gave a thin smile. Suddenly, his new posting looked very attractive.

Twenty-four hours later, he was being driven from Berlin to Grubenmünde. It was a wet day and the road leading to the concentration camp soon deteriorated into a rutted sea of mud churned up by lorry wheels. The driver peered worriedly through the small gap cleared by ineffectual windscreen wipers, trying to steer a firm passage. Suddenly, the car lost traction and slewed to a halt diagonally across the track. The driver cursed, put it into first gear and revved furiously, but it only bedded itself deeper into the mire.

'Incompetent fool!' Otto snarled. 'Go and fetch help.' The driver cast him a baleful look, then got out and started to squelch his way towards some distant buildings. Otto stared out across the dank, uncultivated boglands, interspersed with patches of dark, forbidding conifers. It was country after his own heart. Like the desolate wastes of the Baltic frontiers he had guarded at the end of the war, this was a land where only the fittest survived. No better site could have been chosen for a concentration camp.

Eventually, there was a sound of voices and the driver reappeared, accompanied by several armed SS men, urging forward a motley crew of men with cropped heads, in rough suits made of old sacking — obviously camp inmates. It took them a quarter of an hour to free the vehicle. As the car finally resumed its slithering journey, Otto saw, to his satisfaction, that the prisoners were drenched with mud.

There were no further halts until they drew up outside some gates guarded by two SS sentries. The guards examined their identification cards, saluted and opened the gates. They drove through and stopped. The driver opened Otto's door, then reached into the boot of the car, lifted out his bags and dumped them on the ground outside the guardhouse. With a cursory salute, he jumped back into the vehicle, turned it round and drove back in the direction of Berlin.

'Obersturmbannführer Tobisch reporting to Oberführer Zumstein!' Otto announced to the guards. While one of them telephoned through news of his arrival, he took stock of his surroundings. Sentries, guardhouse and the building immediately ahead of him, undoubtedly the administration block, were all laid out in exactly the same manner as the many army camps in which he had spent much of his life. The only sounds were of hammering and sawing, interspersed with shouted orders. He was on home ground.

'The commandant will see you now, Obersturmbannführer.' The guard led him down several corridors, up a flight of stairs and knocked on a door. There was a brusque, 'Enter!' Telling Otto that his bags would be taken to his quarters, the guard flung open the door and marched away.

Otto entered the room and saluted smartly.

Zumstein, a burly, red-faced, bull-necked man, nodded, waved at him to be seated, then launched into a description of Otto's duties. 'Despite the barbed wire perimeter fence, it's still too easy for inmates to escape. Watchtowers and searchlights are already being erected. Make a tour of inspection and return to me with your findings.'

'Yes, Herr Oberführer.'

'One thing more. I don't need to spell out to you that we are dealing with dangerous criminals. However much they may plead their innocence, nobody is imprisoned here by mistake. Therefore, there is no room for pity, no time for weakness and no place for misguided human understanding.'

Not a muscle twitched in Otto's face. 'I understand.'

Zumstein gave him a piercing glance, nodded and rang a bell. When an orderly immediately appeared, he said, 'Find Scharführer Klinger to escort Obersturmbannführer Tobisch round the camp.'

'Yes, Herr Commandant!'

A few moments later, he was standing in the barrack yard beside Scharführer Klinger. 'This is the administration block and also living quarters for officers,' Klinger said. 'Additional accommodation is being built, but it is not yet completed.' He pointed to some nearby timber sheds on short stilts with central chimneys from which spiralled small columns of smoke. 'Those are the men's quarters. Beyond the barbed wire fence are the sties for the pigs.' He spat on the ground.

The tour lasted two hours, during which Otto made copious notes in his notebook. First Klinger went through the routine for the admittance of prisoners, all standard army procedure. New prisoners were taken to the shower room, issued with camp uniforms, then examined by a doctor. Their personal details were noted and all their personal effects were removed from them, except for a few marks. Their hair was then shorn and they were allotted a dormitory. Reveille was at four-thirty and they worked all day, under supervision of armed guards, on building work within the camp.

It sounded fine, but in practice Otto could see it was less than perfect. By far the worst problem was the lack of discipline. The SS guards were nearly all young men who had grown up in the postwar years without the benefit of conscription and, therefore, had no experience of controlling large numbers of people. Bored with their duties, they stood around smoking and talking, occasionally yelling orders and threatening their charges at gunpoint.

Wherever Otto went, prisoners were huddled idly in groups, breaking off their conversations as he approached. It was clear they were being allowed far too much freedom. Angrily, he scribbled in his notebook: 'Anyone who conspires against the state, by holding meetings, loitering with others, or gives inciting speeches should be hanged.'

'SS pig!' he heard a prisoner mutter, after he had passed.

Otto's pencil moved over the page. 'Anyone who attacks an SS guard or SS man should be shot on the spot, or hanged.'

Finally, they came to a huge derelict timber factory building. 'The camp was originally an explosives works,' Klinger explained.

Otto tapped his stick on the concrete floor and looked around him. Somebody had scratched *LONG LIVE STALIN* on a wall. What punishment should be given for glorifying Bolshevism? Hanging, shooting — or beating? Beating, he decided. Let the bastards feel the lash of a whip on their backs! Then his lips curled in a thin smile. This had once been a factory. Let it be a factory again. Let the communist shit experience for themselves the glories of work they had so long advocated for the masses. They liked slogans. Let them have one of their own! '*Arbeit macht frei*,' he muttered.

'Excuse me, Herr Obersturmbannführer?'

'Work sets free!' Otto repeated. 'That will be our new slogan.'

Late in the afternoon, he reported back to Zumstein. When he had finished speaking, the camp commandant said, 'You have my permission to implement these suggestions. Unterscharführer Fink will type them up. You have done well, Obersturmbannführer. Is there anything else?'

Otto nodded and explained his theory that Grubenmünde should not only be a detention centre but a work camp, and that the prisoners should earn their keep by their labour.

Zumstein's small eyes glinted as he recognized the implications. 'And that would stop any critical tongues from wagging... Work sets free. Very good, Obersturmbannführer.'

'One other matter, Herr Commandant. I request your permission to obtain some guard dogs.'

Zumstein nodded slowly. 'We seem to understand each other very well. Permission granted.'

A few days later, Otto found a Dobermann Pinscher puppy on a neighbouring farm. Even at the age of three months, it had a mean look in its eyes and growled at Otto's approach. Otto named it Wolf, had a kennel erected outside his living quarters and commenced its training.

The dog responded well. Within a week, it followed Otto obediently wherever he went. It would allow nobody else near it. At the sight of any of the prisoners, the hackles rose on its back.

So far as the prisoners at Grubenmünde were concerned, the two were soon inseparable. It was impossible to say which was most feared — SS Obersturmbannführer Otto Tobisch or his dog, Wolf.

With his stocky figure, mane of white hair and piercing brown eyes under shaggy brows, Professor Bethel Ascher was something of a local celebrity in the select suburb of Dahlem. At the grand age of sixty-six, he still lectured at the Friedrich-Wilhelms University on the Opera House Place. He was an amusing conversationalist, a generous host and a fine chess player.

His terraced house in the Königin-Luise-Strasse might be overshadowed by its more palatial neighbours, but it possessed a quaint charm and was kept in meticulous order by Gottlieb and Martha Linke, a middle-aged couple who had been coming in from nearby Wilmersdorf for the past twenty years to tend the small garden, clean, cook and look after Professor Ascher's other domestic needs.

The Linkes had always been proud of their employer. They admired the way in which, after the death of his young wife in childbirth, he had single-handedly brought up his two daughters. They had felt very sorry for him when Pipsi had died from an overdose of drugs, but they consoled themselves with the thought that Sophie's marriage to the wealthy banker, Theo Arendt, compensated for this tragedy. When Theo had sold his bank to

Baron von Kraus and moved to London, they had been greatly saddened by the couple's departure.

But now the Linkes were being forced to reconsider their position, mainly because they were finding it difficult to defend the charge that Professor Ascher was a Jew, at a time when anti-Semitic feeling was mounting, even among the respectable, middle class denizens of Dahlem and Wilmersdorf.

When Martha Linke did the Professor's shopping, she found herself increasingly drawn into conversations about the scandalously expensive clothes and jewellery worn by Jewish women, while their Christian counterparts were having to make do with last year's fashions. Martha began to see Sophie Arendt in a new light and far from being sorry that the Arendts had left Berlin, she began to feel glad they were gone.

Gottlieb Linke was also being pushed into a corner. Many of his cronies at his local bar in Wilmersdorf were unemployed, some compelled into early retirement by the Depression, and they argued that Jews were occupying jobs rightfully belonging to Aryan workers. One Saturday evening towards the end of March, one of them brought the matter to a head. 'Take your Professor, Herr Linke. He's still a lecturer at the University even though he's past retirement age. There must be lots of German teachers who could do his job as well.'

'Or better,' another man muttered darkly. 'Who understands what scientists like Ascher and Einstein are really up to? Einstein's gone to America. I think all the other Jewish witch-doctors should go with him.' He stared curiously at Gottlieb. 'You're not Jewish, are you?'

'God in heaven, no!' Gottlieb exclaimed, appalled that his old friend could even entertain such a thought. He waved to a waiter and ordered another round of beers.

When he returned home that evening, he repeated the conversation to Martha. 'I don't know what to think,' he admitted, scratching his bald head unhappily. 'The Professor's been very good to us, but the fact still remains that he's a Jew. Perhaps we ought to look for another position.'

'Gottlieb, who's going to pay us as well as the Professor does?'

Her husband stuffed some tobacco into his pipe and sighed. 'I don't want to let the Professor down. On the other hand, we don't want people to get the wrong impression of us.'

As his pipe belched out clouds of foul-smelling smoke, Martha had an idea. Every Wednesday, they helped out at the Scheers' parsonage in the neighbouring district of Schmargendorf. Martha cleaned the brass and copper and gave the kitchen a thorough going-over, while Gottlieb did the garden. 'Couldn't you ask Pastor Scheer? He must know all about the Jews.'

But Gottlieb was rather intimidated by the Pastor. 'No,' he said, 'You talk to the Frau Pastor. She'll know what's best.'

Pastor Bernhard Scheer was a tall, thin man, a former army chaplain aged about fifty. Like most Lutheran clergymen, he was a monarchist at heart. In Hitler and the Nazi Party, he saw the possibility, if not of the restoration of the monarchy, at least of a return to the authoritarian values of his youth. Throughout Hitler's struggle to power, he had espoused the Nazi cause, castigating the debauchery, dissipation and licentiousness of the Weimar Republic and vehemently preaching the gospel of a new Germany, positive that it heralded a resurgence of the Lutheran Church.

His fiery sermons were renowned as masterpieces of oratory, some people even claiming that they rivalled any speeches ever prepared by Dr Goebbels or articulated by Hitler. He saw no anomaly in what he was doing, nothing irregular about a pastor involving himself in secular matters. Luther himself had advocated absolute servility on the part of the Church to political authority and, apart from the fourteen dark years of Weimar, Pastor Scheer had never had any reason to believe him wrong.

He was not the only one. The previous year had witnessed the formation of the German Christians' Faith Movement led by Army Chaplain Ludwig Müller, a close friend of Hitler, and Defence Minister General von Blomberg. Pastor Scheer knew that Chaplain Müller was hoping to have his movement recognized as the official State Church, uniting the many denominations of the Lutheran Church into one body.

He was not entirely happy about this, but he did not allow the idea to trouble him too much. There was no personal motivation behind his thinking. He was not seeking preferment to upper ecclesiastical echelons. His concern was for his congregation. His sole desire was to save their souls from damnation.

There was something rather stern and forbidding about Pastor Scheer, but his wife was a very different character. A farmer's daughter from Hesse, Klara Scheer was a plump, rosy-cheeked woman with a heart of gold. Martha Linke could not help feeling curiously uplifted in her presence, as if, through mere contact with her, she had somehow touched the hem of God's robe.

It was to Klara Scheer that Martha Linke confided her worries regarding Professor Ascher. 'He's always treated me and Gottlieb very well,' she explained, 'but I can see now, he's got some strange habits. Like he keeps the sabbath on Friday, not on Sunday like good Christian folk. Frau Pastor, me and Gottlieb have got to consider our reputation. If we continue to work for the Professor, people may start thinking we're Jew-lovers.'

Klara Scheer put down the woollen sock she was darning and stared into space. Eventually, in a troubled voice, she said, 'I have never met Professor Ascher, but from all you have told me, he's a good man who has never done anybody harm.'

Martha scoured extra hard at the greasy deposits inside a large cast iron saucepan. 'But what should we do, Frau Pastor?'

The Pastor's wife smiled gently. 'Frau Linke, that is a decision only you and your husband can make. But never forget that, Jews and Gentiles, we are all God's children. Remember the Professor in your prayers and God will guide your actions.'

It wasn't exactly the answer for which Martha had been hoping, and when Gottlieb asked her later if she had talked to the Frau Pastor, she replied irritably, 'She says God will tell us what to do.'

To her surprise, Gottlieb said, 'Maybe she's right. After all, God must hate the Jews. They murdered Jesus. Perhaps He'll decide to get His revenge one day. Well, we'll stay with the Professor for a bit longer, but I'll still keep my eyes open for another job.'

With a deepening sense of sadness and dread, Professor Ascher watched the attitude of the Linkes change towards him. It was the same in local shops, in cafés, on buses and even at the University. Instead of greeting him cheerfully, people he had known for many years now turned aside pretending not to notice him. Many of his students boycotted his lectures, encouraged by non-Jewish teaching staff.

Most frightening of all, however, was the savage violence of the gangs of stormtroopers who congregated every day outside the University gates, shouting abuse, jeering and chanting: '*Juden'raus! Juden 'raus!* Jews get out! Jews get out!' Missiles would be hurled, stones, bricks, bottles or rotten fruit, sometimes missing his head by inches. Pedestrians scurried past with averted faces, while the police made no attempt to stop the hooligans.

It was scant consolation to know that the University was not the only establishment to be singled out by the stormtroopers. Mobs of brownshirts were picketing and even invading Jewish-owned department stores. In some cities, they had broken into the law courts, dragging Jewish judges and lawyers through the streets. In Chemnitz, armed SA guards had forced Jews to scrub the streets. All over the country, Jews holding important public positions were being dismissed or made to resign. Many were leaving Germany, particularly those with left-wing political convictions, who faced incarceration in one of the new concentration camps if they were arrested.

One by one, Professor Ascher saw his fellow lecturers succumb to threats and violence and feared the dreadful day could come when he, too, would be forced out of his position. But, until that day came, he still had hope that common sense would prevail in the minds of the German people and prove itself stronger than prejudice.

Hitler, however, had no intention of leaving anything to chance. Ostensibly in order to control the crude anti-Semitic demonstrations that had been breaking out, he gave permission for a boycott of all Jewish shops on Saturday, 1 April. To Professor Ascher, it was a dire portent of things to come.

Officially, the boycott lasted a day. In practice, it did not stop. The brownshirted pickets remained with their menacing chant: *'Juda verrecke! Juda Verrecke!* Perish the Jew! Perish the Jew!' And so did the posters warning: *Germans protect yourselves from Jews!*

After that, events moved with frightening speed. When the Professor opened his newspaper on the morning of 8 April, it was to read of new laws passed, the implications of which made his blood run cold. One clearly showed how little faith could be placed in the speech Hitler had made to the Reichstag deputies concerning the Enabling Act. 'The separate existence of the federal states will not be done away with,' he had assured them. Within two weeks he had reneged on this promise. Using the Enabling Act for the first time, Hitler dissolved the state assemblies and appointed Nazi Reich governments for all states.

The second law left few people in any doubt as to the position of the Jews. Entitled the Law for the Restoration of the Professional Civil Service, it banned all non-Aryans and political opponents of the Nazi Party from the civil service, as well as severely limiting the activities of Jews in the legal profession and the judiciary.

So that there should be no confusion, another decree defined a non-Aryan as anybody descended from non-Aryan, especially Jewish, parents or grandparents. The unthinkable had happened. After centuries of coexistence, an organized pogrom had started against the Jews of Germany.

Still Professor Ascher continued to go to the University, braving the pickets on the gates, running the gauntlet of scornful fellow teachers and undergraduates, putting on a bold front before dwindling classes of mainly Jewish students. He recognized it for what it was — a lonely, and rather pointless show of defiance.

Then an event occurred to restore his faith in humanity, to convince him that not all Berliners felt the same about the Jews as did the Nazis, that he still had good, faithful friends. Unexpectedly, he was invited to Stefan Jochum-Kraus's eighteenth birthday party on 28 April.

For a long time after the postman had delivered the invitation, the Professor sat gazing at it, thinking back over his association with the

Jochum family, to whom he had been introduced at the turn of the century by old Isaak Arendt, who had granted Karl Jochum the mortgages to build his hotel. Yes, without Jewish money, the Quadriga, like many other Berlin institutions, would probably not exist. That was what rankled with the Nazis — what they called the financial hold the Jews exacted over Germany. It was ridiculous, of course, but it made wonderful propaganda.

In the olden days, the Professor had often stopped off at the Quadriga bar on his way home from work, but in recent months he had fallen out of the habit. Since Benno had joined the Party, the hotel seemed to have taken on a Nazi flavour and he had sensed that Jews were no longer welcome there. On top of that, there was the decidedly unpleasant fact that Baron Heinrich had bought Theo's bank and villa.

This invitation, however, put a different complexion on things. Perhaps he had been over-sensitive. Baron Heinrich and his son might be staunch Nazis, but that did not mean Ricarda and her two daughters agreed with them. Indeed, the invitation would seem to indicate quite the opposite.

The Professor suddenly decided to call in at the Quadriga on his way home from the University and deliver his thanks in person.

Viktoria was the first to notice Professor Ascher, as he rather hesitantly entered the bar. Immediately, she signalled to a steward and asked that he be invited to their table. After shaking hands with them all and accepting a glass of madeira, he said, 'I wanted to thank you for your kind invitation to Stefan's birthday celebrations. I was very moved, particularly in view of the recent events…'

'Herr Professor, I assure you that we are all very upset at what is going on,' she said firmly, suddenly very pleased that she had overridden Benno's objection that as they had not seen the Professor for a long time, he might feel rather embarrassed at being invited to what promised to be a mainly Aryan gathering.

'You Jews certainly aren't the only ones to be concerned at the way matters are being handled,' the Baron boomed. 'This business is doing us no good at all. The American government is threatening to boycott all German goods if the violence continues. We can't afford to lose that trade.'

Ricarda looked at him askance. 'Heinrich, for once we are dealing with something very much more important than trade! We are talking about human beings. And I, for one, think it disgusting that dear friends like Bethel should suddenly be regarded as aliens.'

'Several of my Jewish schoolfriends have been forced to leave school early,' Stefan said. 'It looks as if they won't be able to attend university. Herr Professor, what will happen to them?'

Professor Ascher nodded sadly. As a result of his teaching, many distinguished physicists had graduated from the Science Faculty who were even now working on projects that would change the world. He was the author of many papers and books recognized throughout the scientific world as definitive works on the quantum theory. Whatever happened to him, those would always remain. But what about the Bethel Aschers of tomorrow? 'That is what concerns me, too, Stefan. I have had my life and made my small mark on the world. But what about the future?'

There was silence for a moment, then Viktoria said, 'I admit that I haven't studied the new laws, but I have the impression that they are meant to protect Jews from the violence of the stormtroopers.'

Professor Ascher raised a sceptical eyebrow, but said nothing.

'Even here at the Quadriga we have suffered an unwarranted invasion of our privacy,' Benno added. 'Do you remember Otto Tobisch, Herr Professor? He and a gang of blackshirts burst in using some flimsy excuse just after the Reichstag fire. Göring can't control the stormtroopers, that's the problem.'

The Baron said, 'Incidentally, I've learned Tobisch has been sent off the active service list and put in charge of security at Grubenmünde.'

'What's Grubenmünde?' Viktoria demanded blankly.

'An internment camp for political detainees, about fifty miles away.'

'An internment camp?' Professor Ascher asked.

Viktoria put her hand on his. 'Don't worry, Professor. At least we know Otto Tobisch is safely out of the way and needn't trouble us again.'

But the confidence in her voice belied her inner feelings. Otto Tobisch and a prison camp seemed an ominous combination.

Before the week was over, she learned something else that, far from diminishing Göring's powers, looked set to enhance them. On 26 April, he established a Secret State Police Office to replace the Prussian political police. Called the *Geheime Staatspolizei*, it was to be known by an abbreviation: the GESTAPO. A new word had entered the German language.

However, Viktoria had more important matters on her mind than Göring's Secret Police. Incredible though it seemed, Stefan was coming of age on Friday. She threw herself into the preparations, determined to give him a birthday party he would never forget.

Stefan's birthday was a splendid occasion. A birthday table was prepared in the Jubilee Room, beautifully decorated with flowers and laden with mysteriously wrapped parcels, in the centre of which stood a magnificent cake bearing eighteen candles. Nearby, wearing a new suit, Stefan received his well-wishers, his parents standing proudly beside him.

First of all, the entire hotel personnel filed in, led by Herr Brandt and his office staff and followed by Herr Fromm and the reception clerks. Impressive in his tall white hat, Maître Vittorio Mazzoni came next, with his fellow chefs, underchefs, commis and kitchen staff; then Hasso Annuschek and the bar stewards; Philip Krosyk and his waiters; the hall porter, Johann Dorn, the page boys, commissionaires and porters; Inge Fiedler the housekeeper, and the chambermaids, laundrymaids and cleaners; Max Knopf and his fellow maintenance men. During the course of the afternoon, the staff of Café Jochum also paid their respects: Fredi Forster and his army of waiters, chefs and kitchen workers. They all shook Stefan's hand and offered their felicitations.

In the early evening, Stefan's guests arrived — only a small number of whom were personal friends of his, most being acquaintances of his parents and the Baron — eager to pay Stefan their compliments on this auspicious day and offer their respects to his family. They came from all walks of life and many Stefan only knew by sight and some he did not know at all. In a daze, he found himself shaking hands with such diverse personages as bankers, civil servants and local government officials, judges, diplomats, generals, merchants and even clergymen. By the time Mortimer Allen arrived, he felt as if his hand had almost been shaken off.

'Quite an august gathering,' the journalist commented, accepting a glass of champagne and looking with interest at the crowded Jubilee Room, echoing to the sound of excited conversation and merry laughter.

'Yes, I feel quite overwhelmed at being the centre of so much attention,' Stefan admitted ruefully, 'but we Germans always make a great thing of birthdays and eighteen is an important age.'

Mortimer laughed. 'Yes, now you can vote, smoke, drive a car — and get married!'

Overhearing this last remark, Viktoria said, 'I hope not, at least not yet! Stefi has a lot to do before thinking of getting married.'

Stefan put his arm round her waist. 'Don't worry, Mama. Voting, smoking and driving should keep me occupied for a while…'

There was something almost unnatural about Viktoria's obsessive love for her son, Mortimer reflected, as he made his way across the room to where Ricarda and Luise were talking to a striking looking gentleman, with a thick mane of white hair and beady black eyes.

Ricarda introduced them. 'Herr Allen, this is a very dear friend, Professor Bethel Ascher. His daughter and son-in-law moved to London last autumn.'

'My son-in-law is the banker, Theo Arendt,' the Professor explained, as they shook hands.

Mortimer raised an eyebrow. 'Didn't he sell his bank to Baron Heinrich?'

'That is so.' The Professor looked as if he would like to say quite a lot more on the subject but, remembering where he was, gave a thin smile and changed the subject. 'I hear you've been unwell, Luise. Are you better now?'

And because she did actually feel brighter that spring day, with her mother and dear Professor Ascher near her, Luise replied, 'Thank you, yes, I'm much better now.'

Mortimer's eyes were roving curiously round the room. 'Who's the Man of God?' he asked Ricarda, indicating a severe-looking cleric, apparently giving a sermon to an admiring audience.

'Don't you know Pastor Scheer?' Ricarda replied in surprise. 'Why, he's very fashionable. Even I have heard him preach!'

'Ah,' the Professor said slowly, 'so that's Pastor Scheer. We share the same housekeeper and gardener — but not the same religion.'

It was a comment that would have embarrassed many lesser people, but not Ricarda. 'I'm not sure that I do either,' she admitted. 'In my opinion, the Church should concern itself with religious matters and leave politics alone. Pastor Scheer will do himself no good in the long run.'

'He's merely following in Luther's own footsteps.'

Ricarda sighed. 'I'm afraid I have never had a very high opinion of Luther. He was such a grim man. He never permitted even himself to be happy, and that seems to me the greatest sin a man can commit.'

The clamour of conversation rose around them, drowning the sound of Christian Engel's small orchestra. The British Ambassador's wife claimed Ricarda's attention. A chess-playing acquaintance of the Professor came to discuss his previous evening's game. An actor, an erstwhile habitué of Café Jochum, sat down beside Luise and started telling her about his current play. Mortimer sauntered away and soon found himself in conversation with Dr Blattner, who had an interesting store of reminiscences about the medical practice he had inherited from his father.

In the middle of the room, Baron Heinrich was deep in discussion with a group of businessmen, with very real worries of their own, for to their unconcealed dismay, the government had announced that the coming Monday, May Day, was to be a public holiday, a 'Day of National Labour'. The Nazis seemed to have effected a complete *volte-face*. Far from disposing with the trade unions, they seemed intent on conciliating the workers.

'I don't understand it,' one factory owner said, voicing the opinion of them all. 'Labour leaders are being flown to Berlin from all parts of the country and there's to be a huge government-sponsored demonstration at Tempelhof Field. Why?'

Rather than admit his ignorance, Baron Heinrich said confidently, 'Hitler doesn't want to alienate the workers. When he has them on his side, he'll deal with their leaders.'

Monika, wearing a new dress for the festivities, was chatting to her best schoolfriend, Beate Weiss, who, as a treat for Monika, was spending the night with them. 'Your brother is so handsome,' Beate sighed.

Monika shrugged. 'I suppose he is, but he isn't interested in girls, Beate. All Stefan thinks about are his studies.'

In the middle of the evening, Benno took Viktoria's arm, called Stefan to his side and clapped his hands for silence. 'As all of you who have children of your own will know, this is a proud day in any father's life. On 28 April 1915, a child entered the world. Today, eighteen years later, he has become a man.' He put his hand on Stefan's shoulder in an unwonted gesture of public affection. 'Stefan, from now on, your life is in your hands. Live wisely and live well, according to the principles your mother and I have tried to instil in you.' He reached into his pocket and pulled out a leather box. 'This is a small gift as a token of our deep affection.'

As his guests applauded, Stefan opened the box to find a heavy gold Jaeger wristwatch. Engraved on the back were his initials and the date. With a lump in his throat, he said, 'Thank you. And, believe me, I do appreciate everything you've done for me.'

His mother kissed him on the cheek and murmured, 'We love you, darling.'

Benno cleared his throat, then said gruffly, 'I mean it. We're very proud of you, son.'

In Monika's room, an extra bed had been made up for Beate. Monika undressed quickly and sat, propped up against her pillows, watching her friend take off her clothes. Six months older than she was, Beate was bigger built and already had well-developed breasts. Monika gazed at them longingly, wondering when her own flat chest would take on similar, grown-up proportions. Then Beate took off her knickers and Monika saw with astonishment that she had a bush of gingery hair at the fork of her thighs. Beate followed her look and smiled. Then she turned off the light and got into bed. 'Good night, Monika. Thank you for asking me to your brother's party.'

'Good night, Beate.' There was silence for a moment, then Monika heard a strange rhythmic sound coming from the neighbouring bed. 'Beate, what are you doing?'

'I'm rubbing myself,' Beate whispered. 'I often do when I'm excited. Don't you ever do it?'

'Rubbing yourself? Where?'

'Between my legs. Why don't you try it? It's fun.'

Monika reached down under her nightdress and tentatively touched her private parts. A kind of electric shock passed through her, making her tingle. She felt hot and moist.

'Rub quite hard,' Beate urged, then she gave a little moan. Suddenly, Monika's exploring hand found an opening. Tentatively, she put a finger into it. 'Beate, I've got a hole.'

'Mmm, that's where a man will put his tail, when you're older.'

'His tail?'

'All boys have tails. Haven't you ever seen Stefan's?' Beate demanded. 'It's what he piddles from. I can't wait until I'm old enough for a boy to put his tail into me.'

Monika spread her legs and rubbed very hard. It was a wonderful, throbbing sensation quite unlike anything she had ever known before. 'Beate, what's it called when a boy puts his tail into you?'

'*Ficken*,' Beate replied succinctly.

One day, Monika determined, she would *ficken*.

A few days later, Monika had another new experience. She started her first period. Her mother explained briefly that it was something that happened to all girls. Monika decided it must have something to do with rubbing yourself and *ficken*.

Never in its history had Berlin witnessed anything to compare with the May Day parades organized by Dr Goebbels to demonstrate the Nazi government's solidarity with the workers, to prove that far from being against the German workers, the National Socialist Revolution was directed in their favour. This was the Day of National Labour.

Led by their union leaders, the workers streamed into the city centre in their thousands, no disorderly rabble marching through the streets demanding their rights, but striding in proud and disciplined lines, flanked by the very stormtroopers against whom they had once waged such bitter war, swastika banners waving above them, already convinced that in Hitler they would find their salvation.

Mortimer followed them to the Lustgarten, the huge square in front of the old Imperial Palace, and listened to Hitler addressing them, registered their roars of approval as he promised them work, bread and security, saw their hands rise up in the Nazi salute, and experienced a moment of enlightenment. So convincing were Hitler's words, so contagious his enthusiasm, so passionate his determination that the workers should help him build a great, new Germany, that Mortimer knew that if he were a German labourer, living in poverty as a result of the Depression and the incompetencies of the Weimar Republic, he, too, would pin his faith on Hitler.

That evening, he attended the night rally at the Tempelhof Field. As far as the eye could see, there were people, probably a hundred thousand of them, massed on the vast airfield, shouting slogans and waving flags, in a fever of excitement. A huge stage had been built, behind which three mighty banners had been erected, over a hundred feet high, two bearing the black-white-red colours of the Third Reich, and, in their centre, the third carrying a giant black swastika in a white circle on a blood-red background, all starkly illuminated by powerful arc-lights.

Speech after speech was made that evening, by trade unionists, Nazi politicians, and eventually by Hitler himself, who vowed that from now onwards, May Day would be celebrated throughout the centuries to honour the workers of Germany. At the end of his speech the cry was taken up: 'Honour work and respect the worker!'

Through the night air it echoed, followed by shouts of '*Sieg Heil! Sieg Heil! Sieg Heil!*'

On a wave of emotion, the people surged home down the streets. Following slowly behind them, Mortimer Allen realized that, in one day, Adolf Hitler had given them more hope than Olga Meyer had in twenty years.

The following day, the very union leaders who had led the workers in their demonstration were arrested, their headquarters occupied and their funds seized. In the Quadriga bar that evening, Baron Heinrich informed Mortimer triumphantly, 'Couldn't have staged the thing better myself.'

'But those trade unionists had, presumably, pledged their support for the Nazis. Why arrest them?'

The Baron shrugged. 'My dear Herr Allen, so long as they were at large, they could have led the workers in a strike against the government. If they are in prison, there's nothing they can do. It's by far the best solution.'

So, Mortimer thought, first it had been the communists, then the Jews and now the trade unionists. Whose turn would it be next?

Up in his room, Stefan was supposed to be doing his homework, but, instead, he was gazing vacantly out of the window, trying to understand the implications of the news he had been given at school that day. A week tomorrow, on 10 May, there was to be another torchlight procession — this time, of students.

Never in his life had Stefan contemplated anything more unwillingly, but his teacher had given the order and the pupils had no choice but to obey. The entire class was to take part in the parade. If they stayed away, the message was plain: no matriculation and no university and in Stefan's case, no Rhodes Scholarship. But what, he wondered, would be the purpose of this particular demonstration?

Exactly one week after Stefan's party Luise celebrated her thirty-third birthday. Although Dr Blattner professed himself satisfied with her progress, Luise herself was aware of the emotional tightrope she was still walking. There were times when her emptiness and loneliness screamed out in her and a black tunnel ahead threatened to engulf her. This birthday seemed to signify not the beginning of a new year or a new era, but the end. Once, like a butterfly, she had flitted from dream to dream and love to love. Now, she had nothing left to dream of or to love.

But there was a surprise in store for her. When she entered her mother's apartment that evening for a small party Ricarda had organized, they were all waiting for her with excited expressions on their faces. There was a chorus of: 'Happy birthday, Luischen.' 'Happy birthday, Aunt Luise.'

Then, from a basket under the table, a puppy emerged, a bundle of silky wool, supported by four wobbly legs, wagging a ridiculously curly tail. It hurled itself across the carpet to Luise, gazing up at her adoringly from bright, beady eyes, its pink tongue hanging out.

Her eyes misted over and she kneeled down to stroke it. 'Oh, isn't it sweet!'

'It isn't an it, it's a she,' Monika informed her.

The puppy scrambled onto Luise's lap.

'She's a Shetland sheepdog,' Stefan said. 'Grandmama had her brought all the way from Scotland.'

'They call them Shelties in England,' Ricarda added.

'We thought she'd be company for you,' Viktoria explained.

'You'll have to train her, of course,' Benno commented.

Luise enveloped the little animal in her arms, burying her face in the long, soft fur. 'I think she's wonderful. You couldn't have given me a nicer present. Oh, Sheltie, Sheltie, I love you already.'

Sheltie gave her the next best thing to a kiss. She licked Luise's nose.

When Luise snuggled down in bed that evening with Sheltie curled up against her stomach, she felt new hope stir within her. For the first time in months, the black tunnel started to recede.

The following morning, the Dean of the University's Science Faculty telephoned to tell Professor Ascher that the Civil Service Law had been extended to include honorary professors, lecturers and notaries. 'Bethel, I'm sorry from the bottom of my heart, but you cannot work here any longer.'

Bethel Ascher listened to the voice echoing through the receiver and knew his old friend was trying to be kind. 'It's all right,' he said dully, 'I'm an old man and due for retirement. But the research work we have been doing? Who will continue it?'

There was a long silence before the Dean replied. Eventually, he said, in a voice little more than a whisper, 'A third of the University's teaching staff was Jewish, Bethel and, as you know, our Science Faculty was staffed almost entirely by Jews. There will be no Science Faculty any more. It simply will not exist.'

The Professor stared unseeingly out of the window. He had devoted his life to the Science Faculty and now, forty-eight years later, it existed in name only. So great was the hatred of the Nazis for the Jews, that they could allow a lifetime's work to disappear without a second thought. If they could do this in the name of patriotism, to what other depths were they prepared to sink?

'My poor, poor friend,' he said, heavily. 'I am truly sorry for you. What blindness, what crass stupidity! Yes, indeed, these are dark and evil days.'

Next morning, he got up at his usual time and took his normal train to the city, intending to go to the University and tidy up his papers. But when he reached the university gates, he was confronted by a dense mob of brownshirts and students, waving banners and chanting, '*Juden 'raus! Juden 'raus!*' They parted ranks to allow an Aryan lecturer through but when they saw the Professor, they surged towards him, screaming fanatically. 'There's one!' 'He's a yid!' '*Juda verrecke!*' The stormtroopers lifted cudgels. Stones and bottles were hurled towards him.

At that moment, Bethel Ascher knew fear greater than any he had ever experienced, certain that if he took another step he would be beaten and trampled to death. With the sound of their mocking laughter and coarse jeers ringing in his ears, he turned back.

In an agony of despair, he roamed the neighbouring streets, until he found himself outside the New Synagogue. He entered it and, going down on his hands and knees, for the first time in years, he prayed. Strangely, his words came not from the Old, but the New Testament. 'My God, my God, why hast thou forsaken me?'

His distinctive student's cap on his head, Stefan marched with thousands of other scholars from the upper classes of the grammar schools and undergraduates from the University past the Hotel Quadriga and down Unter den Linden. The outriders carried flaming torches, which illuminated the tiny buds on the lime trees, as they proceeded towards the Kaiser-Franz-Joseph Platz.

Still known to most Berliners by its former name of the Opera House Place, this was a square steeped in culture, surrounded by historic buildings, most dominant of which was the Opera House itself. To the south was the Catholic Cathedral of St Hedwig, with its massive glass dome and mighty cross, next to which was the Dresdner Bank, then the Palais Kaiser Wilhelm I. On the northern side was the University, virtually adjoining what was the Prussian State Library, founded in the middle of the seventeenth century and housing a magnificent collection of nearly two and a half million books.

It was when they arrived in the Opera House Place that the purpose of the demonstration became clear. In the centre was a massive pile of books, guarded by stormtroopers, into which, at a shouted order, the torchbearers threw their blazing brands. With a mighty whoosh, the books caught light, sending a searing fountain of flames high in the sky, scattering charred fragments of paper and ash over the students and the crowd of fascinated bystanders who had already gathered, cheering and shouting their encouragement: 'Filth!' 'Pornography!' 'Jewish science!'

If it were pornographic books they were burning, Stefan might have understood, but even from where he stood, he recognized many of them as standard reference works, volumes of poetry, plays and classical literature. With a feeling of nausea, he left his classmates and pushed his way towards the fire.

University students and lecturers were bringing yet more cartloads of books across the square to fuel the furnace. The heat was so intense he had to shield his eyes, but Stefan could still read titles and authors' names, as they hurtled before him into the blaze: Thomas Mann, Lion Feuchtwanger, Alfred Döblin, Proust, Heinrich Heine,

Sigmund Freud, Erich Maria Remarque, Zola, Gide, H.G. Wells, Walther Rathenau, Albert Einstein, Bethel Ascher…

'It's like something out of the Middle Ages,' Mortimer Allen's voice said and, with a feeling of relief at discovering at least one friend on such a dreadful occasion, Stefan turned. The journalist was standing nearby, with Professor Ascher beside him.

'No, we've made progress,' the Professor said bitterly. 'In the Middle Ages, they would have burned me. Now they just burn my books.' He shook his fist towards the stormtroopers and students and, for a moment, with his mane of white hair, his flaring nostrils and his eyes fiery with rage, he looked like an Old Testament prophet sweeping down to avenge his people. 'You can destroy my books,' he shouted, 'but you cannot destroy the ideas! They will live on!'

'Shut your gob, Jewish whore-son!' An SA man lifted his truncheon and Mortimer laid a restraining hand on the Professor's arm.

'Desecration!' the Professor muttered. 'Mindless vandalism! What do they hope to gain by it?'

Desperately, Stefan turned to him. 'It's sacrilege! Oh, how can they do it?' To his dismay, he realized there were tears in his eyes and he brushed them away with his hand. 'How can they burn books? Books, of all things? Don't they realize how important books are? Is there nothing we can do to stop them?'

The Professor put his arm round Stefan's shoulder. 'No, my son, there is nothing we can do.'

As the conflagration burned to ashes, Dr Goebbels stepped into the centre of the square. 'From now on, the soul of the German people can express itself again,' he cried. 'These flames light up not only the end of an old era, but illuminate the new. We shall rid the nation of all subversive literature! We shall purify culture!'

As the crowd howled its approval, Mortimer said, 'Stefan, come away. I don't think I can stand any more.'

They turned their backs on the sacrificial pyre and walked up Unter den Linden, past the Kaiser Galerie and the Mercedes House, past the shuttered windows of Friedländer's jewellery shop still picketed by brownshirts, past the Hotel Quadriga and the Russian Embassy, round the Pariser Platz, past the British and French Embassies, the

Academy of Arts and the Brandenburg Gate, until they reached Charlottenburger Chaussee — an elderly Jew, a middle-aged American and a young German, united in their grief.

They made their way across the Tiergarten. 'So finally we have the truth about the Nazis,' Professor Ascher commented. 'They have silenced the communists, the Jews and the trade unions, and now they are destroying our cultural heritage. Everything that is good and fine in Germany is to go up in flames.'

'There's something else you don't know,' Mortimer told him sombrely, lighting a cigarette. 'Earlier today, Göring's police apparently seized all buildings, newspapers and property belonging to the Social Democrats. A few socialist deputies who are willing to go along with the Nazis are still free but most have been arrested.'

'Something must be done to stop them. But what can we do?' Professor Ascher asked despondently. 'I am a Jew. Within a month, I have lost my job and seen my life's work thrown on a bonfire.'

'The strength of the Nazi Party lies in its leadership,' Mortimer said slowly. 'Hitler is succeeding because there is no one person strong enough to oppose him. Alone, the Jews can do nothing, but in conjunction with other persecuted groups, with intellectuals, socialists, artists, with other religious movements, you could achieve a lot. A unified opposition could still topple him from power.'

They had reached the Victory Mall, the avenue lined with marble monuments to German heroes of the past, erected by the Kaiser. Professor Ascher stared at him. 'Where do you stand, Herr Allen? I've read your articles in the *New York News*. Like most foreign journalists, you seem to be toeing the Nazi Party line, faithfully reporting everything Dr Goebbels tells you.'

'There's no point in useless gestures. Any German who speaks out against the Nazis is put in a concentration camp. Any foreigner who criticizes them is sent home. Why should I run that risk?'

'But personally, you are opposed to Hitler?'

'I believe in the freedom of the individual. I detest dictators. I came to Berlin with an open mind to cover an election, only to discover myself in the middle of a revolution of the most obnoxious nature. I will admit to you that what was a journalistic assignment is gradually taking on the nature of a personal mission.'

The Professor gazed down the avenue of huge white statues shining eerily in the darkness, then held out his hand. 'When we met this evening, I was an old man in danger of losing his faith in mankind. You have given me back my faith. Somehow, we shall rid our world of this evil.'

He shook hands with them both, then set off southwards down the Victory Mall, his head held high. Silently, side by side, Stefan and Mortimer returned to the Hotel Quadriga. At the foot of the hotel steps, Stefan said, 'Do you realize that we have formed a kind of new opposition?'

Mortimer smiled ruefully and passed a weary hand through his thick forelock of hair. 'An opposition of three. Well, I suppose it's a start.'

The next day, at school, Stefan's teacher told the class that *Mein Kampf* was to form part of their compulsory reading. So that was how the soul of the German people was to express itself again, Stefan thought, and at that moment, he finally made up his mind that, no matter how much his mother tried to dissuade him or how hard he had to work, he would win a Rhodes Scholarship. He would go to Oxford.

When an advertisement appeared in the paper that Baron Heinrich von Kraus was seeking domestic staff for his villa in Grunewald, Gottlieb Linke came to a decision. Putting on his best topcoat and hat, he took a tram to the Caspar-Theyss-Strasse. He knew the house well, for he had often been here in Theo Arendt's day. He was fortunate. The maid who opened the door said the Herr Baron was in. If he would wait, please. Gottlieb looked around the substantial entrance hall and smiled complacently. A few moments later, he was ushered into the Baron's study.

The interview did not take long. Gottlieb described his responsibilities in Professor Ascher's household, emphasizing his capabilities as a butler and valet and commending Martha as a capable cook and lady's maid. He gave a glossy account of their duties with Pastor Scheer, hinting that it was due to the Pastor's influence that they were forced to seek alternative employment to working for a Jew.

The Baron nodded shrewdly. 'Seems very satisfactory. When can you start?'

'I am at your disposal, Herr Baron.'

'You'll live in, of course. As well as valet duties, I shall expect you to act as my personal chauffeur. I assume you can drive?'

Gottlieb was sure he could learn. 'Naturally, Herr Baron.'

'You'll start on Monday morning. Report here at seven.'

Gottlieb waited for him to mention wages, but the Baron merely said, 'That's all, Linke. You can go now.'

Gottlieb bowed and left. Baron von Kraus was one of the wealthiest industrialists in the country. He was sure to pay well.

When he told the Scheers that he and Martha were going to work for Baron von Kraus, the Pastor politely expressed his regret, but knew he would have no problem in finding another gardener. Klara Scheer, however, showed concern, not on her own behalf, but for Professor Ascher. 'You and your wife have been with him for a long time. How is he going to cope without you?'

Gottlieb gave her the same answer he had given Martha. 'If it was the other way round, he wouldn't think twice about giving us notice. I'm sorry, Frau Pastor, but in this day and age, we all have to put our own interests first.'

'Yes, I suppose so,' she replied doubtfully. But when Gottlieb had gone, she offered up a prayer for a man she had never met. He might be a Jew, but she was sure Professor Ascher was a good man.

Professor Ascher was not surprised at the Linkes' news, for their attitude had become insolent and their work slipshod over recent weeks. But he still experienced a terrible sense of personal disappointment, saddened that a relationship of twenty years' standing should suddenly count for nothing. And when they told him they were going to work for Baron von Kraus, there was bitterness as well. First the Baron stole Theo's villa and now he was taking the Professor's staff. Perhaps, after all, it would have been better to go to England…

Mortimer spent his every waking minute trying to devise a means of alerting a world that did not want to acknowledge the dreadful events that were taking place in Germany. The obvious method of writing truthful reports was out of the question, for they would only antagonize the Nazis. A confidential letter to Bill Wallace, entrusted to a fellow journalist, vividly describing the persecution of the communists, socialists, trade unionists and Jews, had a curt reception. Bill sent a message back saying that his job was to report news, not to write propaganda.

And why should the world want to know? Still suffering from the terrible aftermath of the Depression, there was not a single country without its own dire economic problems, mass unemployment and internal unrest. In the eyes of most people abroad, Germany had found a saviour in Hitler.

This view was enhanced in the middle of May when, in reply to a bid for universal disarmament by President Roosevelt, Hitler made a speech to the Reichstag, which foreign correspondents were specially invited to attend. From the beginning, it was apparent that Hitler wished to assure the world of Germany's peaceful intentions, stressing the fact that Germany did not want war, which he described as 'infinite madness'. 'The mentality of the last century which led people to think that they would make Germans out of Poles and Frenchmen is utterly alien to us. Frenchmen, Poles and others are our neighbours and nothing can change this…'

'Germany is prepared to agree to any solemn pact of non-aggression, because she has no thoughts of attacking, but only of acquiring security for her own people…'

As his pencil recorded Hitler's words, Mortimer's eyes kept returning to the small figure on the stage of the Kroll Opera, speaking so mildly and with apparent sincerity of purpose. Why was Hitler being so conciliatory?

The punchline came so suddenly and was spoken in such a moderate tone that Mortimer almost missed it. 'Germany is entirely ready to renounce all offensive weapons if the armed nations, on their side, will destroy their offensive weapons. Germany would also be perfectly ready to disband her entire military establishment and destroy the small amount of arms remaining to her, if the neighbouring countries will do the same…'

Baron Heinrich was talking to Benno in the Quadriga bar when Mortimer returned. He broke off his conversation to ask, 'Well, Herr Allen, how do you think the Allies will respond to Hitler's offer?'

Mortimer shrugged. 'I can't see England and France being too happy about it. The last war is too fresh in all our minds to agree to disarmament.'

'You heard yourself that the last thing Hitler wants is another war,' Benno said. 'All we are asking is for equality with other nations.'

Baron Heinrich let out an exaggerated sigh. 'Herr Allen, none of us want another war. In fact, it may interest you to learn that I was very opposed to the last war.'

'It's a shame the Kaiser and the Army didn't listen to you,' Mortimer observed caustically.

The Baron gave a thin smile. 'We have suffered far too long from the humiliation of Versailles. The war ended over fourteen years ago. Every other nation has its army. Either they should disband them or they should allow Germany an equal right to defend herself.'

'Provided it is only an army of defence.' Mortimer shook his head. 'Herr Baron, I should like to believe both you and Hitler, but I can't. To stay in power, Hitler needs the support of the armed forces and to achieve this, he has to restore the Reichswehr to its former glory, which means rearmament and the reintroduction of conscription. He can't do that by going along with Roosevelt's peace plans.'

Two days later, Hitler received a unanimous vote of approval in the Reichstag for his declaration on foreign policy. Even the Social Democrats — at least those who still remained — voted in its favour. In his article for the *New York News*, Mortimer was forced to adopt the same tone as everyone else. Hitler had extended the hand of peace and friendship: Germany's claims for equality should be given serious consideration.

After that, the Nazis continued to move with characteristic decisiveness. Further anti-Semitic legislation was passed, increasing the number of professions from which non-Aryans were barred. Non-Nazi cabinet ministers resigned and were replaced by members of the Nazi elite. In the middle of June, the Social Democrat Party was officially dissolved as being 'subversive and inimical to the State'. At the end of the month, stormtroopers seized the offices and assets of the German National Party. At the beginning of July the Catholic Bavarian People's Party and Brüning's Centre Party both announced their own dissolution.

On 14 July 1933, the all-Nazi Reichstag approved a law forbidding the formation of new political parties and stating: 'the National Socialist German Workers' Party constitutes the only political party in Germany'. Within less than six months, Hitler had achieved a one-party totalitarian state.

Surely, Mortimer thought, there must be some reaction to this despotic behaviour, but when he entered the bar that evening, a cheerful hubbub of conversation greeted him, as if nothing out of the ordinary had occurred. Only Hasso Annuschek looked gloomy, but when Mortimer pressed him, he said, 'What can we do, Herr Allen? Everyone who has tried to oppose Hitler has either been forced to flee the country, or has been arrested.'

Mortimer was morosely sipping his Jack Daniels, when Viktoria hurried into the bar, some papers in her hand. Although she was evidently busy, Mortimer could not resist asking, 'Do you realize what has happened today?'

'Happened? What do you mean?'

'This new law.'

'Oh, a new law. For a moment, I thought there had been a catastrophe.'

'In my opinion, it is,' Mortimer said gravely. 'Absolute power now lies in Hitler's hands. He is free to do what he will with the country.'

Viktoria sighed patiently. 'I was brought up as a monarchist in a time when absolute power rested in the Kaiser's hands. After his abdication, we had a republic, which was not a great success. Now, one person is again responsible for all decisions. Perhaps that is no bad thing. As I never stop saying, it is not to Hitler, but to the stormtroopers that I object. Now, if you will excuse me. I must find Herr Brandt…'

Mortimer nodded ruefully. 'Yes, of course.' Seen from her point of view, perhaps events were not so disastrous.

CHAPTER THREE

At the beginning of August, Stefan learned that he had passed all his examinations with flying colours and was accepted by the Friedrich-Wilhelms University to read modern languages and philosophy. 'Does that mean you've given up the idea of going to Oxford?' Viktoria asked hopefully.

'No, Mama. I still want to go to Oxford, but Herr Allen has explained that Rhodes Scholars have to complete at least two years' university studies in their own country before they are considered.'

'Well, a lot can change in two years.' Viktoria brightened, confident that, by 1935, Stefan would have got over the shock of the book-burning and be well and truly settled in Berlin.

Now that the school term had ended for both children and the political situation finally seemed stable, Benno suggested they all take a well-earned holiday at Heiligensee. So they left Herr Brandt in charge of the hotel and set off for the country, Ricarda, Luise and Sheltie in Luise's Opel, the rest of the family in the Mercedes.

The quiet fishing village of Heiligensee lay about fifteen miles north-west of Berlin on one of the lakes formed by the River Havel. Set in about three acres of secluded grounds, the Jochum cottage had been in Ricarda's family for several generations. It formed a horseshoe, with the main building to the south, the stables behind it now converted into living accommodation, and a courtyard in the centre. Its dominant feature was the verandah running the length of its southern aspect, overlooking striped lawns leading down to a spacious boathouse and jetty which jutted into the lake.

The two cars arrived simultaneously and they all got out, laughing joyfully. Smoke was spiralling up from the chimney and the lawns had recently been cut. Fritzi Weber, who looked after the cottage grounds, lifted his cap and hurried across to them. 'Welcome! I shall take your luggage.'

His buxom wife, Hilde, who took care of the domestic side and cooked for them when they were in residence, appeared in the doorway, wiping her hands on her apron. 'Yes, welcome! Frau Jochum, it is good to see you again — and the young ladies and gentlemen.'

Ricarda looked around her in delight. 'Look at my roses!'

'Yes, my Fritzi knew you'd be pleased with them.'

'Can I take Sheltie down to show her the lake, Aunt Luise?' Monika demanded. When Luise nodded, she raced off towards the water, her pigtails flying, the dog darting ahead of her.

Stefan asked, 'Do you think we could take the boat out this afternoon, Papa?'

Benno smiled conspiratorially. 'I had thought of doing a little fishing.'

Fritzi nodded. 'I've overhauled the engine, Herr Benno.'

As Benno and Stefan followed Monika, Viktoria laughed. 'Hilde, you've no idea how wonderful it is to be back here after being in Berlin all winter. It's so peaceful.'

After a plentiful lunch of freshly caught perch from the Heiligensee, accompanied by home-grown vegetables, Benno, Fritzi and the children went fishing, while Ricarda pottered in the garden and Viktoria, Luise and Sheltie sat on the verandah. 'It's like another world, isn't it?' Viktoria sighed contentedly, luxuriating in the warmth of the sun on her bare legs.

Luise glanced at her, suddenly aware of the toll the past few months had taken on her sister as well as herself. Viktoria seemed to have lost weight and new lines had appeared on her face.

She took Viktoria's hand in hers. 'Yes, thank heavens we have this sanctuary. An oasis of sanity in a desert of confusion...' She was looking forward to the quiet of Heiligensee, away from the bustle and clamour of people, stormtroopers and politicians, away from the constant reproach embodied in Café Jochum and the knowledge that she had failed. The others believed that, by giving her Sheltie, they had cured her of her depression, but she knew the dog was only a lifeline. Only time could make her really well again, time — and a reason for living. Heiligensee would give her time. As for the reason for living — well, maybe that would come later...

In the evening, Ricarda said, 'I think I'll do some watercolour painting tomorrow.'

'Sheltie and I will go for a walk.'

'I'm going to do absolutely nothing,' Viktoria told them.

Benno patted her shoulder affectionately. 'You deserve a rest, my dear.'

By ten o'clock, the lights had gone out at Heiligensee. Tall oaks and pines were silhouetted against the sky. A silver moon rose over the silver lake. An owl hooted. Then there was silence.

Mortimer had been in Berlin for nearly half a year and he, too, was due for a holiday. He went home to see his family, determined that, while he was in England, he would try to convince someone of the dangers that faced the world.

The taxi driver drew up in front of the house on the outskirts of Oxford. 'That'll be two bob, mister.'

Mortimer gave him half-a-crown, got out of the taxi, took his suitcase and stood for a moment on the pavement, admiring his home. 'Fairways' was a pretty, detached, three-bedroomed house, built around the turn of the century in mellow Cotswold brick, hung with wisteria and Virginia creeper, set back from the road in a sheltered garden of about half an acre containing ancient fruit trees and luxuriant herbaceous borders.

The front door burst open and Joyce rushed out. 'Mortimer!'

He dropped the suitcase and held out his arms, grinning broadly. She was wearing a pair of old slacks, her straight black hair awry, a daub of oil paint on her nose and a paintbrush in her hand. Whatever else might have changed in the world, Joyce hadn't. In her late thirties now, she still had the figure of a teenager and her face, bereft of make-up, looked very young. He lifted her off the ground, swung her round, then hugged her to him, kissing her long and tenderly. 'Hi, funny face! Pleased to see your old man, then?'

She gazed up at him reproachfully. 'You should have told me you were coming home, then I could have got things ready for you. As it is, I'm in a mess, the house is in a mess, Libby is out somewhere and there are only two chops for supper.'

'Wanted to make sure you hadn't taken a lover in my absence,' he teased, smacking her lightly on the behind.

She put her arm round his waist. 'Of course I haven't got a lover. Apart from anything else, I'm too busy…'

'Daddy!' A human projectile launched itself over the gate, down the path and into his arms. 'I saw the taxi and I knew it was you. I ran all the way from the end of the road.'

An image of a very different family flashed across his mind. In vain, he tried to imagine Viktoria in old slacks and Monika vaulting a gate. He laughed. 'You two don't seem to realize that I'm used to being in the company of elegant ladies in one of the world's most elegant hotels. And look what I'm expected to put up with at home! Untidy hair, grubby faces, scruffy trousers. Why, I've a good mind to go straight back to Berlin.'

Libby disentangled herself from his arms and looked at him aghast. 'Daddy, you can't!'

'How is Berlin?' Joyce asked quietly.

'Berlin is still Berlin — just about.' He picked up his suitcase. 'I'll tell you about it later. First, what I'd really like is a cup of tea. And after that, since there are only two chops, I propose we all gorge ourselves on fish and chips.'

Libby danced up the path ahead of them, very much a miniature version of her mother, her dark hair flying. 'Daddy's home, Daddy's home! And we're all going to have fish and chips! Yippee!'

'And after that?' Joyce glanced at him mischievously.

He bent down and whispered in her ear, 'After that, I'm going to bed with my wife.'

Later, when Libby was asleep in her room and they were lying, Joyce's head on his bare shoulder, Mortimer nestled his face in her hair. 'I love you, funnyface, even if you do smell of turps.'

'I'm sorry.'

'Don't be. Other women wear perfume, you wear turps. It's part of your attraction. You know, I missed you a lot while I was away.'

'Even with all those flaxen-haired Fräuleins to look after you?'

'Mmmm, but none of them smelled of turps.'

'I missed you, too, Mortimer.'

'How much?'

'Let me see. Tuppence-worth?'

'Well, I suppose that will do. After all, we've been married thirteen years now.'

'Fourteen. It was our wedding anniversary a week ago.'

Mortimer groaned. 'Oh no! I forgot again.'

'Darling, you've never remembered.' She rolled over and kissed him. 'Happy belated anniversary.'

'Have you ever regretted marrying me? After all, I'm not much of a husband — never at home…'

'Perhaps that's why I love you so much. So long as you always come back to me, I don't think I'll swop you for anyone else.'

'I'll always come back. Now, why don't you stop talking, woman, and let me have my wicked way?' He ran his hands over the smooth skin of her slim, naked body.

As always when he returned home, they made love in perfect harmony, rejoicing in the rediscovery of each other's bodies, finding forgotten pleasures in the hills and the hollows, the angle of arm, the jut of hip, the touch of lip to lip, of limb to limb, the coming together and the final, abandoned consummation, when everything else in the world seemed to have gone away and there was only the two of them, who now, for an eternal moment, became one.

Then the moment was gone and they lay exhaustedly back on the crumpled sheets. Soon, from her even breathing, Mortimer knew Joyce was asleep. He lit a cigarette and lay awake in the dark, thinking. Curiously, his thoughts were not of Joyce. He was wondering if Viktoria Jochum-Kraus had ever given herself in abandonment to anyone.

Next day, they took deckchairs into the garden and Mortimer told Joyce about Berlin, describing events as they had happened and people as he saw them. Her face growing more and more serious, Joyce heard him out in silence, interrupting only when he told her about Stefan's plans to go to Oxford. 'He sounds a charming young man, not at all like the others. I think it would do him a lot of good to get out of Berlin. You can assure his mother that I'd keep an eye on him.'

Mortimer laughed. 'I think young Stefan is perfectly capable of looking after himself, but thank you, darling.'

She was silent for a moment, watching bees buzzing round the lavender, butterflies flitting round tall, massed delphiniums. 'Of course, we have our problems, but on the whole life is very peaceful. Somehow, it doesn't seem possible that such dreadful things are going on just across the Channel. What do you think will happen?'

He lit a cigarette. 'I don't know. I shall report in at the office sometime and I'll make another attempt to make Bill see that he should take a less partisan stance on German affairs, at least in the form of editorial comment. Then I've decided to try and get an interview with Winston Churchill. He's the only politician I know of who might understand what I'm talking about. But, finally, it's up to the Germans themselves. They are responsible for Hitler coming to power. It's up to them to control his actions now he's there.'

'And do you think they will?'

He inhaled deeply, then shook his head. 'Apart from the exceptions I've told you about, they're besotted with him. And who can blame them? He's going to make Germany great again.'

The interview with Bill Wallace went pretty much as Mortimer expected. After Mortimer had finished his report, Bill said, 'In my opinion, they'd do well to follow Hitler's example over here — and in America, for that matter. Stick all the rabble-raisers in gaol — do them a power of good.'

'It was you who said some of Hitler's policies were rather extreme, remember?'

'And it was you who said the alternative to Nazism was Communism.'

'I'm still convinced that Hitler is determined to rearm.'

'The man's publicly declared himself for peace. You were there yourself. You heard him. In any case, a strong Germany isn't a bad thing for Europe. It will stop Stalin getting ideas above himself. No, Mort, you continue sending me the news. I'll decide how it's interpreted.'

A telephone rang. A messenger hurried in with a cable. Miss Thoroughgood appeared at the door. 'Mr Wallace, there's a man who…'

There was no point in staying any longer. Mortimer put on his hat. 'I'll leave you in peace, Bill.'

'OK, Mort. Enjoy your vacation. Give my regards to your wife.'

As Mortimer passed Miss Thoroughgood's desk, she said reproachfully, 'I thought you said you'd only be gone a month?'

'Hitler doesn't seem interested in my plans,' he told her.

Out on Fleet Street, Mortimer wondered if he should have said more to Bill, but how did one bring across the differences between London and Berlin? To anyone who had not recently been to Germany it must seem as if he were exaggerating. He gazed around him at the news boys and the red double-decker buses. Not a uniform in sight. Not a swastika flag. Not a blare of military music. In a strange way, the very normality was depressing.

His next port of call was to the Arendt Bank on Fenchurch Street. A distinguished man in his early fifties, Theo Arendt received Mortimer in his first-floor office, with portraits of Arendt ancestors hung on dark panelled walls. 'It is good of you to come and see me, Mr Allen. Bethel mentioned you in one of his letters. Reading between the lines, I've gathered things are getting serious. When Sophie and I left, we did all we could to persuade Bethel to come with us, but he refused. He said somebody had to remain in Germany to fight against injustice, intolerance and hatred. He claimed there was nothing Hitler could do to him that he could not face and overcome. I pray that he is right.'

Mortimer told him about his meeting with the Professor and Stefan after the book-burning. Theo Arendt did not smile. 'All of you must be careful. You don't need me to remind you that the prisons and concentration camps are full of people like yourselves. For my part, I shall do what I can to alert my fellow Jews in England and America of the danger that threatens. However, it is difficult for them to believe…'

'What do you think is going to happen?'

'In his Party Programme, Hitler categorically states: "None but those of German blood, whatever their creed, may be members of the nation. No Jew, therefore, may be a member of the nation." I have a dreadful feeling that we are about to witness the end of the thousand year history of the Jews in Germany.'

'There must be at least half a million German Jews! For all their sins, the Germans are a civilized people…'

'So long as President Hindenburg lives, I think the Jews are relatively safe. But Hindenburg is an old man. I am fearful of what will happen when he dies.'

Mortimer nodded soberly. 'I shall keep in touch, Mr Arendt.'

Outside again, he flagged down a cab. 'Paddington Station.'

As the taxi sped along Cheapside and past St Paul's Cathedral, the cabby asked, 'Heard the latest, guv'nor?' When Mortimer shook his head, he said gloomily, 'Looks like Middlesex are going to lose against Yorkshire.'

Yes, London and Berlin were worlds apart.

Mortimer now pinned all his hopes on Winston Churchill, the most controversial of English politicians. Ramsay Macdonald's coalition government did not like him, nor did many of his fellow Conservatives, but still Churchill's voice could be heard from the backbenches arguing against concessions to India and trying to alert his fellow MPs to the threat of German rearmament. Churchill might be nearly sixty now, but he was making it very clear that his political career was far from over.

In a carefully worded letter, Mortimer wrote to him, reminding him of previous meetings and signifying his deep distrust of the Nazi regime.

The very next day, he received a telephone call from Churchill's secretary. 'Mr Churchill thanks you for your letter and wonders if you would come to see him at Chartwell.'

'Yes, of course. When would be convenient?'

'Monday? At eleven o'clock? Oh, and Mr Allen, Mr Churchill would prefer you kept your visit confidential.'

It was a chilly, overcast day and it had started to drizzle when, at exactly eleven, Mortimer drove down the long approach to Chartwell. Dressed in a tweed jacket and Wellington boots, a cigar clamped between his teeth, Churchill met him at the door and immediately led him on a tour of his garden. 'You see that cottage over there. I built that for my daughters, Mary and Sarah. Now, come and see what I'm doing to the valley. Turning the whole area into a rock garden. Satisfying work, Mr Allen.'

At the top of the valley, they stopped. Two workmen were manipulating large boulders in bare, muddy ground. Churchill rumbled, 'I have my writing and painting and I have my garden. Were it not for my anxiety on public affairs, life would be very pleasant.' He took his cigar from his mouth and stared down at it, his forehead creased, his shoulders hunched. 'So you are now Berlin correspondent for the *New York News*. Will you give me your impressions of Berlin?'

Mortimer told his story. Churchill listened attentively, posing occasional questions, nodding his head sagely from time to time. When Mortimer had finished, he said, 'Austria will be the next country to fall to the Nazi menace. Hitler has never tried to conceal the fact that the acquisition of Austria is one of his most cherished ambitions.

'The first page of *Mein Kampf* contains the sentence: "German Austria must return to the great German Motherland." Already members of the Austrian Nazi Party are being introduced into the Austrian cabinet and I've heard the Germans are training Austrian stormtroopers in Bavaria. Chancellor Dollfuss has a hard task ahead of him, if his republic is to remain independent, for both the Nazis and the Socialists oppose him equally. In fact, the only country to which he can turn for protection is Italy, but if he does that, he may well only place himself in greater danger.'

Churchill was silent for a moment, then he continued, 'Mr Allen, it is my belief that we stand on the brink of an almost measureless calamity. It is one that can be avoided if Britain, France, Italy and America are prepared to stand firm against the Germans and enforce the terms of the Peace Treaties. But if we allow Germany to acquire full military equality with her neighbours, while her own grievances are still unredressed and while she is in the unhappy temper she is in, so surely shall we see ourselves within a measurable distance of the renewal of a general European war.'

He confirmed Mortimer's own feelings, but still Mortimer felt forced to comment, 'There are few who agree with you, sir.'

'"A prophet is not without honour, save in his own country",' Churchill quoted grimly. 'I am aware that mine is a lone voice from the wilderness and that the truth I speak is unpalatable to my colleagues in the House.' He jutted his chin obstinately. 'But so long as we are faced with this German menace, I shall never give in.'

The drizzle was turning to rain. The two gardeners succeeded in heaving a huge rock into place and Churchill waved his cigar approvingly at them. Then he turned back towards the house. 'I need information, which you are in a unique position to obtain. As an American, you are free to come and go as you please. As a journalist, you can ask questions. You can get close to the arms manufacturers, generals and politicians. Will you work with me?'

Mortimer had not expected such an immediate, direct response. He cast Churchill a sardonic look. 'You realize what you are doing, sir? You are asking an American to become a British spy.'

'My mother was an American, Mr Allen.' The rain started in earnest, cold as only English summer rain can be. Churchill did not invite him into the house but walked towards Mortimer's car.

To give himself time to think, Mortimer pulled out a packet of cigarettes and lit one under the shelter of his jacket. Then, after a couple of puffs, he said, 'Yes, sir, I'll work with you.'

'Excellent! There's a commercial attaché at the British Embassy in Berlin called James Adams. Give your reports to him and he'll send them across in the diplomatic bag. Good luck, Mr Allen.'

The two men shook hands and Mortimer got into his car. As he drove up the long driveway, his rear mirror reflected the bulldog figure of Winston Churchill standing bareheaded in the rain, the blue smoke from his cigar spiralling stubbornly skywards. When Mortimer turned the corner, Churchill raised his hand in a benedictory gesture.

There was no holiday for Baron Heinrich von Kraus. While the rest of the world frittered away the sunshine hours, the Baron was busy planning for the future. Now that all political opposition to the Nazis had been abolished, the way lay clear for Hitler to fulfil his other promises, chief among them the rearmament of Germany, because, despite everything the Baron had told Mortimer Allen, he knew Hitler had no intention of fulfilling his public promises to disarm.

The first thing he did was to acquire the premises next to the bank on the Behrenstrasse and give orders for the whole block to be converted into a huge new head office for Kraus Industries. Then he telephoned his eldest son, Ernst, in New York. Transatlantic telephone calls were expensive and the Baron wasted no time with pleasantries. 'You've served your purpose in America. I've got a job for you here. I'm opening a new head office in Berlin.'

'And you want me to manage it?' Ernst's voice wavered expectantly down the line.

'No, boy. I'm the head of Kraus Industries and don't you forget it! We've got a big manufacturing programme ahead of us and I need you to go to Essen and take charge of the Ruhr. Hand everything in New York over to Bewilogua and come back to Germany.'

He slammed down the phone impatiently. Ernst was a capable manager, but even at the age of forty-seven, he had no drive or initiative. When the Baron finally handed over the reins, it would not be to him. Ernst would never be the 'Steel King'.

Having organized his son, the Baron's mind turned to the Army. On 20 July, a new Army Law had abolished the jurisdiction of the civil courts over the military and restored to the officer corps all its former powers, clearly showing that Hitler recognized the value of the Reichswehr and was not pinning his country's military hopes on his private armies.

Furthermore, there were changes taking place within the Troop Office, the thinly disguised Army General Staff. The new Reichswehr Minister, General von Blomberg, was pensioning off the old die-hards and replacing them with younger, forward-looking officers.

It was time, the Baron decided, for his nephew, Colonel Count Peter von Biederstein, to return to Germany. An officer in the

Death's Head Hussars, Peter had seen active service in the war and been awarded the Iron Cross, First Class. The war over, he had married Ilse von Schennig, the daughter of his commanding officer. Because of his own and his wife's families' excellent connections, he had been one of the four thousand officers permitted to the depleted Reichswehr under the Versailles Treaty and, shortly after the birth of his daughter, Christa, in 1920, he and his family had been sent to Argentina in a diplomatic capacity. Currently, he was Military Attaché in London.

In a carefully worded, handwritten letter, the Baron wrote to Peter, pointing out the advantages of requesting a transfer to Berlin and indicating that he would be willing to use his influence to obtain him a good post in the Troop Office. He forbore to mention that a nephew on the General Staff could offer considerable advantages to Kraus Industries when presenting tenders.

In August, President Hindenburg made Göring a General of the Infantry. Göring immediately shed his brown stormtrooper's uniform and appeared in public dressed in the resplendent regalia of his new office. The significance of this event was not lost on the Baron. The Minister for Aviation had now become an officer of the Reichswehr. A new air force could not be far off. Baron Heinrich penned a suitable note, offering his congratulations.

Mortimer kissed Joyce and Libby a reluctant goodbye and returned again to Berlin. In an access of generosity, Bill Wallace had authorized him to make the journey by plane from Croydon. Mortimer was both surprised and grateful.

It proved an extremely interesting flight. He flew on a Luft-Hansa monoplane, a Junkers Ju 52, and was seated next to a young German who became very voluble when he realized Mortimer spoke fluent German. He was just returning from his first visit to England. His name was Horst Kleinert and it soon transpired that he was a flying enthusiast. He needed little prompting to launch forth on a vivid description of the properties of Professor Junkers' planes, the superiority of the Luft-Hansa compared to other airlines and the difficulty of being accepted as a Luft-Hansa pilot.

'I obtained my pilot's licence three years ago and have applied to Luft-Hansa each year,' he sighed. 'Each time I have been rejected. Last year, I heard they accepted eighteen out of four thousand applicants. Soon, I'll be too old.'

Mortimer glanced at him. He could have been no more than twenty-five. 'What do you do for a living?' he asked.

'I'm an engineer for Kraus Aviation. I joined as an apprentice at fourteen, when Baron von Kraus started the company at the end of the war. There have been a lot of changes since then. We were building fabric-covered biplanes at that time, now we're making all metal monoplanes similar to this one, with a retractable undercarriage and cantilevered wings. When we have an air force, they'll make excellent prototypes for fighter planes.'

Mortimer's eyes narrowed, but he made no comment, allowing the young man to talk. Göring's name cropped up frequently, for Horst Kleinert did not trouble to conceal his admiration for him. 'He was in command of Jagdgeschwader I, Baron von Richthofen's flying wing, at the end of the war. He understands flying, Herr Allen.'

When they landed at the Tempelhof Field, Horst Kleinert held out his hand. 'I have to take another plane now to Düsseldorf. Thank you for a most interesting journey. I hope we meet again one day.'

It did not occur to him that Mortimer might not share his conviction that Germany should have an air force. All Horst Kleinert cared about was aeroplanes. An air force would mean that instead of a paltry eighteen pilots being engaged each year, every keen young man would stand a chance to fly.

Back in Berlin, Mortimer discovered things to have been remarkably quiet in his absence, apart from Göring's promotion. He went to the British Embassy to introduce himself to James Adams.

He found a Cambridge man of his own age who, for all that he was a commercial attaché, demonstrated a very shrewd understanding of international politics and, when Mortimer pushed him on the subject, confessed to being a socialist. 'At first glance, Mr Churchill and I may seem strange bedfellows, Mr Allen, but we have one thing in common — a great distrust of Hitler.'

'That makes three of us,' Mortimer commented drily.

They discussed ways of keeping in contact and Mortimer suggested the Quadriga bar as a suitable rendezvous. James Adams agreed, then asked, 'Do you know the Taverne?' Mortimer nodded. The Taverne was almost an institution among lower paid foreign correspondents and embassy personnel. 'If you ever have any very urgent information to pass on, ring me, saying you're famished and suggesting a quick spaghetti at the Taverne,' James said. 'Here's my home telephone number.'

At Heiligensee, the days sped past all too quickly, happy, carefree days filled with sunshine and laughter, spent in the garden and by the lake, reading, swimming, boating and fishing, or simply talking lazily against a background hum of bees and a melody of birdsong. All too soon, it was the middle of August and time to return to Berlin, for Stefan to prepare for his first term at university and Monika for a new year at school.

'It seems such a shame to have to go back to the city,' Ricarda said. 'I think I'll stay here a little longer. Will you stay with me, Luischen?'

Unlike her sister and her family, there was no reason for Luise to return to Berlin. 'Yes, I'd like that.'

Slightly envious, Viktoria said, 'I wish I could stay with you.'

'There's no reason why you shouldn't,' Benno told her. 'Herr Brandt and I can manage quite well without you, my dear.'

He meant it kindly, but Viktoria had seen what had happened to Café Jochum once Luise was out of the way and she was not going to run a similar risk with the Quadriga. 'I wouldn't dream of it,' she said briskly. 'A month's holiday is quite long enough.'

So they returned to the hotel, leaving Ricarda, Luise and Sheltie to continue their holiday alone. But as soon as they arrived, the city seemed to close in around them. The tramp of stormtroopers' boots still echoed through the dusty streets. The fear of the Gestapo was still omnipresent. And, one evening not long after their arrival, an even worse threat loomed.

They were sitting in the bar, telling Mortimer about Heiligensee, when the Baron arrived at the hotel. He made no enquiry about their holiday, but announced, 'Ernst is coming back from New York this weekend. I've arranged for Julia, Trudi and the boys to come up from Essen to meet him here. Then Julia will remain in Berlin, while Ernst goes back to Essen.'

Although it was four years since Viktoria had seen Ernst, she had never liked him very much and had much the same opinion of Trudi and the two boys. It promised to be an extremely trying weekend.

The Baron's next words, however, banished all thought of the Krauses. 'Peter and his family are also returning to Germany. He's obtained a post at the Troop Office under General Adam.'

The colour drained from Viktoria's cheeks and, glancing wildly at Stefan, she sank back in her chair.

The Baron turned to Mortimer. 'You may well know my nephew, Colonel Count von Biederstein? Military Attaché in London.'

'Indeed, I do.' Mortimer raised a cynical eyebrow. 'In view of Hitler's apparent willingness to disband the Reichswehr, it seems a rather odd moment for the Count to return…'

The Baron snorted impatiently and Benno asked in a strange voice, 'Is Peter also coming to the Quadriga?'

'Yes, he's arriving on Sunday. We'll have a grand family reunion. The first time we've all been together since 1919.'

Viktoria pushed her glass aside. 'I have a terrible headache. If you'll excuse me, I must go up to the apartment.'

Anxiously, Benno leapt to his feet. 'I'm sorry, my dear. I'll come with you.'

'No, thank you, Benno, I'll be all right.'

'Well, if you're sure…'

As she left the table, she heard the Baron say, 'Modern women haven't got any stamina.'

Shortly after that, Mortimer made his excuses, leaving them to what was, after all, a family affair, but as he went he wondered why on earth the news of Colonel Count Peter von Biederstein's return should have provoked such an extraordinary reaction from Viktoria.

Up in her room, Viktoria lay down on the bed, burying her face in the pillow, unwilling to believe that the nightmare was about to recommence, the nightmare which she had thought was ended when Peter von Biederstein left Germany in 1920. What would happen when he and Stefan met? Would Peter recognize him as his son? Would Benno see them together and realize that, for eighteen years, she had been deceiving him?

Miserably, she thought back to that afternoon at Heiligensee in July 1914, when she had given herself to the handsome young Guards officer. Ever since she was a child she had been in love with Peter, ignoring her mother's warnings that marriage was inconceivable between a humble Jochum and an aristocratic von Biederstein, and Luise's dark comments that Peter would never propose to her anyway.

That very afternoon, she had realized they were right. Peter had taken her body but had spoken no words of love. Upon their return to Berlin, he had gone cheerfully back to his garrison, impatiently looking forward — not to seeing her again, but to the news that the Army would be mobilized. A few days later, his hopes were fulfilled. War broke out. Without a word, he had left for the front.

During the dreadful weeks that followed, she had heard nothing more from him and slowly she had been forced to accept the bitter truth. Theirs had only ever been a one-sided romance. To Peter, she had never been more than a bit of sport, a brief diversion while he waited for the outbreak of war. His very silence proved that he had already forgotten her — that he had never had any intention of marrying her.

Then had come the horrific discovery that she was pregnant. Vividly, Viktoria relived those agonizing moments, as she had stumbled out of the strange doctor's surgery, trying to decide what to do, aware of the shame she would bring upon herself and her family if she had an illegitimate child. Not even Peter's aristocratic background would save her from scandal — indeed, it would only make matters worse.

There had been only one thing to do — marry Benno Kraus. Benno loved her. He had even proposed to her once but, in her infatuation for Peter, she had turned him down.

She had told Benno part of the truth. She had admitted that she had thought she was in love with his cousin, but now she saw she had been deceived. She had spoken in the knowledge that Benno did not like his cousin, that he thought him arrogant and overbearing. She had hoped he would believe Peter had treated her unscrupulously, without guessing the full extent of his caddishness. She had pitched her plea correctly. Passionately in love with her, Benno had been deeply moved by her confidence.

Two weeks later, in a small, civil ceremony, attended only by their immediate families, she and Benno had been married.

Dear Benno, Viktoria thought, he was such a good, kind person, much too good to be deceived. But she had had no choice, for what man knowingly married a woman who was pregnant with another man's child, particularly if that other man was his own cousin?

She had been lucky that he had been so in love with her and too busy, too young and too naive to have any suspicions at her sudden decision to accept his proposal. She had been lucky that Benno and Peter had the same colouring, so that Stefan had grown up resembling Benno as much as his natural father, giving Benno no reason to doubt that this was his own child. And she had been lucky that, in finding a father for her child, she had married a man who would prove to be such a good husband to her.

'Vicki, what's the matter?' Benno entered the room and put a tentative arm round her shoulders.

She must not alert his suspicions any more than necessary. 'I'm sorry. I didn't mean to be rude.'

'You can't really be worried about seeing Peter again?'

She stared mutely at him.

'You must have got over that by now?' His voice was very gentle.

'Yes, but…'

'Vicki, I know you and he had a romantic attachment for a short while, but it was a long, long time ago. I'm sure Peter won't want to embarrass anyone by reminding you of it. Remember, he's married now, with a daughter of his own.'

She looked away. If she confessed to Benno now that Stefan was really Peter's son, she would finally be free of the terrible lie. But she could not bring herself to say the words.

Benno turned her round, so that she faced him. 'It was eighteen years ago, Vicki. We've all been through a lot in that time. But one thing hasn't changed.' He kissed her on the forehead. 'I may not show it very well, but I still love you, my dear. You always have been and always will be the most precious person in my life. Now, why don't you stay here and rest for a while?' He drew the curtains, then stood for a few moments in the doorway, smiling down at her.

Oh, Benno, Benno, her heart cried out. *I want to do what's right for you and Stefan. I don't want to hurt you.* But she did not know how to express her feelings and so she said nothing.

For the first time in months, Benno made love to her that night. But instead of relaxing and enjoying his caresses, she was tense and rather relieved when he reached his climax quickly. She slept badly and her dreams were haunted by Peter von Biederstein.

Benno lay awake for a long time. Ever since Stefan's birth, seven months after his marriage, he had suspected that Stefan was not really his son, but that had never stopped him loving either Viktoria or the boy. During Peter's long absence, there had been whole months when he had never thought about the matter at all. But now, Peter was coming back. Bleakly, Benno gazed into the darkened room and wondered what was going to happen.

The Kraus family made a spectacular entrance on Saturday. Trudi led the procession. A pork-pie hat trimmed with jay's feathers perched primly on the dyed blonde curls framing her plump, pouting face. Around her shoulders was draped a traditional, olive green, loden cape, beneath which her full figure was arrayed in the tightly bodiced, full-skirted regional costume of the Ruhr. White stockings and silver-buckled, black patent-leather shoes completed the picture.

Ernst strutted beside her, his resemblance to Baron Heinrich more conspicuous than ever as he entered his forty-seventh year. After over four years in America, his always corpulent figure was verging now on obesity, thick folds of fat rolling over his stiff shirt collar, while his bald pate shone with perspiration. Gold-rimmed spectacles concealed his piggy eyes above mottled cheeks and a nose riddled with purple veins. True to type, his mouth was rather prim.

Behind them came Countess Julia. Although she and Ricarda were about the same age, life had treated them very differently. A spoiled child, Julia had married the Baron a year after her debut and enjoyed a life of wealth and privilege as a result. Now she appeared a rather bent and brittle shell, enveloped in a long mink coat, her fingers dripping with diamonds. In comparison, Ricarda, who had returned from Heiligensee for the occasion, appeared young and vital.

Werner and Norbert came last, their pudgy figures identically dressed in leather shorts with embroidered braces, loden jackets with velvet collars, knee socks and ankle boots. Viktoria felt a fleeting pang of sympathy, so uncomfortable and out of place did they look in the elegant foyer.

She took a deep breath, assumed a welcoming smile and approached them across the foyer. 'Countess —' she could never bring herself to say Mother or Father to her parents-in-law — 'how nice to see you again.' She kissed the waxy cheek. 'Trudi, what a becoming outfit!' The two women touched cheeks in what passed for a kiss. 'Ernst, how well you look. America obviously suited you.' Ernst's lips brushed hers. She fought an urge to wipe her mouth. 'Werner, I do declare you're almost as tall as Stefan. And Norbert, you're quite a young gentleman.'

Under the supervision of the hall porter, a procession of page boys staggered across to the service lift with Ernst's trunks and the rest of the Kraus luggage. 'Let me take you all up to your rooms,' Benno said smoothly. 'I'm sure you'd like to wash and change. Vicki, maybe we could have tea in the Palm Garden Room in half an hour?'

As the lift doors closed, a voice beside Viktoria murmured mockingly, 'What an amazing scene! If only Hitler had been here as well, they would have made splendid subjects for one of Dr Goebbels' propaganda photographs — *the Chancellor and his adoring subjects from the Ruhr.*'

She struggled to keep a straight face. 'Herr Allen, that is my husband's family.'

The journalist took her hand and kissed her fingers. 'Frau Jochum-Kraus, the last thing in this world I want to do is to offend you. I beg your forgiveness.' He looked up mischievously. 'But you have to admit that hat…'

Viktoria relented. 'I know. Trudi has never had any fashion sense. And those poor boys…'

'I can't wait to see the Herr Baron in a similar outfit!'

The notion was so fantastic, she laughed aloud. 'Herr Allen, imagine those little shorts…'

'And knee-socks… His legs…'

'And a hat like Trudi's, with feathers…' Their laughter rang down the marble foyer. Viktoria wiped her eyes. 'Oh, I can't remember the last time I laughed like this.'

'It's an old Allen remedy. Laughter a day keeps the doctor away. You should try it more often. You're beautiful when you smile.'

'Vicki, dear, have you ordered tea yet?' Benno's voice suddenly broke in. 'The family will be down any minute.'

Her immediate reaction was guilt, as if Benno had discovered her red-handed in an improper situation. Blushing, she said, 'Benno, I'm sorry, I forgot…'

'It's my fault,' Mortimer said, 'I'm afraid I distracted your wife, Herr Kraus.'

'If you'll excuse me, I'll see about it right away.' Afraid that Benno might notice her confusion, she made her escape.

But all the time she was giving her instructions to the restaurant manager, the American's voice echoed disconcertingly in her mind. *You're beautiful when you smile.* A trite remark to cheer her up, nothing more. Or was it? Resolutely, she turned her attention to the Palm Garden Room. However charming he might be, there was no room for Mortimer Allen in her life.

The family reunion was not a success. As the Baron detailed his programme for the future, Ernst's pudgy face grew steadily longer. Only Trudi appeared happy at having Ernst back with her and finally being free of her in-laws. 'So we can have the Fortress to ourselves!'

Viktoria thought of the Baron's stucco and red-brick villa, long ago christened the Fortress by the people of Essen, situated on a hill above the smoke and fumes of the Ruhr. It was one of the ugliest buildings she had ever seen and she could not imagine how anyone, even Trudi, could be excited by the thought of living there.

'I'd like to live in a fortress, or, better still, in a castle,' Monika announced.

'I'd sooner live here,' Norbert piped up boldly. 'Although it's an hotel, it's friendly. I like it much better than the Fortress.' He smiled rather engagingly at Viktoria, little knowing that he could have said nothing better guaranteed to win a place in her affections.

Viktoria regarded him in surprise. He and Monika were both twelve and remarkably similar in looks, with their fair hair, chubby faces and clear blue-grey eyes, but there, apparently, the resemblance ended. 'Do buildings mean a lot to you, Norbert?' she asked.

'I want to be an architect when I grow up.'

'You're going to do what?' Ernst demanded.

'Pfui, take no notice of him. He's only a baby. Doesn't know what he's talking about,' the Baron grumbled. 'The schools feed such nonsense into children's heads these days.'

'Sounds to me rather like history repeating itself,' Viktoria commented, thinking of Benno's unhappy experiences working for his father. 'If Norbert wants a profession outside Kraus Industries, I would encourage him, and architecture is a fine choice of career.'

Ernst glared at her, then turned to Benno. 'I think this is your bad influence. Trudi warned me that you allow your family to be very liberal in their ideas. It comes of living in Berlin. Even in New York, people had nothing good to say about Berlin. It's always been reactionary and, in recent years, it's got worse. It's the communist and Jewish influence. Hitler has a difficult task ahead of him here.'

'Uncle Ernst, are there no communists or Jews in America — or in the Ruhr?' Stefan asked in an innocent tone.

The blood rushed to Ernst's face. 'No Jews in New York?' he spluttered. 'New York's run by Jews! When Hitler talks of a Bolshevik-Jewish world conspiracy, he's absolutely right...'

Stefan narrowed his eyes. 'Some of my best friends are Jews.'

'You needn't worry, Father. I certainly intend to follow your example and work for Kraus,' Werner interrupted obsequiously.

Viktoria looked at him with distaste. Everything was wrong with Werner. His body was unpleasantly fat. His eyes were too close and glowered sullenly under heavy eyebrows. His nose was thin and he had the mean Kraus mouth, which, she was certain, he would conceal under a Hitlerite moustache, just as soon as he could grow one. He was only fifteen, but he gave one the feeling that he had been born an adult. 'Fun' was certainly a word missing from his vocabulary. Life for Werner — as for his father and grandfather — would always be an extremely serious business.

'Only one of my family to show any promise is young Werner,' the Baron growled. 'Reminds me of myself when I was his age.'

The day went from bad to worse. At dinner, had it not been for the Baron, who was only too delighted to have a silent audience, and Countess Julia and Ricarda reminiscing about the past, the conversation might have ceased altogether.

Later, when Viktoria and Benno were getting into bed, Benno sighed, 'I thought four years in America might have improved Ernst, but they haven't. He hasn't changed a bit.'

Viktoria nodded. 'Poor Ernst…'

But neither of them was really thinking about Ernst. Their minds were already on the day ahead and Peter von Biederstein.

As Viktoria stood in the foyer the following morning, she remembered how, as a child, she had impatiently counted off the minutes until the arrival of Peter von Biederstein, never dreaming that, in later years, the same event would fill her with such dread. Worst of all, everyone around her was filled with eager anticipation. There was nobody in whom she could confide.

At last, the dreaded moment arrived and the hotel limousine pulled up at the entrance. The commissionaires opened the doors. The Baron and Benno hurried forward. Viktoria took a deep breath, glanced at Stefan, then resolutely walked across the blue Savonnerie carpet.

Peter had changed little since she had last met him at his wedding in 1919. His dark hair was streaked with silver at the temples and a network of fine lines crinkled the skin around his eyes and at the corners of his mouth, beneath his clipped moustache. Yet strangely, although his face was familiar, it was more because of characteristics that reminded her of Benno and Stefan, than for any individual features of his own. It seemed impossible that this was the father of her son.

Wearing a close-fitting, well-tailored uniform bearing the stripes of a Lieutenant-Colonel, he walked towards her and grasped her hand in his. 'Viktoria…' There was recognition in his eyes, but nothing more.

'Peter…' It was odd to say his name again, but even more extraordinary that it meant nothing. The eyes that looked at her so agreeably, the mouth that smiled so blandly — they belonged to a stranger. Peter no longer had the power to move her, no longer any power to hurt her. As Benno said, their affair had been a long, long time ago…

'You remember my wife, Ilse?' Peter asked.

As if she could ever forget her! But now Viktoria met her again, she could feel no enmity towards her. Shorter than Viktoria, Ilse von Biederstein was neatly and expensively dressed in a tailored frock and jacket. She was, Viktoria thought, rather like a china doll, with a clear, peaches-and-cream complexion and enormous blue eyes, that seemed to look out on the world with the innocence of a child.

'And what do you think of my lovely daughter?' Peter asked, putting his arm proudly round her shoulders. 'Christa, this is Frau Jochum-Kraus.'

The twelve-year-old girl bobbed a curtsy. She had inherited her mother's looks, with blonde hair and bluer-than-blue eyes in a round face, as different from her father and, Viktoria thought fleetingly, from her half-brother Stefan, as it was possible for her to be. 'How nice to meet you, Christa,' she said politely.

'You have a son, don't you?' Ilse asked. 'He came to our wedding. Such a sweet little boy, I remember.'

Viktoria held her breath. Any minute now the dreaded meeting would take place.

'Not so sweet and not so little anymore,' Benno laughed. 'Stefan is just about to start at university. Peter, good to see you again. Ilse, you're even prettier than I remembered! And this must be Christa. Stefan, Monika, come over here and meet your Uncle Peter.'

Despite all her fears, Viktoria felt very proud of her son as he walked towards them with quiet self-confidence, bowing stiffly to

Peter, kissing Ilse's hand graciously and correctly acknowledging Christa's little bob.

'You've certainly changed since I last saw you,' Ilse smiled. 'You must have been four or five then. Do you remember asking me to come to your hotel?'

Stefan's cheeks reddened. 'I do remember actually. Countess von Biederstein, if you will permit me to say so, you had such a lovely smile. And you still do.'

Ilse's laughter tinkled through the room. 'What a gallant thing to say. Viktoria, I congratulate you on your charming son.'

Peter walked away in the direction of the Baron. It was clear he had no interest whatsoever in Viktoria's son.

A few moments later, as Benno was conducting his cousin, Ilse and Christa up to their suite, Mortimer Allen again materialized at Viktoria's side. 'I always knew young Stefan reminded me of someone and now I know who. He's the spitting image of Count Peter!'

Fear gripping her heart, Viktoria turned to face him. 'They are related,' she said slowly.

He grinned. 'Hey, cheer up. If poor old Stefan took after the Krauses, he'd really have problems! Whatever else one may think of Count Peter, at least he's a good-looking bounder.'

They took luncheon in one of the private banqueting rooms. Baron Heinrich sat at the head of the table and Peter at the foot, Stefan next to Ilse, Benno between Christa and Trudi, Monika with Norbert, Ricarda alongside Countess Julia, Viktoria between Ernst and Werner.

Soon, several conversations had struck up. Stefan was telling Ilse about his plans to go to Oxford and discovering with delight that they had an acquaintance in common in the form of Mortimer Allen. Benno was trying to draw out a rather shy Christa. Trudi was informing Ernst how they would reorganize the Fortress. Julia and Ricarda were chatting about their youth. Monika seemed surprisingly interested in Norbert.

Over and above everyone else, the Baron was shouting down the table to Peter. 'Young man, I'll tell you now that Hitler's the best thing to happen since we lost the monarchy.'

Peter fingered his moustache. 'I haven't had the opportunity to form a personal opinion yet, not having met Herr Hitler, but I must admit to reservations. To begin with, he's just some sort of Austrian peasant, and only a corporal when he saw service during the war.'

'How do the English feel about him?' The Baron shovelled a huge forkful of pork cutlet and potato into his mouth, dribbling gravy down the napkin at his neck.

'There is a general feeling of conciliation and also a desire to see the country returned to stability,' Peter replied, his voice carrying effortlessly. 'Interestingly, British public opinion also seems to be in favour of German rearmament. Most people recognize that we were dealt with unfairly in the Versailles Treaty and that it is time to redress inequalities.'

'Whatever they think, Hitler won't pay any attention to them!' the Baron declared.

Viktoria heard the rise and fall of their voices, but the words scarcely registered. She only knew that Peter was not interested in Stefan, nor Stefan in him, and, for the first time since she had learned of Peter's return, she began to relax.

Amazingly, the rest of the day passed much more easily than the previous one. Left to their own devices, the young people seemed to get on quite well together; the men talked business and military matters; and the women discussed more domestic affairs. To her surprise, Viktoria discovered Ilse to be a remarkably down-to-earth person. Were it not for Peter, she could even imagine becoming friends with her.

Over dinner, Peter informed them, 'We'll stay at the Quadriga while we look for a house. Ilse rather fancies a place in Dahlem.'

'You won't have any difficulty finding somewhere,' the Baron said. 'A lot of Jews are leaving Berlin. The villa next door to mine is up for rent. Though I doubt the owner will ever return.'

'You are welcome to stay here for as long as you like,' Benno assured Peter politely.

When they went up to the apartment later, Benno said, 'Christa seems a nice little thing. Did you talk to her at all, Stefi?'

'Not really,' Stefan admitted. 'I didn't know what to say. I mean, she's a girl and she's younger than Monika.'

Viktoria could not care less about Christa. Her heart was singing. Peter and Stefan felt no natural blood ties. Her last fears had been allayed.

Benno saw the triumphant look on her face and knew his worst fears had just been confirmed, for now that he had seen Stefan and Peter together, he was totally convinced that his cousin was the boy's real father. There were certain telltale similarities discernible only to the most sensitive eye: the manner in which they both inflected their upper lip, something Benno could not do; the way their little fingers were arched, a characteristic of Julia, Peter and now Stefan — but not Benno.

This final proof in no way lessened the very deep love he felt for Stefan, because after bringing the boy up for eighteen years as his son, he felt the emotional right to be his father. Neither, strangely, did he feel any strong animosity towards Peter, for he was now sure that brief love affair in the long-ago summer of 1914 had meant little to him. What grieved him was that Viktoria still could not bring herself to tell him the truth.

Benno was not a demonstrative person, but more times than he could recall, he had told Viktoria that he loved her. Never once did he remember her replying, 'I love you, Benno.' Did that imply that he should take her love for granted — or did it mean that she had never loved him? Had she only married him to give her unborn child a father? Was their entire marriage based upon a lie?

Ernst and his family returned to Essen. Countess Julia joined her husband in Grunewald. Ricarda went back to Heiligensee. Only the Biedersteins remained at the Quadriga, but their daily presence was less disturbing than either Viktoria or Benno had feared, for Ilse and Christa were busy house-hunting, and Peter's days were spent at the Reichswehr Ministry in the Bendlerstrasse.

The evenings, however, were rather different. Although the Biedersteins were occasionally invited out to dine, as Peter renewed old acquaintances and made new ones among his military colleagues, on the whole their evenings were unoccupied and common courtesy demanded that Benno invited them to join the family for aperitifs and dinner. Peter assumed an autocratic role, seating himself at the head of the table and treating them to long monologues on his experiences abroad or, more frequently, on the future of the Reichswehr.

Time after time, as she listened to his clipped speech and watched his arrogant features, Viktoria wondered how she could ever have thought herself to be in love with him, and could only console herself with the thought that she had been very young and naive.

Benno, too, found these evenings extremely provoking and could not help hoping the Biedersteins would very quickly find somewhere of their own to live. It was bad enough that his cousin had once seduced Viktoria, but that he should now treat Benno as some kind of social inferior in his own home was infuriating. However, he was wise enough not to show his annoyance.

For all that they tried to appear natural, something of his parents' tenseness transmitted itself to Stefan and he knew it had to do with Count Peter. This did not surprise him. He liked Ilse and considered Christa a pretty little girl, but there was something about the Colonel that he found repugnant. It was a purely instinctive feeling and one he could not have started to describe. Perhaps it was his haughty manner, a legacy of his family's impressive aristocratic and military tradition, but that did not fully explain it. Stefan only knew that whereas he could call the Countess 'Aunt Ilse', he would never be able to bring himself to say 'Uncle Peter' to her husband.

So far as his parents were concerned, this sign of human weakness was rather reassuring. Until then, he had always regarded them as infallible, the secure and unquestionable bedrock of his existence, as solid as the concrete foundations of the Hotel Quadriga itself. Now, suddenly, he saw them as ordinary human beings, subject to the same doubts and weaknesses as himself. Far from shocking him, it made him love them even more.

To the relief of all of them, Ilse quickly found a house, an elegant villa in the Park-Strasse in Schmargendorf, set back from the road amidst well-tended gardens, surrounded by high, protective hedges and not far from an excellent girls' grammar school for Christa. It belonged, the house agent told her, to a Jewish merchant, who was prepared to let it on a long lease. Since it was fully furnished and in immaculate condition, the Biedersteins could move in straightaway.

Pastor Scheer had not been very concerned about the suppression of the Communist and Socialist Parties, or even the trade unions, whose influence, in his opinion, had indeed been subversive. Neither had he been particularly worried by the anti-Semitic legislation. After all, Jews were a race and religion apart. He had even convinced himself that the brutality of the stormtroopers was a necessary adjunct to keeping law and order.

It was when Hitler turned his attentions towards the Lutheran Church that the Pastor's eyes were finally opened. In July, Chaplain Müller's German Christians' Faith Movement had been approved by the Reichstag as the official Reich Church and, with Hitler's public approval, the Chaplain was standing for election as Reich Bishop.

Suddenly, Pastor Scheer realized that, if Chaplain Müller were elected Reich Bishop, the position would place him in absolute power over some forty-five million Protestants and their spiritual leaders and, since the Chaplain had never tried to conceal that his first loyalty was to Hitler, this meant that the Lutheran Church would be Nazified and under the total domination of the State.

Just as the federal states had been abolished and central government established, so now the Church stood in grave danger of losing not only its independent identity, but its authority, and this, Pastor Scheer now saw, with a sickening feeling of despair, was what Hitler had always intended. And, even worse, if that happened, it would be because of the blindness and stupidity of men like himself, who had so fervently preached the Nazi gospel from the pulpit.

He was not the only one to realize this. The leaders of the Church Federation put forward their own candidate for the position of Reich Bishop, a pastor of irreproachable moral rectitude, with no political leanings, a far more suitable head of a Reich Church than Chaplain

Müller. But by now, Pastor Scheer was totally opposed to the very concept of a Reich Church.

As the election day approached, the pressure started, gently enough to begin with, in the form of a visit from his diocesan bishop seeking confirmation that Pastor Scheer supported Chaplain Müller. When he refused to give such an assurance, life became decidedly unpleasant.

Klara was abused when she went shopping. Swastikas were painted on tombstones and on the church doors. Anonymous letters were sent to many of his congregation, claiming that he was practising black magic. On the Sunday before the election in September, a gang of brownshirts gathered outside the church doors, shouting slogans and haranguing the few worshippers who dared to turn up for morning service.

When, trying to conceal his fear, Pastor Scheer strode up the path, they pelted him with rotten eggs and fruit. Throughout the service, they sang bawdy songs, laughing and cracking obscene jokes. One by one, his congregation slipped away, the stormtroopers cheering each one as they left. When only Klara remained, the thugs departed too, with a final resounding threat: Vote for Müller or we'll burn this place down!

'We shall now sing the hymn,' Pastor Scheer said in a shaking voice.

There was no organist, so Klara's sweet soprano led them both, ringing through the empty church:

'A safe stronghold our God is still,

A trusty shield and weapon;

He'll help us clear from all the ill

That hath us now o'ertaken…'

Then, in a most unwonted gesture, Pastor Scheer prostrated himself before the altar, beseeching God to give him courage to do what was right. But the figure of Christ on the cross stared bleakly down at him and God did not say a word.

It was an all too familiar scene that Bethel Ascher saw enacted that Sunday morning in Schmargendorf — the stormtroopers, the frightened people scurrying away to the security of their homes —

except that it was taking place at the church of Pastor Scheer.

He stood in the shade of a huge yew tree and listened to the faint sound of singing emanating from inside: Martin Luther's hymn, *Ein feste Burg...* He watched the Pastor's wife emerge from the building, her head held proudly high — not a woman who would be easily intimidated, the Professor thought, and instinctively he liked her.

She was eventually followed by the Pastor, his face pale, his hands clasped tightly over his cassock. The Professor approached him, his hand outstretched. 'Herr Pastor, my name is Bethel Ascher. May I speak with you?'

Pastor Scheer studied him with a puzzled expression, then said, 'Of course, I remember hearing of you from the Linkes.'

Bethel preferred not to remember the Linkes.

'Will you come over to my house, Herr Professor? I expect my wife will be making some coffee.' Pastor Scheer looked round the churchyard. 'She's rather shaken. We had some — er — unpleasantness here, this morning.'

The Professor suspected the Pastor was rather more shaken than his wife. 'I saw. It was the reason for my approaching you.'

Pastor Scheer glanced at him sharply. 'Yes, how foolish of me. As a Jew you must have experienced quite a lot of that kind of thing, but for us, it has come as a great shock.'

The two men crossed the road and walked towards the parsonage. The front door immediately opened and Klara Scheer hurried anxiously towards them. 'Bernhard, are you all right?'

'Certainly, my dear. This is Professor Ascher.'

She clasped his hand warmly in hers. 'Professor Ascher! You can't know how pleased I am to meet you at last. You have been very much in my thoughts and in my prayers. Do come in.'

They sat down at a freshly scrubbed pine table in the kitchen and, while Klara bustled around making coffee, laying cups and saucers and slicing a golden, crusted apple tart, Professor Ascher asked, 'Herr Pastor, may I ask you if the stormtroopers sought you out today because you are opposed to a Reich Church?'

'I am opposed to Chaplain Müller being made Reich Bishop, that is true. As for a Reich Church…' He shook his head. 'I admit, I do not know what to do.'

Klara poured strong black coffee and placed a thick wedge of apple tart in front of Bethel. 'Cream, Herr Professor?'

'Thank you.' He smiled at her.

'For months, I have been preaching to an overflowing church,' Pastor Scheer continued. 'Now, suddenly, the pews are empty except for a few, faithful souls. I am already in disfavour with my bishop and, if I argue on what really amounts to a point of political, rather than theological dogma, I run the risk of losing my parsonage, or even worse…' He shuddered. 'The concentration camps are filled with Hitler's political opponents. Who is to say dissenting clergy will not go the same route? Such a thing would not be unknown in the history of religion. I have my family to consider. What should I do?'

'Maybe you should think less about Martin Luther and more about God's will,' Bethel suggested drily.

Klara Scheer looked at him quizzically. 'Herr Professor, you are a Jew. Why should you concern yourself with the Lutheran Church?'

He bowed his head. 'Jew and Gentile, we are all God's people.'

The Pastor was silent for a long time, then he replied heavily, 'My heart tells me that Hitler is an Antichrist, that his followers are pagans and that I should do everything in my power to save the souls of my parishioners from a great and destructive evil. But who will listen to me now?'

'Jesus went out and looked for disciples, I believe.'

'And Jesus was hung on a cross,' Pastor Scheer replied.

Klara Scheer touched his hand. 'Bernhard,' she said gently, 'do you need a Jew to tell you your Christian duty?'

Her husband stared at her, shock apparent in his eyes.

Then, slowly, he nodded. 'You are both right. Christ was not afraid, so neither should I be. And you, Klara, are you prepared for all that may happen to us?'

'We were put on this earth to do a task,' she replied simply.

Pastor Scheer stood up, went over to a cupboard and produced a bottle of schnapps. 'Herr Professor, a little Slivovitz to go in your coffee? And I trust you will stay to lunch with us.'

Bethel accepted with alacrity. There was nothing in his empty house in Dahlem to call him home.

The Church Federation was forced to withdraw their candidate and Chaplain Müller was duly appointed Reich Bishop. For several days after the election, the stormtroopers continued to make their presence felt in Schmargendorf and Klara Scheer was the only worshipper at her husband's church. Then the stormtroopers found other targets and the intimidation stopped.

There were some twenty people in the congregation the Sunday Mortimer and Stefan went to church in Schmargendorf. Their minister took as his text the first verse of the first chapter of the Gospel according to St John. '"In the beginning was the Word, and the Word was with God, and the Word was God."' He paused, then continued. 'My friends, I admit to you that I was almost in danger of losing sight of that truth, but God came to me in my hour of need and showed me the path that I must travel, that we all must travel if we are to find salvation.' He spoke for a long time, and they listened with rapt attention. He finished his sermon with the sober assurance, 'The Word of God is greater than that of any man.'

His message was clear. Pastor Scheer had declared himself against the Reich Church and against the Nazis. When the service was ended, Mortimer and Stefan joined Professor Ascher waiting outside the church and were introduced to the Pastor and his wife. Their small resistance movement was growing.

Peter von Biederstein paid little attention to the controversial sermons of Pastor Scheer and the schisms threatening to divide the Lutheran Church. Had he been living at his ancestral home in Fürstenmark, he and his family would naturally have attended church every Sunday, but in Schmargendorf there was no need to set an example.

They were happy in their new home. Ilse had already made several friends in the area, mostly officers' wives, and her days were a constant round of coffee mornings, ladies' luncheons and charity meetings. Christa was settling in well at her new school and seemed to be rather ahead of her class in most subjects. For Peter himself, prospects had never been so good.

The Baron's suggestion that he request a transfer to Germany could not have been better timed. Although under the terms of the Versailles Treaty the Army General Staff, the War Academy and all officer cadet schools had been abolished, the army had never accepted defeat. Before the ink had dried on the papers the international statesmen had signed that fateful June day in 1919, the officer corps had been planning a new Reichswehr, finer, stronger and eventually more powerful than even the Kaiser's Army.

Although so far as the Allies were concerned, the army still consisted of one hundred thousand men and four thousand officers, in reality it was considerably larger and, as Peter knew from his diplomatic experience in London, it was an easy matter to give simplified figures to his opposite numbers in other foreign embassies and in the British Army.

The Reichswehr Minister, General von Blomberg, made no secret of his support of Nazi policies, at least so far as the expansion of the armed forces and the overthrow of the Versailles Treaty were concerned. Although Peter held the view that the army should not ally itself to any political party, and he still had distinct reservations about Hitler as a man, he was already starting to go along with Blomberg.

On 1 October, Peter received gratifying news. He was promoted to full Colonel, and his commanding officer, the choleric Bavarian General Adam, was replaced as head of the Troop Office by General Ludwig Beck. In Peter's mind, the appointment was excellent news.

Twelve years Peter's senior at fifty-three, General Beck had an untarnished reputation. A soldier of the old school, Beck possessed a fine knowledge of military history and held a shrewd, even opportunist, view of the future. Although he, like Peter, believed that the armed forces should stand above politics, there were aspects of Nazi government which he welcomed. He was in favour of rearmament and he hated communism. From the very first, he made it clear to his staff that he would not support another war, except if Germany found herself in danger from the Soviet Union.

That weekend, the Biedersteins dined with Baron Heinrich and Countess Julia at Grunewald. When the ladies had left them, the Baron remarked, 'Things seem to be working out very satisfactorily, don't you think? Blomberg and Beck are sound men and they're bringing in new, forward-looking officers under them.'

Carefully, Peter cut the end off his cigar and lit it. 'Only one thing worries me and that is the SA. I can see a situation arising when Captain Röhm is going to demand a major role for his stormtroopers, not just in internal security but in national defence. It's the Free Corps all over again — veteran revolutionary activists, in command of thousands of badly-trained men. If something isn't done to contain and control them, we could find ourselves in real danger.'

His uncle shook his head. 'I don't think so. The SA has helped get Hitler into power and it forms a useful reserve army, but it will never challenge the Reichswehr.'

Peter exhaled smoke from his cigar, wishing he could feel so certain. The Baron's next words, however, banished all thoughts of the SA from his mind.

'Have you heard that Kesselring has been discharged from the Army and appointed Head of Department of the new *Luftfahrt* Commissariat?'

'I didn't know Kesselring had any experience of flying.'

'He has the Ministry experience necessary to create a new air force, which is what the *Luftfahrt* Commissariat is. Under cover of it, we are going to build an air force, a Luftwaffe.'

Peter absorbed this piece of news in silence. Then he asked, 'Why not put it under control of the Army?'

'Göring has other ideas. He would prefer that it is separate. And, for the moment, rather than raise the suspicions of the Allies, it should be a civilian body.'

'Yes, I see. But what about pilots? Who's going to train them? Nearly all our airmen were killed in the war. Luft-Hansa pilots only have civil flying experience. Kesselring can't fly. Neither can Erhard

Milch, although he is Chief Executive of Luft-Hansa. Göring can, but he's hardly in a position to train new airmen.'

'Do you remember Sepp Nowak?' Baron Heinrich asked. 'Flew with Richthofen, Göring and Ernst Udet? He worked for Kraus Aviation for a couple of years after the war until he got bored and went to California. I've recently succeeded in tracking him down in Kenya. Göring's got in touch with him. I'm pretty certain he'll come back.'

Peter had never met Sepp Nowak, but he remembered his spectacular war record of over sixty victories, for which he had been awarded the *Pour le Mérite*. 'That's the sort of man we need to train a new air force,' he agreed.

That same day, in the Kenyan bush, a dusty Dodge car was bumping over the rough ground to the hangar where Sepp Nowak kept the old biplane in which he flew rich hunters on safari. The driver parked next to Sepp's vehicle, then shouted, 'Sepp! Cable from Berlin! Thought it might be urgent, so I brought it out personally.'

Sepp emerged from the hangar, wiping his oily hands on a piece of rag. A lean man, his face was leathery and burned a dark brown by the African sun. He grinned when he saw the driver and took the envelope. 'Berlin? What the devil...?' He slit it open and read the contents.

Then he gazed out across the open countryside towards the peak of Mount Kilimanjaro shimmering in the heat and thought of two demobbed airmen one rainy November evening in 1918. He heard his voice ask Hermann Göring, 'What are you going to do now?'

'Keep on flying and see this lot to hell,' Göring had replied. 'And you?'

'I've got to find another flying job. The only life for me is in the air.'

Göring had held out his hand. 'If I hear of anything, I'll let you know.'

Sepp looked again at the telegram. 'Found you job as promised. Return Berlin immediately. Minister of Aviation Göring.'

'Not bad news?' the driver asked.

'No, not bad news,' Sepp replied slowly, lighting a cigarette. 'Got time for a beer?'

'Sure.' The driver ran a finger along the biplane's immaculate paintwork and traced the letters painted along her fuselage. 'Unusual sort of name,' he commented. 'Why did you name her *Luise*?'

'Usual reason,' Sepp replied. 'I once knew a girl called Luise.'

'She didn't live in Berlin by any chance?'

'As a matter of fact, she did.'

As Sepp disappeared into the house to fetch the beer, he thought back to his first meeting with Luise Jochum on a train from Nuremberg to Berlin, twenty years ago, just before the war. He could not recall the exact circumstances, but he did remember that his brother Rudi had struck up the conversation with the two young ladies already sitting in the compartment.

Sepp himself had been in army uniform and Luise, little more than a child, had asked, 'Are you in the cavalry?'

'No, I was in the artillery, but now I'm learning to fly.'

'Sepp's going to fly fighter aeroplanes,' Rudi had explained.

'Oh,' Luise had sighed wistfully. 'I'd like to fly in an aeroplane.' She turned to Sepp. 'Would you take me for a flight in one?'

And Sepp had smiled at her, finding her huge green eyes and heart-shaped face oddly appealing. 'Perhaps, one day.'

After the war, he had returned to Berlin and met Luise again, no longer a child, but a very attractive young woman. Although he could not really afford a wife, he had proposed to her and, laughingly, she had turned him down. Later, he had discovered she had already slept with Rudi. Disillusioned with both her and Berlin, Sepp had gone to California. Now, he saw how naive he had been. In the intervening twelve years, he had never forgotten Luise. There was still only one woman for him.

Long after he and the driver had drunk their beers, he remained squatted on his haunches against the hangar wall. His had been an exciting life, full of adventure, answerable to no one. But he was forty-one — soon he would be too old for the nomadic existence. Why not go to Berlin, see Göring and find out what it was all about? And while he was there, call at the Hotel Quadriga and discover what had become of Luise. If she was settled down with a husband and four squalling brats, he would come back to Kenya. If not, there were worse places in the world than Berlin…

The following morning, he drove into Nairobi, cabled Göring to expect his arrival, told the tourist office that he would not be available for any more safaris and informed the air authorities that he would be flying *Luise* up to Europe. Then he loaded his truck with petrol and supplies and drove back through the bush.

All day and for much of the night, he made his preparations for the long journey, giving the biplane a thorough overhaul. When he was satisfied, he patted her undercarriage with a mounting feeling of excitement. '*Luise*, old love, we're going home.' They left the next day, flying north towards Addis Ababa. It was good to be up in the air again, with the wind in the struts and nothing but the birds for company. And soon, they had left even the birds behind.

At Heiligensee, the leaves fell onto lawns carpeted with early morning frost. Copper, russet and gold, they vied with the colours in Luise's hair, as she walked through the garden for the last time that year. Sheltie raced exuberantly ahead of her, tracking scents, scuffling, barking, tossing leaves into the thin sunshine. On the edge of the water there was a fine rime of ice. Soon the fishing boats would no longer be able to go out and there would be skaters on the lake. Luise shivered and turned back towards the cottage.

Along the entire length of the glass verandah and across all the windows, Fritzi Weber had put up the shutters. A blue spiral of smoke still issued from the cottage chimney, but before the day was over it would have been extinguished. Winter was coming. It was time to return to Berlin.

Luise's car, lovingly cleaned and polished by Fritzi for the journey, stood in the courtyard, and into it, under Hilde and Ricarda's supervision, Fritzi was loading their luggage.

'Ready, darling?' Ricarda asked.

Luise smiled ruefully. 'As ready as I shall ever be. The summer seems to have gone so quickly.' She linked her arm through her mother's. 'I've been happy here.'

'We'll come back again next spring.'

'Yes, of course.'

Leaving Ricarda to say her goodbyes, Luise bundled Sheltie into the back seat of her car and started the engine. When Ricarda got in, she drove away without looking back. Physically, Heiligensee had effected its cure. Her skin was tanned and clear; she had regained her appetite and put on a little weight. But mentally, nothing had changed. As they drove through the dappled sunlight of the Tegel Forest towards Berlin, Luise saw only a dark void looming ahead of her. They were going home — but to Luise home was an empty word.

Sepp landed at Tempelhof to what was virtually a hero's welcome, as pilots and mechanics hurried out across the airfield to greet 'Uncle Sepp', who had flown single-handedly all the way from deepest Africa. Reverently, young boys touched *Luise*'s airframe, gazing adoringly at Sepp from big eyes. The pilots, mere boys most of them so far as Sepp could see, shook his hand deferentially. They did not know the man, but his legend had gone before him.

There was no shortage of volunteers to take care of *Luise*. As she was led away to a hangar, Sepp was dragged off towards the airport bar to relate his experiences. His goggles pushed up over his leather flying cap, his scarf still round his neck, he sat on a bar stool and, a beer in one hand and a cigarette in the other, he told them about flying. He talked about triplanes and biplanes, about loops and turns and sideslips and rolls, about forced landings in the middle of deserts and air pockets in mountains, of the time his plane was shot at by bandits outside Buenos Aires and the occasion he flew so low in Kenya he almost hit a giraffe.

He would have talked, and his admiring audience would have listened all night, if an airport official had not come with the message that General Göring had sent a car to take him immediately to the Palace of the Reichstag President. Would Captain Nowak care to wash and change before he went to see the General? Facilities were available…

There was a respectful hush at this and, suddenly, Sepp realized that his old friend had, indeed, become a very important man since they had last met. He glanced down at his leather flying jacket and boots. 'No, thanks. I'll go as I am. Hermann was a flier once. Let's see what he is now.'

Armed sentries guarded the doors to the Reichstag President's Palace and uniformed men accompanied him up to Göring's rooms. An aide led him into Göring's presence. There, Sepp stood stock still in shocked astonishment. Five feet nine, the same height as Sepp, and only one year younger, Göring had become positively gross. Sepp had to fight back an inclination to laugh as Göring waddled towards him, wearing the full dress uniform of an infantry general, complete with a chest full of medals. Sepp understood now why the men at Tempelhof had looked so askance at the thought of him going to the Reichstag President's Palace in his flying kit.

But Göring greeted him effusively. 'Sepp, dear boy, so good of you to come. Have a drink?' He rang a bell and the aide reappeared. 'Still an Asbach drinker?'

Sepp nodded. The last time he had drunk Asbach brandy was twelve years ago in Berlin. 'Pretty impressive place you've got here,' he commented, when they were settled with their drinks.

Göring beamed. 'What do you think of this room?'

Sepp looked round him. It was a large room, hideously decorated with pink roses in bas-relief. 'Dreadful,' he said, cheerfully.

There was silence, then Göring threw back his head and laughed. 'Sepp Nowak, welcome back to Berlin. You're the first honest man I've met for months. Everyone else assures me it's beautiful. Well, I shall shortly be moving out of here into the official residence of the Prussian Minister of Commerce behind the Leipziger Platz. An architect called Speer is going to redecorate it for me.'

For want of anything to say, Sepp lit a cigarette.

'It will provide a splendid gallery for my paintings,' Göring continued blandly. 'You know I collect works of art? It's a relaxing hobby. In my position, one needs to relax as much as possible.'

He went on to explain, at great length, what his position was, describing his duties as Premier of Prussia, as head of the Berlin SA and the Gestapo, and hinting at difficulties with Heinrich Himmler and Captain Röhm.

Chain-smoking one cigarette after another, Sepp listened to him, marvelling at the political deviousness of his mind, but feeling no envy at the power his old comrade now exercised.

Eventually, Göring came to the point. 'The Aviation Commissariat is the first step towards building the Luftwaffe, the greatest air force in Europe. Junkers, Messerschmitt, Kraus and other factories are already beginning production of aircraft. An Air Ministry is being built. But to have an air force, we need trained pilots. Over the years, a certain number have been trained in Russia, but not enough, Sepp, not nearly enough. That's why I asked you back, to train the pilots of our new Luftwaffe.'

'And Versailles?' Sepp asked.

Göring smiled confidently. 'By the time we announce the existence of the Luftwaffe to the world, there won't be a damned thing anyone can do about it.'

Sepp grinned. International treaties meant nothing to him. So long as he could go on flying, he was content to leave the making of them to statesmen and the breaking of them to politicians.

'I hear you flew up here in an old biplane,' Göring sighed reminiscently. 'Those were real aeroplanes, weren't they? Not black boxes like the things they're making now, where the pilot's seated inside. A flier needs to feel the air on his face and hear the wind in the struts to know the speed he's travelling. You can't do that in a Ju 52.'

'I hear they have equipment...'

'New-fangled technology. It will never work! Sepp, we are going to train a new generation of fliers and I want them trained in the same way you and I were — in an open cockpit. Milch and Kesselring will disagree. Messerschmitt, Heinkel and Kraus will try to tell me I'm wrong. But you and I know what it's like.'

Sepp nodded. It was the only kind of flying he knew. For a while they sat and talked about the old days, about Baron von Richthofen and Ernst Udet. 'I keep trying to persuade Udet to come back from America and join us,' Göring said, 'but he won't.'

'Udet's like myself,' Sepp said. 'It's flying and aeroplanes that he cares about, not the political intrigues that are bound to go on while a new air force is being created.'

Göring looked grim. 'I won't tolerate any interference. You'd report directly to me, Sepp. Any nonsense from Milch or Kesselring, you'd let me know. Now, where are you staying tonight?'

Sepp looked at his watch. It was eight o'clock but it felt like midnight. Suddenly the long day had caught up with him. 'Probably sleep in the plane. Won't be the first time.'

'Nonsense, dear boy. My aide will book you in at the Quadriga. Stay there until you find a place of your own. We shall pay your expenses, of course.'

Sepp lit another cigarette. He was going to the Quadriga anyway. Why not at Hermann's expense? 'All right. For tonight anyway.'

Göring rang the bell and instructed his aide to advise the hotel of Sepp's arrival and have his luggage taken there from the airport. When the man had gone, he gazed at Sepp like a small boy who suddenly recognizes the possibility that he may not get his own way. 'You will stay and help me, won't you?' he pleaded.

Sepp realized that the bombast and medals hid an innate sense of insecurity. 'I'll let you know tomorrow,' he promised. There was someone else he had to see before he made any commitment.

He was not the sort of guest one was accustomed to see in the elegant foyer of the Hotel Quadriga. Indeed, under normal circumstances, the Hall Porter would have discreetly intercepted him. On this occasion, however, since his reservation had been made by General Göring, the Hall Porter bowed obsequiously, as the man in the worn leather flying jacket and boots walked through the revolving doors. A page boy reverently led him towards the reception desk. Another begged to be allowed to carry his helmet and goggles. Herr Fromm hurried towards him.

Descending the main staircase to take Sheltie for her evening walk up Unter den Linden, Luise glanced down at the unusual figure. Why so much commotion about an airman? What was an airman doing in the foyer anyway? Then he looked up and she let out a small cry. His skin was deeply tanned, but he had the same laughing, slightly slanting eyes, the same curly hair, the same wide mouth… 'Sepp!'

Sheltie, impatient for her walk, tugged at the lead, pulling her down the stairs.

Sepp spun on his heel. 'Luise!' He held out his arms.

Sheltie barked and together they skidded across the marble floor towards him. Then Luise let go Sheltie's lead and fell into Sepp's embrace, laughing and crying simultaneously.

Her plumed tail wagging, Sheltie jumped round them, barking with almost hysterical delight, evading every effort on the part of Herr Fromm and various page boys to catch her. Guests passing through the foyer stopped to watch and several laughed. Others, not recognizing Luise or her dog, demanded to know what was going on.

Knowing how angry Benno became if the dog made any sound in the hotel, Viktoria hurried out of her office to find out what was wrong.

Sitting with Stefan in the bar, Mortimer Allen heard the noise. 'Sounds like Sheltie…'

Sepp put his arm round Luise's shoulder. 'Let's get out of here. Come for a walk.'

She rested her head against his shoulder, feeling the soft leather give against her cheek. 'Sepp, I can't believe you're real. I didn't think I would ever see you again.'

'Captain Nowak, Captain Nowak…' Herr Fromm wailed.

They ignored him and walked towards the doors, followed by Sheltie, dancing round in circles, tripping over her lead in her frenzied excitement. 'Sheltie, heel!' Mortimer called. She had been well-trained. Reluctantly, she obeyed. Mortimer grabbed her lead. 'Sheltie, you're only a pup. One day, you'll understand that sometimes three are a crowd.'

'What's happened to Luise?' Viktoria demanded.

'If I'm not mistaken,' he said slowly, 'I think she's finally found someone to make her laugh.'

It was so wonderful to see Sepp again, to wander with him, his arm round her shoulder, under the dark trees in the Tiergarten . He told Luise of his travels, of the danger and excitement of life on five continents, and about the aircraft he had flown, including the one he called *Luise*. He told her about Göring's telegram and his meeting that day in the Reichstag President's Palace. And somewhere during his tale, he slipped in the fact that he had never married.

Luise listened to him talk, but did not hear all the words. Like her, Sepp had never married…

They came to a seat and he drew her down on it. 'I've missed you, Luischen.'

She buried her face in his chest and began to cry, softly at first, then with growing wildness.

'Luise, darling, what's the matter?'

Eventually her tears subsided and she lifted a ravaged face to his. 'I'm sorry,' she gulped.

He reached in his pocket for his cigarettes and lit two. 'Why don't you tell me about it?'

She took the cigarette, inhaling on it gratefully. And then, in incoherent disjointed phrases, she described how, after he had left Berlin, she had built the new Café Jochum, discovered Georg's amazing musical talent and of how they had fallen in love. And then Georg had gone to America. She explained how the stormtroopers had frightened all her friends from Berlin. 'They disappeared, as if into thin air. And now Café Jochum's gone…'

'But I've come back.'

'Sepp, I had a kind of nervous breakdown. Mama took me to Heiligensee for the summer, but now I'm in Berlin again, I realize that nothing's changed. I'm a mess. You don't need me in your life.'

Sepp took the cigarette from her fingers and threw it on the ground. Then he cupped her face in his hands. 'Luise, why don't you let me decide that?' he asked softly. 'And, in the meantime, you and I are two lonely people in an alien city. We were friends once. Why shouldn't we be friends again?'

It was strange, the touch of his hands on her face, strange and rather wonderful. 'You really want me for your friend? After all you know about me?'

'Yes, Luischen, more than anything in the world.'

'Sepp, I've been so afraid…'

'But not anymore. I'll take care of you now.'

She smiled and the smile lit up her face. He took her in his arms and kissed her. It was a long kiss, very gentle, very tender, that stirred up strange and almost forgotten yearnings in her. When they drew apart, she whispered, 'Promise you'll never go away again.'

Poor little Luise, he thought, so fragile and vulnerable, so different from the vivacious butterfly he had once known. She made him feel curiously protective towards her and he knew he must make her no false promises. 'Never is a long time,' he said lightly, taking her hand. 'Now stop being so serious. Let's go back to the hotel and get a drink. It's freezing in this park.'

As they walked back towards the Brandenburg Gate, Luise actually found herself humming. It was almost as if with her tears and the kiss, a curtain had fallen over the past and it had lost its power to hurt her. Sepp had not forgotten her. He had called his plane after her. And, even more importantly, he had returned. She squeezed his hand. 'It's so wonderful to have you back again.'

He kissed the top of her head. 'It's good to be back,' he replied, but his thoughts were racing ahead to his meeting with Göring the next morning, and to the weeks and months that would follow, when he taught the young Germans of today how to become the fighter aces of tomorrow.

Unwilling to be beholden to anyone, Sepp did not remain long at the Hotel Quadriga, but found himself a furnished, fourth floor apartment in the central district of Lützow. While he was at work, Luise took pleasure in transforming it from a bachelor flat into a home, and was often still there in the evening with a meal waiting for him. 'Now Sepp's back, it's like the old days,' she told Sheltie.

Sheltie barked joyously. She knew nothing about the old days. She only knew that her mistress was happy.

Within days, Sepp had achieved what Ricarda, Sheltie and Heiligensee had failed to accomplish. Luise changed from a thin, nervous shadow of her former self into a confident young woman. No longer did she lie in bed in the mornings, but was up with the lark, taking an interest in her clothes, her hair and her make-up. Her laughter echoed contagiously through the hotel.

'It's like an answer to a prayer,' Ricarda said.

'Mama,' Viktoria laughed, 'surely you're not hearing wedding bells already?'

Stefan and Monika both adored Sepp and even Benno approved of him. 'I'd be proud to have him as a brother-in-law.'

However, Sepp kissed Luise, but he did not ask her to share his bed. He did not propose and Luise did not push him. They had twelve years to catch up on, twelve years in which they had been strangers, separated by experiences the other had never known. She could not share his passion for flying. He had never known her loneliness. It was sufficient for the moment that they were friends and that her life had a purpose again.

To everyone at the hotel, Sepp gave the same explanation for his return. Aviation was a popular sport in Germany and to encourage the thousands of young enthusiasts who wanted to learn to fly, his old friend Göring — whom he had christened the Fat Man — had asked him to return.

Mortimer knew better. He liked Sepp Nowak as a person. But he also recognized him as a final piece in the jigsaw puzzle.

For Mortimer those days, life in Berlin was like living in a minefield, for Dr Goebbels was flexing his muscles to the full. On 22 September, he had established a Ministry of Culture, with seven chambers responsible for every aspect of the arts. On 4 October, the Press Law was passed, heralding the final end to a free German press. According to it, all newspaper editors had to possess German citizenship and be of Aryan descent, as well as being politically sound. In one fell swoop, the government had rid itself of such venerable Jewish newspaper magnates as the Ullsteins and the Mosses and gained political control of papers such as the *Vossische Zeitung*, the *Berliner Tageblatt* and the *Frankfurter Zeitung*, all renowned for their liberal views.

The law did not stop there. Not only German editors, but foreign correspondents, like Mortimer Allen, had to report to the Propaganda Ministry every morning to receive exact instructions as to what news they might report and how it should be reported.

Regardless of nationality, all journalists working in Germany were subject to censorship.

Now, even the subtle criticisms that Mortimer had slipped into his articles and which had escaped Bill Wallace's eagle eye, had become quite impossible. For the world to find out what was really happening in Germany, he was totally reliant on James Adams at the British Embassy getting his messages to Winston Churchill.

In the middle of October, Hitler announced that a national referendum would take place on 12 November, in which the German people would decide Germany's future by voting for or against the country's withdrawal from the Geneva Disarmament Conference and the League of Nations. Simultaneously, he dissolved the Reichstag and set new elections for the same day, 12 November. The significance of the date — the day following Armistice Day, fifteen years ago — was not lost on Mortimer. Hitler was appealing to German patriotism, and upon the question of Versailles, the entire country had always been united.

He was right. On 12 November, ninety-five per cent of the German population voted its faith in the government and approval for their country's withdrawal from Geneva and the League of Nations. Mortimer was dismayed, but he could not find it in his heart to blame them. They had acted in innocence and good faith. In their minds, the world had refused to take Hitler's ultimatum seriously that it reduce its arms to Germany's level. Now Germany had told the world to go to hell.

Mortimer was one of the few who realized that, whatever the referendum had shown up, Hitler had long since decided to tell the world to go to hell.

CHAPTER FOUR

It was a bitter December day when Olga finally received the travel papers allowing her and Basilius to continue their journey. In a frenzy of excitement, they packed their meagre belongings, said goodbye to their Prague comrades and boarded the crowded, unheated train for Moscow.

Their carriage was full of peasants laden with packages and baskets, many carrying fresh livestock with them, chickens and rabbits. The seats were mere wooden benches. The dirty windows were sealed and a fetid odour permeated the air. But Basili was impervious to his surroundings. He had never experienced any of the luxuries of life and, consequently, he never hankered after them.

He was still short for his age, for his diet had long consisted of hard black bread, watery soup and, occasionally, smoked sausage or ham. His face was pinched and pale. His hands, feet and ears were swollen with chilblains. When the light caught him in a certain way, he looked more like an old man than a boy of fourteen. Only his eyes — clear and grey, like his mother's — betrayed his youth and inner strength. Burning with a fierce intensity of purpose, they looked out uncompromisingly upon the world.

Munich, Berlin, Prague, and now — at last — Moscow. Moscow, Moscow, Moscow — the word echoed in time to the clanking wheels of the train over the rails. Basilius had a mental image of Moscow, of a golden city, the Mecca of the communist world, where all people lived in harmonious brotherhood. He had seen pictures of it, of Red Square and the Kremlin building. With avid attention he had listened to descriptions from comrades who had been there. In his mind's eye, he saw his mother being welcomed by Stalin himself as a heroine of the German Revolution, while huge banners bearing the hammer and sickle waved triumphantly above them.

Every so often during their journey, they were disturbed by officials demanding to see their tickets, passes and travel documents. On other occasions, his mother woke him and he lifted his case down and followed her onto a strange station to wait for the connecting train in a stale, smoky waiting room filled with suspicious-looking strangers. Time lost all meaning. Basilius only knew that the further north they travelled, the colder it got and, once they crossed the border into the USSR, the passengers appeared even poorer and worse dressed than those he had known in Wedding. Moscow, Moscow, Moscow... 'How far is it now?' he asked his mother.

'We're nearly there,' Olga replied, huddled into the shawl she had wrapped round her head and shoulders over her thin grey overcoat. 'Basili, we've nearly reached Moscow!'

But they hadn't. Numb with cold, Basilius stared out of the window at his first sight of the frozen wastes of Russia. Endless open plains, uniformly white, stretched as far as the eye could see, interspersed by occasional villages and trees, almost obliterated by driving snow.

Moscow, Moscow, Moscow... Basilius moved closer to his mother for warmth. From time to time, the train stopped at obscure halts, sometimes for interminable periods and for no apparent reason. Day turned into night and eventually a grey dawn crept up over the bleak white wastelands. They ate the last of their provisions. 'How far is it now?' Basilius asked.

'We're nearly there,' Olga replied confidently. The journey seemed not to have wearied her at all.

Basilius found he needed the comfort of her voice. 'What shall we do when we get there?' he asked, although she had told him their plans so often he knew them by heart.

'They know we're coming, so there may be some kind of reception. Knowing that we'll be tired, they may even have reserved rooms for us in an hotel for our first night.'

'But if the train is very late?'

Olga pulled the envelope containing their papers out of her pocket and extracted a letter from her old friend, Anton Stein, recently arrived in Moscow himself. 'See here, what Anton says. If we are delayed, we should go straight to the lodgings that he has rented for us in the same building as himself. You can go to school and join the Young Pioneers...'

Their fellow passengers studied them impassively, making no attempt at conversation. Outside the train, the wind howled, driving the snow in a blinding vortex across the barren wastelands. Moscow, Moscow, Moscow...

It was early morning when they arrived. There was no reception committee from the *Internationale* to greet them, only grey people, hurrying through the station, with grey, anxious faces and wearing shabby, grey clothes. Even the huge red banners seemed to be tinged with grey. Olga seemed unaffected. Brightly, she asked a station official which bus to take to Anton's apartment. He pointed to an office. 'Intourist.'

'Anton sent instructions. We'll walk,' Olga said.

Basilius picked up his case and followed her across the station concourse into the snow-covered street, bending his head against the icy wind. Occasionally, Olga stopped passers-by and showed them Anton's address. With unsmiling faces, they indicated the direction they should take, then hurried on their way. Dark, grey buildings loomed forbiddingly down on them.

As they left the city centre, their surroundings rapidly grew more drab, the barrack-like apartment blocks and offices more dilapidated, the people more impoverished. They saw children dragging their bare feet through the snow, men wrapped round with old newspapers, women draped with shawls made from rags. Never had Basilius seen such abject poverty as he now saw in Moscow.

At last they arrived at the Steins' building. 'Third floor,' Olga said, pushing open the door. The rickety staircase was dimly lit by small windows. There was a strong smell of cabbage and urine. On the second floor landing, Basilius saw two rats gnawing at an old crust. They did not run away, but gazed at him from mean, calculating black eyes. He hurried up the staircase after his mother.

Olga was hammering on a door. 'Ruth, Anton! We are here!'

'Olga! Basilius! Welcome to Moscow! Come in!' Anton Stein seized their cases and hurried them into the room.

Basilius stared around him. There was no window in the room and the only illumination was a reeking oil lamp, which served also to disguise damp, cracked walls, broken furniture and a single, shabby rug. A stove fuelled by brown coal gave off a faint heat. On top of it, a pot simmered gently.

'Your room is next door,' Anton was explaining. 'Of course, we realize it isn't quite what you were expecting, but there is a shortage of accommodation in Moscow. Comrade Ulbricht has promised to obtain us rooms in the Hotel Lux, but in the meantime we must be thankful to have a roof over our heads.'

'Sit by the stove and I'll make some tea. You must be cold and tired after your long journey.' Ruth bustled round the cramped room.

There was a lump in Basilius's throat which threatened to choke him. Nothing he had read or heard had prepared him for the reality of the city which he had conjured up for so long in his dreams. Never in his life had he been so bitterly disappointed.

On 6 December, St Nicholas's Day, Christmas trees were erected in the foyer of the Hotel Quadriga, decorations were hung in the bar and the restaurant, and huge wreaths made of holly and conifer branches garlanded the length of the portico.

As Christmas approached, the hotel slowly emptied. Some guests, preferring to let others do their catering, spent Christmas at the hotel, but most people preferred to spend those two precious days — Christmas Eve and the First Christmas Day — in their own homes. Baron Heinrich and Countess Julia went to Essen, Peter and his family to Fürstenmark. Mortimer left for Oxford.

At lunchtime on Christmas Eve, Viktoria and Benno handed over the running of the hotel to Herr Brandt, Herr Fromm and their staff, and went upstairs. There, they shut themselves in the living room and decorated their own small tree. Just as it had long been their tradition to enjoy Christmas as a simple, family affair, it was their custom to prepare the tree for the Christchild and the children.

Some of the ornaments were very old: angels made of porcelain dressed in fragile, yellowed lace; stars and coloured balls made of paper-thin glass; and silver candlestick holders, marked with the tallow of candles from Viktoria's and even Ricarda's youth.

Kneeling at the foot of the tree, Viktoria took them from their protective beds of cotton wool and touched them nostalgically, before handing them up to Benno, enjoying this rare moment, shut off from the outside world with its noise and strife, its cares and contentions. 'Perhaps they seem so beautiful because they only come out once a year and we never have time to get tired of them. But they are pretty, aren't they, Benno?'

He stepped down from the stool on which he had been standing and crouched beside her, his arm around her, seized with a feeling of tenderness. 'Yes, they are. And every Christmas we spend together, I think how lucky I am. We didn't have Christmases like this at the Fortress, when I was a child. There was a tree, but it was decorated with electric lights, not candles. And it was the cost of the presents that mattered — not the giving of them. You had a very different childhood, didn't you, Vicki?'

'And so have our children, thank God,' she replied, leaning her head against his shoulder.

A quarter of an hour later, the tree was finished. Benno lit the candles, stood back critically, turned off the electric light, then opened the door and called out, 'Happy Christmas, everyone!'

There were gasps of delight as they filed into the room, bearing gifts in their hands, which they laid at the foot of the tree.

'Vicki, Benno, what a beautiful tree,' Ricarda exclaimed, kissing them both. 'Happy Christmas.'

'Oh, Papa, isn't it pretty?' Monika sighed, standing close to him. 'Happy Christmas.'

'Mama, it's lovely! Happy Christmas,' Stefan said, kissing her on the cheek.

Sepp put his arm round Luise's shoulders. 'Nothing in the world can compare with Christmas in Germany. Happy Christmas, Luischen.'

Viktoria took Benno's hand in hers. 'Happy Christmas, darling.'

His lips brushed her hair. 'Happy Christmas, Vicki, dear.'

Later, when they had opened their presents, they stood around the tree, arms outstretched, fingers intertwined, and sang the old, familiar carols in the flickering candlelight. Benno's strong tenor led them in *Stille Nacht, Heilige Nacht...* Luise's clear contralto took them into *O du Heilige, O du Fröhliche...* Then Ricarda sang the first notes of an

English carol, that she had learned during her youth in London and on which she had brought up her children and her grandchildren: *Oh Little Town of Bethlehem…*

Tears rose in Viktoria's eyes. Everything and everyone who mattered to her was here in this room.

For the officers in charge of Grubenmünde concentration camp, Christmas Eve was a jolly, family festival, for Commandant Zumstein had allowed the married officers to invite their wives and families to spend Christmas with them. Otto had no children, but he had a wife, Anna, whom he had seen only once since his new posting, when he had been home on leave to Traunsee in September.

The prisoners had hauled a large Christmas tree back to the officers' mess and decorated it with glittering tinsel, balls and electric lights. For weeks beforehand in the workshops, they had been making toys for the officers' children and carving wooden ornaments as gifts for the officers' wives. Women prisoners had been plucking geese, peeling potatoes, chopping cabbage, mixing puddings and cakes.

It was a superb evening. Roll-call finished exceptionally early, because everyone wanted to get on with the celebrations. They sat round the long table, the men in uniform, the women in their best frocks, waited on by prisoners. They dined off copious portions of succulent roast goose, stuffed with chestnuts and apples, washed down with an excellent claret. For dessert, there were marzipan *Lebkuchen* and a delicious *Stolle*, topped with whipped cream.

Her face glowing, Anna put her hand on his knee and Otto felt himself stiffen. She was wearing her regional costume, which showed off her plump figure to the best advantage, the deep-cut frilled blouse revealing the cleft between her breasts, the tight bodice accentuating her hips. Three months was a long time for a man to go without a woman. He glanced at the clock. First he must make his evening round and then he could take her to bed.

One of the officers moved over to the piano and started to hammer out a Christmas carol. Otto squeezed Anna's thigh, stood up and put on his cap. 'I'll be back shortly.'

It was bitterly cold outside after the warmth of the mess. From the nearby village came the sound of church bells, summoning the population to worship. Snow lay thick on the marshy plain surrounding the camp, illuminated by the searchlights along the perimeter fence.

Otto strode over to Wolf's kennel and gave a low whistle. Only the jangle of its chain betrayed the dog's presence. He undid the chain and said, 'Heel!'

Their steps silent on the soft snow, they set off round the camp, which had grown quite considerably since Otto's arrival nine months earlier. There had been one hundred and seventy prisoners then. Now there were over two thousand. There had been other changes, too. In October, he and Zumstein had drawn up a Disciplinary and Penal Code, setting out the rules under which prisoners were to be treated and incorporating many of Otto's original suggestions. Discipline had improved beyond all measure — both among the inmates and the guards. Indeed, Grubenmünde was used as a training centre for the other concentration camps that were being built in Prussia.

It was as they approached the east side of the camp that Wolf emitted a low growl. Otto reached down and felt the hairs standing upright on the dog's back. Silently, he pulled his Luger from its holster and stood immobile, waiting, straining his eyes in the darkness. There was a movement and Otto saw a figure crouched beside a hut. 'Who's there?' he shouted.

There was no reply. Wolf gave a little whine. 'Get him,' Otto ordered. The dog bounded across the snow.

The figure raced towards the fence, its prison garb flapping wildly, desperately projecting itself onto the barbed wire. Wolf jumped and a voice screamed in terror. 'No-o-o!'

Immediately the camp sprang into action. Searchlights swung round to silhouette the would-be escaper being knocked down by the Dobermann Pinscher. Alarms were sounded. There was shouting and running footsteps as guards hurried towards them. From the dormitory windows frightened faces of prisoners peered out, ghastly pale. As he had been trained, Wolf went straight for the jugular, pinning the man down in the snow. He paused, waiting for his master's next command. Otto marched over to them and looked down at the man. He was a Jew. 'Kill!' Otto hissed.

By the time the guards arrived, the prisoner was dead, his blood staining the white snow.

'Who is in charge of guard duty tonight?' Otto roared.

An officer stepped forward. 'I am, Herr Obersturmbannführer!'

'This man was trying to escape. How was this permitted?'

'I shall make it my duty to investigate, Obersturmbannführer.'

Otto glared at him. He knew what had happened. Because it was Christmas Eve, discipline had been lax. Under no other circumstances would a prisoner even have attempted to escape at night, certainly not in the prevailing arctic conditions.

'Report to me in the morning. Turn off the alarms and hang this body up on the parade ground! Clear every hut and hold a roll-call until you are certain that every single prisoner is accounted for!'

'Yes, Obersturmbannführer.' He turned to the guards and issued curt instructions. The alarm bells stopped.

Otto waited while the body was dragged away and the guards burst into the huts, shouting at the prisoners. As the first inmates staggered out into the snow in their thin nightclothes, he nodded in satisfaction and walked back towards the mess. There had been no Christmas dinner for the prisoners — on the contrary, their rations had been halved for the occasion. They would be out there half the night and, with any luck, several would freeze to death. 'Well done, Wolf,' he said. The dog licked its lips. It had tasted human blood for the first time.

First Otto reported to Zumstein. Then he returned to the mess to be greeted by a barrage of questions, particularly from Anna, who rushed up to him anxiously. 'They said a prisoner tried to escape. Did you catch him? Are you all right?'

Otto reached for his cigarette case, pulled out a cigarette and lit it with a casualness he did not feel. His pulse was racing and the ache in his groin had intensified. Killing had always excited him. 'Come with me,' he said.

The pianist struck up, 'Silent Night, Holy Night…'

Otto could still hear the tune when he reached his quarters. He seized Anna from behind and lifted up her skirts, forcing her down over the side of the bed, exposing two huge white buttocks. His penis throbbed. *God*, he thought, *I shall come as soon as I enter her*. He did. But ten minutes later, when they were undressed and lying together, her massive, floppy breasts in his mouth, he was ready again. This time, he made it last longer, thrusting at her savagely from above, enjoying her screams.

Much later, he looked out at the parade ground, where the prisoners were still lined up, the corpse of the Jew swinging from the gibbet, silhouetted against the snow. An off-duty officer lumbered back towards his living quarters, swaying drunkenly and singing, '*Stille Nacht, Heilige Nacht…*'. Otto smiled.

For the first time in his life, Professor Ascher spent Christmas with a Christian family. Being the man he was, he did not do it by half. Although he did not join in with the prayers or the hymns, he attended the crowded midnight service held by Pastor Scheer. He admired the nativity crib prepared by children of the parish. He rejoiced in the rich sound of the bells pealing out through the crisp night air.

The following day, he joined the Scheers for a traditional Christmas lunch of roast goose, chestnut and apple stuffing. The entire family was present: the Pastor, his wife, their three married sons and their families. They were decent, simple folk, who took care to involve the Professor in their conversation. Even the children had brought small gifts for him, so that he should not feel excluded.

At the end of the delicious meal, the Professor looked down the table and lifted his glass. 'From the bottom of my heart, I wish you a happy Christmas, my dear friends, and I thank you for welcoming me, a stranger, to your midst.'

Pastor Scheer smiled. 'It is we who thank you for accepting our hospitality, Herr Professor. But I beg you never again to refer to yourself as a stranger, for there have been many occasions this autumn, when I have felt closer to you than to many of my brothers in Christ. And, on that subject, may I ask you to call me Bernhard?'

'And myself, Klara,' his wife added.

'Thank you,' Professor Ascher breathed, aware of the tremendous implications of this apparently simple proposal. 'And my name is Bethel. I hope you will use it.'

'Thank you, Bethel,' Bernhard Scheer replied.

A hum of conversation started again, but Professor Ascher sat silently, deeply moved by this practical, living demonstration of Christianity by people who gained strength from their faith and felt able to share it with others without feeling any need to convert.

Perhaps it was due to his being a scientist, but he had never before been able to believe in God. Yet, during this last year, he had changed, finding himself hankering after the Jewish traditions, to a religious and not just racial identity. Maybe this was what persecution did, he thought. Instead of breaking people's faith, it made them more conscious of it.

In no time at all, Christmas was over and the Hotel Quadriga was preparing for the traditional New Year's Eve ball. If Christmas Eve was one of the quietest days in Viktoria's life, New Year's Eve was one of the busiest. Indeed, from the moment they rose at five in the morning, she scarcely saw Benno or any other members of the family, until they met in the ballroom that evening.

There were endless consultations with Herr Fromm over room reservations, and with Frau Fiedler over laundry, linen and the special requirements of guests. There were discussions with Philip Krosyk over seating plans in the restaurants for the gala banquet, and with Maître Chef Mazzoni over menus for the seven-course dinner.

The parquet floor in the ballroom was waxed and polished to reflect the images of the huge crystal chandeliers suspended from its high ceilings. The mirrors lining the walls were wiped squeaky-clean with fresh newspaper. Maintenance men hung gaily coloured garlands and nets full of balloons.

Benno, too, was fully occupied for, on New Year's Eve, the wine cellars came into their own. Before the night was over, a thousand or more guests would have passed through the glass revolving doors. Between two or three thousand bottles of the most superior champagne would have been consumed. Over a thousand bottles of the finest wine in Germany would have been drunk. Many had to be decanted. All had to be served at the right temperature. And every one had to be accounted for. Benno was in his element.

Throughout the day, limousines drew up at the entrance and, while the commissionaires assisted the guests to alight, page boys hurried to and fro with their luggage. By midday, every suite in the hotel was occupied, every table in the restaurant booked, every seat in the ballroom reserved, and a fever of cheerful excitement pervaded the entire building. In the early evening, people began to gather in the bar for cocktails. At eight, they drifted into the restaurants. At ten, they made their way into the ballroom.

Wearing an off-the-shoulder blue gown, with matching sapphires glinting in her ears and round her throat, accentuating the colour of her eyes and the blondeness of her intricately dressed hair, Viktoria stood beside Benno at the entrance to the ballroom to welcome their guests.

Through the doors they moved, a glittering throng, the cream of society: men, elegant in immaculate evening dress or regimental dress uniform; women, in the latest Paris fashions, necks and shoulders gleaming white, jewels sparkling, exotic perfumes wafting through the air; and children, rosy-cheeked and wide-eyed, wearing sailor suits and taffeta dresses, crisp white socks and polished shoes. As old friends, they all greeted Viktoria and Benno, praising the lavish banquet, exclaiming on the magnificence of the room, reminiscing over former balls, exchanging best wishes for the coming year, before the Master of Ceremonies announced their names and waiters conducted them to their tables.

More waiters, dressed in black frock coats and white gloves wove sinuously between them, silver trays with cut crystal glasses balanced high above their shoulders, popping the corks of champagne bottles, cloaked in starched white linen napkins. In the loge at the far end of the room, Christian Engel directed his small orchestra in the *Emperor Waltz*, the *Blue Danube* and *Tales from the Vienna Woods*. The dance floor filled; a haze of cigar and cigarette smoke drifted above the tables; and the hum of conversation intensified.

It was half-past eleven before Viktoria and Benno were free to join the family at the group of tables near the orchestra, where Ricarda and the children, the Krauses and the Biedersteins had long been seated. Her feet aching in their thin gold slippers and her mind in a daze, Viktoria sank thankfully into her chair and allowed a waiter to pour her a glass of champagne. She took a sip and lit a cigarette.

The men were deep in talk on military issues. Across the table, Viktoria heard the names Reichenau, Blomberg, Fritsch, Schleicher and Beck frequently mentioned. She smiled ruefully. For as long as she could remember, politics and war had formed the staple subjects of discussion for the men at all New Year's Eve balls. It was almost as if, once they were married, they lost all interest in dancing.

'What do you think will happen in Austria, Father?' Ernst asked. 'The situation seems highly inflammatory. Chancellor Dollfuss...'

'Austrians are Germans, boy. They want to join the German Empire,' Baron Heinrich grunted. 'If Mussolini would stop interfering in their affairs...'

'It's a situation that could lead to war, if we're not careful,' Peter interrupted gravely.

The orchestra began to play a slow waltz and Sepp said, 'Thank God I'm not a politician — or a soldier. Would you like to dance, Luischen?'

Luise smiled and took his hand. Golden lights gleamed in her auburn hair, her pale skin was clear, her eyes shone and her slim figure, in an emerald green chiffon gown, moved with lissom grace. *Dear God*, Viktoria prayed silently, *let her be happy this time.*

Their departure onto the dance floor seemed to set an example. Another chair moved and she heard Norbert ask, 'Monika, will you grant me the pleasure of this dance?'

In honour of the occasion, Monika's hair had been curled into shoulder-length ringlets and she was wearing a knee-length pink dress. Why, Viktoria thought, when she smiles, Monika is very pretty!

And Norbert, wearing long trousers and a bow tie, appeared almost grown-up. He had shot up in height and his hair was darker than she recalled. Both children looked questioningly at her and she nodded reassuringly. It was only after they had gone that she saw their glasses contained, not fruit juice, but champagne.

Then she became aware of a silent confrontation taking place at the adjoining small table. Simultaneously, Stefan and Werner had risen and were glaring at each other across Christa's ash-blonde head. Stefan's hand rested on the back of her chair, Werner's on her arm. Werner muttered something to Christa which she could not hear and the girl raised her innocent blue eyes to him, blushed faintly, turned appealingly to Stefan, then stood up and took Werner's arm. Still standing, Stefan glared after them as they joined the dancers.

'Stefi,' Viktoria called softly.

His expression softened and he hurried to her side. 'Mama, would you like to dance?'

He was an excellent dancer, light on his feet and with an innate sense of rhythm. Viktoria let her face brush his cheek. 'Why were you looking like that at Werner? You didn't really want to dance with Christa, did you?'

'Christa?' Stefan said slowly. 'Oh, not particularly. But I asked her first, then Werner barged in. I don't know what it is, but there's something about him that rubs me up the wrong way.'

'Stefi, he's your cousin.'

'Does that mean I have to like him? After all, Mama, you never got on very well with your cousin Olga!'

Reassured, Viktoria laughed and, at that moment, the orchestra stopped playing. The Master of Ceremonies clapped his hands for silence. There was a general movement as people hurried to regain their places, while waiters popped more champagne corks and refilled glasses. Stefan squeezed his mother's hand. 'It's midnight! Happy New Year, Mama.'

Benno strode across to the podium. 'My lords, ladies and gentlemen, on behalf of the Hotel Quadriga, I should like to wish you all a happy, healthy and prosperous New Year!'

There was an outburst of cheering, then glasses were clinked as the hotel's guests toasted each other. 'Happy New Year!' *'Prost Neu Jahr!'* The air was filled with the sound of their excited voices, multi-coloured garlands and floating balloons. On Unter den Linden, cannons were fired and through the windows the first of a magnificent firework display lit up the sky.

Norbert and Monika had slipped, unnoticed, from the ballroom. 'Where shall we go?' Norbert asked.

Monika had drunk two glasses of champagne and was feeling slightly dizzy and extremely daring. 'There's a conservatory where the gardener keeps his tools and things.'

They went through the deserted Palm Garden Room and Monika pointed to where the key was hidden. Norbert lifted her up and she reached it from the hook. Then he unlocked the door, let them in and locked it again. 'I like you,' he said, putting his arm round her and pulling her close to him. 'Can I kiss you?'

Monika closed her eyes and lifted her face to his. The kiss was rather wet and disappointing until something quite extraordinary happened. Norbert prised his tongue between her teeth and licked her teeth and palate. She pressed closer to him and sensed something hard stirring within his trousers. *His tail!* she thought. *His tail's moving.*

Norbert drew his mouth away from hers. 'That's called a French kiss.'

'How do you know?'

'I was shown by a friend of mine's sister.' Monika scowled and he added hastily, 'I didn't like her nearly as much as I like you.'

'Have you ever thought about me?' Monika asked. 'You know…?' She rubbed against him and he drew quickly away.

'Monika, shall we sit down? It would be more comfortable.'

They moved across to the pile of matting and kissed again. His hand came up and fumbled at her chest. She smiled, for since her first period, her breasts had started to grow, although they were still not as big as Beate's. Norbert fumbled with the buttons at the back of her dress. Eventually they were undone and she slipped the frock over her shoulders, pulled up her vest and lay back on the matting so that Norbert could admire her in the dim light. He gasped and ran his fingers over her rounded contours. 'You're beautiful Monika.' She moved her legs and Norbert's hand crept under her skirt. 'Can I touch you there?'

'Yes,' Monika said slowly, 'on one condition. That you'll let me see your tail.'

He seemed to have almost as many buttons as she did. There were buttons on his trousers and on his underpants, but at long last she had undone them and pulled a swollen stump into the open. Monika stared at it in fascination, then tentatively reached out a hand. Suddenly, he lay on top of her, so that it was between her legs and she felt it shudder and sticky wetness flood between her legs.

Norbert fished in his pocket for a handkerchief and mopped at her, an unexpectedly serious expression on his face. 'We shouldn't have done that. You know that's how babies are made?'

She felt suddenly frightened. 'You mean I could have a baby?'

He pulled up his pants and trousers. 'I think it's possible.'

Monika bit her lip and started to right her clothing. 'If I had a baby, would you marry me?'

Norbert looked doubtful. 'We're not old enough.' He put his arm round her shoulder. 'If you do, I'll look after you. Now, we'd better get back to the ball or people will start looking for us.'

The atmosphere in the ballroom had changed considerably by the time they returned. The parquet floor was littered with streamers, the music was louder and the revellers more abandoned.

'Monika!' her mother's voice exclaimed in the low, angry tone she knew so well, 'Where on earth have you been? I've been looking for you everywhere.'

'I was showing Norbert round the hotel,' she replied shakily.

Her mother gave her a piercing stare. 'You're looking very pale.'

'I've got a bit of a headache,' Monika lied.

'I'm not surprised if you've been drinking champagne,' her mother scolded tartly. 'Now, go up to your rooms, both of you. You should have been in bed hours ago.'

They parted at the top of the stairs. 'I probably shan't see you again for a while,' Norbert said awkwardly. 'We're leaving very early in the morning. I hope you'll be all right.'

'Of course I shall,' Monika told him haughtily. 'Good night, Norbert.' At that moment she did not ever want to see him again.

She lay awake for a long time. *Ficken* had been exciting at the time, but now it was over she felt let-down and rather afraid.

The next day, she asked Beate, 'How will I know if I'm going to have a baby?'

'What?' Beate cried enviously. 'You've done it with a boy?'

Her elation totally eclipsed by her fear, Monika nodded and told her what had happened.

Beate gave a knowing smile. 'My married sister's going to have a baby. She told me about it. If you are expecting, you'll miss your period.' She went on to explain the mechanics of menstruation far more explicitly than Viktoria had done.

By the time she had finished, Monika was wiser and even more terrified. She worked out that her period was not due for another two weeks. There was nothing to do but to wait, hope and pray. But if everything was all right, she vowed there would be no more *ficken* until she was old enough to marry.

Two weeks later, to her unbounded relief, Monika's period began. Shortly after that, Beate announced, 'Now I'm fourteen, Mother's agreed that I can join the BdM — the German Girls' League. Why don't you come with me?'

Monika's eyes lit up and the memory of Norbert began to fade. The BdM was the girls' division of the Hitler Youth. Its members wore a special uniform and attended sports meetings, rallies and camps, mixing quite a lot with the Hitler Youth boys. 'Oh yes! I'll tell my parents at supper tonight.'

She was unprepared for the commotion her announcement caused.

'No, Monika,' her mother said adamantly, 'I will not allow you to join any branch of the Hitler Youth. It's a political organization of the worst possible type.'

'Holding sports meetings and going to youth hostels isn't political,' Monika objected petulantly.

'The Hitler Youth are just a bunch of thugs,' Stefan stated.

Monika's eyes flashed and she turned to her father. 'Papa, you're on my side, aren't you?'

Benno hesitated. 'Vicki, I don't see that it can do any harm for her to apply for membership. After all, the BdM is the girls' organization.

She might learn something useful there — how to cook and sew — and the discipline won't hurt her.'

'I have the impression that the Hitler Youth is rather like the *Wandervogel* were in our young days,' Ricarda interjected. 'They used to go for hikes and have singsongs round camp fires. I'm sure it's all quite harmless, Vicki, dear.'

Monika gazed triumphantly at her mother, knowing she had won.

Viktoria sighed. 'All right. You can join. But on one condition — that you do not go to any camps or rallies, and that you do not bring political propaganda into this hotel.'

So Monika commenced her training, applying more effort to it than she had ever done with her schoolwork, determined that by 20 March, her fourteenth birthday, she would be ready to become a member.

'We'll be able to attend the Youth Day at the Nuremberg Rally in September,' Beate said excitedly.

Monika grimaced. 'Mama won't let me. She's only letting me join the BdM on the understanding that I don't go to any rallies.'

Beate smiled slyly. 'Do you know what I do when Mother forbids me to do something? I threaten to tell Father something she'd rather he didn't know. I usually get my own way.'

Monika absorbed this fascinating idea in silence. 'Thank you, Beate,' she said sweetly. 'I'm sure I shall persuade my parents to let me go to Nuremberg.'

Mortimer returned from a quiet Christmas leave in Oxford to an atmosphere of tension and growing discontent in Berlin. To his joy, everyone seemed only too pleased to talk about it.

Hasso Annuschek objected strongly to Hitler's latest piece of legislation — the Labour Charter. 'The Nazis have taken away all our rights — our trade unions and our right to strike, and we're even worse off than we were before, contrary to all Hitler's promises. And now look what he's done! The Labour Charter deprives the workers of the right even to negotiate their own wages.'

'The unemployment figures are falling,' Mortimer commented.

'You tell that to the workers! So's their take-home pay! Of course, being a barman, I get tips, so I'm not so badly off. But you should see all the deductions that are made — income tax, national insurance, sickness schemes. And now there's the Winter Relief!'

'As a socialist you ought to agree with a charity set up to look after the needs of the poor,' Mortimer chaffed him.

'Huh! They just take from the poor. God knows what they do with the money. Probably finance the stormtroopers!'

Rumoured to be four million strong now, the stormtroopers were a bone of contention with everyone. Even Baron Heinrich fulminated against them. 'Röhm is getting above himself, particularly since Hitler made him a cabinet minister. His headquarters in Munich are bigger than the new Kraus Haus, and every wall is covered with works of art. As for his cars…'

'Strange considering the declared ideals of the Party,' Mortimer commented.

'Bah! Röhm cares nothing for ideals.'

Peter von Biederstein was deeply apprehensive for other reasons. When Mortimer questioned him, he was surprisingly forthcoming. 'Röhm's power has to be crushed. Personally, I believe he has hopes of seizing control of the Reichswehr and forming a new people's army, like the Red Army. You must have heard talk of the Second Revolution, Herr Allen? If Hitler doesn't do something to stop Röhm, we may well find ourselves in the throes of civil war.'

'You believe it to be that serious?' Mortimer asked.

Peter nodded grimly. 'Frankly, yes.'

Then there was Austria, where civil war seemed even more imminent. Fear of a socialist revolution had led Chancellor Dollfuss to suspend parliamentary government the previous March, since when he had ruled virtually as a dictator, supported by the Austrian Army. Better organized than their German counterparts, the Austrian socialists had their own private army, the *Schutzbund*, which was in constant battle with the fascist *Heimwehr*, equivalent to the German stormtroopers.

There were rumours that German SA and SS units were stationed on the Austrian border, while Mussolini's troops were waiting on the Brenner. It was a potentially explosive situation.

Finally, there was Poland. Since before Christmas, confidential meetings had been held between Hitler and the Polish Ambassador, the outcome of which everyone awaited with baited breath.

Addressing the Reichstag on 30 January, the first anniversary of his accession to power, Hitler took the opportunity to announce that Germany and Poland had just signed a ten-year non-aggression pact.

The Quadriga bar was packed that evening, when Mortimer returned, everyone vehemently discussing the astonishing item of news. 'Herr Allen! What do you think of this agreement?' the Baron's voice boomed from a nearby table, where he was sitting with Benno and his family. Without giving him time to reply, he went on, 'I can tell you, I don't understand it! I thought the purpose of Hitler's meeting with the Polish Ambassador in December would be to demand Poland back — not to make a peace treaty!'

Mortimer could not resist asking, 'Are you suggesting Germany was considering declaring war against Poland?'

'Of course not, but the fact still remains that Poland is rightfully ours. It was stolen from us under Versailles. Hitler had no right to sign a peace treaty with Pilsudski.'

Mortimer raised an eyebrow. This was the first time he had heard the Baron criticize Hitler — certainly in public. 'It seems to me that, as a dictator, he can do anything he damn well pleases.'

'I think I can understand Hitler's purpose,' Benno said. 'Poland has an alliance with France, so our three countries together now form a strong bulwark against the Soviet Union.'

Mortimer shrugged. 'Alliances. Bulwark against Russia. That's pretty well where the last war started, if I remember correctly. Surely you don't believe Russia is preparing for war, Herr Kraus?'

'I wouldn't put it past her. The communists are capable of anything and, unlike us, they have a large army which they can mobilize at any moment.'

'I think anything that promotes European peace is a good thing,' Stefan said quietly.

'Particularly if Germany is making the opening moves,' Viktoria added.

'What about the League of Nations set up for that very purpose?' Mortimer asked drily. 'I seem to recall Germany rather precipitately withdrew from it last year. Why should Hitler have done that if he genuinely wants peace?'

In an exasperated tone, Benno said, 'Herr Allen, you are, of course, entitled to your opinion, but it seems to me that you will always find fault with Hitler, whatever he does. I assure you again, nobody in Germany wants another war, not even for Poland.'

Mortimer was enjoying himself. 'Hitler isn't just interfering in Polish affairs. What about Austria? I've heard reports that SA and SS units are stationed right along the Austrian border. Why?'

'Herr Hitler does not take me into his confidence,' Benno retorted coldly, 'but Austria and Germany have always been allies. It is our duty to protect the Austrian people from the Bolsheviks.'

'I don't believe you, Herr Kraus. I think Hitler is just waiting for an opportunity to march his stormtroopers into Austria. It's probably the stormtroopers who are causing the disturbances!'

Viktoria gazed anxiously from one man to the other, then at her watch. 'I'm sorry to stop this discussion, but it's time we went in to dinner.'

Benno's face was flushed and he was glaring angrily at Mortimer. 'Yes, I think so too, my dear.' He stood up, pushing his chair back forcefully. 'Father, are you joining us?'

'Women, women, can't think of anything but their stomachs,' the Baron grumbled. 'Well, don't just stand there. Help me up, boy!'

In the ensuing kerfuffle, Viktoria moved to Mortimer's side and said quietly, 'Herr Allen, for your own sake, please be more careful what you say. I know you don't mean any harm, but not everyone sees things your way.'

Suddenly, he became aware of Monika gazing fixedly at him, a knowing expression in her blue-grey eyes, as if she were saying, *Herr Allen, I know all about your little game.* Then she took her father's hand, smirked and walked away.

Slowly, he made his way back to the bar. He had assumed Viktoria was referring to Benno, in whose eyes Hitler could apparently still do no wrong. But what if she had meant Monika? After all, the child was joining the Hitler Youth, and it was not unknown for children to spy on their elders in return for some reward. In fact, it was the despicable sort of trick the Gestapo would play.

In sombre vein, he wrote to Churchill that evening. The Labour Charter, the Polish Pact, Austria, Röhm and the Second Revolution. Whichever way one looked, storm clouds seemed to be gathering on the horizon.

Basilius was young and resilient, and it was not long before his initial feeling of disappointment with Moscow began to fade. Once news of his mother's arrival spread among the German comrades, Olga was able to renew her acquaintance with revolutionaries like Wilhelm Pieck and Karl Radek. She was invited to the prestigious Old Bolsheviks' Cub, and to write articles for the *German Central Newspaper*. She was once again in her element.

Basilius went to a school for foreign children, where he was taught by German émigrés. The only major addition to his curriculum was Russian, which became his first foreign language, with English second. Thanks to Dr Lukas, Basilius had always loved words and he took to Russian like a duck to water.

In February, there began a new influx into Moscow — this time of Austrians, who brought with them chilling stories of a civil war in which, at Dollfuss's instigation, the Austrian Army had fired with machine guns on defenceless socialist workers and their families. Dollfuss was now hated and feared both by the remaining Marxists and by the Austrian National Socialists, who were seeking annexation with Nazi Germany.

By the beginning of March, Basilius was top of his class, not just in languages, but in history, geography, political studies and economics, and was recommended for membership of the Young Pioneers.

Never in his life had he felt more proud than when he attended the enrolment ceremony, standing to attention in the middle of the hall, the ranks lined up ahead of him, a standard-bearer to their fore.

Exactly as on a military occasion, trumpeters played a fanfare, then the local Pioneer leader stepped forward and recited the oath.

In only slightly accented Russian, Basilius repeated it after him. 'I promise to fight loyally and courageously for the cause of the working classes, to keep the holy will of Lenin, to behave always in an exemplary fashion and to fulfil all customs and duties of the Young Pioneers.'

He was presented with a red neckscarf and a badge was pinned on to his jacket like a military decoration. When he got home, his mother gazed at it in admiring adoration. 'Do you know what these symbols mean, Basili? The five logs depict the five continents of the world and the three flames are the Third Internationale!' Then she frowned and tried to pronounce the Russian words inscribed on it. '*Budy gotov! W segda gotov!*'

Basilius winced. 'They say: Be prepared! Always prepared!' He suddenly realized that while he was already becoming a Soviet, his mother would always be a foreigner.

The leader of Monika's Hitler Youth unit was Frau Hedwig Forster, the wife of Fredi Forster, the manager of Café Jochum. Plump and rather prone to tears, she called her girls 'my maidens', painting a glowing, sentimental picture of the future that awaited them in the wonderful world that 'our dear Führer' was creating. Although Beate was rather scornful of Frau Forster, Monika thought she was divine.

At the end of March, Monika was accepted as a full member of the BdM, passing her physical endurance test with flying colours, running sixty metres in twelve seconds, jumping two and a half metres and completing a two hour route march with the greatest of ease. The intellectual side had been a bit harder, but now she knew 'Deutschland' and the 'Horst Wessel Song' off by heart, and could efficiently answer all Frau Forster's questions on Party policy and history.

The initiation ceremony took place in a room hung with swastika banners and dominated by a picture of Hitler. Baldur von Schirach himself was present, the man appointed by Hitler as the Youth

Leader of the German Reich. A handsome figure in his late twenties, Monika found him infinitely romantic.

Her plaits wound round her head, her eyes huge as she gazed from Frau Forster to Hitler's portrait, she swore her oath of allegiance. 'In the presence of this blood banner, I swear to devote all my energies and strength to the saviour of our country, Adolf Hitler. I am willing and ready to give up my life for him, so help me God.'

The occasion became even more emotional as von Schirach made a stirring speech about devotion to their country and the joys of motherhood that awaited them when they married and bore sons to serve the Fatherland. Then he told them all that the Führer was expecting to see them at Nuremberg in the autumn. Eventually, a band started up and they linked arms and began singing. 'Oh, isn't it wonderful?' Monika breathed to Beate.

'Wait till we go to Nuremberg,' her friend said.

Upon arriving back at the hotel in her new uniform, Monika rushed straight to Viktoria's office, her face flushed. Vividly, she described every detail of the ceremony, including the oath.

Viktoria listened with growing dismay, noting her daughter's pupils still dilated with emotion, her voice shrill with excitement. This was far worse than she had feared. 'Monika, how could you swear that oath? Hitler isn't our saviour. He's just a politician.'

Monika's mood changed abruptly. The blue eyes stared back at her coldly. 'Mama, you should be careful what you say. If I reported you to the Gestapo, you'd be arrested.'

For a moment, Viktoria could not believe her own ears. Her own daughter threatening her? Angrily, she smacked her round the face. 'Monika, don't dare talk to me like that!'

With great dignity, Monika stood up. 'If you ever hit me again, I'll tell Papa.'

'He'd agree with me.'

'I wonder if he would.' And with that Monika walked out of the office, slamming the door behind her.

With trembling fingers, Viktoria lit a cigarette. Of course, Monika was right on both points, particularly the last. Benno would be furious if he knew she had hit Monika. 'Oh, my God,' she said aloud, 'what sort of monster have I bred?'

But, when she thought about it, she wondered if she might not be mostly to blame. While Monika was a baby, she had not spent as much time with her as she might, leaving her in Nurse Bauer's care. If she were honest with herself, she had always preferred Stefan. Perhaps Monika realized this and had, subconsciously, always held a grudge against her…

A few moments later, Mortimer Allen knocked on her office door. 'I hope you'll forgive the unwarranted intrusion, but I couldn't help noticing Monika flying out of here like a bat out of hell and I wondered…'

Viktoria let out a deep breath. 'You wondered whether I approved of her taking this appalling oath to Hitler? Well, the short answer to that, Herr Allen, is no.'

Mortimer smiled sympathetically. 'I thought as much.'

'But what can I do? As Monika has just pointed out to me, if I say anything against Hitler, I can be reported to the Gestapo.'

'You're in a difficult situation,' he agreed. He was silent for a moment, then he said, 'May I ask you a rather impertinent favour?'

Viktoria hesitated, some sixth sense warning her that more danger lay ahead. Then she nodded. 'Yes, of course.'

'I know it's usual in Germany to call people Herr and Frau, but I'm an American and I find it rather tedious being called Herr Allen all the time, particularly by someone whom I'd like to think was my friend. Do you think you could bring yourself to say Mortimer?'

It was an innocent enough request, but to use his Christian name meant she should give him permission to call her Viktoria, a transition that would immediately place their acquaintanceship on a much more personal level. Did she want that kind of familiarity? Then she shook her head, irritated by her own stupidity. He was asking her to be his friend — not his mistress. 'Frau Jochum-Kraus is rather a mouthful, I suppose,' she said slowly.

'And Viktoria is such a lovely name. It suits you.'

'Thank you, Mortimer.'

He clasped her hand. 'Thank you, Viktoria.'

She experienced a sudden warmth. She badly needed someone in whom to confide her worries, about her family, her hotel — and her country. 'I'd like to think we could be friends…'

The ice melted on the Heiligensee, small buds appeared on the lime trees lining Unter den Linden and the first daffodils sprang into bloom in the Botanical Gardens at Dahlem. And with the spring, tension in the city grew, as what had been small dissatisfactions took on greater proportions. Angry voices were raised in protest against the State bureaucracy and the growing number of small-minded bureaucrats, against Goebbels' cultural activities, and, ever more stridently, against the stormtroopers. There were calls for an end to the brutality, the arrests, the imprisonments without fair trial, to the intimidation of church ministers and the persecution of the Jews.

Professor Bethel Ascher heard these voices and knew great hope. It had taken them a long time, but at last the people were coming to their senses. And, in the meantime, he had found something to fill his empty existence. He was teaching at a Jewish school in Dahlem. He had been accepted by the Welfare Committee of German Jews, assisting people who wished to emigrate. And he had hopes of becoming involved in Martin Buber's Office for Jewish Adult Education. He was helping the Jews to create their own alternative community.

So, in a spirit of optimism, he prepared to celebrate the *Seder*, the first night of Passover, the Festival of Liberation, commemorating the exodus of the Children of Israel from Egypt before they reached the Promised Land. Among the Orthodox Jews of Berlin — as throughout the world — Passover would last eight days, but Bethel intended his evening to be more of a social occasion, with ritual kept to a minimum, particularly as there would be Gentiles present.

In the morning, he went shopping for *matzos*, the thin wafers of unleavened bread that formed the traditional staple food of Passover; the bitter herbs, horseradish and lettuce, that would be eaten in symbolic memory of the bitterness of slavery; and the special wine that would be drunk four times during the meal.

Then, he brought out the silver dishes and the candlesticks that his own parents had brought with them when they had fled, before his birth, from Russia. Lost in a host of memories, he polished them.

It was almost dusk when his guests arrived: among them, Bernhard and Klara Scheer, Mortimer Allen and Stefan Jochum-Kraus. Bethel Ascher was wearing his skullcap and handed one each to the other men. Then he lit the candles in the seven-branched *menorah* and took his place at the top of the table. He smiled at Stefan. 'It is the custom for a child to ask about our evening's rituals and for the head of the family to reply. Since you are the youngest one present, perhaps you would read the questions?'

Stefan picked up the book in front of him and read aloud, 'Why is this night different from all other nights of the year?'

Bethel Ascher replied, 'This night is different because we celebrate the most important moment in the history of our people. On this night we celebrate their going forth in triumph from bondage into freedom…'

It was midnight when the party ended. On their way home, Mortimer asked Stefan, 'Did you find it interesting?'

'It was like a different world. Mortimer, why do so many people hate the Jews?'

Mortimer was silent for a long time. Finally he said, 'Maybe because they are different. But also because they are the oldest race on earth — God's chosen people. That thought is anathema to men who believe themselves to be chosen by God.'

'Is it really as simple as that?'

'No,' Mortimer replied, 'nothing is ever as simple as that.'

The following morning, Monika asked Stefan, 'Where did you and Mortimer go last night?'

Stefan hesitated for a moment. Then he thought, *Why shouldn't I tell her? It isn't a crime to visit friends.* So he told her where they had been.

Monika stared at him aghast. 'You spent the evening celebrating a Jewish festival? Stefan, how could you? That makes you a Jew-lover. That's even worse than being a Jew. If anyone found out, you could lose your place at the University.'

Stefan's blood ran cold. He had the dreadful feeling she could be right.

'Don't worry,' she went on sweetly. 'Provided you're on my side when I tell Mama I'm going to the Nuremberg Rally in September, I won't tell a soul.'

As spring turned into summer, there was a seething undercurrent of tension and fear throughout Berlin, to which nobody could remain immune. Whenever Viktoria entered the bar, it hummed with rumours of plots and counterplots, intrigues and conspiracies. Göring now had his own *General Göring* police force, stationed at Lichterfelde on the outskirts of Berlin, while Himmler had moved to Berlin and become head of the Prussian Gestapo as well as the SS, with a prestigious headquarters at 8 Prinz-Albrecht-Strasse.

The Second Revolution of which Peter had spoken in January was now discussed as a very real — and terrifying — possibility. In muted voices, people wondered how the Reichswehr could possibly protect itself against four million stormtroopers. Even more importantly, they wondered what their future would be in a country dominated by Röhm's swaggering, vicious thugs.

Then, on 7 June, it was announced on the news that the SA was going on leave for an entire month and that Captain Röhm, suffering from a nervous complaint, was going to take a cure in Bavaria. Everyone breathed a sigh of relief. Hitler had the situation in hand. Feeling happier and more relaxed than she had for a long time, Viktoria prepared for an important landmark in her life.

On the evening of Friday 15 June 1934, she celebrated her fortieth birthday and the fortieth anniversary of the Quadriga's opening. In a splendidly decorated Jubilee Room, she and her guests sat down to a magnificent seven-course banquet, served by waiters dressed in mediaeval costume, entertained by a quartet playing music from the reign of Frederick the Great.

How fortunate she was, Viktoria thought, gazing down the long table at her family and friends: Stefan, so grown-up and handsome; her mother, so beautiful and calmly elegant; Luise, a new person since she had Sepp. And even Monika, in the white blouse and black skirt of the BdM, seemed better behaved since she had joined the movement.

Then there were the Krauses and Biedersteins, no longer so overwhelming since they had moved out of the hotel. And other dear friends: Mortimer Allen, Sepp Nowak, Professor Ascher, Dr Blattner, the family lawyer Dr Duschek, Hilde and Fritzi Weber from Heiligensee... Yes, she was very lucky.

At the end of the meal, Benno stood up and made a speech. 'Ladies are notorious for trying to conceal their age, but in the case of my wife, it is impossible for her to even try, for everyone knows Viktoria Jochum was born on the day His Majesty, Kaiser Wilhelm the Second, opened the Hotel Quadriga forty years ago on 15 June 1894.' Several people laughed.

Forty years — it did not seem possible. She did not feel forty years old. She would have said twenty-five, maybe thirty — but not forty. Why, that was positively middle-aged!

Briefly and amusingly, Benno recounted highlights from the history of the hotel. Then he signalled to Philip Krosyk, who handed him an ornate box on a gold tray. Benno took it and turned to Viktoria. 'Vicki, my dear, I should like you to accept this gift on behalf of the Hotel Quadriga, with love and best wishes for another forty years of happiness from all your family.'

Deeply moved, she opened the lid to find, nestling on a satin bed, a necklace of blood-red rubies, set with sparkling diamonds, with a matching brooch and earrings. Never in her life had she seen anything more exquisite. Tears sprang to her eyes and she shook her head slowly in mute disbelief.

'It appears that, for once, my wife has lost her voice,' Benno laughed, and the entire restaurant burst into tumultuous cheers.

Viktoria reached up and kissed him. 'Thank you, Benno.' Then she turned to her mother and kissed her. 'And thank you, Mama. Thank you for having me forty years ago.' Finally she looked down the long room. 'Thank you, all of you, for your loyalty and your affection during forty years.' More uproarious applause.

Hasso Annuschek moved forward and, with great deference, presented Benno with a decanter of red wine, deeper in colour even than the rubies in Viktoria's jewellery. Waiters bustled round the restaurant filling fresh glasses. Benno cleared his throat and said, 'Karl Jochum laid down this wine forty years ago. I propose that we now drink to the next forty years in the life of the Hotel Quadriga!'

With one accord the guests rose, their arms raised, their voices lifted. 'The Hotel Quadriga!'

Benno put down his glass and smiled ruefully at Viktoria. 'The wine has passed its prime. But you, my dearest, become more beautiful with every passing year. You will never pass your prime.' He fastened the rubies round her neck.

The civilian population might believe that the threat of an SA putsch had been averted, but Peter von Biederstein and his fellow officers were far from convinced. Ernst Röhm was one of Hitler's oldest friends and supporters, one of the few men the Chancellor addressed with the familiar '*du*'. For all Hitler's assurances that he regarded the army as the sole bearer of arms for the nation, there was no certainty that he might not give in to Röhm's demands and incorporate the Reichswehr into the SA, perhaps even appointing Röhm as the new Reichswehr Minister, a thought which was an anathema to officers of the old school like Peter.

Added to this, figures from the past were re-emerging. General von Schleicher was rumoured to be making a deal with Röhm in return for the Vice-Chancellorship, with Brüning promised the post of Foreign Minister. To exacerbate the situation, President Hindenburg was purported to have only weeks to live. He was said to have told Vice-Chancellor Franz von Papen, 'Things are going badly. Do what you can to put them right.'

The Sunday following Viktoria's birthday, Papen made an unprecedented speech to students at the University of Marburg, in which he criticized the Nazis, the terror, the Revolution and ended, 'It is time to join together in brotherly friendship and respect for all our fellow countrymen, to stop destroying the endeavours of serious men, and to silence fanatics.'

Dr Goebbels tried to silence him by forbidding the broadcasting or publication of the speech, but Papen had taken the precaution of releasing copies of it in advance to foreign correspondents and diplomats, and there were few Germans who did not learn of its contents — and of the ensuing feud. Papen threatened Hitler that he would tell Hindenburg of Goebbels' action, upon which Hitler forestalled him by flying to the President's estate in East Prussia, where he was apparently informed by General von Blomberg that Hindenburg was so appalled at what was going on, that he was considering declaring martial law and handing over control of the State to the Reichswehr.

With bated breath, Peter waited to see what happened next. If Hitler wanted to continue in power and keep the Reichswehr on his side, he must take the appropriate action himself. The revolutionary leader must deal with the threatened counter-revolution on his own. He must quash Röhm's Second Revolution before it ever began — and the only way to do it was to rid the SA of its leaders. But the Reichswehr must be seen to take no part in the purge.

Thursday, 28 June was the anniversary of one of the most fateful days in German history. Exactly fifteen years since the signing of the Treaty of Versailles, it was a day of national mourning. When Baron Heinrich von Kraus's private aircraft flew him from Berlin to Essen, the flags were at half-mast at Tempelhof, at half-mast at Essen-Mülheim, at half-mast on the Kraus factories.

Gottlieb Linke helped his employer from the car and, leaning massively on his stick, the Baron stood for a moment listening to the endless snorting and groaning of heavy equipment, the pounding of the power-hammers. He sniffed the soot and sulphur that hung heavily in the falling rain. He saw the jets of flame that illuminated the sky day and night from the Kraus furnaces.

A siren sounded to indicate the end of a shift and a stream of men massed towards the gates, while another crowd clocked in. Work never ceased in these great rolling mills and steel shops, in these vast smelters and forges. And now, more than ever, the workers arrived in a spirit of optimism. The Depression was over. Hitler was going to make them prosperous again.

'Good morning, Father,' Ernst said, hurrying towards him. 'Your visit is most unexpected. Is anything the matter?'

The Baron lumbered towards the main entrance. A porter opened a lift door. They entered and ascended to the first floor. Only when he was stationed at the window looking out across the roofs of the vast gunshops and factories, did the Baron speak. 'Hitler will be in Essen today to attend the wedding of Gauleiter Terboven. In the late afternoon, he will visit our works. See that everything is in order.'

The day passed in feverish activity. Clean overalls were issued to all the staff, flags and bunting decorated the reception hall, offices and workshops. Huge swastika standards were hung from the massive chimneys dominating the town.

The Baron left Ernst to conduct Hitler through the works. He waited to receive him in his suite, for he had a special message for Hitler's ears alone, a message that would be all the more potent after Hitler had seen with his own eyes the immensity of the Kraus empire and understood the power that the Baron himself wielded.

When he and Hitler were finally alone, he did not mince his words. 'The SA is a threat to the security of Germany, Herr Hitler. This Second Revolution must be nipped in the bud.'

'Röhm is not against me,' Hitler objected. The Baron shrugged and had the satisfaction of seeing Hitler look uneasy. *He cannot make up his mind*, he thought. *He is still unused to total power. He is hesitant because Röhm is his friend. He has not yet accustomed himself to the thought that even friendships must be sacrificed when the occasion demands.*

'Herr Hitler, these men are traitors and mutineers. There is only one thing to do with them. They must be exterminated before the canker spreads, before Germany's relations with foreign powers are quite destroyed, before our economy is totally disrupted, before the Reichswehr is forced to take matters into its own hands and attempt its own military coup, in order to preserve the peace.'

Without saying a word, Hitler stared at him for a long time, then, very slowly, he nodded and stood up. 'Thank you, Herr Baron. My visit to Kraus has been most instructive.'

The following day, the army was placed on a state of alert. All leave was cancelled and all troops were confined to barracks. General von

Blomberg published a signed article in the *Völkischer Beobachter*. 'The Army,' he wrote, 'considers itself in close harmony with the Reich of Adolf Hitler… The role of the Army is clearly determined: it must serve the National Socialist State, which it recognizes. The hearts of the Reich and the Army beat in unison…'

The Baron permitted himself a thin smile, in no doubt as to what would happen next. Hitler could not afford fo ignore the challenge extended to him first by the Baron and now by the Reichswehr, for his continued survival depended upon them. Now, he would be forced to act.

On Saturday, 30 June, dawn came early in a haze of grey mist at Grubenmünde concentration camp, where Obersturmbannführer Otto Tobisch was in charge of the morning rollcall, a long and tedious business, because there were now over three thousand prisoners in Grubenmünde.

Wearing the insignia of the SS Death's Head Division and with Wolf at his side, he watched the prisoners march in groups of ten from their blocks onto the parade ground. The Block Senior gave the commands. 'Stand to attention! Caps off!' Then he reported the number of prisoners present, those sick, those at work. SS men counted the prisoners present and confirmed the names against the Senior's list. 'Caps on! At ease!'

Zumstein's aide appeared at Otto's side. 'Obersturmbannführer, you are to report to the Commandant's office immediately.'

Otto signalled to another officer to take over and marched up to Zumstein's office, where five of his colleagues were already gathered.

'I have just received orders from Standartenführer Heydrich in Berlin,' Zumstein announced. 'By order of the Führer, a state of emergency has been declared. You are to report to Lichterfelde Barracks immediately — your task to put down the Second Revolution.'

At last, the moment had arrived for which the SS officers at Grubenmünde had been waiting, when the blackshirted elite would show their superiority over the brownshirted rabble.

At the Hotel Quadriga, that weekend began like any other. The first hint they had of anything out of the ordinary was when Mortimer tried to ring Joyce and was informed that all international telephone services had been stopped until further notice. Visits to the Foreign and Propaganda Ministries elicited no information, but an English reporter told him, 'There's something funny going on and I think it's to do with the SA.'

'You mean Röhm is staging his putsch?'

His English colleague shook his head. 'I don't think so. The Standartenstrasse has been closed off, with armed police guarding both ends.'

'The Standartenstrasse? That's where the SA headquarters are.'

'There seem to be a heck of a lot of police cars about, particularly from the General Göring squad.' One rushed past them at that moment, preceded by a screaming SS motorcycle unit.

Chuck Harris joined them. 'The Tiergarten is full of SS troops and there's a hell of a traffic jam on the Charlottenburger Chaussee.'

Baffled, Mortimer asked, 'What the devil is happening?'

It was afternoon before he found out, when a telephone call summoned him to a press conference at the Propaganda Ministry, where an official explained that Dr Goebbels had been summoned by the Führer to accompany him to Bavaria. In his absence, General Göring would address the foreign press corps.

Accompanied by a retinue of aides, Göring walked onto the podium, dressed in his blue aviation uniform with white tabs, carrying a mediaeval-looking sword and wearing a tragic, almost funereal expression. He read from a prepared statement, explaining that the Führer had entrusted him with special powers to strike at those who thought they could overthrow the State, whether on the Right or the Left.

Everywhere the operation had been successful. In Munich, Röhm and the other leaders had been arrested. Those who had offered resistance had been killed, while others had committed suicide. Quite emphatically, he declared, the SA as a whole, and especially the Führer's devoted SS, were absolutely loyal, as were all State servants.

It was just that some of the SA rank and file had been led astray by unworthy leaders.

There was a stunned silence, then an excited buzz of conversation. Göring turned to leave the room and one reporter called, 'Herr General, I have heard that General von Schleicher was among those who lost their lives.'

Göring stared at him icily. 'General von Schleicher was plotting against the regime. I ordered his arrest. He made the mistake of trying to resist. He is dead.'

Mortimer took a deep breath. So this was a purge not just of the SA, but of other opponents of the Party. If Schleicher were dead, how many others had perished in Göring's operation? He took a text of the official communiqué from a Reichswehr officer, but it gave him no more information. Slowly, he made his way back towards the Hotel Quadriga in the hot afternoon sun. Berliners were strolling under the dappled shade of the lime trees, still unaware that anything untoward had taken place.

Special late editions of the newspapers carried an announcement that some SA leaders had been executed for treason. In the Quadriga bar, guests discussed the news in quiet groups, their overwhelming feeling one of relief that the hold of the stormtroopers had been broken. Benno summed it up when he told Mortimer, 'Now we can get on with our lives in peace.'

'It doesn't worry you that the SA leaders have been summarily executed, that they were given no trial?' Mortimer asked.

'Herr Allen, they were traitors, plotting a putsch. There is only one way to deal with treason.'

'What about General von Schleicher?'

Benno looked round the bar cautiously. 'I have heard that he was in league with Röhm. If that was so, he was also guilty and deserved to die.'

Long into the night, Lichterfelde Barracks reverberated to the sound of gunfire. The grey walls of the courtyard were splashed with blood and pieces of flesh, as members of the Second Revolution were lined up and shot.

'Load! Aim! Fire!' Otto Tobisch felt no compunction as he issued his staccato orders to the firing squad. These men were traitors to the Reich. They were getting their just deserts.

Not even when Karl Ernst, the leader of the Berlin SA and a former colleague of Otto, was dragged into the courtyard, his elegant figure dishevelled, one of his eyes blacked and a bloody bruise across his forehead, did Otto experience any unease. The guards threw Karl Ernst forward and he stumbled and fell.

The SA man staggered to his feet, stared dazedly about him, then recognized Otto. 'Comrade, what's happening? I was going on honeymoon. We were just outside Bremen, when they stopped my car and knocked me out. They said there's been a putsch…'

'Shut up!' Otto ordered. Whether or not he had participated in the putsch, Ernst was an enemy of the Reich. And for that he must die. He drew his Luger from his holster. 'By your treachery, you have forfeited all right to life.'

The SA leader stared at him disbelievingly. 'Tobisch, we were comrades…'

Otto lifted his Luger to Ernst's temple and a nine millimetre bullet splattered the man's brains over the grey prison wall.

This was what they should do at the concentration camps, he thought. Rather than keep the traitorous Bolshevik and Jewish scum alive, they should simply exterminate them.

It was only as Sunday wore on that disquieting stories began to circulate through the Quadriga. It appeared that not only General von Schleicher, but his wife too, had been shot. Neither was he the only army officer to have been killed. His close friend, General von Bredow, was also dead. Franz von Papen had been placed under house arrest — ostensibly for his own safety. His *Chef de Cabinet*, Herr von Bose, who had written the famous Marburg speech, and several other members of his staff, had lost their lives.

'The suppression of the SA is one thing,' Viktoria told Mortimer with a troubled expression, 'but it's beginning to look as if Hitler is getting rid of everyone who has ever opposed him.'

Mortimer had spent the morning trying to glean information from his various contacts throughout the city. 'I think you're right,' he told her gravely. 'From what I can gather, many more people have been killed than has been reported. One of my informants who lives near the Lichterfelde barracks says there has been a constant stream of SS lorries driving in. He claims the sound of gunfire was so loud that it kept him awake last night.'

Viktoria bit her lip. 'In other words, you believe the SS has been carrying out this purge?'

'It appears so.'

In the afternoon, the state of alert was cancelled and troops paraded past the Chancellery, receiving Hitler's salute. In the evening, Peter von Biederstein entered the Quadriga bar in the company of two fellow officers and ordered a bottle of champagne.

He was no sooner seated than Mortimer approached him.

'Herr Colonel, are you able to give me any information on this weekend's events?'

Peter gave a bland smile. 'Herr Allen, you probably know more than I do. What has gone on this weekend was an internal struggle within the Nazi Party. Naturally, the Reichswehr had to stand ready, in case things became violent, but the matter seems to have been resolved peacefully.'

'And the murder of Generals von Schleicher and von Bredow?'

Peter grimaced. 'Yes, I have heard of these unfortunate incidents, but if the Generals resisted arrest, I suppose they were to blame.'

'The role played by the SS does not concern you, Herr Colonel?'

'The SS?'

Mortimer took a deep breath. 'By standing aloof from the weekend's carnage, the army has kept its integrity and honour intact. But, in my opinion, like Faust, it has in reality sold its soul to the devil. From now on, the real military masters of Germany will be the SS.'

Peter stared at him in genuine bewilderment. 'Herr Allen, you are wrong. The SS is a negligible force. By breaking the power of the SA, Hitler has demonstrated very clearly that he regards the Reichswehr as the sole bearer of arms for the nation.'

In the streets of Essen, that Monday evening, a massive parade took place. It was headed by SS bands and followed by rank upon rank of blackshirted SS men. They marched through streets bedecked with flags and lined with fanatically cheering crowds. The band played, 'We are marching through the Ruhr.' Kraus workers massed at the entrance waved their flags and screamed their applause.

At his office window, Baron Heinrich watched the scene with supreme satisfaction. Once again, at a vital moment in German history, he had not only influenced events but proved himself to be a very real power behind the throne. He turned to Ernst. 'Well, boy, it's time I returned to Berlin. Tell the pilot to have the plane ready in an hour's time. I have an appointment to see Himmler tomorrow.'

Ernst's fat face stared at him in bewilderment. 'Himmler?'

His father ground out his cigar. 'As a result of this fiasco, Himmler has become the second most powerful man in Germany.' He almost added smugly, 'after myself', but avoided the temptation. That private conversation with Hitler was no business of Ernst's.

It did not occur to the Baron that Hitler might have learned from his moment of weakness and would never again ask for or listen to advice from anyone.

The next morning saw the Baron in Himmler's office in the Prinz-Albrecht-Strasse. They sat across the desk from each other, two physically quite disparate men, except for their spectacles — the Baron huge and florid of face, the Reichsführer-SS, forty-two years his junior, slight of figure, with a pale complexion.

'You may have heard of the society called the Circle of Friends of the Reichsführer-SS,' Himmler said. 'It looks after the cultural, social and charitable activities of the SS. Its members are entitled to become officers in the SS and to wear the uniform of the Death's Head troops. Herr Baron, I should be privileged if you would join my Circle of Friends…'

The Baron waved his hand expansively. 'Delighted, Herr Reichsführer. And I'm sure you would appreciate a small financial contribution to your social fund…'

Himmler's bloodless lips formed what passed for a smile. 'I look forward to a mutually profitable friendship…'

A couple of weeks later, Hitler announced, 'In view of the great services rendered by the SS, particularly in connection with the events of 30 June, I promote it to the status of an independent organization within the framework of the Party.'

In an impressive ceremony at Himmler's headquarters in Berlin, Otto Tobisch was promoted to Standartenführer. Zumstein was posted to another camp and Otto became the new Commandant of Grubenmünde.

That same day, Baron Heinrich von Kraus zu Essen visited his tailor for a second fitting of his new SS officer's uniform. The black jacket and trousers were strangely flattering to his corpulent figure.

In the middle of July, schools and universities broke up for the summer holidays and there was a general exodus from Berlin. Viktoria, Benno, Luise and the children joined Ricarda at Heiligensee. Mortimer returned to Oxford, looking forward to spending long hours with Joyce and Libby in a sunny, flower-filled English garden.

But it did not turn out like that. For one thing, leisure was foreign to his nature. For another, although his wife and daughter made him welcome, they also made it clear that, in his absence, they had developed their own lives.

Libby was twelve now and beginning to grow up. She was pleased to see her father again, but once the initial excitement of his return wore off, she renounced him for her best schoolfriend, with whom she had much more in common.

Joyce was still the same, black-haired, scruffy and smelling of turps, but she had her own career. One of her landscapes had been hung at the Royal Academy summer exhibition and, on the strength of its success, commissions were pouring in. Her days were spent in her studio. In the evenings, they sat together, but she asked him nothing about himself — and so he did not volunteer any information. He found himself thinking of Viktoria. In some ways, he felt closer to her than to his own wife.

He had not been home a week when, on 25 July, the world was shattered by news of an attempted Nazi coup in Vienna and the assassination of Chancellor Dollfuss. Mortimer listened to the announcement, then told Joyce, 'I'm going back to Berlin.'

She smiled ruefully. 'It doesn't seem to be turning into a very good holiday, does it?'

But he was already telephoning his editor.

Bill Wallace laughed grimly. 'I've booked you a flight for tomorrow morning, Mort.' He filled him in with a few more details of the day's events, then said, 'Incidentally, it may interest you to know that the German News Agency seems reluctant to admit that Germany was responsible for the putsch. I'll ring you if I hear any more.'

Tense with anxiety, Mortimer remained all evening within earshot of the phone, but it was midnight and Joyce had long since gone to bed before Bill rang back. 'The official German version seems to be that the putsch and Dollfuss's murder are a totally Austrian affair, nothing to do with them. We've also heard that Mussolini has mobilized four divisions on the Brenner, which must be causing alarm in Berlin. Good luck, Mort. And sorry to break up your vacation.'

Mortimer grunted and hung up the receiver.

Almost immediately, the telephone jangled again. 'Mr Allen? Churchill speaking. In view of the grave news from Vienna, I assume you will now be returning to Berlin. I merely wished to apprise you that, in my opinion, this will not be Germany's last attempt to win Austria into the Greater German Reich.'

For a long time, they spoke about Austria, Poland and France, about Germany's territorial and military aims, and the perils inherent in Hitler's kind of dictatorship. It was evident from Churchill's voice that he was still filled with grave foreboding for the future. Finally, he said, 'I am indebted to you for the invaluable information you send me, Mr Allen. Continue your good work and your vigilance.'

There was a click and the phone went dead. Mortimer lit a cigarette and quietly let himself into the garden. The sky was bright with stars. The air was heavy with the perfume of night-scented stocks. And in Vienna, Dollfuss had been left to bleed to death from gunshot wounds.

181

There was a movement behind him and Joyce slipped her arm round his waist. 'Mortimer, I'm sorry. I didn't realize this business with Dollfuss was so serious.'

'The assassination of a European Chancellor not serious?'

'From what one reads in the papers, people seem to be being killed all the time in Europe, particularly in Germany.' Her voice shook a little. 'I read the editorial in the *New York News* after the Röhm putsch. It said, "Life is cheap in Germany nowadays." Somehow, I assumed you had got used to it and that you didn't care any more.'

'Is that why you haven't asked me about it?'

She nodded.

He sighed and kissed the top of her head. 'Oh dear, the problems we create for ourselves by the inability to communicate. Bill wrote that editorial, not me. I care, all right. That's why I have to go back.' He threw his cigarette stub onto the lawn and watched it glow in the dark until its little light expired.

Joyce shivered in her thin nightdress.

He put his arm round her. 'Come on, let's go to bed.'

But as he lay beside her, he wondered if he was telling the whole truth about his reason for returning to Berlin. Was it just the political situation? Or was there a deeper and more personal motive that even he did not fully understand?

In the early morning, Mortimer packed his bags, telephoned for a taxi, took Joyce and Libby a cup of tea in bed and then he was gone.

The Wednesday following his return, at nine o'clock in the morning, the death was announced of President Field Marshal von Hindenburg. Throughout Berlin, men doffed their hats and women dressed in black in salute to the passing of this great figure. He was eighty-seven and his health had long been ailing, but he was the Grand Old Man of Germany, one of the few remaining links to the good old days of the monarchy. And, now he was gone, the question that hung on everyone's lips was, who would be the next president?

Hitler did not leave them long in their uncertainty. At noon, exactly three hours after Hindenburg's death, it was announced that there would be no new president. In accordance with a law enacted the previous day — thus implying that it had the late President's approval

— Hitler had become absolute Head of State and Commander in Chief of the Armed Forces. He would henceforth be known as the Führer. Instead of an election, a plebiscite would be held on 19 August, at which the people could demonstrate their approval.

What kind of skulduggery had gone on behind the scenes to get that piece of legislation passed, Mortimer wondered. But at the final count, it made little difference. Hindenburg was dead and Hitler had become Führer. With the result of the plebiscite a foregone conclusion, his dictatorship was complete.

To officers of the old order, like Peter von Biederstein, Hindenburg had been less the President of the Reich, than the venerable Field Marshal who had led them through the Great War. Coming so soon upon this sad news, the announcement that Hitler had become Commander in Chief of the Armed Forces stunned them.

But they were given scant time for reflection or discussion, for within the course of the next twenty-four hours, at the Reichswehr Ministry in the Bendlerstrasse and in parade ground ceremonies at barracks throughout Germany, every officer and soldier made an oath of allegiance to Hitler, vowing:

I swear by God this sacred oath, that I will render absolute obedience to Adolf Hitler, the Führer of the German Reich and Commander in Chief of the Armed Forces, and will be ready as a brave soldier to sacrifice my life at any time for this oath.

Drums rolled and trumpets sounded a triumphant fanfare. Shortly after Peter had returned to his office following the ceremony, there was a knock at the door and General Beck entered. Peter stood to attention and saluted. 'Herr General!'

The general signalled Peter to stand at ease. His face lined and grey, he walked to the window and stared out at the summer sky. 'There was no warning. One moment, the old Marshal was alive, the next moment he was dead. Biederstein, I fear that, with him, has died the last soldierly ideal. Now Hitler possesses powers formerly undreamed of.'

To give himself time to think, Peter pulled his cigarette case from his pocket and laid it on his desk. 'Field Marshal von Hindenburg approved Hitler's appointment, Herr General.'

'So it is said, but I find it hard to believe that he approved an oath of allegiance to Hitler in person.'

For the first time, Peter considered the full implications of the words he had just sworn. Slowly, he asked, 'You are concerned in case there should ever be a conflict between obedience to the Führer and duty to the nation?'

Beck sighed heavily and turned to face Peter. 'Yes. I have the feeling that I have betrayed my class and my country by taking that oath.'

'Hitler may not come from our class, but he is indubitably a patriot. I cannot believe that he will ever do anything against the interests of Germany.'

Beck nodded and moved towards the door. With his hand on the knob, he said, 'Nevertheless, this is the blackest day in my life.'

After he had gone, Peter lit a cigarette. He respected General Beck as an excellent Chief of General Staff, a man of sound reason and utter integrity. Beck had long sympathized with Nazi policies and agreed with all Hitler's plans for the Reichswehr. Why was he now suddenly having reservations?

On the morning of 18 August, an officious young man in semi-military uniform and wearing a Party badge came to the cottage at Heiligensee. Hilde Weber had not yet arrived, so Viktoria opened the door to him. He raised his right arm, fully outstretched, to eye level, and bellowed, 'Heil Hitler! My name is Toll and I am Blockwart for this district.'

Viktoria did not return the salute. Whoever he was, this distasteful little man had been well named. Toll meant mad — and that he undoubtedly was. 'Blockwart? What does that mean?'

Affronted, he pulled a bulging file from a large briefcase. 'I am the warden responsible for this block of houses. It is my duty to ensure that you go to the polling station tomorrow and vote in the plebiscite.

Now, if I may see the head of the household, I must check the names of all the residents against my register.'

At that moment, Benno appeared on the scene. He saluted Toll with an abrupt, 'Heil Hitler!' Then he said, 'There are six of us here: my wife and myself…'

Soberly, Viktoria went into the house. She had thought she was free at Heiligensee. She had been wrong.

Next day, a Sunday, they went to the village hall, temporarily transformed into a polling station. Three SS men stood at the doors and saluted as they entered. Benno saluted back. For a moment, Viktoria hesitated, then raised her own arm.

Inside, against a backdrop of swastika banners with a portrait of Hitler in place of honour, an election committee sat behind an enormous table. Blockwart Toll hovered nearby. Their names were checked twice: against an alphabetical list and Toll's residential index. Then they were handed voting papers and filed into the booths. It was very simple. They either had to tick 'Yes', indicating that they approved the Führer's rule, or 'No', to show their disfavour.

Viktoria's pencil hovered over the paper. Her main objection to the Nazis had always been the stormtroopers, but now the SA had been brought to heel, the worst people like herself had to fear were petty bureaucrats like Blockwart Toll.

There were, of course, other matters of which she disapproved: censorship, the Nazification of education and culture, the treatment of the Jews, concentration camps, the Hitler Youth. But already, she was learning to live with them.

And Hitler, as Benno had so frequently pointed out, was a patriot. He had come to power when there were six million unemployed and the country was threatened by a communist revolution. Already half those unemployed now had jobs and the economy was gradually righting itself. He was making Germany strong again. Prosperity seemed to loom on the near horizon — so long as Hitler was given an opportunity to complete what he had started. And hopefully, when this occurred, the initial fervour of the Revolution would die down and there would be a growing laxity in other areas of everyday life…

To vote 'No' seemed a negative action. It was to condemn without suggesting any alternative. To vote 'Yes' was the mark of a generous spirit, prepared to give the government a chance. In a sudden moment of decision, Viktoria ticked 'Yes'. She folded her paper, placed it in the sealed urn in the centre of the room and walked out, past the SS guards, into the sunlight and to the sound of church bells ringing.

Stefan linked his arm through hers, as they made their way back to the cottage. 'I'm going to watch when they count the votes tonight,' he said. 'I want to see if the figures are rigged.'

'How will you know?'

'Well, at least two people voted no — you and I.' Since the book-burning, Stefan had remained steadfastly anti-Nazi.

Viktoria could not bring herself to admit that she had betrayed his trust.

Stefan and Benno both went to watch the public counting of the votes that evening. The results were immediately announced. Fourteen per cent of the people of Heiligensee had voted against the Führer. The remaining eighty-six per cent were overwhelmingly in his favour.

Next morning, Fritzi brought them a newspaper giving the results for all Germany. Over thirty-eight million had voted yes; four and a half million had said no. 'What did you vote?' Viktoria asked Luise as they wandered across the lawn.

'I'm certainly no heroine. I've no desire to spend the next few months in a concentration camp, as I would if Blockwart Toll discovered that I was against his beloved Führer. So I voted yes. Didn't you?'

Viktoria nodded. She had believed she had voted yes from conviction. But now, she realized, it had also been from fear. Then a dreadful thought occurred to her. 'Stefi voted no!'

'He'll be all right,' Luise said consolingly. 'It won't be long before he goes to Oxford. Perhaps it's a good job he's going.'

'If he wins his scholarship...' For the first time, Viktoria found herself hoping he would. He might be a long way away from her in England, but at least he would be safe.

CHAPTER FIVE

That afternoon, Sepp packed a small travelling bag, jumped into his open-topped sports car and set off for Heiligensee. The traffic was thick and he drove slowly, enjoying the warm wind in his hair and on his face. Driving wasn't flying — but it was the next best thing. And it was certainly better than the interminable meetings in which he seemed to be constantly involved nowadays at the Air Ministry.

With an ease born of long practice, he ducked towards the windscreen and lit a cigarette. Milch, Kesselring, Wever and Stumpff — all of them army men, staff officers, administrators! And, more than anything, all of them politicians, squabbling for priority in finance, manpower, buildings, equipment and personal prestige, with their armies of clerks, executives and engineers, few of whom had any experience of flying — or any desire to learn.

The traffic started to clear and a long straight stretch of road opened up across the Jungfernheide beside the canal. He double-declutched, changed down into second, then accelerated past a huge black chauffeur-driven Mercedes containing two uniformed Party officials. Bah! Officialdom! For a couple of pfennigs, he'd say good riddance to the lot of them — including the Fat Man, General Göring — and return to Kenya. There had been no politics, phoney putsches or plebiscites in the bush, and he had been his own man, free as a bird...

He shook his head, knowing he would not go back to Kenya, for no sane man walked out on a dream when it was coming true. Despite all the little men, the Luftwaffe would be created: it would become the finest air force in the world, with machines of the most advanced design and pilots of the highest calibre, keen young daredevils trained in the mould of Sepp Nowak, fighter ace.

He lit a new cigarette from the butt of the last and entered the Tegel Forest. But he was damned if he was going to join the Air Ministry staff, as Secretary of State Erhard Milch kept insisting to Göring that he should. Milch! He had never met anyone whom he detested quite so much. Rumour had it that he was a Jew, although Göring denied it and it seemed unlikely in view of the man's fawning admiration for Hitler.

However, one thing was sure — Milch disliked Sepp every bit as much as Sepp disliked him, and Sepp believed he knew why. Milch was jealous of his ability, his popularity and his friendship with the Fat Man. He resented his independence and his non-conformist attitude. Milch liked everything to be neat and under control — which Sepp, in his old flying jacket, a cigarette in his mouth and a joke on his lips, certainly was not. By bringing him onto his staff, Milch hoped either to tame or to break Sepp Nowak. But Sepp wasn't having it...

He drove down the Heiligenseestrasse and into the village, no longer as small and rural as he remembered it, nor as remote. There were flags outside the village hall and various self-important officials bustling around. He turned down a winding drive banked with dense shrubs. Suddenly, the cottage came into sight and he caught his breath. What a place! What a view!

'Sepp! Sepp!' Luise was running across the lawn, her hair streaming out behind her, preceded by an excited Sheltie.

Sepp stopped the car and, without bothering to open the door, stepped over it. Sheltie jumped up at him, licking his face. He laughed. 'Hey, Sheltie, calm down.'

Breathlessly, Luise took both his hands in hers. 'Sepp, I thought you were never going to arrive!'

He laughed, suddenly realizing that he had not consciously thought of her once during his journey, but she had been there, all the time, at the back of his mind, the biggest reason of all for him to stay in Berlin — the only woman he had ever wanted to marry.

Yet, after nearly a year, he had still not been able to bring himself to propose to her. Indeed, the closer they had grown, the greater the gap had appeared between them. Sepp looked again at the elegant house standing in its immaculate grounds. He thought of the Hotel Quadriga and Café Jochum. What could he offer to compare with them? A second-hand sports car, a battered biplane, a rented apartment — and himself, forty-two years old, with no real career and a reputation for nonconformity. Not much of a bargain for a woman in Luise Jochum's position.

Luise drew away from him and took his hand. 'Come and have some coffee, then I'll show you round.'

Sheltie raced ahead of them and Sepp grinned ruefully. That dog had everything. It was beautiful, almost flying through the air with a streamlined grace no aeroplane would ever achieve. And, unhampered by considerations of money, job, morals or wedding rings, Sheltie shared Luise's life more intimately than he could ever hope to.

Because they all liked Sepp, they made him feel at home. Stefan and Monika took him down to the boathouse to inspect the yacht. Luise picked a bouquet of fresh flowers for his room. Viktoria asked Hilde to make his favourite dish of green eels with dill sauce for supper. Fritzi washed his car. Over aperitifs, Benno sympathized with Sepp's problems at the Air Ministry. During the meal, they all vied with each other in describing the beauty spots around Heiligensee. Only Luise sat quietly.

When Sepp had first returned, she had been happy to let events take their own course, grateful for his friendship. But since then, she had grown to love him — not with the wild passion she had once felt for Georg Jankowski — but in a much deeper fashion. Most importantly, perhaps, she liked Sepp. She enjoyed his sense of humour. She respected his achievements. When she was in his company, there was a warmth in her she had never experienced before. This was a man with whom she could happily spend the rest of her life, maybe even raise a family... But did Sepp feel the same? Or was he so wedded to his bachelor ways that he had decided against the commitment of marriage for ever?

It was dusk when supper ended. 'I should like to play Halma,' Ricarda announced. 'Stefi, will you fetch the board? Monika, you can be my partner. Vicki, you'll join us, won't you?' She looked meaningfully at Luise, and Luise knew her mother was deliberately occupying the family so that she could be alone with Sepp.

She took Sepp's hand. 'Let's stroll down to the lake.'

Sheltie rushed across to the door. 'I think that dog is a bit off-colour,' Ricarda said. 'She'd better stay here, where I can keep an eye on her. Come, Sheltie.' Tail between legs, Sheltie obeyed.

It was a gloriously mild evening, quiet and still. Little waves lapped softly on the shore and against the jetty. In the centre of the lake, a rowing boat drifted, its single occupant silhouetted against the skyline, trailing a fishing line. Luise led Sepp over to the fallen oak tree and, kicking off her sandals, sat down on the warm grass. He squatted beside her. 'Luischen, what's wrong? You've hardly said a word all evening.'

Ten years ago, when she had been a supremely self-confident twenty-four year old, Luise would not have hesitated to propose to him herself, resolving the issue one way or the other, once and for all. But now she was thirty-four and she had lost too much to run the risk of rejection. She bit her lip and shook her head.

Sepp cupped her chin in his hand, drawing her face towards him. 'Come on, Luischen. What's up?'

She closed her eyes tightly. 'Sepp, do you love me?'

'Love you…? Oh, my God, what a fool I am! Luischen, of course I love you. You're the only person I've really loved in my whole life.'

She opened her eyes. His face was very near to hers, so that its every feature seemed magnified. She raised her hand and wonderingly, with her finger, traced its contours, the lines that crinkled round his tilting eyes, the sharp ridge of his cheekbones, the day's stubble on his upper lip and chin, the scar across the bridge of his nose, his mouth, wide and generous, where even now the beginnings of a smile were appearing. 'Sepp, I…'

'Sssh.' He silenced her with a kiss, infinitely tender and gentle. Then he released her, pulling her to her feet and seating her on the oak trunk. 'In case you haven't realized, I'm an old-fashioned man and I believe in doing things in an old-fashioned way.' Solemnly, he knelt down before her and bowed over her hand. 'Fräulein Jochum, I am only a humble flier with very poor prospects, but I love you more than any other woman in the world. May I request the honour of your hand in marriage?'

A lump rose in her throat and her eyes blurred with tears. She felt his lips on her fingers and myriad images of his face danced hazily in front of her. Yes, yes, yes, she wanted to say, but no words would come.

'Luischen, how much longer must I stay down here?' He was grinning up at her. 'For goodness sake, put me out of my agony. Are you going to say yes or no?'

'Oh, Sepp!' She threw her arms round his neck.

'Do I take it that means yes?'

She nodded against his shoulder, her tears soaking into his shirt.

'Women are very strange creatures,' Sepp commented. 'Last time I proposed to you, you laughed and said no. This time, you are crying and saying yes. I suppose I'll understand you one day.'

When they eventually returned to the house, the Halma game was just finishing with Ricarda and Monika the victors. No trace of her weeping left, Luise faced them with a radiant expression. 'Sepp and I are engaged to be married!'

After they had all congratulated them and Benno had hurried down to the cellar to fetch a bottle of champagne, Sepp added, 'We've decided to get married early next summer. By then, my position should be more settled — and it will be a good time for a honeymoon.'

Sheltie crept across the room and looked up with mournful eyes, her tongue lolling out. Sepp laughed. 'Yes, you can come too.'

It was at the end of their holiday that Monika dropped her bombshell. 'Papa, it will be all right if I go to the Youth Day at the Party Rally, won't it? Nearly all our unit is attending. A special coach has been reserved in the train and we have hostel accommodation at Nuremberg.'

Angrily, Viktoria burst out, 'You remember I gave you permission to join the BdM on the condition that you went to no rallies?'

Monika looked at her knowingly and suddenly Viktoria recalled that scene in her office when she had slapped her daughter's face. 'If the Gestapo knew…' Monika had stated. 'If Papa knew…'

Monika smiled and turned to her brother. 'Stefi, you think I should be allowed to go, don't you?'

Looking distinctly uncomfortable, Stefan muttered, 'I suppose so, if you really want to.'

Triumphantly, Monika turned back to her mother. 'Parents who forbid their children to attend Hitler Youth functions can be heavily fined — or even put in prison.'

'Monika, don't be ridiculous!' Benno snorted. 'Nobody's forbidding you to do anything. We're just concerned for your safety. One hears dreadful stories of what happens at Hitler Youth camps.' He looked rather uncomfortable. 'You're only fourteen — you don't understand the dangers...'

'Why do you want to go?' Viktoria asked.

'It will be so spectacular — the flags, the parades, the music. Frau Forster has told us such wonderful stories. Baldur von Schirach will be there. He's so handsome,' Monika said dreamily. 'But most importantly, I shall see the Führer himself...'

Viktoria sighed. She would never accustom herself to the rituals of Führer worship, the adoration Hitler sparked in the hearts of women like Trudi and girls like Monika.

'Of course, it would be a great privilege for you to see the Führer and hear him speak,' Benno said slowly. 'Vicki, perhaps she should go. It's the opportunity of a lifetime.'

Viktoria nodded weakly. It seemed she had no alternative but to give in. But when she went outside, it was as if a dark cloud had settled over Heiligensee.

Mortimer also received an invitation to the Nuremberg Rally. Curious to experience this, the greatest festival in the Nazi Party calendar, he accepted with alacrity. Even he, however, was unprepared for the near hysteria of the crowds who lined the narrow streets to catch sight of Hitler, streets so hung with flags that the ancient timbered houses, and even the sky, almost disappeared from view.

He had seen parades and rallies in Berlin, but nothing to compare with the sheer immensity of Nuremberg: the vastness of the Zeppelin Field; the massive platform where Hitler and his colleagues sat in state, against a backdrop of swastika banners that reached up like sails on huge galleons; the mighty eagle, towering a hundred feet above the crowds.

The rally opened with a meeting in the Luitpold Hall, the massive auditorium a sea of flags, the stage spotlighted. When Hitler and his aides entered, the orchestra struck up the *Badenweiler Marsch* and, as one, the crowd rose to its feet, arms outstretched. When Hitler was seated on the platform, against a backdrop of some five hundred SA standards, the orchestra played Beethoven's *Egmont* overture.

The ceremony began, as grandiose and awe-inspiring a ritual as any observed in the Kaiser's day. Rudolf Hess read out the names of Nazi martyrs who had been killed in the struggle for power. Gauleiter Wagner of Bavaria read his Führer's proclamation. 'The German way of life is determined for a thousand years to come. The crises of the nineteenth century have ended with us. There will be no other revolution in Germany for the next thousand years!'

The room rose to its feet with ecstatic shouts of 'Heil! Heil! Heil!'

The Rally lasted five days, a masterpiece of organization, a tribute to the genius of Goebbels and Speer, who had arranged it, and a breathtaking indication of the changes that had taken place in Germany since his arrival. Virtually everyone was in some kind of uniform, be they SS officer or Gauleiter, local party official, Labour Front leader or Hitler Youth. They goose-stepped proudly, in strict military formation, standing in straight lines, their arms held uniformly high as they gave the Hitler salute.

An emotional, patriotic fervour charged the ceremonies and conferences attended by hundreds of thousands of delegates, stretching as far as the eye could see. They came from every part of Germany and from every walk of life, but every single one of them belonged to a Nazi organization.

Most staggering of all, however, was the presence of the Reichswehr, the first occasion the Army had ever attended any political party congress. Before an ecstatic crowd of three hundred thousand spectators, they fought a mock battle, which showed that German militarism was a far from forgotten art.

Yes, Mortimer reflected soberly, there might still be malcontents in the country — as had been witnessed by the plebiscite — but the majority of the people were now solidly behind Hitler. He had led them down a road lined with violence and stained with blood, but he had imbued them with a sense of purpose and direction. He had restored their pride in their country and themselves. And he had given them himself — their Führer — their leader.

The Day of German Youth was the greatest event Monika had ever experienced. Parade officials instructed them how they should enter the vast arena, marching in even tempo, their standards held proudly aloft, their eyes right towards the platform where the Nazi hierarchy was seated, and how they must stand to attention listening in silence to the words of Baldur von Schirach and finally to those of the Führer himself.

That day was pervaded with an almost religious ardour: it impressed Monika, it inspired her and, above all, it gave her a feeling of belonging. So mesmerized was she by the pageantry, the uniforms, and the magnificence of the spectacle, that she hardly heard the words of the speeches, but their sentiment reached deep into her soul.

In the youth of today, Hitler said, was the Germany of tomorrow. Upon their shoulders rested the responsibility of a Reich that would last a thousand years. And they would be the victors, they would inherit the earth. 'He who wishes to fight will fight,' Hitler declaimed in ringing tones, 'and whoever does not wish to fight in this world of eternal struggle does not deserve to live.'

He sat down, his eyes glowing with a fanatical light and Baldur von Schirach stepped forward. A Hitler Youth leader raised high the flag and Schirach declared, 'Let this flag be your honour.' Then he chanted, 'Germany, holy word,' and the young people joined in the familiar lines, 'thou who art infinite, may you be glorified for all time. Holy are your lakes, holy your forests, and the garland of your quiet mountain heights as they reach towards the green ocean.'

After this, they sang:

'See in the east the red of the morning,
A symbol of freedom, of sun,
We stand together, whether living or dead,
No matter what shall befall us.

German, awake and stand in line,
We're marching towards victory!
Work should be free, and we must be free
And brave and defiantly daring.

Young and old, man and girl,
Are embracing the swastika banner,
Whether burgher or peasant or working man,
They are swinging the sword and the hammer.

For Hitler, for freedom, for work and for bread.
Germany awake and end the distress!
People, stand to arms! People, stand to arms!'

Across the Zeppelin Field the words echoed, then sixty thousand Hitler Youth lifted their arms in the Hitler salute and screamed their ecstatic approval: '*Sieg Heil! Sieg Heil! Sieg Heil!*' Tears streamed down Monika's face.

Next morning, they returned to Berlin. Monika was still in a vaguely trance-like state and, to start with, paid little attention to the unit of Hitler Youth boys from Pomerania who were travelling in the same carriage, but, when Hedwig Forster and the boys' leader went to the buffet for refreshments and she and Beate found themselves surrounded by an admiring group, she gradually came back to earth.

On the whole, the boys were older than the girls and several of them had already left school. They were big country lads, with broad, open faces and hands rough from work on the land, who clearly found their travelling companions from Berlin extremely glamorous. When Monika told them that her parents owned the Hotel Quadriga, one asked, 'Are you related to Baron von Kraus?'

'He's my grandfather,' she replied nonchalantly.

'He often comes to our village.'

'Where do you live?'

'Fürstenmark.'

Monika gazed at him in amazement. 'Relatives of mine live in Fürstenmark — the von Biedersteins…'

The young man looked suitably impressed. 'My father is the pastor. Let me introduce myself. My name is Hans König.'

Monika studied him more closely. He was probably a year younger than Stefan, tall, with light-brown hair and the beginnings of a fair moustache. Unlike his colleagues, he spoke with an educated accent and his hands were smooth. 'Are you still at school?'

'I've just started college. I'm training to be a teacher. When I'm qualified, I shall teach at Fürstenmark school. Ludwig Schmidt, who runs the school at the moment, will be retiring in a few years' time. And you, what do you want to do?'

A job was not something to which Monika had given any thought. She assumed her parents would keep her until she married and had a home of her own. 'I don't know,' she admitted.

'So you're not one of these emancipated women who want a career and financial independence?'

She was so flattered at being called a woman, she forgot they had only just met. 'No, I want to get married.'

By the time they arrived at Berlin, Monika and Hans had become firm friends. Hans promised to write to her from college and Monika promised to reply immediately. As Hans left her to catch another train for the next stage of his journey, Monika saw her life stretching idyllically ahead of her. As soon as she was old enough, she and Hans would marry and live at Fürstenmark and have lots and lots of babies.

That winter, the Revolution over, everyday life took on a pattern of normality and, wherever she went, Viktoria sensed a growing feeling of confidence. The unemployment figures were going down, as production was increased and new factories were opened. New roads, including the first Autobahn, were under construction.

In the country, the peasant was coming into his own, as a glowing *Blut und Boden* — blood and soil — propaganda campaign announced him to be the salt of the earth. Holiday camps for the workers were provided through the *Kraft durch Freude* — Strength through Joy — movement. Gone were the half-starved waifs who had haunted the slums throughout the last decade and, in their place were the fit, bronzed children of the Hitler Youth.

Yet, despite the optimism that surrounded her, Viktoria felt a stirring of uneasiness. These were the positive aspects of Nazi policy — but there were negative sides too, not least of which was her children's education. Since all teachers had been forced to join the Nazi Teachers Association, there seemed to be less regard for facts than for political propaganda. Because there was little the authorities could do to tamper with English and French, the modern languages Stefan was studying, this affected him less than Monika.

But Monika worried her greatly. Never as clever as Stefan, Monika unquestioningly accepted everything she was taught, with the result that there were large gaps in her knowledge, particularly in literature, biology and history, and corresponding biases towards Party dogma.

When Viktoria tried to correct these imbalances, Monika fobbed her off irritably. 'What does it matter?' she asked on one occasion. 'Nothing they're teaching me is going to be any use to me later, when I'm married. Domestic science is my favourite subject and I'm doing very well at that.'

Rather than argue with her, Viktoria discussed the matter with Benno one evening, when they were getting ready for bed. He listened patiently, then said, 'I understand what you're saying, Vicki, and if Monika were a boy, I'd agree with you. But, as it is, she's an attractive girl and she probably will marry soon after leaving school. It's better that she knows how to run a home, than have her head stuffed full of useless facts.'

'She might want a job as well as a marriage. After all, I do.'

'Yes, you do.' With his back to her, Benno placed his trousers in the press and hung his jacket over a hanger. 'But aren't you unusual — and, in fact, rather selfish? You work, not from necessity, but from choice. As a result, you haven't spent as much time with your children as most mothers.'

'I don't think they've suffered as a result!' Viktoria replied hotly, but even as she spoke, she wondered if there might not be more than a grain of truth in what he said, particularly so far as Monika was concerned.

Benno laid out clean underclothes and socks on a chair. 'A woman's place is really in the home with her husband and children. If that's what Monika wants, I think it a very natural desire.'

Viktoria sat down at the dressing table and unplaited her braids. She had the feeling that they were actually talking about more than Monika. 'Do you resent the role I play in the hotel?'

Benno buttoned up his pyjama jacket. 'How could I resent it? The Quadriga belongs to your family. However, now that you've mentioned it, I do think that you sometimes ignore the fact that you are a woman in a man's world. And I know the staff are sometimes rather confused. The other day, Herr Brandt said he wasn't quite sure whether he was supposed to see me or you about some matter or other.'

'We've never had that sort of problem in the past.'

'I don't know. But I do know that we are entering a new era.' He walked across to her and laid his hand on her shoulder. 'Vicki, I know you mean well and I appreciate all you do. But don't take yourself too seriously, my dear. Running an hotel is a business profession and you are not a businessman.' Lightly, his lips brushed her hair. 'For one thing, you are far too beautiful.'

Stung to the quick, she opened her mouth for an angry retort, but he had gone into the *en suite* bathroom and shut the door behind him. With quick strokes, she brushed her hair. If Benno thought he could exclude her from the running of the Quadriga, he had another think coming!

But during the days that followed, she realized that, without her noticing, certain responsibilities had already been taken from her. A lot of the paperwork, particularly that relating to registration formalities, was no longer brought to her for checking. When she asked Herr Fromm about it, he said, 'There are new regulations, Frau Viktoria. Herr Brandt told me that Herr Benno should approve the forms before sending them off to the authorities. After all, Herr Benno understands these things better…'

'Yes, of course.'

When she commented on this to Benno, he sighed. 'We're in a bureaucratic jungle. In fact, I'm taking on another assistant just to deal with government forms. If you really want the headache of coping with them, you can, but I think your time would be better used making sure our guests are comfortable.'

With this, Viktoria had to be content.

In January 1935, a plebiscite was held in the Saarland, and the population of that small mining and industrial district voted by an overwhelming majority to be ruled by Germany. The first of the old territories of which the humiliating Versailles Treaty had tried to rob Germany had returned to the Reich.

On Saturday, 16 March — the day before Heroes' Remembrance Day, the national day of mourning for two million dead from past wars — Hitler took another huge step towards shaking off the chains of Versailles by passing a new law reintroducing conscription and announcing the formation of a new army comprising thirty-six divisions and some half a million men. Simultaneously, he announced the existence of the Luftwaffe and Kriegsmarine.

Next morning, Sepp Nowak arrived at the Hotel Quadriga in a new blue uniform with yellow piping on his epaulettes, his visored cap worn at a jaunty angle. On it was the national rosette, flanked by oak leaves and spreading wings, surmounted by a flying eagle. Mortimer, on his way to the State Opera House for the Remembrance Day ceremony, did not recognize him as they passed in the foyer. It was only when Sepp called, 'Hey, Mortimer, don't you greet old friends any more?' that he stopped, stared incredulously, then reached out his hand to shake Sepp's.

Sepp laughed. 'Oberst Nowak at your service, Herr Allen. Yes, I've succumbed! The Fat Man made me an offer I couldn't refuse. Chief Training Officer of Air Fleet One, Berlin.' He reached in his pocket. 'Have a cigarette and stop looking so surprised. It's not the first time I've sported a uniform, you know.'

Mortimer accepted the cigarette, but before he could say anything, Luise appeared. Sepp swept off his cap and bowed low before her. 'Gracious lady, you see before you, no longer an impecunious civilian, but an officer in the Luftwaffe. From now on, the sky's the limit. There's nowhere to go but up!'

'Oh, Sepp, I'm so pleased for you!'

But Mortimer felt unable to share their happiness and, filled with misgivings, continued on his way.

His feeling of mistrust increased when he entered the Opera House. Across the spotlit stage curtains hung a massive Iron Cross, in front of which officers from the armed forces stood in formation holding war flags. The tiered seats of the auditorium were filled with military uniforms: the grey of the old army, the brown of the new, the blues of the Luftwaffe and the Navy, every one of them bearing the swastika insignia. Hitler and his aides sat in the royal box. The orchestra played Beethoven's *Funeral March*.

General von Blomberg spoke: 'The world has been made to realize that Germany did not die of its defeat in the World War. Germany will again take the place she deserves among the nations. We pledge ourselves to a Germany which will never surrender and never again sign a treaty which cannot be fulfilled...'

When the ceremony was over, Mortimer succeeded in falling in step with Peter von Biederstein. 'Good morning, Colonel.'

The Count saluted. 'Herr Allen, I am pleased that you were able to witness this great and historic occasion.'

Mortimer's eyes moved from the Iron Cross Peter wore so proudly at his throat to the swastika carried by the outstretched wings of an eagle on his right breast and, not for the first time, he wondered what this man was made of.

'You are looking pensive, Herr Allen. Does this new law trouble you?' A sardonic smile played on Count Peter's lips beneath the clipped moustache.

'As an American, I am, of course, wondering what the Allies will do.'

Peter tapped his polished black boot with his swagger stick. 'We have volunteered to disarm, but the Allies have refused our proposals. In my opinion, rearmament and conscription are our only option. Indeed, they are our right!'

Mortimer nodded. Yes, a former Austrian corporal had achieved what Field Marshal von Hindenburg had never even tried to do. He had recreated a navy, established an air force and restored the German army to its former prestigious status! To Sepp had been given the freedom of the open skies, to Peter the challenging prospects of promotion and glory. Why should either suffer misgivings?

But the member countries of the League of Nations must surely react! Hitler had thrown down the gauntlet. He had openly defied the Allies. Mortimer waited to learn world reaction to this flagrant breach of the Versailles Peace Treaty.

To his amazement, almost as if nothing untoward had occurred, the British Foreign Secretary, Sir John Simon, and the Lord Privy Seal, Mr Anthony Eden, accepted a longstanding invitation from Hitler to visit Berlin, reporting back to the Commons in due course that the Luftwaffe was already of equal strength to the Royal Air Force, a fact received with apparent equanimity by everyone except Churchill.

The League of Nations met. The French reluctantly agreed to extend compulsory military service from one year to two. Mussolini, whose Italian troops had, for several months, been stirring up trouble on the border between Somaliland and Abyssinia, gave veiled hints that he would side with England and France, provided he were given free rein in Africa. From America came benign good wishes that Europe should sort out its own affairs.

In due course, nineteen countries formally protested against Hitler's breach of the Versailles Treaty but, other than protest, they did nothing to stop Germany from rearming.

On 21 May, news of further changes emerged. The Reichswehr was renamed the Wehrmacht, with General von Blomberg the Commander in Chief, and each of the services was appointed its own commander in chief and general staff. General Beck, instead of being head of the Troop Office, became the official Chief of Army General

Staff.

That evening, Mortimer was again present at the Kroll when Hitler addressed the Reichstag. It was a long, impassioned and well-reasoned speech, in which Hitler offered to conclude non-aggression pacts with all Germany's neighbours and again and again impressed upon the deputies — and the world — Germany's desire for peace. 'We renounce all claims to Alsace-Lorraine, a land for which we have fought two great wars... We shall adhere unconditionally to our non-aggression pact with Poland... Germany neither intends nor wishes to interfere in the internal affairs of Austria, to annex Austria, or to conclude an Anschluss...'

In return for his assurances of peace, Hitler demanded justice and equality for Germany and, primarily, he asked that the military conditions of the Versailles Treaty be done away with.

Mortimer's pencil sped across the pages of his notebook, but his mind was looking beneath the words. This, he was convinced, was a bid for time. Hitler had already demonstrated his blatant disregard for Versailles. While the nations of the world convened and discussed, pontificated and debated, his Wehrmacht would continue to grow in size until it was simply too late for anyone to do anything about it.

And, in the meantime, his war would continue against the enemy at home — against the Jews, the Church, the socialists and all other so-called enemies of the Reich.

This was the essence of the accompanying note he sent to Bill Wallace with his report, but the editorial in the *New York News* of 23 May contained no hint of Mortimer's reservations. Instead, it read: 'Herr Hitler's speech should give men everywhere hope that Germany, now once again a strong and united nation, can help us protect the peace we all so desperately desire.'

Mortimer then knew the added frustration of having this pointed out to him by Benno. 'I am pleased to see that you are finally becoming convinced that the Führer is sincere, Herr Allen.'

Mortimer bit back angry words. Benno, Bill, Peter, Sepp, they were decent, law-abiding men, but they were all blinded by their own dreams and delusions.

Next day, when he went to the British Embassy, James Adams handed Mortimer an envelope sent from London in the diplomatic bag. The sheet of notepaper inside bore the address, 'Chartwell, Kent' and some handwritten lines of verse:

Who is in charge of the clattering train?
The axles creak and the couplings strain,
And the pace is hot, and the points are near,
And Sleep has deadened the driver's ear;
And the signals flash through the night in vain,
For Death is in charge of the clattering train.

Mortimer read them and did not know whether to laugh or cry.

Luise and Sepp were married on 1 June 1935. Luise looked beautiful as she walked up the aisle of Schmargendorf church on Benno's arm. Tall and very slender, she wore the dress her mother had worn forty-six years earlier when she had married Karl, a cloud of handmade lace yellowed slightly with age, with a fitting bodice and full skirt and a flowing train held up by two bridesmaids, Monika and Christa. Sprigs of syringa garlanded the veil covering her auburn curls. In her hand, she held a spray of pink carnations and lily of the valley.

The organist played Wagner's *Wedding March* and the congregation rose. Sepp, elegant in his Luftwaffe uniform, and Stefan, who was his best man and quite resplendent in a pearl-grey morning suit, stepped forward to meet them at the altar. Pastor Scheer commenced the service. So nervous was she that Luise hardly heard the words until he asked, 'Wilt thou, Luise, take this Man to be thy wedded husband, to live together after God's ordinance in the holy estate of Matrimony? Wilt thou obey him, and serve him, love, honour, and keep him in sickness and in health; and, forsaking all others, keep thee only unto him, so long as ye both shall live?'

Luise gazed lovingly at Sepp. 'I will.'

'Who giveth this Woman to be married to this Man?'

Benno took her hand, placed it in Sepp's and they plighted their troth. And then they were giving each other rings and saying, 'With this Ring I thee wed, with my body I thee worship, and with all my worldly goods I thee endow…'

Pastor Scheer joined their right hands and said, 'Those whom God hath joined together let no man put asunder.'

There were prayers and hymns, an address from Pastor Scheer, the signing of the register and eventually Luise and Sepp were walking back down the aisle, between pews filled with brightly dressed people with smiling faces, to emerge into the sunshine. Sepp stopped and tipped her face towards his. For once, his tilted eyes were serious. 'I love you, Luischen. I shall try to be the husband you deserve.' Then, ignoring the congregation spilling out of the church, he took her in his arms and kissed her.

In a stately procession of limousines, they travelled back to the hotel, where virtually the entire staff was waiting on the steps to greet them. Herr Brandt stepped forward to open the door of the bridal car and hand Sepp and Luise out. Then, bowing deeply, he said, 'Frau Nowak, on behalf of the personnel of the Hotel Quadriga and Café Jochum, I wish you and the Herr Oberst a long and happy marriage.'

'And many little *bambini*!' Chef Mazzoni stepped forward, swept his white hat from his head, took Luise's hand in his and kissed it.

There were cheers, laughter and a few surreptitious tears from female members of staff.

'Oh, thank you all so much,' Luise said. Then Sepp took her arm and, preceded by Herr Brandt, led her into the Jubilee Room, where aperitifs and cocktails were being served before the wedding luncheon. Luise said little, but her radiant face spoke for her.

Throughout the meal, prepared and served in the very best tradition of the hotel, and accompanied by the very finest of wines from the cellars, an atmosphere of excited suspense permeated the room. Much of the conversation centred round other weddings.

'Karl and I went to Heiligensee for our honeymoon,' Ricarda sighed nostalgically. 'It's a tradition in our family.'

A shiver ran down Viktoria's back as she remembered her own wedding day at the beginning of the war and the dreadful knowledge that she had already been pregnant with Peter's child. Then she shook the thought away. That was a long time ago. And today was a happy day.

Countess Julia asked, 'Are you and Sepp spending your honeymoon at Heiligensee, Luise?'

Luise glanced shyly at Sepp. 'As Mama says, it's a tradition.'

Sepp just grinned.

The ladies looked conspiratorially at each other and smiled.

Luise saw them smile and was wondering why, when Professor Ascher asked, 'Are you planning to set up home here at the hotel?'

'Benno and Viktoria very kindly offered us an apartment here at the Quadriga, but Luise says she'd prefer to move into my flat, sir,' Sepp replied. 'It's very small, but there's still room for the three of us.'

'Three?' Mortimer asked, startled.

'Don't forget Sheltie!' Sepp laughed.

The young people were seated together. 'I shall be eighteen this year,' Werner told them proudly. He grew to look more and more like his father and grandfather. 'That means I shall be conscripted in the autumn — one of the very first. What about you, Stefan?'

'I hope I shall be exempted until I've finished my studies,' Stefan replied stiffly, wondering when the long-expected telegram would arrive from the Rhodes Scholarship selection committee.

'You don't want to do military service?'

'Not very much.'

'I don't mind,' Norbert said, 'but a year in the Army isn't going to help me become an architect.' Fifteen now, it was more than ever apparent that he was not a typical Kraus. His was a rebellious nature, with the added charm of a lurking sense of humour...

Monika and Christa, both looking very pretty in their pale pink bridesmaid's dresses, were seated opposite them. 'Do you think Aunt Luise has guessed — about her surprise?' Monika demanded.

'What surprise?' Norbert asked.

Monika looked at him disdainfully. Since meeting Hans König, she chose to forget their brief experience in the conservatory. 'Norbert, you are stupid sometimes!'

Norbert flushed.

'Oberst Nowak has a special present for her,' Christa said shyly.

Christa was a sweet little thing, Stefan thought, but childish compared to Monika.

At the end of the meal, speeches were made and toasts were drunk, then, still early in the afternoon, Sepp turned to Luise. 'Do you mind leaving your wedding early?'

If Sepp had suggested they should go swimming in the Havel, Luise would not have objected, so happy was she. 'Whatever you want.'

'I'll come up and help you change,' her mother said.

Sepp grinned. 'Put on something warm. It may be a bit chilly travelling all the way to Heiligensee in a horse-drawn carriage.'

'Sepp, how romantic! Are we really going by Droschke?'

'You know me,' Sepp laughed. 'I'm an old-fashioned chap.'

There was indeed a horse-drawn carriage waiting on Unter den Linden when Luise and Sepp reappeared, and all the guests were waiting on the hotel steps to wave them goodbye. Amid a shower of rice and rose petals, they set off towards the Brandenburg Gate with Sheltie sitting between them. Sepp put his arm round Luise's shoulder. 'Are you happy, Frau Nowak?'

'It's the most wonderful day of my life.' But instead of going straight ahead, through the Pariser Platz, the driver turned left down the Wilhelmstrasse. 'Sepp, he's going the wrong way.'

'I thought we'd take a long route. You don't mind, do you?'

Mind? So long as she was with Sepp, Luise didn't mind where they went or how long it took to get there.

The moment the Droschke disappeared from view, the wedding guests, with much laughter, hurried out to the waiting line of limousines that had conveyed them to and from the church. Chauffeurs opened doors and hustled them inside. In a splendid cavalcade, they drove right along Unter den Linden, then right again down the Kanonierstrasse, parallel to the Wilhelmstrasse, along which Sepp and Luise were making their leisurely journey.

In the leading car, Viktoria turned to her mother. 'Do you think she's guessed?'

Ricarda shook her head. 'She's so happy, she's no idea in which direction she's travelling. It's a pity they're not keeping up the tradition, but it's a lovely idea.'

'What an amazing day!' Benno said. 'I never thought I'd live to see Luise married. And this honeymoon…'

Similar conversations were taking place in all the other cars, as they sped through the Belle-Alliance-Platz, down the Belle-Alliance-Strasse towards Tempelhof.

Sepp tapped the driver on the shoulder and said, 'Will you turn into the airfield?'

'Certainly, Herr Oberst, sir.' The driver looked over his shoulder at Luise and winked.

The horse trotted smartly across the concrete toward some distant hangars, in front of which a number of cars were parked and people were standing in a large group, waving. Sheltie stood up, wagging her tail joyfully.

Luise stared incredulously, recognizing Viktoria and Benno, her mother, the massive figure of the Baron in his SS uniform, Peter in his Wehrmacht uniform, Pastor Scheer and Professor Ascher. 'Sepp? What are they all doing here? What's going on?'

Amidst loud cheers, the Droschke drew to a halt in the centre of the group and then she saw it, a small biplane, superbly camouflaged with white roses and, on both sides, picked out in pink carnations, her own name: Luise.

Sepp grinned. 'You may not remember, but when I first met you, twenty-two years ago on a train from Munich, you asked if I would take you up in an aeroplane. Finally, I'm going to keep my promise.'

A quarter of an hour later, dressed in a leather flying suit, goggles over her eyes and a helmet concealing her curls, Luise clambered into the passenger seat of the plane with Sheltie on her lap. Sepp strapped them both in, then climbed into the open cockpit behind her. Various uniformed airport ground staff, all obviously enjoying the adventure, prepared the machine for take-off. While two men held down the wings, another turned the propellor, and others removed the chocks from under the wheels. At a signal from Sepp, they moved away and the plane taxied down the runway, strewing roses and carnations in its wake.

Cradling Sheltie in her arms, Luise felt the wind on her cheeks and heard the roar of the engine and the rattle of the wooden struts. In a moment of pure exhilaration, they left the ground. They circled round the airfield and below them, she saw her family and friends, all gazing skywards, still waving their arms. Then Sepp righted the plane and they flew away into the clear blue of the afternoon.

Below them was Berlin, a criss-cross pattern of streets and houses, parks and gardens, filled with very small and insignificant motor cars, buses, trains and people. To the north was the wide avenue of Unter den Linden, the Hotel Quadriga, the Brandenburg Gate and the green expanse of the Tiergarten and the zoo, like a pocket handkerchief from their vantage point in the sky, beyond it the tenement blocks of Wedding and the tall chimneys of Kraus Chemie, belching clouds of black smoke into the air. To the north-west lay the Tegel Forest and a tiny patch of water Luise identified as the Heiligensee.

They flew south-west over Schmargendorf, Dahlem and the botanical gardens, Grunewald, Schlachtensee and the Wannsee, over the Pfaueninsel with its bijou castle, Potsdam and its barracks. Like little lead soldiers, she could see men lined up on the parade ground. Then they left the city behind and were over open country, dotted with lakes, the shadow of their plane reflected on the ground.

It was a strange sensation to feel nothing around her but the fragile airframe and the open sky. She twisted in her seat and looked at Sepp, almost unrecognizable in his flying helmet and goggles, the tearing wind contorting his face. And then she realized it was not just the wind. His expression was one of sheer, unadulterated happiness. Sepp was in his element.

They did not go far that afternoon, landing at a small airfield outside Magdeburg, where a crowd of young men hurried towards them to hold down the plane and help them out, excitedly examining the aircraft and asking Sepp a host of questions. He pushed his goggles up onto his helmet, revealing a white patch in a blackened face and, one arm resting on the biplane's wing, laughingly answered them.

For a while, Luise stood nearby, accustoming herself again to the sensation of having solid ground beneath her feet, to the stillness after the rushing wind and the roar of the engine. She looked curiously at the young men, at their expressions of rapt, almost reverent, attention as they listened to Sepp.

Sheltie tugged at her lead and Luise wandered slowly towards the small hangar, feeling suddenly excluded from his world. He had married her, but his first — and greatest — love would always be flying. He might name his plane after her — but he would always be the captain and she the passenger.

In the air, Sepp was a complete person. He needed nothing and nobody else. But she was not a complete person. To be complete she needed other people — and most of all, she needed Sepp. That was the difference between them.

'Luischen, I'm sorry, darling.' Sepp appeared beside her. 'I didn't mean to ignore you, but those boys were so fascinated by the plane. If you don't mind waiting a few moments while we wheel her into the hangar and lock her up for the night, one of them has promised to drive us over to the inn.'

'I understand.' She took his hands in hers and smiled. 'Sepp, thank you for planning such a wonderful honeymoon.'

He looked at her searchingly. 'Do you mean that? I wasn't sure. After all, just because flying is the great love of my life doesn't mean you have to enjoy it. If you don't want to go on, we can still go to Heiligensee instead. I promise I won't be upset.'

She reached up and kissed his sooty face. 'Thank you, but no. I haven't waited twenty-two years to turn back now! Come on, hurry up and put that plane away. If I look anything like you, I need a bath.'

He grinned mischievously. 'You look beautiful, gogglepatch and all.'

Later that evening, after a long, hot bath and a good meal, they stood together in their room, looking out of the open window onto a moonlit night. Sepp drew her close to him and kissed her. 'My little wife, my Luischen. What fools we were to waste so many years that we could have shared together.' Then he pulled the curtains. Gently, he undid her negligée and ran his fingers over her bare shoulders. 'I love you so much.'

'And I love you, with all my heart.'

He carried her over to the bed and with great tenderness started to make love to her. As their naked bodies pressed together, intertwined and were finally united, Luise had the sensation of flying high into the sky towards some blue mountain of infinite happiness. And with Sepp's arms around her, carrying her safely towards this unknown peak, her earlier moment of loneliness was quite forgotten. Sepp was hers and she was his, and nothing could ever separate them.

A week after Luise's wedding, Herr Fromm handed Stefan the long-awaited telegram. Stefan ripped it open, read the few words, then rushed into his father's office. 'Papa, look! I've been accepted for a Rhodes Scholarship!'

Benno read the telegram, then stood up and shook his hand. 'Well done, son. I can't say how proud I am. One of only two German students to be awarded a Rhodes Scholarship this year. What an achievement! My congratulations. We must tell your mother at once!'

They found Viktoria with Ricarda and Mortimer in the Palm Garden Room. She took one look at their excited faces and exclaimed, 'Stefi! You've done it! You've got your scholarship! Well done, darling.'

Ricarda took him in her arms and kissed him on both cheeks. 'Congratulations, Stefan.'

Mortimer pumped his hand. 'Well done, old boy. I certainly recommended you, but the rest was due entirely to you.'

'This warrants a celebration!' Benno glanced at his watch. 'I don't think it's too early for some champagne.' He called a waiter and asked him to bring a bottle of Krug.

In an unparalleled break from routine, they held an impromptu party. Stefan plagued Mortimer with questions about Oxford, while Viktoria and Ricarda sat listening attentively. 'I think it might be a good idea for Stefan to come with me when I go home on leave in

August,' Mortimer suggested. 'That would give him an opportunity to find his way about and generally acclimatize himself.'

Stefan looked expectantly at his mother.

'Of course, darling,' Viktoria said. But although she was pleased and proud for him, she could not help thinking how much she was going to miss him.

There was one other matter to be resolved. Currency restrictions had recently been imposed on foreign travellers, who were only allowed to take fifty marks with them. Benno waved the problem aside. 'Father can arrange Stefan's allowance through the Liegnitzer Bank.'

Luise, Sheltie and Sepp returned from their honeymoon in high spirits and moved into Sepp's small flat in Lützow. Stefan took his final examinations and, with a sense of relief, said goodbye to his fellow students at the University and got ready for Oxford. His air ticket was bought. His trunk was sent on ahead by rail. Then he went to bid farewell to Pastor Scheer and Professor Ascher.

The Pastor was increasingly optimistic these days. His arch enemy, Dr Müller, had been ousted from his position and a lawyer, Dr Kerrl, had been appointed Minister for Church Affairs. 'He's a much more moderate man than Müller,' the Pastor assured Stefan. 'He recognizes the need to unite the Protestant Churches. And he also sees that we have our parishioners on our side.'

This last statement certainly seemed true. Every Sunday, the little church was overflowing, and a record number of baptisms and marriages had been registered. When Stefan left the Scheers, it was with the confident feeling that when he returned it would be to an even happier pastor and his wife. As far as Professor Ascher was concerned, he felt less certain. Throughout the summer, the picketing of Jewish shops had increased and there had been many ugly incidents in an atmosphere dreadfully reminiscent of the boycott in April 1933, which had led up to the first anti-Semitic laws.

'Herr Professor, won't you come with me to England?' he implored.

'No, Stefan, I have work to do here. My pupils at the Jewish school and my students at the adult education college need me. There are my positions on the Jewish Presidium and the Welfare Committee. And there is my unfaltering belief that things cannot continue as they are. People are not stupid or blind. One day, they will see that Hitler is evil and they will rise up against him.'

Stefan tried once more. 'Please come with me.'

'If I were your age it might be different, but I am an old man and my duty to my people is to stay with them in their moment of need. They are not as fortunate as you. Even if they could get to England, how long could they live on fifty marks?'

When he got home that evening, Stefan repeated the gist of this conversation to his parents. 'I think the Professor should go to England,' he said. 'I'm sure there are no signs outside shops in London warning people not to buy from Jews, and no SS men marching through the streets. And they certainly have no such organization as the Gestapo — or concentration camps!'

His father took a deep breath. 'England doesn't have our problems. The SS and the camps are necessary to maintain peace and order. As for the Jews, I don't like what's going on either, but what can I do about it?'

'People like Professor Ascher have done nothing to harm anyone!'

Benno sighed. 'I know. I like the Professor, but…'

'I don't see what all the fuss is about,' Monika said spitefully. 'In my opinion, Stefi pays too much attention to Mortimer Allen and Professor Ascher. I think it's a good job he's going to England. If he stayed here much longer, he'd probably be arrested.'

'It's our last evening. Please don't let's argue,' Viktoria pleaded.

Stefan looked from one to the other of them. 'I'm sorry, but you'll never make me change my mind. I've seen my whole world alter in the last two years and I don't like it all.'

'*We* are still the same, Stefi,' his mother said.

Stefan nodded. 'Yes, of course you are.' But they weren't. They had all changed. And, suddenly, he couldn't wait to get away.

Two days later, they were at the international terminal at Tempelhof airport, the concourse decorated with swastika banners and blackshirted SS men on patrol. *This is the moment I have been dreading*, Viktoria thought, as she fussed around Stefan. 'Are you sure you have everything you need? Your passport, your ticket?'

Stefan nodded patiently.

'Promise you'll write to me often. I want to know everything you do. Write long, long letters.'

'Your studies are the most important thing,' Benno said gruffly. 'But we're going to miss you, son, so keep in touch.'

'I'll make sure he writes,' Mortimer promised.

Viktoria looked at him appealingly. 'Your wife will keep an eye on him, make sure he's all right, won't she?'

Stefan shuffled uncomfortably. 'Mama, I'm not a child any more.'

But you are, she thought, *to me you will always be my child, my baby*...

The London flight was announced and, with obvious relief, Stefan said, 'Come on, Mortimer, we must go.' He embraced Viktoria awkwardly. 'Goodbye, Mama. Don't worry about me. I'll be fine.' He shook hands with his father, gave Monika a peck on the cheek, picked up his luggage and followed Mortimer through the gates.

They saw him once more on the tarmac, walking towards the Luft-Hansa aircraft. He turned and waved, then walked up the gangway and into the plane.

Benno put his arm round Viktoria's shoulder. 'He's not going away for ever. He'll soon be back.'

She fought back her tears. 'It feels like for ever.'

'All baby birds fly the nest,' Benno said gently. 'If you truly love him, you must allow him to test his wings.'

On the tarmac, the plane's engines roared into life. The gangway was removed and the aircraft taxied down the runway. Then, a distant speck, it rose from the ground and started towards England.

There were no flags at Croydon airport and no SS men. They passed through passport control and customs to find two figures waiting impatiently — Joyce in a flowered shirtwaister, her bobbed black hair sleek and shining, and Libby, with skinny brown arms and legs in a white cotton dress. They flung themselves into Mortimer's arms, with cries of, 'Mortimer!' 'Daddy!' Then they turned to Stefan. 'So you're Stefan,' Joyce said, holding out her hand.

Stefan clicked his heels together and kissed her fingers. 'Stefan Jochum-Kraus, at your service, gracious lady.'

Then he did the same with Libby. To his surprise, she giggled. 'Do you always do that in Germany?'

No, we fling out our arms and say, 'Heil Hitler!', Stefan thought, but he replied, 'It is the custom.'

'And a very charming one,' Joyce commented. 'Stefan, we're very pleased to meet you. Now, come along both of you. The car's just outside.'

Mortimer drove the Morris 8 with Stefan sitting beside him, Joyce and Libby in the back talking non-stop. They decided that London deserved a separate sightseeing trip, so after passing through endless towns on the city's peripheries, crossing the Thames at Kingston and meandering down the river to Windsor, they eventually reached the open countryside. Stefan gazed out of the window in fascination at the lush pastures of the Thames Valley, very different from the sandy heathlands, lakes and forests surrounding Berlin; at people, walking, riding, driving about their business and not one of them in uniform.

They came over a hill and Mortimer slowed down. Before them lay the city of Oxford, shimmering in the haze. Stefan stared at it in delight. 'I'm really here at last!'

They entered Oxford over Magdalen Bridge, with Magdalen College on the right and everyone was speaking at once, pointing things out to him. 'That's the Cherwell and Cherwell Walks.' 'Down there is Merton. Its library is the oldest in England.' 'That's the Radcliffe Camera.' 'The Bodleian...' 'Corpus Christi...' 'Christ Church...' There were tantalizing views through ancient stone archways of quadrangles of green grass, of massed delphiniums and roses, of valerian growing on grey walls, of the occasional figure in flowing robes, flat cap on head, strolling, books under arm.

'Of course, it's only August. When the students return, it's quite different,' Joyce said.

'Do you think you're going to like it here?' Libby demanded.

Stefan twisted in his seat. 'Oh, yes,' he breathed.

They left the city centre and drove through narrow streets with small shops and terraced cottages, which broadened after a while into a suburban area with semi-detached and detached houses, all with their own neat gardens. 'Nearly there,' Mortimer told him and a few moments later they drew up in front of a house set back from the road, with wisteria and Virginia creeper clambering over its walls. A cat lay sunning itself on the front step.

Taking the key from her mother, Libby jumped out of the car, vaulted over the gate and ran down the path to open the front door. Mortimer laughed fondly. 'Little tomboy!'

Stefan looked at him questioningly. 'Tomboy?'

'A new word for your vocabulary. Now, come in. I'm longing for a cup of tea.'

The house was small, much tinier even than Heiligensee, with just three bedrooms, Stefan's being only big enough to hold a single bed, a wardrobe and a table, but it had a fine view over the neat garden. Libby danced round, pulling open doors and drawers. 'I'll help you unpack, once we've had tea. Oh, and you must watch out. The cat likes sleeping in this room. She gets under the bedclothes if she can. Do you like this picture? Mummy painted it.'

'Stefan! Libby! Tea's ready!' Joyce called.

'Come on!' Libby said. 'We've got treacle tart. I made it.'

Whatever tomboy meant, Libby was a new phenomenon! His mind in a whirl, Stefan followed her downstairs into a lounge that ran from one end of the house to the other, with French windows opening into the garden. The furniture was chintz-covered and had a lived-in look about it. Books and magazines were piled on low tables and spilled onto the floor. The walls were covered with pictures and, from somewhere, came a smell of turpentine and linseed oil.

Joyce appeared beside him and took his arm. 'I hope you'll feel at home with us, Stefan. And remember, even when you move into your rooms at college, you're welcome here whenever you want to come.'

'Thank you. You are very kind.' Stefan had the strange sensation that this was the first real home he had ever lived in.

In a curious way, having Stefan at his house made Mortimer feel as if he had brought a bit of the Quadriga to Oxford with him. With great pleasure, he watched the boy begin to relax. By the time his fortnight's leave was over, Stefan had discarded his formal clothes for casual slacks and an open-necked shirt. Despite the disparity in their ages, he and Libby had become good friends and his English was improving from day to day. At her suggestion, he had even anglicized his name to Stephen. 'By the time term starts, he'll be able to hold his own,' Mortimer told Joyce in satisfaction.

'I've got a feeling he's going to end up more English than you will ever be,' she laughed. 'It's odd. I've never imagined German boys to be like him.'

'Most of them aren't,' Mortimer replied grimly.

Before he returned to Berlin, he made a visit to Chartwell and once again, he and Churchill strolled through the fine grounds.

'They are beginning to recognize the dangers,' Churchill rumbled. 'They are imagining what would happen if we quarrel with Herr Hitler, hence the policy of appeasement. They are beginning to accept the possibility of a European War, in which England, France and Belgium are attacked by Germany. There is now an Air Defence Committee, on which the Prime Minister has been good enough to invite me to sit.'

'An Air Defence Committee?'

'I believe Germany to be preparing for war regardless of whether we upset Herr Hitler. It will be two or three years at least before her Army and Navy are ready for a three service war, but if some authority thinks they can take us by surprise from the air and beat us to our knees in months, or even weeks, by violent, mass-bombing attacks, such an event may happen very much sooner.'

Mortimer tapped his cigarette ash onto the grass. In view of everything he had seen and heard in Germany, what Churchill said was logical yet, in the peace of Chartwell, still scarcely conceivable.

'The more our defences are respected, the greater will be the deterrent upon a war fought purely in the air. However, as I am constantly inculcating upon the House and the ministry officials, our strategy must not be merely defence, but attack, and we should impose a similar policy on our enemy as he will impose on us. He will be aiming for our dockyards, our technical establishments, our factories, our railways, our assembly points. So we must prepare to immobilize our enemy. The Ruhr, for instance, is easily accessible to long-distance bombers. The Kraus gunshops in Essen…'

Later that afternoon, as he flew across the Thames estuary, Mortimer stared down, grim-faced, at the shipping threading its way out of the Port of London and thought how vulnerable London would be in the event of a war. Not for the first time, he wondered how he could so mistrust the German race yet like some individuals so much.

That summer, several major changes took place in the life of Basili Meyer. In July, the Steins moved out of Moscow to Saratov on the Volga. And in August, Basili left the one-room flat he shared with his mother across the landing from the Steins' former apartment and moved into a home for foreign children near the Nikitsky Gate in the city centre.

It was the beginning of a new and wonderful existence, the kind of life he had always expected to live in Moscow, but which had evaded him until then. The director of the home was a German. The children all wore special clothes. Their own cook prepared them German meals. The home possessed its own clinic, with a German doctor and German nurses. A coach was at their constant disposal to take them to the theatre, opera and concerts. Wherever they went, they were feted as though they were members of a visiting foreign delegation.

Very quickly, Basili adjusted to his new life, convinced the Russians had finally recognized the true value of the new generation of communists, of children such as himself, born of the revolution.

Every Saturday, he went to see his mother, but he grew to dread his visits, for she never ceased to complain about her squalid surroundings and about the lack of prestige accorded to her. In vain, Basili repeated what he was taught at school. 'We are at the beginning of a new era. These remnants of the past will soon disappear. We have lived through the worst.'

'No,' Olga said, 'if we are not careful, there will be worse to come!'

Basili sighed impatiently, knowing he would now be treated to a lecture on the iniquities of Stalin's regime. The previous December, Stalin's closest friend, Sergei Mironovich Kirov, had been murdered in Leningrad. Stalin's reaction had been terrifying. Throughout the country, hundreds of thousands of people were arrested by agents of the NKVD, the Secret Police, and thousands were brutally killed. Former party officials suddenly disappeared, never to be heard of again. In May, the Old Bolsheviks Club was dissolved, its buildings and its funds seized. In Olga's mind, it was incomprehensible that Bolshevik should turn on Bolshevik. 'Their terror tactics make the Nazis seem amateur in comparison,' she said in horror.

But worst of all was the realization that Stalin held the international communists in scant regard. Her vision of the Soviet Union was proving a fantasy.

At the beginning of September, Basili changed schools and started attending the Karl Liebknecht School, one of seventy-two new schools built that year in Moscow. To a boy brought up in the slums of Wedding, it was a revelation. A modern, four-storey building, it had big, sunny classrooms and possessed every conceivable teaching facility. In its entrance hall, stood a massive statue of Stalin on the base of which was engraved, 'There is no fortress which the Bolsheviks cannot storm'. Across its main corridor hung a red banner containing Lenin's famous words, 'Learn, learn and learn again!'

Sixteen now, Basili entered the eighth class, the pupils of which were already marked out for college or university. He was in little doubt as to what his future held. He would continue to work hard and pass all his examinations. He would go to college and then be offered a place on the Comintern alongside other leading German émigrés, like Walther Ulbricht and Wilhelm Pieck. And when the German workers overthrew Hitler, he would return to Germany to help govern the country.

At this point Olga threw all caution to the wind. Basili urged her to be careful, but fear was an emotion foreign to Olga. 'Stalin's is not the regime that Lenin wanted,' she told everyone she met. 'Stalin's policies are subversive. He will push us into an abyss from which we shall never recover.'

If they agreed with her, they did not say so, but increasingly avoided her company. So, too, did Basili. She might be his mother, but he was not going to have her putting his future in jeopardy.

No sooner had Mortimer returned with glowing tales of how well Stefan was adapting to English life, than the Nuremberg Congress commenced, and there was a mass exodus from Berlin, not just of the Party hierarchy, but also senior officers from the armed forces, including Peter and Sepp, and the SS, including Baron Heinrich. On this occasion, Viktoria made no attempt to discourage Monika from attending, although she suspected it was less the rally itself, than the thought of seeing Hans König again that excited her daughter.

It wasn't Monika who concerned Viktoria, but Stefan. She was pleased that he was settling in so well at Oxford, but, at the same time, she felt a slight pang of jealousy. Since so much of her paperwork had now been taken over by Benno's new assistant, she had ample opportunity for letter-writing. She started a screed that was twenty pages long by the time it was despatched, the first of many such missives that Stefan was to receive, asking him about his new life and relating episodes from her own.

Monika returned from Nuremberg in excellent spirits. She had seen Hans again. 'He's been conscripted and he starts his year's military service in October. He's promised to visit me when he's on leave. Oh, it must be wonderful to be a man and be a soldier...'

If Stefi were not at university, he might have been conscripted. Wasn't it better that he was in England and out of danger?

'And the rally?' Benno asked. 'Did you see the Führer?'

An ecstatic light shone in Monika's blue-grey eyes. 'Papa, he was wonderful! We were given photographs of him, signed by him personally. I'm going to put mine beside my bed.'

'I'll get it framed for you,' her father promised.

That was one incident Viktoria did not repeat to Stefan.

Mortimer saw that Nuremberg Rally in a very different light. Hitler used the conference to legalize the pickets, the terrorism and the intimidation of the summer against the Jews in a new piece of legislation.

Like all previous racial laws, it was very simple. Marriage and extra-marital relationships between Germans and Jews were forbidden. Jews were forbidden to employ Aryan servants under the age of forty-five. In an accompanying law, the old German flag was abolished and the swastika was adopted as the official national emblem. Jews were forbidden to fly it.

The rally ended with a military display such as Mortimer had never witnessed. One hundred thousand soldiers participated in a massive parade of armoured vehicles, tanks, mechanized artillery and anti-aircraft guns and, as a grand finale, there was a flying display in which over one hundred fighter and bomber planes from the Luftwaffe participated in aeronautical feats and mock battles.

He returned home from Nuremberg in grim mood.

Wherever one looked, there were placards reading: *Jews not wanted here! Germans do not buy from Jews! Germany awaken! Perish Judah!* With law on their side, the stormtroopers stepped up their campaign of hatred, marching through the streets shouting slogans and chanting songs:

'When Jewish blood spurts from the knife

We shall have a better life…'

In the cafés lining the Kurfürstendamm, they had a captive audience. In the balmy warmth of a mid-September afternoon, Mortimer sat on the terrace of Café Jochum and watched the ugly scene. There were still Jewish customers in the café and Jews walking along the street, but most were Aryans. Although some people joined the brownshirts, most paid little attention to them, but it was impossible to totally ignore them.

Fredi Forster came and stood on the terrace, his arms folded over his huge stomach. 'Ach, Jews,' he said complacently to the world at large, 'why don't they take the hint and get out? We don't want them here.' He had the satisfaction of seeing a couple leave the café. Their places were immediately taken by a middle-aged Aryan couple. Mortimer paid his bill and went too.

With a heavy heart, he made his way to Dahlem. 'Where does this place you now?' he asked Bethel.

'Better that this canker comes out in the open. Berliners won't put up with it, Mortimer. They have always lived in friendship with us and they have their own truculent pride. If a Berliner has a Jewish girlfriend, he won't forsake her just because the Nazis tell him to. Berliners dislike the Nazis as much as we Jews do.'

Mortimer sank down in a chair, lit a cigarette and gazed through the smoke at the Professor, sitting upright behind his desk, the sun framing his flowing white hair like a halo. Sadly, he noted Bethel no longer thought of himself as a Berliner — but as a Jew.

'But in view of the Nuremberg Laws, can there be a viable Jewish community in Germany, a state within a state?'

Bethel Ascher sighed deeply. 'What choice do we have? I am on the committees of the Jewish Presidium and the Welfare Association of German Jews. Perhaps better than anyone, I know the problems of would-be emigrants. If we leave Germany, where are we to go? The answer should be Palestine, but the British limit the number of entry visas, and the Jewish settlers already there impose their own stringent restrictions.

'England, France, Sweden, Switzerland, the United States — yes, these countries will accept a few Jewish immigrants if they are young, well-trained and have jobs to go to. But they have dire economic problems of their own without adding to them by taking in refugees. And, finally, do not forget, we are still German citizens.'

Not for long. On 14 November, while the eyes of the world were focused far away on the Italian invasion of Abyssinia, the Reichstag passed the National Law of Citizenship and Jews officially became subjects instead of citizens. They were forbidden to call themselves Germans.

The next time Mortimer saw him, the Professor said, 'From now on, you must take care when you visit me. There have been many instances of the Gestapo watching Jewish meeting places and arresting Jews on trumped-up charges of conspiring against the government. I do not want you to attract attention to yourself and get into trouble.'

'But there is no law yet forbidding two friends meeting and trying to put the world to rights,' Mortimer retorted indignantly.

Bethel shook his head wearily. 'Perhaps that is the trouble. What do we do but talk? I have always maintained that we had time, that Hitler would not last, that a miracle would occur, but now I am beginning to fear time is running out like sand in a glass. Ah me, I have a dreadful feeling that we have left it too late. Too late…'

Stefan came home for Christmas, his hair rather longer than when he had left and wearing a tweed sports jacket, baggy trousers and a cravat knotted casually at his neck. This was a new Stefan, who walked with a confident, jaunty step, held his head nonchalantly high and whose voice had an assurance not present before. With fervent enthusiasm, he talked of his rooms, his tutors, his fellow undergraduates, of quads, and pubs, and rags, and bicycles, of punting on the Cherwell and tea at the Randolph Hotel. Oxford, he said without any regret, was quite, quite different from Berlin.

Viktoria hung on his every word, wanting to know every detail of his life. For the first few days, Stefan was only too happy to talk. He had feared that, because of the drop in teaching standards at the Friedrich-Wilhelms University, he might be below the standard of the other undergraduates, but that wasn't the case. In philosophy, he had had to do quite a lot of reading to catch up. 'But at least the books are there, Mama, every sort of book you can want to read, by every author under the sun!'

There had been a tricky moment at an Oxford Union meeting when the motion of compulsory military service had been debated. His fellow students had assumed that, as a German, he must be in favour of it. 'I don't know if they believed me, but I assured them the last thing Germany wanted was another war.'

He could not speak too highly of Joyce and Libby Allen. 'They've been so kind to me, made me feel at home from the first moment I arrived. Joyce is about your age, but very different from you. She's terribly untidy and the first thing you notice when you go into their house is the smell of turps and linseed oil and pictures everywhere.'

Viktoria frowned. 'It sounds a rather unusual household.'

'I like it. I often spend the weekend at "Fairways", studying, watching Joyce paint and helping Libby get lunch. Although she's only thirteen, Libby's great fun!'

At this vision of English domestic life, Viktoria felt a sudden pang of jealousy. Did Stefan portray life at the Hotel Quadriga in such glowing colours to his English hosts? Did he talk about herself and Monika with the same enthusiasm? She changed the subject slightly. 'Tell me about your roommate, Trevor Neal-Wright.'

'Oh, he's all right. Serious sort of chap with glasses. His father's something in the British Foreign Office. TNW's going into the FO himself when he goes down.'

Viktoria shook her head. TNW. FO. Go down. The abbreviations and expressions were a different language from a different world. 'What do they call you? SJK?'

Stefan laughed. 'No! Callearn christened me Cross when I arrived. He said I was evidently the cross he had to bear through life. It's stuck! Even the dons call me Stephen Cross. I quite like it.'

The Honourable Anthony Callearn, second son of the Earl of Chanctonbury, had featured in several of Stefan's letters. There was a photograph of them both wobbling down the High Street on bicycles, gowns flapping in the wind, Stefan dark and serious, Anthony Callearn blond, athletic-looking, with an open, smiling face.

'Mr Callearn sounds a nice boy. Maybe he'd like to come back here with you during the next holidays.'

Stefan looked a bit uncomfortable. 'Actually, Tony's already asked me to his place in Sussex. I'd rather like to, if you don't mind. It should be good sport.'

'I see,' Viktoria said faintly.

After Christmas, when the novelty of being home had worn off, Stefan went to see Professor Ascher and the Scheers. Both visits left him feeling very depressed. From Professor Ascher, he learned the full implication of the Nuremberg Laws. From Pastor Scheer, he heard about the neo-pagan rituals with which the Nazis were trying to replace the Christian faith.

He returned to the Quadriga upset and indignant. 'Why doesn't somebody do something to stop this stupidity?' he asked his mother bitterly. 'Or don't any of you care any more?'

His words stung her. 'Of course we care, Stefi. Even if their legal status has altered, Jewish people will always be welcome at the Quadriga. As for the Church, I don't think anybody takes these new ideas seriously.'

He looked at her doubtfully. 'I'm pleased to hear it.'

Then she realized the implications of the question he had asked: 'Don't any of you care?', as if they were on two different sides, as if she had somehow failed him. 'Stefi, you must understand how things are here. To criticize anything is to attract the attention of the authorities and, even worse, the Gestapo. I am sorry, but if your friends are unhappy with their position, they must seek to rectify it themselves.'

'Yes, I see.' But she knew he didn't see. He had become infected by the freedom of England.

With the exception of Countess Julia, who was unwell, the whole family attended that New Year's Eve Ball. 'Julia's like all women,' the Baron snorted, 'a hypochondriac!'

'We must go and see her,' Benno said. But, in the meantime, he had more than enough to do without going to Grunewald.

As usual, Baron Heinrich dominated the party. He was full of Dr Schacht's plans, as Minister of Economics, for stabilizing the economy and financing rearmament. There was talk about General Ludendorff's recently published book, *The Total War*, and a lot of discussion on the Abyssinian War, with most people approving Mussolini's action.

'The League of Nations is impotent against him,' Peter remarked, 'while Geneva and London lack the courage and the power to drive him out by force. If the *Duce* wins, I can foresee an alliance between us and Italy which will greatly strengthen our position in Europe.'

Baron Heinrich laughed grimly. 'One way or another, everyone is playing into our hands. Did you know that the British made their agreement with us over battleships without even consulting the

League of Nations? And I've heard they won't tell France how many they have agreed for us to build! Not that we're telling the British anyway!'

Sepp joined in, 'And in the air, we're much stronger than any of the Allies.'

There was laughter and more confident, self-congratulatory comments. The music became louder, the pall of smoke over the room denser, the dancing livelier, and Stefan's face grew longer.

'Stefan,' Christa asked shyly, 'have you enjoyed your holiday?' She looked quite entrancing in a turquoise frock that enhanced the blue of her eyes, her ash-blonde hair coiled in plaits round her ears.

Stefan seemed hardly to see her. 'Thank you, yes,' he replied, mechanically, then turned his attention back to the men.

At midnight, the band stopped and Benno stepped onto the podium. 'On behalf of the Hotel Quadriga, I wish you a happy and prosperous new year. Now I ask you all to be upstanding and drink to our beloved Führer.'

With one accord, they rose to their feet and, arms stretched out, called out in unison, 'The Führer! Heil Hitler!' Some voices were less strident than others and some merely mouthed the words, but Stefan did not notice this. His vacation had clarified his mind: he detested Hitler and everything he stood for. He remained obdurately seated.

When they eventually reached their apartment, Benno demanded angrily, 'What on earth were you thinking of not joining in the toast to the Führer?'

'Why should I drink to him?'

Benno took a deep breath. 'Stefan, you are pushing my patience too far. All we have heard since your return is how wonderful England is compared to Germany. However, much as you appear to dislike the idea, you are a German and you owe it to your country to be a loyal citizen. And that includes honouring the Führer! Now, raise your arm and say, Heil Hitler.'

Stefan eyed him calmly and said nothing.

'Stefi, what does it matter? Do what your father asks. They are only words, after all,' Viktoria implored. 'It's the beginning of a new year. Please don't let's start it off at war with each other.'

'You must be the only person who doesn't want war then! Didn't you hear them this evening? They all want war!'

'Stefan, that is enough!' Benno said coldly. 'If you cannot be polite to your mother, you can go to your room immediately and stay there until you see fit to apologize.'

Stefan cast them both a pitying glance. 'I didn't mean to be rude and if I was I apologize. And from the bottom of my heart, I wish you both a happy new year. But Hitler, no! I wish him to perdition!' Before they could react, he marched out of the room.

Benno's face was white. 'The boy is a fool! I shouldn't be surprised if someone reports him to the Gestapo for this! So far as I'm concerned, he can go back to England and stay there.'

Viktoria grasped his sleeve. 'Don't be hard on him. He's young and idealistic, that's all.'

'He'll have us all in a concentration camp!'

'Benno, he's your son…'

He pulled away from her and strode across the room. 'Yes.' There was a strange, almost empty quality to his voice. 'Yes, he's my son and I love him.' For a long time, the room was silent, then he said, 'Go to bed, Vicki. I'll join you shortly. I need a few moments on my own.'

The episode was not mentioned again, but Stefan continued to make his mute disapproval felt. When, a week later, he left for England, Viktoria felt almost relieved to see him go. She could not bear the accusation in his eyes.

CHAPTER SIX

Once New Year was over and Stefan gone, the future stretched bleakly ahead of Viktoria. Each day, when she went to her office, there were fewer and fewer things for her to deal with and her meetings with Herr Brandt seemed ever briefer. Herr Fromm assured her the reception clerks were coping excellently. Chef Mazzoni hustled her out of the kitchen. Philip Krosyk found no need to discuss banqueting or table arrangements. One afternoon, in desperation, Viktoria asked Benno, 'Can I help you in any way?' The offer cost her dear, but she could not bear to be inactive.

Benno, however, was too busy to give any thought to her sensitivities. 'If Helga has time, perhaps she could type this letter for me.'

There had been nothing for her secretary to do, so she had sent her home early. 'Helga's gone for the day.'

'Confound it. My secretary already has more than she can cope with. Vicki, would you mind typing this out?'

Viktoria bit her lip, then took the handwritten sheet back to Helga's office and settled down at the typewriter. After all, she had offered to help. But never again! Giving vent to her anger and mortification, she banged the keys so hard they locked up. 'Oh, damn!'

'Hey, that's no way to treat a typewriter!' Mortimer's voice laughed.

Dismayed that he should discover her doing such a menial task, she tried to untangle the metal bars.

'Here, let me do it. I've had more practice than you.' He turned the machine round and, with a deft movement, freed the keys. 'There you are.'

'Thank you.'

'Helga gone home?'

'Yes.' She smiled weakly. 'This letter is rather urgent...'

Mortimer glanced at the sheet of paper from which she was typing, clearly marked: FROM THE OFFICE OF BENNO KRAUS. He reached in his pocket for his cigarettes and offered them to her. 'I didn't realize you doubled as Benno's secretary.'

Viktoria took the cigarette and, in a most unfeminine gesture, clamped it between her lips. 'I don't.' Then, with a sigh, she removed it, propped her head on her hands and said, 'I'm sorry, Mortimer. You've caught me at a bad moment. Did you have a special reason for wanting to see me?'

'It will wait. Finish your letter first.'

She gritted her teeth and recommenced typing, promptly making a mistake. Using the eraser tied with a piece of ribbon to the platen knob, she rubbed at the offending character and made a hole in the paper.

Just in time, Mortimer suppressed the chuckle that rose in his throat, as he realized the implications of the scene he was witnessing. When he had arrived in Berlin, Viktoria had been the undisputed mistress of the Quadriga. In the course of three years, her power had gradually been eroded, so that she was now relegated to being little more than her husband's personal assistant and social secretary.

Now he thought about it, he could see how it had happened. Women were not encouraged to work in the male-dominated Germany of today, but urged to lead a domestic existence. From the government's point of view, this achieved two important goals: it helped the unemployment figures and, with the generous financial incentives for mothers, produced more sons for the Führer. For a man like Benno Kraus, who must often have smarted under the knowledge that his wife wore the trousers in the house, it was a godsent opportunity to seize control of the reins.

Quietly, Mortimer lowered himself onto a chair and watched while she finished typing the letter. Poor Viktoria, he reflected. Within a short space of time, the Nazis had taken from her the two things she loved best in the world: her son and her hotel.

Snatching the paper out of the typewriter, she looked at it critically and said, with a trace of her old spirit, 'Well, he won't ask me to do that again in a hurry. It's only an order to a supplier. It didn't need to be typed. Will you wait while I take it in to Benno?'

'On condition that you let me buy you a drink.'

She gave a rueful smile. 'I think I need one.'

Five minutes later, they were seated in the bar. 'I really came to tell you that I've had a note from Joyce,' Mortimer said. 'I gather Stefan and his father had a bit of a tiff at New Year and that he left here under a bit of a cloud. Joyce asked me to reassure you that Stefan is all right and filled with remorse. I gather he's going to write to you.'

Viktoria bit her lip, then related the scene. 'It was dreadful. By the end of the holiday, I could hardly wait for Stefi to go — but now he's gone, I miss him so much…'

He nodded. 'You and I are very similar in many ways. We are gregarious and get on well with most other people. Yet, we are essentially solitary types. Of course you miss Stefan. He's your only real friend.'

She looked down at her finger tapping ash from her cigarette in the ashtray. 'He is my son…'

The simple statement moved Mortimer more deeply than he would have imagined. Impulsively, he put his hand over hers. 'A long time ago, I told you that I should like to be your friend. I still mean that. We've known each other three years now. They must count for something?'

A hint of a smile played on her lips. 'Of course our friendship means a lot to me, Mortimer. As you have just pointed out, I don't have many friends.'

A group of people entered the bar, reminding Mortimer that they were not alone. Reluctantly, he took his hand away from hers and, as he did so, he realized that his feeling towards her was much deeper than that of friendship. It was not just pity for her or affection for Stefan that drew him to her. No, the truth that he had been hiding from himself was that, ever since he had met her, he had been slowly but surely falling in love with Viktoria.

The realization stunned him. He was a married man, with a wife and daughter to whom he was deeply attached. He had never been unfaithful to Joyce. But during the past three years he had seen far more of Viktoria than Joyce and as a result, felt closer to her than he did to his wife.

Yet to embark upon an affair with her would certainly be the height of folly. If her attraction were merely physical, it would be easy to ignore it or, if he were ruthless enough to take advantage of her momentary imbalance, have his fling and forget her. The trouble was, he liked and respected her as a person... He stubbed out his cigarette and thought ruefully, *There's no fool like an old fool.*

After that, a subtle new quality entered their relationship. Mortimer never indulged in untoward familiarities and never presumed upon their friendship, and Viktoria grew to depend upon him being there, solid, sensible, wryly humorous. He took an interest in Stefan. He was concerned about her well-being. He was her friend.

When he informed her at the end of the month that he was going to Garmisch-Partenkirchen for the Winter Olympics, she knew she was going to miss him badly.

In the event, however, she had little time to think of him, because at the beginning of February, Benno's mother died.

Martha Linke discovered Countess Julia collapsed on the floor while Gottlieb was out with the Baron. She telephoned Dr Blattner, then rang Benno. By the time he arrived at Grunewald, the doctor had completed his examination. 'I can assure you your mother suffered no pain, Herr Kraus. We shall have to conduct a post-mortem, but she almost certainly suffered a cardiac arrest.'

'Where is she?' Benno asked.

The doctor hesitated. 'In her bedroom. It might be better if you didn't see her. She has been dead quite a long time and rigor mortis has set in. She is not — er — as you will remember her.'

Benno disregarded him and, upstairs in her room, gazed down at the woman who had been his mother. Her once beautiful features were grossly contorted and her hooded eyes stared lifelessly at him. How many hours had she lain alone before Martha Linke found her? He touched her frail, thin hands laden with heavy rings. 'I am sorry,' he murmured. 'I didn't realize you were so ill. Can you forgive me?' There was no answer, only the reek of death. Benno turned and left the room.

Downstairs, Martha and Gottlieb Linke were wringing their hands. 'I am so sorry, Herr Kraus,' Martha said. 'She was all right when I took up her hot milk yesterday evening.'

'I drove the Herr Baron to Kraus Haus,' Gottlieb added. 'Since then, I have been doing errands for him.'

'And I have been busy in the kitchen,' Martha went on.

Benno nodded. He could blame neither of them for their neglect. It was over three months since he himself had last been to see her. 'Do you know where the Herr Baron is?'

'He is attending a meeting at the Air Ministry,' Gottlieb replied, fingering the Party badge on his lapel.

Benno picked up the phone and asked the operator for the Air Ministry. After impressing upon a number of adjutants the urgency of his call, he was eventually connected to his father. 'Father, it's Benno. I'm afraid I have bad news for you. Mother is dead.'

'Good God! How did that happen?'

'Dr Blattner believes she had a heart attack. He says death was almost certainly instantaneous. I'll send Linke over with the car to bring you home.'

'Why? What can I do? We're in the middle of a very important meeting. Just tell Blattner to do whatever's necessary. Get in touch with Duschek to sort out the legalities. I'll talk to you later.' The receiver went dead.

Slowly, Benno put down the phone.

Dr Blattner cast him a sympathetic look. 'I'll call an ambulance to take the Frau Countess's body to the mortuary,' he said quietly.

The funeral took place ten days later in Essen. Countess Julia might have died alone, but the Baron ensured that her body did not make its final journey unescorted or unnoticed. From all over Germany, the mourners assembled at the railway station, where the coffin arrived from Berlin in a special coach with a police guard.

As well as the Krauses and Jochums, Countess Julia's remaining older sisters, their husbands, children and grandchildren were present, but Count Johann was too ill to make the journey from Fürstenmark. Peter's father had long been suffering from arteriosclerosis and there were doleful murmurs among the family of,

'It will be Johann next, you know…' Many people cast curious glances at Peter, as the heir apparent to Fürstenmark.

Among the other mourners were high-ranking officers from the three armed forces and the SS; Gauleiters and Party officials from the Ruhr, Berlin, Silesia and Wilhelmshaven; managers from all Kraus factories; workers' representatives and old family retainers.

A band played Beethoven's *Funeral March* and the pallbearers, all Kraus employees, walked forward to transfer the coffin, draped with a swastika flag and covered with flowers, to a waiting gun-carriage drawn by six horses. Then, through streets lined with silent people, the cortège started its long journey past the Kraus factories into the foothills and up the winding road to the Fortress.

There, the coffin was taken deep into the grounds, where a mausoleum had long been built. In his SS uniform, Baron Heinrich headed the solemn procession of mourners, with Ernst and Benno, Werner and Norbert, walking in pairs behind him.

At the mausoleum, the band played the funeral march from the *Götterdämmerung*. A pastor conducted a service, which seemed to bear little relationship to the normal funeral rites. He ended, 'Julia Kraus, you have fought with a brave spirit and you have suffered for your country at your husband's side, but you have rejoiced in it even unto death. Go now, ardent soul, enter the great hall of Valhalla!'

After her earthly remains had been entombed in the sepulchre, the mourners made their way to the house. 'I don't understand why Julia should enter Valhalla and not heaven,' Ricarda murmured unhappily.

Even Benno was uncomfortable. This was the first time he had personally witnessed the neo-paganist rites that were so upsetting Pastor Scheer and other priests.

Perturbed, he entered the house where he had lived as a boy, a cold, forbidding building, with dark panelled walls and doors, small windows and bulky furniture. The immediate entrance hall was hung with guns. The long dining room in which they gathered was decorated with heavy oil paintings depicting battle scenes. A huge sideboard was laden with silver plates and trophies. A small fire burned in a massive grate. A uniformed butler obsequiously handed round minute glasses of sherry and tiny open sandwiches.

Benno shivered. In forty-six years, nothing had changed at the Fortress. It still represented money and the very worst in taste.

People stood awkwardly in small groups, glancing surreptitiously at their watches. Benno moved over to where his father and Ernst were standing in front of the fire, keeping what little heat it gave off from the other guests. 'Retire?' the Baron was demanding. 'What makes you think I should retire, boy?'

'I thought maybe, now Mother is dead...' Ernst stammered. 'You seem to forget, Father, that I shall be fifty this year. I could take a lot of responsibility off your shoulders. You should relax more...'

The Baron's face turned puce. 'You're as bad as the bloody doctors! I may be seventy-seven, but I've no intention of visiting the inside of that mausoleum for a very long time!'

Benno walked away again. Perhaps he had been unfair to Stefan at Christmas. He had certainly never wanted to be as tyrannical with his son as the Baron was with both of his. He tapped Viktoria on the shoulder. 'Come on, let's go home. I don't think I can take much more today.'

Mortimer returned from Garmisch, tanned and relaxed from the Alpine air, and resolved to keep his feelings for Viktoria well under control in the future. When Benno asked about the Olympics, he replied tersely, 'I was impressed by the organization and depressed by the military nature of the Games — and the fact that most foreign visitors are still unaware of what is actually happening in Germany.'

Benno sighed. 'Herr Allen, you have a morbidly unhealthy imagination. I shall be interested to see what you make of the Summer Olympics.'

That August, Berlin was due to host the Summer Olympics, an occasion greeted with great joy by most people, for it would mean a vast influx of visitors, with a corresponding increase in business. The Hotel Quadriga was already fully booked for the entire month, with a long waiting list.

In order to stage the Olympic Games, fundamental changes were being made to the city. The stadium at the Grunewald Racecourse, on the road to Spandau, was being rebuilt. A wide bridge was being constructed to link the Pfaueninsel in the Wannsee to the mainland, so that visitors to the Italian gala night Dr Goebbels intended to hold there could cross on foot instead of by ferry.

To impress and accommodate the visitors, a new North-South underground line was being constructed to connect the Stettiner and Anhalter main line railway stations, with a new S-Bahn station on Unter den Linden itself, within a stone's throw of the Hotel Quadriga.

Soon, they were awakened each morning by the sound of massive excavators, as a huge pit was dug in the central promenade, with mountains of sand to all sides. Then, to their dismay, the trees were felled. Drawn to the spectacle in dreadful fascination, they stood on the hotel balcony and watched them fall, maples, planes and the linden trees that gave the avenue its name.

'Couldn't they have spared the trees?' Viktoria cried.

'They were old, weren't they?' Mortimer asked, standing beside her and Ricarda.

'Nearly three hundred years old,' Ricarda replied. 'Thank God Karl isn't alive to see this.'

'You know how the old song goes?' Viktoria said.

Mortimer looked at her questioningly.

'*So long as the old trees bloom on Unter den Linden,*
Nothing can befall us. Berlin will stay Berlin.'

Several people turned and nodded gravely. 'And when the old trees are gone?' Mortimer asked.

She shook her head sadly.

Day after day, the desecration continued. In order to make way for the railway tunnel, blocks of lovely old houses were demolished. The central avenue itself was made narrower, the carriageways to either side of it wider, so that troops could march twelve abreast along them. The old lamp standards were taken down. The trees continued to be felled. The piles of sandy earth grew.

Mortimer had other things on his mind than linden trees. To the unconcealed dismay of the Nazis, the French Government had finally agreed a mutual assistance pact with the Soviet Union. On 7 March, the Reichstag was convened.

An atmosphere of tension pervaded the packed auditorium of the Kroll Opera. Hitler commenced his long speech with an hysterical hymn of hate against Bolshevism. 'I will not have the gruesome communist international dictatorship of hate descend upon the German people! This destructive Asiatic ideology strikes at all values! I tremble for Europe at the thought of what would happen should this chaos of the Bolshevist revolution prove successful!' The deputies cheered.

Hitler continued that, by signing the Soviet Pact, France had invalidated the Locarno Treaty. 'Germany no longer feels bound by the Locarno Treaty. In the interest of the primitive rights of its people to the security and defence of its frontier, the German Government has re-established, as from today, the absolute and unrestricted sovereignty of the Reich in the demilitarized zone.'

The deputies leaped to their feet, arms outstretched, and burst into a frenzied paroxysm of, 'Heil! Heil! Heil!'

Hitler raised his hand for silence. 'Men of the German Reichstag! In this historic hour, when in the Reich's western provinces German troops are at this minute marching into their future peace-time garrisons, we all unite in two sacred vows.'

Mortimer gasped. The Kroll Opera went wild. German troops were at that moment marching into the Rhine…!

Hitler waited until silence again prevailed, then he continued, his voice low with emotion. 'Firstly, we swear to yield to no force whatever in restoring the honour of our people, preferring to succumb with honour to the severest hardships rather than to capitulate. Secondly, we pledge that now, more than ever, we shall strive for an understanding between the European nations, especially for one with our western neighbours.' His voice rose to a crescendo. 'We have no territorial demands to make in Europe! Germany will never break the peace!'

While the frenzied cheering continued, Mortimer observed some figures in military uniform make their way up the aisle towards the exit, among them General von Blomberg and Peter von Biederstein. Their faces were white and strained.

And well they might be, for if the French mounted a counter-attack, crossed the border and tried to force them into retreat, under the terms of the Locarno Treaty that Hitler had just repudiated, Britain would have to support her — and Germany could suddenly find herself plunged into war.

But the French did nothing except hold talks with the British. And the British did nothing either. Their attitude was summed up by Lord Lothian, who said, 'The Germans, after all, are only going into their own back garden.'

The mood in the Hotel Quadriga, in Berlin, indeed in the whole of Germany, was ecstatic. 'Even the Allies realize that it is time we were freed from Versailles,' Benno said triumphantly.

'The Führer was quite right. The Rhineland is our territory. We should be allowed to do what we like in it,' Ricarda added.

'Including building fortifications?' Mortimer asked quietly. 'Because that is undoubtedly what Hitler intends to do.'

'And why not?' Benno demanded. 'The French still have the Maginot Line. Herr Allen, you still seem to ignore the necessity for our country to defend herself.'

Unwilling to become involved in a pointless argument, Mortimer shrugged. 'I know. Germany will never break the peace.'

'We have all seen enough of war. We none of us want another one. I promise you,' Viktoria assured him, her face pale.

But none of you are Adolf Hitler, Mortimer thought.

Berlin continued to change. What was once the Reichskanzler Platz was now the Adolf Hitler Platz. What had been the Königgrätzer Strasse, then the Friedrich Ebert-Strasse, had now become the Hermann Göring-Strasse. It was there, right in front of Dr Goebbels' residence, that a crowded tram plunged through the weakened road surface into the new underground tunnel. Never had the city known a similar tragedy. From all over Berlin, people came to stare at the site of the disaster and muttered among themselves, 'Before long, we shall all collapse in front of Goebbels' house in the Hermann Göring-Strasse — and that will be the end of us.'

Perhaps to still such rumours, the authorities planted new trees, four years old and sixteen feet high, along Unter den Linden. They erected new lamp posts, which were taller than the trees. And they lined the avenue with towering white columns, bearing massive gilded eagles and swastika symbols.

Stefan wrote: *Dearest Mama and Papa, I was sorry to hear about the trees. I hope you won't mind if I spend the summer holidays with Tony. His people have taken a place in Scotland for the grouse season from August 12th and invited me to go with them…*

'Why doesn't he bring Herr Callearn here first for the Olympics, then go to Scotland?' Benno suggested. 'The Chanctonburys are an excellent family. I've looked them up in the *Gotha Almanach*. The line goes back to William the Conqueror…'

Viktoria wrote back: *Darling Stefi, we understand that you want to go to Scotland, but couldn't you and Mr Callearn come home first? After all, this is the first time Berlin has hosted the Olympics….*

Stefan replied: *Dear Mama, Tony agrees with me that when Hitler stops persecuting innocent people, then will be the time for us to visit Germany…*

She showed the letter to Mortimer. 'For God's sake, tell him to be careful what he writes,' he exclaimed. 'I hate to think what would happen if that letter got into the wrong hands!' He ran his fingers through his hair. 'It's close in here. Feel like a stroll?'

Although it was a warm May evening, it was not close inside the hotel. But Viktoria knew what he meant. Outside, they would be free from curious eyes and listening ears.

They walked towards the Pariser Platz. Mortimer took Stefan's letter and set fire to it, throwing the blackened ashes into a waste bin. 'I've learned today that hundreds of pastors from the Confessing Church have been arrested for signing a letter of protest against the government's anti-Christian and anti-Semitic policies. Fortunately, our friend Pastor Scheer was not among them. Possibly, they were worried about the repercussions. After all, he's very well-known.'

'Do you think Stefan knew about that? Is that why he…?'

'I doubt it. Dr Goebbels doesn't allow us to report such items of news. And anyway, who's interested?'

'But several hundred pastors…!'

Mortimer gazed sombrely towards the statue of the Quadriga above the Brandenburg Gate. 'Viktoria, there are now over a hundred concentration camps filled with people who have dared to protest. Who does anything about them?'

'What can we do? If I demanded to know why several hundred pastors had been arrested, the Gestapo would simply arrest me.' She shivered. 'Mortimer, it's dreadful. We all live in fear. It's as if the whole country has become one huge concentration camp.'

'No, there is no barbed wire fence around Germany. Unlike the Soviet Union, this is still a free country. There are no travel restrictions. You can come and go as you like and foreign visitors are welcomed, which is one of the main purposes of holding the Olympics here. No, Viktoria, you are imprisoned by your own fear — and by the ambitions of ruthless and greedy men.'

They entered the Tiergarten and sat down on an empty bench.

'And Stefi?' Viktoria asked. 'Mortimer, he's changed so much since he's been away. You saw in that letter, he hates Germany now.'

'No, he doesn't. On the contrary, he loves his country with a very deep, unfaltering love.'

'Then why...?'

'Because, more clearly than any of you, who are here all the time, he can see what is happening to it. I think he always had reservations, but after the book-burning he knew something had to be done. That was why he was so determined to go to Oxford. Books are very precious to Stefan — like the linden trees are to you.'

She was silent, watching children playing in the lush grass under the watchful eye of their nannies. Yes, the trees and the tram disaster. 'You mean, we will all put up with so much, but it takes something that affects us personally to open our eyes?'

'Yes. To return to the Lutheran pastors, they can see the authority of the Church being undermined and possibly even destroyed.'

Countess Julia's pagan funeral... *You are imprisoned by your own fear — and by the ambitions of ruthless and greedy men.* Baron Heinrich... Even Benno. The hotel staff no longer reported to her, guests no longer came to her with their requests. They called her Frau Viktoria — but

Benno was the Herr Generaldirektor. It had taken place so gradually, she had hardly noticed it happening. So it must be with the pastors…

As if he could read her thoughts, Mortimer took her hand, smiling ruefully. 'I'm sorry. I didn't mean to depress you. I really wanted to tell you that you are not alone, that I *do* understand what you are going through, and to reassure you that, although Stefan isn't coming home, he *does* still care for you. Come on, let's walk a bit.'

It was lunchtime when they arrived back at the hotel. Benno had not even noticed her absence.

After that, Mortimer frequently contrived to meet her, as if by coincidence, and walk with her up Unter den Linden, through the Tiergarten or along the Spree embankment, and these meetings, innocent though they were, began to take on a great importance. Viktoria did not tell Benno about them. Benno had taken enough away from her. He was not going to take Mortimer as well. So, if he asked where she had been, she just said she had been for a walk, and Benno, busier than ever as the Olympics approached, accepted her explanation without question. But increasingly, seeing Mortimer gave a sense of purpose to Viktoria's life.

In the middle of July, Monika left school. She had poor grades in all subjects except needlework, sport and domestic science. She showed absolutely no aptitude for arithmetic and her spelling was not very good. The only books she read were romantic novels.

'We must talk about your career,' Viktoria said.

'I don't need a career. I'm going to marry Hans and have lots of children.'

'I don't understand you, Monika. At your age you should want to have a job, to be independent. Yet all you want is to get married.'

'Surely that's a very natural ambition?'

'I suppose so. But you hardly know Hans — and your father and I haven't even met him yet. We may not like him.'

'I like him. That's all that matters.'

'Has he finished his studies yet?'

'No. When he finishes his military service in September, he still has another year at teaching college.'

'I suggest we discuss the matter again then.'

'Whether you approve or not, I shall marry Hans.'

When Viktoria told Mortimer about this conversation, he said, 'If her mind is made up, I fear you've got no choice but to go along with her. She's doing exactly what Hitler wants. Why else do you think the Nazis have defined the role of women so rigidly as wives and mothers? Hitler wants women to breed new little Nazis as quickly as possible.'

'But why?'

'To grow up into soldiers and conquer the world.'

'Mortimer, what a dreadful thought...' But she did not argue with him, for gradually, under his influence, she was beginning to see the world through his eyes.

He talked to her now as he might to a man about international events and, although she learned nothing from him that she could not have read in the papers, she saw things in a clearer light.

There was Abyssinia, for instance. At the beginning of May, the Italians had occupied Addis Ababa and now, two months later, the League of Nations had lifted the economic sanctions against Italy. 'Very foolish,' Mortimer said. 'After this, the League can no longer be an effective institution. In many ways, it has played straight into Mussolini's and Hitler's hands.'

Then there was the Austro-German agreement, which Dr Schuschnigg and Hitler signed on 11 July. Mortimer said, 'Ostensibly, Hitler has agreed not to interfere in Austrian affairs. Well, we shall see...'

And there was Spain. On 18 July, an anti-socialist revolt, led by General Franco, broke out in Spain and, not long after, Germany sent ground troops and an experimental air force unit called the Condor Legion, under the command of General Hugo Sperrle, to Spain to assist Franco's troops.

'What has Spain to do with us?' Viktoria asked, meeting Mortimer outside the British Embassy.

'Ideologically, Hitler is on Franco's side in a war against communism. But there is more to it than that. If Mussolini also joins in the fray, it will mean France is surrounded by three alien powers. It will also give Hitler a chance to test the strength of the Wehrmacht and the Luftwaffe. A trial run for war, if you like.'

'You really believe that there will be another war?'

He nodded. 'I hope not, but I fear so. Once Hitler has secured the territories to the west, it is my belief that he will look towards the east, towards Austria, Poland, Czechoslovakia and the Baltic States, to the countries that will provide the *Lebensraum* — the living space — he has always vowed to win for the German people.'

'And the British? What do they think about Spain?'

'Strictly neutral. They are far more concerned about the relationship between the King and an American divorcee called Mrs Wallis Simpson. Certain informed sources seem to think love is in the air.' She gave him a quizzical look. 'The English constitution does not permit the monarch to marry a divorced person. What would you do if you were King? Would you renounce the throne for the woman you loved — or would you see your first duty to be to your country?'

'Mama! Mama!' Monika ran down Unter den Linden towards them, her plaits flying, waving a letter in her hand. 'Mama! I've had a letter from Hans. He's coming to Berlin for the Olympics!'

'Mustn't love be wonderful! When I'm older, I'll fall in love too,' Mortimer murmured, sardonically repeating an old saying. 'Ladies, I must leave you for a meeting at the Propaganda Ministry.'

Monika frowned at his departing back. 'Doesn't he know sarcasm is the lowest form of wit? Mama, Hans can stay with us, can't he?'

'Yes, of course,' Viktoria replied absently. 'He can have Stefan's room.'

As they walked into the hotel, Monika asked, 'What were you and Herr Allen talking about?'

'The King of England,' Viktoria told her, truthfully.

There was no time to think of Mortimer, or the King of England, or Spain during the weeks that followed, because at the end of July, in an atmosphere almost reminiscent of the glorious days of the Kaiser, Berlin gave itself over to the Olympic Games.

'Vicki, if you could spare the time, I could use your help,' Benno said.

He could have phrased his request better, but she was so happy to be needed, she said nothing.

The streets were a mass of flags and banners — and not just the swastika. From tall white flagpoles, flags of every participating nation fluttered in the breeze. In every colour and every language under the sun, Germany bade its visitors welcome.

With an eye made more observant since she had grown closer to Mortimer, Viktoria noticed that the signs saying *Jews not permitted!* were quietly put away. The stormtroopers, who had for so long entertained their captive audiences on the terraces of Café Jochum and other cafés along the Kurfürstendamm with their repulsive rendering of *When Jewish blood spurts...* returned to their barracks.

Representatives of the royal houses of Europe assembled in Berlin. There were the King of Bulgaria, Crown Prince Umberto of Italy and the Crown Princess, Umberto's sister — the Princess Mafalda — and her husband, Prince Philip of Hesse. The Crown Prince of Greece came, as did Count Bernadotte, heir to the Swedish throne. England was represented by Lord Halifax.

With the visitors from every part of the country and every nation of the world came Hans König, tall, blond and bronzed, in a brown army uniform with sergeant's tabs. He saluted them correctly and he spoke respectfully. 'Thank you for inviting me here. I do appreciate it, particularly at a time when you are very busy.'

Benno nodded. 'We're very pleased to meet you, young man. We hope you'll feel at home with us and enjoy your stay here.'

The Olympic Bell was carried in ceremony through the Brandenburg Gate. In the Lustgarten, against a background of tall swastika banners, the Olympic Flame was lit from the Olympic Torch that had been carried 1,800 miles by three thousand runners through seven countries, and the 1936 Olympic Games began.

They were heady days that followed, exhilarating and stirring. In glorious sunshine, in 'Führer weather', the world's greatest athletes competed in the finest stadium in the world. There was only one sour note, regarding the black American athlete, Jesse Owens. The German press was indignant about what it called, 'the use of black auxiliaries', claiming that black men had stronger physiques than whites, and they offered unfair competition, and they applauded Hitler when he refused to shake hands with Owens.

But most people either agreed with or ignored the Owens incident. They strolled beside the little linden trees, discussing sporting events and the fact that things here did not seem nearly so grim as they appeared from the newspapers. They were lavish in their praise. Never before, they asserted, had any country offered such excellent organization or such spectacular entertainment as Germany did that summer. There were special performances at the opera. There were lavish receptions, balls and gala dinners, hosted by Hitler, Göring and Goebbels. There was an Italian Night for some three thousand guests on the Pfaueninsel.

That evening, Hans requested a private interview with Benno, in which he asked his permission to marry Monika when he had finished his teacher training. 'Of course I said yes,' Benno told Viktoria later, as they got ready for bed. 'I approve of Hans. He's a very sensible young man. He'll make Monika a fine husband.'

Viktoria sat down at the dressing table and unplaited her hair. It appeared that yet another decision had been taken out of her hands. Monika's future was decided.

The Games ended. Monika proudly wore an engagement ring. Hans König went back to his barracks and the Quadriga's aristocratic guests returned home.

Mortimer typed out a long article on the Olympics and sent it to Bill Wallace. After depicting the event in glowing colours, it ended: 'The spectacle was so overpowering that it was almost oppressive. Germany was not just demonstrating to the world its achievements in economic recovery, in its ability to host a display as grandiose as this one. No, there was a much deeper message. These Olympic Games were a symbol of Germany's new power, a means of showing the world how far she has advanced, a symbol that should be a warning to us all of how far she can go.'

In the published article, this final paragraph was omitted. Mortimer hammered his fist on the table in exasperation and wondered why Dr Goebbels didn't simply employ Bill Wallace on his staff.

Mortimer was not the only one to suffer disappointment in the wake of the Olympics. Benno told Viktoria, 'Thank you for your help, but I don't think there's anything more for you to do. Herr Brandt and I can manage now.'

Hurt and angry, she said, 'Benno, you seem to forget that this hotel belongs to Mama, myself and Luise, not you.'

The colour drained from his cheeks. 'I realize that and I'm certainly not taking it from you. On the contrary, I'm endeavouring to run it efficiently. Stop thinking emotionally and be sensible! No woman can manage an hotel on her own, not even you!'

'But I've enjoyed the last month so much...'

'Of course you have. You've been acting as hostess to princes and dukes. But they've gone, and now I have to catch up on the paperwork, on forms and requisitions. You've no idea how to do these things. So stop wasting my time and let me get on with it.'

Tears of anger welled up in her eyes. So, all the time she had run the hotel for her father during the war and the years when she and Benno had worked together during the Weimar Republic now counted for nothing. Coldly, she said, 'Thank you, Benno. You could not have spelled out my position more clearly if you had tried.' She stalked out of the office.

Mortimer was collecting his mail from the reception desk. '"The tumult and the shouting dies, the Captains and the Kings depart..."' he quoted, when he saw her.

It was hard to believe Fate had not deliberately placed him there. She strode through the foyer and out of the hotel.

'Viktoria, what's the matter?'

'I've just realized that Benno has succeeded in taking over the Hotel Quadriga. Mortimer, the Krauses have finally won!' Her voice trembled.

He grabbed her arm and propelled her into the first café they came to. 'Two double cognacs,' he told the waiter. Then he turned to Viktoria. 'First you're going to get a drink inside you, then you can tell me what's happened.'

The brandy stopped her shaking and, rather incoherently, she recounted the scene with Benno.

His mouth hardened. His sympathies lay entirely with Viktoria. However, being a cautious man, he said diplomatically, 'Don't be too hard on poor old Benno... He means well.'

Viktoria was not interested in hearing excuses for Benno. 'We've been married for over twenty years. If you were in Benno's position, would you treat me like he did today?'

He prevaricated. 'It's a bit difficult to imagine myself in the delightful situation of being married to you...'

'Seriously...'

'Well, I hope I should have employed a little more tact...' Her eyes blazed. 'To think I once felt grateful to him for marrying me! What a fool I've been! At the final count, Benno is just like his father. To hell with him! He can manage without me! Let him do so! I can get on very well without him, too!'

Mortimer's trained ear did not miss that extraordinary comment about being grateful to Benno for marrying her, but now was not the moment to ask what she meant. 'You've still got me,' he said quietly.

Many times, it was on the tip of Benno's tongue to apologize for having spoken so harshly to Viktoria, but because he knew he had right on his side, he could not bring himself to do so. And, as the days went by and Viktoria did not mention the matter, he decided to let sleeping dogs lie. He had enough on his mind without inviting another emotional scene.

Therefore, that day marked the beginning of a strange new existence, in which they all seemed to live on several planes. Superficially, nothing changed. Living in the same hotel and with so many acquaintances in common, it was inevitable that Benno, Viktoria and Mortimer should meet at dinners, banquets, musical evenings at the Biedersteins and functions held at the Quadriga. On such occasions, they conversed with a studied politeness, almost like strangers.

For Viktoria, it was Benno who was becoming the stranger. All day long, she scarcely saw him. In the evenings, they were usually in company. At night, they slipped into their own sides of the bed and slept.

She saw far more of Mortimer and yet, their meetings, too, had a quality of unreality, for they were never really alone. Their meetings always took place in public, in parks or on café terraces, where they could never be sure of not being recognized.

Because it was undefined, their intimacy introduced an awkwardness into their friendship. Was Mortimer in love with her? If so, he said nothing. And was Viktoria in love with him? She did not know. In many ways, he had replaced Stefan as the focal point in her life. There was scarcely a moment when she did not think of him, wondering what he was doing and whether he was thinking of her. When she was away from him, she yearned for him.

But she could not forget that she was a married woman and that, whatever her feelings towards Benno, an affair was not something to be lightly undertaken. One day, one of them would do something, take the final, irrevocable step that would tip the fine balance of their relationship. In the meantime, there was a great deal to be said for leaving things as they were. She had made one mistake in her life. She was not going to leap precipitately into another.

That summer, Basili made a decision which would affect his whole life. At seventeen, he had just completed the eighth class at the Karl-Liebknecht School and was given the alternative of continuing his studies there or transferring to a Russian school. He chose the Russian school.

Many factors influenced his choice, not least of which was his ambition to be selected for the Moscow Teacher Institute in two years' time, where he wanted to qualify in foreign languages. He was now fluent in Russian and top of his class in English. When he wasn't in class, he was in the library reading all the German, Russian, English and American books he could consume. But the atmosphere in the Karl-Liebknecht School was still predominantly German and some sixth sense told Basili he stood a better chance of success as a foreigner if he integrated himself as completely as possible into his Russian surroundings.

Apart from this, the atmosphere at the Children's Home and the Karl-Liebknecht School had changed within the last year. Conditions were deteriorating rapidly. The private coach suddenly disappeared. The food became simpler. The home's German director was replaced by a Russian. Basili was not surprised, for unaccustomed as he was to luxury, it had always seemed too good to be true. The foreign children were still feted wherever they went. Important visitors still came to inspect and admire them. But Basili had the feeling that they were no longer a showpiece that the Soviet authorities wanted to display. They were beginning to lose their importance.

These were the arguments Basili put to Olga when he told her of his decision. She was appalled and angry. 'Have you already forgotten that you are a German, that your first loyalty should be to your homeland, not to Russia? Don't you understand what is happening here? The proletariat does not rule. Just as Hitler has established a dictatorship in Germany, Stalin has set himself up as a dictator over the Russian people!'

As Basili stared at her in horrified silence, Olga continued, with the old, fanatical gleam in her eye, 'Europe is heading for a crisis. In France, the Popular Front, led by Leon Blum, has achieved power. In Spain, the Popular Front will triumph over the fascist military. In Germany, the workers are increasing their resistance to the Nazis. Hitler's government will fall any minute. And here, too, the Trotskyites and Zinovievites will lead the people in a revolution against Stalin.'

'How do you know this?'

'From old comrades like Karl Radek, from Sokolnikov and Piatkov.'

Basili's stomach churned. Even within the sheltered atmosphere of the children's home, they knew of these men, supporters of the exiled Trotsky, who believed in permanent revolution and made no secret of their opposition to Stalin's policies.

'When we succeed,' Olga cried, 'we shall return to Germany…'

Experience, reason, logic or, perhaps simple intuition, told him she was living in a dream that was doomed to failure. When he left her that evening, his resolution to become an integral member of Russian society was stronger than ever.

That September, at the Nuremberg Rally, Hitler announced the Four-Year Plan, the purpose of which was to make Germany self-sufficient within four years. Göring was put in charge of it.

When his father came to the hotel shortly afterwards, Benno said, 'I didn't know General Göring was an economist, Father. Why on earth was he given the job?'

For once, the Baron looked distinctly nonplussed and Benno had the feeling Hitler had not consulted the industrialists on this major piece of policy, and that Göring's new position had taken them unpleasantly by surprise.

Göring wasted no time in introducing measures which left nobody in any doubt as to the true purpose of the Four-Year Plan. For the first time, people heard the slogan, *Guns before butter!* 'Guns will make us powerful. Butter will only make us fat,' he said, at which there were a number of sarcastic comments that Göring should take his own advice. Dr Goebbels' Propaganda Ministry urged them to develop a 'political stomach'. Once a month, they were compelled to eat a 'one-pot meal', donating the savings to the State.

At the same time, shortages started to become noticeable in the shops and imports were reduced to essentials. Imported fruits became a luxury, while the quality of tea, coffee, cheese and meat deteriorated rapidly. Bread was made with more potato than wheat or rye. The butter that could make them fat tasted more of water than cream. Price and wage controls were introduced, limiting buying power. Newspapers devoted considerable space to instructing housewives in the art of preparing nutritious meals from unappetizing, but cheap and home-grown, ingredients.

One of Berlin's showpieces, the Hotel Quadriga suffered less than the ordinary household. The government still wanted to encourage foreign visitors and starving them would be bad publicity. So the Hotel Quadriga did not have to sacrifice its high international standards, but it had to pay in other ways, in massive donations to Party charities and in taxes.

Having, in theory at least, organized the domestic economy, Göring turned his attention to heavy industry, where he immediately identified a crucial weakness. Iron ore, essential to the metal industry, was imported mainly from Sweden. 'There is plenty of iron ore in Germany,' he announced blandly, 'but the industrialists do not want to mine it.'

So he ordered that the largest metal works in the world be built at the foot of the Harz Mountains at Salzgitter, where there were plentiful deposits of iron ore. It was to be called the Hermann Göring Works.

At this preposterous idea, not even Baron Heinrich could contain his tongue. 'Göring's a bigger fool than I took him for! We all know there's ore at Salzgitter, but it's substandard. We shall still have to import magnetic ores to mix with it. So much for making Germany self-sufficient! Then there's another factor Göring seems to have forgotten. The ideal site for a metal works is near a coal mine and an iron ore mine. Why else does he think Kraus operates in the Ruhr and Silesia? There isn't any coal at Salzgitter! The Hermann Göring Works is going to be nothing but an extremely costly white elephant!'

Viktoria repeated his words to Mortimer. 'You see, I understand what Göring's Four-Year Plan is all about. Germany is mobilizing its production to war. I've lived through one war. I don't ever want to live through another. But what can we do about it?'

Mortimer smiled reassuringly. 'I shouldn't worry too much. It doesn't sound as if Göring's plans are going to be very successful.' However, without telling Viktoria, he included this information in his report to Winston Churchill.

The first year of Luise's married life was supremely contented. Her entire world revolved around Sepp. Morning, noon and night, his face was before her eyes, his name on her lips. She ate, drank and slept Sepp. She planned treats and surprises for him; she bought him small presents; she spent hours preparing his favourite meals.

Unlike many men, whose personalities change when they put on a uniform and gain a title, Sepp's altered status made no difference to his character. He remained as he had always been — a heavy-smoking, hard-drinking, irreverent and independent spirit.

As the Luftwaffe grew, he was forced more and more into the company of the Secretary of State for Aviation, Erhard Milch, for

Sepp possessed an innate knowledge of aviation Milch would never have. To a man as ruthlessly ambitious as Milch this was in itself an anathema. Coupled with his intense disapproval of Sepp as a person, it inevitably turned their meetings into tense confrontations.

Yet Sepp remained blithely unperturbed. Indeed, he took a certain delight in deliberately provoking Milch. Unlike his superior, he was adored by the airmen. Manufacturers and engineers respected him. Most importantly of all, he enjoyed Göring's protection.

'The Fat Man can't stand Milch,' he explained to Luise. 'That's why he leaves me alone to run my department my own way.'

Sepp maintained his unswerving affection for Göring, despite all his posturing extravagances. 'We were fliers together,' he told Luise simply. 'We understand each other.'

Although she understood little of his world, Luise loved to listen to him talk. While she sat in a big armchair, with Sheltie cradled in her arms, he would stride restlessly up and down the apartment, a glass in one hand, a cigarette in the other, talking about Focke-Wulfs, Heinkels, Dorniers and Messerschmitts; about the pros and cons of open cockpits; about aerodynamics, wing-loadings, engines, airspeeds and fuel consumption.

His current involvement was with the prototypes of the Messerschmitt Bf 109. 'It's a far better machine than the Heinkel. It's manoeuvrable: it rolls, dives, turns and climbs much more efficiently. It's a real flier's machine!'

In the autumn of 1936 an aviation display was performed in Göring's honour at the Luftwaffe Test Centre at Rechlin on the Baltic. Sepp came home very happy. 'We had a mock air battle. I flew the 109 and "destroyed" four Heinkel fighters and four bombers!' He poured himself a glass of brandy, slumped into a chair and continued enthusiastically, 'That's the equivalent of destroying a whole formation! The Fat Man was beside himself with joy!'

As usual, Luise listened with only half an ear, revelling in his cheerful mood.

'With the new cannon, we could undoubtedly shoot down even more enemy aircraft...'

Sheltie's cold wet nose nudged against her hand and, with a start, she took in what Sepp was saying. 'Cannon?'

'The 109 isn't being built for joyrides, sweetheart. It's a fighter plane.'

For the first time, Luise realized that Sepp's job was not about flying for pleasure, but preparation for war.

Sepp yawned and looked at his watch. 'Let's get an early night.'

They went to bed, but it was a long time before they slept. Sepp undressed and lay in bed watching Luise take off her clothes. 'Don't bother to put on a nightdress!' She slipped between the sheets beside him and he drew her to him. 'You're the most beautiful woman in the world and I love you.'

'Better than a Messerschmitt Bf 109?'

His hands moved up her body, stroking her flat stomach, the little hills of her breasts. 'You're softer than a Bf 109.'

'I love you so much.'

'Stop talking and kiss me.'

Still elated by the day's events, Sepp made love to her that night with an ardour she had not experienced since her honeymoon and slowly, her fear ebbed away. Carried in Sepp's arms, she was transported up through a clear white sky towards the peak of the blue mountain. They were flying, flying, flying, just the two of them, and then they were united and became one person. Not just their bodies, but their spirits were irretrievably interwoven. Nothing and nobody could ever separate them.

Shortly after that, there was a new and frequent visitor to the Nowak apartment — another veteran of the Richthofen Squadron, Ernst Udet, now head of the Development Section of the Air Ministry. Night after night, long after Luise had gone to bed, Sepp and Ernst Udet sat on in the smoke-filled living room, ashtrays piled high with cigarette butts, empty wine bottles on the table, talking about aeroplanes and Spain.

Sometimes, when the door was left ajar, words filtered through to Luise in the neighbouring room. 'The Fat Man...' 'The He 51 is totally outdated...' 'We're sending three to Spain in December...'

As the weeks passed, they grew impatient. '"Iron Annie" is fine as a transport plane, but as a bomber she's only an interim measure.' Udet's voice, tense and urgent. 'Wait till Junkers finish developing the Stuka. I tell you, Sepp, the Stuka will be the greatest dive-bomber ever built. I can't wait to see it in action in Spain...'

Laughter. Glasses tinkling. 'The Russian planes won't stand a chance...'

Luise buried her head in the pillow, but still the words echoed in her mind. Fighters. Bombers. Spain. Sepp and Ernst Udet were like children, seeing the Spanish Civil War as a tremendous adventure, which they were itching to join in. But she could still remember the horrors of the last war and the millions who had perished. She clung to Sheltie. 'Oh, Sheltie, don't they realize war isn't a game?'

The leaves fell from the little linden trees. Frost rimed the grass and the shores of the lakes. The first nip of snow was in the air. When Viktoria and Mortimer met, they both knew that something had changed in their relationship, but neither was quite sure what the next move should be.

Apart from anything else, things were happening in the world around them, which boded ill for the future.

At the end of October, Count Ciano, Mussolini's son-in-law, went to Hitler's mountain eyrie, the Berghof, above Berchtesgaden. In a public statement in Milan on 1 November, Mussolini said, 'This Rome-Berlin Line is not a diaphragm, but rather an Axis.' It was evident that some kind of alliance had been formed between the Italian and German governments.

Less than a month later, the new German ambassador to London, Joachim von Ribbentrop, announced in Berlin that he had concluded an Anti-Comintern Pact with Japan, declaring their mutual hostility to international communism. The pact's purpose was to defend western civilization against Russia, should she unprovokedly attack either country. The Charlottenburger Chaussee was re-named the East-West Axis.

And from the Soviet Union, rumours emanated of a reign of terror more brutal, more horrifying than anything experienced even in

Germany. To purge the Bolshevik Party of all possible rivals to power, Stalin had ordered the NKVD to arrest all opponents to his policies and leadership. Many former heroes of the 1917 October Revolution were said to be awaiting trial, while hundreds of thousands were believed to have been shot or exiled to Siberia.

In Spain, General Franco's Nationalists, supported by German and Italian troops, continued their battle against the Republicans, the Basques, the Catalans and the International Brigades.

In the Rhineland, the Germans had commenced the construction of a massive line of fortifications along the French and Belgian borders. It was being called the Siegfried Line or the West Wall.

In Austria, the Nazi Party was gaining in strength.

In England, on 10 December, King Edward VIII chose to abdicate rather than give up the woman he loved.

When Mortimer went home for Christmas, it was with the feeling that all of Europe was a seething cauldron, bubbling with scarcely suppressed tensions, including that of his own love for a German woman called Viktoria Jochum-Kraus.

It was very strange suddenly to be without Mortimer, but his absence was more than compensated for by Stefan's return, by a Stefan who was clearly determined that there should be no repetition of the ugly scene which had marred his holiday the previous Christmas. He came home, cheerful, affectionate and laden with gifts. He was tactful in his references to Oxford, making no contentious comments to Benno about Berlin. Because of this, Viktoria and Benno seemed to recover a little of their old closeness, although a sense of estrangement still persisted beneath the surface. That scene following the Olympics had left a permanent scar.

Sepp had been given a week's leave between Christmas and New Year, which he and Luise spent at the Quadriga. To Monika's delight, Hans also came to Berlin. He had finished his year's military service and was now back at teaching college in Stettin.

'How lovely to have the whole family together,' Ricarda exclaimed happily, as they stood round the tree on Christmas Eve.

But the following day, the first painful note made itself felt. At Ricarda's request, Stefan accompanied her and Viktoria to church at Schmargendorf, a beautifully traditional service with a nativity crib and carols, after which the Scheers invited them into their home for coffee and cakes. 'One of the pastors arrested in May has died at Sachsenhausen concentration camp,' Pastor Scheer told them, after they had caught up on each other's news. 'He was murdered. Stefan, do you think people in England realize how bad things are over here?'

'Very few,' Stefan admitted. 'They are much more concerned about the abdication crisis.'

'I don't think there are many Germans who realize either,' Viktoria said. 'If it hadn't been for Mortimer, I should never have known.'

'Such things never appear in the papers,' Ricarda added in a troubled voice. 'If one isn't personally involved, one has no idea what is really going on. It wasn't until Julia's funeral…'

'I'm very worried about Professor Ascher,' Pastor Scheer continued. 'I keep trying to persuade him to go to his daughter in London, but he won't listen to me. He is doing very useful work here, but he is no longer a young man. Stefan, you will go and see him while you're home, won't you?'

'Of course.'

They drove back to the Quadriga in sombre mood. The signs were back over shops: *Jews not admitted, Jews not wanted here.* 'It's all so distasteful,' Ricarda sighed, 'so undignified…'

'Somebody must be able to do something!' Stefan said.

Viktoria took his hand. 'When you see the Professor, tell him he is always welcome at the Quadriga.'

Stefan looked at her gratefully. 'Thank you, Mama.'

So far as Luise was concerned, those few days were very happy. Sepp was at his most considerate: loving and affectionate; drinking and smoking less than usual; taking long walks with her and Sheltie; going to bed early and making love to her each night. He did not once mention Spain, nor did they see Udet. By the time New Year's Eve arrived, Luise was all but convinced that her fears had been nothing but crazy figments of her imagination.

For once, the Biedersteins were not present at the New Year's Eve ball, because they were spending the holiday at Fürstenmark. Viktoria was not sorry. Although she had got used to having Peter around by now, she still felt slightly uneasy in his presence.

She was not the only one. Stefan, growing more pacifist every year, made no effort to conceal his dislike for him. 'He epitomizes the very worst of the officer classes,' he said, when Viktoria cautiously asked him why he didn't like his uncle. Relieved, she did not even attempt to argue with him. It was much better he felt like that than that he should hold him in too high regard.

Consideration for Count Johann did not take the Krauses to Fürstenmark, however. They came from Essen not only to celebrate New Year at the Quadriga, but also so that Ernst could familiarize Werner and Norbert with the Kraus Chemie works at Wedding. Nineteen now, Werner, like Hans, had completed his year's conscription and was being trained in all aspects of Kraus Industries. Upon Werner, Viktoria and Stefan were still in total agreement. He was quite simply the most insufferably dull and pompous prig they had ever met.

And they both agreed they liked chubby Norbert, although Monika, for some unfathomable reason, did not have any time for him at all. But then, Monika was in love with Hans.

'What's your opinion of Hans?' Viktoria asked Stefan.

'All right,' he replied noncommittally.

'Oh, Stefi, it's so wonderful to have you home again. I've missed you so much.' But even as she spoke, she realized that she had missed him less than she would have done had she not had Mortimer.

The New Year's Eve ball that year was, as always, a spectacular event, with many prominent politicians and military officers present, the dance floor a swirling mass of dapper uniforms and colourful evening gowns. 'Mama, have you noticed how drab most of the women have become?' Stefan asked, as he led her in a quick waltz.

'Drab? Everyone looks very nice to me.'

'You do and so does Aunt Luise. But look at all the others. No powder. No lipstick. Have the Nazis banned cosmetics?'

'It's the new, fashionable clean-and-scrubbed look,' she laughed.

But now that Stefan mentioned it, she could see what he meant. *So having taken away all our rights, they are now taking away our femininity*, she thought despondently.

Midnight came and the ballroom echoed to hundreds of voices. 'Heil Hitler! Heil! Heil! Heil!' Outside, the air reverberated with the booming of mighty cannon.

Stefan got over the situation by kissing his mother. 'Happy New Year, Mama.'

'And to you too, Stefi, darling.'

He raised his glass. 'To absent friends.'

'You're thinking of the Allens?'

'They seem to have become part of my life,' he replied simply.

And mine, Viktoria thought.

In Oxford, an hour later, because of the time difference, Mortimer raised his glass. 'To absent friends,' he proposed.

Joyce smiled. 'Yes, to Stephen. Libby and I miss him. He's become part of the family.'

And I miss his mother, Mortimer thought.

Next day, when Sepp and Luise returned to their own apartment, Sepp announced, 'I didn't want to spoil the holiday, but now you'll have to know. I'm being posted to Spain to join Sperrle's Condor Legion. We're taking the first Bf 109s out there.'

Luise struggled to keep her voice even. 'How long will you be away?'

'It depends on what happens, but probably no longer than six months.' He chucked her under the chin. 'Don't worry, Luischen, I'll be all right.'

She smiled bravely, determined not to let him see her fear and, when he left two days later, she waved him goodbye with a cheerful confidence to match his own. That afternoon, however, when Ricarda came to see her, she admitted, 'Mama, I know I should feel proud of him, but I can still remember the last war so clearly. I couldn't bear it if anything happened to Sepp.'

Ricarda took her hand. 'Sepp knows how to take care of himself. But I understand how you feel. It's always harder for those who are left behind. Would you like me to stay here with you for a while?'

Luise looked at her gratefully. 'That would be nice. It would stop me brooding.'

Count Johann von Biederstein died on 25 January 1937. His funeral took place a week later.

Three limousines conveyed the party from Berlin to Fürstenmark. They trundled over the cobbled village street, lined with peasants who raised their caps as they passed, under an archway and joined others already parked in the courtyard in front of the castle. The chauffeurs hurried to open the car doors and help their passengers alight. The Baron, his massive bulk supported by Ernst and Trudi, followed by Werner and Norbert, made his way into the castle to join the rest of the family.

Monika watched them enviously. 'Can we go into the castle later?'

Benno took her hand. 'What's so special about a castle? The Quadriga is much more comfortable.'

'But less romantic,' his daughter informed him.

Fürstenmark Castle dated back to the first Biederstein knight who had settled there in the thirteenth century. In the intervening years, a church had been built, peasants' cottages erected, an inn, a few shops and a school had been opened. So far as the eye could see, the surrounding countryside, flat, arable land, interspersed with marsh and forest, belonged to the von Biederstein estate. To the east, it was bounded by the marshy banks of the River Oder. To the north it extended almost to the Baltic Sea.

They walked towards the church standing adjacent to the castle. 'Imagine having your own church,' Monika breathed.

Ushers guided them to their pew. The organ played quietly. A choir, among whom Hans could be identified, sang an anthem under the direction of the schoolmaster. Then there was silence and they all stood, as, preceded by Pastor König, pallbearers carried the coffin containing the mortal remains of Count Johann up the aisle and laid it in front of the altar. At least Hans's father conducted no neo-paganist rites. 'I am the resurrection and the life...' he chanted. Behind them, came the Count's family.

Leaning heavily on a stick, Countess Anna came first, with Peter beside her. The rest of the cortège passed: Ilse and Christa; Biederstein sisters, husbands and offspring; Baron Heinrich and his family; the estate manager, Gerhardt Bischof; family retainers and tenant farmers, uncomfortable in their stiff black suits; local councillors and officials; cooks and servants from the castle; grooms and farmhands.

His face flushed red with importance, Pastor König took his stand at the front of the church. 'Lord, thou hast been our refuge: from one generation to another...'

From one generation to another... Thankful Stefan had been spared this ordeal, Viktoria wondered what he would say if he knew that he represented another generation of Biedersteins. *Oh God*, she prayed, *I love Stefan so much. Do what you will to me, but please never let Stefan discover what he really is...*

When the service was over, they filed out into the churchyard and gathered round the grave. The wind was bitingly cold and snow was rimed on the barren earth. The Pastor was well into his stride. 'Man that is born of a woman hath but a short time to live, and is full of misery. He cometh up and is cut down, like a flower; he fleeth as it were a shadow, and never continueth in one stay... Thou knowest, Lord, the secrets of our hearts...'

Viktoria stared at Peter's bowed head. Had he loved his father? Had he ever loved anyone? Was he upset at his father's death or was it merely an incident, as their brief love affair had been?

When the final blessing had been said, the congregation walked across the courtyard into the castle, where maids relieved them of their coats. The raftered hall was cold and draughty, the tapestries and carpets frayed and faded. From the hubbub of conversation, it was evident that most of those present had discarded their mourning with their outdoor garments. 'The king is dead. Long live the king,' Benno whispered, as they made their way towards Countess Anna.

The cruel Pomeranian climate and the years had treated Peter's mother less than kindly. Her face was deeply etched with lines and her sparse hair, imperfectly concealed by a black hat, trimmed with a black veil, was quite white. Yet, despite her loss and her infirmities, she accepted their words of condolence with dignity. 'Thank you, Benno. Viktoria, you were a mere scrap of a girl last time I saw you. So this is Monika.'

Monika gazed at her with big eyes. 'Frau Countess, I've heard so much about Fürstenmark — and now I'm here, I think it's beautiful.'

The Countess patted Monika's arm with a gnarled hand. 'You're a dear girl. Young König has told me about you. Stay with me, child, and keep me company.'

So, while servants handed round glasses of hot mulled wine and the mourners drifted into groups around the inadequate fire, Monika remained at Countess Anna's side. In the late afternoon, Peter called Viktoria and Benno into the old Count's study. 'As you can see, my mother is very frail. Ilse and I are very reluctant to leave her here on her own and she adamantly refuses to come and live with us in Berlin. In view of Monika's engagement to young König, I wonder if you would consider allowing Monika to stay here with her as her companion? Mama has taken quite a fancy to her.'

'Companion?' Viktoria asked sharply. She had no intention of allowing her daughter to become a servant in the Biederstein household.

'A highly respectable position, my dear Viktoria, quite in keeping with her upbringing and background,' Peter said, a trace of amusement in his eyes. 'Monika would be expected to read to my mother, accompany her on visits to local gentry and perhaps play the piano on occasions.'

'To tell you the truth, Peter,' Benno said, 'we've been a bit concerned about Monika. She gets rather bored at the hotel all day.'

Peter nodded. 'I know. We're sending Christa to finishing school in Switzerland in September.'

They summoned Monika, who was overjoyed at the idea, showing not the slightest regret at leaving home. So it was agreed that they should all return to the Quadriga for Monika to collect her belongings and that Benno should return with her in a few days' time to make sure she settled in all right and also to get to know the Königs.

A week later, the hotel limousine took Viktoria, Benno and Monika to the Stettiner Station. 'I doubt I'll be gone longer than a week,' Benno said. 'I'll let you know when to expect me back.'

'Don't expect to see me back ever, except on holiday,' Monika announced complacently.

Viktoria kissed them both goodbye. The steam train pulled out of the station and Monika's white handkerchief became just a distant speck and finally disappeared. She pulled her coat collar round her throat and made her way slowly across the crowded station concourse. Benno and Monika were gone, Stefan was in England, Ricarda in Lützow with Luise. She was free to do what she wanted.

Out of the crowd, a figure approached, lifted his hat in an elaborate gesture, bowed deeply and said, '*Gnaedige Frau*, may I have the honour of inviting you to take luncheon with me?'

'Mortimer!'

'I've taken the liberty of booking a table at the Schildhorn. I hope that meets with your approval?'

In the Grunewald forest, on the edge of the lake, it was not a restaurant she and Benno ever frequented. 'It sounds lovely.'

'I have my car, if you want to send yours back to the hotel.'

She laughed. 'You seem to have thought of everything!'

Mortimer placed his hand under her elbow. 'I've been waiting four years for this opportunity.'

Undisturbed, they ate their meal at a corner table in the window, gazing out across the frozen lake. 'It's so peaceful,' Viktoria sighed. 'Do you ever wonder why we choose to live in cities when we could have the peace of the countryside?'

'How long will Benno be away?'

'About a week.'

'Let's spend it in the country.'

The sun was a huge red ball on the horizon when they left the restaurant, the air sharp with frost. 'Shall we walk for a bit?' Mortimer asked.

Arm in arm, they strolled beside the lake, the silent forest around them. The sun dipped behind a small hill and darkness crept out from the forest. Mortimer stopped and put both hands on Viktoria's shoulders. 'I think you know that I'm in love with you?' His breath steamed in the icy air.

It was strange now that the moment had come, strange and rather wonderful and not at all frightening. 'Yes, I know.'

'And you love me too?'

'Yes, I love you too.'

He drew her to him and kissed her, very tenderly. Then he released her and said, 'We have a week. Let's be happy.'

She looked away from him across the lake, where the sun was reflected blood red upon the ice. 'Mortimer, I…'

He put his finger to her lips. 'Hush. I don't want you to do anything that you will later regret. Let's take each day as it comes.'

She was silent for a long time. The ice turned magenta and then deep blue. The sun disappeared. Finally, she said, 'Yes, let's take each day as it comes. And let's make them happy.'

Mortimer took her hand in his, led her back to the car and drove home towards the bright city lights.

CHAPTER SEVEN

For a whole week, Viktoria and Mortimer were seldom out of each other's company. Viktoria conferred every morning with Herr Brandt on the hotel's programme, explaining to Mortimer, 'I'm not going to have Benno claiming I let things slide in his absence.' Mortimer also reported daily to the Propaganda Ministry, but, for once, all was calm in the capital.

On their first day, muffled up in gloves, hats and scarves, they drove north to the Mecklenburg lake district around Feldberg. It was a magical, snow-covered landscape, flat and white, crisp with hoar frost under an Alpine blue sky, out of which an orange winter sun shone down upon them. Not a breath of wind rustled the branches of the trees, encrusted with sparkling icicles.

'Let's hire a sleigh!' Mortimer suggested. He turned into the courtyard of an inn, returning shortly with the news that a horse-drawn sleigh could be made available from a neighbouring farm. 'And I've asked the landlord to prepare a picnic.'

'A winter picnic!' Viktoria exclaimed. 'What a lovely idea!'

Half an hour later, they were huddled under a huge fur rug, skimming across a track of virgin snow to the jingling of bells from the bridles of the two horses. As far as the eye could see there was no living creature, no sign of man or beast to disturb the white desert landscape broken only by the black ice of the lakes.

The cold made Viktoria's eyes water, but it was a stimulating coldness that blew the cobwebs from the mind, even if it numbed the feet. She felt as if they had been transported back into the fairytale world of childhood.

Mortimer turned to her, just his nose and eyes visible above his woollen scarf and under his Cossack hat. His hand in a thick fur glove reached for Viktoria's and squeezed it.

Under an arch of trees, they entered a forest and there, in a sheltered glade, the driver halted the horses. Mortimer jumped down and helped Viktoria out of the sleigh, then he took her arm and led her along a path through the wood. 'Happy?' he asked.

'It's an enchanted land.'

For a quarter of an hour or so, they wandered in contented silence until their hands and feet were tingling hot again. When they returned, the driver had covered the horses with rugs and was walking them slowly up and down the far end of the clearing. Mortimer spread the picnic on the seat of the sleigh — a steaming vacuum flask of soup, chunks of brown rye bread and home-cured sausage. 'No knives or forks and only the lid of the thermos to drink out of,' he laughed.

'Who needs knives and forks in a place like this?' But it was too cold to remove their gloves and so they ate bread and sausage, garnished with bits of fur, and took it in turns to drink the welcomingly hot soup. When they had finished, Viktoria sank back against the seat. 'That was the most delicious meal I have ever eaten!'

The driver re-harnessed the horses and they followed their tracks back towards Feldberg. Long shadows fell across the land. The moisture from their breath froze on their scarves. The snow crackled under the runners and the horses' hooves. The bells jingled.

In the car going back to Berlin, they sang, '*So ein Tag, so wunderbar wie heute...*' 'Such a day as wonderful as this one. Such a day should never, never end...'

As she walked into the hotel, Viktoria was sure that people must remark upon the colour in her cheeks, the sparkle in her eye, the magic of the forest that still seemed to surround her like an aura. It was difficult to telephone Benno at Fürstenmark and listen to his news about Monika and the Countess and sound interested when he said, 'We've been invited to coffee with the Königs tomorrow.' And it was harder still to say, 'I've had a usual sort of day. You know, shopping and tea with friends. Incidentally, Benno, Mortimer Allen has invited me to a Beethoven concert at the Philharmonie tonight.'

'That's very decent of him. Did someone let him down?'

'Something like that.'

'Well, enjoy yourself.'

She took as much care with her toilette as if she were a young girl going on her first date. Remembering Stefan's comments about drab women, she smoothed powder over her skin, brushed her eyebrows, darkened her eyelashes with mascara and put on lipstick. From her wardrobe she selected the black evening dress most flattering to her slim figure and round her throat and in her ears she fastened the rubies she had been given for her fortieth birthday. Then, after dabbing perfume on her wrists, she pulled on long black lace gloves and slipped into an ermine coat with a huge, fluffy collar.

Mortimer was waiting at the foot of the stairs, strikingly elegant in a stiff shirt and evening suit, even that wayward lock of hair neatly brushed back. For a moment, he just stood, shaking his head in smiling admiration, then he hurried up towards her. 'You look ravishing! I don't know that I dare take you to the Philharmonie. Everybody will be so busy gazing at you they won't pay any attention to the music.'

The ornate foyer of the Philharmonie was full when they arrived to join the couples and families promenading before the concert. Viktoria was glad she had told Benno she was going, for, inevitably, there were many people she knew. She caught looks of surprised admiration in their eyes. *It isn't just my clothes*, she thought. *I look different because I feel different, because I am happy.*

Music was the art that was suffering least under the Nazis: modern composers might be banned; the Jewish Mendelssohn might be forbidden; Bruno Walter, Otto Klemperer and Erich Kleiber might have emigrated; but Berlin still possessed magnificent concert halls, opera houses and orchestras. It still had its musical heritage of Bach, Mozart, Schumann, Schubert, Wagner and Beethoven. The concert that night, directed by Wilhelm Furtwängler, was wonderful.

Afterwards, they dined in the candlelit Weiss Czarda restaurant, served by waiters in Hungarian national costume and entertained by a violinist playing vivacious folk tunes. They ate spicy goulash with boiled potatoes and green salad, washed down with red Hungarian wine. And they talked about happy, amusing things, about holidays and travel, poems, pictures and dreams.

It was only when they walked back into the Quadriga and up the main staircase, that Viktoria felt a moment of trepidation. What was going to happen now? Was Mortimer expecting her to invite him into the apartment for a nightcap? She suddenly felt awkward. Part of her wanted to stay with him — and part of her was afraid. Apart from anything else, this was her family home…

As if he could read her thoughts, Mortimer lifted her fingers to his lips and murmured, 'Good night, Viktoria, and thank you for a lovely day.'

She relaxed. He understood. He had meant it when he had said, 'I don't want you to do anything you will later regret.' 'Thank you,' she said. 'I can't remember a day I have enjoyed more.'

Next morning, Mortimer said, 'Let's go to the Spreewald.'

'Let's…' As the week passed, Viktoria realized this expression was typical of Mortimer, of his infectious enthusiasm and his desire to share things. 'Let's climb to the top of that hill…' 'Let's see what's down that road…' 'Let's have lunch at that inn…' 'Let's take a toboggan…' Everything they did took on an air of adventure and, above all, it was fun.

They pelted each other with snowballs. They took turns pulling each other along on a sledge. They built a massive snowman. They pretended to be yetis. They tumbled down snowy banks into drifts and emerged white and wet. The woods and fields echoed to their laughter. Viktoria could not recall ever being as happy as she was that week, or feeling so at ease in someone else's company as she was with Mortimer.

Yet, all the time, there was an undercurrent of almost electric tension. Each evening, when they said goodnight, their hands remained entwined a little longer. And when she got into her lonely bed, Viktoria felt such longing for him that it required all her strength of mind not to pick up the phone and ask him to come to her.

On Saturday, Mortimer said, 'Let's go skating.'

It was their last day together. Tomorrow Benno would return and her brief holiday from life would be over. She could not let it end on such an inconclusive note. With a calmness she did not feel, she suggested, 'Why don't we go to Heiligensee?'

Mortimer gave her a searching look. 'If you're sure…'

She did not tell the Webers they were coming, so the windows were shuttered and no welcoming spiral of smoke issued from the chimney, but for all that, the cottage was beautiful in its mantle of snow. 'Some cottage…' Mortimer breathed in awe.

She unlocked the door and led him into the living room, flicking a switch to light a table lamp. 'Brr, it's freezing. Let's light the fire before we go out.' There were kindling papers and logs already in the grate. She knelt down on the hearthrug, struck a match and set fire to them.

Hand in hand they went down to the lake. Mortimer laughed and joked as he fitted her skates and found a pair for himself. Then they were skimming across the ice, their scarves flying out behind them. They skated along the edge of the shore and, all the time, Viktoria knew that soon the moment would arrive which she had been waiting for and postponing for so long.

Clouds passed over the sun. The wind grew chill. 'The weather's changing,' Mortimer said. 'You're cold. Let's go back to the cottage.'

The fire was burning brightly. They took off their outdoor clothes, then sat close to each other on the settee. Mortimer took her hand in his. 'You look so beautiful in the firelight. Will you do something for me? Will you take down your hair?'

With trembling fingers, she took out the pins and let her braids fall down in front of her shoulders. Mortimer removed the bands that secured them and unplaited them, so that her hair rippled loose, almost to her waist. He ran his fingers over it. 'Like ripe corn,' he whispered and then his mouth was on hers, bruising her lips as he kissed her with a fierce, hard passion, his hands caressing her body.

A feeling of liquid heat consumed her, almost frightening in its intensity. She felt light-headed with desire.

'I want you, Viktoria.' It was the tone of his voice and the touch of his hands on her skin that triggered off that distant memory of a summer's day in 1914. So many things had happened in the intervening years, that she had almost forgotten being in this same room, alone with Peter for the first time.

Now, vividly, she remembered how he, too, had drawn her close to him and she had been filled with an almost unbearable longing to feel and to be felt, to hold and to be held, to possess and to be possessed. The same hunger was consuming her now…

Oh, no, I made one mistake. I must not make another…

But love was not something that could be switched on or off at will. Desire could not be banished just because it was uncomfortable. She had embarked upon this week with Mortimer in the full knowledge that he loved her and that she loved him. And it was so long since she had felt like this, so young, so beautiful, so alluring.

His lips pressed down again on hers, while he undid the buttons at the front of her dress, his hand creeping inside, cupping her breast. She lay back yieldingly and his other hand stroked her thigh, working upwards until it found those few inches of bare flesh above her stocking top. Huskily, he whispered, 'Let's go to bed. I need you, Viktoria…'

I need you, Viktoria. The same words as Peter had spoken before he had carried her up to the bedroom…

At that moment, Viktoria knew she could not go through with this. Love and desire were not enough to make up for the pain of knowing that, after they had made love, they would have to dress again and go their separate ways. And certainly not enough to banish the agony of an old memory…

Shakily, she re-buttoned her frock. 'Mortimer, I'm sorry if I've given you the wrong impression, but I can't do it. I love you, but…'

He did not get angry, merely stood up, moved across to the fire and lit a cigarette. 'The last thing I want to do is make you unhappy.' His voice was very gentle, his grey eyes very kind.

Viktoria looked away.

Mortimer said, 'A long time ago, I wondered if you had ever given yourself in abandonment to anyone. I think I know the answer now. It is my guess that this week was the first time in your life when you have literally cast care to the wind and allowed yourself to be happy. I wanted to make that happiness complete. To show you that love between a man and a woman is a beautiful experience, that loss of control is not loss of soul…'

She was silent. *A long time ago*, she wanted to say, *I brought someone here and gave myself to him in abandonment and for the past twenty-two years I have been paying the price. That is a long penance to pay for a few moments' beautiful experience.* But she did not trust even him enough to confess her secret.

'Such a waste,' Mortimer said. 'So much loveliness hidden away — wasted. We only have one life. We owe it to ourselves to live it to the full.'

'But, this week, we have lived. I have been so happy. I shall never forget it.'

He strode across to her and knelt in front of her, seizing her shoulders, forcing her round so that she must look at him. 'Viktoria, why are you afraid? Are you worried about deceiving Benno?'

Viktoria nodded. It was the easiest explanation, even if it was not the whole truth. 'I'm sorry. You must think I am very naive, but I didn't realize…'

He sank back on his heels. 'We're two grown-up people. It doesn't really matter whether we sleep together or not. What is important is that we don't misunderstand each other, that we don't lose this very special thing that exists only between ourselves.'

She stared mutely across his head to the fire. He was not pressing her for a closer explanation. He was not forcing her to do anything against her will. He really did love her. And, because of this, she loved him more than ever.

He kissed her lightly on the forehead. 'Do your hair. Let's go to Tegel and have some lunch.'

They put out the fire, locked the cottage door and drove away. In Tegel, they found a crowded restaurant, full of high-spirited skaters, where an accordionist was playing folk songs. Mortimer ordered a bottle of wine, steaming *Bratwurst* and jacket potatoes. Then, trying to put her at her ease, he launched into a stream of amusing anecdotes. At the end of the meal, he lit two cigarettes and handed one to her. 'I once heard it said that friendship between a man and a woman is only possible if they could have had an affair, or if they have had an affair. Don't regret our week, Vicki.'

'Such a day, as wonderful as this one,' the accordionist played. Everyone in the restaurant linked arms and swayed to the rhythm. 'Such a day should never, never end…'

Tears rose in her eyes. 'I don't regret it. I don't want it to end. I don't know what I want…'

Mortimer was not one to waste time crying for the moon. He smiled gently. 'It's probably better it ends this way. We would never have been satisfied with just one day. Instead of simply meeting for walks in the park, we would have been constantly seeking opportunities to go to bed with each other, for journeys to Heiligensee or assignations within the hotel, which, sooner or later, would have aroused Benno's suspicions…'

Miserably, she said, 'I know all this, but I can't bear the thought of losing you.'

'I'm not so easy to lose!'

But whatever Mortimer said, she knew that nothing could ever again be the same between them as it had been before.

The following afternoon, Benno returned. Monika was so well settled at Fürstenmark, that he and the Biedersteins had felt quite confident at leaving Countess Anna in her hands and had travelled back to Berlin together. 'I met several times with Pastor König. I liked him and his wife. They agree that Hans and Monika should wait until Hans is earning a salary before they get married.'

He was not interested in how she had spent her week. Only once did he refer to it and that was when they went to the bar for aperitifs before dinner. Seeing Mortimer in his usual seat, Benno said, 'Incidentally, did you enjoy the concert at the Philharmonie?'

'Very much.'

'Good, good. Now, if you'll excuse me for a moment, my dear…'

Mortimer did not so much as glance at them, but continued chatting to Hasso Annuschek. It was almost as if the past week had never been.

That night, she dreamed of Mortimer. They were gliding in a sleigh through a snow-covered landscape towards a city of golden spires and palm trees, where the sun always shone and people lived happily ever after. She awoke with tears streaming down her cheeks.

Benno was lying on his back, snoring.

Luise wrote long letters to Sepp every day, describing every moment of her life, but Sepp's replies, when they came, were terse, telling her nothing of his. Still she treasured them. To see his handwriting was almost like hearing his voice. It was a part of him.

Then hope grew in her that maybe Sepp had left even more of himself behind. At the end of January, she missed her period. A few days later she was sick when she got up. Of course, it could be nervous reaction to him going to Spain. Or it could mean she was pregnant. In the middle of February, to Luise's incredulous joy, Dr Blattner confirmed the latter.

'Mama, Mama!' Luise rushed into the flat at Lützow. 'I'm going to have a baby!'

'Luischen, darling!' Ricarda took her in her arms.

Sheltie danced round them in crazy circles, her tail wagging. It was the happiest they had been since Sepp had gone to Spain.

That afternoon, they went to the hotel to tell Viktoria the wonderful news. Viktoria kissed her on both cheeks. 'Luischen, I'm so pleased for you. Have you told Sepp?'

'We've just sent him a cable.'

'When's the baby due?'

'At the end of September. Oh, I just can't believe it's true. I'm still getting used to being married. I never believed I would be a mother as well. I do hope Sepp will be happy.'

'Of course he will,' Ricarda said briskly. 'Now, Vicki, could you order some tea? We must look after Luise.'

'Mama, please don't fuss. There are another seven months yet.'

'The first three months are the most dangerous. I think it's a very good job that I'm staying with you.'

Viktoria signalled to a waiter and ordered tea for them all, then asked Luise, 'When did you last hear from Sepp?'

'A week ago. He doesn't say much in his letters, but his squadron appears to be moving towards the Basque provinces in the north of Spain.' Luise leaned forward. 'Vicki, you're so lucky having Benno here with you all the time. It's dreadful being separated from the person one loves.'

A sadness flitted across Viktoria's face. Luise saw the expression and misunderstood it. 'Vicki, I'm sorry. I forgot about Stefan for a moment. But at least you know he's safe. He isn't fighting a war, like Sepp is.'

The waiter came and Viktoria was saved from answering.

Life had become progressively harder for Pastor Scheer, as the activities of the clergy were increasingly hampered by the Ministry for Church Affairs. On 13 February, the Minister, Dr Kerrl, made a speech to a select gathering of churchmen, which included the following astounding assertions:

Christianity is not dependent upon the Apostles' Creed... True Christianity is represented by the Party, and the German people are now called by the Party and especially by the Führer to a real Christianity... The Führer is the herald of a new revelation...

Pastor Scheer was not present when this speech was made, but it was not long before he found out about it. 'To allow this statement to pass unnoticed, is to give it my tacit approval,' he told Klara. 'I must speak out against it.'

She took his hand and smiled her sweet, gentle smile. 'Yes, Bernhard, you must.'

From dawn the following Sunday, people started to make their way to Schmargendorf and by ten every pew was crammed tight. People were standing in the aisles, packed into the porch and massed in the snowy churchyard.

In his white gown and black cassock, Pastor Scheer stood in the pulpit. 'On very many occasions, you have gathered in this small church and repeated the Apostles' Creed, the foundation upon which the Christian church was built, the foundation which the secular authorities of our country are now trying to undermine by telling us that Christianity is represented by the National Socialist Party. Brethren, this is heresy!

'These days, we all go in fear of what will happen to us if we say the truth that is in our hearts. However, if Christ was prepared to die for his faith, so must we be, too, in the certain knowledge of life everlasting. We, his disciples, shall be silent no longer. Affirm your faith by saying with me, *I believe in God, the Father Almighty…*'

The congregation rose and repeated the Apostles' Creed.

That evening, Bernhard asked Klara, 'You realize that they will come for me tonight? I must pack my bag in readiness.'

'No, Bernhard!'

'You must be brave, my dear, very brave.'

For the first time, she understood what she had done by encouraging him to speak the truth. 'Can't we go away somewhere?'

'Klara, I haven't fought for so long in order to run away. Now, help me with my packing.'

So they packed a small case and left it standing beside the front door. They washed and took off their outer garments and got into bed. They did not sleep, but lay side by side in the dark, their hands clasped together, waiting…

At three o'clock in the morning, the parsonage reverberated to a thunderous knocking on the door. Pastor Scheer switched on the bedside light and kissed Klara on the forehead. 'Thank you for being a good wife.'

'I shall pray to God to keep you safe.'

The knocking was repeated, longer and harder. A voice shouted, 'Open up in the name of the Gestapo.'

They got out of bed. Pastor Scheer pulled on trousers and a jacket. Klara put on a dressing gown. Then, they went downstairs and opened the door. Snow was slanting hard across the garden. To either side of the porch loomed two figures in black, who seized the Pastor by the arms. 'You are under arrest.'

Angrily, he demanded, 'Is it a crime to preach God's word?'

The Gestapo men stared at him disinterestedly. 'Get moving, Scheer. You can plead your case to the judge.'

Klara picked up the suitcase with trembling hands. Bernhard took it from her and kissed her again. 'God bless you, my dear.'

'And you, Bernhard.'

He was propelled down the path and pushed roughly into the back of a black van waiting in the road. Through the silent white streets of

Berlin, he was driven to the Moabit prison, where his suitcase was seized from him and he was thrown into a small, dark, bitterly cold dungeon, furnished only with a straw mattress and a bucket. As his cell door slammed shut, the Pastor struggled to his knees. 'Our Father, which art in heaven... Thy will be done...'

Klara stood in the porch until the lights of the police van had disappeared, then went back into the house. By the kitchen table, she knelt down. 'Forgive us our trespasses, As we forgive them that trespass against us...' But, after that, the words would not come. Crouched on the floor, she wept and wept and wept. 'Oh, God, he has done no wrong. Please send him back to me...'

Day was dawning over Schmargendorf when Klara's tears finally exhausted themselves. Bernhard's life depended upon her now. But what could she do? To whom could she turn? Then she thought of Mortimer Allen. She picked up the telephone and asked for the Hotel Quadriga.

Half an hour later, Mortimer was in Schmargendorf, listening grimly to Klara's account of the night's events. When she had finished, he said, 'The first thing is to find out what prison he's in.'

They took a taxi to Gestapo headquarters, a grey, forbidding building in the Prinz-Albrecht Strasse with armed sentries outside, who demanded to see their identity cards and know their business. Inside, they were directed into a crowded waiting room full of silent, anxious people like themselves. They had to wait for a long time before anyone attended to them, but eventually their names were called and they were taken into the presence of a black-uniformed official, seated behind a desk. There was nowhere for them to sit.

'We are here regarding Pastor Scheer, who was arrested this morning,' Mortimer began.

The Gestapo man stared at him coldly. 'When in the presence of a government official, it is necessary to make the Nazi salute.'

Mortimer took a deep breath, glanced at Klara Scheer and they both held out their arms. 'Heil Hitler!'

'You were saying?'

'We are here regarding Pastor Scheer...'

It was a long and uncomfortable interview, during which Mortimer had the feeling that, any moment, they too would be arrested and guards summoned to march them away. But at the end of it, the Gestapo man said, 'Bernhard Scheer is in Moabit prison.'

'May I visit him?' Klara asked.

'No visitors are permitted.'

'When will he be brought to trial?' Mortimer demanded.

'The courts are extremely busy. It is impossible to say.'

'What is he charged with?'

'If he has been arrested, he is guilty of a crime. That is all I can tell you.' The Gestapo man pressed a bell on his desk and an aide appeared at the door. 'Show these people out.'

On the pavement again, Mortimer said, 'At least we know where he is now.' Sleet drove into their faces.

'Thank you, Herr Allen.'

He had done nothing except bring himself to the notice of the Gestapo. What Klara Scheer really needed was the help of a lawyer, who, while deemed 'politically reliable' by the Nazis, still believed in justice. And where did one find a man like that in Berlin? 'I'll take you home now, Frau Scheer.'

She shook her head. 'It's all right. You must have a lot to do and I must get used to being on my own. Think of poor Bernhard...'

Mortimer was thinking of Bernhard, so he did not argue. 'I'll keep in touch,' he promised. Then, having seen her into a taxi, he pulled his collar round his ears and walked swiftly to the Quadriga. He knew only one person who might know of a suitable lawyer and that was Viktoria. But since their week together, he had the feeling that she was avoiding him. Would she be prepared to let bygones be bygones in order to help Frau Scheer?

He strode briskly through the foyer, past Helga Ruh's temporarily vacated desk and into Viktoria's office. Startled, she looked up. 'Mortimer...'

He closed the door and leaned against it. 'Viktoria, I need your help.'

After only a moment's hesitation, she said, 'Mortimer, I will always do anything I can for you. Nothing has happened to change my feelings towards you. You will always be my friend.'

It was said so simply that he felt an overwhelming sense of affection and admiration for her. 'You are a quite remarkable woman, Viktoria.'

She gave a thin smile. 'What is it you want me to do?'

Briefly he told her what had happened and asked, 'Can you recommend a lawyer?'

Shaken, she exclaimed, 'How dreadful! Poor Frau Scheer. Of course you must do everything you can for her. But I only know Dr Duschek, our family lawyer.'

'Do you think he is trustworthy?'

She did not reply, but picked up the telephone and asked for a number. When she was eventually connected with Dr Duschek, she said, 'Dr Duschek, it's Viktoria Jochum-Kraus. A friend of mine wonders if you would consider taking on a rather unusual case. Someone has been arrested...'

A few moments later, she put down the receiver and told Mortimer, 'Dr Duschek will see you in half an hour. His office is above Café Jochum.'

Mortimer leaned across the desk, kissed her on the cheek, then left the room.

For a long time after he had gone, Viktoria sat gazing into space. Somehow, Frau Scheer's troubles put her own into perspective.

In his early fifties, grey-haired and of medium build, Erwin Duschek was the sort of man who passes unnoticed in a crowd. He did not make the Hitler salute when Mortimer entered the room. Instead, he shook him firmly by the hand, offered him a coffee and said, in fluent English, 'It's a pleasure to meet you, Mr Allen. I read your articles in the *New York News* with great interest. How can I help you?'

It might be wise to keep the conversation in English. If there were listening ears, they were less likely to understand. Factually, Mortimer told the story of Pastor Scheer. When he had finished, Dr Duschek leaned back in his chair and shook his head. 'Mr Allen, why are you so interested in the Scheers?'

'Perhaps, like Don Quixote, I enjoy tilting at windmills.'

'A dangerous occupation in Germany — even for an American.'

'It appears that being a pastor is a dangerous occupation, too.'

Dr Duschek gave a thin smile. 'If sufficient attention is brought to bear on the case of Pastor Scheer, it is possible that he will be tried, as a political offender, before the Special Court.'

'Would you be prepared to act in his defence?'

'Being a defence lawyer can also be a dangerous occupation. Lawyers representing clients before the Special Court have to be approved by the authorities and, even then, it is not unknown for them, too, to end up in a concentration camp.'

Disappointed, Mortimer said, 'So even though you recognize the iniquities of the system, you are scared to do anything!'

'You jump to very rash conclusions, Mr Allen. I said earlier that, if sufficient attention is brought to bear on the case of Pastor Scheer, he may be tried. If you are prepared to alert people abroad, I will make waves within judicial circles here.'

That evening, Mortimer wrote out an exact account of the persecution of the Lutheran and Catholic churches in Germany, terminating with a graphic account of Pastor Scheer's arrest. He then painstakingly typed it out with several carbon copies and, when he was finished, put each copy into separate envelopes. Next morning, he took them to James Adams at the British Embassy. 'Is there any way of seeing these get to the right people?'

James Adams raised an eyebrow. 'Interesting correspondence you're having these days, Mr Allen! The Archbishop of Canterbury, the Catholic Archbishop of Westminster... Yes, I'm sure I can arrange for these to be sent in the diplomatic bag.'

When Mortimer rang Klara Scheer, he mentioned nothing of what he had done. He did not want her to be disappointed and he thought it very likely that her telephone would be tapped from now on.

These days, Olga was living in fear. Basili seldom came to see her and she did not dare visit him at the Russian students' home. She stayed alone in her room, seated in front of an archaic stove in which a few inferior briquettes of brown coal gave off an inadequate heat. Forty-six now, she appeared frail, dressed in a ragged frock and thin grey coat that she had been unable to replace since the flight from Germany and never felt warm enough to take off.

In January, her old friend Karl Radek had been among the many arrested and tried for treason. The valiant Pole, who had, like herself, devoted his life to the cause of international communism, had been condemned to ten years in prison. He and other members of the Trotskyite movement were publicly branded as spies and traitors to the homeland. They were accused of wanting to restore the capitalist system within Russia and of having made secret deals with Hitler's Germany. It was said that they had organized fires, explosions and railway accidents; that they had tampered with food supplies, injecting bacteria into them which had killed innocent Soviet workers and peasants; that they were the leaders of terrorist groups, whose aim was to kill all Party leaders.

The headlines in *Pravda* read: THE ENEMIES OF THE PEOPLE MUST BE EXTERMINATED! SHOOT THE MAD FASCIST DOGS!

Since then, Moscow was full of stories of German teachers, writers and artists being arrested — never to be seen again. It was no longer just Stalin's Russian enemies who were the quarry, but foreigners like herself. Therefore, she, too, was in danger. She made no secret that she considered Germany her homeland. One day, in the early hours of the morning, the NKVD would knock at her door and she would be taken away...

But why? That was the question that plagued her during those long days when she sat alone in her squalid room. Why, when she had fled from Hitler's stormtroopers to the sanctuary of Stalin's Russia, was she now in constant danger of being accused of being a fascist? Surely the Russians did not really believe that because she was a German she must be an enemy of Mother Russia?

And yet, Radek was in prison... Trotsky was in exile... Sokolnikov, Serebriakov, Piatkov — all the old revolutionary heroes were suddenly spies and traitors.

It was a long time before the solution burst upon her in an illuminating flash. Stalin did not want the German communists to return to rule Germany any more than Hitler did. Stalin wanted world revolution. But when it succeeded, the world would be ruled from Moscow — by Stalin.

They came for her at three in the morning of 3 March, breaking the lock on her door and seizing her as she lay huddled under the thin blankets covering her bed. 'Who are you? What do you want? Let me go!' she shouted, struggling as they pulled her to her feet.

'Shut up, German sow!' One of them struck her across the mouth, knocking her back against a wall.

While he stood guard over her, two others systematically searched her room. Her guard ordered her to get dressed, staring at her mockingly while she did. Then they marched her downstairs. 'Where are you taking me?' she demanded. Surely one of her neighbours must hear her, must come out and help her. But every door remained closed.

For reply, the guard hit her again. Then they were on the street and she was thrown violently into the back of a waiting van. Olga heard the crack as her head hit some metal object, then she passed out.

When she regained consciousness, she was lying on a stone floor in almost total darkness. Her head ached so much she could hardly lift it, but, eventually, with great difficulty and in considerable pain, she succeeded in getting to her knees. There was a thin line of light, presumably from beneath a door, and it was towards this that she crawled. Eventually, she reached it and pulled herself upright. Then she began hammering on it. 'Let me out! Let me out!'

Nobody came. Olga sank back onto the floor and cradled her head in her hands. For the first time in her life she understood why people needed a God to whom to pray. But she had given her life to an ideal and now that had gone, she had nothing at all except the silence of a dungeon cell, somewhere deep under Moscow.

When Basili arrived at his mother's flat a fortnight later, the entrance was barred with planks of wood. For a long time, he stood looking at it, unwilling to acknowledge the truth. Then he knocked on the door of the room opposite, where a Russian family now lived. 'Do you know where my mother has gone?' he asked, when a man eventually opened the door a crack.

The Russian shrugged. 'She's probably been sent on a command. It happens, you know. We were in Kharkov. Then we were suddenly sent to Moscow. It's directional labour.'

'Why is her door barred?'

'Don't ask too many questions, son. If she wants you to know where she is, she'll get in touch with you.' With that, the man firmly shut the door on him.

With lagging steps, Basilius made his way back downstairs. Perhaps his mother was on a command. Maybe she was, in fact, on some secret mission for the German Communists. But it was far more likely that she had been arrested...

There was only one person he trusted sufficiently to ask what to do — Dr Renz, the German teacher at his school, an émigré like himself and his mother. Dr Renz, however, looked terrified when he heard Basilius's news. The colour drained from his face and his hands began to shake. 'You must do nothing,' he muttered. 'It's too dangerous.'

'She's my mother...'

'You must forget her.'

A few days later, Dr Renz disappeared. Gradually, Basilius heard from other fellow German children that their parents had disappeared. They all pretended to each other that there was a natural explanation, but in their hearts, they knew they would never see them again. They had seen what had happened in Hitler's Germany and they knew the same thing was happening here. Once again, they were living in fear.

Soon, there were few people who did not know of the circumstances of Pastor Scheer's arrest. It was not easy or safe to buy foreign newspapers in Berlin, but they were obtainable and in them were accounts of the Church of England's censure of the Nazi regime, deploring the treatment of the German clergy, particularly the conditions under which Pastor Scheer was being detained.

'I think he will be allowed to stand trial,' Dr Duschek told Mortimer. 'The authorities don't like this sort of bad publicity.'

But, when Mortimer went to Schmargendorf to tell Klara, it was to learn that the Ministry of Church Affairs had given her two days' notice to leave the parsonage. 'Where will you go?'

'Don't worry, I'll rent a room somewhere.'

'You must come to the Quadriga.'

'Thank you, Herr Allen, but I'm sure that won't be necessary.'

It wasn't. As soon as Professor Ascher heard of her fate, he asked her to share his small house in Dahlem. Deeply moved, Klara Scheer accepted. 'I'll be able to cook for him and maybe help him in his work,' she explained to Mortimer, adding with an unusual asperity, 'and nobody can object. I shan't be contravening the Nuremberg Laws. I'm over forty-five, too old to be in any danger.'

Mortimer admired her courage, but he could not help feeling uneasy. The campaign against the Jews was hotting up again. There were more and more signs in shops and cafés reading: *Jews and dogs are not permitted!* More Jewish businesses were taken over by Aryans, outside which notices proclaimed: *This firm is German-owned!*

Klara Scheer had lost her husband and her home. How long would the small ménage in Dahlem be permitted to exist in peace?

In Moscow, the terror continued. It became a common sight to see people being pushed into the green cars belonging to the NKVD. It was rumoured that several members of the Politburo and half the generals in the Red Army had been arrested and executed, that millions of civilians had been sent to labour camps or to build new towns in Siberia, that millions had died.

The fortunate ones who were spared called themselves the survivors. To survive was an art. It was not telling anybody one's secret thoughts. It was exercising caution when writing political essays. It was trying to judge exactly which way the wind lay during interminable sessions of criticism and self-criticism. It was recognizing that whoever was in power today might be out of favour tomorrow.

In June, the trials took place of Marshal Tukhachevsky, Chief of the General Staff and seven other Red Army generals. Five whole pages of *Pravda* were devoted to the outcome and on all six pages of the newspaper were huge headlines reading: SPIES, TRAITORS TO THE HOMELAND AND THE RED ARMY — DESPICABLE FASCIST MERCENARIES — SHOOT THEM! Like Radek, six months earlier, they were accused of collaborating with Hitler's Germany.

'Tukhachevsky was one of Stalin's closest comrades...' 'He was a hero of the Civil War...' In small groups, with pale faces, the students tried to understand what was going on. Their teachers, as perplexed and frightened as their pupils, had to adapt their lessons to the new circumstances from day to day.

At the end of June, the Director of the children's home summoned Basili to his office. Heart in mouth, Basili obeyed, certain that he would find the NKVD waiting for him there. But the Director was alone. Silently, he handed Basili a card. It read: 'Meyer, Olga. Died pneumonia, Vilyuysk, 5 May 1937.'

Basili looked from it to the Director. 'Thank you.'

There was a hint of sympathy in the man's eyes. 'You are how old, Basilius?'

'I shall be eighteen in July, Comrade Director.'

'You hope to enter the Teaching College for Foreign Languages?'

Basili nodded.

'As a German, you may find that difficult. Why do you not call yourself by the Russian Vasili? After all, this is your home now.'

His dormitory was deserted when he entered it. For a long time, he stared at the card that was all he had left of his mother, vowing that, one day, he would see her and his father's dream fulfilled and the hammer and sickle flying over Berlin. In the meantime, Moscow was his home and it was his duty to survive.

Vasili Meyer tore up the card into minute fragments.

Those days at the end of June hung heavily on Luise. For the last two months, Sepp's letters had been very infrequent and when they came, they said very little. She was getting big now and she slept badly and moved awkwardly. Every morning, she was awake long before the postman arrived, waiting for a letter notifying her of Sepp's return.

He arrived on the evening of Saturday, 3 July. While Sheltie tore round in ecstatic circles, Luise threw herself into his arms. 'Sepp, Sepp, you're back!' Ricarda stayed only to welcome him home, then, knowing better than to intrude on their reunion, went back to the Quadriga.

Sheltie soon settled down to sleep and, for a while, Sepp sat beside Luise on the settee, asking after her and the baby, then, refusing anything to eat, he went over to the sideboard and, with trembling hands, poured himself a large brandy. Glass in one hand, cigarette in the other, he began pacing restlessly up and down the room. Luise watched him anxiously. He was thinner than when he had left and his hair was streaked with silver. The laughter had gone from his eyes. 'Tell me about Spain,' she implored.

He gave a short, hollow laugh. 'It was all right to start with, when we were transporting troops, but in combat the Ju 52 was a disaster, totally inaccurate and useless for bombing. And, just as I've always told the Fat Man, the He 51 was no good. The Russian planes were vastly superior.'

On and on, he talked, explaining the qualities of the different aircraft used by each side, the turn-around times required at air bases, air-to-ground and air-to-air communications. It meant little to Luise, but she listened to him intently. Something had happened in Spain, something Sepp could not bring himself to tell her.

The clock struck midnight. Sepp refilled his glass for the sixth time. His hand had almost stopped trembling, but he looked dreadfully tired. She stood up and put her arm round him. 'Come to bed.'

'Yes, let's go to bed.' There was a note of despair in his voice. He lit yet another cigarette and allowed her to lead him into the bedroom. Wearily, as if each movement cost him a tremendous effort, Sepp took off his uniform, switched off the light and got into bed. 'Luischen,' he said, and his voice was very quiet, 'in April, we murdered a whole town of people. It was called Guernica.

'Time after time, German planes went in and dropped bombs on civilian houses. Not military bases, not ammunition depots or

282

barracks, but houses like this one, where ordinary people were sheltering with their children. And each time they came back to base, our bomber pilots cheered, totting up the number of roads they had set fire to, the number of homes they had demolished.'

'Oh, my God...'

'I flew over Guernica afterwards. There was hardly a house standing. Just rubble, blackened shells, smouldering ashes. I saw photographs of little children who had lost their arms and legs, sitting helplessly beside their mothers' corpses. Luischen, they weren't enemies of Spain and certainly not of Germany...'

The room was silent. In the darkness, Sepp lit another cigarette from the butt of the last one. 'Is there something the matter with me?' he demanded harshly. 'Is there something I can't see — but everyone else can? It was regarded as a tremendous victory. The Fat Man even sent a telegram of congratulation...'

She took the cigarette from his lips, felt in the dark for the ashtray and stubbed it out.

'Luischen, I'm no coward. I fought in the last war and had over sixty victories. But they were in air combat. I'm a fighter pilot — not a mass murderer. And that's what Guernica was — mass murder. Those people were killed by pilots I helped train...'

'Sepp, darling...' She put her arms round his neck.

He buried his head in her breasts, his hands clutching at her stomach, his tears scorching her skin. 'I thought it could have been you, I kept thinking it might have been you...'

She cradled his head in her arms, rocking him as though he were a child, her face hidden in his hair. 'Hush, Sepp, hush. You're home now. Everything is all right.'

For a long time, Sepp cried the ugly, shuddering tears of a man who has never wept before in his life. Sheltie crept onto the bed and lay down beside him, one paw protectively on his chest. When Sepp eventually lifted his face, she gently licked the salt from his cheeks. Sepp laughed shakily and put a hand down to stroke her. 'You understand, don't you, dog?'

The four of them slept in close embrace that night — Sheltie, Sepp, Luise and their unborn child.

Gradually, Sepp recovered from his shock and his exhaustion. After his six months in Spain, he was given four weeks leave, which they spent with Benno, Viktoria and Ricarda at Heiligensee. For the second summer in succession, Stefan was taking his holidays with Tony Callearn, while Monika stayed at Fürstenmark.

Luise was very big now and could not do very much, so while Ricarda worked in the garden, and Benno and Sepp went sailing, she and Viktoria sat on the sun-drenched verandah or sauntered beside the lake. 'Sheltie seems to have adopted Sepp these days, doesn't she?' Viktoria commented one day, as they watched her leap onto the boat with the two men.

'Yes, it's happened since he came back from Spain.' And then, while Viktoria listened in shocked horror, Luise told her about Guernica.

During one of their sailing expeditions, Sepp described to Benno the war in Spain. Benno listened to him with a troubled expression. 'My father and my cousin Peter make little secret of the fact that they both see Spain as a training ground for our troops. Sepp, do you think this is the pattern of a future war?'

Sepp lit a cigarette. 'I hope not, but I fear so.'

'Kraus is developing tanks that can travel at up to thirty miles an hour. If your planes can demolish whole cities from the air and the artillery can move at such speed, we seem certain of victory.'

'At the cost of the lives of millions of innocent civilians?'

The two men looked at each other. 'I voted for Hitler because I agreed with him over the Versailles Treaty and because I believed he was the only man capable of saving Germany from the Bolsheviks,' Benno said, slowly. 'Now, we have shaken off Versailles and we can defend ourselves against Russia. We have a viable economy. And we have recovered our national pride. We don't want another war.'

'I don't believe we are prepared for another war. Franco's troops are succeeding in Spain because the Republicans cannot defend themselves, not because of our superior abilities.'

'The Luftwaffe still destroyed Guernica...'

Despite the heat of the sun, Sepp shivered. 'Yes. Our attack came as a surprise.' He changed the conversation abruptly. 'Benno, did you bring rods? Let's fish.'

One evening, towards the end of their holiday, they discussed names for the baby. 'If it's a boy, I should rather like him to be called Manfred, after von Richthofen,' Sepp said.

Ricarda smiled. 'Viktoria and Luise were both named after royalty. If it's a girl, why don't you call her Elizabeth in honour of the new English Queen and her eldest daughter?'

'Elizabeth, that's a nice name.' Luise nodded. 'We could always shorten it to Lili. Sepp, what do you think?'

'I suppose there's no reason why a girl shouldn't learn to fly.'

They all laughed.

A few days later they returned to Berlin. To his dismay, Sepp found himself deskbound at the Air Ministry, his job analysing and collating the reports that poured in every day from Spain with comments and suggestions for improved ground and air support for the bomber command from the fighter arm. 'I'm a pilot for God's sake, not a bloody bureaucrat,' he fumed to Luise. 'This is Milch's doing!'

Luise placed a restraining hand on his arm. 'If you say anything, Milch will only send you back to Spain.'

Sepp sighed. 'All right. I'll be patient until Manfred makes his appearance.'

That summer, in Moscow, Vasili Meyer passed all his examinations with distinction and was accepted by the MUIIJA, the Moscow Teaching Institute for Foreign Languages. He began his studies there in September. At Oxford, Stefan started his third year as a Rhodes Scholar. At Stettin, Hans König commenced his final year at teacher training college. In Essen, Norbert Kraus entered into his last year at school. To his great joy, his father had agreed that, provided he worked well, he could enter the Todt Organization as an architectural apprentice. In the middle of the month, Ilse von Biederstein took Christa to her new finishing school at Lausanne.

On 25 September, Mussolini paid his first visit to Germany, an illuminating experience for him — and for Mortimer, one of the horde of reporters who accompanied the trip. No holds were barred to make it a visit the Italian dictator would remember. Wherever they went, black-uniformed SS men lined the streets, where frenzied civilians cheered their enthusiasm. There were parades, rallies, military displays by the armed forces and visits to armaments factories, including the Kraus works at Essen and Kraushaven.

The visit culminated in a spectacular reception in Berlin. Virtually the entire city crowded onto balconies and pavements to watch the Führer and *Il Duce* head a magnificent motor cavalcade. A million people packed onto the Maifeld to hear the two leaders speak. 'The *Duce*,' Hitler declaimed, 'is one of those lonely men on whom history is not tested, but who are themselves the makers of history.'

'Heil! Heil! Heil!' screamed the crowd.

In vain, Mussolini tried to reply, but when he began his speech, in German, the cheers of the crowd drowned his reply. So, too, did the thunderstorm that chose that moment to break.

Cynically, Mortimer suspected it would take more than that to dampen Mussolini's ardour. *Il Duce* was susceptible to flattery. The Berlin-Rome 'axis' had been strengthened.

Luise's baby was born in a Lützow nursing home on 4 October 1937. 'A baby girl, Herr Oberst,' Dr Blattner announced. Suddenly, Sepp didn't give a damn that Manfred was Elizabeth. 'Is Luise all right?'

The doctor nodded reassuringly. 'She'll be fine, provided she takes care of herself. Your wife is thirty-seven, and that's late to have a first child. She's going to need time to recuperate.'

'Yes, of course. And the baby?'

The doctor laughed. 'Never seen a healthier-looking girl in all my life! Come and look!'

Sepp followed him into the room. Luise was lying propped up against the pillows, her eyes huge in a face totally drained of colour. 'Sepp, I'm sorry, she's a she.' She smiled weakly.

He kissed her tenderly. 'Provided her hair is the same colour as yours, I'll forgive you. I have a weakness for redheads.'

'Sepp, I love you so much.'

'I love you, too and I'm very proud of you.'

'Go and look at her.'

Elizabeth was lying in a cradle beside the bed. Wrinkled and red-faced, with a downy fuzz of sandy hair, she opened her eyes as Sepp approached and he saw them to be a bright green. 'She's going to be a character,' the doctor chuckled. 'Look at that determined chin.'

'Just like her mother,' Sepp grinned. 'Hello, Lili.'

Lili formed a strong bond between Sepp and Luise, making them into a real family. Sepp cut back on his smoking and drinking and resigned himself to life at the Air Ministry. He still found opportunities to fly and these few precious hours of freedom in the air compensated to a certain extent for the miseries of his squabbles with Milch and the indecisive bureaucracy of politicians and government departments. Guernica he never mentioned, but sometimes he woke in the night screaming. He would not tell Luise what his nightmare had been about. Only he knew the ghastly images the night conjured up of Luise, Lili and Sheltie buried under a pile of rubble.

Lili changed Luise's life dramatically. For the first time, she had somebody who was totally dependent upon her. Her first love would always be Sepp — the never completely attainable — but Lili, small and helpless, fulfilled a different kind of need in her.

Lili also achieved something else: she gave Luise social respectability. The ladies of Berlin no longer regarded her as Luise Jochum of the controversial Café Jochum on the Kurfürstendamm, but Frau Oberst Nowak, mother, whose husband held an important post in the Luftwaffe.

Ilse von Biederstein was the first to adopt Luise into her circle. Four years older than Luise, plump and cheerful with a lively outgoing nature, she welcomed Luise to her home and introduced her to her friends. Soon Luise was being asked to coffee mornings and becoming involved in charity functions. To her surprise, she found she enjoyed her new life.

'I always thought these sort of women were boring,' she told Viktoria, calling in at the Quadriga one morning. 'But, in fact, most of them are cultured people, who take a caring, intelligent interest in the world.' She glanced at her sister's desk. 'Why don't you come with me sometimes? It would do you good to get out of the hotel.'

Viktoria hesitated. As she had realized at the time, her relationship with Mortimer had changed after the incident at Heiligensee and their meetings in street and park had ceased. Since then, she had developed a new working routine which, although it did not satisfy her, kept her mind occupied and stopped her feeling sorry for herself. And after she had been able to arrange Mortimer's introduction to Dr Duschek, she had felt less awkward when they met. Indeed, they had virtually reverted to their original easy-going friendship. But there were still many occasions when she felt lonely.

So, although she had never been a woman's woman, she reluctantly complied with Luise's suggestion and the two sisters became part of the Berlin subculture of wives, whom the State prevented from taking any active participation in its running and whose status did not necessitate them to work for their living. For Luise, they were new friends who opened up new vistas. For Viktoria, they gave some sense of purpose to a rather barren existence.

Through Ilse and during their rounds of coffee parties and charitable functions, they met many other officers' wives. One whom Viktoria particularly liked was Gertrud Oster, wife of Colonel Hans Oster, an officer in the Abwehr — the Military Intelligence Service.

Colonel Oster was a handsome man of fifty, with an eye for the ladies that had once nearly ruined his career. Before the Osters came to Berlin, he had indulged in a brief love affair with the wife of a senior army officer, which had ended in the lady's divorce and Oster's dismissal from the cavalry. That Oster's own marriage had survived was due to his wife's remarkably broad-minded understanding. That his career had survived was due to the unswerving loyalty of influential officers who had helped him obtain his new post in the Abwehr.

Soon, the Osters became frequent and popular visitors to the Quadriga, Colonel Oster in particular endearing himself to everyone. Despite the past scandal attached to his name, Benno could not speak highly enough of him, while Ricarda thought him most gallant.

To Viktoria's surprise, Mortimer also seemed to get on very well with Colonel Oster. On several occasions, she noticed them drinking together in the bar. Once, she entered the hotel just as they were shaking hands on the steps. Colonel Oster bowed to her courteously, then got into his waiting car. Mortimer accompanied her into the hotel. In a low voice, he said, 'That's an intriguing man, very different from most army officers.'

'He's certainly more charming...'

Mortimer looked at her with barely suppressed excitement. 'More than that, Viktoria. From little things he has let drop, I get the feeling that, unlike the Count Peter von Biedersteins of this world, Colonel Oster is deeply mistrustful of Hitler and is not prepared to blindly toe the Party line.'

'What do you mean?'

Mortimer's eyes twinkled and he lifted her fingers to his lips. 'I mean that I am once more in your debt for effecting a very useful introduction.'

At the end of November, nine months after Pastor Scheer's arrest, Dr Duschek told Mortimer that the Pastor was due to appear before the Special Court. 'They're going to try him for sedition — and they are allowing me to appear in his defence. A breakthrough, Mr Allen — and mainly due to your untiring efforts!'

'Any chance of reporters being allowed into court?'

'Not at the Special Court! But I would suggest you wait outside. I believe there is actually a chance that he may be freed.'

It was a long morning for Mortimer, Klara Scheer, Professor Ascher and the other bystanders outside the courtroom building, who were patiently awaiting the outcome of the trial. Then, suddenly, the doors opened and Pastor Scheer appeared with Dr Duschek at his side. There were cheers from the small crowd. 'Bernhard!' Klara called and rushed towards him.

The Pastor smiled. 'Klara!' He was noticeably thinner than when he had been arrested and his suit hung loosely from his shoulders, but otherwise he appeared unchanged.

'Well I'll be damned,' Mortimer muttered.

At that moment, two Gestapo men emerged from the court. One drew his gun warningly at Klara and she stopped still in her tracks. The other placed his hands firmly on Pastor Scheer's shoulder. Dr Duschek turned angrily. 'My client has just been released.'

'And we are taking him into protective custody so that he can't get into any further harm.'

'No!' Klara shouted. 'No, you can't do that…'

Bernhard Scheer looked sadly at his wife then turned back into the building he had just left. The door slammed behind him. Silently, the small crowd dissolved.

Dr Duschek hurried towards Klara. 'I'm sorry, Frau Scheer.'

'What will happen to him now?'

'He'll be taken to a concentration camp.'

'How can they do it?' Mortimer demanded.

'Under the Law for the Protection of the People and the State, very easily. The Court fined him on the charge of sedition and sentenced him for nine months for abuse of the pulpit, then declared him free since he had already been nine months in Moabit. Now the Gestapo has re-arrested him. Mr Allen, in case you haven't already realized, the SS and the Gestapo are a law unto themselves.'

The Pastor's watch had long since been removed from him, but he guessed it was about midnight when he was taken from his cell and driven to a goods yard outside Berlin, where he was pushed into a stinking, airless cattle truck with about a hundred other prisoners. For a long time, the train clanked through the night, its frightened inmates jolted and bruised.

Eventually, they stopped, the doors to the cattle trucks were opened and armed SS men waiting outside shouted orders for the prisoners to get out. It was dawn, the beginning of a damp, cheerless day. A painted sign on the station building read: Grubenmünde.

'At the double! Run!' A bayonet prodded the Pastor in the back. He followed the others up a pitted track, along which stood more SS men with whips and dogs. Taunting comments followed them. 'Look at that one! What kind of bitch bore him? Gee up, old monkey!'

'Prisoners, stop! Stand in line!'

Gasping for breath, they stopped in front of huge iron gates bearing the maxim: *Arbeit macht frei!* Sentries stared mockingly at them. A clock on an archway beyond the gates said six. It began to rain. Their guards pushed them roughly into groups, counted them and recounted them. The gates opened. 'At the double!' Together with some five hundred other prisoners, Pastor Bernhard Scheer ran into Grubenmünde concentration camp. Behind him, the gates slammed shut.

They stood in line in a square resembling an army parade ground. Beyond them were wooden barracks on stilts. For an interminable period, nothing happened. Occasionally, prisoners asked if they could go to the lavatory. Singly, at the end of a bayonet, they were allowed to step out of line and relieve themselves within sight of the others. Before long, the rain was coming down in torrents. One of the prisoners collapsed. When his neighbours stooped to help him, they were curtly ordered to leave him where he lay.

He was still lying unconscious in the mud when the guards gave the order for them to form into alphabetical groups, inevitably a long and complicated business. Those whose names began with 'A' were taken — at a run — into a building. Pastor Scheer's legs began to shake. In his head he recited, 'I believe in God the Father…'

Eventually, it was the turn of the S's. Inside the building, an SS officer took his personal details. 'Why were you arrested?'

'I don't know. I have committed no crime.'

The thongs of a whip cut across his hands. Pastor Scheer had learned his first lesson.

The formalities continued. The prisoners queued up again to have their photographs taken; to have their heads shorn by barbers with blunt tools; to take ice-cold showers, after which they were sprayed with disinfectant. Naked, they were taken to another chamber, where the men who sat behind the table were dressed not in SS uniform, but in trousers and jacket of striped canvas. If anything, their attitude was even more brutal than that of the SS guards. To his dismay, Pastor Scheer realized they were prisoners like himself.

He was allowed to keep a picture of Klara and a little money, but apart from these few precious belongings, he had to hand over everything he owned. He was issued with a ragged striped suit, boots, a chipped mug, a bowl, knife, fork and spoon. Still naked, he went to another room where he was cursorily examined by an SS doctor.

It was dark when, dressed in his new ill-fitting clothes, he found himself again on the parade ground. The minutes turned into hours and still they waited. The Pastor was bitterly cold and faint with thirst and hunger. 'Solf, Scheer... At the double!'

Clumsily, they ran into the indicated hut where they were greeted by a scarfaced prisoner who described himself as the Block Senior, who asked Pastor Scheer derisively, 'Who were you?'

'I am Bernhard Scheer, Pastor of Berlin-Schmargendorf.'

He was handed a red cloth triangle and a cloth badge bearing a number. 'Not any more. You're prisoner 814318. Category political. Sew these on your uniform. At the double!'

There was worse to come. Sometime during the evening, prisoner orderlies brought a pot of insipid bean hash, enough for only half of the ninety prisoners in the hut. At lights out there were only about sixty straw mattresses. Pastor Scheer found himself lying in a bunk with two other men. He was still awake at four, when the door burst open and a voice snarled, 'Get up, pigs!'

A frenzied activity broke out, as the prisoners made the bunks and tidied the room. SS men marched in, jeering at and beating some of the inmates, disarranging the bunks, throwing objects round the room, deliberately creating chaos from order. Following the inspection, the prisoners ran to the washrooms, where there were not enough basins or towels. There was a mad rush for the latrines and back to the block for coffee, which was little more than tepid water.

At five, they were back on the parade ground for roll-call. It was still pouring with rain. The old hands were dismissed into work commandos. The newcomers were kept in line. Suddenly, the guards stood to attention and saluted. An officer accompanied by a Dobermann Pinscher marched to their fore. He was a blond man in his early forties with a scar across his forehead and chilling blue eyes.

'I am the Commandant of this camp. *You* are criminals. Since there is no hope of reforming you, you will learn how to work here, something you have undoubtedly never done before. In your block you will find a list of camp regulations. They are to be obeyed. The penalty for disobedience is death.'

The first few weeks at Grubenmünde took the form of an induction period. Since Pastor Scheer had been a chaplain in the Kaiser's army, the routine of drill, singing, parades and roll-calls was not new to him. But it took its toll. He was no longer a young man, the conditions were infinitely poorer and he was not a conscript, but a prisoner, constantly subjected to the brutality and offensive taunts of the SS men and the trusties.

Pastor Scheer was not put to work in one of the camp factories, but outside on a building site. The guards took a merciless delight in maltreating him, goading him to work miracles, beating him with barbed wire, forcing him to carry heavy beams, shouting, 'Christ carried a cross. You can't even carry that twig, heaven dog! You'll soon see your maker. You'll never get out of here alive.'

For over a quarter of a century, Pastor Scheer had preached against the horrors of hell. Now he knew hell's actuality. If he were to survive, it was going to take more strength than he alone possessed. Weak from lack of food, crippled from being thrashed and too exhausted to sleep even when night came, he prayed: 'O Lord, have mercy upon us, miserable offenders…'

Shortly before Christmas, Commandant Tobisch informed the prisoners that Reichsführer-SS Himmler would be accompanying some important visitors to the camp, an announcement which heralded a period of intense activity and sadistic cruelty, as Grubenmünde was transformed. Every floor was scrubbed and polished until it shone. The outside of the administration block was painted, the inside totally redecorated.

On the great day, all prisoners deemed too sick or too old were locked out of sight in the quarantine block. For prisoner 814318 and his fellows, roll-call came an hour earlier than usual. New uniforms were issued. A band assembled by the gates. The commandos were sent out with strict instructions to look happy at their work.

At eleven, a cavalcade of black Mercedes swept through the iron gates with their motto: Work sets free. The band burst into a ragged version of 'Deutschland', followed by an even more discordant

'Horst Wessel Song'. Strains of music reached prisoner 814318 as he wheeled barrowloads of sand and cement — at a run — from stores to the site of a new factory building. A dog growled at his heels. An SS officer running beside him, goaded him, 'Christ's faith moved mountains. Move that bloody cement, heaven dog.'

Only when Tobisch, Himmler and his important guests hove into view did he stop his heckling, but prisoner 814318 knew better than to stop running. The guard saluted. Tobisch said, 'See how keen our inmates are to get on with their work.'

'Most impressive,' a familiar voice intoned.

Slipping on the mud, sweat pouring down his forehead nearly blinding him, prisoner 814318 could not help but recognize the massive figure of Baron Heinrich von Kraus.

'Of course, these are the dregs of humanity, but they are political prisoners, not common criminals, and we are beginning to suffer labour shortages in our factories.' The Baron made no effort to lower his voice. 'Herr Reichsführer, have you considered hiring out your prisoners? It could be a mutually profitable business.'

Prisoner 814318 slowed down a little, willing Baron Heinrich to recognize him. But he had lost two stone in weight during the three months he had been in Grubenmünde. His head was shaved and he was dressed as a convict.

'The SS is rapidly becoming a viable commercial organization,' Himmler said. 'As the number of prisoners increases, we may find ourselves with surplus manpower, in which case we shall consider your propositions, Herr Baron.'

They turned away. The guard's whip lashed across prisoner 814318's hands. 'Keep moving, heaven dog.'

Baron Heinrich dined at the Hotel Quadriga that evening. Espying Mortimer Allen in the bar, he summoned him to his table. 'Now listen to me, boy. I know you're responsible for a lot of the hoo-ha being kicked up about Pastor Scheer. Well, I was at Grubenmünde today and I can assure you there's nothing the matter with conditions there. The barracks are almost as good as rooms at this hotel, the kitchens are spotlessly clean and the food of excellent quality.'

'Did you see Pastor Scheer?' Mortimer inquired.

'We didn't visit the chapel. No doubt that's where he was, conducting a service.'

Mortimer raised an eyebrow.

The Baron fingered the decorations on his black uniform. 'If anything, the prisoners are looked after too damned well. Waste of SS funds. I was rather surprised that an old campaigner like Tobisch should be so lax.'

At Grubenmünde, they finished work at dusk. Miraculously, only one prisoner had collapsed during the day, but, as always, that necessitated an even longer roll-call than normal. Eventually, they were fed their ration of dry bread, spread with foul margarine. The weals on prisoner 814318's hands swelled and throbbed. When the Block Senior's back was turned, one of his fellow prisoners slipped him a tube of ointment. 'I took this last time I was in the sick bay. Rub it in, Pastor. It should help.'

'Dear God,' Pastor Scheer prayed that evening, 'you are indeed bountiful in your mercies…'

CHAPTER EIGHT

Stefan came home at Christmas evidently decided to be at his least critical and his most charming. The only bad moment was when he learned of Pastor Scheer's fate. Then his face went very pale and he clenched his fist into a hard ball. 'They are swine, pigs, offal…'

On this occasion, the Osters joined the Krauses and Biedersteins at the family table at the New Year's Eve Ball. Christa was spending the holiday skiing at St Moritz with a friend from finishing school and Monika was at Fürstenmark. 'It's disconcerting to realize one's children don't need one any more, isn't it?' Ilse commented to Viktoria, as they took their places in the ballroom.

'It is indeed,' Viktoria replied, although she did not miss Monika very much and was feeling on top of the world because Stefan was home again.

Nevertheless, in view of Stefan's pacifist views and dislike of the military, she was slightly apprehensive when he was introduced to Colonel Oster. The Colonel was at his most elegant and gallant, his monocle in his eye, his conversation suavely amusing. But when he learned Stefan was a Rhodes Scholar, his attitude changed subtly. Drawing his chair a little to one side, he questioned him closely on his studies and impressions of England, becoming engrossed in a long and intense conversation.

Later, Oster remarked to Benno and Viktoria, 'You must be proud of your son. An articulate and extremely intelligent young man.'

Benno did not conceal his pleasure. 'Thank you, Herr Colonel.'

Colonel Oster looked thoughtful. 'When he leaves Oxford in July, he'll be called up for military service. Would you consider my trying to get him posted to the Abwehr? He is very much the calibre of recruit we are trying to attract and I think Military Intelligence work would suit his temperament better than active service.'

'Herr Colonel, you would be doing us a great honour.'

To Viktoria's surprise, instead of being dismayed at Oster's proposal, Stefan appeared quite excited at the prospect, but all he would say was, 'We seem to have quite a few things in common.'

When Mortimer learned about Oster's proposition, he was rather perturbed. In view of Stefan's convictions, Military Intelligence seemed the very last place that he should work — unless Oster had some special role in mind for him. Because he was fond of the lad and did not want him to get into unnecessary trouble, he decided to tackle Oster on the subject. Next time he saw the Colonel, he said quietly, 'I've heard that you are considering recruiting young Jochum-Kraus into the Abwehr. You know he has become rather — er — anglicized in his views since he's been at Oxford?'

Oster gave a thin smile. 'He made his feelings very clear. He also intimated that you have encouraged him in his dislike for Emil.'

'Emil?'

'Emil is my private name for our glorious Führer.' The scorn in his voice was unmistakable. 'Herr Allen, I distrust that man to the depths of my soul. I am filled with a great fear that he is going to lead Germany into disaster, unless somebody stops him.'

'You believe you can stop him?'

'I am building up a cell of oppositionists within the Abwehr.'

'That is why you are interested in Stefan?'

'He has English friends with fathers in high places. The day may come when we shall need his contacts.'

Mortimer averted his face to light a cigarette, while he considered the implications of this statement. 'You would ask him to betray his own country?'

'I shall ask him to do nothing that I would not do myself — in the cause of justice and to prevent Emil starting a war which Germany can only lose.'

Mortimer nodded heavily. 'Let's hope it doesn't come to that. In the meantime, Colonel, you know you can count on me, too.'

In the middle of January, with Hitler and Göring as witnesses, the War Minister, General von Blomberg, remarried. Peter von Biederstein was slightly surprised, particularly since Blomberg's new bride was considerably younger than himself and from a much lower class. However, when he learned that the woman had been a prostitute, who modelled for pornographic photographs, Peter — and the rest of his fellow officers at the War Ministry — were horrified. The highest-ranking soldier in the German Army married to a whore! That was a disgrace to the whole officer class! When Blomberg's dismissal was announced on 26 January, there was a general feeling of relief.

The following day, however, a fresh scandal broke out when General von Fritsch, Commander-in-Chief of the Army, was accused of a homosexual offence and of having been paying hush money to an ex-convict for the past two years. He was taken for interrogation to Gestapo headquarters, after which he was sent by the Führer on indefinite leave, tantamount to suspension from service. Peter's superior officer, General Beck, was made Acting Commander-in-Chief of the Army.

Peter's immediate reaction was not concern for Fritsch, but eager anticipation for the future. If Beck's new position were made permanent, it could mean promotion for himself, possibly even to Beck's post of Chief of General Staff. He requested an interview with Beck and, in the General's impressive, high-ceilinged office overlooking the Bendlerstrasse, offered his congratulations.

Beck, however, looked at him gravely. 'Biederstein, I know General von Fritsch well and I do not believe he is a homosexual. Neither do I believe General von Blomberg's wife was a prostitute.'

Peter had long ago learned not to let his emotions show. Impassively, he asked, 'What do you mean, Herr General?'

Heavily, Beck replied, 'I am convinced this is an SS conspiracy to discredit the general officers. I am demanding that the Führer give Fritsch a chance to clear his name before a military court of honour.'

If Beck's suspicions were correct, he was right to demand that Fritsch be given a chance to clear his name. Realizing his congratulations had been premature, Peter murmured a few words of support and withdrew to his own office.

After that, Peter guardedly discussed the Fritsch affair with other close associates. Admiral Canaris made no attempt to conceal his distress, while Colonel Oster — a long-standing friend of Fritsch — was appalled. 'Fritsch may be a bachelor, but he isn't a homosexual. He's been framed. General Beck is absolutely right in believing that these are not just attacks on Blomberg and Fritsch, but attempts to undermine the power of the Army. Remember how Schleicher and Bredow were murdered in June 1934.'

'They were plotting against the State.'

'Perhaps. However, they should still have been allowed to stand trial. It is my belief that Hitler wants Blomberg and Fritsch out of the way so that he can put his own men in charge of the Army.'

It was a grave accusation, but one that Peter heard repeated several times during the troubled days that followed, together with rumours that Hitler was considering placing either Göring or Himmler in command of the Wehrmacht. He learned that Fritsch's friends, including Colonel Oster, were urging him to lead a military putsch against the government when the Reichstag met to celebrate Hitler's fifth anniversary on 30 January. Several officers sounded Peter out, asking whether he would side with them against the government and the SS.

Deeply perturbed, he requested another interview with General Beck, who admitted, 'I, too, have been approached by certain generals, but although I will defend Fritsch's innocence, I will not take part in any military coup. That would be mutiny and mutiny is a word which does not exist in the vocabulary of a German soldier.'

'However, if the Führer placed the Wehrmacht under the command of Göring or Himmler...?'

'I do not believe he will.'

Upon consideration, Peter did not think he would either. During the five years he had been in power, Hitler had clearly demonstrated his belief in the Wehrmacht: siding with the Army against Röhm's stormtroopers; reintroducing conscription; re-occupying the Rhineland; and allowing the Wehrmacht to test its strength in Spain.

The anniversary ceremony at the Reichstag was indefinitely postponed, but, as one top secret meeting after another took place at the War Ministry and the Chancellery, Peter became convinced that Beck's was the star to follow. Whether or not the General was genuinely concerned about Fritsch's honour or was merely safeguarding his own future, he appeared to stand high in the Führer's regard.

Cold-shouldering Colonel Oster and Fritsch's other friends, Peter let it be known that he would have nothing to do with any military coup.

He was soon extremely glad of his decision, because on 4 February, Hitler announced extensive changes within the Wehrmacht, beginning with the statement that he, personally, would take over Blomberg's position as Commander-in-Chief of the Wehrmacht and War Minister. The War Ministry would be abolished and a new establishment created in its stead: OKW, the *Oberkommando der Wehrmacht* — the High Command of the Armed Forces — in overall command of the Army, the Luftwaffe and the Navy. General Keitel would be Hitler's deputy and Colonel Jodl, his Head of Operations. The new Commander-in-Chief of the Army was to be General von Brauchitsch. The retirement of sixteen generals was announced — many of them, Peter noticed, men who had been advocating a military coup — and Göring was promoted to the position of Field Marshal.

The following morning, Peter was among the officers summoned to a meeting in the Great Hall of the Chancellery. He listened to Hitler, unusually pale and clearly exhausted, explain his bitter disappointment over Blomberg's behaviour, especially since he and Field Marshal Göring had been witnesses at the wedding. In the light of this experience, he had been forced to suspend General von Fritsch, but he was prepared to allow a military court of honour, presided over by Göring, to determine Fritsch's innocence or guilt.

To Peter, it seemed an eminently satisfactory solution. Although General Beck had not been promoted, he still had command of the General Staff and Peter's reputation remained untarnished. He commented on this to Beck, as they returned to the War Ministry. To his surprise, the General shook his head morosely. 'No, Biederstein, we have been hoodwinked. But now it's too late, much too late, to do anything about it.'

Suddenly, Peter was reminded of the occasion, nearly four years earlier, when Beck had said, after swearing his oath of loyalty to the Führer, *This is the blackest day of my life.* And just as he had been bewildered then, so he was puzzled now.

Colonel Oster was one of the four assessors appointed to hear Fritsch's case. When Peter next met him, he remarked, 'As the General's friend, you must welcome this opportunity to see justice done.'

Oster gazed at him bleakly. 'It is too late, Biederstein. General von Fritsch has not only lost his position — but also his honour.'

The following weekend, Peter happened to be driving through the Tiergarten, when he passed General Beck and Colonel Oster riding together. As such, there was nothing sinister in this, for it was well-known that both officers were keen horsemen. However, Peter could not help but notice their expressions, as instead of enjoying a brisk canter they held their mounts back to a gentle walk, while they engaged in what seemed to be serious, almost conspiratorial conversation.

Continuing his journey, Peter pondered the significance of this chance sighting. What had the two men been discussing that they could not talk about at the War Ministry or the Abwehr offices? The more Peter thought about it, the more convinced he became that they had been plotting something. In view of Oster's poorly concealed distrust of the Nazis and Beck's recently expressed misgivings, he could only conclude that Oster had not renounced all ideas of a military putsch and was trying to involve Beck in his schemes.

However, since Peter had no proof, he kept his suspicions to himself, merely resolving not to get involved with them in any way.

So far as the civilian population and the press were concerned, Generals Blomberg and Fritsch had retired for health reasons and the changes within the Wehrmacht were purely routine, as were the various cabinet and diplomatic changes that had been announced at the same time. Although Mortimer thought the whole thing smacked rather of a purge, he had no proof and, in any case, other events intervened to distract his attention.

On 20 February, Hitler made his long-awaited address to the Reichstag. There was little new in it. For three hours, he boasted of the country's economic and military successes. He described industrial and mining output, financial and commercial turnover. He passed a few derogatory remarks about Jews and Bolsheviks.

Then, just as Mortimer felt his eyes closing, Hitler said, 'Over ten million Germans live in two of the states adjoining the frontier.' It was the duty of Germany, he went on, to protect these fellow-Germans and to secure them general freedom — personal, political and ideological. Mortimer sat bolt upright. Hitler did not mention them by name, but there was no doubt which two states he meant — Austria and Czechoslovakia.

Hitler then told the deputies that at a recent meeting with the Austrian Chancellor, Dr Schuschnigg, at Berchtesgaden they had agreed that the Reich and German Austria were bound together, 'not only because we are the same people, but also because we share a long history and a common culture.'

The only way Dr Schuschnigg would have agreed with Hitler over anything was under extreme pressure, Mortimer reflected grimly, and he felt an overwhelming sympathy with the Austrian Chancellor.

Hitler's speech caused a furore in Austria, sparking off massive pro-Nazi demonstrations, although these were countered to a certain extent by pro-Schuschnigg demonstrations. Addressing the Bundestag in Vienna, Schuschnigg vowed Austria would never give up its independence, but as the Nazi demonstrations increased in strength and violence, he began to weaken. On Wednesday, 9 March, he announced a plebiscite to be held that Sunday, in which the Austrian people could pledge their vote for an independent Austria under his chancellorship or say 'Yes' to an *Anschluss* with Germany.

Mortimer telephoned Bill Wallace in London, then told Viktoria, 'I'm off to Vienna.'

'Vienna? Do you think these disturbances could be serious?'

Mortimer looked at her grimly. 'I think the whole situation is very serious indeed.'

Viktoria was reminded of his words, when she saw the German newspaper headlines on Saturday morning: GERMAN AUSTRIA SAVED FROM CHAOS. There followed horrific stories of violent communist attacks on the innocent civilians of Vienna, of fighting, looting and shooting on the streets of the capital, and a copy of a telegram sent by the Austrian Nazi leader, Dr Seyss-Inquart, requesting the German government to send troops to Austria's aid as soon as possible, in response to which Army and Luftwaffe troops had crossed the border and were rapidly restoring order.

Despite this latter assurance, the atmosphere was tense. As Benno said, a communist revolution in Austria might spread to Germany if it was not put down immediately. At his request, Hasso kept the bar radio on low all morning, waiting for news flashes.

These grew progressively more encouraging, as radio reporters described the enthusiasm with which the Austrian people were welcoming the German troops. That same afternoon, Hitler broadcast from Linz, the city of his birth. 'If Providence once called me forth from this town to be the leader of the Reich, it must, in so doing, have charged me with a mission, and that mission could only be to restore my dear homeland to the German Reich. I have believed in this mission, I have lived and fought for it, and I believe I have now fulfilled it.'

Instantly, the mood at the Quadriga changed. Several people in the bar cheered and Hasso was inundated with orders for bottles of champagne. Benno put his arm round Viktoria. 'Thank God for that. I had a dreadful feeling that Austria might find itself in the throes of civil war.'

Luise, Sepp and Lili joined them for dinner. Sepp admitted, 'When I heard the news this morning, I thought I was missing out on something, but obviously the Bolsheviks aren't going to put up a fight. I gather our chaps over there are just dropping leaflets reassuring the people. Someone even told me they are dropping flowers!'

Later still, Peter and Ilse dropped in for a drink after the theatre. Sepp laughed when he saw Peter. 'So you missed out on the fun, too!'

Peter was not amused by Sepp's flippant attitude. 'This could have been another Sarajevo — leading to another world war. Fortunately, we had been warned and were able to move troops to the border in time. And, of course, most Austrians want an *Anschluss* with Germany.'

Viktoria suddenly remembered the plebiscite and asked Peter if it would still be held the following day.

'It's been postponed,' Peter told her. 'In some cities, street battles are still raging. A plebiscite can hardly be held under those conditions. But, once peace is fully restored, I am sure it will take place.'

'In any case,' Benno commented, 'the result must be a foregone conclusion. Germany and Austria are traditional allies. As Hitler said the other week, we share a long history and a common culture — and, of course, the same language. If it hadn't been for the Treaty of Versailles, none of this nonsense would ever have happened.'

The next day, Austria was proclaimed a province of the German Reich and a new date was set for the plebiscite. On Monday, Hitler made his triumphant entry into Vienna. He spent the next four weeks in Austria, making election speeches, ranting against Schuschnigg and urging the people to vote 'Ja' in the plebiscite. Photographs showed streets lined with joyful people, waving the swastika flag and cheering, throwing flowers and laughing, clearly overcome with pleasure at being united with Germany.

On 10 April, over ninety-nine per cent of the Austrian population voted for Austria's inclusion in the German Reich. No longer was the country called Österreich, but the Ostmark, and its nine provinces became *Gaue* of Greater Germany. In Berlin, the news was hailed with delight, but with little surprise.

Most important of all was the fact that Austria had been annexed without a drop of German blood being shed. As Sepp laughingly said, it had been a 'campaign of flowers'.

Mortimer returned to Berlin, with a rather different picture of Austria than that painted by the German papers. Finding an excuse to meet Viktoria outside the hotel, he said bitterly, 'Yes, thousands of

Viennese stood cheering on the streets to welcome Hitler. Church bells rang. Flags were waved. What you did not see in the newspapers, Viktoria, were the thousands who dared to resist the Nazis and who are now already in concentration camps — including Schuschnigg.'

She shuddered. 'So it was just like here.'

'But much, much swifter.' Mortimer took a deep breath. 'Worst of all, was the treatment of the Jews. The SS tried to keep foreign correspondents away, but we couldn't help but see. Stormtroopers broke into hundreds of Jewish homes, hurling bricks through windows, shooting open locks on doors, forcing the Jews out onto the streets, stealing their valuables and smashing their furniture.

'Those who were not arrested were made to go down on their hands and knees and scrub the pavements, cleaning the Schuschnigg plebiscite slogans from the walls and washing out public toilets — watched, needless to say, by soldiers and non-Jewish civilians, jeering, "Look! The Jews are working! The Führer's created work for the Jews!"'

Viktoria gazed at him in horror. The anti-Semitic demonstrations they had witnessed in Berlin were bad enough, but she had never seen anything to equal what Mortimer was describing. 'Are you able to do anything?' she asked.

'Not much. I sent a confidential report to my editor with an English reporter who managed to get a flight back to London, but even if he wanted to kick up a fuss, nobody will pay any attention to him. The only way to stop what is going on in Austria is to use force and no government is prepared to risk going to war.' He gave a harsh laugh. 'The editor of the London *Times* summed up the situation when he said that, two hundred years ago, Scotland chose to annexe itself to England. Who were the British to condemn the same course of action in another country?'

'Seen like that, I suppose he is right. But that doesn't help the Austrian Jews. Mortimer, what will happen to them?'

'God knows,' Mortimer said heavily, 'but I'm sure we'll soon find out.'

He was right. Very soon, the first Austrian Jews arrived in Berlin. Among the wealthier of them, who could afford to stay at the Quadriga, was an elegant, middle-aged Viennese called Nathan Roth, his wife and two children. It did not take Mortimer long to get into conversation with him, although not within the hotel. Mortimer was very much a fresh air fiend these days.

'What are you by profession?' Mortimer asked him, as they strolled along Unter den Linden.

'A lawyer. I had a fine practice in the Inner City. My clients came from the cream of Viennese society — aristocrats, landowners, professional people like myself…'

'Why have you come to Berlin of all places?'

Nathan Roth stared sightlessly at the little linden trees. 'Have you heard of Adolf Eichmann?'

Mortimer shook his head.

'But you know of Reinhard Heydrich — head of the SS Security Service?'

'Indeed I do.'

'Well, Eichmann is Heydrich's "Jewish expert" and he is now in Vienna setting up the Reich Emigration Office — the task of which is to coordinate the expulsion of Jews from Austria. Forced emigration, Herr Allen. Well, I preferred to leave of my own volition — and I was fortunate: I had the money to do so, even though it meant selling our house at a ridiculously low price and leaving many of our possessions behind. However, I was able to bribe the right officials and get our documents through quickly.'

'But why Berlin?'

'I have a cousin here, who assured me I would be safe while I tried to get an immigration visa for England. However, it seems that my problems are only just beginning. I've been to the British Embassy, but they say I must first have a job to go to.'

Impressed by and sorry for the man, Mortimer went to the British Embassy and explained Nathan Roth's predicament to James Adams.

The diplomat ran his fingers through his hair. 'Mr Allen, we're in a devilish awkward situation. The House of Commons has voted overwhelmingly against a Private Member's Bill to give the Home

Office wider powers for admitting Austrian refugees. The Home Secretary has, however, agreed to examine sympathetically all applications from refugees working in the arts, sciences, business or industry, or those of independent financial means.'

'Dr Roth is a lawyer and he can afford to stay at the Quadriga.'

'Then he should be able to get a job in England.'

When Mortimer pursued his enquiries further afield, he learned that Czechoslovakia had immediately closed its borders to all Jews upon announcement of the *Anschluss*. Paul-Henri Spaak had announced there could be no wholesale admission of Jews into Belgium. The American Secretary of State, Cordell Hull, suggested setting up an international committee to debate the question of political refugees, but, in the meantime, the numbers allowed into America would remain severely restricted.

'And because Germans don't need visas to enter Switzerland,' Professor Ascher told Mortimer heavily, when he went to see him at Dahlem, 'the Swiss police are demanding that a large red J be stamped on all Jewish passports. So much for Swiss neutrality.'

Mortimer repeated Nathan Roth's story.

The Professor nodded. 'If he's a lawyer, Theo can probably help. It's the others I'm sorry for, those who are still in Austria and have no money.'

A couple of weeks later, Theo Arendt wrote offering Nathan Roth a clerical position in his bank. Far from being grateful, the lawyer exclaimed indignantly, 'I am a doctor of law, Herr Allen, not a bank clerk. I would rather stay in Berlin than be subjected to such a humiliation. What will people think?'

Something in Mortimer snapped. 'They'll think, like I do, that you're a fool if you don't accept.'

'But Berlin is quite different from Vienna. I've been here nearly a month now and realize my cousin was right. Berliners don't hate the Jews at all. Oh, yes, there are notices saying JEWS NOT PERMITTED and one hears the occasional anti-Semitic comment, but, by and large, I feel as if I have escaped from Hitler.'

'Have you found a job?' Mortimer asked acidly.

'Well, actually, that has proved rather difficult. However, there are still Jewish lawyers practising here.'

A couple of days later, another anti-Jewish decree was passed, according to which every Jew had to report all his domestic and foreign property if it exceeded five thousand marks. A cryptic paragraph advised that the Plenipotentiary of the Four Year Plan would ensure that use made of the property would be in keeping with the interests of the German economy.

Dr Roth saw that what remained of his property was in danger of being seized. He swallowed his pride, accepted Theo Arendt's offer, received his entry visa to England, paid his bill at the Quadriga and left Berlin.

Viktoria was considerably encouraged by Dr Roth's success. 'If he has obtained a visa, others will too,' she told Mortimer.

Mortimer nodded doubtfully. She was doing all she could in making the Jews welcome. There was no point in depressing her by describing the problems they were facing.

Times had never been more propitious for Baron Heinrich von Kraus zu Essen. In Germany, for a fraction of their real value, he was buying companies from Jews only too thankful to take what they could get and leave the country. From a concern comprising some four hundred subsidiaries when Hitler came to power, the Kraus empire was now six hundred companies strong.

It encompassed vast mining interests in the Ruhr and Silesia. The Kraushaven shipyard was constructing massive battleships financed by the government. The Essen factories were producing tanks superior to any ever built; heavy artillery, infantry rifles, machine guns and mine-throwers. Kraus Chemie in Wedding was developing new gases, explosives, synthetic rubbers and resins.

Kraus Industries' financial arm, which had started with the Arendt Bank, now included insurance companies, commodity brokers, mortgage lenders, import-export and discount houses. In recognition of the Baron's services to the Party, Göring allowed him to have first pick of the Jewish businesses in Austria. He not only acquired a famous Austrian bank, but as part of the deal, he obtained the Jewish banker's castle near Innsbruck, Schloss Waldesruh, a turreted, fairy-tale structure, set high on a mountainside, filled with priceless antiques, furniture and paintings.

The Baron's association with Himmler was also beginning to pay dividends. In his efforts to create a business organization within the SS, the Reichsführer had come up against a sticky problem. He had production space and he had labourers, but he lacked technical know-how. So Kraus Industries entered into a joint venture with the SS. At Grubenmünde concentration camp, a factory was being built, financed by the government, to be supervized by Kraus engineers and to be staffed by the prisoners.

At Grubenmünde, a new perimeter fence was erected, trebling the size of the camp site and on this terrain the prisoners dug foundations, then began to build a vast factory complex. Conditions were the cruellest they had ever known. Their meagre ration of bread was stale and often mouldy. The evening gruel was so thin as to be almost transparent. But despite the fact that they were nearly starving, they were driven to ever harder exertions.

An atmosphere of frenetic urgency prevailed throughout the camp. Every day, Commandant Tobisch, accompanied by his dog Wolf, came to inspect progress, snarling bad-tempered criticism at the guards and the inmates. Shouts of *'Tempo! Los! Los!'* echoed throughout the camp all day. Prisoners who collapsed were mercilessly flogged and frequently killed. They were replaced by trainloads of new arrivals, many of them Jews from Austria.

Prisoner 814318 was scarcely recognizable as Bernhard Scheer, Pastor of Berlin-Schmargendorf. There was not an ounce of spare flesh on his body. His hands were hard and calloused. His eyes were deeply sunk. But he had survived seven months in Grubenmünde and was now one of the old lags.

As a special privilege, he was allowed to write to Klara. It was the most wonderful day of his life when he received her reply. Very brief and much fingered, the pastor was sure it had been looked at by many Gestapo officials before it had reached him. 'Your cousin and I are well,' she wrote, 'and working hard for the family's welfare.' Wisely, she ended, 'Heil, Hitler!'

That day, as his guards goaded him to greater efforts while he ran with his barrow from the pile of bricks to the rising factory building, his heart was singing:

'Now thank we all our God
With heart and hands and voices...'

'Move your arse, heaven dog!' the SS man growled. With a superhuman effort, prisoner 814318 obeyed.

In his mind, Mortimer heard a man in a Kent garden rumble, 'Mr Allen, it is my belief that we stand on the brink of an almost measureless calamity...' There was no doubt which country must be next on Hitler's list. Surrounded on three sides by Germany and Austria, Czechoslovakia was highly vulnerable.

The Republic of Czechoslovakia had been created in 1918 from the former western Slavonic provinces of the Austro-Hungarian Empire. Its minority German population of three million was concentrated in the industrial area of the Sudetenland. Free from the shackles that limited German industrial expansion in the 1920s, these people had enjoyed relative prosperity until the Depression. Now, while Germany was booming, they were continuing to experience severe unemployment and chronic hardship.

In the election campaign currently being conducted, the Sudeten-German Party, led by Konrad Henlein, was demanding autonomy and an alliance with the Fatherland. Like Austria, the Sudetenlanders wanted to join the Reich.

Czechoslovakia was equally determined not to give in to their demands. In 1924, President Masaryk had signed a Treaty of Mutual Guarantee with France. In 1936, shortly after the French-Soviet Pact, his successor, Eduard Beneš, had gone to Moscow for confidential meetings with Stalin. Now Beneš made it clear that, rather than grant the Sudetenland autonomy, he was prepared to risk war. Czech troops were mobilizing.

In May, the newspapers were full of accounts of Czech atrocities against the Sudeten Germans, of civilians being shot in the streets, of babies being butchered, of rape and looting. 'It could mean war...' Suddenly, the words were on everyone's lips. The Siegfried Line — the West Wall — was not completed. Germany was still virtually unprotected if France should decide to side with Czechoslovakia and attack from the West. It certainly could not hope to defend itself in a war on two fronts. Konrad Henlein, leader of the Sudeten-German Party, came to Berlin, begging for protection, pleading that, like Austria, his people be allowed to join the Reich.

Although there was sympathy with their plight, there was also a distinct antagonism towards the Sudetenlanders. 'They aren't real Germans,' Viktoria said. 'They have never been ruled by Germany. If the situation can be resolved diplomatically, all well and good, but I don't believe we should be forced into a war because of them.'

Benno was very worried. 'As the Führer said in February, it is the duty of Germany to protect her fellow-Germans. We are the same people, Vicki. But I, too, hope war can be prevented.'

Only Baron Heinrich was smugly complacent. The industrial regions of Czechoslovakia offered rich pickings.

On 18 May, Ilse visited Luise in Lützow. 'Peter believes it could mean war. He's so certain that he's sending me to Lausanne to be near Christa. Luise, will you and Lili come with me?'

She shook her head. 'No, I can't leave Sepp.'

'Luise, he's a Luftwaffe officer. If war breaks out, he won't be in Berlin. He'll be at the front.'

'Yes. That is why I must stay here.'

Sepp would always be, first and foremost, a flier. When he came home, there was an excited glint in his eye and he admitted, 'Yes, it's true. I've been put on active service again, in charge of Fighter Arm A. I'm leaving for the Czech frontier first thing tomorrow morning.' He did not attempt to conceal his delight at being released from his desk.

Luise leaned down and patted Sheltie's collar to hide her fear.

Sepp poured them both drinks. 'Luischen, don't worry. Just because I hated the wanton destruction of Guernica doesn't mean I'm scared of war. I've seen aerial photographs of the Czech fortifications. They're nothing. If it does come to war, I think we'll pull it off. But I'm pretty sure the matter will be resolved politically.'

Luise wished she had his faith, but she could not help feeling that men like the Führer, Göring and Milch, would be more than ready to risk valuable men's lives out of a vainglorious belief in their own invincibility.

In the Quadriga bar that same evening, a page boy brought Mortimer Allen an envelope. Mortimer slit it open to find a terse handwritten note: 'Emil is up to his tricks again. Meet me in the Preussen Park at eight.'

He stuffed the note in his pocket, drained his Jack Daniels and slipped off the bar stool, showing no outward sign of his inner excitement. At last, he had made a breakthrough — Colonel Oster had information for him! Careful of watching eyes, Mortimer walked to the Potsdamer Platz, where he took a cab to the Fehrbelliner Platz, then strolled casually into the small Preussen Park. He immediately saw Colonel Oster — out of uniform — on a bench. Lighting a cigarette, he sat down next to him. 'Good evening, Herr Colonel.'

'Good evening, Herr Allen. Thank you for coming so promptly.' He stared into the twilight for a moment, then said, 'If he can't get the Sudetenland any other way, Emil means war. The code name for the operation is Case Green. It has already been extensively planned. There are twelve German divisions on the Czech frontier ready to march within twelve hours. We have to get this information urgently to British Military Intelligence. Can you help me?'

Mortimer thought quickly. He dared not telephone such sensitive information to London personally, but James Adams could probably do something. 'Yes, I can help you,' he replied confidently.

Back in the Fehrbelliner Platz, he found a public telephone kiosk and telephoned James's private number. 'James, it's Mortimer. I'm famished. Fancy a quick spaghetti at the Taverne?'

There was a moment's hesitation, then James said, 'Feeling a bit peckish myself. See you there in fifteen minutes.'

The Taverne was crowded when Mortimer arrived and, as always, there was a fair sprinkling of foreign correspondents and diplomatic staff present. He and James did not appear conspicuous. After they had ordered, Mortimer passed over Oster's information, not mentioning its source. James gave a low whistle. 'Thank you, Mortimer. I'll make sure the news reaches Churchill first thing tomorrow morning.'

Next day, upon receipt of James Adams' message, Churchill told Prime Minister Neville Chamberlain, 'There are twelve German divisions mobilized on the Czech border.' After a long discussion the Prime Minister agreed to send the British Ambassador to Berlin to see the German Foreign Minister, Joachim von Ribbentrop, and warn him against German aggression.

Two days later, the German papers reported that Czech troops were definitely mobilizing. All Europe was in uproar. There was frenzied diplomatic activity. But, finally, the Foreign Office in Berlin assured the Czech envoy that Germany had no aggressive intentions towards his country. The crisis seemed to have been averted.

Air Fleet A under the command of Oberst Nowak returned from Senftenberg. Ilse von Biederstein came back from Switzerland.

'It's given us breathing space,' Oster told Mortimer, 'but that's all. Now we must hope that the generals will come to their senses and realize the dangerous path along which Emil is leading them.'

Exactly one week later, on 28 May, General Beck was among the commanding officers summoned by Hitler to the Chancellery. Upon his return, he called his senior officers to a meeting. His face grey, he informed them, 'The information I am about to give you is highly confidential. The Führer has just given orders that Case Green has only been postponed. Unless Czechoslovakia grants autonomy to the Sudeten-Germans, we are to prepare for an invasion to take place by 1 October at the latest. There will be no time for England to mobilize by then and France will undertake nothing without England, so the operation stands every chance of success.'

Heads nodded in agreement and Beck went on to outline their specific areas of responsibility. When he had finished, he asked whether there were any questions. There was only one, from an officer who asked whether Russia was likely to intervene on Czechoslovakia's behalf.

Beck shook his head. 'The Führer considers it unlikely. As a result of Stalin's purges, the Russian army is virtually bereft of officers.'

Peter stared at him curiously. There was a grey tinge to Beck's face, a strange note in his voice. Something was obviously worrying the Chief of Staff.

During the weeks that followed, it grew increasingly difficult to obtain an interview with Beck. Whenever Peter and his fellow officers made an appointment through his adjutant, they were inevitably kept waiting, often for several hours. When they pressed for an explanation, the adjutant explained, 'The General is in an important meeting with Colonel Oster of the Abwehr.'

Most of Peter's colleagues accepted the necessity for close cooperation between the General Staff and Military Intelligence and saw nothing strange in these endless meetings. However, Peter could not forget the horseback encounter he had witnessed in the Tiergarten. Although rather overshadowed by the Austrian *Anschluss*, a Court of Honour had heard General von Fritsch's case, in which it had transpired that the Gestapo witness had made a mistake of identity and the ex-convict had been blackmailing a Captain Frisch, not General von Fritsch. Although he was not offered back his old position, the General had been acquitted.

From things both Beck and Oster had let drop, Peter knew the Fritsch affair still troubled them, and he could not help suspecting some hidden purpose behind their current, private discussions, but what it could be he had no idea.

Instead of dying down, the tension and unease intensified in Berlin. The first air-raid shelters were built and anti-aircraft searchlights erected. Many foreign guests stayed away from Germany that summer, so the Hotel Quadriga was unusually empty of tourists and overseas businessmen. Several waiters and kitchen staff, who had already completed their military service, were ordered to report to their units for summer exercises.

At the beginning of July, when everyone's nerves were becoming decidedly frayed, an event occurred which took their attention away from Czechoslovakia. A scant year after her husband's death, Countess Anna von Biederstein died.

It was the first time anybody close to Monika had died, and she found it difficult to come to grips with the idea that the sickly old Countess had been alive one evening and dead the next morning. Even more worrying, however, was her own future. Hans was just finishing his final year at teacher training college and was promised the post of village schoolmaster from September. There seemed no reason why they should not be married. However, if the country did find itself at war, the situation could change dramatically.

Once again, the family gathered in Fürstenmark churchyard, Pastor König intoned the familiar words of the burial service and Countess Anna was laid to rest next to her husband.

After the ceremony, they went to the castle for refreshments and, to her relief, Monika found herself the centre of attention. Everybody praised her devotion to the Countess and condoled with her upon her loss. She had almost become a von Biederstein as a result of her long stay at the castle.

This sensation was enhanced when she discovered that she was mentioned in the Countess's will. In gratitude for her companionship, Countess Anna had left Monika an empty cottage on the estate for her and Hans to live in once they were married.

With difficulty, Monika fought back her joyful excitement. War or no war, she could stay at Fürstenmark!

Her father, however, received the news with misgiving. 'I think you should wait a little longer. If there is a war, Hans will be called up.'

Hans put his arm round Monika's shoulder and she looked appealingly at his parents. Pastor König cleared his throat. 'Gerda and I have been discussing the matter, Herr Kraus. So far as we are concerned, Monika is welcome to stay with us until the Czech crisis is resolved. Then we hope the young people can be married.'

'Monika will be quite safe with us,' Gerda König added. 'And, thanks to the Countess's generosity, she will have plenty to do getting the cottage ready, while Hans settles in at his new job.'

It seemed the most sensible solution. Benno expressed his gratitude and acquiesced. As they drove home, he said to Viktoria, 'I hope to God everybody comes to their senses in time. These young people deserve happiness. We're just recovering from the last war. We don't want another.'

In London, the Foreign Minister, Lord Halifax, told the Commons, 'I do not believe that those responsible for the Government of any country in Europe today want war.'

To his constituents, Winston Churchill said, 'I must tell you that the whole state of Europe and of the world is moving steadily towards a climax, which cannot be long delayed... War is certainly not inevitable. But the danger to peace will not be removed until the vast German armies, which have been called forth from their homes into the ranks, have been dispersed...'

The students at Oxford called Churchill a warmonger. They agreed with Chamberlain's policy of appeasement. If the Sudeten-Germans wanted to join Germany, let them. The Czech government should allow them self-determination. Anything rather than have Europe plunged into another war. They had been born in the wake of one world war. They wanted to live the rest of their lives in peace. In any case, what was Czechoslovakia? It was a small country, a very long way away.

Cramming for his finals, Stefan Jochum-Kraus, commonly known at the university as Stephen Cross, agreed with them. The last thing he wanted was war between England and Germany.

Still the Austrian Jews arrived in Berlin. Unlike Dr Roth, these were poorer people, who had waited until they were sacked from their jobs and thrown out of their apartments by Aryan landlords; who could not bribe officials, but had to queue for days outside embassies and government buildings, waiting for papers that never arrived. They could not afford to stay at the Hotel Quadriga, but took cheap rooms in the suburbs and immediately applied for help from Bethel Ascher and his colleagues at the Welfare Association for the Jews of Germany.

They brought with them dreadful stories of intimidation, violence and of Eichmann's Reich Emigration Office. Eichmann's system was working very smoothly now. Exit visas were granted to all Jews, provided they parted with virtually all their worldly possessions. The problem was that no country in the world would then grant these penniless refugees an entry visa. They were offered the choice of leaving Austria within two weeks or being thrown into a concentration camp as vagabonds. So they came to Berlin.

In July, all Jews were ordered to carry identification cards with them at all times. Jewish doctors were forbidden from practising, although, with special permission, they could — calling themselves orderlies — treat Jewish patients. Violence, looting and picketing of Jewish shops increased. Groups of rowdies — mainly Hitler Youth — marched through Berlin chanting: '*Juden 'raus! Juden 'raus!* Make room for the Sudeten-Germans! The Sudeten-Germans are real Germans! *Juden 'raus!*'

Professor Ascher was seventy-two and Klara Scheer fifty that summer. Every day, they worked unremittingly from first light until well after midnight. They formed part of a vast network that spread across the European continent and throughout the Americas, whose sole purpose was to help those persecuted by the Nazis in Greater Germany.

Throughout the world, Jewish companies tried to find jobs for German Jews, so that their governments would issue that precious entry visa, but all too frequently families were split in the process, for it was the young who were wanted, not their parents, and certainly not their grandparents.

'What will become of us who are left behind?' Bethel Ascher asked Klara one day, after they had witnessed yet another tearful separation at Tempelhof. 'In all so-called civilized societies, the old are obsolete. In Nazi eyes, I have a dreadful feeling that the old — certainly the Jewish old — are expendable.'

By August the new factory at Grubenmünde was completed. Engineers from Kraus Chemie moved in and supervised the installation of machinery for the manufacture of synthetic rubber. Then they interviewed prisoners for fitness and suitability to work the equipment — and came up against a dreadful problem. The camp inmates were little more than bags of bones, verging on starvation.

Such men could not work effectively.

Following an exchange of memoranda, the SS agreed to feed the prisoners better provided Kraus paid for their upkeep. Baron Heinrich agreed. For each prisoner employed in the rubber factory, Kraus Industries would contribute four marks.

Among the factory workers was prisoner 814318. He grasped the opportunity as a passport to life.

Stephen Cross, BA (Oxon), cycled for the last time through the narrow streets of Oxford. He sold his bicycle, packed his gown, cap and books. He shook hands with Tony Callearn and Trevor Neal-Wright. He kissed Joyce and Libby Allen goodbye. The happiest three years of his life were over. With very real regret, he left for Berlin.

At Tempelhof, two grim-faced men, one passport control, the other Gestapo, studied the details on his entry card, examined his passport and grilled him about the nature of his visit to England and the duration of his return to Berlin. On learning that he was home for good, they stamped his passport. Stefan took a deep breath, collected his luggage and eventually emerged into the airport concourse.

Nothing had changed. It was still decorated with swastika banners and the portrait of Hitler still hung in its place of honour. The area swarmed with uniforms. 'Heil Hitler!' echoed everywhere.

'Stefi, darling!' His mother rushed towards him and took him in her arms, smothering him with kisses. 'Stefi, welcome home!'

'Yes, welcome home, son,' his father said gruffly, taking his hand. 'It's good to have you back. Did you have a good journey?'

At that moment, he noticed a strange scene taking place nearby. A couple with two very pretty daughters were saying a sad goodbye to an elderly man. 'I'm sure you'll be able to join us soon, Papa,' the woman was saying. 'You'll get an entry visa.'

The old man was obviously putting on a brave front. 'Yes, I'm sure I shall. Now, hurry along, children, before they change their minds and try to stop you going.'

'Stefi, what's the matter?' his mother asked anxiously.

'I was watching those people.'

A sad expression flitted across Viktoria's face. 'A lot of Jews are leaving Berlin now.'

The Jewish family kissed the old man and moved towards emigration. The old man watched them go, tears streaming down his cheeks. An SS man seized him roughly by the shoulder. 'Clear out of here, dirty Jew!'

'Come along, the car is waiting outside,' Benno said.

Viktoria linked her arm through his. With an unnatural brightness, she said, 'Yes, come along, darling, let's go home.'

He nodded. Stephen Cross no longer existed. He was Stefan Jochum-Kraus — home again in Germany.

The next couple of weeks passed quickly as Stefan renewed his acquaintance with old friends and struggled to come to terms with the fact that war was very much nearer, here in Berlin, than it had seemed in Oxford. 'I know,' Mortimer laughed grimly, when Stefan told him this, 'Czechoslovakia is a small country, a very long way away.'

Next day, he received a letter telling him to report to Abwehr headquarters on the Tirpitz Ufer at ten o'clock on Friday.

Considering the nature of the organization, an extraordinary atmosphere of informality surrounded Stefan's acceptance into the Abwehr. Naturally, he had to complete extremely detailed forms about himself and his family, as well as providing the necessary documentation to prove his Aryan ancestry and his scholastic record, but when this was done, he was led into an interview room where Colonel Oster was waiting. When he raised his arm in the Hitler salute, Oster shook his head smilingly. 'Not in my presence, Herr Jochum-Kraus. Please take a seat. So I understand you got your degree. My congratulations. Are you happy to be back?'

Stefan smiled ruefully. 'Yes and no, Herr Colonel.'

'Within these four walls, you can speak freely. Elsewhere in the building, it is advisable to be more careful. After all, we are in the espionage business and, however careful we try to be, we can never be sure that we have not been infiltrated. Now, suppose I begin by explaining briefly the functions of the Abwehr.'

'Thank you, Herr Colonel.'

'Firstly, you should understand the difference between ourselves and the Gestapo. We are concerned with military intelligence, not poking our noses into the lives of private citizens. Our purpose is threefold. We collect information from agents abroad regarding the military activities of other countries. We try to provide against sabotage inside Germany and to identify enemy spies operating in this country. We are also responsible for all German military attachés abroad and for supervising all foreign military attachés on embassy staffs in Berlin.

'I see your role as falling within the first category and specifically dealing with England. You speak fluent English — something, unfortunately, I do not myself. Places and people mentioned in our agents' reports would be familiar to you.'

Stefan stared down at the tabletop. This was not the job he had envisaged being offered. For three years, he had lived in England. He loved the English. He did not want to spy on them. It seemed like betrayal of the worst kind.

'Is something wrong?'

Within these four walls, you can speak freely. 'Herr Colonel, if Germany should find itself at war with Czechoslovakia, we could also find ourselves at war with England. If such a situation arose, I should find myself very torn in loyalty.' He took a deep breath. 'Particularly since Germany is the aggressor.'

Oster gave him a piercing stare through his monocle. 'Apart from your love for England, do you have any other reasons for believing Germany should not go to war?'

Stefan clenched his hands tightly in his lap, aware that what he was about to say could cost him his freedom or even his life if he had misjudged Colonel Oster. 'I believe there are two issues at stake, Herr Colonel. One is the Führer's territorial aims, his determination — as expressed in *Mein Kampf* and in subsequent speeches — to reoccupy all the territories lost through Versailles, if necessary by means of war. Flower war is one thing. Total war is another. And something, I believe, few Germans want.'

'And the other issue?'

'The German people themselves must be liberated.'

'How would you suggest doing this?'

Stefan looked at him helplessly. 'I don't know how. I only know that the rule of the Nazis must be broken and, if necessary, that Hitler must be removed from power.'

Oster leaned back in his chair and smiled. 'I agree with you. Herr Jochum-Kraus, we must stage a *coup d'état*.'

We must stage a coup d'état... Stefan was not shocked or even unduly surprised. He felt only overwhelming relief that a man in Oster's high position understood the situation.

'I ask you to trust me,' Oster continued. 'Accept the position I offer you here in the Abwehr. It will be routine work and you may have to put in long hours. But it will provide a camouflage for other duties I may demand of you, duties that I believe will conflict neither with your love for England nor with your love for Germany.'

As preparations for the invasion of Czechoslovakia continued, Peter experienced his first moments of doubt. War with Czechoslovakia would commit all Germany's troops to the east and leave the western front undefended. No matter what the Führer said, to attack Czechoslovakia was deliberately to risk war with Britain, France and Russia — and that meant a war on two fronts. Trying to fight on two fronts had been Germany's downfall in the Great War. If she attempted it now, it would be her downfall again.

Despite all the efforts of Kraus Industries and other arms manufacturers, it would be at least another two years — or, according to Baron Heinrich, even longer — before the German armed forces were fully equipped. And, even then, Germany still lacked vital raw materials. Göring's Four-Year Plan had failed to make the country self-sufficient. She was still very reliant on imports, which would immediately stop if the country were at war.

Just as Peter reached these conclusions, General von Brauchitsch convened a meeting of commanding generals and senior officers at the War Ministry and, for the first time, Peter gained an inkling of the nature of Beck's discussions with Colonel Oster. Brauchitsch opened the meeting by expressing his dismay at the Führer's directive dated

30 May 1938, which stated: 'It is my unalterable decision to destroy Czechoslovakia in a military action.' He then read from a memorandum Beck had sent him in the middle of July.

'The Chief of General Staff wrote to me as follows: "In full consciousness of the magnitude of such a step, but also of my responsibilities, I feel it my duty urgently to ask that the Supreme Commander of the Armed Forces call off his preparations for war, and abandon the intention of solving the Czech question by force until the military situation is fundamentally changed. For the present, I consider it hopeless…"'

There was a hum of agreement and Peter realized he was not the only one to entertain doubts. Yet, although all of the officers present agreed with Beck, they could not agree what action to take and the meeting ended inconclusively.

Peter's office was situated a short distance from Beck's and they returned together. When they reached Beck's door, the General asked heavily, 'Can you spare a few moments, Biederstein?'

'Of course, Herr General.'

In the privacy of his own room, Beck said, 'It is not only the prospect of war that disturbs me, but the fact that Hitler has destroyed everything that is decent in Germany. Our people have no freedoms…'

Peter stared at him aghast. 'But Hitler has achieved much good, Herr General.'

Beck sighed. 'So not even you are on my side, Biederstein. Well, so be it. But I shall not give up my fight. The General Staff should be the conscience of the Army. History will burden those military leaders with blood-guilt who fail to act according to their professional knowledge and their conscience. I can no longer keep my oath to the Führer. I cannot lead my country into ruin, so I have no choice but to resign and hope others will follow my example. With no generals, the nation cannot go to war.'

On 18 August, Beck resigned as Chief of Army General Staff, but no other officers followed his example. Peter knew a moment of grudging admiration for the General, but he still believed him to be being unnecessarily defeatist.

322

General Franz Halder, a Catholic Bavarian, became the new Chief of Army General Staff. Peter put Beck to the back of his mind and concentrated on gaining influence with his new commanding officer.

Stefan was given an old desk in a small cubbyhole near Colonel Oster's office, with a threadbare carpet on the floor and littered with piles of scruffy files. His work was extremely interesting — but it was very depressing, as it became increasingly clear that the British government and the British people were in favour of letting Hitler have his own way.

Stefan soon realized how privileged he was. In a country where the reading of foreign newspapers and listening to foreign broadcasts was actively discouraged, he was given English language newspapers to read and sat tuned into the English news broadcasts, as well as reading reports that came in every day from German agents in England.

He was privileged in another way. Frequently, Colonel Oster asked him to attend meetings, on some occasions to take minutes, on others merely to listen. Usually, these were held at the Tirpitz Ufer, but sometimes they were held in cafés, hotel lounges or even in private homes. They involved people from many different walks of life, who had two things in common. None of them — not necessarily for the same reason — wanted war. All of them wanted the end of the Third Reich.

Gradually, Stefan became aware of how widespread the opposition was to Hitler and the number of prominent men it included, most of whom had lost their jobs because of their outspokenness. Dr Hjalmar Schacht, so unsparing in his efforts to help Hitler to power, had resigned as Minister of Economics because of his disillusionment with what he called the 'Nazi quack economy'. Carl Goerdeler, the former mayor of Leipzig, had resigned because of Nazi anti-Semitism and the policy of rearmament. Ulrich von Hassell, Ambassador to Rome until Hitler had recalled him that February, loathed the violence and brutality of the Nazi regime. Other civilians included the lawyer, Hans von Dohnanyi, one of Oster's fellow assessors at the

Fritsch trial, and his brother-in-law, Pastor Dietrich Bonhoeffer, an old friend of Pastor Scheer.

There were several trade union leaders, who had so far succeeded in slipping the Gestapo net; various groups of intellectuals and young aristocrats; even two Gestapo officials, who had become disillusioned with Nazi tactics and who, although unwilling to give up their jobs, were able to provide Oster with invaluable information.

Although Admiral Canaris, Chief of the Abwehr, did not overtly participate in this side of Oster's activities, he was aware of them and gave them his tacit approval. Among the staff of the Abwehr there were several others like Stefan, young men with impeccable family backgrounds, whose education and experience suited them absolutely for Abwehr work. Oster's principal reason for recruiting them, however, was their implacable hatred for the Nazis.

With General Beck's resignation came a link with the Army vital for any *coup d'état*. The Army possessed the manpower, the arms and the organization which individuals like Stefan and other civilian groups — like the Jews, the Church, intellectuals, socialists, even the aristocracy — lacked.

General Beck might have left the Wehrmacht, but he retained many contacts — and old friends. Released from his oath, he could do far more than previously to urge them to obey their consciences rather than the Führer. He was able to give Oster the names of generals who were opposed to Hitler's military policies. These included General von Witzleben, General Hoepner and General Halder, Beck's replacement as Chief of Army General Staff and the man who had recommended Oster's reinstatement after his scandalous love affair.

One of General Halder's first actions after taking office was to ask Colonel Oster to report immediately to the War Ministry. Peter von Biederstein was not present at the meeting. Had he been, he would have been very surprised to hear Halder expressing total disapproval of Hitler's war plans and demanding to know what preparations had been made for a *coup d'état*.

After that, events moved quickly and a plan was set up. General Halder arranged for OKW, the military High Command, to give him advance notice of Hitler's attack on Czechoslovakia, whereupon the conspirators would arrest Hitler and bring him before the People's Court, on the charge that he was exceeding his powers in leading Germany into a European war and was, therefore, unfit to govern.

Within a matter of weeks, Stefan's life had become more exciting and more dangerous than he could ever have envisaged. Five years after the book-burning, his hopes seemed finally to stand a chance of coming true and, what was more, he was at the centre of the plot to rid Germany of Hitler for ever. He spent every waking hour in his new office and it was often past midnight when he returned to the Quadriga. Sometimes he did not come home at all, but slept on a camp bed in his office.

That autumn of 1938, which had promised such happiness with Stefan's return, was turning into a nightmare for Viktoria. Far from having her son to herself, she had lost him already to the Abwehr. Night after night, she lay awake, waiting for the sound of his footsteps, fearful for his safety.

Benno had no patience. 'For God's sake, Vicki, he's a grown man and he has a job to do. We may find ourselves at war any moment.'

'That's what I'm afraid of. Benno, Stefi's right at the centre of things.'

'Of the administration, maybe, but not of the fighting. Be thankful for that. At the Tirpitz Ufer, he's in no physical danger, not as he would be if he were on active service.'

In her heart of hearts, Viktoria knew he was right, but that did not stop her worrying.

The Nuremberg Rally commenced in the new stadium designed by Speer. Thousands of soldiers, airmen and sailors paraded through the streets and onto the Zeppelin field, followed by the Hitler Youth, brownshirted SA men and black-uniformed SS. The narrow streets of Nuremberg shook with the passage of heavy tanks, whilst overhead, wave after wave of the new Luftwaffe flew by in perfect formation. At night, a hundred and thirty searchlights pierced the heavens to a height of twenty-five thousand feet. It was the most massive and spectacular demonstration yet of German strength.

While the world held its breath and waited to learn Hitler's intentions, there was frantic activity in political, diplomatic and military circles, a frenetic crossing of borders, exchanging of letters and telephone calls.

On 12 September, the last day of the Rally, Hitler spoke.

He demanded justice for the Sudeten-Germans and vowed that if his demand was not met, Germany would see that justice was done. But, abusive and warlike though his words were, pouring vitriol on the Czech State and its President, Hitler did not make the feared declaration of war.

The atmosphere grew ever more tense. Two days later, diplomatic and intelligence circles hummed with the news that Neville Chamberlain was going to Berchtesgaden to meet Hitler. His mind in a whirl, his eyes red from lack of sleep, Stefan encountered Mortimer in the hotel foyer when he got home early on the morning of the 15th. 'Mortimer, do you think Chamberlain will succeed?'

Mortimer's face, too, was haggard. 'He's no match for Hitler. He's the wrong man — and he comes too late. He should have given Hitler an ultimatum back in May.'

More soldiers were called up and trainloads of troops moved towards the east, among them Hans König. To Luise's dismay, Sepp again flew off to the Czech border. Chamberlain returned to London and, a week later, went back to Germany, this time to meet Hitler at Bad Godesberg on the Rhine. Mortimer went there to report on the outcome of the meeting.

On Friday, 23 September, the headlines screamed: GODESBERG TALKS FAIL! CZECHS MOBILIZE! The hotel guests scanned the papers anxiously, gathering in small, worried groups, talking in muted voices. Later editions reported that there was hope, after all, provided the Czechs pulled their troops out of the Sudetenland by 1 October and ceded the territory to Germany. If not, Germany had no alternative but to march in and take it by force. Faced with this ultimatum, Chamberlain returned again to London.

It was a beautiful weekend, the last hot weather Berlin would know until the spring. Many people drove out to the countryside or strolled through the parks. Longingly, Viktoria thought of Heiligensee, but neither Stefan nor Benno would accompany her while such danger hung in the air.

On Monday evening, Hitler addressed a huge rally at the Sportpalast. 'I have assured Herr Chamberlain that the German people want nothing but peace. I have further assured him, and repeat it here, that, if this problem is solved, there exists no further territorial problem for Germany in Europe. And I have assured him also that I shall then have no further interest in the Czechoslovak State. And that will be guaranteed. We don't want any Czechs!' He spat out this last dismissive comment in a tone of utter contempt.

On Tuesday, Chamberlain addressed the British people. At the Hotel Quadriga, people huddled in their rooms, their ears close to their radio receivers, listening to the clear, well-modulated voice of the Englishman, contrasting so strongly to Hitler's histrionics the previous evening.

'I would not hesitate to pay even a third visit to Germany if I thought it would do any good. I am myself a man of peace to the depths of my soul. Armed conflict between nations is a nightmare to me; but if I were convinced that any nation had made up its mind to dominate the world by fear of its force, I should feel that it must be resisted...'

It was clear that Hitler was pushing the peace-loving Chamberlain too far.

That evening, a military parade took place in Berlin. From Unter den Linden came the rumble and clank of tanks lurching through the Brandenburg Gate, the all too familiar strident brassy sound of military music accompanying the regular crunch of marching boots. People hurried to the windows, anger and dismay clearly etched on their faces. One or two even raised their fists. The soldiers themselves did not look happy as they passed.

It was almost midnight when Peter arrived in the bar with a couple of fellow officers. They, too, looked tired and worried. When questioned about the probability of war, Peter replied, 'This is a war nobody wants — certainly not the Army.' His colleagues nodded.

'Can't it be stopped?' Viktoria asked desperately.

'Only the politicians can stop it now,' Peter told her soberly.

At the Tirpitz Ufer, reports flooded in from Abwehr agents all over Europe. British children were being evacuated to the country, trenches were being dug and there were rumours that the British Fleet had been mobilized. French armies were moving towards the French-Italian border, where the Italians were doing nothing to stop them. Not even Mussolini apparently supported Hitler. Yugoslavia and Rumania were threatening to attack Hungary if she helped Germany against Czechoslovakia. President Roosevelt made a personal appeal to Hitler to keep the peace.

In Czechoslovakia an army of a million men was preparing for action. The first refugees from the border provinces reached Berlin.

Hitler's deadline of 1 October was three days away. Among Oster's conspirators there were frenzied meetings. That night, nobody slept. In the morning, they learned Hitler had refused Chamberlain's latest offer. General Halder agreed that this was tantamount to proof that Hitler wanted war. The time had come to act.

Then Mussolini intervened with an offer of mediation. On Thursday, 29 September, Chamberlain flew to Germany for the third time and met with Hitler, Mussolini and the French Prime Minister, Edouard Daladier, at Munich.

Next day, the world learned the terms of the Munich Agreement. The Sudetenland was to be evacuated within ten days and an international commission would determine the final borders.

Throughout Germany — throughout most of the world — there was jubilation. Newspapers showed photographs of a radiant Neville Chamberlain, with his now famous bowler hat and furled umbrella, returning to London to be hailed as a conquering hero. From a window at Number 10 Downing Street, he addressed the cheering crowds beneath him with the triumphant words, 'I believe it is peace in our time.'

In Berlin, the mood was ecstatic. It was as if a tremendous weight had been lifted from everyone's shoulders. War no longer threatened. Germany had won another great victory. With not a drop of German blood being shed, the Sudetenland — like Austria — had become part of Greater Germany. Within six months, the Third Reich had grown by ten million inhabitants. And, far from opposing Germany's actions, Britain and France had helped Hitler.

That Saturday, 1 October, the day the German troops had been due to cross the borders, the city gave itself over to wild abandonment. There were demonstrations and processions and, at night, anti-aircraft searchlights sent arced beams twenty-five thousand feet into the air, forming a cathedral of light over the entire city. At the Hotel Quadriga, everyone crowded onto the balcony to watch the spectacle.

Standing behind his family, his face in shadow, Stefan tried to understand what had happened. He had the feeling that Mussolini and Chamberlain had somehow played straight into Hitler's hands. Of course, he was glad war had been averted, but, because of the foreign politicians' actions, Colonel Oster and General Beck had been robbed of the opportunity to arrest Hitler. The Sudetenland might have been liberated — but Germany was still enslaved.

At the end of the week, the English papers printed extracts from a speech made by Winston Churchill to the House of Commons, a speech which his fellow MPs had greeted with boos and jeers. 'We have sustained a total and unmitigated defeat... We are in the midst of a disaster of the first magnitude... And do hot suppose that this is the end. This is only the beginning. This is only the first sip, the first foretaste of a bitter cup which will be proffered to us year by year unless, by a supreme recovery of moral health and martial vigour, we arise again and take our stand for freedom as in the olden time.'

Stefan showed the paper to Mortimer. 'No one wants to hear him, but he is right!'

Mortimer nodded bleakly. 'He once said to me, "A prophet is not without honour, except in his own country." One day, they will wish they had paid more heed.'

CHAPTER NINE

Baron Heinrich's eightieth birthday fell on the Saturday exactly two weeks after the liberation of the Sudetenland. Freed from the threat of war, the Hotel Quadriga prepared for a party to surpass all previous functions ever held within its prestigious portals, for the guest of honour at the banquet was to be the Führer himself!

Stefan was dreading it and attended only because Viktoria begged him not to let her down. 'There are some things one has to do whether one wants to or not,' she said. 'It is your grandfather's birthday. Like me, you must put on a brave face and forget your prejudices.'

From all over Germany, the elite of society thronged to Berlin. All day long, visitors poured through the revolving doors and were received in the Jubilee Room, where the Baron, in his SS uniform, sat enthroned in his massive, carved oak winged chair, Gottlieb Linke hovering subserviently behind him, Ernst and Benno to either side.

Trudi, Werner and Norbert came with Ernst from Essen. Trudi had grown very fat and prefaced every sentence with, 'The Führer says…' Werner, twenty-one now, was a photo image of his father and grandfather at the same age. He was showing a keen financial acumen, and, after the party, was going to stay for a while with the Baron.

Norbert was eighteen. Very much a Kraus in looks, his rather plain features were redeemed by a mischievous smile and grey eyes which, most unusually for a Kraus, positively twinkled. Just completing his first year with the Todt Organization, he was involved in building the West Wall in the Rhineland.

Monika and Hans came from Fürstenmark. It was the first time Stefan had seen his sister for nearly two years and he was pleasantly surprised at the change in her. Fürstenmark seemed to have quietened her down and, instead of being the spiteful little girl he remembered, she was really quite grown-up, although she still persisted in an almost idolatrous Hitler-worship which he found quite nauseating.

The rest of the birthday guests arrived towards seven. They gathered in the Palm Garden Room, where they paid their respects to the Baron, then as the glass-roofed room reverberated to a clamour of excited voices, they waited for the high point of the evening — the Führer's arrival.

Field Marshal Göring was the first of the Nazi hierarchy to appear, beaming effusively and looking more than ever like Baron Heinrich's son, as he almost burst out of his flamboyant uniform. The Propaganda Minister and his wife were next: Dr Goebbels, small, dark and dragging his lame foot, Magda Goebbels unexpectedly elegant.

Then there was a volley of loud Heil Hitlers from the foyer and all conversation stopped in the Palm Garden Room. A forest of arms shot into the air and the room echoed to strident shouts of 'Heil Hitler!' Gottlieb Linke and Ernst prised the Baron out of his chair and, followed by his SS bodyguard, Hitler approached him. 'Congratulations on your birthday, Baron.' There was no warmth in Hitler's voice or in his eyes.

'Thank you, mein Führer. I am honoured that you could spare some of your precious time to share in our celebrations.'

The birthday guests thronged closer in fawning admiration. From the back of the room, Stefan observed the scene. It was the first time he had ever been in the same room as the Führer; had ever seen at close quarters the man whom he held guilty above all others for the terrible ills that had beset his country; whom, a few short weeks ago, he had been conspiring to arrest. Nothing he saw made him like Hitler any better. The Führer's smile was forced and he seemed ill-at-ease in his elegant surroundings. He glanced impatiently at his watch.

Benno noticed the gesture, withdrew from the crowd and murmured something to Philip Krosyk. A few moments later, the restaurant manager intoned, 'Mein Führer, Herr-Feldmarschall, Herren Generale, Herren Admirale, Herren Offiziere, lords, gentlemen and ladies, dinner is served.'

They proceeded into the restaurant and took their places, Hitler and the Baron at the head of the horse-shoe formation of tables, the others seated according to their rank. To his relief, Stefan found himself in a family group with Sepp, Luise, Ilse and — he stared in amazement — a ravishingly beautiful young woman in an ivory gown, with thick, waving, ash-blonde hair and the biggest, bluest eyes he had ever seen.

After that, the banquet passed in a daze. One course followed another, but Stefan had no idea what he ate. Different wines were served, but he scarcely tasted them. All around him, people were talking, but Stefan was aware only of this utterly transformed Christa von Biederstein, too far away for him to talk to, but smiling at him occasionally across the table.

The only time he paid any attention to the rest of the company was when the meal eventually finished and the Baron rose to make his speech. 'Many of you were present at my last birthday celebration here at the Quadriga a decade ago. Shortly after that, the world suffered a Depression and Germany knew the misery of having six million people out of work. But that is ancient history. Today, we have become again one of the most prosperous nations in Europe, if not the world, the envy of our neighbours, so much so that they are begging to join the glorious Third Reich!

'Two things have combined to make Germany great again. One is industry. We, the German people, have never ceased to work. Work is our religion! But hard work without leadership is nothing. In our hour of greatest need, there was given to us the greatest leader the world has ever known, our Führer, Herr Hitler!'

With one accord, the Baron's guests rose to their feet and raised their arms, shouting, 'Heil Hitler! Heil Hitler! Heil Hitler!'

When the cheering ended and Gottlieb Linke had helped his employer be seated again, Hitler stood up. 'It is seldom that I find myself in agreement with anything a certain Mr Churchill says, but on this occasion, I am going to repeat his exact words from a speech he made recently to the English House of Commons. "Do not suppose this is the end. This is only the beginning. This is the first sip."'

Again, the room surged to its feet. 'Heil Hitler! Heil Hitler! Heil Hitler!' Stefan glanced at Christa. Her lips formed the words, but to his joy, she was looking not at the Führer, but at him.

Hitler glanced at his watch again, said something to the Baron and stood up. With obvious reluctance, Göring followed suit. Dr Goebbels explained, 'Pressing matters of state still await us.' To loud applause, they made their exit, escorted by Benno and Ernst.

Soon after this, the rest of the guests moved back into the Palm Garden Room, where Christian Engel and his small orchestra were playing light music. Mortimer appeared at Stefan's side. 'We couldn't have been given a clearer warning than that,' he murmured in a low voice. '*This is only the beginning...* Presumably he was referring to the rest of Czechoslovakia.'

At that moment, Stefan couldn't care less about Czechoslovakia, the resistance, Germany, or even Hitler. 'Yes, I suppose you're right,' he muttered and hurried towards Christa, who was standing with her mother just inside the entrance to the Palm Garden Room.

Remembering his manners, he greeted Ilse first, then he took Christa's lace glove in his hand and bowed over it, clicking his heels together. 'Christa, how nice to see you again.'

'And you, Stefan. It's such a long time since we last met.' Her even teeth gleamed white against her tanned skin.

She was very petite, reaching only to his shoulder and he had to lean over slightly to catch her words. A tantalizing fragrance of gardenia hung about her hair.

'Ilse, you're back from Switzerland at last!' a woman's voice screeched. 'Just in time for the little concert I'm giving in aid of the Winter Relief. You will play the piano for us, won't you, dear?'

'Hedda! Yes, of course I'll play.' Ilse turned her back on Stefan and Christa.

'You've been in Switzerland?' Stefan asked Christa.

'At finishing school in Lausanne.'

'When did you come back?'

'A fortnight ago.' A natural shade of lipstick accentuated her rosebud mouth. A thin dusting of powder tried, in vain, to conceal a few light freckles on her nose. 'Did you enjoy your time in Oxford?'

He did not want to talk about Oxford. He wanted to take her in his arms and kiss her. 'Yes, very much.'

'It's very interesting to travel. But it's nice to come home, isn't it?' She gazed up at him from those amazing eyes and smiled. 'I missed Berlin while I was in Lausanne.'

Stefan felt — hoped — wished with all his heart — that what she was really saying was that she had missed him. But why should she? The orchestra started to play a waltz. 'Would you like to dance?'

'Thank you.'

He put his hand under her elbow, her skin silky soft to his touch, and guided her across the crowded room on to the parquet floor. Then his arm was circling her slim waist and her hand was in his and they were floating away to the sound of the music.

Mortimer smiled ruefully and turned to discover Viktoria standing beside him, gazing at Stefan and Christa with an expression almost akin to fear. 'Viktoria, what's the matter?'

She did not reply, but reached into her purse with trembling fingers and pulled out her cigarette case. 'Allow me.' Mortimer lit her cigarette. She did not even look at him, but continued staring at Stefan and Christa. Then she turned on her heel and strode across the foyer. Poor Viktoria, he thought. It had never occurred to her that her son would fall in love, that she must one day lose him to another woman.

Christa was not the first woman in Stefan's life. Tony Callearn, titled, wealthy and extrovert, had made sure of that. 'Make hay while the sun shines,' had been his favourite motto and, where Tony was concerned, the sun was always shining. Very few of the women to whom he had introduced Stefan would have met with the approval of either set of parents — for the most part they were hospital nurses, secretarial students and even, occasionally, shopgirls — but they were good dancers and amusing company.

At college balls, Stefan had met several of his fellow undergraduates' sisters and even believed himself to be in love with one, a pert little brunette called Molly Harris. As the first flush of dawn had come up over Oxford, he had walked with her beside the

Cherwell and taken her in his arms and kissed her. Then she had discovered he was German and the romance had abruptly ended. Later, he had learned she was Jewish.

But all his Oxford adventures were paled into insignificance by Christa. The day after the Baron's birthday party, he took her to the Botanical Gardens, where in the late autumn sunshine they strolled arm in arm, paying little attention to the plants and trees, but learning a lot about each other. They started with the advantage of having England in common and, although Christa had only been a little girl during her father's posting there, she still remembered London very well. It transpired she was also very fond of reading and art and the afternoon sped quickly by talking about books and art galleries. All too soon, dusk fell and reluctantly they made their way back to the Park-Strasse. 'There is a recital of Schubert's *Winterreise* on Wednesday,' Stefan said. 'Would you like to come to it?'

'I should enjoy it very much.'

'I'll call for you at seven.'

That evening, too, was a great success and when they arrived back at Christa's home, Ilse invited him in for coffee. 'I am so pleased you two are becoming friends,' she said fondly, as they sat next to each other on the settee. 'Peter, dear, don't you think it's nice that Stefan and Christa have so much in common?'

Peter grunted noncommittally behind his newspaper and Stefan knew a moment of misgiving. Christa's father had always made it very clear that he considered Viktoria and Benno his social inferiors. Once, Stefan had even heard him refer to his mother as a mere sweetmaker's daughter, not realizing that he had been overheard. Then he consoled himself that Peter's opinion was unimportant. All that mattered was that Christa should love him. And, by the way she gazed at him, he was sure she did.

That weekend, however, he was in for a shock. 'I'm taking Christa to the National Gallery this afternoon,' he told his parents on Saturday morning at breakfast. 'I'd like to invite her to dinner afterwards. May we join you and Grandmama here at the Quadriga?'

The colour drained from Viktoria's face. 'I don't know what you see in Christa,' she snapped. 'She's just an empty-headed chit of a girl with big blue eyes.'

Stefan stared at her in amazement. 'Mama, why on earth do you say that? Far from being empty-headed, she's very intelligent...'

Benno cleared his throat. 'I think your mother means that Christa is very young. She's only just out of school.'

'You wouldn't know it to talk to her. Perhaps it's because she went to finishing school. That's why I hoped we could dine with you — so that you could get to know her better.'

Viktoria poured herself some coffee, her fingers shaking so much that the coffee pot rattled against her cup. Benno glanced at her anxiously, then said, 'Yes, son, of course Christa can come to dinner.'

In the event, the evening went off quite well. Although Viktoria said very little, Benno was a courteous host and Ricarda was clearly captivated by Christa, helping the conversation considerably by reminiscing about her old memories of Fürstenmark and London.

However, when Stefan returned from taking Christa home and went up to his room, he found his mother waiting for him. 'Stefi, I beg you, please don't get too fond of Christa.'

Stefan sighed. He knew his mother did not really like Peter and could only assume she was extending her antagonism to Peter's daughter. Rather than get embroiled in an emotional argument, he said, 'Don't worry, Mama. After all, I've really only known her a few days.'

She bit her lip, then nodded. 'I'm only warning you because I love you, Stefi. I don't want you to be hurt.'

The following afternoon, Stefan took Christa to the Grunewald. Hand in hand, they walked through the forest to the edge of the lake and there, Stefan told Christa in faltering tones that he loved her. 'It's as though you have always been a part of me and I have only just recognized it. When I saw you at Grandfather's birthday party, everything seemed to fall into place and a bit of me that had always been empty was suddenly filled — and I became a complete person. I love you, Christa. I love you now and I shall love you for ever.'

She gazed innocently up at him. 'I love you, too, Stefan.'

He took her in his arms and gave her a chaste kiss. 'My darling Christa, I promise you I shall do everything I can to make you happy.'

After that, everyone and everything — even his work, that had seemed so vitally important — took second place to Christa. He did not work any less diligently or any fewer hours, but he was no longer doing it for Germany or England's sake, but because he wanted to make the world a safer place for Christa.

The age they lived in was not a romantic one. At school and in the Hitler Youth, children were taught that the purpose of sex was to have children. There was an institution called *Lebensborn*, whose sole function was to find suitable partners for SS men to breed blond Aryan boys for Hitler. Monika and Hans were true products of their time.

Stefan and Christa were different. Both were romantics, who had the advantage of having lived outside Germany in a world where people still believed in old-fashioned love. They had read the great romantic novels. Unlike most of their contemporaries, they knew *Anna Karenina*, *Madame Bovary* and *Jane Eyre*. Amongst the ugly uniformity surrounding them, they aspired to the sublime — and found it in each other's company.

When the day was over, Stefan rushed out of his office, where Christa was usually waiting for him outside. Then they wandered through the streets, over carpets of russet leaves. The perfume of gardenia. The soughing of the wind through the pine trees in Dahlem. The damp smell of autumn earth under a silver moon. Two figures walking, hand in hand...

Stefan held her hand, but no more. Christa was the daughter of Colonel Count Peter von Biederstein, a ranking General Staff Officer. Much though he longed to, he did not kiss her again, and he made sure she was always home by ten. But after that altercation with his mother, he did not bring Christa to the hotel or mention her name in his parents' presence. On the evenings that he took Christa out, rather than invite a row, he intimated that he was working late.

In the pathetic hope that her words had had some effect, Viktoria convinced herself that her fears had been for nothing. Benno hoped the same. It had been an infatuation. As was the way with young people, there had been a spark that had fizzled and then died.

His parents and the von Biedersteins were not the only ones to be upset by the affair. Because Stefan confided in him, Mortimer knew the romance was far from over, but although he sympathized with young love, he was also impatient with it. Mortimer was more convinced than ever that Hitler was hurtling down the road to war. Why on earth did Stefan have to choose this moment to fall in love — and with Biederstein's daughter?

There were moments that autumn when Professor Ascher felt near to despair. On the slightest pretext, Jews were arrested and sent to concentration camps. Some were released only on the condition that they immediately left Germany. But emigration became even more difficult when a new law, passed in October, ordered that all Jewish passports were stamped with a big red J. There was no hope of sending people across frontiers any more in the hope that neighbouring countries would take them for Aryan tourists. The Jews were marked. They were refugees. Nobody wanted them.

Not only did the Jewish Presidium have the German and Austrian Jews to look after, from September onwards they had to contend with a mass exodus of Jews from Czechoslovakia. Then they were confronted with another problem. In March, the Polish government had passed a law annulling the citizenship of all Jews who had lived abroad for longer than five years, unless they received a special stamp from the Polish consul in their country of residence by 31 October. In Germany, Polish consuls refused to issue that stamp.

When this dreadful piece of information came to the Professor's ears, he was extremely concerned. There were some fifty thousand Polish Jews in Germany. Now they were stateless.

It was dusk on the last Sunday in October and the Professor was walking swiftly down the Kurfürstendamm, when he saw a shuffling procession of men being led along the pavement, handcuffed together in pairs, guarded by police and SS officers. He stepped back into a shop doorway to let them pass.

Beside him, a man asked his companion, 'What have they done?'

'Ach, they're Polish Jews. They're being sent home. And good riddance to them, too.' He spat on the pavement.

Feeling utterly helpless, Professor Ascher stood there a long time after the Poles had disappeared. Stateless men had no home to go to. What would happen to them?

A week later, the newspapers had a sensational story to tell. In Paris, a young student called Herschel Grynszpan had taken the law into his own hands. His parents had been amongst the Polish Jews deported from Hanover and, in revenge, young Grynszpan had tried to assassinate a diplomat at the German Embassy. The diplomat was still alive, but he was seriously injured.

Bethel Ascher read this report and buried his head in his hands. The Nazis would not allow an event like that to pass unnoticed. They would take their revenge somehow.

Two days later, on 9 November, the German diplomat died.

9 November — an historic date. 9 November 1918, a black day, when the Kaiser was overthrown and the first socialist republic was declared in Germany. 9 November 1923, the date of Hitler's Munich Putsch, the first time he had tried to seize power, the beginning of the National Socialist Revolution. 9 November 1938 — the fifteenth anniversary of that great day, when stormtroopers everywhere celebrated their Führer's ultimate victory.

9 November was not a night for peace-loving souls to venture forth. Even Stefan did not see Christa that evening, but stayed home. After supper, he went to his room and wrote a long overdue letter to Tony Callearn. About eleven, there was a knock on his door and his mother came in, her face pale. Stefan waited for her to start lecturing him again about Christa, but instead, she said, 'Stefi, something dreadful is happening. Come and look.'

He followed her through the first floor corridors to the doors leading onto the balcony, where a small group was already gathered. Immediately he heard the noise rising from the street below, a blare of distorted voices through loudhailers, shouts of *'Juda verrecke! Juda verrecke! Juda verrecke!'*, the crash of breaking glass, men chanting: *When Jewish blood flows from the knife...* He peered over the edge of the balcony and saw, a hundred yards up the street, a mob of Hitler Youth and stormtroopers massed in front of a Jewish jewellery shop, throwing bricks at its plate glass windows. 'Has somebody called the police?' he demanded.

'The police are already here,' a man told him heavily. 'Look!'

Stefan looked where he pointed. In the central avenue, looking on and doing nothing, were several policemen.

'Juden 'raus! Juden 'raus! Juden 'raus!' From a neighbouring apartment block came the sound of more breaking glass and a sudden blast of gunfire. The front doors opened and some SS men emerged, dragging a man down the steps and into a waiting van. 'Herr Jakobsohn,' Viktoria muttered.

Suddenly, a beacon of light flared up to the east, from just behind the Castle. 'Fire!' someone called. 'A building's on fire!' 'There's another one over there!' somebody else exclaimed, pointing north. Soon, in all directions, flames were spiralling up into the night sky. Beneath them, the yelling and jeering continued, mingled with screams, shattering glass and the occasional shot. In the distance could be heard the sound of sirens.

'We've got to do something!' Stefan shouted, pushing his way back towards the door.

A hand came down on his shoulder and Benno said, 'No, Stefan, stay here. There's nothing any of us can do.' His face was white and etched with deep lines in the eerie light. 'I think we should go indoors. It's not safe out here.'

Benno gave orders for the bar and public rooms to be closed and the doors to the hotel locked and barred, and requested all guests to go to their rooms. When only the night staff was left, he stood alone in the foyer, listening to the muted sounds of violence permeating the thick glass doors and looking up at the portrait of Hitler.

The Führer was in Munich, celebrating the anniversary of the Beer Hall Putsch. Did he know what was going on in Berlin? Encouraging the Jews to leave Germany was one thing. Arson and shooting was another. No, the Führer could not know. It was just a few hotheads celebrating 9 November. When the Führer found out, heads would roll...

Hasso Annuschek came and stood behind him. 'Herr Benno, I never thought I'd ever see anything like this. Hitler's gone too far this time. Next thing we'll find *our* houses being burned.'

Benno said nothing. Deep in his heart of hearts, he feared Hasso was right, that Hitler not only knew what was going on, but condoned the action. With heavy steps, he ascended the staircase. For ten years, he had placed his faith in Hitler. For the first time, he wondered if he might have made a mistake.

In Dahlem, Klara Scheer read a book, while Professor Ascher played a game of solitary chess. At ten o'clock, they turned off the lights and retired to their respective bedrooms. Bethel lay awake in the dark, listening to a distant clock strike the hours — eleven, midnight, one… He had just dozed off when Klara shook him awake. 'Bethel, listen! Can you hear them?'

In the distance were chanting voices: '*Juda verrecke! Juda verrecke! Juda verrecke!*' There was the sound of broken glass, of people screaming, of men shouting.

He reached out to turn on the bedside light, but Klara restrained him, whispering urgently, 'Bethel, you must hide.'

He was already out of bed, pulling on his outdoor clothes over his pyjamas. 'No, I won't hide! I won't run away from these louts.'

'Bethel, I stood by and watched my husband be arrested. I will not allow the same thing to happen again. Your people need you.'

He saw the sense in what she was saying, but he didn't like it. 'And you?'

The shouting drew closer. 'I am an Aryan,' Klara said bitterly. She grabbed hold of his arm and pushed him into a wardrobe. Then she made his bed and, with pounding heart, waited for the stormtroopers.

They announced their presence by ramming the front door and immediately started to lay about the furniture in the hall. Klara heard the sound of a mirror shattering. She picked up her handbag, belted her dressing gown tightly, emerged from her bedroom, turned on the lights and, standing at the top of the stairs, demanded authoritatively, 'What on earth is going on?'

She was in time to see two brown-uniformed thugs disappear into the living room. In the hall, a knife poised, ready to slash into one of the Professor's prized Expressionists was a tall young man of about twenty in black SS uniform. 'Get out of the way, Jew-whore.'

Klara Scheer descended the stairs, her head held high, her hands clenched in her pockets, so that he should not see them trembling. 'Be careful what you say, young man. I am not a Jew.'

She looked exactly what she was — a well-built, Aryan, farmer's daughter from Hesse. Doubt flickered across the SS man's face. 'That's not what we were told!' he growled, his knife poised level with her capacious bosom.

'Put that knife down, young man. If you don't get out of here immediately, I shall report you to the police.' She strode purposefully towards him, hands on hips.

Through the open door, outside in the road, she could see a policeman standing motionless, surrounded by a few horrified spectators. She pushed past the SS man, screaming, 'Help! I'm an honest, God-fearing woman! My house is being destroyed! I've done no wrong! I'm not a Jew! I'm an Aryan! Help! Help! Help!' The SS man came after her, knife in hand.

'Here, Officer, that's Frau Scheer!' one of the bystanders said. 'She's no Jew.'

'No, Frau Scheer's not a Jew.' There was a faint chorus of agreement. There was a crash and a huge porcelain vase hurtled through a window, smashing into smithereens on the stone path.

Klara brandished her handbag and turned hysterical. 'I've got my papers. I shall report you all. I shan't let you get away with this!'

'Once the police protected German citizens,' an onlooker jeered.

'Maybe you'd better move along,' the policeman told the SS man.

The SS man hesitated for a moment, then went back into the house. A few moments later, he re-emerged with his two henchmen. As the small crowd watched in silence, they marched on up the road.

'It's disgraceful, that's what it is,' a man muttered. 'Smashing up people's houses and the police just look on.'

'Get back to your homes,' the policeman ordered, 'or you'll all be arrested. Hurry up!'

The people moved away into the darkness. Klara walked up the path, through the battered door and, treading over pieces of broken china, books and furniture, went upstairs to release the Professor. It was dawn before they finished clearing the wreckage. Then, blinds drawn, they sat in the kitchen, sipping coffee, wondering what to do.

Mortimer scarcely slept that night. He got up at dawn, dressed, went downstairs, past a morose hall porter and out into the bleak Berlin morning. He wanted to see what had gone on during the night and, even more importantly, he had to find out if Professor Ascher was all right. Not trusting the hotel's switchboard, he preferred to make his telephone call from a public box.

He crunched his way over pavements strewn with broken glass and goods from Jewish shops. The smell of smoke still hung acrid in the air. The first trams were clanking through the streets, and people were emerging from underground stations on their way to work. They picked their way over the debris, staring down at the ground. Nobody even attempted to take any of the shop merchandise lying about.

He found a telephone kiosk and rang Professor Ascher's number. Klara Scheer answered. Yes, she replied guardedly, they were both all right. There had been some disturbance in the night, but she and her cousin had not been hurt. Relieved, Mortimer promised to come and see them soon and returned to the hotel.

In the restaurant, a few people sat in silence, placing their breakfast orders in muted voices, hiding behind their morning papers. Nobody seemed quite able to look another in the face. The newspapers reported similar scenes to that which they had witnessed on Unter den Linden as having taken place throughout Germany. They called the night's events a spontaneous demonstration of the German people to the news of the diplomat's murder in Paris.

Mortimer had no appetite. He gulped a cup of coffee, lit a cigarette and made his way into the foyer. Small groups of people gathered near him. Voices muttered: 'It's bad.' 'It's a disgrace.' 'Spontaneous demonstration of the people. What people, I'd like to know?' 'It was

343

the SS.' 'It makes me feel ashamed to be German.' 'But what could we have done…?'

Viktoria and Stefan appeared, both showing signs of sleepless nights. 'Mortimer, do you think Professor Ascher is all right?' Stefan asked anxiously.

'Yes, I've just telephoned him.'

Viktoria said, 'Mortimer, if there is anything we can do for the Professor, you will tell me, won't you? And I mean that — anything.'

'Does Benno say the same?'

She was silent for a moment. 'It's as if last night opened Benno's eyes to what has been going on. He's dreadfully shocked.'

'I seem to remember him saying he approved of Hitler's anti-Semitic policies,' Mortimer commented drily.

Kristallnacht — the Night of Broken Glass — was how that 9 November became known. On this occasion, Bill Wallace did not attempt to water down Mortimer's report. In fact, he added his own biting editorial comment, utterly condemning what he described as a totally unwarranted and bestial attack on German Jewry. President Roosevelt recalled the American Ambassador to Washington, where public opinion raged against the Nazis. At long last, the world was waking up to the realities of Nazism. But, Mortimer thought angrily, apart from making futile token gestures, they were still doing nothing about it.

The initial shock over, two vital questions immediately came to the fore. At a rough estimate, repairing the night's damage was going to cost some twenty-five million marks, five million of it for broken glass. Who was going to pay for the damage incurred? And where were the replacement glass and other building materials going to come from? German industry was already having problems satisfying the quotas of Göring's Four-Year Plan. It could not cope with this extra demand.

Baron Heinrich fulminated at length on the subject to Benno. 'The insurance claims we've already received are sufficient to bankrupt our insurance companies if we have to pay out on them. And the cost of importing glass and other materials is going to be prohibitive. Göring's got to do something.'

Göring did. Two days after Kristallnacht, two new laws were passed. One eliminated the Jews from German economic life. They were no longer allowed to run their own businesses or have an executive role in any German company. The second decreed: 'The hostile attitude of Jewry towards the German people and Reich, which does not shrink even from committing cowardly murder, necessitates determined resistance and harsh penalty.' It demanded from the Jews a payment of one billion marks compensation for Kristallnacht.

Benno was still suffering misgivings about Kristallnacht. 'The Jews suffered the damage,' he said dubiously. 'They didn't cause it.'

'Well, *I* certainly didn't!' his father stated. 'So I don't see why I should pay for it.'

'Apart from any moral implications, I don't see how the Jews are going to raise a billion marks, especially after the recent legislation.'

The Baron looked at him coldly. 'That's their problem. Those who had any sense got out long ago.'

A few days later, two senior Gestapo officers arrived at the hotel. In Benno's office, they explained to him that a new law had been passed banning Jews from a number of public places, including hotels and restaurants. 'You will put a notice up to that effect,' he was ordered. 'If any Jew tries to break the law, you will notify us immediately.'

To argue was pointless, so Benno duly put up the notice and was immediately attacked by Viktoria and Stefan. 'This is a private hotel,' Viktoria stated angrily. 'We should be allowed to have who we like here as guests!'

'We don't ban dogs — but now we suddenly ban Jews!' Stefan added furiously. 'Jews are people, Papa! How can you do such a thing?'

Helplessly, Benno retorted, 'I don't want to do it, but what choice do I have? If I refuse, the authorities can take away our licences and force us to shut down. In any case, we have had no Jewish guests for a long time.'

It was true. Since the departure of Herr Roth and other wealthy Austrian Jews, there had been no Jewish guests. Since Kristallnacht, no Berlin Jews had been near the hotel. So the notice remained, although they were all uncomfortable about it.

Kraus Industries profited greatly from Kristallnacht. Not only were most of its insurance losses covered by reinsurance, but through the Aryanization Programme it acquired some more extremely viable Jewish businesses.

Benno's conscience was still troubling him. 'Will you keep the employees on, even though they are Jewish?' he asked his father.

'Why not? I've got nothing against Jews. They need work and I need workers. It's the best possible deal. We all profit from it.'

Benno felt rather better.

The Baron did not bother to tell him that he was paying his Jewish workers a fraction of the wages he was paying Aryans.

Gradually, names reached the Jewish Presidium of Jews who had disappeared during Kristallnacht. The lists grew ever-longer, soon reaching ten, twenty thousand men, whom the Gestapo had taken away to concentration camps, leaving terrified wives and children behind. Then the Gestapo returned and seized what possessions the families had left — car, jewellery, camera, antiques, savings.

Bethel Ascher knew he had been fortunate to have Klara Scheer to protect him. Compared to incarceration in a concentration camp, selling his Passover silver and his other valuables to raise money for the billion dollar fine did not seem too high a price to pay. It was the first time Jews had ever had to finance a pogrom — but, with it, those who remained had bought freedom.

That this freedom was an illusion soon became apparent. More legislation was swiftly passed, banning Jewish children from all schools, public swimming baths, parks and recreation grounds. Jews were forbidden to go to theatres, concert halls and art galleries. They were not allowed to eat in public restaurants or stay in hotels. Their businesses were taken away from them and those who still had jobs were appallingly treated. A series of special dues, taxes and fines were imposed, systematically robbing them of their remaining assets. And without any money, they could not hope to pay the necessary levies to obtain emigration visas.

All remaining power was taken away from the Jewish Presidium. The Jewish leaders were informed that their activities would be placed under Heydrich's authority and would come under the supervision of the Gestapo. The Jews had lost control of the fate of their own people.

Now, more than ever, Mortimer's help was needed. With Bill Wallace finally on his side, he was more successful in finding homes and jobs abroad for the emigrant Jews. In a massive ADOPT A JEWISH CHILD campaign in the *New York News*, Bill managed to find homes for five hundred children.

But their parents were forced to stay behind. For them, a link was established between the Arendt Bank in London and Mortimer's Berlin bank. Nobody could touch monies paid into the American's account, nor could they prevent him spending his cash drawings how he liked, provided valuable marks did not leave Germany. Uncontrolled by the Gestapo, financial assistance continued to be given to the Berlin Jews who could not leave the country.

At the end of November, Bethel Ascher's landlord served notice on him to leave his house in Dahlem. One of Klara's sons provided her with an apartment in Wilmersdorf — but the Professor could not accompany her. Both Mortimer and Klara did their best to persuade him to join the emigrants, but the Professor adamantly refused.

Survival, in his mind, meant more than saving his own skin — it meant saving others, particularly those who were younger than himself, whose lives were still ahead of them. Too many people were taking the easy way out — either fleeing with the few possessions they could salvage or by committing suicide from desperation. 'If I go to England it means one entry visa less for a more worthy person.'

'But you can do more in London by alerting the English to what is happening here,' Klara said.

'Others are already doing that better than I. My concern is for those who are left behind.'

She put her hand on his. 'You are a very good man, Bethel Ascher.'

'I am a very fortunate one. It is not given to many men in my position to have friends like yourself and Mortimer Allen. You have endangered your own lives for me. And for that also I must stay. So long as you remain in Germany, I shall too. You go to your new apartment, Klara. I shall find a home.'

He learned of two rooms to rent in the Jewish district near the Hackescher Markt and, within a week, he had sold the furniture he did not need and moved into the Rosenthaler-Strasse.

Mortimer brought Stefan news of the Professor and Frau Scheer, but Stefan did not go to see them. 'Why not?' Mortimer asked bluntly.

'I'm kept very busy at work,' Stefan muttered.

'There is always the evening.'

'I see Christa then. I could hardly take her with me.'

'Are you ashamed of the Professor?'

'No, of course not, but…' In fact, Stefan was embarrassed. He was one of the fortunate ones — a Jochum-Kraus, an Aryan. He could come and go where he pleased. Whether he liked it or not, he was one of the master race. But a sign suddenly prevented Professor Ascher, a guest of forty years, from entering the Hotel Quadriga.

He' imagined that the Professor must blame him for what was happening and felt guilty because he was doing nothing to stop the excesses against the Jews. But what could he do? He was still fond of the Professor — but now they were separated by a great divide.

Mortimer sighed. 'I think I understand. However, remember one thing. Good friends like Bethel and Klara are hard to come by.'

Mortimer's words increased his feeling of guilt and, after this brief conversation, Stefan found himself avoiding his company as well. Only with Christa did he feel totally at ease. She seemed to know how he felt without him needing to explain things to her. She made no demands on his conscience. She accepted and loved him exactly as he was.

Monika and Hans were married on 17 December. They made a handsome couple, Viktoria thought, as she watched them stand before the altar. Hans wore army uniform, while Monika, bigger built than Luise and therefore unable to wear Ricarda's wedding dress, was a froth of white lace and taffeta. She had asked Christa and her old schoolfriend, Beate, to be her bridesmaids and they looked quite delightful in peach sateen, with garlands of mock orange blossom in their hair.

Pastor König had obtained permission to conduct the ceremony and gave a stirring address on the union of true love and patriotic duty, ending with the fervent hope that the marriage would be very fruitful and that Monika would be awarded with the Motherhood Cross.

From the pew behind her, Viktoria heard a slight snigger, which changed into a cough, and turned in time to see Norbert burying his face in his handkerchief. Then Lili started to cry and Pastor König cleared his throat pointedly, while Luise tried to quieten the little girl. Stefan whispered, 'It seems the Pastor prefers the theory of babies to the reality,' and it was Viktoria's turn to stifle a laugh.

Eventually, Lili grew quiet and the service continued and then they were all streaming out of the church into the frosty Berlin afternoon. A photographer took some pictures, but it was too cold to stand around long, so they got into the waiting limousines and drove back to the Quadriga.

Unlike other functions, Viktoria had made sure she had a say in the arrangements for her daughter's wedding reception. The hotel was already festively decorated for Christmas, so in contrast, she had asked Herr Krosyk to arrange the tables in the Jubilee Room to form a heart with a heart-shaped bank of pink and white flowers as a centrepiece.

Against the silver decor, the room looked stunningly attractive and there were many appreciative murmurs from the guests as they entered. Even the Baron managed a grunt of approval, while Ilse and Christa were most effusive in their praise. Luise, carrying a now sleeping Lili, laughed, 'Why, Vicki, you must have hidden artistic talents.' And Monika, for whom Viktoria had made so much effort, kissed her mother and said, 'Thank you, Mama. It looks absolutely beautiful.'

After an excellent dinner, the guests moved into the ballroom. Viktoria followed them slowly and stood for a moment at the doorway, watching the dancers swirling round to the music. Mothers were supposed to feel sad when their daughters married, but she had never really understood Monika. Indeed, her main feeling was relief that her daughter was now Hans's responsibility.

'It's strange when one's children grow up, isn't it?' Ricarda said.

Viktoria nodded. How shocked her mother would be if she knew her true thoughts.

'It will be Stefan's turn next,' Ricarda went on. 'It's funny how times have changed. Do you remember when you were a little girl and so infatuated with Peter? A marriage between a von Biederstein and a Jochum would never have been permitted then. But now, nobody can object to it. Yes, I think they'll make a fine couple. Look at them dancing together. Stefan always was a handsome boy and Christa is a very pretty girl.'

Viktoria followed her mother's glance and the blood drained from her face. They were dancing together, Stefan's hand possessively round Christa's waist, so that she was pressed closely against him. The top of her head scarcely reached his chin and her face was tipped back so that she gazed up at him. Stefan was looking at her as if nobody else in the world existed.

Ricarda moved away. Other people came up to Viktoria, telling her how pretty Monika looked and what a nice young man Hans seemed. Waiters wove their way between tables carrying trays laden with glasses. The music changed tempo and grew louder. Dancers changed partners. Stefan said something to Christa and she smiled. Her hand still in his, he led her from the dance floor into the Palm Garden Room.

Viktoria watched them go. She had believed it to be a passing infatuation. Stefan had not seen Christa for weeks. He had been working late at the Abwehr. He had had no opportunity to meet her. Then the dreadful truth occurred to her. Rather than face her criticism, Stefan had lied to her. He had said he was working late, but, in fact, he had been meeting Christa.

As if it were yesterday, she remembered how she had deceived her own parents. She had met Peter without their knowledge. In those few glorious days of roses after Sarajevo, just before war had broken out, she had danced with him, kissed him and — finally — she had taken him to Heiligensee and gone to bed with him.

How far had this romance gone? She made her way towards the other entrance to the Palm Garden Room. The wide doors were open, the room dimly lit and empty except for the figures of Stefan and Christa silhouetted against the glass at the far end.

His arm was round her and they were talking in low voices, too quietly for Viktoria to hear what they were saying, drowned by the sound of the orchestra wafting in from the neighbouring ballroom, by the conversation and ringing laughter of the wedding guests. Christa laid her head on Stefan's shoulder. His lips brushed her hair.

'Vicki, come away, come with me.' Luise took her arm. 'Vicki, you mustn't stay here. Please, come upstairs.'

A lump rose in her throat and Viktoria allowed her sister to lead her through the foyer and up to the apartment. Luise locked the door behind them, sat down on the settee beside Viktoria and put her arm round her shoulders. 'It's Stefan, isn't it? He's Peter's son?'

Viktoria closed her eyes. 'How did you know?'

'I wondered for a long time, but I wasn't sure. You seemed so in love with Peter, then you married Benno in such a hurry. I know I was only fourteen at the time, but I wasn't entirely ignorant of the facts of life. And I could never understand how you could be taken in by Peter. It was clear he was just using you. Then, when you had Stefi seven months later...'

'Yes,' Viktoria said hollowly. 'Stefan is Peter's son. He and Christa are brother and sister. I thought of everything — but I never thought Stefan and Christa would fall in love. What am I going to do?'

It was very quiet in the room, the silence broken only by the ticking of a clock. Finally, Luise asked, 'Vicki, does Benno know?'

'No, Benno doesn't know.'

'Can't you tell him the truth?'

Viktoria buried her face in her hands. 'What good would that do? If I tell anyone, it must be Stefan — and I just can't bear it. I tried to protect him by marrying Benno. Although he and Benno don't always agree, he loves Benno. And Benno adores him. You know that.'

'Yes, and Stefan doesn't like Peter any more than I do,' Luise said slowly. 'He likes Ilse. He loves Christa. But he takes no pains to conceal the fact that he doesn't like his real father at all.'

Viktoria's blue eyes were huge in her face as she turned to stare at Luise. 'If Stefi ever learned the truth, I would lose him. Luischen, I can stand the thought of anything else that might happen to me. I can bear losing the hotel. I could even live without Benno. But, without Stefan, I might as well be dead.'

There was another long silence. Eventually, Luise said, 'Perhaps it won't last. After all, she's six years younger than him. Maybe Stefan will get bored with her.'

'Maybe...' But Viktoria knew he wouldn't.

'We'd better go back to the wedding,' Luise said gently. 'It will look strange if we disappear for too long. Put some powder on your nose. And don't worry. Something will happen to solve your problem. It usually does.'

In the Palm Garden Room, Stefan drew Christa closer to him and kissed her long and very tenderly.

Standing where Viktoria had stood earlier, Benno watched them and his heart turned to stone. With leaden steps, he turned away and rejoined his daughter's wedding.

To Ricarda's delight, Monika and Hans were spending their honeymoon at Heiligensee, but it was too late for them to leave that evening, so they spent a rapturous night in the bridal suite, departing for the cottage the following morning. Almost the entire hotel crowded onto the steps to wave them on their way, Chef Mazzoni beaming happily, maids wiping their eyes on their aprons and the commissionaires unbending sufficiently to smile stiffly as they opened the doors to the Mercedes.

Radiant-faced, Monika and Hans came down the steps. Hans was wearing a smart civilian suit and Monika a brown and cream travelling costume, a leather handbag over her arm, her wedding bouquet in her hand. They said goodbye to their families, Hans shaking hands and Monika kissing everyone in an unusual display of affection. 'Thank you for a lovely wedding,' she told her parents. 'I know I'm going to be gloriously happy.'

'I hope so, darling,' Viktoria said.

'I'm sure you will,' Benno told her gruffly.

Monika paused before entering the car, a little smile on her face. Then she tossed her bouquet into the air. A host of female hands shot up, but it was caught by Christa. As she blushed, Monika laughed. 'That means you'll be the next bride!'

That evening, Benno came to Stefan's bedroom. 'I don't want to pry, but how serious are things between you and Christa?'

There was a defiant glint in Stefan's eyes. 'I'm very fond of her, Papa. She's a lovely girl.'

Benno nodded. 'She's charming, I agree. But she's still very young. Stefan, don't rush into anything, will you?' There was no censure, only concern, in his voice.

Stefan glanced at him, then nodded. 'Don't worry, Papa. I know what you mean. I've only just started work and I can't afford to take on any commitments yet.'

With that, Benno had to be content.

During the following days, Stefan sensed a general easing in the attitude of people towards him and Christa, which he took to indicate a tacit approval of their romance. His father's words seemed to mean that he accepted it and his grandmother went out of her way to make kind comments about Christa.

Ilse had always made it clear that she approved of Stefan, but now Peter, too, seemed to view him in a more favourable light. The Biedersteins invited him to spend Christmas Day with them and, after lunch, Peter took him into his study for a long masculine discussion over cigars and port.

Only Viktoria continued to make her dislike of Christa very clear. She changed the subject whenever Christa's name was mentioned and made disparaging comments about her age and inexperience. 'Well, of course the child would think that,' was typical of her statements, dismissing Christa as if her opinion were worth nothing.

At the New Year's Eve Ball, she was almost rude, ignoring Christa and pointedly devoting all her attention to Monika and Hans.

Hurt by her behaviour, Stefan apologized to Christa, but she said wisely, 'She's frightened of losing you.'

'If that's true, she's going the right way about it!' Stefan commented angrily. Then, as midnight chimed, he forgot his annoyance and took Christa in his arms. 'I love you, my darling.'

Viktoria watched them and thought her heart would break.

Herr and Frau Hans König returned to Fürstenmark and Mortimer came back from his Christmas holiday in England. Stefan tried to talk to him about Christa, but Mortimer had far more important things on his mind than young love.

During his leave he had spoken to Churchill, who had been dishearteningly full of foreboding. 'Munich is dead, but no new, real effort is being made to arm our nation. Even this breathing space, purchased at a hideous cost, is being wasted. Mr Allen, at a time when Germany is working to a war economy, France has just reduced its working week to forty hours. And despite all my efforts, we, the British, are lamentably unprepared for war.'

Mortimer was also quite convinced that the prospect of war still loomed. In what remained of Czechoslovakia, a now familiar pattern of events was taking place. Separatist movements in Slovakia and Ruthenia were demanding independence. There were reports of shooting and dreadful atrocities being committed against Nazi sympathizers. A feeling of unease emanated from Poland, too. Newspapers reminded their readers that Danzig was German territory and should be allowed to return to the Reich.

In the course of his speech to the Reichstag on his sixth anniversary, Hitler discoursed at length on the bloodless victories of the previous year and spoke about the friendship between Germany and Poland, calling it 'one of the reassuring factors in the political life of Europe.' In the press gallery, Mortimer pursed his lips, in no doubt which country's fate hung in the balance after Czechoslovakia.

Then Hitler turned his attention to the Jews. 'I have often been a prophet during my life and was often laughed at. During my struggle for power, the Jews primarily received with laughter my prophecies that I would some day assume the leadership of the State and thereby of the whole people and then, among many other things, achieve a solution to the Jewish problem. I suppose that the then resounding laughter of Jewry in Germany is now choking in their throats.

'Today I will be a prophet again: If international finance Jewry within Europe and abroad should succeed once more in plunging the peoples into a world war, then the consequence will be not the Bolshevization of the world and therewith a victory for Jewry, but on the contrary, the destruction of the Jewish race in Europe.'

Unanimously, the Reichstag deputies rose to their feet, their arms outstretched. The auditorium of the Kroll Opera echoed to shouts of '*Sieg Heil! Sieg Heil! Sieg Heil!*'

The taste of bile rose in Mortimer's throat. Suddenly, he could stand no more. Grabbing his coat, he pushed his way through his colleagues and left the building.

From Fürstenmark, Monika telephoned excitedly, 'I'm going to have a baby. The doctor says it will be born in September.'

Benno was delighted with the news, momentarily forgetting all his misgivings about Stefan. 'Imagine that, Vicki, we're going to be grandparents.'

Viktoria pulled a face, as the full implication of Benno's statement hit her. 'But I'm only forty-two. I'm not old enough to be a grandmother.'

Ricarda laughed indulgently. 'Vicki, dear, you were little older than Monika when you had Stefan and made me a grandmother. I can assure you, it won't be as bad as you think.'

Mortimer merely laughed grimly. 'So Monika is bearing sons for the Führer. She'll get a Motherhood Cross yet.'

Stefan felt an odd pang of envy when he heard Monika's news. It seemed unfair that his parents should welcome her marriage to Hans, but frown upon his romance with Christa. However, he was not daunted by their attitude. Although it would be a long time before he could afford to rent an apartment and keep Christa in a fashion of which her parents would approve, he was saving as hard as his meagre salary allowed.

In the meantime, he spent his every free moment with Christa. They went to theatres and concerts, sat on café terraces and, if the weather was fine, went for long walks through Berlin's parks or took the S-Bahn out to the forests and lakes. When darkness fell, they kissed, long, passionate kisses, that made them yearn to fulfil their love.

Much as he longed to, Stefan was not prepared to allow impatience to jeopardize his future happiness. He respected Christa too much to take advantage of her. Whatever his parents felt about it, one day they would marry and she would be his for ever.

Towards the middle of March, newspaper reports whipped public indignation into a frenzy against Czechoslovakia. Headlines read: GERMAN FAMILIES FLEE CZECH MONSTERS. There were horrific accounts of German women being raped and having their breasts cut off, of babies being murdered in their cradles, of whole villages being destroyed.

On Monday, 13 March, the situation suddenly changed. The secret order 'War alert' was issued from OKW. Ground and air troops were swiftly moved east and told to prepare for the possibility of hostile action against Czechoslovakia. In an atmosphere of almost unbearable tension, Stefan spent the night at the Tirpitz Ufer, receiving telephone calls from Abwehr agents and monitoring BBC reports to learn whether the British were going to intervene on Czechoslovakia's side.

On Tuesday, President Hacha and Foreign Minister Chvalkovsky of Czechoslovakia arrived in Berlin to a full military guard of honour. Early on Wednesday morning, they departed again and Hitler made a triumphant radio broadcast. After explaining that the Czechoslovak President had confidently placed the Czech people and country under the protection of the German Reich, he announced, 'Czechoslovakia has ceased to exist!' German troops moved over the border to effect a peaceful occupation and Hitler himself flew to Prague.

Stefan could not understand it. Tired and confused, he came home to the Quadriga and went straight to Mortimer's room. 'Last September, Hitler categorically promised Chamberlain that he had no more territorial demands. Doesn't Chamberlain realize that Hitler has broken his word? Is he really going to allow such a gross breach of faith to pass uncontested? Are the British really going to do nothing?'

Suffering from a streaming cold, Mortimer looked even worse than Stefan. 'Czechoslovakia is a small country, a long way away,' he reminded him bitterly.

'You're not going to Prague?'

Mortimer shook his head. 'I was invited to, but I pleaded ill health. Perhaps I'm getting too soft to be a journalist, but I can't face the thought of seeing poor, beautiful Prague under these circumstances. Anyway, what good would it do? I shan't be allowed to report the truth…'

Elsewhere in the Quadriga, the mood was very different. The predominant feelings were relief that war had again been averted and pride that more former German territories had been returned to the Reich. When Stefan arrived in the bar that evening, it was in time to hear his father explaining to Viktoria and Ricarda, 'For a thousand years, the provinces of Moravia and Bohemia were intrinsically German…'

'The best thing is that not a drop of German blood has been shed,' Ricarda added. 'I've heard people calling it political warfare…'

Sepp and Luise joined them for dinner. 'Another flower war,' Sepp laughed.

Luise smiled at him teasingly. 'Poor Sepp. All your Luftwaffe does is drop leaflets!'

Stefan listened to their happy voices and wished he could share their pleasure, but he knew too much to be complacent. Only his mother sat silent and withdrawn. But whether this was because of Czechoslovakia or for other reasons, Stefan did not know. Ever since he had started courting Christa, she had been acting very strangely.

A week later, there was further rejoicing when it was announced that Lithuania had handed back to the Reich the former German territory of the Memelland. Again, England and France did not so much as register a protest.

When Stefan went to supper with Christa and her parents, Peter told him, 'In my opinion, this ends all threat of a European war. Without any doubt, our military strength is a deterrent to other nations. England and France now recognize that a strong Germany is in their own interests to protect Europe against Soviet aggression.'

Stefan lacked the knowledge and the self-confidence to argue with a Staff officer of Peter's standing, so he merely murmured agreement. In any case, when he was in Christa's company, he found it difficult to think of anything but her.

Before the month was over, however, Stefan had reason to hope that Chamberlain was not as easily fooled as he had feared and Peter had believed he was. No sooner had Czechoslovakia been absorbed into the Reich, than a storm started to brew in Poland. The Poles claimed German troops were converging towards the Danzig Corridor. Abwehr agents reported Polish troops mobilizing round Danzig.

On 31 March, Stefan monitored a speech by Chamberlain broadcast to the British nation. 'In the event of any action which clearly threatened Polish independence and which the Polish government accordingly considered it vital to resist with their national forces, His Majesty's Government would feel themselves bound at once to lend the Polish Government all support in their power. They have given the Polish Government an assurance to this effect.'

He immediately requested a meeting with Colonel Oster to report this momentous piece of information and, when he had finished, Oster leaned back in his chair with a smile. 'So Chamberlain has finally been pushed too far. He's prepared to go to war for Poland. I wonder what Emil is going to think about that.'

During the weeks that followed there was again much frantic diplomatic activity, but not until Friday, 28 April, did Hitler respond publicly to Chamberlain's announcement, with a speech to the Reichstag, broadcast with simultaneous translations throughout the world. It happened to be Stefan's birthday and in the evening the family gathered in the bar to celebrate. Luise, Sepp, Lili and Sheltie came from Lützow. Gottlieb Linke drove Baron Heinrich over from Grunewald. Peter, Ilse and Christa arrived from Schmargendorf.

As always on such occasions, Hasso turned the volume of the radio up loud when the speech began and silence fell over the bar as Hitler began to speak. Stefan did not mind the fact that attention was diverted from him. The future of the world might depend upon Hitler's words.

After repeating the iniquities of Versailles, but declaring his friendship for England, Hitler denounced the 1935 Anglo-German Naval Treaty. He then went on to deal with Poland. 'The worst is that now Poland, like Czechoslovakia a year ago, believes under the pressure of a lying international campaign, that it must call up troops, although Germany has not called up a single man and has not thought of proceeding in any way against Poland.' After more protests of a similar nature, he declared, 'I therefore consider the Agreement to have been unilaterally infringed by Poland and thereby no longer in existence.'

No sound could be heard in the bar, as people digested the fact that Hitler was, apparently, reneging on two agreements, until Peter said, 'The British can't do a thing. We must already have naval parity with them. As for Poland, what right do they have to interfere in our affairs? Poland is German territory.'

Then, in a conciliatory tone, Hitler said that he was willing to negotiate replacements for the two treaties, so long as they were on equal terms. Baron Heinrich chuckled. 'He's shrewd, very shrewd. He knows he's arguing from a position of strength.'

Hitler then proceeded to attack and ridicule President Roosevelt, explaining that the American President had sent a telegram requesting Germany's assurance that she would not attack or invade any of thirty-one listed countries, including Poland. He deliberately read out the name of each country, making pertinent comments on many of them, and, while the Reichstag rocked with laughter, Hitler ended up by assuring Mr Roosevelt that he had no intention of invading the United States.

Stefan frowned and looked quizzically at his family, but apparently none of them, not even the Baron or Peter, had noticed that Hitler had not mentioned Poland.

The rest of Hitler's speech was a brilliant summing-up of his own achievements. 'I once took over a state which was faced by complete ruin... I have conquered chaos in Germany, re-established order and enormously increased production... I have succeeded in finding useful work once more for the whole of seven million unemployed... Not only have I united the German people politically, I have also rearmed them... I have brought back to the Reich provinces stolen from us in 1919. I have led back to their native country millions of Germans who were torn away from us and were in misery ... without spilling blood and without bringing to my people, and consequently to others, the misery of war...'

When he eventually finished, there was a spontaneous outburst of applause in the Quadriga bar, and as Hasso turned the radio down, people excitedly began to discuss the speech, their morale boosted by this description of their own strength.

Stefan sat quietly, wondering how they could be so gullible, how so many intelligent people could fail to see through Hitler's words.

After that, newspaper headlines became larger, telling of Polish atrocities perpetrated against innocent German citizens, whipping up a storm of public hatred against the long-detested Poles who were refusing to hand over what was rightfully German territory.

Stefan knew a new fear. What if war broke out and his duties separated him from Christa? Last October, when they had met, there had seemed so much time. Now, it was inexorably running out. When he took Christa in his arms, it was to kiss her with an almost unbearable urgency and a sense of growing desperation.

Towards the end of May, it was announced that Prince-Regent Paul and Princess Olga of Yugoslavia were to pay a state visit to Berlin and the tension eased. The Hotel Quadriga threw itself energetically into preparations for the visit, for although the Prince-Regent and Princess Olga were staying at the Bellevue Castle, many of their attendants and the diplomats accompanying them were to be accommodated at the Quadriga.

Suddenly, there was no shortage of supplies. Benno bustled around with a contented expression and even Viktoria began to look happier. 'It's just like the old days,' Ricarda sighed nostalgically.

Only Stefan could not enter into the spirit of things. He could not help wondering whether Yugoslavia was the Führer's next territorial aim or whether this was the beginning of a new alliance.

The day before the Yugoslavs arrived, Colonel Oster summoned him to his office. 'I think it's time you took a holiday. What would you say to a short break in England in about a fortnight's time?'

Something in the Colonel's voice made him realize this was more than a granting of leave. 'I should like that, Herr Colonel.'

'Some of your old friends from Oxford have pretty important positions now. Trevor Neal-Wright is in the British Foreign Office. Tony Callearn's father, the Earl of Chanctonbury, is on one of the Defence Committees. Are you prepared to use your contacts to try to stop Europe going to war?'

'Of course, Herr Colonel.' But Stefan could not help wondering what they would be able to do.

Colonel Oster studied him gravely. 'Before we go any further, you should understand one thing. Until now, you have been working as an Abwehr agent, in the official interests of the State. If you do what I request, you will be placing yourself in great danger. If the Gestapo catch you, you will be arrested as an informer — a traitor. I needn't spell out what that would mean.'

Stefan experienced a brief moment of apprehension, then he cast it from his mind. It was fear that had stopped other people from doing anything. 'I understand, Herr Colonel, and I am prepared to run the risk.'

'I believe that stiff opposition from England could still frighten Emil from provoking a war that we can only lose. My main fear is that the British will get cold feet and back out of their promise to support Poland. They have to be made to keep to that guarantee.'

Oster explained the complicated alliances that were being formed throughout Europe and went on to describe the great significance of Russia. 'We know that the British and French have been making tentative moves towards Moscow. A triple alliance with Russia is the one thing that might put the fear of God into Hitler.' He frowned. 'But they must hurry. There have also been highly secret discussions between the Wilhelmstrasse and the Kremlin. If Hitler and Stalin make any kind of pact, heaven help us all.'

Stefan stared at him in amazement. 'Surely Hitler wouldn't make a treaty with the Bolsheviks?'

Oster laughed cynically. 'Emil is capable of anything. Surely you know that by now!'

That evening, Stefan told his parents that he had decided to take a holiday in England. 'It's a year since I last saw Trevor, Tony and my other friends from university,' he explained. 'I thought I might arrange a reunion.' Immersed in last-minute preparations for the royal visit, Benno said, 'An excellent idea, son, I hope you enjoy yourself.' Viktoria smiled at him for the first time in months. 'It will do you good to get away from Berlin.' He knew she actually meant Christa.

CHAPTER TEN

It was Führer weather. A brilliant sun shone from a clear blue sky. The streets were lined with dense crowds, waving flags and cheering as the Prince-Regent and the Princess drove through Berlin. The foyer of the Hotel Quadriga thronged with elegant ladies and uniformed gentlemen, the cream of European society: dukes and counts, generals and admirals, government ministers and heads of industry.

Everything possible was done to make the visit a memorable one for all concerned and Viktoria allowed herself to be carried along by the heady atmosphere. Feeling almost like her old self, she mingled with the guests, many of whom she had not seen since before Hitler came to power. She and Benno attended banquets and balls and, as the high point of the royal visit, were among the guests invited to a gala performance of *Die Meistersinger* at the State Opera.

It was a spectacular evening — a lavish performance given to a resplendent and discerning audience. In the centre box, Hitler sat with the royal couple. In neighbouring boxes were Field Marshal Göring, Dr Goebbels and Foreign Minister von Ribbentrop. With other public figures in the dress circle were the Biedersteins and the Krauses. Viktoria and Benno were towards the back of the stalls with Sepp and Luise.

It didn't matter. Viktoria felt as if a huge weight had been lifted from her shoulders. Stefan's visit to England could only mean that he and Christa were drifting apart and that he wanted to put distance between them while he sorted out his emotions. Her worries of the past eight months had been for nothing. The danger was over!

The royal visit ended on 5 June with an awesome military parade, in which not only full battalions of infantry, cavalry and — for the first time — parachute troops participated, but also huge tanks and heavy artillery.

This was Baron Heinrich's moment of glory. Standing on the balcony of the Hotel Quadriga, he proudly pointed out to the foreign military attachés that half the tanks and most of the weapons they could see had been manufactured by Kraus Industries. Often his words were drowned by the thunder of the tanks he had built. By now, Berliners were used to this kind of demonstration of their own military strength, but the Yugoslavs were not.

The royal couple were still in Berlin the following day, when the Condor Legion staged its Victory Parade through the swastika-hung Brandenburg Gate, in open celebration of Germany's role in the Spanish Civil War and Franco's overwhelming victory. Twenty thousand Legionnaires, including Sepp, marched along Unter den Linden and down the Wilhelmstrasse past Hitler at the Chancellery window.

That evening, the hotel swarmed with even more uniforms and glittered with gold braid, as German, Italian and Spanish officers mingled triumphantly. Very quietly, but with great dignity, the Yugoslavs made their departure.

Mortimer watched them go and murmured to Stefan, 'What chance do they stand? What chance do any of us stand against that?'

The royal visit over, Ricarda left Berlin to spend the summer at Heiligensee. Letters from Tony and Trevor arrived for Stefan, expressing delight at seeing their old friend again. Stefan applied for and received a travel permit; was given his final instructions by Colonel Oster; and, on Sunday, left Tempelhof for Croydon.

A couple of days later, a telegram arrived for Mortimer from Bill Wallace, instructing him to return immediately to London. 'Bloody editors!' he fumed. 'Why can't he leave me in peace?'

His assumed indignation took everyone in. His fellow journalists laughed and Viktoria was concerned enough to ask if he had upset his editor and if there was a possibility that he might not return. 'I should miss you if you left Berlin, Mortimer. Even if I don't show it very well, I'm still very fond of you.'

She wouldn't be if she knew what he was involving her son in, Mortimer reflected wryly, if she knew that the telegram was set up so that he could personally introduce Stefan to Winston Churchill.

His first two days in London were intensely disappointing for Stefan. Tony Callearn, working at a merchant bank in the City, of which his father was a director, greeted him warmly, took him for a long lunch at his club and shook his head pessimistically when he heard Stefan's mission. 'No problem arranging for you to meet the old man, but you know nobody over here believes all this nonsense about war.'

The Earl of Chanctonbury saw him for tea in the House of Lords. 'Of course, I'm only a committee wallah, Stephen. But what Hitler gets up to in the east is really no problem of ours. We'll begin worrying if he attacks France. And I can't see that that's very likely!'

Stefan spent the night at Tony's club and made an appointment to see Trevor Neal-Wright at the Foreign Office the next morning. Serious behind his horn-rimmed spectacles, his old room-mate said, 'I think these things are best left to the diplomats, Stephen. But I don't think there's any real likelihood of war.'

With difficulty, Stefan persuaded him to take him to see his father, who held a very much more senior position. He found the elder Neal-Wright dwarfed by a massive empty desk in a huge office and felt his heart sink still further. Berlin was preparing for war and the English were sitting in empty offices doing nothing! Vividly, he described the Yugoslav visit, the military parade, the return of the Condor Legion. 'Hitler means war, Mr Neal-Wright,' he stated earnestly. 'But we, the German people, don't want war. Please can you give me some assurance…'

Trevor's father shook his head wearily. 'There's no point talking to me in London, Stephen. You should discuss these things with our Ambassador in Berlin, Sir Nevile Henderson. Mind you, Henderson isn't the brightest of people…'

Stefan listened to an extraordinary tirade against Sir Nevile and eventually left the office and Whitehall with the dreadful feeling that he was simply wasting his time. But when he arrived back at Tony's club, he found a message waiting from Bill Wallace, Mortimer's editor, instructing him to hire a chauffeur-driven car and meet Mortimer at Croydon Airport the following morning.

The journalist emerged from customs grinning broadly and dressed in his favourite sports jacket and baggy trousers, a cravat knotted round his neck. 'Hi, Stefan,' he called, in English. 'So you got my message. How's tricks?'

'Not very good, I'm afraid.'

Mortimer listened sympathetically to his tale of woe, then said, 'I think you'll get a different reception from Churchill.'

'From Churchill?'

Mortimer grinned. 'That's where we're going next! Did you hire a car? Right, let's get moving.'

Their journey was taken up with going over the points Mortimer and Oster wanted Stefan to make and Mortimer began to feel very confident about the outcome of the meeting. Wearing one of the well-tailored suits he had had made at Oxford, with his clean-cut features and unfalteringly honest brown eyes, Stefan made a good impression. He spoke excellent English and he was used to dealing with influential people. Whatever else Churchill thought of him, he could not take him for a fool.

It was noon when they entered a narrow country lane, crunched over a long gravel drive banked with glorious rhododendrons in full blossom and drew to a halt at the front entrance. Mortimer grinned and held out his hand. 'Good luck.'

Stefan grasped it warmly. 'Thank you, Mortimer.'

They got out of the car and made their way towards the house. Mortimer knocked and almost immediately a butler opened the door. 'Good morning, Mr Allen. Good morning, sir. Will you come this way, please? Mr Churchill is expecting you.' He showed them into a waiting room, then closed the door behind them. Mortimer was just lighting a cigarette, when the butler returned. 'If you will come to the study, gentlemen, Mr Churchill is on his way.'

Mortimer went first, his cigarette dangling from his lips, his wayward forelock of hair flopping into his eyes. Stefan followed, his hands clasped behind his back. He was well aware of the lack of formality in England compared to Germany, but he still could not help wondering at Mortimer's casual approach to a famous politician.

They were left standing for a few moments in the study, looking at a huge desk and leather chair, shelves full of books, a portrait of the Duke of Marlborough. Then the French doors opened and Churchill appeared, foursquare and balding, shorter than Stefan had imagined him, but no less imposing for that, despite the ancient gardening clothes he was wearing.

He paused for a moment on the threshold, studied them both and gave an almost shy smile. 'Good morning, Mr Allen.' He waved a cement-covered hand in the air. 'I am building another wall. Seems to be a fashionable occupation at the moment — building walls.'

'Mr Churchill, may I introduce Stefan Jochum-Kraus?'

Churchill extended a dusty hand towards Stefan. 'Herr Jochum-Kraus, I'm pleased to meet you.'

'And I'm honoured to have the opportunity to meet you, sir.'

Churchill nodded. 'Sit down, sit down, both of you.' He rang a bell and, when the butler reappeared, asked him to bring sherry. Then he reached into a humidor and extracted a large cigar, cut off the end, lit it and gusted a cloud of blue smoke into the room. The butler brought the sherry and left the room.

'So you're from Germany, Herr Jochum-Kraus?' Churchill rumbled in that distinctive voice. 'And you don't think much of your country?'

'On the contrary, I love my country very much,' Stefan said firmly. 'But I don't like what's happened to it since Hitler came to power and I am very frightened indeed about what is going to happen in the future.'

Churchill leaned back behind the desk. 'That makes two of us. Well, what do you think we can do about it?'

Stefan shook his head ruefully. 'I wish I knew, sir. I am certainly not the only German to feel as I do about the Nazis. However, in a one-party state, where all opposition is banned and critics of the regime are dealt with extremely harshly, either by imprisonment or by death, it is very difficult to organize the kind of united resistance movement necessary to remove the Nazis from power.'

'And that is what you would like? To stage a *coup d'état*?'

'You know I work for the Military Intelligence? Last September, there was a plot to arrest Hitler if he declared war over the Sudetenland. However, Mr Chamberlain came to Munich...'

Churchill gave a hacking cough. When he had finished, he asked, 'And if you had succeeded, who would have taken charge of

Germany? The military? Have you won the generals over to your side?'

'I only began my job last August. I am not involved in high-level meetings. However, I think possibly General Beck.'

'Hmmm…' Churchill stared shrewdly at Stefan. 'Mr Allen has told me a certain amount about you. You were a Rhodes Scholar. Your family owns one of the most famous hotels in Europe. You are the grandson of Baron von Kraus. You are connected to Colonel Count von Biederstein. You have everything to gain — and nothing to lose — from Herr Hitler's plans. Why should I trust you, Herr Jochum-Kraus?'

The question took Stefan momentarily aback. Then he replied, 'If the Gestapo learns that I have been to see you, I shall be arrested — and probably shot — as a traitor. None of my family connections will help me then.'

There was silence in the room, then Churchill leaned forward and picked up the bottle the butler had left on a silver tray. 'Have some more sherry, young man, and tell me how you think I can help you in your dangerous mission.'

Stefan took a deep breath. 'The most important thing is that Britain keeps her promise to Poland. Then that she and France form a triple alliance with Russia…'

They were two hours at Chartwell, by the end of which time Stefan had given Churchill all the information he could about the general mood in Germany; propaganda, education and state organizations; the Church and the Jews; the concentration camps; Colonel Oster's views on Poland and Russia; the members of Oster's resistance movement; the locations and production capacities of Kraus factories; troop movements, so far as he knew them from his work at the Abwehr; and the ambivalent feelings of the officer class towards war, particularly one on two fronts in which Russia was involved.

When he had finished, Churchill pursed his lips round his fat cigar. 'Mr Jochum-Kraus, I am greatly indebted to you and, I promise that if this disastrous war occurs, despite all appearances to the contrary, England shall not be found missing.'

He rang the bell for the butler, stood up and came round to their side of the desk. As the butler appeared in the doorway, he shook both their hands. 'Goodbye, Mr Allen. Goodbye, young man, and good luck. Now I'm going to tackle a bit more of that wall.' He lumbered out through the French windows into the garden.

As the car conveyed them back up the drive, Mortimer asked, 'Well, what did you think of him?'

Stefan said slowly, 'I think he is one of the greatest men I shall ever meet.'

That afternoon, after reporting to Bill Wallace, they went to see Theo Arendt. After they had caught up with family news from both sides of the Channel, the banker asked heavily, 'Have you heard about the White Paper on Palestine that's just been passed by Parliament? The British are giving in to the Arabs just as they are giving in to the Nazis. As a result, Jews won't be allowed to purchase land in Palestine any more and Jewish immigration into Palestine is to be limited to seventy-five thousand people a year for the next five years, then stopped for ever.'

'What does that mean?' Stefan asked.

'It means the end to dreams of a Jewish homeland.'

'Just when the Jews need it most,' Mortimer added. In a burst of anger, he slammed his fist down on the table. 'God damn it! How much longer is this policy of appeasement going to continue? When are people going to wake up to how life actually is in Germany today? It makes me sick to think of men like Bethel risking their lives by remaining in Berlin, when nobody else in the world lifts a finger to help the Jews — indeed, deliberately hinders all the efforts!'

'I hate to think of my father-in-law living in such squalid conditions in the Hackescher Markt,' Theo Arendt said. 'Is there any chance of him changing his mind and coming to England?'

'No,' Mortimer replied. 'So long as there are Jews in Germany, he will remain. And he does a lot of good. As well as providing financial assistance, he is a symbol of hope to many.'

Theo Arendt gave a thin smile. 'Yes, he's an obstinate man.'

They took the six o'clock train to Oxford and spent the next day with Joyce and Libby, walking beside the river, picnicking in long grass under a clear blue sky, while dragonflies skimmed over the placid water. Both Mortimer and Stefan were preoccupied and it was Joyce and Libby who kept the conversation going, Joyce telling them about her forthcoming exhibition, Libby chattering about school.

On Friday morning, Joyce brought Stefan a cup of tea in bed. She walked over to the window, drew the curtains and looked out over the back garden. 'Mortimer's told me why you are here, Stephen, and I want you to know that, if ever you decide to leave Germany, there is always a home for you with us.'

'Thank you, Mrs Allen.'

'Mortimer's told me about Christa, too. If you want to bring her, she will be welcome.'

He thanked her again, but, try as he might, when he looked round the small room he thought of as his, he could not imagine Christa sharing it with him.

That afternoon, he and Mortimer returned to Berlin.

Stefan reported every detail of his visit to Colonel Oster and, in the course of the next few weeks, several other men went to England on similar missions, one or two of them to meet Churchill. All came back with identical accounts to Stefan's. Churchill believed them. Nobody else wanted to know. Some were prepared to take the German emissaries more seriously if they could offer help from within the country, but without the Wehrmacht on their side, they had little to offer. Most of the British Foreign Office officials and politicians refused to believe that Hitler would attack Poland and, if he did, they were unconvinced that the British would help the Poles to defend their country.

Stefan soon realized that the same attitude prevailed among the officer corps in Germany. Christa's father was typical of them, maintaining a blinkered view that political warfare would resolve the problem of Poland, because the British would not issue an unconditional guarantee of support. 'There will be no second world war,' he told Stefan confidently.

Few tourists came to Berlin that summer. Such guests as there were at the Quadriga were businessmen and military personnel. Sepp was rushing hither and thither throughout the country helping supervise what virtually amounted to a complete reorganization of a rapidly expanding Luftwaffe with vastly increased personnel and new planes. In his absence, Luise would not leave Lützow and not even Benno and Viktoria spent their usual month at Heiligensee with Ricarda.

As the summer went on, the newspapers continued to scream out messages of hatred against Poland, but soon found an additional object of loathing — England. 'Gentlemen and Bolsheviks!' ran one headline in red ink. London was described as being the centre of the international Jewish-Bolshevik conspiracy. Regardless of any kind of truth, scorn was heaped on the heads of all British politicians, particularly Chamberlain and Churchill.

The fear of war and his frustration at being unable to prevent it, grew in Stefan like a tumour. It haunted his dreams and poisoned his days. He found it difficult to concentrate on his work. He had little appetite and picked at his food. His sole release was on Sundays, when he and Christa borrowed the hotel Opel and drove out of Berlin into the country — usually to see Grandmama at Heiligensee.

At the beginning of August, Mortimer finally decided to snatch a brief holiday and flew back to England. Next day, Colonel Oster asked Stefan if he would pay another visit to London. When Stefan agreed, he said, 'I suggest you go next Monday. They're clamping down on permits, so this may be one of the last opportunities we have.'

'You believe war is that near, sir?'

Oster nodded grimly. 'Yes, I do.'

Stefan went home more depressed than ever.

While he was changing, his father knocked and came into his room. Sitting down on the bed, he asked, 'Stefan, what's the matter? Is it something you can talk over with me? You know, we fathers have our uses sometimes.'

Stefan pulled his shirt over his head. 'Thank you, Papa, but there's nothing you can do.'

Benno cleared his throat. 'Is it something to do with Christa?'

'Christa? Good heavens, no. Christa's the only thing that's right with this lousy world!'

'Stefan, please don't get too fond of her. As I said before, she's very young, not long out of school. I know your mother isn't happy about the relationship...'

Stefan's voice cut coldly through his. 'It isn't Christa I'm worried about, Papa. It's war. I can't bear the thought of war — and certainly not one between Germany and England!' Before he knew what he was saying, the words came out. 'But at least I'm trying to do something to stop it, unlike most other people.'

The colour drained from his father's face. 'What do you mean?'

Stefan was too upset and too angry to stop now. 'I'm going to London again on Monday to tell the British what Hitler is planning and to beg them to sign a treaty with Poland, to make an agreement with the Soviet Union...'

Benno stared at him in horror. 'You're going to do what? Is that why you went to England in June?'

Stefan nodded. 'Papa, do *you* want war — and a war, moreover, that Germany can only lose?'

'That's not the point! Stefan, do you realize what you're doing? You're acting as an informer against Germany. That's treason!'

'No,' Stefan informed him coolly. 'You may think I'm a traitor, but I consider myself a patriot.'

'Who else knows the purpose of your visit? You can't tell me that Colonel Oster...'

Stefan's lips clamped shut.

Incredible though it seemed, Stefan must be acting with the knowledge of Colonel Oster. Maybe the Abwehr officer had serious reason to believe he could prevent war by sending Stefan on this mission. Benno stood up. 'Naturally, I shall tell nobody of this conversation. But I beg you to remember that, if you continue with this crazy plan, you run the risk of being found out by the Gestapo. You will be putting not only your own life at risk, but those of many other people — including Christa!' Without waiting for Stefan's reply, he let himself out of the room.

In the sanctuary of his office, Benno poured himself a stiff brandy. First Christa and now this dreadful revelation. What should he do? He swallowed his brandy in one gulp. *Papa, do you want war?* The answer to that was no. Benno knew he could do only one thing: say nothing to anybody and pray that Stefan's mission would be successful.

Stefan watched the door shut behind him and sank down on the bed. His father was right. He was endangering other people's lives. Perhaps he should go to England and never return. But he would not go alone. On Sunday, when he next saw Christa, he would ask her to be his wife — and they would go to Oxford together.

The rest of the week dragged by. His father's attitude was aloof and his mother scarcely addressed a word to him.

Sunday was hot and stuffy. He and Christa drove out to Heiligensee along streets jammed with traffic heading into the country. The heat rose shimmering from the road surface and, despite the open windows, the car soon felt like an oven. It was almost noon when they arrived at the cottage.

As always in Christa and his grandmother's company, Stefan felt some of the tension seep out of him. Hilde Weber had prepared fresh crayfish with dill sauce and a delicious home-grown salad for lunch, which they washed down with a light white wine. Then Ricarda said, 'I usually sleep for a couple of hours in the afternoon. Fritzi's put a couple of deckchairs down by the lake. Why don't you two digest your lunch, then have a swim?'

But Stefan was still restless. As they made their way across the lawn, he said to Christa, 'Old people always worry about their digestion. I'd like to swim now. Would you?'

'I certainly still feel hot and sticky,' Christa admitted.

Their swimming costumes were in the boathouse. Stefan changed first, then ran out along the jetty and jumped into the lake with a splash. A few moments later, Christa joined him, wearing a navy-blue sailor costume, her hair concealed in a petalled bathing hat. She entered the water more decorously from the shore, and soon they were swimming leisurely, side by side, towards the glade where Fritzi had placed the deckchairs.

They left the water and sat down on the hot grass, out of sight of the cottage and the lake. Christa lay back luxuriantly, her eyes closed. It was very quiet. Around them was a hum of insects. Overhead, a skylark sang. From the distance came the hum of traffic and the faint roar of an aeroplane.

Stefan gazed at Christa with an almost unbearable longing. Drops of water sparkled on her bare legs and arms. Her breasts, clearly defined under the thin material of her bathing dress, rose and fell with her breathing. He leaned over and kissed her. 'Christa, I love you.'

She put her arms round his neck and drew him down to her. 'Mmm, and I love you, too, Stefi.'

Stefan put a hand on her breast. It swelled to his touch. Her fingers stroked his bare back. 'I want you so much,' he said, huskily. 'Do you want me, too?'

Almost inaudibly, she whispered, 'Yes.'

He slid the straps of her swimsuit from her shoulders and gently peeled the damp garment down her body until his mouth was pressed between her breasts. 'Oh, my darling, you are so beautiful.'

He slipped off his bathing trunks and drew her to him, naked flesh against naked flesh, his lips on hers, his hands wonderingly exploring the hills and hollows of her smooth body, while her hands caressed his warm skin gently. They rolled over on the grass and he was lying on top of her, her thighs embracing him.

Suddenly, the world ceased to exist. He was aware only of a delirious frenzy, a searing white heat unlike anything he had ever known in his life. It was such a wonderful sensation, he wanted it never to end, although he knew it must: it was too ecstatic, too agonizing to last. In an earth-shattering explosion of stars and suns and silver moons, Stefan reached his climax.

For a while, they lay together, hushed and shaken by the immensity of what had happened to them. Christa was the first to move. Drawing away from him, she said, in a strange voice that did not sound like her at all, 'Stefi, we'd better get dressed again.' With trembling fingers, she put on her bathing costume and Stefan pulled on his trunks.

Then he took her hand in his. 'Christa, will you marry me?'

A troubled expression flickered across her face. 'Before I say yes, can I ask you something?'

'Of course.'

'When you went to England, it wasn't on holiday, was it? It was to see your friends over there to ask them to do something to stop Hitler going to war against Poland.'

'What makes you think that?' he asked fearfully.

Her huge blue eyes were watching him steadily. 'Something Papa said. He didn't actually mention you by name, but he was talking about the clandestine activities of General Beck and Colonel Oster. Knowing how you feel about England, I put two and two together.'

Stefan's heart seemed to stop beating. 'If that were the case, what would your reaction be?'

'I don't really understand anything that is going on, but I do know that not even Papa wants another world war.'

Stefan took a deep breath. 'If I went to England, would you come with me, Christa?'

At this, she looked away. Eventually, she said, 'I don't know. If war does break out, we should be in an enemy country and I shouldn't like that. And if we were not at war, there would be no point in going.'

'But you will marry me, won't you?'

Again, she hesitated. 'Yes. But let's wait a little longer. Stefi, if war *does* break out, everything will change.'

Stefan stared out across the lake. 'Do you regret what we've just done?'

There was no doubting the sincerity of her reply. 'What we just did was — how can I put it? — the ultimate expression of our love.'

'Then why won't you marry me now?' he asked miserably.

She might be six years younger in age, but she was older in wisdom. Very gently, she said, 'People don't have to get married just because they make love. That's a very old-fashioned idea.'

Stefan nodded, but it was not what he had wanted to hear. He grasped her hand very tightly. 'Christa, if for any reason, I found I could not return from England, would you join me there?'

She forced a laugh. 'Stefi, stop being so serious. Come on, let's have another swim.'

As soon as Viktoria saw Stefan that evening, she knew what had happened. He was her son, flesh of her flesh, a part of herself. However hard he tried, he could have no secrets from her. All night, she tossed and turned in her bed, waking, drenched with sweat, from nightmares in which Stefan was arrested for incest, and a jury, composed of her family, cried accusingly, 'It's your fault! You knew! You should have done something about it!'

He came home from work unexpectedly early the next afternoon. Benno was out and Viktoria was sitting in the apartment, pretending to read a book, when Stefan came through the door. Looking at her rather awkwardly, he said, 'I've got to pack. I'm going to London for a couple of days.'

'Stefi, sit with me for a moment. I want to talk to you. It's a long time since we've had an opportunity to be alone.'

He glanced at his watch. 'I haven't got much time, but…'

'Stefi, why are you going to England?'

Stefan gave a harsh laugh. 'Papa knows. Christa knows. What does it matter if I tell you too? I'm going to London to try to make the British understand that Hitler is determined to go to war and to force them to do something to stop him.'

It was the last thing she expected him to say. She had no idea that he was taking his crusade against the Nazis that far. For a moment, she almost forgot Christa at the thought of the appalling danger he was placing himself in. 'But, Stefi…'

He interrupted her. 'What's more, I may not come back.'

'You may not come back?'

'If I can persuade Christa to join me.'

'What do you mean?'

He spun on his heel and faced her. 'I mean that I have asked Christa to marry me.'

So, after all this time, it had finally happened. Viktoria sank back in the chair. 'No, Stefan, I cannot allow you to marry Christa.'

'Can't allow?' Stefan repeated scornfully. 'Mama, I am twenty-four. I can marry whom I like.'

'We could disinherit you…'

'I have never expected anything from you. Other couples start with nothing. We can too. For the last year I have been saving. Soon I shall have enough for an apartment.'

Viktoria felt light-headed, unable to sense the various parts of her body, all seemingly disjointed and floating away from her. Only the knowledge remained that she was about to hurt the person she loved most in the world, the one person she had sought to protect from the day he was born and whom she had now so utterly and dismally failed. She forced herself to be strong. 'Stefan, you cannot marry Christa.'

'Mama…!'

'Sit down, and I will tell you why not.' When he was seated, she went on, 'A long time ago, I made a terrible mistake.'

'You're not going to tell me *you* married the wrong man?'

'I made my mistake before I married Benno. I fell in love with someone else and got pregnant by him.' She took a deep breath. 'Stefan, Benno is not your real father.'

'Papa isn't my real father…? Does he know that?'

'No, Benno thinks you are his son.'

'But how could you do such a thing?'

'Because your real father wouldn't marry me and, in any case, at that moment, war broke out and he was sent to the front. Benno had already proposed to me so, when I discovered I was pregnant, I accepted him. I had to have a father for my child.'

'But did you have to deceive him all that time? Couldn't you have told him the truth? God, what a despicable thing to do!'

Viktoria nodded. 'Yes, it was a despicable thing to do. So many times, I nearly told him, but what purpose would it have served other than to cause trouble and unnecessary pain? He loved you. He believed you were his son and, in all but one thing, you were. There was no need for him to know. There was no need for anyone to know.'

'Then why do you suddenly find it necessary to tell me? Why give your dirty little secret away now? Do you think Christa might be worried about marrying a bastard?' He did not attempt to conceal the loathing in his voice.

'Because you have to know who your real father is.'

'I don't want to know! I've lived without the knowledge all these years and I can go on doing so.' He strode across to the window. 'Christa will still marry me. She loves me because of who I am, not who my father is. You can't win, Mama. Your sordid little confidences don't alter anything, other than to make me feel very, very sorry for Papa.'

Her fingers were clasped so tightly together that the knuckles were white and bloodless. 'Stefan, your father is Peter von Biederstein.'

Now the words were out and she could feel them hanging in the air between them. She reached out through them with her hand, imploring her son to come to her, wordlessly beseeching him to understand and grant her absolution.

In a choking voice, Stefan asked, 'You mean Christa is my half-sister? Oh, my God…'

'Stefi, darling, I'm sorry…'

'Why the hell didn't you tell me before? Why did you let me fall in love with her, when you knew all the time she was my sister?'

'I tried to warn you,' she whispered, 'but I didn't want to hurt you. You see, Stefi, I love you so much.'

'You love me so much that you'd allow me to commit incest?' The words cut at her like a knife.

There was nothing more that she could say.

In a daze, Stefan crossed the room to the door. 'Well, there is only one thing for me to do now, isn't there?' His face was white as a sheet, his hand trembled on the doorknob. In a shaking voice, he said, 'I'll go to England and I'll stay there. Oh, my God…'

'Stefi, you will be careful? You won't — you won't do anything stupid?'

'*You* ask me that?' he said witheringly. The door slammed behind him and, a short while later, she heard him leave the apartment. Stefan, her son, the love of her life, Stefan had gone.

Viktoria was still sitting motionless when Benno returned an hour later. He took one look at her and asked, 'Vicki, what on earth has happened?'

In a dull voice, she replied, 'Stefi's left.'

'What do you mean — left?'

'He's gone to England. And he's never coming back.' She stared at him wildly, then buried her head in a cushion, her body racked with shuddering sobs.

'Vicki, darling, of course he's coming back.'

'No!' She gave a stifled scream. 'He's gone for ever.' She started to weep the wild, desperate tears of a woman who has lost everything that ever meant anything to her in her life.

He put his arm round her. 'Vicki, come and lie down.' He took her into the bedroom, laid her on the bed and covered her with a blanket. Then he pulled up a chair beside the bed and took her hand in his. When her tears had subsided a little, he asked, 'Why is he never coming back?'

But his question merely brought on a fresh paroxysm of hysterical weeping. Helplessly, Benno smoothed his hand over her forehead. 'Vicki, darling, please stop crying. You've made a mistake. You misunderstood him. Of course, Stefi will come back. I know he's involved in some hare-brained scheme with the English to try and stop a war breaking out. But that doesn't mean he's going to stay there for good.'

She gazed up at him from swollen eyes. 'He is,' she gulped. 'We had an argument...'

'An argument?' Benno thought he began to understand. 'You mean you told him that you didn't like what he was doing?'

'I couldn't allow...' Words failed her again and more passionate tears flooded from her eyes. Benno looked at her worriedly. Her head was fiery hot under his hand. When, after half an hour, her crying had still not abated, he quietly left the room and telephoned Dr Blattner's surgery.

The doctor arrived very quickly and spent about ten minutes with Viktoria. He emerged looking puzzled. 'She's in a state of very severe shock. Herr Kraus, have you any idea what brought it on?'

Benno took a deep breath. 'Stefan has gone back to England. He told his mother that he wasn't going to return.'

Dr Blattner sighed. 'She loves that boy, doesn't she? Well, I've given her a sedative and I recommend she is kept in absolute quiet. I'll call again tomorrow and have another look at her.'

Benno accompanied him downstairs and sent the chauffeur to Heiligensee to bring Ricarda back to the hotel. Then he returned to the darkened bedroom and pulled a chair up beside the bed. Viktoria was staring blankly at the ceiling. He took her limp hand in his and said quietly, 'Vicki, I'm sorry about Stefan.'

Her eyes closed and her breathing became more even. Benno bent over and kissed her on the forehead. 'I love you, my darling. That's always been the trouble. I love you more than anyone else in the world, but I never seem to have loved you in the right way.'

Her eyelashes flickered, but she did not say a word.

Ricarda arrived, very upset to learn what had happened, but still calm and serene. 'Benno, dear, don't worry. I'll stay with her.'

Benno went into Stefan's room and sat down on his son's bed, remembering the scene that had taken place so few days before. Why had Viktoria and Stefan argued? Was it because of his mission to try and stop war breaking out? Or was there some other, hidden reason? But, whatever had occurred, he, Benno, was not entirely blameless. He had helped drive Stefan away, alienating him with his dogmatic views. He, too, had argued with him — although, God knew, he didn't want another war...

He gazed around the room that was so distinctively Stefan — shelves overflowing with books, including a number banned since 1933, one of Ricarda's watercolours of Heiligensee, a framed family group, a photograph of Christa... Benno buried his head in his hands. 'Oh, Stefan, what have we done to you, my son?'

The journey to Oxford seemed interminable. Stefan telephoned

Mortimer from Croydon airport and Mortimer was waiting at Oxford station when he finally arrived. He took one look at Stefan's face and bundled him into the car. 'You look dreadful, kid. What on earth's happened?'

Incoherently, Stefan told him everything. Mortimer heard him out without interrupting, but, as he listened, a number of things became clear. He understood Viktoria's almost unnatural love for her son and her horror when she realized Stefan was falling in love with Christa. And he also understood finally why she had been unable to consummate an affair with him.

When Stefan finally finished talking, he started the car engine. 'Come on, son, let's get you home.'

Libby was in bed when they reached 'Fairways'. Joyce hugged Stefan to her, then said, 'By the look of you, you need a strong cup of tea.'

'I think a brandy might be more to the point,' Mortimer said, pouring him a stiff measure.

Stefan sank wearily back on the settee. 'What am I going to do?'

'We'll talk about that tomorrow,' Joyce said, firmly. 'First, you're going to have a good night's sleep.'

Stefan gave a wan smile and allowed her to take him up to his room. Without washing, he undressed, slipped between the sheets and closed his eyes. The cat jumped on to his bed, but he did not feel it. Physically and emotionally exhausted, he fell into a deep sleep. Only in his subconscious mind, the name kept repeating itself, 'Christa, Christa, Christa...'

When he got up, it was noon. Joyce was in her studio and Mortimer was reading the paper in the kitchen. He put the kettle on the hob, spooned some tea into a pot and placed some bread under the grill. 'How are you feeling?'

'A bit shaky...'

'Have something to eat, then we'll talk.' He prepared Stefan's breakfast and sat in silence while he drank and ate. Then he asked, 'Have you made up your mind not to go back to Berlin?'

'I shall never go back. England is my home now.'

'Mmm,' Mortimer exhaled a cloud of cigarette smoke and studied him gravely. 'In that case, we must go to the Home Office and try to obtain a residency permit for you.'

Stefan looked at him aghast. 'You mean…?'

Mortimer nodded. 'Yes, you're a refugee now.' He drummed his fingers on the table. 'I've been giving your situation a lot of thought. Does anyone other than Colonel Oster know why you were coming to England?'

Stefan hesitated. 'My father and mother.' He pronounced their names awkwardly. 'And Christa.' He repeated what he had told them.

'So, on the assumption that your mother won't have told them the truth about Peter, your father and Christa will assume you've left Germany for political reasons?'

'I suppose so.'

'And so will Colonel Oster. I think you should write him a formal letter, sending in your resignation. It would be the decent thing to do and will also convince the Home Office of your integrity.'

Under his supervision, Stefan wrote a carefully worded letter to Colonel Oster, saying that, for ideological reasons, he had decided to make a new life in England. Together, they went to the Post Office to mail it. As the clerk took the envelope and stamped it, Stefan knew his fate was sealed.

It was two days before they could obtain an appointment at the Home Office, two days during which Mortimer, Joyce and Libby were very kind and patient, listening to him as he went over again and again that dreadful half-hour with his mother. On the train journey to London, Mortimer said, 'Stefan, I want to ask just one thing. Don't be too hard on your mother. She meant well — and I'm sure she's suffering very badly as a result.'

Stefan stared out of the train window. Let her suffer. He hated her. She had destroyed his life.

The Home Office official received them with considerable scepticism. 'You were at Oxford, Mr Kraus? You know the Earl of Chanctonbury and Mr Neal-Wright? You've met Mr Churchill? You worked for German Military Intelligence? And you, Mr Allen? You are an American national living in Oxford, but working in Berlin? I'm sorry, but in the eyes of His Majesty's Government you are both aliens. So far as you are concerned, Mr Kraus, we're going to have to look very carefully into your story. For all we know you could be a spy.'

Stefan was about to break into an angry tirade when Mortimer threw him a warning glance. The official pulled open a desk drawer and handed him a sheaf of forms. 'Now if you'll complete these.' With a deep sigh, Stefan complied. When he had finished, the official consulted a folder on his desk, then handed him a card. 'You may stay for the time being. You will take this card to Oxford Police Station, where you will be required to report every week. You may not move around the country without our express permission.'

'But what about a work permit? Your country will need my services when war breaks out.'

The Home Office man looked at Stefan in undisguised horror. 'I don't think it will come to that. There won't be a war.'

For the first few days after Stefan's departure, Viktoria did little but sleep. The pills prescribed by Dr Blattner deadened her senses, so that she passed her nights and much of the day in a state of blessed oblivion. Only when she awoke, did the anguish return: the memory that Stefan had gone, the dread that he would never forgive her, the fear that she would never see him again. Whimpering like a small child, she cried, 'Stefi, oh Stefi...'

Ricarda sat all day beside her bed, sewing or reading, waiting for time and nature to do their work. Very kind and very patient, she knew from her own experience the pain of losing the person dearest to one. She knew that brief moment between sleeping and waking, when dreams seem more real than actuality. She knew the piercing agony of the reality that followed, the sense of desolation and despair. She knew how much courage was required to conquer that feeling of doom, that nothing could ever, ever be the same.

Luise, remembering only too well her own breakdown, brought flowers and terribly expensive fruit, and sat, Lili on her knee and Sheltie at her feet, gazing anxiously at her sister. 'How much longer can she go on sleeping?' she asked her mother.

Ricarda was an essentially practical person. 'Sleep is nature's remedy, but when nature has done all it can, it's up to the patient to complete the cure. If only we knew what really happened that afternoon. I know Vicki says that Stefan was part of an underground resistance movement, trying to prevent war with Poland, but I can't help feeling there was something more than that.'

Luise had a very shrewd suspicion as to what had occurred and when Ricarda was out of the room and Viktoria was awake enough to talk, she asked, 'You told Stefan about Peter, didn't you?'

Viktoria nodded weakly. 'I had to. He'd asked Christa to marry him. Oh, Luischen, what am I going to do? Even before I confessed, Stefi had been thinking of staying in England. Even if he gets over his shock, he won't return while Hitler is still in power. I have wondered if there is some way that I can continue his fight, but I can't. I'm powerless to do anything. All my rights have been taken from me. Never in my life have I felt more helpless...'

In the meantime, Benno had got over his immediate shock and had begun to think about the ramifications of Stefan's precipitate departure. When his subordinate did not return from England, Colonel Oster was going to become concerned. At some point, somebody was going to discover the purpose of Stefan's visit to England and the fact that he had decided to stay there.

Inevitably, questions were going to be asked and the repercussions could be extremely unpleasant for everyone. Well, there was nothing he could do to help Stefan, but he could protect Viktoria and the hotel. Benno's shrewd Kraus mind started to work out a plan of campaign.

When the hotel was asleep, he emptied his son's desk and took the contents, along with all but the most uncontentious of Stefan's books down to the basement and burned them in the incinerator. Then, in the rather spartan room, he prepared a story.

On Friday, a distinctive English airmail letter arrived at the Abwehr offices, addressed to Colonel Oster and marked 'Personal'. After reading its contents, the Colonel stared at it for a long time, disappointed but not altogether surprised by Stefan's decision to stay in England, then he made his way to the office of Admiral Canaris.

For the next hour, the two men weighed up the consequences of Stefan's action. 'During the time he has been working for the Abwehr, he can't have learned sufficient to greatly damage the organization,' the Admiral said eventually.

'There are other aspects of our work, however, of which he has quite considerable knowledge,' Oster commented meaningfully. 'If the wrong people learned that I had sent him to England, we could find ourselves the very unwelcome target of the Gestapo's attention.'

'Legally, he is a defector and a traitor. We have to report his disappearance. But, in my opinion, the whole matter should be kept as quiet as possible. It's in nobody's interests to broadcast it.'

'What about his family and friends? He was very close to the Biederstein girl. And don't forget his connection with Herr Allen.'

Canaris gave an enigmatic smile. 'I think I can make Heydrich see reason. So far as the boy's family is concerned, it isn't in the interests of the SS to upset Baron von Kraus. As for Herr Allen — he is an American and, as such, safer than the rest of us.' He picked up the telephone. 'Get me SS-Obergruppenführer Heydrich.'

By Saturday morning, five days after Stefan's flight, Benno's nerves were getting decidedly frayed. When Herr Fromm came to his office with a routine enquiry, he snapped at him in a most uncharacteristic manner. 'For God's sake, Fromm, don't bother me with trivialities! Get someone to bring me some coffee.'

Herr Fromm looked at him, startled. 'Certainly, Herr Direktor.'

A few moments later, the door was flung open. Benno glanced up, expecting to find a waiter. Instead, he was confronted by two strange men in leather coats. One sat down in the chair across the desk from him, while the other, hand in pocket in a manner suggesting that it contained a gun, took up station by the door. 'Who are you?' Benno demanded. 'How dare you enter my office without…'

There was a knock and a waiter entered with a tray. He did not get very far. The door was slammed in his face. Benno had a brief glimpse of him careering backwards, coffee flying everywhere.

The seated man pulled a wallet from his pocket and flashed an identification card in front of Benno's nose. 'Oberführer Kuhn — Gestapo. Herr Kraus, where is your son?'

'My son? He's on holiday in England.'

'On holiday?'

'He studied in England. He has a lot of friends there. What the devil is this about? I'm a busy man — I've got an hotel to run...'

The Gestapo officer eyed him closely. 'You have heard nothing from him?'

'Not a word. But he's only been gone for a few days...'

'Herr Kraus, your son is not on holiday. He has defected.'

'Defected...?'

'He has sent a letter to the Abwehr, resigning for "ideological" reasons. We believe that he was recruited by the British Secret Service while he was at Oxford and has been working here for the last year as a British spy.'

Benno sank back in his chair and covered his face with his hands. 'No, no... I don't believe it.'

'Do you sympathize with your son's views?'

Benno uncovered his face and half rose in his chair. Indignantly, he said, 'I have been a member of the Nazi Party since 1932. I am a Kraus, a respected name in Germany...'

'Where is your son staying in England?'

'I have no idea.'

'He is at the house of the American reporter, Mortimer Allen.'

'You mean Herr Allen is aware of Stefan's activities?'

'We believe he has encouraged him. Allen's left-wing sympathies have long been known to the Gestapo.'

'When Allen returns, he'll find no room under my roof,' Benno blustered.

'On the contrary,' Oberführer Kuhn said. 'When Allen returns, we want you to appear grateful to him for looking after your son, and to report to us anything about him that strikes you as suspicious.'

'You want me to spy on Herr Allen?'

'It is in your own interests to do so, Herr Kraus, if you want us to believe that you are not a traitor like your son.'

Benno let out a long breath, shaking his head in disbelief. 'I can't believe it. Not Stefan…'

'I am telling you the truth.'

'Then I no longer consider him my son,' Benno said slowly. 'I disown him. If he ever returns, I shall tell him so.'

'If he ever returns, he will be executed.'

'Oh, you dear God…'

Oberführer Kuhn stood up. 'That is all. I am sure you realize that, if you are discovered to have been lying, the penalty will be extremely severe.'

When they had gone, Benno went to the cupboard where he kept his emergency supply of brandy and poured himself a very stiff measure.

That same morning, all remaining evidence of Stefan was cleared from the apartment. His clothes were given to the Winter Relief. All photographs of him were burned. If the Gestapo ever checked, Benno was keeping his word. He no longer considered Stefan his son.

Viktoria thought her heart would break. The future stretched ahead of her, barren and comfortless. It was as if Stefan had never existed. And she had only herself to blame.

Benno's ordeals were far from over for the day. At noon, his father telephoned. 'I've just heard Stefan has defected! I don't suppose you've given a thought as to how this is going to affect me? You've always mollycoddled that boy. He's never had any discipline. Too much study has addled his brains. Well, it's good riddance to bad rubbish as far as I'm concerned. I never want to hear his name mentioned again. He is not — and never has been my grandson. I disown him.'

After several minutes more in a similar vein, the Baron slammed down the phone, without allowing Benno a word in edgewise. Benno rubbed a weary hand across his forehead and poured himself another brandy. There was nothing surprising in his father's reaction.

An hour later, there was a knock on the door and Herr Fromm entered very hesitantly. 'I am sorry to disturb you, Herr Direktor, but

Colonel Count von Biederstein and Fräulein Christa are asking to see you urgently.'

Resignedly, Benno said, 'Show them in, Herr Fromm.'

Peter wasted no time in preliminaries. Angrily, he said, 'Canaris has told me the news. Stefan has gone over to the British. It appears he was a member of some resistance movement. What the devil were you thinking of, allowing him to get mixed up in something like that?'

At that moment, years of pent-up emotion exploded inside Benno. He could take such accusations from his father, but was damned if he was going to take them from his cousin. 'If it wasn't for men like you, there would have been no need for Stefan to do what he did!' he shouted. 'You and your kind glory in war, with no thought for anybody else. Whether or not Stefan was right to act as he did, at least his motives were good. He was trying to keep the peace.'

Peter's eyes narrowed. 'Don't try to glorify him, Benno. Your son is a traitor.'

'So the Gestapo informed me,' Benno said acidly.

Peter went white. 'The Gestapo? Did they mention…?'

For an instant, Benno was tempted to put the fear of God into him, then he remembered Christa. 'No. They said nothing about you.'

Christa gazed at him with appealing blue eyes. 'Uncle Benno, is it true? Is Stefan really not coming back?'

Poor child. The most unwitting and innocent victim of the whole, ghastly affair. 'Yes, Christa,' he said heavily. 'It's true.'

Christa studied her fingernails. 'He warned me this might happen. Perhaps you don't know, Uncle Benno, but last time we went to Heiligensee Stefan asked me to marry him.'

'Stefan asked you to marry him?' Benno gasped, sinking back in his chair. And, suddenly, the complete picture dropped into place. That was the reason for Stefan's precipitate departure and Viktoria's distress. Stefan had told her that he had proposed to Christa, at which she had been forced to tell him the truth — that he was Peter's son and Christa's half-brother.

But what about Christa? Did she entertain some crazy notion about running away to join Stefan in England? Benno asked, 'And how did you reply?'

Again, she hesitated. 'I told him we should wait, that if war broke out, everything would change. He was rather disappointed, but I think I was right — particularly in view of what's happened now.'

'You can forget any notion you may be entertaining of marrying this blackguard,' Peter remonstrated.

Oddly self-contained, Christa said, 'I don't love Stefan less for what he's done, although I could never have gone with him. I'm going to miss him dreadfully, but at least I know he's safe and where he wants to be.' She turned to Benno. 'I have a feeling that, however much it hurts, the only way of showing someone that you love them is to allow them their freedom. Does that sound very strange, Uncle Benno?'

'No,' Benno said slowly, 'but it is sometimes very hard to do.'

For a long time after they had gone, Benno sat in his office, staring blindly at the photograph of Viktoria on his desk. He was not lying when he told people that Stefan was not his son. Viktoria had told Stefan the truth. Why could she not tell *him*?

Was it because she did not love him, or was she frightened as to how he would react? He gave a thin smile. It really did not matter. He still loved her and her son. Whatever they said or did, nothing would ever change that. He had given his heart — he could not take it back.

Mortimer returned to the Quadriga on Monday. When he reached the reception desk, Herr Fromm picked up the internal phone, dialled a number and said, 'Herr Direktor, Herr Allen has arrived. Yes, certainly.' He turned to Mortimer. 'Will you go to the Herr Direktor's office immediately?'

Mortimer grimaced, in little doubt that he was about to be thrown out of the hotel. He knocked on the door to Benno's office and entered. 'You wish to see me, Herr Kraus?'

Benno motioned him to be seated and asked, 'How is Stefan?'

Warily, Mortimer replied, 'He's all right, under the circumstances.'

'Is he determined to stay in England?'

'Yes.'

Benno glanced down at his desk, took a deep breath and asked, 'Will you tell me what reason he gave you for leaving so hurriedly?'

At that moment, Mortimer knew that Benno had guessed Viktoria's secret and he felt a sudden, unexpected surge of sympathy for him. 'He has never liked Hitler's Germany, Herr Kraus...'

'Did he mention Christa?'

Mortimer chose his words very carefully. 'Yes, he said that he had realized she was not the right girl for him. He decided it was better to make a clean break.'

Benno's shoulders sagged and he rubbed his hand across his eyes. 'I had a visit from the Gestapo. They have ordered me to keep you under observation. But you needn't worry. While your family is looking after my son, I shall not betray you.'

Mortimer felt ashamed. He had tried to seduce Benno's wife and had been partly to blame for Stefan's action. 'Thank you, Herr Kraus. I shall try never to do anything against your interests.'

Benno was silent for a moment, then he said, 'Word is going to get round about what has happened and your part in it. It will look very strange if any of us continue to treat you as a family friend. If my wife tries to talk to you about Stefan, I must ask you to dissuade her. It is for her own safety.'

Mortimer nodded. 'I understand.'

Benno stood up and held out his hand. 'Thank you, Herr Allen.'

After Mortimer had left, Benno went up to the apartment, where he found Viktoria and Ricarda sitting on the balcony. 'Mortimer Allen has returned. Stefan is safe and well. But he is determined to remain in England. So long as Hitler is in power, he refuses to come back to Germany.'

He could not help but see the relief on his wife's face as she realized he was accepting the explanation that Stefan's reasons for leaving were purely political. 'Thank you for telling me, Benno...'

During the days that followed, Benno was quickly proved right about Mortimer. The journalist provided the perfect scapegoat for Stefan's defection. Because he was of German extraction and spoke fluent

German, people had accepted him as one of themselves. Now they saw how they had been deceived. He was married to an Englishwoman. His home was in England. His sympathies lay with England. He had met Stefan when the boy was at a vulnerable age and deliberately exerted influence over him to make him betray his country.

From being the most popular of the foreign correspondents in Berlin, Mortimer became *persona non grata*. Guests snubbed him when they encountered him in the bar. Conversations stopped short when he entered the vicinity. Only his fellow journalists continued to keep company with him. The Americans found his situation rather amusing. The English, already suffering from the anti-British campaign, were more sympathetic.

Mortimer tried to take his new status philosophically — but it was decidedly frustrating. Men in brown raincoats — presumably Gestapo agents — followed him through the streets or sat in the bar pretending to read a newspaper and making a glass of beer last several hours. His work on behalf of the Jews was hampered, because he was frightened of drawing attention to Bethel and Klara by visiting them.

His principal sources of information dried up overnight. There were no more titbits from the Biedersteins and the Krauses. He no longer dared communicate with Colonel Oster. He had become like every other member of the foreign press — dependent upon communiqués from Goebbels' Propaganda Ministry.

So far as Viktoria was concerned, he kept his word to Benno. The first time she tried to talk about Stefan, he said abruptly, 'I am sorry, there is nothing I can tell you about him.'

'Mortimer, we were friends once…'

'That was a long time ago. Things have changed.'

Hurt and mortified, she nodded bleakly. 'Please understand. I acted like I did because I loved him.'

He understood better than she knew and had never felt more sorry for her than he did at that moment.

CHAPTER ELEVEN

Although Christa was rather subdued after Stefan's departure, she did not seem as upset as Ilse had feared. 'Either modern girls are tougher than my generation,' Ilse told Peter, 'or Christa was not as in love with Stefan as he was with her.'

Peter frowned. He had not really approved of the romance in the first place and the revelations of Stefan's treachery had shaken him to the marrow. He considered they had all had a very narrow escape. 'I hope she takes considerably more care in choosing her next suitor,' he commented sharply.

However, Christa was not interested in other young men or in invitations from girlfriends to go to dances or the theatre. Even now, she knew Stefan to be a unique experience in her life. She had never really understood him and, perhaps, as her mother said, she had not loved him with the same passion as he loved her. But she had cared for him deeply and now he was gone, she missed him much more than she showed.

Although she did not say so, she hoped that one day he would return and they could start again. In the meantime, she had been brought up on the English and Prussian principle of a stiff upper lip and had never been prone to overt demonstrations of emotion, so she kept her feelings private.

But the time hung emptily on her hands and when she saw an announcement in the paper that a part-time secretary was needed at the Foreign Office, she decided to apply. She was ideally qualified. She had learned shorthand and typing at school, spoke fluent French and English, and came from an excellent family. To her delight, she was immediately offered the position.

Her mother took the news calmly. 'If it makes you happy, dear, then I see no reason why you shouldn't accept the job.'

Her father was less pleased. 'I never envisaged my daughter working as a secretary. Don't you think it's rather undignified?'

But Christa had made up her mind. 'On the contrary, Papa, I think I am setting a good example, as well as serving my country.'

'Well, if you find it too tiring, you can always leave, I suppose,' Peter said grudgingly.

Christa began her new job on Monday, 21 August. Far from overtiring, she found it very routine, assisting another secretary in the office of a very junior official, but it was certainly more interesting than being at home with nothing at all to do.

She and her parents were just preparing to go to bed that evening when the light music playing on the radio was interrupted and a news flash was announced. The newsreader said, 'The Reich government and the Soviet government have agreed to conclude a pact of non-aggression with each other. The Reich Minister for Foreign Affairs will arrive in Moscow on Wednesday, 23 August, for the conclusion of the negotiations.' The music resumed.

Suddenly, Christa became a very important person in the household. Her father asked, 'Now, why should Hitler want a friendship pact with Stalin? Christa, did you hear anything about this at the Foreign Office?'

Christa smiled. 'Papa, I'm only a junior secretary. Minister von Ribbentrop is hardly likely to confide in me.'

Early next morning, Peter accompanied General Halder to a military conference at the Führer's spectacular mountain eyrie, the Berghof, above Berchtesgaden in Bavaria. They were met from their plane and driven at high speed along hairpin bends, past countless sentries and into the great hall of Hitler's fortress, where many of their colleagues from the Army, Luftwaffe and Navy were already gathered.

The Führer began by outlining the current political and military situation in Europe. *Il Duce* was on Germany's side. Franco would assure Spain's neutrality. 'As for the other side,' Hitler sneered, 'there is no outstanding personality in England or France.' Therefore the showdown had better take place now. And where better to start than in Poland, where the Army would experience actual battle before the big, final showdown in the West?'

Peter glanced around him and saw the same misgiving displayed on the faces of his fellow officers as he felt in his own mind. This time, there was to be no political solution. Hitler had determined upon war.

The purpose of the Nazi-Soviet Pact became clear. 'The enemy had another hope, that Russia would become our enemy after the conquest of Poland. The enemy did not count on my great power of resolution. Our enemies are little worms. I saw them at Munich... The day after tomorrow, Ribbentrop will conclude the treaty. Now Poland is in the position in which I wanted her... The way is open for the soldier...'

After lunch, Hitler went into greater detail. 'The destruction of Poland has priority. The aim is to eliminate active forces, not to reach a definite line. Even if war breaks out in the West, the destruction of Poland remains the primary objective...

'I shall give a propagandist reason for starting the war — never mind if it is plausible or not. The victor will not be asked afterwards whether he told the truth or not. In starting and waging a war, it is not right that matters, but victory...

'Things will happen in Poland which will not be to your taste. You should not interfere in such matters, but restrict yourselves to your military duties. Close your hearts to pity! Act brutally! Eighty million people must obtain what is their right... Be harsh and remorseless! Be steeled against all signs of compassion...'

Used as he was to Hitler's furious tirades, Peter could not help feeling uncomfortable. There was something degrading about such outbursts — and the sentiments contained in them. He stared at his hands rather than look at the Führer's bulging eyes and purple face.

General Halder was silent as they flew back to Berlin. Only as they came in to land, did he say, 'I think it will be all right. With Russia on our side, we shall easily overrun Poland.'

'England and France won't intervene,' Peter added confidently.

'Even if they do, Hitler won't permit a world war. He knows we're not strong enough. He knows it would be our ruin.'

Peter glanced at him curiously. There was a note in Halder's voice that reminded him of his predecessor, General Beck.

Next day, at Army High Command, the War Ministry, the Air Ministry and the Admiralty, meetings were held and orders issued. In four years, the Wehrmacht had developed from a hundred-thousand-man army to over three million, seven hundred thousand trained soldiers, sailors and airforcemen. Within the Army, there were five heavy and four light armoured divisions, with over three thousand panzers and seven thousand guns. From having virtually nothing, the Navy now possessed two battleships, two battlecruisers, three pocket battleships, eight cruisers, twenty-two destroyers and fifty-six U-boats. From being virtually non-existent, the Luftwaffe now numbered over a quarter of a million men and a fleet of over four thousand planes, including bombers, fighters and the unique Stuka dive-bomber.

These were the forces and the weapons with which Germany prepared to launch its Blitzkrieg against Poland, which was known to possess only four hundred outdated planes, four ancient destroyers and no tanks at all.

As the mammoth German war machine was set into motion, Peter felt supremely confident of victory. He did not believe that Britain and France would risk unleashing a world war on behalf of Poland any more than they had done for Czechoslovakia. Before they had time to react, Poland would, once again, be returned to the Reich.

In Moscow, displays of anti-Fascist books in the bookshops disappeared overnight and on Wednesday the terms of the German-Soviet Non-Aggression Pact were announced. Mikhail Geruschke stared at the newspaper headlines in stunned bewilderment, then turned to his roommate, Vasili Meyer. 'I don't understand it. Why should Stalin make a pact with Hitler? It's a betrayal.'

Vasili produced a battered packet of Dukats. 'Like a cigarette?' Mikhail was an Austrian émigré, whose parents, like Olga, had disappeared in the purge. He was attending the same course at the Teaching Institute as Vasili.

Mikhail took a Dukat. 'It doesn't make sense. My parents, your mother, Radek, the generals — they were all arrested because they were supposed to have been negotiating with Germany, and now…'

Vasili seized the newspaper and read the small print, his forehead creased in a frown of concentration. Finally, he said, 'Mikhail, I don't believe this is a pact with Hitler and the Nazis. In fact, I don't think it is a betrayal. Quite the opposite. This is a pact with the German proletariat and its purpose is to support them in their fight against imperialism and capitalism.

'It's clear that Great Britain, France and the other imperialist nations are preparing for war and they intend to use Poland as an excuse to attack Germany. We have no desire to be dragged into an imperialist war so, by signing a non-aggression pact with Germany, Stalin has secured peace and security for the Russian people.'

Mikhail nodded. 'Yes, I think I understand,' he said slowly. 'And when the smaller countries, including Nazi Germany, have burned themselves out, we shall be able to establish communist rule.'

'Stalin is a remarkable man,' Vasili went on, admiringly. 'If war breaks out between Germany and the capitalist powers, it will be the beginning of the World Revolution. The Soviet Union was born out of the wreckage of the last imperialist war. When this war is over, the Soviet Union will be the only country not to have been involved. Our armies will march through Europe and we shall be able to return home.' He ground out his cigarette. 'My father's dream will come true. The communists will rule in Berlin!'

Thursday was hot and stuffy and, as the day wore on, an uneasy atmosphere permeated the Hotel Quadriga. All day long, the skies reverberated to the sound of bombers flying in formation towards Poland, and Luise telephoned to say that Sepp had been sent east on a reconnaissance exercise. Several young waiters from the hotel and Café Jochum were called up for reservist duties. Anti-aircraft guns were installed in the Tiergarten and on the roofs of high buildings. Baron Heinrich confirmed that flak guns were also being erected in the Ruhr and on the North Sea coast.

In the evening, all British and French journalists were suddenly ordered by their embassies to leave for the nearest frontier. They packed their bags quickly, settled their bills and, with a few brisk handshakes, departed. One of them said cheerfully, 'We'll be back in a few days. This is just another false alarm. Chamberlain will negotiate another Munich.'

Nobody knew whether to believe him or not. The following day, the British Ambassador, Sir Nevile Henderson, had two meetings with Hitler. At the same time, however, all telephone and telegraph communications with the outside world were cut off. There were rumours that an invasion of Poland was planned for dawn. Then, just as suddenly, the telephone lines were reinstated. New rumours abounded that Mussolini and the Pope were trying to mediate between Hitler, Chamberlain and Daladier.

On Saturday morning, Henderson left for London. All weekend, the weather continued overbearingly hot, adding to the tension. Most Berliners escaped to the country, including Ricarda, Viktoria and Benno. Mortimer spent his time trying to glean information from the grim-faced, harassed officials bustling along Unter den Linden and the Wilhelmstrasse between the various ministries and the Chancellery.

A rally due to be held at Tannenberg the following day was cancelled. The Nuremberg Party Rally due to start in a week's time was also called off. The American Embassy asked all Americans whose presence was not absolutely necessary to leave Germany. Mortimer arranged with Bill Wallace that, if war did break out, he would route his reports via the *News* office in Zurich.

Sunday's newspapers proclaimed: WHOLE OF POLAND IN WAR FEVER! ONE AND A HALF MILLION POLES MOBILIZED! UNINTERRUPTED TROOP TRANSPORT TOWARDS THE FRONTIER! CHAOS IN UPPER SILESIA! On Sunday afternoon, a secret session of the Reichstag was held. The official communiqué was brief to an extreme, stating that the Führer had outlined the gravity of the situation.

'He can't make up his mind what to do,' Chuck Harris said.

'If only Britain would sign that damned guarantee to Poland,' Mortimer muttered.

'Perhaps that's what's keeping Henderson in London.'

Viktoria and Benno arrived back from Heiligensee in time to hear a news bulletin announcing that rationing of coal, soap, textiles, food and shoes was to take effect from the following day — the first real intimation that war was closer than anyone had really believed. Faces everywhere were glum.

They grew even longer on Monday morning, when more staff received mobilization orders. Hastily equipped, they joined colleagues marching through the streets or being conveyed in a hotchpotch selection of vehicles. In the afternoon, Philip Krosyk issued his waiters with scissors to clip the new ration cards and Chef Mazzoni frantically worked out new menus conforming to the regulations.

Next day, the Blockwart for the Quadriga's section of Unter den Linden arrived to detail blackout and air raid procedures. A reception clerk and the Hall Porter were appointed air-raid wardens and were made responsible for ensuring that the entire hotel was blacked out at night and that all personnel and guests were issued with gas masks. Finally, the question of an air-raid shelter arose.

Benno personally conducted the Blockwart past the kitchens and through heavy doors leading into the basement. First they inspected the area where the boilers and electricity generators were situated, with laundry and workrooms adjacent and beyond them the living quarters for the maintenance men, page boys and other menials. The Blockwart nodded. 'And the rest of the cellars?'

Benno selected a key from the huge bunch he carried with him at all times and unlocked the door to the wine cellar. Gangways separated the racks of wine, wide enough for them to walk four abreast through the interconnecting arched rooms. Benno pointed upwards. 'We are beneath the portico now, but the cellars extend underneath Unter den Linden itself. I keep my less valuable vintages there, because of vibration from the traffic and the underground. Herr Blockwart, this is the most priceless collection of wine in the whole of Germany. It numbers about a million bottles.'

Even the Blockwart was impressed. 'A million bottles, Herr Direktor… However, part of this cellar must be cleared to make an air-raid shelter. Your guests must have somewhere to go.'

They returned upstairs and Blockwart Sachs took his leave. Benno came into Viktoria's office, angrier than she had ever known him. 'Who the devil do they think they are, telling me what to do with my cellar? And who the hell have we got in charge of this country, leading us into a war where Berlin is in danger of getting bombed? Why isn't someone doing something to prevent it happening?'

Viktoria looked at him coldly. 'That is exactly what Stefan was trying to do. But you wouldn't listen to him! Well, you voted Hitler into power — and now you're going to have to put up with what he does, war and all.'

'Vicki, that isn't fair. Never once have I said I wanted another war. Quite the opposite...'

But Viktoria was not interested in Benno's opinions, past or present. She needed an outlet for her pent-up emotions and anger was better than weeping. 'It isn't your cellar, it's our cellar. It isn't your wine, it's our wine. And since we seem to be on the brink of war, rather than moan about it, I suggest you get on and take adequate precautions, so that, if we are bombed, we and our quests will suffer as little as possible.'

She got up from behind her desk and marched out of the room, experiencing a perverse satisfaction in seeing Benno discomfited.

Under Benno's reluctant supervision, the cellar was reorganized and a space cleared for people to shelter in the event of a Polish air raid. Blackout blinds were installed at all hotel windows and outside doors. The house wardens distributed gas masks — grotesque, foul-smelling, claustrophobic objects that brought home even more clearly the dangers that might lie ahead. All cars were fitted with headlight shields. Workmen painted white stripes on the kerbstones to guide vehicles in the dark.

Three more days went by, each hour bringing fresh rumours, including ones that Mussolini had fallen out with Hitler and that Hitler was trying to negotiate an alliance with Great Britain, but nobody, not even Mortimer or the Baron, could discover what was actually happening, other than that there was a lot of frantic diplomatic activity, that the Poles were mobilizing and that German troops were still moving towards the Polish border.

At nine o'clock on the evening of Thursday, 31 August, Hitler broadcast to the nation. He had tried to reach an agreement with Poland. He had demanded only the return of Danzig and suggested that the fate of the Corridor be settled by a Plebiscite in twelve months' time. Whoever then received the Corridor would allow the other country road and railway rights through it, and he was happy that Poland should continue to have access to the Baltic through the sea port of Gdynia. An exchange of population should take place and each country should accord full rights to the nationals of the other.

In the hotel bar, everyone looked at each other hopefully. What could be more reasonable than these proposals?

But, Hitler continued, despite his offers to negotiate, the Poles refused to send a negotiator. 'In these circumstances, the German Government regard their proposals as having been again rejected, although they consider that these proposals, in the form in which they have been made known to the British Government also, are more than loyal, fair and practicable.'

Hasso Annuschek turned down the volume of the radio. 'Why wouldn't the Poles negotiate?' Benno asked hollowly.

'Or the British?' Viktoria added.

Mortimer stared blankly into space, wishing he knew what the hell was going on, but the British Embassy staff seemed to have as little idea as he did, while the Americans appeared to be totally in the dark. It was impossible to get through on the telephone to London, Paris or Warsaw. Only after a long wait, did he succeed in sending his report to the *New York News* via Zurich.

Night fell over Germany. In the small town of Gleiwitz on the Polish border, a company of SS men stole through the dark. Waiting for them, near the German radio transmitting station, were about a dozen concentration camp inmates, dressed up in Polish army uniforms, smeared with blood and scarcely conscious. The SS men rushed into the radio station, broadcast an inflammatory speech in Polish against Germany, fired a few revolver shots at the prisoners, left their corpses lying on the ground and then disappeared back into the night.

News reached OKW, Armed Forces Command, of the Polish Army attack on Gleiwitz and other similar incidents along the border. From the office of Adolf Hitler, Führer and Supreme Commander of the Armed Forces, came the order to invade Poland. While telephone and radio wires hummed and staccato instructions were barked out, Peter remembered Hitler screaming, 'I shall give a propagandist reason for starting the war — never mind if it is plausible or not.' But, as the German war machine sprang into action, he pushed the memory to the back of his mind.

A grey dawn came up over Germany. At Schneidemühl air base, a few miles west of the Polish border, Sepp's orderly knocked on the door and hurried excitedly into his room with a jug of tepid water. 'Herr Oberst, wake up, sir! General Kesselring has called a briefing for 0400 hours. It's started, sir!'

Sepp prepared to turn over for another fifteen minutes' sleep, then the implication of his batman's words sank in and he leaped out of bed, snatched a cigarette and performed the miraculous feat of washing his face and smoking simultaneously.

The briefing room was full when he arrived, an air of tense expectancy hanging over the men. Kesselring and his aides entered and strode onto the podium. Standing in front of a large and, by now very familiar map of Poland, the General said, 'During the night, a series of violations have taken place on the frontier. The Führer has given the order that force must be met with force. Gentlemen, it is our task to immobilize the Polish air force.'

As he stood back to allow the Area Commander to issue exact instructions, there was a ripple of hushed excitement. Intelligence showed that, in aircraft numbers and quality, the Polish air force lagged far behind the Luftwaffe. German victory was a foregone conclusion.

The Major's baton pointed at a map reference. 'Fighter Wing 101 will rendezvous with Bomber Squadron 52 in Berta-Ludwig six at 0535. You will cover the Stukas to their targets at Posen.'

Five minutes later, Sepp and his colleagues from Fighter Wing 101, popularly known as the 'Nowak Wing', were running across the airfield towards their aircraft, now a scene of frenetic activity as mechanics prepared the planes for take-off and pilots settled themselves in their cockpits.

A member of the ground crew helped Sepp into the cockpit of his Messerschmitt Bf 109. On the panel was a caricature painted in Ernst Udet's distinctive style, of himself with a cigarette in his mouth and a bottle in his hand. He looked across to the next plane at his wingman, Andreas Müller. 'You stick close on my tail,' he yelled. Andreas nodded and grinned.

Through Sepp's earphones came the crackled order, '101, prepare for take-off.'

'Viktor, viktor,' he acknowledged. Automatically, he glanced over the instrument panel, checked flaps and rudder. He signalled to the ground crew and the engine fired, flashes of flame and blue smoke spurting from the plane's stub exhausts. Sepp pulled his goggles over his eyes, but did not close the cockpit hood. Flying was not flying unless one had the wind on one's face.

The signal was given and he taxied along the runway, then he was airborne. Behind him, plane after plane rose into the air, flying east towards Poland, silver in the early morning light. Shortly afterwards, he and the forty Messerschmitts of the Nowak Wing had rendezvoused with their Stuka formation and were settled at a comfortable height above the bombers. Sepp looked at his airspeed indicator. The 109 was capable of some 350mph, but he was limited by the top speed of the laden Stukas of 230mph. However, Posen was only sixty miles distant. They should reach their target in a quarter of an hour.

Ahead of them, the skies were strangely empty. Beneath them there was no movement in the flat countryside except the minute shapes of German panzers lumbering down narrow roads. No fighter planes came up to intercept them, and there was no anti-aircraft fire. Considering the Poles were the aggressors, it was a very curious start to a war.

'Where are all the bandits, Uncle?' Andreas's voice laughed down his earphones.

'Perhaps they don't realize there's a war on, Andreas.' Sepp encouraged an atmosphere of informality in his wing. He had no patience with officers who considered themselves superior to their men. In deference to his age and experience, his fliers called him

Uncle. He knew them all by their first names. It made them unique in the Luftwaffe and it also made them a cohesive team. Only battle experience would prove whether his philosophy was correct and the team held together under stress, battle experience which would hopefully be forthcoming very shortly.

'If that's Posen coming up, it certainly doesn't look as if it's awake yet,' Andreas commented. 'There's no flak at all.'

Sepp grunted, cursing the lack of radio contact between bombers and fighters, which meant that the navigator in the lead Stuka was unable to communicate with his fighter escort. As the Stukas began to dive, Sepp issued a staccato order to his men to separate and increase altitude to ten thousand feet. As he had discovered in Spain, it was not unknown for a Stuka rear-gunner to shoot down his fighter escort in mistake for the enemy. Apart from this, the Stuka was most vulnerable when it pulled out of its dive. Were he a Polish fighter pilot, that would be the moment to attack.

Automatically, Sepp had assumed that the Stukas' target would be the Posen airfield, but when he looked down, he saw they were over the town centre itself. His heart contracted as puffs of black smoke ascended, where buildings exploded. So this was the kind of war it was going to be — another Spain... 'Shit,' he exclaimed.

'What's that, Uncle?' Andreas asked.

A voice broke in on the radio. 'Uncle, bandits approaching from the south.'

There they were, far below them, six little PZL P11s, gull-winged metal monoplanes, sturdy but obsolescent by German standards, heading straight for the first Stukas now clambering slowly up to regain their former altitude of four thousand feet. 'After them!'

'Viktor, Uncle!'

Like eagles, forty Messerschmitts swooped out of the clouds towards the six P11s, which were now flying wildly and firing madly at the Stukas. Sepp hesitated for a moment, then dived towards the Poles. Gazing through his gunsight, finger hovering on the firing trigger, Sepp aimed at the fighter leader. Although not within optimum range, he fired a quick burst from his machine guns. Ridiculous though it was, he wanted to give the Polish pilot a chance.

He wanted a fair fight — not mass slaughter. His bullets only punctured the Pole's metal wings.

'Bad luck, Uncle! My turn now!' Andreas yelled over the R/T.

Outnumbered nearly seven times, one after another the P11s were tumbling to the ground, exploding like fireballs or trailing smoke and metal debris in their wake. Attacking again, the Polish leader banked his plane violently towards the last of the Stukas, which was now diving towards the rising pall of smoke over Posen. Sepp could not refuse. 'Viktor, Andreas.'

His wingman's bullets raked across the Pole's fuselage and engine, which erupted in a cloud of smoke, sending a stream of black oil across its windscreen. Erratically now, the P11 continued on its course, guns still blazing at its target. Sepp felt a surge of admiration for his unknown adversary. Obviously severely wounded, and his plane badly damaged, he was not going to give up.

Then he caught his breath in horror as the Pole's intentions became clear. Instead of avoiding the Stuka's path, he was deliberately flying straight at it. For a split second, he caught sight of the Pole's face, his mouth open in a lunatic grin. Then the two planes collided, burst into flames as the Stuka's bombs exploded and, scattering pieces of tangled metal through the sky, spiralled to the ground.

'Did you see that?' Andreas gasped.

Sepp did not reply. His opponent had chosen death rather than defeat. He raised his hand in salute to a brave flier, lifted the nose of his 109 and turned to accompany the remaining Stukas back to Schneidemühl. Reaching into his pocket, he pulled out his hip flask, expertly unscrewing the top with his teeth, hoping against hope that the brandy would settle the nausea rising from his stomach.

Mortimer slept badly that night, waking early and pouring with sweat. Pulling on his dressing gown, he went to the window and looked out into the grey dawn, where workers were already scurrying to their offices. A newsvendor shouted, 'Poles attack! German troops move into action!' At breakneck speed, Mortimer dressed and, without waiting for a lift, raced down the four flights of stairs to the foyer.

Guests and hotel personnel were gathered in grim-faced groups, scanning the papers. 'It's true. Polish soldiers came over the border and attacked German troops.'

Foreign correspondents were invited to listen to Hitler address the Reichstag at ten. As usual, Mortimer walked to the Kroll Opera. The streets were virtually empty. There were no crowds waiting to cheer Hitler when he arrived. The Reichstag deputies were in sombre mood. Hitler himself spoke in a subdued manner and seemed to feel a strange need to justify his actions. 'For two whole days I sat with my Government and waited to see whether it was convenient for the Polish Government to send a plenipotentiary or not... But I am wrongly judged if my love of peace and my patience are mistaken for weakness or even cowardice... I have therefore resolved to speak to Poland in the same language that Poland for months has used towards us...

'This night for the first time Polish regular soldiers fired on our own territory. Since 5.45 a.m. we have been returning the fire and from now on bombs will be met with bombs... Whoever fights with poison will be fought back with poison. Whoever deviates from the rules for the humane conduct of war can expect nothing else from us, but that we will take the same steps...' The deputies cheered — but with none of the fervour of the past.

Hitler went on to announce other edicts. As from that moment, listening to foreign radio stations and reading foreign newspapers were crimes punishable by death. A curfew was imposed upon the Jews. In the event of anything happening to Hitler, Göring was to succeed him, with Hess next in line.

Mortimer spent the rest of the day going from embassy to embassy trying to glean information. In the evening the British press attaché issued a communiqué: 'Unless the German Government are prepared to give His Majesty's Government satisfactory assurances that the German Government have suspended all aggressive action against Poland and are prepared promptly to withdraw their forces from Polish territory, His Majesty's Government will without hesitation fulfil their obligation to Poland.' A little later, Mortimer learned that the French Government had given an identical assurance.

405

The Quadriga bar was doing a very healthy business when he returned to the hotel, packed with anxious-faced people drowning their worries in drink. Suddenly, a new sound filled the air: the shrill, spine-chilling, ululating wail of a siren. Pandemonium broke loose. People grabbed their gas masks and tore into the foyer. 'It's the Poles!' 'They'll kill us all!' A page boy shook his fist heavenwards. 'Don't you bomb us! I'll give you what for!'

Johann, the Hall Porter, steel helmet and armband indicating his new important role of air-raid warden, blew a piercing blast on a whistle. 'Everyone down to the cellar! Please proceed in an orderly manner. There's no need to panic.'

Benno was standing beside him, pale but composed, directing people through the baize doors. Mortimer stood back, more interested in their reactions than fearful for his own safety. Then Viktoria and Ricarda came down the main staircase and he felt a pang of sympathy. There was a defiant gleam in Viktoria's eyes, but Ricarda appeared suddenly older than her seventy-two years. He hurried towards them and took Ricarda's arm. 'I'm sure it's just a practice,' he said consolingly.

Her green eyes looked at him anxiously, but her voice was even, as she replied, 'Yes, of course, Herr Allen.'

'Will you look after Mama, while I help Benno?' Viktoria asked.

Eventually, they were all down in the cellar and Johann started to do a roll-call, ticking off names on a register, but with so many non-residents present and so many guests elsewhere, he had an almost impossible task. Maids were crying hysterically. Men's voices fulminated against Hitler and Poland. People milled about in sheer terror, adding to the confusion.

Eventually, the all-clear sounded and they returned upstairs. Mortimer saw Ricarda back to her rooms, then went out into the moonlit night. The Biedermeier lamps on Unter den Linden were all extinguished. He groped his way in darkness towards the German News Agency building, where he was told that the country's defences had prevented Polish bombers reaching the capital.

When he got back to the Quadriga, people seemed intent on getting very, very drunk. He could not find it in his heart to blame them.

At Fürstenmark, Hans König received his call-up papers, ordering him to his nearest army camp. 'This is it!' he exclaimed excitedly. 'We'll teach those Poles a thing or two!'

Monika was huge, her baby due any day. 'But what about me?' she wailed. 'You can't leave me on my own!'

Hans's blue eyes shone, as he clasped her hands. 'Monika, don't you see? We are both doing our duty for the Fatherland. While I am away at war, you will bear the first of many sons, who will grow up proud in the knowledge of the glorious deeds their father is doing.'

The whole village turned out to watch the soldiers depart, of whom Hans was easily the most handsome. Monika shed a few tears, but she was actually very proud of her husband. The band played. The church bells rang. Monika waved her handkerchief ecstatically.

Every able-bodied man of military age at the Hotel Quadriga and Café Jochum received his call-up papers. Within a matter of hours, the personnel had been almost halved.

Herr Brandt told Benno resignedly, 'Herr Direktor, we should recruit replacements immediately, preferably older, married men who are less likely to get conscripted. As for Café Jochum, I suggest I manage both establishments now that Forster's gone.'

'Certainly for the moment,' Benno agreed. 'After all, although the British and French have promised their support to Poland, they haven't actually done anything. Perhaps there won't be a war with them.'

All day long, there was no word from London or Paris. From Poland came news of glorious German victories, of naval attacks on coastal garrisons, of bomber attacks on Polish airfields, of panzers smashing their way through Polish defences. It was another moonlit night, but still no Polish bombers appeared in the skies over Berlin.

Sunday came, another warm, sunny day, and the atmosphere relaxed. The Polish campaign — if not a flower war — would be quickly over. Roads and trains were crowded with people heading for the country to enjoy the last of summer. Not from the Hotel Quadriga, however. Benno, Viktoria and Ricarda were very wary about leaving, even for a day, while Mortimer was beating a constant path from the French Embassy in the Pariser Platz to the British Embassy and the Chancellery in the Wilhelmstrasse.

Suddenly, just before noon, loudspeakers boomed forth their message: Great Britain had declared war on Germany. The few people gathered outside the Chancellery listened in silence, then, shaking their heads in stunned bewilderment, moved away.

On his way back to the hotel, Mortimer passed the British Embassy. Under police guard, the Ambassador and his staff were moving their belongings to the nearby Hotel Adlon. Mortimer crossed the road and fell in step with James Adams. 'Where are you going?'

'I gather we're being taken to Switzerland in due course. Mortimer, get back to the Quadriga quickly. Chamberlain is due on the radio any minute.'

Mortimer took his friend's hand in a firm grasp. 'Good luck, James, and thanks for all your help. If you get a chance, give my wife a ring when you get back to England and tell her I'm okay.'

A policeman rapped him on the shoulder. '*Los! Los!*'

A newsvendor shouted: 'England declares war!' He shoved a paper into Mortimer's hand. The headlines read: BRITISH ULTIMATUM TURNED DOWN! ENGLAND DECLARES A STATE OF WAR WITH GERMANY! BRITISH NOTE DEMANDS WITHDRAWAL OF OUR TROOPS IN THE EAST! THE FÜHRER LEAVING TODAY FOR THE FRONT!

Mortimer turned into Unter den Linden, hurried up the steps of the Quadriga and into the quiet foyer. Instantly, he was confronted by Viktoria. 'Mortimer, is it true? Has England really declared war on Germany?' The anguish in her voice was unmistakable.

'Go up to your room and listen to the BBC. Chamberlain's about to broadcast.'

Quickly she summoned Ricarda and Benno, then tuned into the BBC. With the door securely locked and the volume turned down low, they listened to Chamberlain's broadcast. 'I am speaking to you from the Cabinet Room at 10 Downing Street. This morning the British Ambassador in Berlin handed the German Government a final note, stating that, unless the British Government heard from them by eleven o'clock that they were prepared at once to withdraw their troops from Poland, a state of war would exist between us. I have to tell you now that no such undertaking has been received and that consequently this country is at war with Germany.'

Ricarda shook her head incredulously. Benno's face was ashen. There were tears in Viktoria's eyes. Chamberlain went on, 'This is a sad day for all of us and to none is it sadder than to me. Everything that I have worked for, everything that I have believed in during my public life, has crashed into ruins... I trust I may live to see the day when Hitlerism has been destroyed and a liberated Europe has been reestablished.'

For a long time after the speech was over, the radio reset to a German station and turned off, they sat in silence. Viktoria buried her face in her hands. 'Oh, Stefi…'

Benno put his arm round her shoulder, brushing her hair with his lips, knowing no words with which to console her.

With Chamberlain's words still echoing in their ears, Joyce, Libby and Stefan sat around the kitchen table. 'Well, that's it,' Joyce said quietly. 'This country is at war with Germany.'

Improbable though it had seemed, Stefan had still been praying for a miracle, hoping that last-minute diplomacy would succeed in averting disaster. He had been in England nearly four weeks, a long period of nothingness, during which he had tried to reconcile himself to the broken fragments of his life. Every morning when he awoke, he remembered Benno was not his father and Christa was his sister. He waited for the postman to bring a letter from his mother, saying she had lied to him. No letter came. He waited for word from the Home Office. No word came. He listened to the radio, waiting for news that war had been averted.

But there was to be no miracle. He buried his face in his hands. 'I'm sorry.'

'Stephen dear, it's not your fault. You did everything you could. You mustn't blame yourself.' Joyce put her arm round his shoulder.

'My family, Christa, Colonel Oster, Admiral Canaris — none of them want war. The only people who want it are men like my grandfather, who will make a lot of money from it — and Hitler himself. Nobody else in the world wants war.'

Libby came round to his other side, kneeling on the floor beside him, placing her cheek next to his. 'You tried to tell them. It's not your fault that they wouldn't listen.'

'No, I failed.' His voice came out as a strangled cry. 'I've failed everybody. I've failed you and Mortimer and Christa and... Oh, I can't bear it.' He began to weep in great, shuddering sobs.

Libby couldn't bear it either. She was seventeen and a kind-hearted girl, who had grown very fond of the young German. 'No, you haven't failed any of us. We love you, because of what you've done — because of who you are. We love you, Stephen.'

But Stefan hardly heard her.

Peter von Biederstein had spent all that day at the War Ministry. In the late afternoon, he received orders that he was to accompany General Halder to new General Headquarters in East Prussia. He telephoned Ilse to pack his bags and sent a driver to collect them. Apart from the fact that he had no time, it did not seem worth going home to say goodbye. Despite the British announcement, he still did not believe the war would last long.

Later that same evening, listening to the BBC — a privilege accorded to Mortimer as a foreigner, but not the German population — Mortimer learned that Winston Churchill had been appointed First Lord of the Admiralty and given a seat in the War Cabinet. It was the first bright spot in a black, black day. But, now that a state of war existed between the two countries, there was no way he could contact him — all telephone, telegraph and postal communications with England were stopped for the duration of the war. Mortimer was as effectively cut-off from home as Viktoria was from her son.

That night, no enemy planes — whether Polish, French or British — crossed the German borders and during the next few days, it seemed that the principal impact war was going to have upon the lives of Berliners was financial. A fifty per cent surtax was imposed on income and big tax increases were put on beer and tobacco. Petrol was rationed and restrictions imposed on civilian motoring. A new decree forced workers to accept new jobs even if they were paid lower wages than they were already receiving.

Newspapers told of glorious conquests in Poland. The German armies crossed the River Vistula, capturing Cracow, Bydgoszcz and Sulejow.

It appeared that the Anglo-French promise to defend Poland had been mere empty words. The first British planes entered German air space. They bombed Wilhelmshaven, but did not get very far before anti-aircraft guns shot at them. For the rest, they dropped — not bombs — but propaganda leaflets. The French, whom it had been feared would sweep in from the West while the German forces were occupied in Poland — sent only a few timid divisions and planes across the Maginot Line. They were swiftly repulsed before they reached the West Wall.

The British did attempt to blockade ports so that supplies could not reach Germany by sea, but this was a game two could play. In retaliation, U-boats attacked Royal Navy ships in the North Sea and British merchant vessels in the North Atlantic, with the aim of cutting off vital British supplies from America. America officially declared her own neutrality on 5 September. On 7 September, the Polish government fled from Warsaw to Lublin. Next day, German troops reached the outskirts of Warsaw.

There was another air-raid alarm in the early hours of Saturday, 9 September, but no planes appeared. Göring broadcast to the nation, heaping scorn upon the RAF leaflet raids and calling for a peace agreement between England and Germany. His boast — that if a single bomb fell on the Ruhr or an enemy bomber reached Berlin, 'then my name is not Hermann Göring, but Meier!' — was not only amusing but infinitely reassuring.

'There will soon be peace,' Benno stated confidently. 'The Poles have learned their lesson. The French have no will to fight. And the British want to remain friends with us, just as we do with them.'

411

'I hope you're right,' Viktoria said fervently.

Monika's baby was born on 10 September 1939. Gerda König telephoned Viktoria to tell her the wonderful news.

'It's a sweet little boy and Monika has decided to name him Heinrich after her grandfather, the Herr Baron von Kraus. Just imagine! He weighed ten pounds! It's such a shame poor Hans isn't here, but we've sent him a telegram, which we hope he will receive.'

When she eventually stopped to take a breath, Viktoria asked Gerda to give her love to Monika, and handed the phone over to Benno. She had yet to see Heinrich König, but she hoped he wouldn't turn out like his namesake.

By 8 September, there was little more for the Nowak Wing to do. The valiant Polish air force was all but destroyed and the Stukas no longer needed fighter protection when they flew their lethal sorties against the few remaining pockets of resistance — the Bzura, Gdynia and Warsaw.

General Kesselring transferred the Nowak Wing to the Rhineland. Sepp's spirits lifted. He had fought the British and the French over France in the last war, when the British, in particular, had proved worthwhile adversaries. Unlike the Poles, the RAF had modern planes. To fight them would mean an honourable battle, not the massacre that had taken place in Poland.

But, to his amazement, he was told the Nowak Wing's role on the Western Front would be purely defensive. One way and another, he reflected, as he flew back in his Bf 109 over the Danzig Corridor and West Prussia, it was a very odd and extremely depressing war.

Peter von Biederstein's task was the administration of General von Bock's Army Group North. He and his men travelled to the rear of the infantry, establishing a long-term military presence in Poland — setting up communications networks, reorganizing troops, ordering supplies, ammunition and mail.

Peter was not a sentimental man, but when he was driven through the streets of Danzig on his way East, a lump rose in his throat. It was to Danzig he had gone as an eighteen-year-old officer cadet and where he had met Ilse. It was to Danzig that he had returned in November 1918 and from Danzig that his regiment had been ousted in the summer of 1919 after the Allies had dictated to Germany the peace terms of Versailles.

Twenty years later, he returned as a conquering hero. The streets were lined with ecstatically cheering crowds. Swastika flags hung from every flagpole, banners were slung across the streets. Church bells peeled. Danzig had returned to the German Reich.

By 10 September, they were twenty miles north-east of Warsaw. Overhead, the air was sundered by the screaming of Stukas flying continuous sorties towards Warsaw. From the distance, they heard thunderous explosions, as bombs dropped over the beleaguered city. A pall of dust hung over the horizon.

Processions of people, carrying shabby suitcases and trundling handcarts, made their way along the muddy roads. Many were Jews, easily distinguishable by their long coats and queer hats, side curls and beards. As their car sent another lot scurrying for a ditch, Peter's ADC, Captain Schatz commented, 'Look like carrion crows, don't they? Look at them, running away, shit-scared. They think they'll be safe from the bombs if they hide in the country. But they're mistaken. The SS Einsatzgruppen have been ordered to kill them. They take them off into a remote spot and shoot them.'

Peter stared at him with scarcely concealed repugnance. Schatz was a typical example of the new breed of soldier. He might be competent, but he lacked all social and cultural graces, was crude and totally without human sensitivity. 'Captain, those are civilians leaving the war zone. Of course they are not being shot.'

Captain Schatz looked insolently at him. 'They're Polish Jews, the scum of humanity, little better than animals. Best thing to do with them is kill them and leave their carcasses for the wolves.'

Peter took a deep breath. 'Do you have any proof of this?'

'No, but everyone's talking about it. It's true.'

That day, they arrived at Castle Podsiadli, already teeming with German soldiers, its once beautiful park massed with tents, army lorries and tanks. Inside, Peter marched along stone corridors lined with tapestries and family portraits and crude, hand-painted German signs. His office was the Count's study, light and airy, with French windows overlooking the wooded grounds.

At dinner that evening, an officer laughed, 'Did himself all right, didn't he, Count Pod? Too bad he won't see this place again!'

Peter stared at him from narrowed eyes. 'What do you mean?'

'Haven't you heard? The castle appeared deserted when we arrived here. Then we found the old Count hiding in a cowshed. When we handed him over to the SS, he tried to run away. So the SS pumped a few bullets into his back.'

Trying to hide his revulsion, Peter pushed his plate away and lit a cigarette. As soon as possible, he left the mess. At the top of the staircase, he was confronted by a portrait of a distinguished man, resplendent in full dress uniform, his hand grasping his sword. For a moment, Peter was arrested by the soldierly stance and aristocratic bearing, then strode on towards his room.

He awoke that night for no apparent reason. Outside it was still dark and the night was silent. Before his eyes, he seemed to see the portrait of Count Podsiadli, the nobleman's eyes boring disdainfully into his. Peter could almost hear him saying, 'How would you feel if this situation were reversed?'

Peter suddenly remembered the famous words of Count Yorck, spoken on the eve of the Battle of Liberation in 1813. Courage, endurance and discipline were a soldier's virtues, he had declared, then added, 'But the Fatherland expects something more sublime from us who are going into battle for the sacred cause: noble, humane conduct, even towards the enemy.'

Commandeering Count Podsiadli's castle was one thing. But Peter knew Count Yorck would not have described shooting an old man in the back as noble and humane conduct.

After a few days at Castle Podsiadli, he sensed a change in the mood of his fellow officers. One evening, he found several of them talking in low voices in the mess. 'There were some Jews repairing a railway bridge under the supervision of an SS artillery division. When they had finished, they were taken into a synagogue and shot.'

'In Posen, SS men got into the prison, where some prostitutes were being held. They raped the women, then shot them.'

'Near Thorn, the SS shot about a hundred people in the main square — nearly all Jews.'

'In Bromberg, the SS strung a Catholic priest up from a tree.'

'It was the SS who shot Count Podsiadli…' Nobody was laughing any more.

Peter wondered to whom he should report these stories. It must be somebody in very high authority, who could use their influence to stop the SS continuing to commit such atrocities. Of course, the Polish Jews were different from the German Jews, but they were still people… Finally, he resolved upon General Halder.

The following day, Peter succeeded in talking to the General on the telephone. Succinctly, he repeated the rumours and demanded, 'Are these reports true, Herr General?'

By Halder's sharp intake of breath, he knew immediately that they were. But the General replied sharply, 'Colonel von Biederstein, the Führer's orders to the SS do not concern you.'

'But if civilians are being indiscriminately killed, the Wehrmacht must intervene. We cannot condone murder.'

'Colonel, have you personally witnessed the murder of a civilian by an Army officer?'

'No, Herr General, but Count Podsiadli was shot in the back…'

'By an Army officer?' General Halder interrupted him coldly.

'By officers of the SS.'

'I suggest, Colonel, that you remember the Führer's words at the Berghof, that we should concern ourselves with military matters. Leave the SS to carry out its duties while you carry out yours.'

The message was explicit. The Army knew what the SS was doing, but was choosing to ignore it. For the first time, Peter von Biederstein experienced apprehension for the future.

Considering the black marks against his name, Mortimer was surprised to be invited to join a group of American correspondents allowed to enter Poland in the wake of the German armies. 'They need a good press,' Chuck Harris laughed, when Mortimer commented on this. 'They want to keep us sweet.'

'And in any case, we shan't be allowed to report the truth,' Mortimer added ruefully.

They were not permitted to travel alone, but were accompanied by Captain Lau, a press attaché from the Propaganda Ministry. A fervent proponent of Blitzkrieg, Captain Lau treated his small audience to detailed lectures on military tactics. 'The speed of the Luftwaffe and the panzer forces, operating as an undivided whole, is the deciding element of this campaign. Our troops moved into Poland from three directions: front Germany, from East Prussia and from Czechoslovakia. Now we are in the process of encircling and isolating the last pockets of resistance. The war will soon be over.'

They passed through devastated villages, patrolled by German soldiers, where the swastika flag blew in the wind. Terrified peasants stared at them from cottage doorways and a few chickens scratched in the dust. Fields were pitted with bomb craters. The roads were lined with bodies of Polish soldiers. In the fields, they saw the blackened wrecks of planes. 'Those planes were never any match for the Luftwaffe,' Chuck Harris muttered.

In a forested area of the Danzig Corridor, they came across carcasses of horses and corpses of dead Polish cavalrymen, crawling with flies and bluebottles. 'The remains of the Pomorska Brigade,' Captain Lau informed them scornfully. 'How foolish of them to think they could win against General Guderian's Panzer Division!'

How foolish indeed. The stench of death rose in nauseous waves around them. One of the cavalry officers was lying on his back, staring glassily at the sky, his lance still clasped in his hand, his bloody cloak partially covering a gaping hole in his abdomen. The barely recognizable remains of his steed were splattered around him. Sick at heart, Mortimer thought, *Horses against tanks... Poor, brave Poland...*

Captain Lau brought his journalists to a halt well behind German lines, some thirty miles north-east of Warsaw at a roadside inn, where there was no electricity or running water. They were the only guests and neither the landlord nor his wife spoke German or English. After a supper of coarse rye bread with smoked sausage, consisting more of fat and potato than meat, washed down with neat vodka, they spent the night three to a room on lumpy horsehair mattresses.

On Sunday afternoon, Captain Lau announced, 'Gentlemen, you have been summoned for briefing to the field headquarters of General Küchler's Third Army.'

The reporters looked at each other hopefully. It would be their first contact with the Army since leaving Berlin. Until now they had had to rely on the evidence of their own eyes, releases dictated to them by Captain Lau and news bulletins on the radio.

Field headquarters was a rambling castle. German sentries stood guard at once ornate iron gates, which had been knocked down to allow entry for tanks and lorries. The tyres of Army vehicles were ruining a long, curved drive, lawns and flowerbeds. Ancient trees were being chopped down for firewood.

After showing their passes, they were conducted into a raftered hall, crowded with German officers. Staggering news awaited them. In a dry voice, an Army spokesman announced that Russian armies had entered Poland from the east and were advancing towards Brest Litovsk. There was a stunned silence.

The journalists were not the only ones to be astonished. It was clear from the puzzled expressions on the faces of the officers that they had been taken totally by surprise. As they moved out of the hall, Mortimer heard several men mutter, 'Why have the Russians intervened? We've got the Poles beaten. We don't need their help.'

At lunch, in the officers' mess, Mortimer encountered Peter von Biederstein. The Count's handsome face was pale and showing signs of strain, which Mortimer put down to the punishing campaign and the news of Soviet intervention. But as they stood for a few moments in the courtyard before Mortimer's departure, Peter suddenly said, 'Herr Allen, there are strange stories going around. If they reach your ears, I want you to know that these occurrences are nothing to do with the Army and that we do not approve of what is happening.'

'What occurrences?' Mortimer asked sharply.

'I am sorry, Herr Allen, I can say nothing more.'

The following day was spent travelling back to Danzig, where Hitler was due to make a speech. In vain, the journalists tried to get Captain Lau to explain why Russia had invaded Poland. The press attaché seemed rather put out, too, and could only say, rather lamely, that it was to protect Germany and Russia's common interests.

Once, they passed a group of peasants being herded along by SS men. 'They're Jews, aren't they? Where are they going?' Mortimer demanded.

Captain Lau frowned. 'The Jews are poisonous parasites. They are the enemy not only of us Germans, but of all peoples. Our fight against world Jewry is a moral fight for the health and purity of all God's people. We are fighting for a new and just order in the world.'

'Cut the rhetoric. Where are they going?'

'For resettlement with other Jews.'

Next day, in Danzig's Guild Hall, in a speech otherwise full of hatred, Hitler announced, 'I have no war aims against Britain and France.' The journalists glanced at each other questioningly. Was it a bid for peace? But then he added, 'We will never capitulate.'

To go from Poland to the Western Front was to enter a different world. *Sitzkrieg*, they were already calling it — sedentary war. Ground troops were stationed right along the West Wall, ready to defend the industrial Ruhr from French attack, but although the French crossed into no-man's-land between the Maginot Line and the West Wall, it was clear they had no intention of coming much further. Sepp and his men lazed in the autumn sunshine, smoking and playing cards. Loudspeakers broadcast light music, regularly interspersed with propaganda. The Nowak Wing made occasional sorties to drop leaflets over the French border, reading, 'Frenchmen, do you want to die for Danzig?' 'We don't want war with France. You stay in France. We'll stay in Germany.'

On one occasion, the boredom was alleviated slightly when two Bristol Blenheims actually crossed the West Wall into German airspace, heading towards the Ruhr, obviously on a reconnaissance mission. Forgetting their pamphlets, the Messerschmitts swooped down on them. The British planes' guns blazed, but they stood no chance against the 109s. Guenther Harding shot down one, Sepp another.

Including Sepp's kills in Spain and Poland, it was his tenth victory, but he felt no satisfaction in it. Like all the others, it had been no test of skill between equally matched opponents. He returned to base, frustrated and impatient. '*Sitzkreig*,' he sighed, lighting a cigarette. 'Come on, boys, let's have a drink.'

Baron Heinrich was at Essen that Wednesday, chairing a management meeting of Kraus Industries. He sat at the head of the conference table, with Ernst and Werner to either side, while the departmental managers deferentially filed in, made their reports, answered a few sharp questions, then departed again.

At the end of the day, the Baron summed up the situation. 'Unless something is done quickly, we face disaster. We had labour shortages before war broke out. Now, as a result of mobilization, we have lost about half our manpower. Within three weeks, production, instead of being increased to cope with increased orders from the military, has gone down by a third. Valuable machinery is lying idle, because we lack workers. Ernst, how do you propose to resolve this problem?'

Ernst shifted awkwardly on his chair. 'The men are working overtime. Many are already putting in an eighty-hour week. I don't see what else we can do.'

'I don't see…' the Baron mimicked impatiently. 'We need more men, boy. Where are you going to find them?'

'Do they have to be men, Grandfather?' Werner asked. 'Why don't we employ women?'

Baron Heinrich rubbed a pudgy hand over his chin. 'Women? I suppose we could if all else fails. But women are unreliable, always having time off to have babies. Besides, Hitler's got a bee in his bonnet about women being kept out of the workplace.'

'We seem to have a good arrangement with Grubenmünde concentration camp,' Werner said. 'Could we take on more prisoners?'

'When war actually starts on the Western Front, we could have French prisoners of war,' Ernst commented.

'We could well find ourselves with a damn sight more!' his father snorted angrily. 'The *Sitzkrieg* is the only thing that's going in our favour at the moment. Has it occurred to you, boy, that Essen is going to be the first place the French and British are going to head for? Knock out our gunshops and they've won the war! I know all this business about Göring calling himself Meier if bombs drop on the Ruhr, but I know what I'd do if I were the British War Minister.'

'The Polish campaign is almost over. Perhaps there will be peace.'

'Perhaps pigs will fly!' The Baron flew back to Berlin that evening, his problem still unresolved.

The most dreadful ramification of war for Bethel Ascher was the loss of contact with England. There were no letters from his daughter, Sophie, and no money from Theo. Overnight, hope had gone. The Jews of Berlin were utterly dependent upon their own resources.

On 23 September, there were new, reduced ration cards and a law forbidding Jews to own radio sets. The reason given was that the military needed them, but clearly, it was intended that the Jews should be further cut off from the outside world.

The Blockwart for the Rosenthaler-Strasse, accompanied by a posse of Hitler Youth, personally supervised their handing over at the local collecting centre. As Bethel Ascher's radio was snatched from his hands and thrown carelessly onto a growing pile, he knew he would miss it less for the news than for the concerts, the only thing that had kept him sane. Blindly, he made his way out onto the street. A world without music… Could anything be more intolerable?

'Professor Ascher,' a voice said quietly. 'It's Hasso Annuschek. Herr Allen has sent me. Don't turn around. Just keep walking.'

The Professor did as he was told. Hasso went on, 'Herr Allen will be waiting for you at the entrance to the St Hedwig Hospital at three this afternoon.'

'Move your arse, Jew-pig!' a Hitler Youth thug snarled. Bethel did as he was told.

That afternoon at the hospital, it was visiting time, the entrance hall full of people and, for a moment, Professor Ascher stood bewildered by the bustle. Then Mortimer strolled across to him. 'Bethel, old friend, how are you?'

'I live — and I pray — but my heart is heavy. And you, Mortimer? It is a long time since I have seen you.' It was a statement made without reproach.

'I have just come back from the war zone, where I learned something I think you should know. In Poland, Jews are being forcibly resettled into ghettos.'

The blood drained from Bethel's face. 'So it is beginning…'

'Bethel, I am sorry and I wish there were something I could do.' Mortimer handed him an envelope. 'All I can give you is money…'

On 28 September, Warsaw fell and rumours of peace abounded. Mussolini was calling for European peace. Molotov and Ribbentrop signed a German-Soviet Friendship Treaty in Moscow, dividing Poland between them, and issued a joint declaration for peace, stating that if their efforts proved fruitless, 'this would demonstrate the fact that England and France are responsible for the continuation of the war.'

At the Hotel Quadriga, Benno prophesied, 'There will soon be an armistice.'

'The English are gentlemen,' Ricarda commented.

'Chamberlain never wanted war,' Viktoria added hopefully.

In Mortimer's mind it meant only one thing. By giving Russia half of Poland as a sop, Hitler had won a formidable ally. By launching a peace offensive, he could have his war against England without being blamed for it.

At the end of the month, Admiral Canaris paid an unannounced visit to Castle Podsiadli. His face was etched with tiredness when Captain Schatz showed him into Peter's office. 'Well, Biederstein,' he said, sinking down in one of the Polish Count's leather chairs, 'how sweet the smell of victory, eh?'

Although he had known him for years, Peter never quite knew where he stood with the Abwehr chief. A short man in his early fifties, with kindly features, thoughtful eyes and white hair, Canaris reminded him of the Kipling story he had read as a child of the cat who walked by himself.

'Been to Warsaw?' Canaris asked.

'Not yet.'

'It was a beautiful city once. Unrecognizable now. You must have seen the smoke and flames from here. They burned the city centre to the ground.' Canaris narrowed his eyes. 'And Kesselring still maintains that the Luftwaffe's attacks were strictly limited to military targets.' He took a deep breath. 'General von Fritsch killed himself. Did you know that?'

Peter stared at him, appalled. 'Suicide?'

'Not exactly. He allowed himself to be killed. He couldn't live with his shame — or with the war we are waging here in Poland.'

Peter felt Canaris's eyes boring into his. Was this an invitation for him to speak? Slowly, he said, 'There have been rumours circulating about the SS Einsatzgruppen. The Count who owned this castle is reported to have been shot in the back. There are other stories concerning Jews...'

'They are true,' Canaris replied bleakly. 'Do these incidents disturb you, Biederstein?'

'They seem incompatible with the code of honour of a German officer. I spoke to General Halder...'

'I, too, have spoken to General Halder and to General Keitel. I am also in possession of some other facts. On 19 September, Heydrich issued an official directive to the Einsatzgruppen concerning the Poles. All Jews are to be concentrated into urban areas — basically ghettos — as a first step towards the final solution. Their leaders, as well as leaders of other non-Jewish groups, are to be cleaned out.'

'Cleaned out?'

'Exterminated,' Canaris answered succinctly.

Peter fumbled for a cigarette. 'Is OKW aware of this?'

'Oh, yes,' Canaris said grimly. 'Although the Einsatz squads receive their orders directly from Heydrich, they are subordinate to High Command, which has received a copy of Heydrich's memorandum.'

'And hasn't Keitel contested the order?'

'The General has obtained the concession that Heydrich's "house-cleaning" operations will be postponed until after the military has withdrawn and a civil administration is set up in Poland. Apart from anything else, if news leaked out to the foreign press, particularly the Americans, it could have most unfortunate repercussions.' Canaris paused, then asked, 'Well, Biederstein, now you know the truth, what are you going to do?'

Peter shook his head. 'What can I do? I have no authority, except over my own men and, even then, I must act on General Halder's orders. If he agrees with what the Führer is doing, it is my duty to obey him.'

'And you still believe that you should obey the Führer, right or wrong?'

Shocked, Peter replied, 'But, of course.'

Canaris stood up and moved towards the door, an enigmatic smile playing on his lips. 'So long as you realize that, one day, when the dreadful truth emerges, the world will hold the Army responsible for these atrocious deeds.'

'But we have no part in them...' However, he was speaking to an empty room. As suddenly as Canaris had arrived, he was gone.

In England, there was suddenly a lot of talk about fifth columnists. Special tribunals were set up to investigate fifty thousand enemy aliens registered in the London area — fifty thousand people who had escaped from Nazi Germany and were now suspected of being spies.

On the street, Stefan sensed people looking at him suspiciously. Once, they had accepted him as Stephen Cross. Now, they remembered he was Stefan Kraus. He even received some anonymous letters addressed to him as S. Kraut, accusing him of unmentionable atrocities.

Libby, in her final year at school, tried to console him. 'You mustn't take it personally. You're not a typical German.'

Miserably, Stefan replied, 'I don't know what I am any more.'

Children dressed up in toy steel helmets and marched with toy rifles. They sang, 'Ven der Führer says ve ist der Master Race, then ve heil fart, heil fart, right in der Führer's face...' To the tune of *Colonel Bogie*, they chanted, 'Adolf has only got one ball, Göring's got two but they're too small, Himmler has got something similar, But poor old Goebbels got no balls at all...' On the radio, they played, '... Have you got any dirty washing mother dear? We're going to hang out the washing on the Siegfried Line, if the Siegfried Line's still there!'

Despite promises from Trevor and Tony to intervene on his behalf, there was no residency permit, no work permit.

An impassioned plea to Winston Churchill, not unexpectedly, received no answer. Stefan still had to report to the local police station every week. To live he was dependent upon the Allens' charity. He prayed for peace, but he knew that so long as Hitler refused to give up Poland, there could be no peace. The days passed very, very slowly.

On 5 October, exactly thirty-five days after the Polish campaign had begun, Hitler flew to Warsaw to review a parade of the victorious German troops. Through streets lined with rubble, past huge craters where ancient buildings had once stood, past houses whose roofs gaped open to the sky, they marched in triumphant procession: rank upon rank of soldiers in field grey uniforms and airmen in Luftwaffe blue and SS men in black, the black insignia of the swastika upon the blood-red standards borne before them. In steady tempo, burnished black jackboots goose-stepped over the cobbled roadways, thousands upon thousands of them, hour after hour after hour.

Military bands played patriotic songs and marches: *Deutschland, Deutschland, über alles...* The 'Watch on the Rhine'... The 'Horst Wessel Song'... 'When Jewish blood spurts from the knife, We shall have a better life...'

Marching, eyes right, to the front of his men, Peter saluted Hitler, Führer and Supreme Commander. At the end of the parade, General Halder informed him that, for his part in the campaign, Hitler was promoting him to the rank of Major-General. Only a month into war and promotion! Peter decided, once and for all, to ignore this business about Heydrich's house-cleaning. He pushed his misgivings to one side, thankful he had paid no attention to Canaris's innuendos.

A demarcation line now cut Poland in half, dividing the captured territories between Germany and the Soviet Union, but it was clear the Government trusted the Soviet Union no more now than in the past. A strong military presence was remaining to keep the new frontier secure. Peter was appointed to General Blaskowitz's Military Government in Warsaw.

Next day, Hitler addressed the Reichstag. After boasting about Germany's triumphs in Poland, he announced the formation of a Polish State and admitted that he still had to decide upon a solution to the Jewish problem. He talked vaguely about population exchanges. Then he turned to his proposals for peace. 'Germany has no further claims against France… At no time and in no place have I ever acted contrary to British interests…'

I think I've heard this before, Mortimer reflected wearily, as Hitler's words flowed on, holding his audience spellbound. *Surely the British won't fall for it?*

'Why should this war in the West be fought?' Hitler demanded, in a tone of righteous indignation. 'For the restoration of Poland? Poland of the Versailles Treaty will never rise again…'

No, Mortimer thought sadly, *Poland is as dead as the cavalry officer in the Danzig Corridor.*

Well into his stride, Hitler offered concessions to the British and French. He wanted a peace conference. He was willing to discuss reduction of armaments, to settle minority problems in Europe, to have regulations regarding air warfare, poison gas and submarines. 'If, however, the opinions of Mister Churchill and his followers should prevail, this statement will have been my last… There will never be another November 1918 in German history!'

The newspaper headlines read: GERMANY'S WILL FOR PEACE!

Back at the Quadriga, opinion was unanimous. 'The British and French Governments have got to accept the Führer's offer,' Benno said for all of them.

'And Poland?' Mortimer asked.

He got the answer he expected. 'We have only taken what is rightfully ours. What is the point of millions more men dying just for a matter of principle?'

What indeed? Mortimer wondered. As he got into bed that evening, he suddenly felt very glad that he was not a British or

French politician, trying to read Hitler's mind, with the responsibility of the future of Europe weighing upon his shoulders.

The Warsaw Victory Parade over, Hans König returned with his company to their camp on the outskirts of Lublin, where the men were told that they were to remain in Poland while order was restored. The special task allotted to them was assisting SS Einsatzgruppen with Jewish resettlement.

Hans had been brought up with a superstitious dread of Jews. His father, a strict Lutheran, had never made any secret of his loathing for them and Hans, with no personal experience to the contrary, believed that they were indeed Germany's misfortune.

Until he went to Poland, he had never met a Jew. There were none in Fürstenmark, none in the Army and none at his college in Stettin. Possibly, he had seen some in Berlin, but if so, he had not recognized them, so Aryan did they look. Certainly, he had never encountered anyone remotely resembling the rabbis and other pious Jews of Poland, frightening in their strange tall hats and flowing black caftans, with their outlandish side curls and beards.

It was not hard to believe the stories of Jewish sorcery he had heard, or to believe that the Jews were in league with the devil. Not only did they look different, they spoke another language, ate strange food, killed their meat with sadistic ritual and had heathenish customs, like the circumcision of their boy children. They were usurers and parasites. They were vermin.

During the bombing of Poland's major cities, thousands of these Jews had escaped and were now hiding in small villages or scurrying to safety with their Bolshevik comrades in Russia. It was the task of Hans König and his fellow soldiers to rout them out and bring them back to Lublin, where they could be collected into a Jewish reservation and kept under the supervision of the Gestapo.

They set about their job with gusto. Driven out into the countryside in army lorries, they rampaged through Polish villages, tearing apart barns and cattlesheds, searching farmhouses and cottages, terrorizing peasants into revealing the whereabouts of any

Jews they were concealing. Having found them, they herded them into the village square or the local school for the SS to deal with.

Sometimes, they heard the sound of gunfire and learned later that the Jews had been shot. Hans never actually witnessed this happening and when one of his friends squeamishly commented on it to him, he said, 'I think it's the best solution really. After all, there are three million Jews in Poland. There isn't room in Lublin for all of them. Isn't it better just to get rid of them?'

Once the Jews were accounted for, baby Germans — like Heini König — could sleep safely at night without fear of falling victim to the evil eye.

As the days passed, hope grew stronger and rumours increased. On the morning of the 11th, a German radio broadcast announced that the British Government had fallen and that there would be an immediate armistice. Unable to believe it, Mortimer sat with his ear glued to his radio, waiting for confirmation on the BBC, but from London came only an ominous silence.

In the meantime, Berlin threw itself into an orgy of celebration. Benno invited everyone in the Hotel Quadriga to drinks on the house. Luise, Lili and Sheltie rushed over from Lützow for the impromptu party, bringing Ilse with them.

Her morning's duties at the Foreign Ministry over, Christa arrived in time for luncheon. It was the first occasion she and Viktoria had met since Stefan's abrupt departure and Viktoria felt very embarrassed at seeing her again. But Christa harboured no ill-will. Although she knew Viktoria had been against her romance with Stefan, she had no idea of the role she had played in Stefan's sudden flight and, far from holding a grudge, sympathized with her loss.

Taking Viktoria's hand in hers, she said, 'I know how you must miss Stefan, Aunt Viktoria. I miss him, too.'

There was nothing for Viktoria to do but accept the proffered olive branch with good grace. 'Yes, of course you must.'

Christa gave a sweet little smile. 'But if there's an armistice, then maybe Stefan will return.'

Before Viktoria could react to this, Mortimer entered the bar, grinning broadly. 'It was a propaganda hoax! I've just heard that someone put the rumour out to see what public opinion would be to an end of the war.'

There was a stunned silence, then Viktoria said bitterly, 'Well, whoever that someone might be, he must be clear now as to our feelings.'

The following day, their hopes were dashed even further when they learned that Chamberlain had called Hitler's proposals vague and uncertain. They contained no suggestions for righting the wrongs done to Czechoslovakia and Poland. If the German government wanted peace, he said, 'acts — not words alone — must be forthcoming.'

On Friday, 13 October, an official statement announced that, by turning down Hitler's offer, the British Government had deliberately chosen war. With heavy hearts, Berliners reconciled themselves to the fact that, from now on, there would be no turning back.

Yet, still, the greatest reality of war was rationing and shortages of petrol, soap, leather and shoes. As wars went, it could be far worse. But better still, would be no war.

On 8 November, Hitler made his annual visit to Munich to celebrate the 1923 Putsch. The following morning, a shocked nation learned that, shortly after he and his colleagues had left the beer hall, a bomb had exploded, killing seven people and injuring sixty-three others. The blame was laid upon the British Secret Service.

There was a wave of public indignation and a surge of hatred against England, the first Mortimer had witnessed since hostilities had commenced. Benno seemed to speak for them all, when he demanded, 'What did the British hope to achieve by such a dreadful thing?'

The foreign correspondents were sceptical, agreeing that the affair stank to high heaven. 'How could British agents have got past Hitler's guards to plant the bomb in the first place?' Mortimer asked. 'Sounds like a repetition of the Reichstag fire. A put-up job.'

The assassination attempt shocked Peter to the marrow, convincing him that no time should be lost in launching the western offensive. Impatiently, he waited for orders to return to Berlin, but, to his dismay, no orders came.

In the meantime, the first convoys of Polish slave labourers departed for Germany, to work in factories and mines and an edict made forced labour compulsory for all Jews between the ages of fourteen and sixty. As Peter travelled through Poland, he saw Jews scrubbing pavements and moving rubble, clearing forests and digging ditches, obviously half-starved and many near death from the unaccustomed labour. He could not help witnessing the barbarities of the SS guards, goading them to work with insults and whips, burning their religious scrolls and setting fire to their synagogues.

Himmler's resettlement programme also slowly got underway. Once again, the roads were filled with unwieldy processions of people, trundling handcarts and barrows, heading miserably towards the Generalgouvernement, forced along by SS men and army troops. Peter consoled himself with the knowledge that they were nothing to do with him and his staff.

Then, in early November, driving through a small village on his way back from Lublin, a terrible event occurred. They passed a school, surrounded by SS men armed with machine guns. His driver slowed down to look and, with a sickening feeling of dread, Peter opened his mouth to order him to pick up speed again, when Captain Schatz, sitting with the driver, asked, 'What do you think is going on there, sir? Should we stop and help?'

The driver glanced over his shoulder, waiting for Peter's order. Still he hesitated, then, as he sensed Schatz staring at him curiously, he nodded. 'Driver, stop the car.' Stiffly, he got out and walked back down the street to the commanding SS officer, Schatz close behind him.

As he approached, the officer shouted, 'Attack!'

About half a dozen men kicked open the door to the building and fired a blaze of bullets into the room. Peter waited for the returning fire, but there was none. The SS men charged into the building and started dragging bodies out onto the deserted street. Among them was a rabbi, his singed side curls still recognizable under his smashed and bloodied skull. Beside him lay a boy of no more than twelve years.

'Leave them!' the SS officer shouted. 'Fire the building!' Cans of gasoline standing nearby were tipped over the floorboards and a blazing rag thrown into it. Moments later, the schoolhouse was ablaze.

The smell of burning flesh clawed at Peter's nostrils and made his stomach heave. 'What the devil are you doing?' he demanded.

The SS man turned to him, looked insolently at his stripes and said, 'General, I have my duties to perform, just as you have yours. Those men were Jewish intellectuals plotting to overthrow the Government. Now, if you will permit me to continue...'

There was nothing Peter could do. Abruptly, he turned away and walked back to his car. A rabbi and a child... So the stories were true. The Jews were being slaughtered before they ever reached the special compounds in the cities.

To his surprise, he found Schatz already back at the car, his face green. 'Well, Captain,' he snarled, 'now you've seen what happens to the sub-humans.' Schatz retched and Peter looked at him in disgust. 'If you're going to throw up, don't do it in my car.' Clasping his stomach, Schatz ran behind a neighbouring barn.

When Peter next saw General Blaskowitz, he reported the incident, omitting Schatz's indiscretion. The Military Governor nodded soberly. 'But what can I do? My hands are tied.'

'You could protest to the Führer.'

'And provoke his rage to no avail? Remember, he told us to be steeled against all signs of compassion.' He ran his hand across his forehead. 'Maybe I shall write to General von Brauchitsch. He is closer to the Führer than I am.'

But even if he did, Peter knew Brauchitsch would do nothing. That night, he got very, very drunk. A week later, to his relief, he was informed that his duties in Poland were over.

CHAPTER TWELVE

Peter returned to Berlin and a different world. Apart from the blackout and flak guns, everything looked just as it had for the last two years. The horrors he had just experienced suddenly took on the unreal aspect of a nightmare. Ilse greeted him as if he had been away on holiday and arranged a series of dinner parties to celebrate his promotion. One of the first was at Grunewald with Baron Heinrich.

The Baron was in superb form. 'Poland's resolved a lot of my problems,' he told Peter. 'Had a terrible labour shortage when war broke out, but now they're sending us Polish workers, production has increased considerably. Don't you worry, boy. By the time you find yourselves at war with France and England, you'll have all the tanks and guns you need.'

Ilse frowned. 'I've thought about taking a Polish maid, but one hears such dreadful stories about them. They don't wear underclothes, they can't speak German and they're very lazy.'

'Lazy! All workers are lazy. Just have to show them who's boss. If any of our Poles are found slacking, they don't get their rations.'

'Where do you house them?' Peter asked.

'In camps. Their conditions are probably better than they were in Poland.'

'Yes, I suppose so.' There was a strange hesitation in his voice.

Ilse glanced at him curiously. His face was drawn and it suddenly occurred to her that he had aged since the summer. When they got home, she asked, 'Peter, you didn't sound as if you agreed with Uncle Heinrich about the Poles. Why not?'

But Peter could not tell her the truth about Poland, although he wished he could, if only to ease his conscience.

At Zossen, some twenty miles south of Berlin, where Army High Command had moved since the outbreak of war, there was a very different, very troubled atmosphere and Peter soon learned the reason. Several of the generals, including General Halder and General von Brauchitsch, had been trying to dissuade Hitler from waging war in western Europe. Flying into a rage, Hitler had accused the Army of being too scared to fight.

'But it is not fear that holds us back,' Halder assured Peter. 'It is because none of us believe the offensive has any prospect of success. Blitzkrieg worked in Poland, but it will not succeed in France. And to go to war at the onset of winter is sheer folly.'

On 23 November, the commanding generals and General Staff officers were summoned to a meeting at the Chancellery. Hitler treated them like naughty schoolboys, boasting about his own brilliant achievements and admonishing them for their defeatism. Then he outlined his plans for the future, stressing the importance of the fact that, due to the treaty with Russia, the next campaign would be fought on one front, although, he added meaningfully, 'Treaties are kept only so long as they serve a purpose.'

Equally blandly, he announced, 'My decision is unchangeable. I shall attack France and England at the most favourable and earliest moment. Breach of the neutrality of Belgium and Holland is of no importance. No one will question that when we have won.'

He ended: 'As long as I live I shall think only of the victory of my people. I shall shrink from nothing and shall annihilate everyone who is opposed to me…'

It was clear he was referring not only to the enemy abroad, but to those who attempted to oppose his policies at home. Not a person moved, not a voice spoke, and Peter knew that just as the atrocities in Poland would continue, so would the attack on the West take place. And, although he regretted the atrocities, he could not regret the victories. He, too, could not help feeling that General Halder was being unnecessarily defeatist.

Yet the weeks passed and Hitler gave no order. The sea war went on, the British Fleet unfortunately showing itself to be considerably stronger than the German Navy. Russia invaded Finland. And on the Western Front, *Sitzkrieg* continued.

The Lieutenant marched purposefully into the Hotel Quadriga, his collar biting into his neck and his eyes gleaming with grim determination. He saluted to Herr Brandt and announced, 'I must speak to the Hotel Director on a matter of utmost importance.'

Herr Brandt returned the salute. 'I'll fetch Herr Kraus.'

Benno emerged from his office, with Viktoria close on his heels. 'Lieutenant, how can we help you?'

With great self-importance, he handed over an official order and announced, 'The fourth floor of this hotel is to be vacated within the next twenty-four hours and will be taken over by a department of Army High Command.'

Benno stared at him, open-mouthed.

'Army High Command?' Viktoria echoed hollowly.

The officer's glance flickered briefly in her direction, then returned to Benno. 'We no longer have room in our existing offices. This time tomorrow, officials from the Todt Organization will come to decide upon the necessary structural alterations.'

'Who's going to pay for them?' Benno asked grimly.

'The Army will cover all costs. Because of the confidentiality involved, Gestapo agents will arrive shortly to examine your records, to ensure that none of your staff pose a security risk.'

'The Gestapo?' Viktoria exclaimed faintly.

Benno shot her a warning glance. 'I don't think they will find anything amiss, Herr Lieutenant.'

'I shall be back at nine tomorrow morning.' With a salute, the Lieutenant was gone.

Viktoria seized Benno's arm. 'How can they take over a whole floor of our hotel?'

'They did it in the last war, so I suppose they can do it in this one.'

'And the Gestapo?'

Benno threw her a strange glance. 'My dear, you are just going to have to lie. But it won't be the first time you've lied for the sake of Stefan and your hotel, will it?'

Before she could react to this, two Gestapo officers were marching through the foyer.

Inevitably, their first question regarded Stefan. Viktoria had no choice but to follow Benno's lead and say that she no longer considered him her son. Quite truthfully, she could say that she had heard nothing from him since his departure.

The two men stayed four gruelling hours, during which they went through the registration documents of all guests, past and present; the workbooks of all employees, including those on active service; and conducted a thorough search of all rooms, including staff quarters and the cellars. They left with the terse communication that, once the alterations were completed, guards would be stationed permanently in the foyer and outside the hotel.

That evening, Norbert telephoned, cheerful and excited. 'Uncle Benno? Wonderful news! I'm being sent to Berlin as Site Manager in charge of the alterations to your hotel. I'm flying up tomorrow morning for a site meeting.'

'Norbert seems so young, but at least he knows the hotel,' Benno commented, as he put down the phone.

'Yes,' Viktoria agreed. 'He won't spoil its character.'

Norbert had changed little. His luggage was taken into the Kraus suite on the first floor, then he tucked into a huge breakfast, moaned about his brother and father and ogled a pretty brunette sitting on the other side of the restaurant. He had just finished eating when Air Ministry and OKW officials, together with his superior from the Todt Organization arrived.

The rest of the day passed in a daze, as the plans of the hotel were examined, measurements taken, calculations made, costs and timetables discussed. In view of the important people who were going to move into the fourth floor, adequate air-raid precautions had to be made. The cellar must be converted into a proper air-raid shelter.

Once again, Benno pleaded for the safety of his wine.

Norbert came up with an excellent suggestion. 'Divide the wine cellar into two. Since you've lost quite a few staff through conscription, move the downstairs staff up into the attic and put your oldest vintages in the staff quarters. The rest will have to go under Unter den Linden. Then make the shelter itself into a restaurant. Personally, if I were being bombed, I think I'd rather like something to eat. You could get quite a lot of outside trade.'

'Yes, I suppose so,' Benno said doubtfully.

The Air Ministry official shrugged. 'I don't see why not. To be honest with you, gentlemen, I think it quite improbable that Berlin will ever be attacked from the air. You might as well put the space to good use.'

'What about cooking?' Viktoria asked.

'Build a kitchen,' Norbert said brightly. 'You've got water and electricity down there. The cost would be negligible.'

'Such additions would not be paid for by OKW,' the Lieutenant pointed out hurriedly.

After that, everything happened at high speed and with unwonted efficiency. With a great deal of grumbling because they would be far less secure in the attic, the staff moved upstairs and, under Benno's supervision, the wine was transferred into their rooms. Guests living on the fourth floor were given superior rooms on the third floor at the same price. 'Who's moving in?' Mortimer asked Viktoria after a maid had moved his belongings from room 401 to 301.

'It's something to do with the military,' was all she could tell him. She looked so depressed, his heart went out to her.

The very next day, builders arrived. Working night and day, they sealed off all access to the fourth floor, except for one lift. Steel doors were erected at all exit points from the fourth floor and were barred so that they could be opened only in an emergency. All telephone communications with the rest of the hotel were severed and new lines installed.

The roof and walls of the cellar were reinforced and a thick dividing wall constructed between the two halves with an interconnecting door. Immediately beneath the existing kitchen, a smaller kitchen was installed, with a lift so that food could be conveyed down from the ground floor and dirty dishes returned for washing-up. A new staircase into the cellar restaurant-cum-air-raid shelter opened off the foyer next to the present restaurant. A rest room was built for the Gestapo guards.

Benno had expected there to be a problem in finding decorators, but Norbert had a solution. 'Jews,' he said, succinctly. Twenty middle-aged Jews turned up next morning and were pathetically grateful to be rewarded for their labours in food.

To everyone's amazement — so used had they become to bureaucratic delays — the fourth floor was ready for habitation and the cellar had been transformed in exactly two weeks. Desks, chairs, filing cabinets and chests of papers were taken up to the fourth floor. Viktoria watched them despondently.

Then, through the revolving doors, an urbane smile on his face, strolled Colonel Oster, the first time he had visited the hotel since Stefan had gone. Hope flared in Viktoria's heart. He must have news of Stefan! She glanced towards the Gestapo men. 'Colonel Oster...'

He bowed low over her hand and said, 'My dear Frau Jochum-Kraus, how delightful to see you. And from now on, I think we shall be seeing very much more of each other.'

'What do you mean?'

He waved his hand towards the lift. 'I shan't be working here personally, but I shall often be visiting. The Abwehr is taking over your fourth floor.'

'The Abwehr?'

'It was Canaris's idea. When we ran out of space on the Tirpitz Ufer, an hotel seemed to have certain advantages, including anonymity and camouflage.' He twinkled at her through his monocle, then took her arm and, casually, led her onto the street. 'Viktoria, I am sorry about Stefan, but we could not risk arousing the suspicions of the Gestapo. We had to denounce him as a traitor.'

'I understand,' she said quietly.

Surprisingly, the new inhabitants of the fourth floor caused little disturbance. The hotel's guests were nearly all military or civilians connected with the war. Used to dealing with important people on confidential business, the hotel personnel took the Abwehr's presence in their stride. Even the Gestapo guard stationed in the foyer and the guards patrolling the portico soon became as much a part of the furniture as the portrait of Hitler in its gilt frame.

There were even advantages to having them there. The military was exempt from rationing and so the hotel's kitchens were given special food dispensations. 'I suppose we should consider ourselves lucky,' Benno commented drily. 'We have the most secure hotel in Germany, and what's more, we're never going to starve.'

The cellar, however, remained unused, both as an air-raid shelter and a restaurant. Although the blackout continued, no enemy bombers threatened Berlin.

The close proximity of the Abwehr made Mortimer's situation more frustrating than before. He dared not resume contact with Hans Oster for fear of incriminating him and thwarting his activities. In any event, even if Oster were able to pass him information, Mortimer still lacked the means of passing it on.

But Christmas was approaching. He applied for a travel permit and booked a train ticket to Holland. Soon he would get home, see his family and re-establish contact with the outside world.

Christmas and New Year's Eve were subdued occasions. Instead of roads sparkling with thousands of candlelit trees, Berlin was shrouded in darkness. It was cold and wet, with snow in the rain. There was a shortage of coal and a shortage of traditional Christmas gifts in the shops and, finally, there was Himmler's directive that, instead of staying open all night, all cafés and bars had to shut at one a.m. on New Year's Day.

Possibly, the only person to be truly happy was Luise, for Sepp was home on leave. He grumbled about the quietness on the Western Front, but Luise was simply delighted that he was in no danger. For the rest of them, there was a forced gaiety to their celebrations.

Everyone drank far more and danced far less than usual at the New Year's Eve Ball and when the police arrived at one to make sure that the bar was shut, they discovered quite a few people had passed out in the Palm Garden Room and even on the foyer floor.

'What shall we do with them?' Hasso asked.

Benno shrugged. 'Let them sleep it off. After all, who can blame them? It hasn't been much of a Christmas, has it?'

In Oxford, the blackout curtains were up and in the hall gas masks hung ready on hooks with the coats. Despite steadily rising prices and food shortages, Joyce had saved her ration stamps to prepare Mortimer's favourite meal of roast beef, Yorkshire pudding and Brussels sprouts.

As the hands of the clock approached midnight, Mortimer opened the bottle of champagne he had managed to buy at ridiculous cost in London. The cork hit the ceiling with a resounding bang, causing the cat to dive under the table in fright. Mortimer poured the foaming wine into the waiting glasses and grinned. 'Happy New Year and to hell with the enemy!'

Joyce, Libby and Stefan raised their glasses and repeated the toast, then Joyce said quietly, 'And to absent friends.'

Stefan hesitated for a moment, then, after glancing sheepishly at Mortimer, said, 'Yes, to absent friends.'

The next day, he handed Mortimer a sealed envelope. 'Will you give this to Mama?' In the afternoon, the precious letter stitched inside his coat lining, Mortimer started his arduous journey across the Channel to the Hook of Holland and on to Berlin.

He stayed one night in Amsterdam, in a very different environment from Oxford or Berlin. The street lights were on. There was food in abundance. And the Dutch people were supremely confident that they would be able to continue their way of life. As Mortimer crossed the border, he could not help but notice the number of German troops, tanks and armoured trucks in the area.

Mortimer was waiting for Viktoria as she left the Quadriga. Casually, he fell into step with her, opened the newspaper and pointed to an article. Stefan's envelope was resting on it. 'Take the paper,' he said.

She took it, glancing at him unhappily. 'Has Stefi forgiven me?'

'I think so.'

'He told you the whole story?'

'Yes. Naturally your revelation came as a great shock to him, but he's young and resilient. He's getting over it.'

A biting wind gusted down Unter den Linden and Viktoria shivered. 'If Hitler went and the war ended, do you think Stefi would come back?'

'There's a fair chance. But, in the meantime, Hitler is still here and the war continues, albeit in a very strange way.'

'I keep thinking there ought to be some way I can continue Stefi's fight, but there is nothing I can do.'

Mortimer looked cautiously around, but the pavement was empty. 'You can tell me if you hear anything odd, for instance from the Baron or Peter. But apart from that, you've just got to be patient.'

'I feel so helpless.'

'We all are. Try to remember that, one day, things will change.'

'Mortimer, do you understand why I have acted as I have?'

'Yes, I understand and, you may not believe me, but I admire you for it. But then, I have always thought you a remarkable woman.'

With that, he was gone, striding towards the Wilhelmstrasse. As she watched him, a new courage took root in Viktoria's heart. Whatever horrors lay ahead, she would survive them. When Stefi returned, he would be proud of her. One day, he, too, would think her a remarkable woman.

She rushed to her bedroom to open his note. It was very short, but it said everything she needed to know: 'I am beginning to understand and I am sorry. Love, S.' After reading and re-reading it, she reluctantly tore it into pieces and flushed them down the lavatory. Then, head held high, she went to face the world.

Hans also came home on leave that Christmas for a joyful reunion with his parents, Monika and baby Heinrich. Three months old, Heini was a handsome baby with a fat face, a few blond curls and blue-grey eyes. He was a very contented child, not given to crying, and sleeping soundly after copious feeds. Hans felt inordinately proud of him.

Motherhood suited Monika, lending a bloom to her cheeks and a flattering fullness to her figure. While Heini slept in his cradle, Hans drew his wife to him in their big double bed. 'Let's make lots and lots more babies,' he said, 'one every time I come home on leave.'

Monika giggled. 'How often can you get leave?' she asked.

All too soon, Hans returned to Poland. Scarcely had he arrived in Lublin, than winter really set in, freezing and more bitter than any he had ever experienced. Fierce blizzards swept across the plains, as temperatures plummeted to as low as forty degrees below zero. Rivers and canals froze solid, bringing all transport to a halt. Dense banks of snow piled high on roads and city streets, where Jews, wearing the yellow Star of David on the right sleeves of their thin coats, shivered as they shovelled.

Despite the biting cold, the resettlement of Jews, Poles and ethnic Germans continued. In all major cities, ghettos were created, special residential areas into which the Jews were crowded behind barbed wire fences or brick walls, guarded by SS men. And through the snow drifts, weary processions of Polish men, women and children, urged on at gunpoint by SS men, dragged themselves towards railway stations and trains that would convey them to the Reich. Sometimes, they tried to escape and were shot as they ran. Many simply perished *en route*, their corpses left in the snow.

Crossing the border the other way came ethnic Germans, angry and confused at being uprooted from their homes and forced to move to an alien country. Often, once they arrived, there was nowhere for them to live and they were shoved into makeshift camps.

This vast movement of people might be a dreadful administrative headache for the authorities, but it was not Hans's problem. Prevented by the weather from getting out, he and his fellow soldiers huddled round the cast-iron stove in their billet, playing cards, listening to the radio and drinking beer, waiting for the spring.

In the middle of February, Monika wrote, telling him that she was pregnant again. Hans threw an impromptu party. 'I'm going to have a son a year,' he boasted.

Since the outbreak of war, prisoners' conditions had deteriorated considerably at Grubenmünde concentration camp. Numbers had been swollen by an influx of Polish prisoners and rations had correspondingly diminished. The outside working parties put in twelve hours a day at the Kraus synthetic rubber factory, work which took its toll of many during the excruciatingly cold period that January.

Many of the SS guards had been called up on active service and replaced by newly trained SS recruits, young thugs, who were not wanted by the Wehrmacht or the Waffen-SS, but were considered good enough for concentration camp guard duty. Punishments increased and became more sadistic. Death became an everyday occurrence. Corpses were piled in a huge pit, covered with lime and left to rot.

Bernhard Scheer was an old lag now. Because of his experience, he was made a Block Senior, responsible for organizing his barrack's march to the parade ground each day, roll-call, suitability for work, food distribution and discipline. He administered his Block with as scrupulous a fairness as was possible under such dreadful conditions. Equal shares — of food and of work — was the Pastor's maxim, and it was rigorously applied.

There were some things, however, over which Bernhard had no power and this included the punishments frequently inflicted upon no more than a whim of the Camp Commandant or an SS officer. During his three years in Grubenmünde, he had witnessed every conceivable kind of torture. He saw men flogged until their bare bones shone out under the skin. They returned from the punishment block with their fingernails pulled out, their testicles burned by cigarette ends and their toes amputated. From solitary confinement, they came back gibbering wrecks, emaciated and frozen with fear.

Bernhard sat with them, tending their wounds as best he could from his meagre first-aid supply, praying to God to give them strength, but there were times now when he doubted God's existence. What God could permit the existence of men such as Otto Tobisch, who was capable of inflicting barbarities so extreme that they escaped human understanding?

What God could permit the atrocities that were taking place in Poland, blood-curdling accounts of which the Polish prisoners brought with them, stories of the mass persecution of the nobility, the intelligentsia and the Jews, of whole Jewish communities being shot in schools and synagogues?

Then, like a blinding flash of light, Bernhard had an image of Christ on the cross, a sign over him reading, 'This is the King of the Jews.' And he seemed actually to hear Christ's voice saying, 'Forgive them, for they know not what they do.' And, again, he heard Christ's voice: 'O thou of little faith, wherefore didst thou doubt?'

SS Oberführer Richard Glücks, head of the Concentration Camp Inspectorate, discovered the town of Glacow in March 1940. Situated on a railway line near Katowice, it consisted of some two hundred houses, a school, an ornate but dilapidated Catholic church and a huge, disused factory, originally an army garrison.

It was this building which interested Oberführer Glücks. It stood, isolated, outside the town at the end of a straight, muddy lane, surrounded by a forest of mainly silver birch trees, which stretched as far as the eye could see. It was in good condition, the perimeter fence and the guardhouses still intact. The parade ground, although overrun by weeds, could easily be cleared. Oberführer Glücks took his Leica camera from its case, screwed in a wide-angle lens, and proceeded to photograph the garrison from all sides.

A couple of days later, Baron Heinrich was studying the resulting black and white prints in Reichsführer-SS Himmler's office. Briefly, Himmler described the problems the SS were encountering in Poland, principally the threat of insurgence from left-wing political leaders, Jewish-Bolsheviks and the intelligentsia. Almost plaintively, he explained, 'To put them into concentration camps here in the Reich is not only costly, but extremely dangerous, for they may contaminate the existing inmates with their foul ideas. No, Herr Baron, they must be kept in quarantine, while we sort out the chaff from the grain.'

The Baron nodded shrewdly, leaned back and lit a fat cigar. 'I think our little experiment at Grubenmünde has worked extremely well and, apart from a few initial problems with Polish slave labour at Essen, things are going very smoothly. Glacow is only a hundred miles from our Silesian mines. It would seem an excellent site to which to move our tank and lorry chassis production, which is ideally suited to unskilled labour. After all, if Essen were bombed...'

Himmler's pale eyes twitched nervously behind his pince-nez. 'How long would it take to get a new factory running?'

Baron Heinrich examined his pudgy fingers. 'It depends upon the labour available and it would facilitate matters considerably if there were railway access directly into the camp.'

'Herr Baron, all these things can be easily arranged.' Himmler was sweating slightly, as he listed the assistance the SS could offer Kraus Industries. He ended, 'We are renaming the town. From now on, it will be called Schlachtenhausen. SS-Oberführer Tobisch will be in charge of the camp and the slave labour. We'll need some of your technicians on hand, of course, but once you have installed your equipment, you won't need to concern yourself any further with the running of Schlachtenhausen.'

'Except for the profits,' Baron Heinrich pointed out coldly.

Himmler gave a thin smile. 'Naturally, Herr Baron.'

'Three months,' the Baron said. 'There is no reason why we should not be in production by June.'

The following day, a letter reached Otto advising him that he was shortly to be transferred to Poland to superintend a new quarantine camp housing fifty thousand Polish prisoners, ten thousand of whom would be assigned to Kraus Industries' steel fabrication works.

In Poland, where there were nearly three million Jews, Otto's particular talents could be exploited to the full and to the greatest benefit of the Reich. At the mere thought, Otto felt a stiffening at the groin.

When he gave Anna the good news, she had a surprise of her own. Gazing at him from cow-like eyes, she said, 'Otti, that is wonderful. Perhaps this is the start of a new era. You see, I am pregnant.'

'Pregnant?' Otto stared at her in utter disbelief. Although he had long since grown bored with her conversation, he never tired of her body. She was a massive woman now, with thighs like tree trunks and pendulous breasts that hung to her stomach. However, she was also forty-nine, two years older than himself and theoretically past childbearing age. 'You are sure?'

She rubbed a hand over her stomach. 'Oh, yes, the doctor confirmed it today. And he says because I am healthy and have wide hips I should have no trouble having a baby. It is due in November.'

Otto's mouth went dry. 'Did the doctor say anything about…'

Anna smirked knowingly. 'Yes, I asked him about *ficken*, and he said it will not hurt until the seventh month. Otti, do you want…?'

Three million Polish Jews and an Aryan baby... If he did not take her now, he could come inside his trousers. He fumbled at his buttons and pulled out his swollen, throbbing penis. Anna gazed at it, licked her lips and lifted her skirts. Underneath she was naked. On the farm in the Salzkammergut where she had been raised, she had not worn knickers, nor had Otto ever encouraged her to.

Otto took her over the table, ramming into her like a bull. When he had finished, he poured himself a beer then, with Wolf at his heels, went back into the camp. Evening roll-call was just starting. He decided to make it one the prisoners would never forget.

At Schlachtenhausen, hundreds of Poles camped in freezing and unsanitary conditions in the old garrison, constructing their own prison. High barbed wire perimeter fences were erected, with watchtowers for SS guards. Under the supervision of local railway officials, they started to build a new railway line right into the camp, along which rolling-stock soon conveyed bricks and timber for new barracks and the Kraus factory.

The inhabitants of Glacow town showed no curiosity as to what went on at the camp. They were still getting used to the fact that their town had a German name and was under German administration. They kept themselves to themselves, the only thing to do under the circumstances.

That long, bitterly cold winter of waiting was the worst Mortimer had ever experienced. There were food and fuel shortages, causing very real hardship to many people. Often, Mortimer thought of Bethel Ascher, but he dared not visit him and he lacked any means of ameliorating his conditions, so all he could do was hope the Professor was all right.

The American Undersecretary of State, Sumner Welles, visited Berlin for talks with Hitler, but refused to give the American correspondents any hint as to how they went. Lord Haw-Haw, the nauseating British turncoat, continued to broadcast pro-Nazi propaganda. Ribbentrop went to Rome to see Mussolini and the Pope.

Such action as there was took place elsewhere. The Finnish war ended with a Russian victory. German bombers raided the Royal Navy main base in the Scapa Flow and, in reprisal, British bombers attacked the Sylt seaplane base.

Then, suddenly, as spring approached, an atmosphere of tense expectancy pervaded the city. True to her word, Viktoria passed him little titbits of information. Ilse was complaining that Peter was rather snappish. Luise was happy because Sepp was coming home. Monika had written that Hans's duties in Poland were over. Baron Heinrich was complaining that the British were mining the Baltic to stop supplies of Swedish ore reaching Germany.

Sepp returned and immediately left again. Hans, too, after a week's leave, departed with his regiment for an unknown destination. Generals who had spent the winter on the Western Front appeared in Berlin, spent a few nights there, then travelled north. Trainloads of Alpine troops from Bavaria and Austria passed through Berlin on their way north. Mountain troops going north? There was no information forthcoming from the Foreign Ministry, but Mortimer was in no doubt where they were heading. Hitler had set his sights on Scandinavia.

On the evening of Sunday 7 April, he noticed a Norwegian diplomat with whom he was vaguely acquainted sitting in the hotel bar. Taking a seat next to him, he offered him a drink and asked, 'Herr Stang, do you get the feeling that something is in the wind?'

Stang looked at him in a strange manner, then, after glancing cautiously round, replied, 'Yes, Herr Allen. We have heard rumours that the English are going to land in Norway.'

'The English?' Mortimer asked, dumbfounded. 'No, Herr Stang, I think you've got it wrong, and you should warn Oslo accordingly. When an invasion occurs, it will be by German troops.'

Stang shook his head confidently. 'Oh, no. It is of the English that we Norwegians must beware.'

The following day, the Abwehr men on the fourth floor were confined to quarters. All food was taken up to them by waiters accompanied by Gestapo men. The guard in the foyer and outside the hotel was doubled. Something was imminent.

On Tuesday 9 April, Mortimer and his colleagues were summoned to a press conference at the Foreign Ministry, where they were informed by Ribbentrop that, 'Germany has occupied Danish and Norwegian soil in order to protect those countries from the Allies, and will defend their true neutrality until the end of the war. Thus an honoured part of Europe has been saved from certain downfall.'

Deeply depressed, Mortimer walked up the Wilhelmstrasse towards his office. He had seen the signs. He should have done more.

Before the day was over, it was triumphantly announced that Denmark had become part of the Reich. However, although the airports of southern Norway and the country's most important military depots and ports had fallen to the Germans, it appeared that Norway was not going to give in easily. To the dismay of the Wilhelmstrasse, the Norwegians were putting up quite a fight and British warships were approaching Bergen.

To his surprise, there was no great rejoicing at the Hotel Quadriga. Despite blazing newspaper headlines and histrionic radio flashes, people seemed almost uninterested. It was not that they were particularly concerned that Hitler had violated Scandinavian neutrality. It was more as if they didn't care.

Mortimer sat down at the bar and asked Hasso for a Jack Daniels. Suddenly, close beside him, Colonel Oster's voice murmured, 'I hear you talked to Stang.'

'How on earth…?'

'I have a friend on the Dutch legation. He approached Stang, too, and got the same answer as you. Stang is pro-Nazi. Most diplomats are who are still in Berlin.'

'And your Dutch friend?'

'An exception to the rule. But how long he'll be here, I don't know.' Oster's monocle twinkled, but the eye behind it was sombre. Then he turned and walked out of the bar.

Mortimer stared after him. Oster's comment could mean two things: either that his Dutch friend was falling foul of the Nazis, or that Holland was next on Hitler's list.

When he tried to hint at the latter in his reports to the *New York News*, the German military censor to whom he had to submit all his articles struck through his words, saying, 'Herr Allen, this is absolute nonsense!'

A cavalcade of cars swept through Schlachtenhausen town and up the long roadway leading to the new quarantine camp. In the first car rode Otto and Anna Tobisch and their dog Wolf, with two SS officers. Anna looked round her anxiously. This new home was very important to her, for it was where her baby would be born.

The original garrison building was still recognizable. Beyond it, behind the high perimeter wall topped with barbed wire and broken glass, overlooked by watchtowers, were line upon line of wooden barracks and, in the distance, the new Kraus steelworks. Surrounding the whole complex was forest, stretching as far as the eye could see. Diverging from the road, a branch railway line led towards the factory. There was a small station and a siding, in which goods trucks were parked.

The car stopped outside high wrought iron gates, bearing the familiar motto WORK SETS FREE. Sentries leaped to attention and saluted. Passes were examined, the gates opened and the new Commandant and his colleagues were permitted entrance. They drove through a high brick archway into a courtyard and drew to a halt.

Everyone got out except Anna. 'Take Frau Tobisch to our quarters,' Otto instructed the driver.

Their house was newly constructed, with its own fenced-in, as yet uncultivated garden, away from the main camp and the houses of the other officers. It looked bare and comfortless, with sparsely furnished rooms. By the time Otto arrived, Anna had made several decisions. 'Otti, can I have shutters and window-boxes?'

Otto's mind was full of more important matters. 'Of course.'

'And furniture like we had at Traunsee, made of white wood and painted with roses and edelweiss?'

'So long as you stay out of the camp, I don't care what you do.'

Anna gave a sigh of contentment.

Next morning, under supervision of an SS guard, a detachment of Polish prisoners arrived at the Commandant's house. Some were given the task of making and erecting wooden window-boxes and shutters with hearts carved in them. Others set about turning the muddy terrain in front of the house into a complex arrangement of flower beds and vegetable gardens. Anna decided to keep chickens and geese. One prisoner was given the job of looking after them.

In the workshops, furniture was made: tables, chairs, beds, wardrobes, dressers, chests, kitchen implements, breadboards and cutlery with blades of best Solingen steel, all intricately carved and hand-painted with Alpine flowers. Seamstresses made thick feather quilts for the Frau Commandant's bed and embroidered curtains and cushions for her boudoir.

Having seen to her and Otto's immediate comforts, Anna turned her attention to the nursery. She had it decorated in blue and furnished with a wooden carved cradle on rockers and miniature chairs and tables. Delicate Polish fingers stitched baby clothes, napkins and shawls. In everything but its surroundings, the house resembled a chalet in the Salzkammergut. Anna was delighted.

At the beginning of May, there was another sudden influx of officers into Berlin, all needing rooms, attending dinners, sitting in close groups in the bar and the Palm Garden Room, holding confidential discussions in quiet voices. Then, just as suddenly as they had arrived, they were gone.

On 9 May, the occupants of the fourth floor were once more placed in solitary confinement, but Viktoria told Mortimer that, on this occasion, not even waiters or chambermaids were permitted access. Food was taken up to them by the Gestapo. Their rooms remained uncleaned. Their windows were hermetically sealed. The Abwehr's sole contact with the outside world was by telephone.

The guard in the foyer and outside the Quadriga quadrupled. The papers of everyone entering the hotel were closely scrutinized and all registration documents and passports taken away. Any guest who had wished to leave would have found it impossible. The claustrophobic atmosphere was intolerable. Mortimer toyed with his dinner, then decided to go out for a breath of air. But when he reached the revolving doors, an armed Gestapo man turned him back.

He went up to his room, lay down on the bed and lit a cigarette, convinced that the long-awaited attack on the Low Countries was about to take place. Imprisoned within the hotel, what could he do? Then he had an idea. Perhaps he could telephone a message to Zurich or New York. But, when he asked the telephone operator to connect him, he was told all communication with abroad was forbidden for an indefinite period. Mortimer could only hope that Oster had warned his friend in the Dutch legation and that he had managed to get a message through to Holland.

He was woken in the morning by a telephone call summoning him to a press conference at the Foreign Ministry. Nobody tried to prevent him leaving the hotel. It was a fresh spring morning and he walked along Unter den Linden with other people going to work.

But, for all the semblance of normality, it was no ordinary morning. With an inane smile, Ribbentrop informed them that German troops had crossed the border at dawn into Holland, Belgium and Luxemburg, to protect the Low Countries from an imminent invasion by the British and French, whom he claimed had been about to march through them to seize the Ruhr.

Sick to the depths of his soul, Mortimer went out into the May sunshine. For the second time, he had seen the signs but been unable to do anything about them.

That day, a fanfare of military music preceded the first of the Army Command 'Special Bulletins', amplified through loudspeakers in the streets and which every bar, café and restaurant was compelled to broadcast. It announced the progress of German troops, sweeping through Luxemburg and the Ardennes, an airborne landing at Fort Eben-Emael. Key airfields and bridges had been seized. Dutch ships had been sunk. The Anglo-French Army situated in Belgium was already surrounded.

Far from being jubilant, the Berliners appeared nearly as depressed as Mortimer. Benno admitted in a low voice, 'We had no right to invade those countries.'

Viktoria looked at him disdainfully. 'So you're suffering the first pangs of conscience?' As he flinched, she turned to Mortimer. 'It can't go on like this. One day, someone must retaliate and what's going to happen then?'

It was a question to which he had no answer.

Late that night, a news broadcast announced that Neville Chamberlain had resigned and Winston Churchill was the new British Prime Minister. Three days later, Churchill presented his new War Cabinet to the House of Commons and addressed the British people. In Oxford, Stefan listened to the familiar, dauntless voice. 'I have nothing to offer but blood, toil, tears and sweat... Victory — victory at all costs, victory in spite of all terror, victory however long and hard the road may be...'

In the meantime, German panzers had crossed the River Meuse, virtually destroying the French Ninth Army. In no time at all, they would reach the Channel. Next day, Stefan read that the War Office was asking for Local Defence volunteers to combat possible German parachute landings. 'They won't permit me to have a job, own a car or join the Army. Do you think they'll allow me to volunteer for civil defence?' he asked Joyce.

She was making tea. 'I don't know, dear. I suppose you could always ask.' At that moment, there was a ring at the door. 'Libby, see who that is. I expect it's Mrs Pettit. I won't be a moment.'

Libby pushed her exercise books to one side and went to the door. She returned looking puzzled. 'Mum, it's not Mrs Pettit. It's a man asking about Stephen.'

'From the Home Office?' Stefan asked, excitedly.

'I don't think so.'

Joyce dried her hands on her apron and went into the hall. There was a low murmur of voices. Then she called, 'Stephen, can you come here, please?' From her tone, he knew it was not good news.

The man standing on the doorstep was wearing a blue serge suit and bowler hat. His car was parked directly in front of the house. 'You are Mr Stefan Kraus?' he asked.

Stefan nodded.

450

'I'm from the Oxford Constabulary, sir.' The man drew his identification card from his pocket. 'I have orders to take you into custody as an enemy alien.'

Despair welled in Stefan's heart. 'Oh, no…'

'There must be some mistake, Inspector,' Joyce said firmly. 'Stephen left Germany because of his hatred for the Nazi regime. The Home Office have his particulars. Can't you check with them?'

'My instructions come from the Home Office, Madam.' The policeman looked rather embarrassed. 'Listen, sir, you're not being charged with any crime, nor are you the only one in this situation. I have a list of hundreds of people — not only Germans, but Poles, Austrians and Czechs. Now, would you be good enough to come along with me quietly?'

'Where are you taking him?' Joyce demanded.

'I'm not allowed to say, Madam.' The policeman shuffled impatiently. 'Look, I've got a lot to do before today's out. Can we hurry up, please? I assume you want to bring a bag with you? Well, if you could pack as quickly as possible…'

Stefan went mutely into the house and upstairs, swiftly followed by Libby. 'Why don't you escape out of the window?' she whispered. 'I'll say you attacked me and left me unconscious on the floor. While they're finding out if I'm all right, you could be miles away.'

Despite his misery, Stefan had to smile. 'You're sweet, but they would still catch me.'

She threw her arms round him and burst into tears. 'Oh, Stephen, I'm so sorry. I'm going to miss you.'

'I'm sorry, too,' he said bitterly. 'I thought it was only in Germany that things like this happened.'

'Mr Kraus?' the policeman called.

'I'm just coming.' Stefan gently disengaged himself from Libby's embrace and reached up to the top of the wardrobe, pulled down a small case and rammed a miscellaneous collection of clothing into it. Then, with a quick look round the room, he went back downstairs.

Joyce kissed him on the cheek. 'Don't worry, Stephen. We'll soon have you free again.'

Stefan nodded with a confidence he did not feel then, head held high, got into the back of the waiting car and allowed himself to be driven away.

He spent that night in a police cell. Just as he was going to sleep on his hard mattress, a policeman stomped across to him and demanded, 'Have you heard what your lot have just done? You've bombed Rotterdam. The Dutch offered to surrender, but, oh no, you Huns weren't interested in that. You dropped your bombs just the same and now the whole city is in flames. They say thousands of innocent people have died already.' He spat derisively.

As the steel doors clanged shut, Stefan buried his face in his hands.

The following day he was taken to a former racecourse in Surrey. Wooden barracks had been erected on the track and soldiers stood on guard outside the high wire fence surrounding it. As a babble of Central European and German voices greeted him, Stefan knew he had arrived at an English internment camp and that, once again, all the wrong people were imprisoned.

When, five days after the German invasion, the Dutch Army capitulated, Baron Heinrich placed a telephone call to Kok van der Jong in Rotterdam. Kraus Marin had more orders than it could cope with. Now, more than ever, it needed the Dutch firm's shipbuilding facilities. Kok van der Jong was a staunch Nazi. The Baron was sure he would welcome the incorporation of his family company into the Kraus empire.

He was not mistaken. Although the line crackled badly, he could hear Kok's voice quite clearly as he said, 'Heil Hitler, Herr Baron! This is a great day for all of us.'

'Herr van der Jong, can you come to Berlin?'

'Certainly, Herr Baron, provided I get the travel authorization.'

'I shall arrange it.'

The Baron put down the phone with a grunt of satisfaction. Kok could be useful in many ways. Not all Dutchmen or Belgians were sympathetic to the Nazi cause and there were many Jewish companies in the Low Countries. As their owners were arrested, Kok could take over and administer these companies on Kraus Industries' behalf.

Later in the day, the radio reported that German troops had broken through at Sedan and that civilians were fleeing from Paris in their thousands. The Baron added France to Kok's future activities.

A branch railway line went through the Kraus works at Essen and out to the labour camp on the outskirts of the town, a huge encampment of makeshift barracks housing some fifty thousand people, surrounded by barbed wire fences, overlooked by watchtowers manned by the SS.

That Wednesday, 15 May, Dr Eugen Dietrich stood on the platform as the latest freight train from the East drew in. Metal bolts were released on the cars and the doors slid open. 'Out! Out!' the SS guards shouted and the emaciated inmates tumbled out. So often had Dr Dietrich seen this happen, he had lost count. The sight, however, never ceased to appal him.

This consignment was no different from any of the others — cold, suffering from malnutrition and many already dead. Most would prove to be verminous with fleas and lice, which carried already rampant diseases further into the work camp. At a glance, he could see the signs of tuberculosis and spotted fever.

With whips and clubs, the SS men urged the prisoners up the platform and through the gates. Dr Dietrich took a deep breath, left the station and got into his small car to drive down to Kraus Haus. Every time he saw Ernst Kraus, he tried to persuade him to do something about the conditions of the camp. Today he was determined to succeed.

For as long as Ernst could remember, he had been working at least twelve hours a day. He was not a young man — he would be fifty-four that summer. Neither was he a very fit one. He took little exercise and for three years he had had no holiday. Now he was suffering from pains in his chest, which he was convinced heralded angina or, even worse, a heart attack.

Dr Dietrich put down his stethoscope. 'There is nothing the matter with your heart. What you are suffering from is over-acidity, causing chronic indigestion.' Then, taking advantage of Ernst's half-naked state, he added, 'Herr Ernst, I must insist that something be done about the Polish labourers. Another trainload has just arrived in the most appalling condition, with nothing to wear but the rags on their backs. Some are already dead. The rest need immediate treatment. But I have no sanatorium and no medicaments.'

If there was anything guaranteed to make Ernst feel the symptoms of a heart attack, it was the Poles. He looked at the doctor coldly. Dr Eugen Dietrich was a young man, not long out of college, still filled with student idealism. 'Have you any idea how many Poles there are in Poland? There are millions, enough to keep our factories supplied with labourers for the next century. For those who die, there will always be more to replace them. But there is only one Ernst Kraus, Dr Dietrich. If you want to keep anyone alive, make sure it is me. Otherwise…'

Dr Dietrich stuck obstinately to his guns. 'The Poles are also human beings.'

'Not in my book or in Herr Himmler's.'

'Have you any idea what conditions are like in that camp?' Dr Dietrich persisted. 'There are ten latrines per thousand people, their condition defying description. For days on end, the water supply does not function. And food rations are totally inadequate.'

'You're not trying to tell me they are starving? The company pays seventy pfennigs a day towards their upkeep.'

'Herr Direktor, what can one buy for seventy pfennigs? These people are living on mouldy bread and watered-down soup. Not even the meanest animal could exist long on that. Whether or not you care about the slaves as people, you should be concerned for the efficiency of your business — and that is suffering because the Poles are simply too weak to work.'

Ernst gave a deep sigh. 'You mean well, so I will be honest with you. In my opinion, the slaves are more bother than they're worth. Kraus Chemie in Berlin uses a lot of Jewish labour and I would willingly exchange six Poles for one German Jew. Better still, I would like to employ women, as they do in England and America.'

'Local women would seem a very sensible solution,' Dr Dietrich said eagerly. 'They wouldn't need housing…'

'They'd be more expensive. We pay the SS four marks a day for the slaves. We'd have to pay women a far higher wage. Still, I suppose I could suggest it to my father.'

Dr Dietrich stood up. He had always suspected Ernst was totally under the old man's thumb. Now he knew. If Ernst had to refer the matter to the Baron, nothing would change. But he added, 'In the meantime, can you also request that the camp conditions be improved?'

'To increase productivity,' Ernst said. 'I suppose I can try. Now, give me some tablets. I have work to do.'

It was getting dark when Ernst left his office. He sank back into the cushioned rear seat of his Mercedes and ordered the chauffeur to drive him home to the Fortress. Only a thin pencil of light shone from the car's headlights, just enough to illuminate the phosphorus strip along the kerb. They left Essen and started up towards the low hills. Ernst looked back. Apart from an occasional shower of sparks from a factory chimney, the whole town was in darkness.

Only noise betrayed the fact that under its shroud of blackout blinds and camouflage nets, Essen was still very much awake and at work. There was a clanking of couplings in railway marshalling-yards, the hissing of steam engines, the snorting and groaning of heavy equipment. Twenty-four hours a day, seven days a week, the Ruhr laboured to produce the coal, the steel and, above all, the guns that Germany needed to continue her victorious war.

Ernst closed his eyes as a pain shot through his chest. He knew it was the first symptom of a heart attack. Quickly, he swallowed a pill. All Dietrich cared about was the Poles…

When he reached the Fortress, Magnus Rudel, immaculate in black frock-coat and white gloves, opened the door, took his briefcase and relieved him of his coat. Magnus was a constant comfort to Ernst. About sixty now, he was a family retainer of the old school. He anticipated all his master's wishes. He only spoke when spoken to. He ran the large house punctiliously. And he never seemed to sleep.

'Good evening, Herr Ernst. Madame, your wife, is indisposed with a headache and has retired early.' Nothing unusual in that. Ernst and Trudi seldom met these days. 'And Cook has your supper ready.'

Ernst went straight into the dining room. It was his favourite meal: roast knuckle of pork, potato purée, braised cabbage with caraway seeds and bacon, followed by a large jam pancake. He ate hungrily, washing it down with several tankards of beer. The pain was already receding.

He had just finished eating when his father rang from Berlin. 'Schlachtenhausen is ready. Tobisch has arrived. You've moved all the plant over there, haven't you, boy?'

'Yes, Father. It went this weekend, with the engineers.'

'The sooner we can move more of our operations out of the Ruhr, the safer I'll feel. I don't trust Churchill an inch.'

'The British won't dare attack us. They know how heavily fortified we are.'

'Hmph. Never underestimate anybody.' Before Ernst could mention slave labourers, the Baron slammed down the phone.

Ernst went to his study, a first-floor room at the front of the Fortress, overlooking the valley. The pain was returning. It always did when he spoke to his father. He belched and rang the bell for Magnus, who entered the room, bowing obsequiously. 'Bring me another beer and a Steinhäger.'

'Yes, sir.'

Ernst sat down to the evening paper. His eyelids drooped. His head sagged on the leather chair. Suddenly, the air-raid sirens wailed. He woke with a start, switched off the light and pulled the curtains. Although the sirens had been sounding regularly, ever since Allied planes had been crossing the West Wall to drop their propaganda leaflets, they never failed to send a tremor down Ernst's back.

One moment, the valley was in darkness. The next, it was lit up with searchlights flickering high into the clouds, moving in an ever-changing pattern. And, into this circle of light, came the unmistakable black shapes of enemy bombers. Ernst stared at them, mesmerized. Ten, twenty, fifty…

The valley echoed to the heavy thunder of anti-aircraft fire. Still the bombers flew on in perfect formation. From the Fortress, Ernst could hear the drone of their engines. Muffled thumps and spurts of flame momentarily illuminated the town. The bombs were well off target, falling away from Kraus factories, oil installations and marshalling-yards.

'Ernst, what's happening?' Trudi burst into the room, her hair dishevelled, her dressing gown clasped round her fat body. Behind her, servants crowded in the doorway, their faces pale and frightened.

'Turn out the light! Shut the door!' Ernst shouted.

A flak gun succeeded in shooting down a bomber. The plane lost a wing and burst into flames, spiralling down through the searchlights, leaving a trail of debris and oily smoke in its wake.

The pain in Ernst's chest was the worst it had ever been. 'The impossible is happening,' he said slowly and in utter disbelief. 'British bombs are falling on the Ruhr.'

Peter was at Army General Headquarters at Münstereifel, from where Hitler himself was directing the campaign. On the huge board in the operations centre, the coloured indicators representing the different German Armies moved rapidly forward. They entered Brussels. Antwerp was captured. Rommel's Seventh Division crossed the Meuse and pushed forward a narrow salient into France, breaking through the Maginot Line and heading swiftly towards Arras.

In the meantime, Guderian's Nineteenth Panzer Corps raced towards the Channel: Boulogne, Calais and Dunkirk. His panzers sealed off the Calais pocket and suddenly, the Belgians, the British Expeditionary Force and three French armies were trapped.

The mood at General Headquarters was ecstatic. The Führer was lavish in his praise of the Army and its leaders. He spoke openly of the Peace Treaty he would make which would return to the German people territory of which they had been robbed for over four hundred years.

And then, on 24 May, on the threshold of the greatest victory of the campaign, Hitler issued an extraordinary order to halt the advance. For two days, the troops were forced to kick their heels while interminable meetings took place among the top leadership as to who should carry out the decisive battle. Göring was adamant that it was a role for the Luftwaffe, while Brauchitsch and Halder were emphatic that success was dependent upon a land encirclement by ground troops.

Two days later, the advance recommenced, but those two days had given the British time to redeploy their troops, and it was hard going for the German panzers. The weather was so bad that the Luftwaffe was virtually grounded. Still they pressed forward, confident the encircled armies were doomed, that the British Army numbering a third of a million men, compressed into the territory around Dunkirk, was facing its destruction.

It was not until the afternoon of 30 May, after Belgium had capitulated, that they realized the truth, that the armada of little boats which had been noticed plying backwards and forwards across the Channel, was evacuating the British Army. On 4 June, the Germans finally captured Dunkirk. It was not the victory they had hoped for — but the fact remained that the British had retreated.

That same day, Churchill spoke to the British people. Peter and his colleagues listened to his speech on the radio, confident that Churchill could have little desire to continue this unequal battle.

They were mistaken. Across the airwaves came the distinctive, sonorous voice: 'Even though large tracts of Europe and many old and famous States have fallen or may fall into the grip of the Gestapo and all the odious apparatus of Nazi rule, we shall not flag or fail. We shall fight in France, we shall fight in the seas and oceans, we shall fight with growing confidence and growing strength in the air, we shall defend our island, whatever the cost may be, we shall fight on the beaches, we shall fight on the landing grounds, we shall fight in the fields and in the streets, we shall fight in the hills; we shall never surrender, and even if, which I do not for a moment believe, this island or a large part of it were subjugated and starving, then our Empire beyond the seas, armed and guarded by the British Fleet, would carry on the struggle, until, in God's good time, the New World, with all its power and might, steps forth to the rescue and the liberation of the Old.'

'You don't win wars by retreating!' one officer shouted. 'Try to attack us in France and that will be the end of you!' another added. 'Come over to our side, Winnie!' Peter called. Like most of his colleagues and, he suspected, Hitler himself, he had great admiration for the English. They were essentially a Germanic people and it was wrong that two countries with so much in common should find themselves at war. Much better that they should be allies.

Next day, Hitler launched a massive attack on the Somme and the Battle for France began. Unlike the British, the French were traditional enemies. 'One good skirmish with the French', had been Peter's Uncle Ewald's ambition. 'In six weeks, we'll have taken Paris,' young Peter had told Viktoria in July 1914. Instead, the war had ended in Germany's defeat. On 11 November 1918, in a railway carriage in a clearing of the Forest of Compiègne, German emissaries had been forced to sign the ignominious armistice.

Twenty-six years later, the German armies swept through France, determined to redress all past iniquities. The French had lost their best units in Belgium. Their air force was virtually non-existent. And their allies, the British, could do little to help them.

On 10 June, Mussolini finally entered the fray by declaring war on Britain and France, and the Italian, French and British fleets engaged in their first sea battles in the Mediterranean. On 14 June, exactly five weeks after the beginning of the western offensive, General von Küchler's Eighteenth Army occupied Paris. General von Bock reviewed victory parades in the Place de la Concorde and at the Arc de Triomphe. The swastika waved from the Eiffel Tower.

A week later, in the very same railway carriage in the Forest of Compiègne, another armistice was signed, under which Germany occupied two-thirds of France, including Paris, Alsace-Lorraine, the Channel and Atlantic coastlines. The French Navy was to be demobilized and the French were to pay the cost of a German army of occupation.

The railway carriage itself was moved, in triumph, to Berlin.

Hans König had discovered a hero, a man for whom, far beyond the bounds of duty, he would go out and die — but General Rommel engendered that kind of loyalty in all his men. He was not an arrogant Prussian type. He knew all his officers personally and all his men by name. He never expected anyone to do anything he would not personally do himself. He was always on the front line. In every attack, his tank led. He took amazing, but calculated risks and his boldness always paid off.

By the time the Seventh Panzer Division captured Cherbourg on 19 June, it had taken nearly a hundred thousand prisoners and captured a vast number of enemy guns, tanks and vehicles. Despite the extremely heavy fighting they had experienced, their own losses were remarkably small. General Rommel might take risks, but he was parsimonious with the lives of men.

As a result of the campaign, Hans was promoted to Captain. He remained in France as part of the army of occupation, but he now had one fixed ambition: to follow General Rommel to the ends of the earth.

At the beginning of July, the Nowak Wing was transferred to Dallot in the Pas de Calais, just south of Cap Gris Nez. On a hot afternoon, they flew through a shimmering blue sky, landing on the airfield of a former French airbase overlooking the hazy Channel. As the noise of their engines died down, a murmuring quiet hung over the meadow. In a neighbouring field, peasants were cutting a second crop of hay. From a nearby copse, a thrush burst into song.

Sepp followed the others towards the administration block, stopping at the entrance to light a cigarette. Suddenly, war seemed a long way away. Poland, Norway, Rotterdam, Dunkirk, became somehow unreal in this pastoral setting. For a moment, he wondered if he could have imagined the devastation he had left behind.

Andreas Müller interrupted his chain of thought. 'Do you think we have earned a holiday by the sea, Uncle?' he laughed. 'If so, I'm not going to object.'

Sepp gave a tired smile. Andreas would never understand his antipathy for the kind of war they were engaged in. He would never share his disgust at having to provide escort for bombers, particularly over civilian targets. But he had turned into a capable fighter pilot. 'We'll soon find out,' he said.

The atmosphere changed as they reached the base buildings. Armed sentries and a camouflaged tank guarded the main entrance. Flak guns, pointing towards the Channel, were in sandbagged emplacements. Uniformed ground personnel hurried from one office-block to another, papers in their hands. The feeling of war returned.

Sepp asked his way to the base commander's office and a sentry accompanied him down a narrow corridor, knocked and announced, 'Oberst Nowak is here, sir.'

'Sepp, good to see you!' Oberst Theo Osterkamp came from behind the desk and reached out his hand. The two men were old friends. Like Sepp, Osterkamp was a First World War veteran and holder of the *Pour le Mérite*. 'Welcome to your new office.'

'My new office?'

'It's only a small base, but you're in command here now. My congratulations. You and your men have been doing a good job.'

Sepp gave a wry smile. 'Thank you, Theo. Where are you stationed?'

'A few miles up the coast.'

For a few moments, they exchanged pleasantries, then Osterkamp said, 'England's the next target, unless the British change their minds and surrender which, judging by the defences they're erecting along their beaches, they have no intention of doing.'

Sepp nodded. He had no personal animosity towards the English — indeed, he had an abiding respect for their pilots. That was what made the prospect of the forthcoming campaign so exhilarating. At last, he would be pitting his skills against a worthy adversary. 'War against England must be a fighter war?'

'Perhaps, but our orders are to cover bombers from KG2 based at Cap Blanc Nez while they attack British shipping. The British convoys must be stopped. Too much food and too many supplies are getting through.'

'That should bring the Spitfires and Hurricanes out! They can't just ignore our bombers and let their ships be sunk.'

'When we have gained air superiority over the Straits of Dover and starved the British into submission, our way will lie open for a seaborne invasion.'

'Don't underestimate the strength of the RAF...'

'Don't worry, Sepp. You'll get your chance to become an ace again. In the meantime, I suggest you and your men relax for a few days. Enjoy the lull. I doubt it will last long.'

'And if we should happen to find ourselves over England?' Sepp asked.

'I'm not going to object. However, you don't need me to remind you that the 109 only has a range of four hundred miles. If you run out of fuel over the Channel, it's a long swim home.'

Sepp grinned. He and Osterkamp understood each other. Provided the fighters fulfilled their escort duties, they were free to spread their wings a little.

The Nowak Wing quickly settled in at Dallot. The weather continued fine, with a few gentle showers to sweeten the air. Sometimes they only made one sortie a day, a welcome relief after the arduous spring campaigns. There was even an element of sport in going after the British convoys.

Best of all, were those occasions when the Messerschmitts left the bombers and swept across Kent, taunting RAF fighters up into the summer skies for free fights gloriously reminiscent of those heady days in the last war when German and English aces had vied with each other for supremacy of the skies. This was the fighting Sepp loved best: one-to-one combat, fliers and machines jousting in the air like birds of prey, in which skill was the ultimate victor. But very few British fliers rose to his challenge. The RAF was being cautious and conserving its strength.

In England, fear grew that the British Isles were Hitler's next target for an invasion. Once again, the enemy aliens became the focus of attention. Who knew what spies and saboteurs were concealed in their midst?

Stefan and his fellow internees were put in a train under police guard and taken north to a derelict cotton mill outside Burnley in Lancashire. High barbed wire fences, patrolled by guards, surrounded the mill, while within, it was evident that the only inhabitants in the last twenty years had been rats.

They were crowded into large, makeshift dormitories, allowed no books, newspapers or radios. Medical facilities were minimal, the food inadequate and their contact with the outside world virtually non-existent.

Stefan's mattress was between an Italian and an Austrian Jew. 'I've been running my small restaurant in Wardour Street in London for twelve years,' the Italian complained angrily. 'My children were born here and still they lock me up, as if I were some kind of criminal. Just because Italy has declared war on Britain. I got out of Italy because of Mussolini. Now they say I'm a fascist spy.'

The Austrian was clearly terrified. 'I don't understand. I fled Vienna because I was a Jew. And now the English lock me up because I am an Austrian. Have I escaped death in a concentration camp in Germany only to die in one in England?'

Day after day, the same arguments were heard, until Stefan found himself growing weary of them. Each detainee loudly protested his own innocence. Everyone thought himself a special case. Stefan remembered his own meeting with Churchill when the great man had asked him why he thought he should be trusted. 'Churchill must be under a tremendous strain,' he said hesitantly. 'He probably realizes most of us are anti-Nazi, but he can't be sure that there aren't some fifth columnists among us.'

'Then why not give us a trial or a chance to prove our innocence? He's employing the same tactics as Hitler.'

'I'm certain we shall be given the opportunity, but surely the Government's first priority must be to defend England? And, let's face it, our conditions could be far worse.'

Another German sitting nearby said, 'The young man is right. If Hitler succeeds in invading us, it's natural to think we Germans might collaborate with our own countrymen. It's happened elsewhere. After all, the Austrians didn't put up much of a fight.' The Jew's eyes glittered dangerously. 'And most Italians have been quick enough to side with Mussolini.' The Italian spluttered indignantly. 'And look at the Dutch and the French. They gave in pretty swiftly, didn't they?'

The Jew turned on him. 'We Jews have always been anti-Nazi. Can't the British differentiate between Jews and Aryans?'

'That is what Hitler is doing and you are complaining about it,' a Dutchman joined in the fray. He turned to Stefan. 'If you Germans had opposed Hitler in the first place, we should none of us be in the situation we are in now.'

As a fierce argument broke out, Stefan drew back into a corner. What purpose would it serve to explain the dreadful road he had travelled to try to set Germany free?

But, as the days went by, he remained convinced that Joyce and Libby would not forget him and that Churchill was an essentially just man. One day, he would be freed and allowed to serve his adopted country.

When Otto Tobisch left Grubenmünde to take up his new posting, Bernhard Scheer had not believed his replacement could be any more callous. He was swiftly proved wrong. According to rumours emanating from the guards, Commandant Zimmermann had spent his late teenage years in a psychiatric hospital. Some said he had tried to murder his parents; others that he had run amok in a children's recreation ground. Whatever the truth about Zimmermann's background, Tobisch now seemed almost angelic in comparison.

Zimmermann's sadism knew no limits. He began by instituting a reign of terror over the guards, who took out their aggression on the prisoners. From twenty-five lashes, the standard beating became fifty. At least a hundred prisoners were suspended from trees every day. The tortures that took place when men were placed in solitary confinement defied description, but betrayed the perverted nature of Zimmermann's mind. Men who returned told of being made to stand for hours on end without food or water, either in total darkness or stark light, with shots being fired outside the door and guard dogs barking. But, more often than not, such men never returned.

For a while, Bernhard tried to keep count of the death toll within his block, but it was impossible. As the Reich increased in size, so the camp grew. Germans and Poles still accounted for most of the prisoners, but there were also Belgians, Dutch, French, Austrians, Czechs and Jews of all nationalities. There was also a constant moving of prisoners from one camp to another. Grubenmünde would suddenly experience an influx of Austrians from Mauthausen, Poles from Dachau or Jews from Sachsenhausen. Just as suddenly, detachments of Grubenmünde prisoners would be sent away. Nobody knew where.

In the resulting confusion, barracks became overcrowded. New diseases became rife. Epidemics sometimes broke out. Disciplinary rules had to be explained to the newcomers and enforced when necessary. A contagious atmosphere of fear and suspicion hung over the camp. Bernhard Scheer found his spiritual resources stretched to their utmost limits in trying to alleviate the misery surrounding him.

At the same time, the prisoners were expected to work even harder and even longer hours. New industries were introduced to the camp. Besides the Kraus synthetic rubber plant, there was a textiles factory, employing mostly female labour and making SS uniforms. So far as food was concerned, Grubenmünde was almost self-sufficient. A slaughterhouse and a butchery, a bakery, and a market garden growing vegetables and herbs, supplied most of their food requirements.

The prisoners saw little of it. After Zimmermann's arrival, rations were cut drastically and the quality of food deteriorated. From having had just enough to survive on, they were now existing well below subsistence level. There was no need for executions. Men began dying like flies.

In Berlin, on 18 July, they celebrated the victory over France. It was Führer weather. From a high stage in the Pariser Platz, Dr Goebbels reviewed the troops in their Victory Parade. Through the Brandenburg Gate, decorated with flags, laurel wreaths and banners, they marched, rank upon rank of the finest, most victorious soldiers, sailors and airforcemen in the world. Thus, in 1871, had their forefathers marched after the Franco-Prussian War. Thus, sixty-nine years later, another generation marched again.

Standing on the balcony of the Hotel Quadriga, Viktoria gazed down on the crowds lining the pavement, waving, cheering, singing the National Anthem: *Deutschland, Deutschland über alles...* Germany, Germany, above all... Their voices swelled when they came to the lines, 'From the Meuse to the Memel, From the Etsch to the Belt...' Now, thanks to Hitler, the German Empire reached that far.

But would Hitler be content with that, or would he find himself compelled to pit his strength against the British? Viktoria knew she should feel pride in her country's triumphs, but she felt only fear for the future. Glancing at Mortimer, she saw the same fear registered on his face. She turned and went into the cool quietness of the hotel.

The following evening, Hitler addressed the Reichstag, in a ceremony broadcast live on the radio. He spoke with the quiet confidence of a man who holds the world in the palm of his hand. 'From Britain,' he declared, 'I now hear only a single cry — not of the people, but of the politicians — that the war must continue... Believe me, gentlemen, I feel a deep disgust for this type of unscrupulous politician who wrecks whole nations. It almost causes me pain to think that I should have been selected by fate to deal the final blow to the structure which these men have already set tottering... For millions of other people, however, great suffering will begin. Mr Churchill ought perhaps, for once, to believe me when I prophesy that a great Empire will be destroyed — an Empire which it was never my intention to destroy or even to harm...

'In this hour I feel it to be my duty before my own conscience to appeal once more to reason and common sense in Great Britain as much as elsewhere. I consider myself in a position to make this appeal since I am not the vanquished begging favours, but the victor speaking in the name of reason.' Slowly and deliberately, he stated, 'I can see no reason why this war must go on.'

The ornate auditorium echoed to the shouted acclaim of his audience. Hitler quieted them and announced that he had honours to distribute. A hushed air of expectancy fell over the Kroll Opera, then the Führer read out the names of new generals — twenty-seven of them. Mostly, they were field commanders, but at least one was from the General Staff — Peter von Biederstein, promoted from Major-General to Lieutenant-General.

Twelve new field marshals were named, nine from the Army and three from the Luftwaffe. And, finally, Göring was given the newly created rank of Reich Marshal of the Greater German Reich and awarded the Grand Cross of the Iron Cross.

It was an evening of celebration. Certain after Hitler's peace offer that no enemy planes would attack the capital, the lights shone out on the streets of Berlin. Since the conquests of Denmark and the Low Countries, food had become very much more plentiful. There seemed to be almost an abundance of vegetables, dairy produce and meat. The Hotel Quadriga swarmed with uniforms, glittering with medals. The Biedersteins were present: Peter taking no pains to control his pride at yet another promotion.

Sepp had also returned for the occasion. 'So far as the Fat Man is concerned, I'm delighted,' he said. 'Reich Marshal and a king-size baton to go with it! That pleased him no end. And I suppose Sperrle and Kesselring have earned their promotions. But Milch! Why the hell did Hitler make that fat, pop-eyed little creep a Field Marshal?'

Luise laughed, her arm through his, gazing at him adoringly. Viktoria went around with a smile on her face and Benno was at his most charming. Even the Baron was in good humour. Toasts were proposed and healths were drunk. Everyone was sure the war was over.

Suddenly, a junior officer hurried through the room, saluted to Peter and spoke swiftly in a low voice. 'Thank you,' Peter said and turned to them with a dazed expression. 'Apparently the British have given an unconditional "No" to the Führer's offer of peace.'

Suddenly, the papers were full of accounts of British air-raids of which nobody had been aware before. It appeared that Hamburg, Bremen and the Ruhr had all been badly hit, with mainly women and children killed. CHURCHILL'S ANSWER — COWARDLY MURDERING OF A DEFENCELESS POPULATION, read the headlines. The propaganda campaign against England had started.

Distraught, Viktoria asked Mortimer, 'Are we really about to invade England? Is there nothing we can do to stop this madness?'

Mortimer was in no doubt as to his answer. Through two invasions he had sat back and done nothing. Now, not only Viktoria's son, but his home, wife and daughter were under threat. It was time to throw caution to the wind and act. 'I can't do anything to stop Hitler. But I'll do my damnedest to make sure the English know what's going on,' he replied vehemently.

It was not going to be easy. Like all Hitler's campaigns, the invasion of England would be kept a close secret until the very last moment. On top of this, the Propaganda Ministry no longer sought to appease the American journalists: they had outworn their usefulness.

On 20 July, Roosevelt had been renominated for his third term as American President and an anti-American campaign that had long been simmering began to boil up. Several American correspondents were ordered to leave Germany. At the slightest excuse, they would kick Mortimer out, too. He might just as well go with a bang.

After that, he missed no opportunity to openly scoff at the possibility of German troops landing in England and the British giving in without a fight. He pretended knowledge of British defences, claiming them to be inviolable. He emphasized the strength of the RAF, as yet virtually untested and therefore undepleted by war.

He knew his strategy had worked when he encountered Colonel Oster after one of his periodic visits to the Abwehr offices on the fourth floor. They sauntered out together to the street. 'Herr Allen, I have the impression that you are weary of your assignment in Berlin. You may be interested in learning that my colleagues at the Foreign Ministry and the Gestapo also think you have been here long enough.'

'I've certainly no desire to stay if England is the next target.'

Oster nodded. 'When you return to England, would you care to take with you some information about the invasion?'

'Do you need to ask?'

Succinctly, Oster told him the little he knew. Code-named Operation Sea Lion, the plan was that the Luftwaffe should eliminate the RAF. Once German planes controlled the skies, the Navy would convey the Army across the Channel. 'General Jodl estimates the whole operation should take about nine weeks to complete.'

'When is it due to commence?'

'The closest I am able to ascertain is somewhere around the middle of August, with the sea landings taking place a month later. However,' Oster paused meaningfully, 'it might interest Herr Churchill to learn how great a toll the Norwegian campaign has taken upon our Navy. We now possess only one heavy and two light cruisers, six destroyers and only a handful of U-boats.'

Mortimer let out a long breath. 'In other words, you mean Operation Sea Lion is unlikely to ever take place?'

'It seems to be based more upon wishful thinking than reality, unless we can acquire some more ships in a hurry.'

Mortimer nodded and held out his hand. 'Thank you, Colonel. I shall make sure your information reaches Herr Churchill.'

Colonel Oster stepped into his car and drove away. Mortimer went back into the hotel and up to his room. All that remained now was to obtain an exit visa and get the hell out of Berlin. The Foreign Office was only too pleased to see the back of him. His passport was stamped and he was promised a seat in a passenger plane to Portugal. He packed his bags, paid his bill and bade farewell to Hasso Annuschek and other hotel personnel whom he had got to know well.

He found it harder to say his goodbyes to the family. In her apartment, Ricarda took his hand and he suddenly realized how much older and frailer she had become since his arrival eight years earlier. 'I have enjoyed knowing you, Herr Allen, and I hope we meet again under happier circumstances. It's going to be strange not having you around, but I understand that you want to be at home with your family.'

Impulsively, Mortimer kissed her smooth cheek. 'Frau Jochum, it has been a great privilege knowing you. *Auf Wiedersehen.*'

She smiled sadly. 'Yes, *auf Wiedersehen* — until we meet again…'

Benno was less sorry to see Mortimer go, but he gave a polite smile. 'Under different circumstances, we might have been friends, Herr Allen. I hope we do not part as enemies. At the final count, we both want the same thing — the end of this dreadful war…'

As he shook Benno's hand, Mortimer thought grimly, *Well, I'm doing my best…*

He succeeded in seeing Viktoria alone in her office. For the first time since their week at Heiligensee, he took her in his arms and kissed her. Her body trembled and he stroked her hair. 'Hush, Vicki, please don't cry.'

She buried her face in his chest. 'Mortimer, do you have to go?'

'Darling, I'm afraid so. But I'll come back one day and I'll bring Stefan with me.' Gently, he lifted her head, so that she was made to look at him. 'Vicki, I fear we are all going to have to endure a lot before this war is over, but I know you will be very brave.'

Mutely she nodded. She did not feel very brave.

'Smile for me. You look so beautiful when you smile. That is how I want to remember you while I'm away.'

There was a knock on the door and the Hall Porter's voice said, 'Herr Allen, the car is waiting to take you to the airport.'

Viktoria's lips trembled, but she forced a little smile. Mortimer kissed her again. 'Dear Viktoria…'

And then he was gone and she was left alone in her office with her memories and her fears.

In Lisbon, the lights were on and there was a direct telephone link with England. Fighting the desire to hear Joyce's voice again, Mortimer rang Bill Wallace to explain his whereabouts and to pass on Oster's information. Perhaps it was due to his excitement at being free again that his native caution forsook him. It did not occur to him that there were Nazi spies in Portugal and that his line was tapped.

Next, he spoke to Joyce and heard about Stefan. He contemplated sending a message to Viktoria, but immediately dismissed the idea, as serving no purpose. Better that she remained in ignorance. In the morning, he obtained a berth on the *Guinevere*, a merchant ship bound for England. 'You travel at your own risk,' the captain said.

It was one he was prepared to take and, in the event, they arrived without incident in Falmouth. Two days later, Mortimer heard the *Guinevere* had been sunk by an enemy bomber off the Isle of Wight on the last lap of her journey to Portsmouth.

CHAPTER THIRTEEN

Two nights after Mortimer left Berlin, Benno was woken by a screeching of tyres and a screaming of sirens. He leaped out of bed and looked down onto the road to see several police cars outside the hotel, their occupants spilling out onto the pavement.

'What's the matter?' Viktoria asked sleepily.

'God knows!' He pulled on his dressing gown and hurried out of the apartment.

The foyer was black with SS uniforms when he arrived. Among them, he espied a familiar face — Oberführer Kuhn, the Gestapo officer who had interviewed him after Stefan's departure. Belting his dressing gown more tightly, Benno strode towards him. 'Herr Oberführer, what is the meaning of this?'

The officer gave a nod of recognition. 'Heil Hitler, Herr Kraus. We must inspect your guest lists. We believe there is — or has been — an enemy agent living in your hotel.'

Benno ran his fingers through his hair in exasperation. 'You have guards on the door and the Abwehr on the fourth floor. Surely this is the last place from which an enemy agent would operate?'

Kuhn narrowed his eyes. 'Somebody has succeeded in getting hold of confidential military information and passing it to London. I am sure you do not need me to remind you that it is in your interests to cooperate. Show me your records.'

It was pointless to protest. Armed men stood at the entrances to all lifts and at the foot of the stairs, while Oberführer Kuhn and a colleague went through the hotel records. Finally, Kuhn said, 'So the American journalist, Mortimer Allen, occupied room 301 directly below the Abwehr offices, until two days ago?'

'That is correct.'

'The room must be searched.'

Fortunately it was still empty. Benno stood helplessly by while the room was ransacked — the carpets pulled up, floorboards lifted, wallpaper torn off, walls tapped and the bed ripped apart. Nothing was found. Without another word to Benno, Oberführer Kuhn strode angrily to the lift, called his men together and left the hotel.

When Benno got back to the apartment, Viktoria was sitting up in bed. 'Benno, what's wrong? What are all those police cars doing outside?'

Benno got back into bed and told her what had happened.

Viktoria stared at him aghast. 'Do you think Mortimer is all right?'

'I assume so, or they wouldn't have needed to search the hotel.'

Yes, he must have got away. Feeling better at that thought, Viktoria asked, 'Do you think that's why he left in such a hurry? So that he could pass his information on to the English? Benno, what do you think he can have learned that is so important? Do you think it will stop the war?'

Benno leaned back against the headrest. 'I've no idea,' he said heavily. 'What concerns me far more are the likely repercussions upon the hotel. Well, there's nothing we can do tonight. Let's try and get some sleep.'

They turned off the lights, but it was a long time before they slept. Viktoria was wondering whether Mortimer had got back to England and whether he had seen Stefan yet, and Benno was worrying what Oberführer Kuhn's next move would be.

It did not take him long to find out. Just before lunch, there was an electricity failure. Benno gave orders for the standby generator to be activated and sent the head maintenance man down to the cellar to identify the fault. He came back scratching his head. 'Can't see what's wrong, Herr Benno. I think we should call in an electrician.'

Benno was just picking up the telephone when Herr Fromm knocked on his office door. 'Some engineers have arrived from the electricity company. They say our fault is to do with the mains supply, but they have to go down to the basement to sort it out.'

'Take them down there, Max,' Benno told the maintenance man.

Soon Max was back with the chief electrician, who informed him that before the fault could be rectified, some of their cable needed renewing. 'It looks as if it's been here since the hotel was built,' he said gloomily.

'It probably has,' Benno replied tartly. 'How long will it take you to sort it out?'

'Provided I can get enough men to help me, we should be able to do the job today. We'll have to get to the cable ducts and put in some new wiring on the ground floor. Going to cause a bit of a mess, I'm afraid. We'll have to seal off the rooms concerned.'

'Can't you do the work at night?'

'What's the point? You'll still be without electricity all day. No, sir, better let us get on with the job straightaway.'

It seemed Benno had no choice. For the first time in the hotel's history, signs were put up saying: RESTAURANT CLOSED. BAR CLOSED. An hour later, an engineer arrived from the telephone company. 'Seems you have a fault on some of your telephone lines.'

Benno sighed. 'As well as a fault in the electricity supply?'

'They could be connected. Better let me have a look.'

Benno detailed a page boy to accompany the telephone engineer. From time to time, he went down to the cellar and into the public rooms to see how the job was progressing. A veritable army of men were hard at work with great coils of wire. 'Shouldn't be long now,' the electrician informed him. 'You leave us to it, Herr Direktor.'

The telephone engineer returned to say he had looked at all the phones and everything seemed to be in order. At six, power was restored to the upper floors of the hotel. The lifts began working again. Then the lights in the foyer and the bar came on, swiftly followed by the restaurant, Palm Garden and Jubilee Rooms. The electrician came to Benno with a pad. 'If you'll just sign here that the work has been carried out to your satisfaction, sir.' He duly signed and the workmen departed.

A few moments later, there was a knock on the office door and Colonel Oster entered. After first putting his fingers to his lips, he unplugged the telephone, then he turned to Benno. 'I gather strange things have been taking place at the Hotel Quadriga. A visit from your old friend Kuhn, a power failure and a telephone fault.'

He pointed to the phone. 'Herr Kraus, I think you'll find that as from today your phones are being tapped. It's a comparatively simple matter to switch a couple of wires to make the microphone live, so that not just telephone conversations, but everything else that takes place in the vicinity can be overheard.'

Benno stared at him, appalled. 'And the power failure?'

'Let's go and look.'

They entered the restaurant and Colonel Oster walked across to a radiator. Without saying a word, he pointed to a concealed microphone, measuring about an inch by half an inch, a thin wire leading from it into the wainscot. Behind the next radiator was another. Wired into a table lamp at a corner table was another. The colour drained from Benno's face.

They returned to Benno's office. Oster took his monocle from his eye and cleaned it. 'What happened last night?' After Benno had described the night's events, he nodded. 'So they believe Herr Allen obtained his information from the Abwehr, although they are not sure how. Herr Allen will be safe in England. But we are less secure. These microphones mean that the Gestapo's suspicions have been aroused. They distrust not only you and your guests, but the Abwehr.'

'The Abwehr?'

Oster hesitated for a moment, then murmured, 'Suffice to say that we are rival intelligence services.'

Benno sank back in his chair. 'Now they have planted these microphones, the Gestapo must have some means of listening to them.'

'For the telephones, there is a central monitoring station, in the local exchange probably. I imagine the rest of the microphones are linked to the guards' rest-room here on the ground floor.' Colonel Oster stood up. 'Believe me, it was never my intention to bring so much misfortune on you and your family.'

'I don't blame you, Herr Colonel. I just don't understand what is going on any more.'

'We are pawns in a game, Herr Kraus, a very deadly game.' The Colonel reconnected the telephone and, with a sympathetic smile, left the room.

With shaking fingers, Benno lit a cigarette. He must talk to Viktoria. But where? Ruefully, he realized that the only place he could speak to his wife in certain privacy was in the street. He took a deep breath, lifted the phone and asked to be put through to his apartment. When Viktoria answered, he asked her to come down.

They walked up Unter den Linden towards the Brandenburg Gate. When he finished explaining, Viktoria said in incredulous horror, 'Yes, the telephone engineer came to our apartment. I thought nothing of it. Do you mean there are listening devices in every room? Can't we do anything about them?'

'Under extreme circumstances, we can unplug the telephones, but to do so too often will rouse the suspicions of the Gestapo, which could have really serious repercussions.' He looked up at the statue of the Quadriga and put his arm round his wife. 'Vicki, I'm sorry.'

She leaned back against his shoulder. 'I'm sorry too, Benno. Sorrier than I can say.'

But sorrow wasn't enough. Action was needed to protect them and their guests. When she was in bed that night, she had a sudden inspiration. As she was plumping up her pillow to make it comfortable, it occurred to her that its feathery bulk must effectively muffle sound. Holding her finger to her lips, she nudged Benno, then placed the pillow over the telephone.

He gave a smile. 'Well done.'

After that, Viktoria resumed her old job of welcoming guests to the hotel. Those who were old friends she personally escorted to their rooms and, after the page boy had left their luggage, she demonstrated the new properties of their pillows. Without exception they understood and nodded their thanks.

When they left, Herr Fromm was quite surprised at the number of guests who commented on the comfort of the beds. 'I don't understand it,' he told Viktoria. 'The beds are just the same as they always were.'

Viktoria dared not explain, not because she did not trust Herr Fromm, but, since the outbreak of war, they had taken on many new staff, some of whom were doubtless in the pay of the Gestapo. It needed only one careless word and they could all be in very serious trouble. The only member of staff in whom she did confide was

Hasso Annuschek and it was truly surprising the number of drinks that were accidentally spilled over the microphones in the bar.

A few days later, workmen started to build huge stands in the Pariser Platz in front of the Brandenburg Gate. First they painted them, then they erected two massive golden eagles. Finally, they added two enormous Iron Crosses. Word spread that they were in preparation for the Victory Parade that would be held when Germany conquered England. Whatever information Mortimer might have passed on to the English, Hitler was clearly supremely confident of winning his next battle.

That evening, they heard that the greatest air battle of the war had been fought out along the coast of England, in which over a hundred British planes had been shot down. After that Viktoria scanned the papers in a fever of anxiety for mention of Oxford, terrified in case Stefan should be killed in an air-raid. Her sole consolation was that Mortimer was home and must, therefore, be looking after Stefan.

On the northern coast of France, an atmosphere of relaxed optimism prevailed among the Luftwaffe pilots, their ground and air crews. During the past month, bomber divisions had won superiority over the Straits of Dover. For days, no British destroyer or coastal convoy had dared venture into the English Channel. When, on 8 August, twenty-five merchant ships had steamed out of the Thames Estuary, twenty-two of them had been destroyed — albeit at the loss of thirteen Stukas. The British Merchant Navy had not ventured forth again.

On 11 August, a record thirty-two British planes were shot down, two by 'Uncle Sepp', on his way to becoming an ace for the second time, with fifteen kills to his name.

On 12 August, the fighter squadrons were ordered to deliberately provoke the RAF into the air and move the battle east, away from the coast. In their wake, a formation of Bf 110 fighter-bombers approached Dover, their mission to bomb the radar towers strung out along the coast. Behind them came Stukas to bomb the shipping in Dover docks. The raid was very successful for, with the radar out of action, the English did not know they were coming.

Morale at Dallot had never been higher when Sepp briefed his men that evening. 'Tomorrow, 13 August, is Eagle Day! At dawn, we shall launch our all-out attack on the airfields of England! Our orders are to drive the RAF from the skies of southern England!'

A cheer went up. Sepp raised a hand to quieten his men and pointed to the map of England. 'At 0700 hours we shall rendezvous with KG 202 over Cap Gris Nez. Our own target is the forward airfield at Lympne. Now the radar network has been put out of operation, our attack should come as a total surprise.'

He paused, then continued. 'However, once they have got over the shock of our attack, the English won't sit around waiting to be bombed. They'll come up to meet us. Contrary to everything our Field Marshals tell us, they're not going to give in easily. Our machines are better than theirs, but they are good fighters and hard fighters. Do not underestimate them. They'll fight to the last breath and with a skill you have yet to experience. Gentlemen, you are now dismissed. I wish you good luck.'

Sepp's orderly woke him at five the next morning. He pulled the curtains and commented gloomily, 'Looks like a storm brewing, sir.'

Sepp rolled out of bed. Black clouds glowered over the Channel. 'So the weather men have got it wrong again.' Half an hour later, he was in his office when the telephone rang. 'Regional Command here. Orders have just been received from the Reich Marshal's headquarters that, due to weather conditions, Eagle Attack has been postponed.'

Sepp ordered his adjutant to call the men to the operations room and informed them of the change of plan. Tensed for the long-awaited raid, they received the news grouchily and returned to the mess to while away the morning. As Sepp sat down to breakfast, he heard the sound of bombers flying north. Gazing through the window, he glimpsed a formation of Stukas heading towards England. If the attack was off, what the devil were they doing?

Two hours later, his telephone rang again. It was Johannes Enderle, the commander of KG 202. To Sepp's astonishment, he demanded, 'Where the hell were you? We were over Gris Nez at 0700. Not a damned fighter in sight.'

'You weren't notified that the attack has been postponed?'

'Postponed? What the hell are they playing at? Don't they realize how long it takes a bomber squadron to get across?'

'Did you reach Lympne?' Sepp asked hesitantly.

'Overflew it, couldn't see a damned thing through the clouds. But we got another airfield, could have been Hawkinge, where we ran into a squadron of Hurricanes. Intelligence says we put the British radar out of action yesterday. So how was it that those Hurricanes were expecting us? Wait until I reach Kesselring! I've lost five planes and their crews through his bungling ineptitude.'

Sepp waited until the tirade finished, wished him luck and put down the phone. Bungling ineptitude! Criminal negligence would be more like it!

Grimly, he went over the morning's events: the weather the experts had failed to predict; the incomprehensible failure on the part of Regional Command to notify the bombers of the change of plan; the sobering information that the British radar network had not been destroyed. Finally, the vital element of surprise had been lost. Eagle Day was a disaster before it had even begun.

During the morning the weather improved somewhat, thick cloud alternating with sudden brilliant sunshine. Orders came through from Regional Command that the Nowak Wing was to rendezvous with Enderle's bomber squadron over Gris Nez at 1400 hours. Their target was still Lympne. No mention was made of the morning's disaster.

At 1400 hours, the Nowak Wing successfully rendezvoused with the remaining ten bombers of KG 202 over Cap Gris Nez, but the euphoria of the previous evening had gone. Sepp could sense a certain tenseness among his fliers. Even though radio silence was maintained over the Channel, the feeling persisted.

Suddenly, they were crossing the English coastline and a barrage of flak came up to meet them, no menace, just puffs of white smoke at their high altitude. As the first Stukas began to dive, Sepp issued a sharp command for the wing to separate.

Then, through a break in the cloud, he saw them: some twenty Spitfires climbing from the east. '*Achtung!* Spitfires approaching from the east! After them!' The Spitfires were lost momentarily in cloud as they banked and dived, and the Messerschmitts swooped after them through the clouds into the murky grey afternoon. A Stuka was hit, tumbling towards the earth in a pall of black smoke. The bombs from the second Stuka succeeded in hitting the airfield. A fountain of chalky dirt and smoke erupted.

As the Spitfires continued towards their targets, the Nowak Wing peeled off into pairs. Andreas got a Spitfire in his gunsight, flew nearer until he was within range and fired. With a trail of glycol, the Englishman spiralled earthwards.

'I've got him!' Andreas yelled, excitedly.

'*Achtung*, Andreas, there's one on your tail!' Sepp shouted urgently through the R/T, diving towards the Spitfire.

Andreas banked violently, but the Spitfire could turn even more tightly. However, he was no match for Sepp, swooping in from the sun. He pressed his trigger and a line of bullets punctured his wing. A second cannonade and the Spitfire followed its colleague towards the fields of Kent.

Soon, the sky was a milling whirl of metal and white vapour trails, Spitfires and Messerschmitts weaving a complex, dancing pattern in the deep blue sky. A 109 was hit. As it hurtled towards Kent, its cockpit hood opened and the pilot baled out, his body twisting and rolling, as he jerked frantically at his parachute ripcord.

Their bombs delivered, the Stukas clambered for altitude, heading towards the Channel, where another Messerschmitt squadron was waiting to escort them home. Sepp glanced at his fuel gauge. Enough for one final skirmish. A Spitfire was flying towards a straggling Stuka. Sepp headed into a near vertical dive. The engine screamed and the wings quivered. Sepp laughed aloud. This was the flying he loved. The Spitfire was more manoeuvrable than the 109, but Sepp knew he was the more practised pilot. All his flying instincts came to the fore. His finger hovered over the trigger until he was within range. Then, still in mid-dive, he pressed the button. The aircraft shuddered as the heavy calibre cannon fired. The Spitfire exploded in a burst of orange flame and the wreckage spiralled into the grey waters below.

Either the remaining Spitfires were in no mood to continue the fight, or they were out of ammunition or fuel. They turned landwards, as the Messerschmitts likewise headed towards France. Back at base, they were debriefed by an Intelligence officer and reported their victories. Sepp had shot down two Spitfires, Andreas one and other members of the wing claimed three more. But against that, four of their own planes were missing, the pilots and crew either dead or taken captive, there was no way of knowing which.

In the early hours of 14 August, the air-raid sirens wailed in Berlin for the first time in months. Benno staggered out of bed, muttering, 'It must be a false alarm, but we'd better go downstairs.'

Rubbing her eyes sleepily, Viktoria followed him, stopping at her mother's room to take her with them. They joined a crowd of people making their way, grumbling, down the stairs to the cellar, where the all-important, steel-helmeted air-raid wardens were ticking off names on their registers.

For a long time, they listened in silent apprehension for the sound of aircraft, the thunder of exploding bombs. But there was nothing. Eventually, the all-clear sounded and they returned to their beds.

The incident lessened their feeling of confidence. Berlin was surrounded by a massive circle of anti-aircraft guns, with another inner ring protecting the city centre, which, Göring vowed, made it impenetrable to enemy bombers. On top of that, it was impossible that British bombers could ever get as far inland as Berlin. However, somebody must have thought it possible, otherwise the sirens would not have sounded.

'What the hell's going on?' Andreas Müller muttered.

'God knows.' Sepp lit another cigarette and squinted impatiently into the sky as if seeking enlightenment. Unlike Eagle Day, that morning of 15 August was perfect flying weather, the skies over the Channel a clear, brilliant blue, yet all along the French coast not an aircraft had left the ground. The planes were fuelled, the crews were ready, the pilots were waiting.

It was mid-morning before the telephone jangled and Sepp's adjutant called, 'Herr Oberst, Oberst Deichmann's office!' Sepp leaped up the steps and ran down the corridor to his office, where he listened attentively to the crisp orders issued by Oberst Deichmann, Chief of Staff of the Second Flying Corps. Then he returned to his men. 'Rendezvous with KG 203 at 1145 hours! Destination Rochester!'

Already bombers were droning overhead as they left their inland bases, the blue sky reverberating to the sound of their engines. The men of the Nowak Wing pulled on their parachutes and ran towards their machines. A few moments later, Sepp was taxiing down the runway and was airborne, followed by the other thirty-five 109s. KG 203, a formation of ten twin-engined Junkers 88s, was just passing over Gris Nez as they arrived and soon they were part of the vast tidal wave of aircraft sweeping across the Channel towards Kent.

They crossed the coast just east of Hythe and could clearly see renewed attacks taking place over Lympne and Hawkinge airfields, the smoke rising from their bombs and the enemy's flak guns, flames as fuel drums and stationary planes exploded. Avoiding Ashford, over which they could see barrage balloons, they followed the hump of the North Downs. More heavy fighting was taking place over Headcorn, Detling and West Mailing aerodromes. No RAF planes came up to intercept the Nowak Wing.

A quarter of an hour after leaving Dallot, they were over Rochester and the Junkers were dropping their bombs on the flying boat factory. Soon a dense cloud of black smoke hid the city from view. Cumbersomely, the bombers flew on over the marshy lands round the Medway estuary, while their escort hovered protectively above them, scanning the skies for the RAF. 'Uncle, bandits on the left!'

'Viktor, viktor! After them!'

There were six Hurricanes, hopelessly outnumbered by the Messerschmitts. The ensuing dogfight lasted about a quarter of an hour, at the end of which the one remaining Hurricane limped towards the west. By now, the bombers had disappeared from sight. Because there was no radio contact between them, Sepp had no idea exactly where they were.

They caught up with them five minutes later, east of Ashford, just as a dozen Defiants appeared as if out of thin air, beneath and to the rear of the Junkers, their machine guns aimed unerringly up at the bombers' undercarriages.

Shouting an order, Sepp fell from the sky like an eagle, followed by half his flight. The Defiants scattered but not before two of the Junkers had been hit. The Defiants were no match for the 109s, but they were not going to give up easily. Soon, Sepp was involved in a gladiatorial battle with one of them. Its rear gunner's bullets raked his wings. His bullets punctured its fuel tank. Flames were dancing along its fuselage but still its pilot and gunner fought back.

'Uncle!' Andreas's voice burst anxiously into his earphones. 'Red light showing!'

Sepp glanced down at his instrument panel. There, too, the red warning lamp was glowing, showing that he was dangerously low on fuel. Fifteen minutes' flying time remained at the most, just sufficient to see them back to France, if they were lucky.

It would require only one last blast on his guns to send the Defiant to its death. Sepp took his finger off the trigger, levelled the 109 and headed south-east towards the coast. Whoever he was, the English flier had earned the right to live.

Cap Gris Nez was in sight when Andreas shouted, panic-stricken, 'I've run out of fuel.'

'Rock her from side to side,' Sepp yelled urgently.

For a moment, he glimpsed Andreas's face through the cockpit, then his plane began to lose height. 'Bale out,' he ordered. 'We'll send a rescue plane for you.'

Andreas's plane dropped. The cockpit opened and he saw the young man jump out. As his parachute blossomed, Sepp's own engine began to misfire. He was pouring with sweat. 'Come on,' he urged. 'Come on.' A few moments later, he was over the shore. He touched down on the beach, his engine stuttering as the plane rolled to a halt just below the airbase. Shaking in every limb, he clambered out and fumbled in his pockets for his cigarettes. Leaning against the fuselage, he lit one.

'Put that damned cigarette out!' a voice shouted.

Sepp looked up and saw an Army sentry. He threw him a withering look. 'How can a plane catch fire when it's out of fuel?' Then he pulled himself together. 'My wingman had to ditch in the Channel a few minutes ago. I saw his parachute open. Did you see it? Are the rescue boats out?'

Coming closer, the sentry recognized him. 'Glad you made it, sir.' He shook his head ruefully.

A shaken group of fliers gathered outside the operations room. Out of thirty-six planes, only twenty-eight had returned and, of those, only twenty were still serviceable. Several pilots were so badly wounded that it would be a long time before they could fly again, if ever. Until reserves and spares were sent in, Nowak Wing was down to half-strength. The remaining planes were refuelled and immediately sent on another sortie.

As they crossed the place where Andreas had gone down, Sepp thought he saw the remains of a 109 airframe bobbing in the water, but he was too high to be able to identify a white parachute.

A fishing boat found Andreas that night. Tangled in the folds of his parachute, he had drowned.

Not all the victories the Luftwaffe had scored could compensate for the losses it had endured on what became known as Black Thursday. Osterkamp confided to Sepp that, in all, seventy-five planes had been lost that day — against which only thirty-five RAF planes had been shot down.

'What's more, they fell on their own home ground,' Sepp said angrily. 'We have no chance of recovering either machines or pilots. And I hate to think how many more men we're going to lose in the Channel. We shouldn't be babysitting bombers — we should be bringing the RAF fighters up into the air. When we've dealt with them, the way will be open for the bombers.'

Osterkamp sighed. 'Göring doesn't see it that way, although I think he is finally beginning to realize that, despite the fact that the Stuka is an excellent short-range bomber, it won't win the Battle for Britain. However, from now on, he is insisting that there should be more fighters covering every bomber.'

'Which means that half our bombers are going to be grounded for lack of escort, while we fighter pilots make ourselves sitting targets for every Spitfire. Osterkamp, that's not lunacy, that's murder!'

'Try telling Göring…'

'If I have the chance I shall.'

Three days later, to Sepp's surprise, the opportunity arose. He made his twentieth kill. A telephone call from Field Marshal Kesselring's headquarters advised him that he was being awarded the Knight's Cross and that the Reich Marshal wished to present his medal to him personally. He was to fly to Berlin the following morning, where a car would be waiting to take him to Karin Hall.

At Karin Hall, Göring's magnificent, thatched hunting lodge north of Berlin, a manservant showed Sepp into the vast banqueting hall where Göring was reclining at the end of a copious meal. 'Herr Reich Marshal, Oberst Nowak.'

For a moment, Sepp stood rooted to the spot. Not since their meeting at the Palace of the Reichstag President in 1935 had Göring singled out Sepp for a private interview. All their subsequent meetings had been of an official or semi-official nature, with Göring dressed in one of his many flamboyant uniforms. Now, he resembled a character from an operetta, arrayed in a green suede hunting jacket over a white shirt with big puffed sleeves, thigh length boots over leather breeches, and a massive hunting knife in his belt.

'Sepp, take a seat. Have a drink. Asbach is your tipple, isn't it?' Göring waved a languid, manicured hand. There was a gleam of nail lacquer.

With a sudden feeling of misgiving, Sepp approached.

The manservant poured him a large brandy and left the room. Sepp raised his glass. 'Happy landings.'

'Your first visit to Karin Hall, I believe? I must show you round.' Göring raised his massive bulk and Sepp thought, *He looks so decadent. What has happened to my old comrade?*

Their tour took a long time. Every wall was covered with pictures and Göring had to explain the provenance of each one. 'This is from Rome — a Botticelli. This one is from The Hague — Rembrandt, of course. This sculpture is by Rodin — erotic, isn't it? From Paris, of course. Yes, here at Karin Hall, I have works of art from every country within the Reich. People just love giving me presents.' He smiled, his teeth an unnatural, dazzling white.

Sepp shuffled uncomfortably. Art was more Luise's province than his, but he still recognized many of the paintings. It seemed scarcely credible that national art galleries should have donated them to Göring — far more likely that he had simply appropriated them.

'And now for the *pièce de résistance*!' Göring opened the door to a sumptuously appointed bedroom and pointed to a life-size nude dominating the ceiling. 'Isn't that exquisite? Every morning when I wake, I gaze up at Europa and remember that Europe belongs to me.'

A long time ago, Göring had been a cocaine addict. Looking at his slightly dilated pupils, Sepp was sure he was back on drugs.

They returned to the banqueting hall and their brandies. Göring sank back in his leather armchair and gave a theatrical sigh. 'Now, back to business. Sepp, dear chap, this is a very different war from the last one we fought in. Ach, those were the days in our old biplanes — the freedom of the open sky, wind in the struts, the dogfights…' His tone changed sharply. 'But those days are gone. You have earned your Knight's Cross. But it isn't enough. The whole fighter effort isn't good enough. From now on, things are going to change. There must be better co-ordination with bomber units.'

'Damn it all, we shouldn't be escorting bombers,' Sepp exclaimed hotly. 'Hermann, you don't know what it's like out there. For one thing, we're limited by the speed of the bombers. For another, we have no radio contact with them. How the devil are we supposed to co-ordinate…'

Göring flushed and broke in, 'I'm not interested in excuses. Furthermore, I am giving an order. From now on, fighters will stay with bomber formations all the way to their target and back again, no matter how much the RAF tries to deflect them.'

'What the hell are we supposed to do? The only way we can attack the RAF is to leave the bombers.'

'Then you will not attack.'

Sepp tried a new approach. 'You realize the bomber range will be limited by the range of the 109? The battle will be confined to Southern England. For God's sake, Hermann, we'll never wipe out the RAF Fighter Command that way! The British have got all the rest of the country to build and repair their planes, while we...'

Göring banged his fist on the table. 'That's enough! How old are you, Sepp?'

'Forty-eight.' It was one year older than Göring.

'Forty-eight,' Göring said scathingly. 'Combat flying shouldn't be left in the hands of old men like you. You've outlived your time. You lack the necessary aggression to fight a modern war. Well, from now on, that's going to change. The maximum age for Geschwader commanders has been set at thirty-two. No wing leader will be more than thirty, no squadron commander older than twenty-seven.'

Sepp glared at him in disbelief.

There was a cruel twist to Göring's lips. 'However, I don't want you to think that I'm unaware of your talents or your loyalty. I have decided to make you Technical Director for Fighters, a new post, but one which I am sure you will find satisfying. You'll be stationed at Kesselring's headquarters at Blanc Nez.'

'I don't want a new post. I want to keep my wing. I want to go on flying...'

'I don't care what you want. Your flying days are over.'

Slowly, Sepp rose from his chair, knowing it was pointless to argue. 'Yes, Herr Reich Marshal.'

Göring could now appear magnanimous. He beamed expansively, reached in his pocket and took out a small box. 'Before you go, you must have your medal. The Knight's Cross of the Iron Cross. A fitting reward for a brave pilot. My congratulations.'

Sepp took the box, but did not open it.

'While you're back, why not spend a night with your family before returning to the front. I'm sure — Lisa is your wife's name, isn't it? — will be pleased to see you.' Göring rang a bell and the manservant reappeared. 'Show Oberst Nowak to his car. Goodbye, Sepp. Enjoy your leave.'

Luise was just putting Lili to bed, when Sepp let himself into the flat. Sheltie raced round in ecstatic circles, Lili cried, 'Papa! Papa!' and Luise threw herself into his arms. 'Sepp! What are you doing home?'

'I've just been to see the Fat Man at Karin Hall.'

Luise drew away from him. 'What's happened?'

'I've been awarded the Knight's Cross.' He flung the box onto Lili's bed.

'Sepp, what's the matter?'

'I've been grounded, that's what's the matter.'

'Grounded?'

'According to the Fat Man, flying is for young men. Experience doesn't count any more. Twenty enemy aircraft shot down means nothing. I'm too old to fly. I've been made Technical Director for Fighters.'

Lili opened the box and took the medal from its bed of silk. 'Lili, put that down!' Luise admonished.

Sepp shrugged. 'Let her have it. It's only a bit of old tin.'

That evening was the most miserable Luise had spent with Sepp since their marriage. Nothing she said did any good. He withdrew into himself, toying with his dinner, smoking packet after packet of cigarettes and seeking mute solace in the brandy bottle.

They were just going to bed when the sirens wailed. Sepp peered through the windows at the searchlights probing the sky, then asked, 'Has this happened before?'

'Yes, a few nights ago.'

'Presumably you have some kind of drill?'

'We're all supposed to go down to the cellar.'

'Then you'd better go.'

'Sepp, you don't think the British will really bomb Berlin?'

He shrugged. 'We're doing our best to knock out England.' Then he gave a thin smile. 'Go down to the cellar. I'd rather you were safe.'

In the distance there was a brief burst of anti-aircraft fire, then silence. Luise took his hand. 'Come with us, Sepp.'

He shook his head. 'I'd rather see the bomb that's going to get me.' He went into Lili's room, lifted the little girl from her bed, carried her down to the cellar and returned upstairs. An hour or so later, the all-clear sounded. No bombs had dropped on Berlin.

On the radio and in the papers the next morning, there was no mention of the alarm, but there was a photograph of Sepp taken several years earlier, standing beside his plane, cap set at a rakish angle, bearing the headline: KNIGHT'S CROSS FOR 'UNCLE' SEPP. He threw the paper into a bin, kissed Luise and Lili goodbye and set off for France.

Miserably, Luise picked Lili up and buried her face in the little girl's soft hair. 'Oh, Lili, darling, why couldn't Göring have let him go on flying? I worried about him, but at least he was happy…'

On 23 August, Göring announced that it was unnecessary to go down to the cellars when the sirens went. Only if the anti-aircraft guns sounded near their homes should people seek shelter. The implication was clear. Whatever else happened, the centre of Berlin was the safest place on earth.

Nobody including Kesselring, seemed to know what Sepp's new post should entail so, rather than remain entombed in the subterranean depths of Kesselring's headquarters, nicknamed the 'holy mountain', he took upon himself a roving commission, inspecting all the fighter bases along the French coast. At best, he could make a fairly accurate assessment of their fighter strength. At worst, his visits boosted the morale of the fliers.

Following Sepp's visit to Karin Hall, Göring did indeed order all fighter planes to bomber protection duties, meaning that when the German fighters met a similar number of RAF fighters, they not only had to engage them, but cover their bombers as well. Sepp witnessed a steady demoralization among the pilots. Few of them believed any more that the battle would be over in a few days.

It was the same old story: the rivalry and ambition of ruthless men. Göring, in faraway Karin Hall, had no understanding of the realities of the battle. Milch, piloting his own Storch liaison plane, was prowling around France, ostensibly on inspection visits, in reality, Sepp had no doubt, compiling a dossier to further his own career. Sperrle was living in great style in Paris.

Kesselring, at least, was on the front line, but Sepp would never see eye-to-eye with the Field Marshal, particularly since he was advocating an all-out bombing raid on London, similar to those on Warsaw and Rotterdam, which had decided the fate of Poland and Holland.

On the night of 24 August, Kesselring almost got his own way, although not by design. A round-the-clock offensive was being carried out over England now and, that night, a bomber crew heading for the oil refinery on the Thames estuary erred too far westwards and jettisoned their bombs on the City and East End of London.

All day long the telephone wires hummed furiously between Blanc Nez, Karin Hall and Hitler's headquarters. In retaliation for the bombing of Rotterdam, Churchill had loosed his bombers on the Ruhr. What were the likely repercussions for what could well be seen as a deliberate attack on London? No word was released to the press and the public about the night's events.

Sepp's depression deepened.

In the early hours of Monday, 26 August, the air-raid sirens wailed again in Berlin, followed almost immediately by sounds of anti-aircraft gunfire from very near by. Benno leaped out of bed and peered through the curtains at the sky lit up by arcing searchlights. He cocked his ear. The faint drone of aircraft engines could be heard. 'Vicki! Those planes are coming this way!' There was the distant sound of an explosion. 'That was a bomb! Vicki, for God's sake, hurry!'

Viktoria had never moved so quickly in her life. Ricarda appeared at her bedroom door and they joined the crowd hurrying downstairs. There was none of the casual confidence of six days before. Panic-stricken, guests were running for their lives, through the foyer and into the cellar. From the service entrance, staff were rushing pell-mell, knocking against each other in their urgency. The lift descended from the fourth floor, carrying a few night staff from the Abwehr. The Gestapo officers had already deserted their posts.

The distinctive crack of anti-aircraft fire continued, as the bombs fell nearer. The planes could be heard very clearly now. It sounded as if they were directly overhead.

In the cellar the noise was much more distant. Apart from the crying of one or two women, there was silence as the air-raid wardens conducted their roll-call. Then they stood, looking at each other in apprehension, trying to face the fact that the impossible was happening. Bombs were falling on Berlin.

They were in the cellar three long hours, during which a host of thoughts ran riot through Viktoria's mind. Now that the first raid was actually taking place over Berlin, she had to face the fact that German bombs might have been falling on civilian England. She clenched her hands in a private prayer. *Dear God, please keep Stefi safe. If somebody has to be hurt, let it be me…*

When the all-clear sounded, they could return to their rooms. Viktoria's first action was to telephone Luise. To her relief, her sister sounded very calm. 'Of course, it was a bit frightening,' she said, 'but then I thought of Sepp and knew I had to be brave — for him.'

The only mention in the papers about the raid was a six-line paragraph saying enemy planes had dropped some incendiary bombs in two suburbs, damaging one garden hut. During the day, however, word got around that three streets had been roped off where whole houses had been destroyed.

Overnight, the atmosphere changed. Five weeks earlier, Berlin had been celebrating victory, confident that England would surrender. Now, that hope had gone. With their bombs, the British had dropped leaflets reading, 'The war which Hitler started will continue and it will last as long as Hitler does!' Despite all Göring's promises, the RAF had not been driven from the skies. Despite all Göring's promises, bombs had fallen on Berlin.

People finally began to take adequate precautions, equipping their cellars with provisions and emergency lights, shoring up ceilings and sandbagging walls. For the first time since it had been created almost a year ago, the Quadriga's cellar restaurant opened for business and quickly proved very popular.

Three nights later, the British came again and the population of Berlin spent another long, uncomfortable night underground. On this occasion, ten people were killed and about thirty injured. The newspapers waxed highly indignant, calling the British 'Night Pirates' and accusing them of brutal and cowardly attacks on defenceless women and children.

Two nights later, on 1 September, the first anniversary of the outbreak of war, they were back again, the resounding thud of exploding bombs felt even deep in the cellar beneath the Quadriga. The next day, although a whole area of the Tiergarten was roped off, there was an Army Command 'Special Bulletin' announcing that the British fliers had been unable to drop any bombs, because of the efficacy of the city's anti-aircraft guns. 'But we heard the bombs. We felt the vibrations,' Viktoria said.

She spoke for everyone. At the Hotel Quadriga and throughout Berlin, there were puzzled, worried faces. If High Command perpetrated so obvious a deception, about what else had it been lying? Was it possible that casualties in the air battle over England were higher than reported? Was it possible that far from being nearly over, the war was only just beginning? Not even a report in the evening papers admitting to bomb craters in the Tiergarten could dispel their fears.

The British Night Pirates returned again the following night. When the cellar restaurant closed for the evening, preparations were immediately made for the night's siege. Blankets were stacked ready. People slept half-dressed, one ear open for the sirens.

On the evening of 4 September, Hitler opened that year's Winter Relief Campaign at the Sportpalast, his speech broadcast two hours later. 'Mr Churchill is demonstrating his new brainchild, the night air-raid. Mr Churchill is carrying out these raids not because they promise to be highly effective, but because his Air Force cannot fly over Germany in daylight ... whereas German planes are over English soil every day... We are now answering night for night. When the British Air Force drops two or three or four thousand kilograms of bombs, then we will in one night drop 150-, 230-, 300- or 400,000 kilograms.'

The applause from his unseen audience was hysterical and Hitler had to wait until it died down before he could continue.

'When they declare that they will increase their attacks on our cities, then we will *raze* their cities to the ground. We will stop the handiwork of these Night Pirates, so help us God! The hour will come when one of us will break and it will not be the National Socialist Germany!'

'Never! Never! Never!' screamed his audience.

At the Quadriga, Hasso Annuschek turned down the volume on the radio. Nobody commented on the speech. Some were too tired and too depressed. Others, including Viktoria and Benno, were filled with a fear too deep for words. Punctually, at a quarter to midnight, the British bombers arrived. Another sleepless night awaited Berlin.

The following morning, a cable arrived from Fürstenmark, saying that Monika had safely given birth to a little girl, whom she was calling Senta. 'Would you like to go and stay with her for a while?' Benno asked Viktoria. 'I'm sure she'd be pleased to see you — and you would be safer there than here.'

Viktoria stared at him, appalled. 'Apart from the fact that I really don't like babies, I couldn't leave the Quadriga now!'

Benno gave a tired smile. 'No, I suppose not...'

On Saturday, 7 September, Göring himself arrived at Blanc Nez in his personal train, with a great entourage of aides and reporters. Impressively posed with binoculars to his eyes, he stood with his commanding officers grouped around him, gazing out to sea as a vast bombing formation set off across the Channel.

Never in history had anything been seen to compare with this spectacle. Wave after wave of aircraft rose into the air, one thousand two hundred bombers and fighters, darkening the sky, until they formed a dense cloud two miles high and hundreds of miles long, all flying with one destination — London.

Göring turned to a radio reporter and announced with a beaming smile, 'I personally have taken over the leadership of the Battle for Britain ... for the first time we have struck at England's heart... This is an historic hour.'

As the afternoon progressed, the smile slowly faded from Göring's face. Although returning pilots claimed that London had been virtually undefended, and gave vivid descriptions of the city burning from end to end, flames and smoke billowing high into the sky, nevertheless, the results that came into Kesselring's headquarters showed the cost of the operation to the Luftwaffe. Bomber losses crept up until they reached forty.

Göring's fury knew no bounds. Incapable of admitting that his own judgement might be at fault, he looked for a scapegoat and found it in the fighter pilots. Sepp was the first to suffer the whiplash of his tongue. 'Do you realize we have lost nearly five hundred fighter planes so far in this campaign? Now, in one day, we have lost forty bombers! How do you explain that?'

Angrily, Sepp retorted, 'The fighter pilots are tired out. They are making up to five sorties a day, always with the fear that they won't have sufficient fuel to return. All too often, the bomber squadrons are late departing or the fighters lose them in the cloud, squandering precious fuel in the process. The 109 is built for attack, not defence. It's like holding back a racehorse to keep pace with a donkey!'

'As Technical Director of Fighters, your duty is to infuse the men with courage, not make excuses for their cowardice.'

Stung to the quick, Sepp shouted, 'Don't you dare call these men cowards, Hermann! They've seen five hundred of their colleagues die! Are you calling the dead cowards, too? What do you understand of flying? It's twenty years since you last flew.'

'Nowak, be careful...'

But Sepp no longer cared. 'Bombing London isn't going to do any good either. Apart from the moral aspects, you won't be able to keep up today's intensity and, while you're bombing London, you're giving the RAF the very respite they need to recoup their strength...'

'If I want your advice, I'll ask for it, Nowak.' Purple in the face, Göring roared to his adjutant, 'Bring the fighter group commanders here. Let's hear what they have to say for themselves!'

While Sepp stood by, trying to contain his impotent rage, Göring lined his commanders up like naughty schoolboys and continued his tirade. Finally, he asked them scathingly what they thought they needed for victory. As angry as Sepp after Göring's accusations of cowardice, one replied, 'More powerful engines for the 109.' Very quietly, Adolf Galland said, 'A squadron of Spitfires.'

Göring cast them all a look of utter contempt and stormed back to his train.

That night, in the solitude of his room, while the night sky continued to echo to the roar of engines, Sepp drank a whole bottle of brandy — but he did not succeed in getting drunk. Göring was nothing less than a murderer. What was taking place was a massacre, not just of enemy airmen, but of innocent civilians and, almost worse, of Luftwaffe pilots themselves.

For the next week, the bomber raids on London continued, albeit on a smaller scale than that of 7 September. Although Luftwaffe losses continued, it almost looked as if Göring and Kesselring's philosophy might be right. Such opposition as the RAF put up was uncoordinated and scrappy. English casualties, too, were very high. Göring decided one last onslaught was all that was needed to bring England to her knees, either suing for peace or open for invasion.

It took place on Sunday, 15 September, a sunny day, with high white clouds. So confident was Göring of success that he did not come to France to watch his armada depart, but directed the battle from Karin Hall.

Sepp saw the planes leave and knew the bitter truth they carried with them: the exhaustion of the pilots; the fear of being shot down over England or having to ditch in the Channel; the knowledge that, if they did return, there were few spares or reserves; and, above all, the grim fact that, contrary to Göring's belief, the RAF was far from beaten.

Just how far England was from defeat the events of that day quickly proved. Returning pilots told of whole squadrons coming to meet them as they crossed the coast, of the skies over Kent filled with British planes, of London so strongly defended that most bombers had to turn back. Even had they been permitted to attack, there was little the German fighters could have done against such mighty concentrations of RAF fighters. As it was, like the bombers, they were sitting ducks. Many bombers, recognizing the hopelessness of their situation, simply jettisoned their bombs in the Channel or over Kent without even trying to reach their target.

On each successive wave, the RAF, instead of growing weaker, seemed to increase in strength. New squadrons appeared from nowhere, their pilots flying with a breathtaking audacity that could only mean they were confident of victory. By the end of the day, at least sixty planes had been lost and hundreds more so badly damaged as to be beyond repair. Hundreds of men had been killed, wounded or taken prisoner.

From Göring came the order that all fighter group and wing commanders, including Sepp, should report the following day to Karin Hall. Dejected and resentful, they duly presented themselves. His massive bulk swollen with fury, Göring accused them of being the cause of the failure.

Theo Osterkamp pointed out again that Göring was expecting the fighters to fulfil a role for which they were unsuited, but Göring wanted to hear nothing of this, insisting that in future smaller bomber formations would have even bigger fighter escorts.

Sick to the depths of his soul, Sepp could stand it no longer. He had known Göring when they were both raw subalterns at the outbreak of the First World War. Göring had brought him back to Berlin to help build the Luftwaffe. He was not going to stand by and watch it bleed to death. Knowing this could be his last opportunity, he forced himself to sound calm. 'Herr Reich Marshal, if you will permit me to say so, our entire strategy is wrong. From the very beginning, the British have allowed our fighters to fly unmolested while using their fighters to attack our bombers. If we...'

Göring allowed him to go no further. 'Oberst Nowak, you seem to forget that I am in command of the Luftwaffe. How dare you criticize me? If you were anyone else, I would have you court-martialled. As it is, I will give you the benefit of the doubt and assume that two and a half months of battle have unsettled your brain. You are hereby relieved of your duties and will take a month's sick leave while I decide what your future is to be.'

While the others cast him sympathetic glances, Sepp gave Göring a stoney look, then walked out of the room.

The Berlin to which Sepp returned had changed in his absence. Many buildings had holes in their roofs, shattered window panes, doors fixed with planks of wood or even whole walls fallen away to reveal half-furnished rooms. Craters gaped in parks, gardens and roads.

Tall poles had been erected along the East-West Axis, from which wire netting had been suspended, over which artificial grass had been laid so that, from the air, it would merge with the Tiergarten park to either side. The RAF had yet to stage their first daylight attack, but it was clear the city authorities did not rule out the possibility. When Sepp looked up towards the statue of the Quadriga, it had been obscured from view. Victory was no longer in sight.

For Luise, living with the new Sepp was like sharing her home with a stranger. He had grown very thin and moved with a shambling gait. He was totally uninterested in food and seemed to exist on cigarettes and brandy. He told her that Göring had sent him on sick leave, but refused to see a doctor. 'Unless a doctor can prescribe oblivion, it's a waste of time.'

Luise was at her wits' end to know what to do with him. More often than not, he seemed unaware of Lili's existence and, although Sheltie nuzzled his hand affectionately, he did not stroke her. When, a fortnight after his return, Ilse invited them to dinner, Luise accepted, less through any desire for their company, than in the hope that seeing fresh faces would jolt Sepp out of his apathy.

The dinner party was not a success. Impervious to Sepp's mood, Peter insisted upon talking about the battle for Britain. 'In my opinion, it never stood a hope of success,' he stated blandly. 'In any case, the seaborne invasion has been postponed indefinitely, although that isn't public knowledge, of course. As a propaganda exercise, it's useful for the British to continue to live in fear.'

'What about the thousands of airmen who have been killed? What about the air-raids on Berlin and London? Are they also part of a useful propaganda exercise?' Sepp demanded bitterly.

'There are rather unfortunate aspects to the whole affair, but then, that's what comes of leaving a campaign in the hands of someone like Göring. I'm afraid the Reich Marshal has lost his touch.' Peter fingered his clipped moustache. 'Personally, I'm more interested in the ramifications of the Tripartite Pact. Bringing Japan in on our side is a very shrewd move, certainly strengthening our position should America be entertaining any thoughts of entering the war. I also find it intriguing that the Soviet Union does not form part of it...'

On the way home, Sepp said, 'Luischen, I know you meant well, but I don't think I can stomach any more evenings like that. Perhaps the Fat Man was right and I have outlived my time.'

Luise leaned across and kissed him on the cheek. 'I'm sorry, darling, I had forgotten how dreadful Peter can be. He really is one of the most arrogant and self-opinionated men I've ever known. I've never liked him and after what he did to Vicki...' She stopped, suddenly realizing Sepp did not know what Peter had done to Viktoria. 'I mean, to listen to him talk you'd think he actually relished the thought of the war continuing.'

Luckily, Sepp appeared not to have taken in the reference to Viktoria. 'There are a lot like him in the Luftwaffe as well as in the Army. They are so blinkered, they can only blindly obey orders. They can't see that we are all being led down the road to destruction...'

The British raids over Berlin not only continued, they grew more accurate and more frequent. They did not cause a lot of damage, but they did have the effect of robbing everyone of a good night's sleep.

Gradually, thanks to Luise's patient ministrations, Sepp put on a little weight and cut down on his drinking and smoking. When his month's leave was up, he reported to the Air Ministry, where Field Marshal Milch received him with a sneering, 'So you've decided to grace us with your presence again, Herr Oberst? I trust your rest has done you good?'

Sepp knew better than to rise to the bait. He merely said, 'Yes, thank you, sir.'

It did not take him long to realize that, in his absence, Milch's powers had been extended considerably. He had started on a programme to expand the Luftwaffe to four times its current size, which, in a moment of great originality, he had named the Göring

Programme. The Fat Man had little to do with it, however. Aviation power now lay firmly in Milch's hands.

For Sepp, this was the very worst thing to have happened. His value to the Luftwaffe was his flying ability and his knowledge of fighter planes. Milch, their long enmity never forgotten or forgiven, moved him sideways into a staff job, dealing with clerical work regarding trainee fliers.

Never had Sepp felt so lonely. His old friend Ernst Udet, who would have understood, was ill. Most of his former friends were dead or English prisoners-of-war. Younger men, like Galland, were suffering their own problems with the hierarchy. Few of his present colleagues shared his concern that the Fat Man and Milch were leading the Luftwaffe — and Germany — down the road to self-destruction.

On 12 November, the Soviet Foreign Minister, Molotov, arrived in Berlin. On the second evening of his visit, the air-raid sirens began to wail, the flak guns to thunder and the searchlights to thread their criss-cross patterns across the overcast night sky. From above the clouds came the unmistakable drone of British bombers. The following night, while the RAF gave a repeat performance, German bombers staged a massive raid on Coventry. Triumphantly, the newspapers announced that the city centre had been razed to the ground, the fourteenth-century cathedral totally destroyed and a dozen vital aircraft components factories rendered inoperable.

A new word entered the German vocabulary — Coventrisation. Sepp's old nightmare returned. He saw Luise buried beneath a pile of rubble, flames licking up around her. He awoke, screaming, drenched in perspiration.

The air-raids brought both hope and despair to the heart of Bethel Ascher. When he heard the British bombers overhead, he knew there was a chance that Germany might lose the war and that the Jews might be liberated. At the same time, they brought fresh dangers, for Jews and Aryans were forbidden to share the same cellar.

Only one Aryan couple lived in the Professor's tenement block — but there was only one cellar room. During the raids, the Jews had to huddle in the entrance hall — the most dangerous place to be if a bomb landed in the street. So far, however, they had been fortunate. Several people had been injured by bomb splinters, but nobody had been killed.

The air-raids also effected another change in the Professor's life. At the end of September, one of his two rooms was taken from him and a Jewish family moved into it whose flat had been bombed. Sorry though he was to lose half his precious accommodation, he soon grew very attached to his new neighbours.

The Levis were an elderly couple who had married late in life and suffered from ill health. Their daughter, Sara, was a beautiful girl in her early twenties. Although she could have emigrated before the war, she had refused to leave her parents and was now a munitions worker at Kraus Chemie, a very poorly-paid and extremely arduous job, but one which gave her a certain financial and personal security.

It was not so much the parents, as Sara, who concerned the Professor. He worried about the long hours she worked and the fact that she never had enough to eat. Because the Jews were given no clothing points, her clothes were badly worn, her winter coat threadbare. With the scant means available to him, he did what he could to alleviate her hardships. He did this for two reasons: firstly, because her black hair and lustrous dark eyes reminded him of his daughters at that age; and secondly, because she was one of the few young Jews left in Berlin. It became vitally important to him that she survived the dreadful times through which they were living.

It was not just the present, but the future, that worried Bethel. More and more Jews were being deported from Germany into Poland. Nobody knew what happened to them. Some said they were resettled in ghettos in Warsaw and Lublin, but Polish Jews who had succeeded in escaping from Poland told of vast new camps, called Schlachtenhausen and Auschwitz. The name Otto Tobisch surfaced again...

These Polish Jews themselves posed a terrible problem, for they possessed neither identity papers nor ration cards, as well as representing great danger to anyone caught giving them shelter. A tenuous underground escape route had been established with the help of courageous Berliners like Klara Scheer. Under cover of darkness the refugees would be taken to her apartment or the houses of other Aryans like her, where they would be given shelter for a few days while they recovered their strength, then given the addresses of other safe houses in the country. The only way out of Germany now was through Switzerland and unoccupied France to Spain, but the Professor doubted that many succeeded in making it, while any who were caught were shot on the spot or sent straight back to Poland.

Otto Tobisch was a very worried man, for the problems of administering Schlachtenhausen were beginning to overwhelm him. Built to accommodate fifty thousand, the camp now held seventy thousand inmates, only ten thousand of whom could be employed at the Kraus steelworks. Apart from anything else, the condition of most rendered them totally unfit for work. After a week or more in a train without food or water, often in contact with contagious diseases, they arrived more dead than alive.

At the same time, the quality of Otto's staff was deteriorating. Without any doubt, the best men were being sent to the front, and he was given the dregs. The new guards took no pride in their work. They drank too much and had little understanding of discipline.

The 'trusty' system therefore had to be expanded, with disastrous results. Crime was rampant among the inmates. They stole food from each other, fought and even murdered their fellow prisoners, something that had never occurred among the German prisoners at Grubenmünde.

Thousands of Jews arrived at Schlachtenhausen already dead. Others died shortly after their arrival. Their corpses were taken by prisoners to huge burial pits to the south-east of the camp, where they were covered with quicklime to speed decomposition and neutralize the soil for future agricultural use. It was a foul job in a foul area, but the Jews did not seem to mind.

The vast burial pits in themselves constituted another problem. Dead bodies, besides taking up valuable space during the process of disintegration, were a considerable health risk. What was needed were proper crematoria, where the corpses could be burned.

What was needed, Otto privately believed, was a proper system to deal with the Jews. Those who were fit and healthy should be used as slave labour. The rest — the very old, the very young, the maimed and the sick — should, quite simply, be exterminated.

But, for one day, in the middle of November 1940, Otto forgot his problems. The flags were run high. The band marched through the camp playing stirring German folk songs. The kitchens prepared a feast of wild boar with chestnut stuffing, roast potatoes and braised cabbage. The pastry cook made a splendid cake, dripping with white icing.

For most of the prisoners, it was a day like any other, except that roll-call was shorter than usual and the Commandant gave a speech. Since few could speak German, they had no idea of its content.

In the evening, the SS officers gathered for their celebration, waited on by camp inmates. Towards the end of it, before they were too drunk and the revelries became too boisterous, Otto despatched an aide to his quarters. A few moments later, the man returned, carrying a squalling baby in his arms.

Otto took the child and held it up for everyone to see. 'This is my son!' he shouted above the din. 'This is Adolf Alois Tobisch!'

The SS men stood up and raised their glasses. 'Adolf Alois Tobisch!' they shouted. Then they threw their glasses over their shoulders to shatter on the stone floor.

By the beginning of December, Bernhard Scheer resembled nothing more than a walking skeleton. His hair had completely fallen out, his fingernails had flaked away. Folds of leathery skin hung over his ribs and hip bones. His arms and legs were brittle sticks. It was only by dint of superhuman determination that he shuffled to the Kraus factory. His energy was all but spent. One more day and he knew he too must die.

He reached his machine, put out his hand to move the lever — and fainted.

He regained consciousness in the sick bay. A voice was saying, 'Try this broth. Sip it very slowly.'

It was beef broth, made with real beef. There were even pieces of meat and potato in it. Greedily, Bernhard gulped it down, its welcoming warmth soothing his stomach, giving him strength again. When he had finished, he turned to see who had held out the cup.

To his amazement, it was an SS doctor. 'We have a new camp commandant,' he explained in an even tone. 'Commandant Knopf is very experienced in camp administration. He understands that certain standards must be kept if a camp is to be run efficiently and profitably. It is a waste of manpower to allow our prisoners to die.'

The doctor continued to do all he could for Bernhard, the first sign of kindness from an SS man that he had ever experienced. Not until two weeks later, when Bernhard was strong enough to leave the sick bay, did the doctor confide in him that he had been confirmed into the Lutheran faith and that his wife had attended Schmargendorf church. 'Why did you join the SS?' Bernhard asked.

The doctor looked away. 'My brother joined and threatened to denounce me to the Gestapo. What choice did I have?'

The same day as he was reported fit for normal duties, Bernhard was told he was being transferred to Dachau.

At Dachau, Bernhard Scheer was put in Block 26 and, for the first time since his arrest, found himself in the company of other clergymen. In striped uniforms, heads shaven, emaciated bodies covered with sores, their eyes unnaturally huge in sunken eye-sockets, they did not look at all like Monsignore or bishops, like deacons, priests or curates. They were all creeds and nationalities and from every ecclesiastical level — although, Bernhard realized sadly, there was not a Jew among them.

Each had his own dreadful story to tell. But one thing soon became clear. Although they were in prison, the world had not forgotten them. Untiring intervention by the Vatican and the Reich Church had finally succeeded in bringing them together and, to a certain extent, alleviating their circumstances.

From now on, they were to be allowed to conduct services in a room made into a chapel, to own breviaries and to perform lighter manual labour. When Bernhard heard this, he could scarcely believe it and fell down on his knees. 'O Almighty God, who art a strong tower of defence unto thy servants against the face of their enemies; We yield thee praise and thanksgiving for our deliverance from those great and apparent dangers wherewith we were compassed...'

In a communal service, they celebrated Christmas. Bernhard Scheer, former Pastor of Schmargendorf, was invited to read the Gospel. 'In the beginning was the Word, and the Word was with God, and the Word was God... And the light shineth in darkness, and the darkness comprehended it not...'

For the first time since his captivity, he was filled with a deep certainty that he would survive the horror and live to tell the world the truth of what went on within the concentration camps of Germany.

For the first ten weeks of 1941, the Night Pirates stayed clear of the skies over Berlin, concentrating their efforts on ports, military installations, industrial areas, and on France. The Luftwaffe continued their raids over England, but although they inflicted considerable damage on major targets, they did not achieve another Coventry.

Sepp was becoming convinced that neither the Fat Man nor Milch had any real interest any more in the war against England, which was directed with no proper strategy and no hope of a conclusive victory. By scattering his bombs over large areas, instead of concentrating them on specific targets as the British were now doing over Germany and France, the Fat Man was simply dissipating his efforts to small effect — and losing valuable fliers and planes in the process.

There was nobody to whom Sepp could talk, nothing he could do. In the middle of February, when a group of hand-picked men was moved from the Aviation Ministry to the Gatow Air Academy to work on a top-secret project supervised by Göring himself, Sepp was not included.

He finally acknowledged to himself that he was tolerated only for his past achievements, not for any real contribution he might make in the future. From thirty a day, his cigarette consumption slowly crept up to fifty, then sixty. He started hitting the brandy bottle again. It did nothing to change the facts, but it dulled the pain.

CHAPTER FOURTEEN

Although Hans was unable to spend Christmas and the New Year with his family, he was granted leave at the beginning of February. The weather was cold and snowy, but the cottage was snug and inviting. Monika was plumper and homelier than on his last visit, for she had kept most of the weight she had put on during her pregnancy but, to Hans, she was much more attractive than the swarthy French women, who were all he saw in Brittany.

For the first time, he met his baby daughter, now five months old. More delicately built than Heini, Senta showed signs of taking after Ricarda in looks rather than either Monika or Hans. There was a reddish tinge to her hair and her eyes were an unusual greenish-blue. To Hans, she was a strange phenomenon. Never having had a sister, he found it difficult to relate to a girl child, especially one as delicate as this.

With Heini, he felt much more at ease. A year Senta's senior, his son was a very solid little fellow. Once he had got over an initial shyness, Heini was fascinated by his father's uniform and followed him around on chubby legs, an adoring expression on his face. Whenever he saw his sister, he tried to hit her on the head. Hans laughed. 'There's no doubt what he's going to be when he's grown up — a soldier!'

That night, in bed, he asked Monika, 'Do you remember agreeing to make a son for the Führer every time I came home on leave?' His hands crept up under her nightdress.

Monika sighed contentedly. Although her days were more than filled looking after her children and helping her mother-in-law with charitable works in the village, she had sorely missed her man's body at night and, on occasions, had succumbed to the self-satisfaction that Beate had taught her many years before. But, as she had known then, it wasn't the same as *ficken*.

Soon, the double bed was creaking to the rhythm of their bodies, while the signed photograph of the Führer gazed benignly down on them. However, after Hans returned to his regiment a week later and Monika was once more alone with Heini and Senta, she was not so sure that she really wanted to become pregnant again and she was not altogether sorry when her period started. Two young children were quite enough to cope with.

Hans did not return to France. Instead, he was sent by train through Italy and then across the Mediterranean to Libya. To his joy, he was again under the command of General Rommel. Because of security, he could not let Monika know where he was, but he succeeded in outwitting the censors by mentioning the heat in his letter and enclosing some grains of African sand in the envelope.

The Mercedes carrying Lieutenant-General Count Peter von Biederstein swept up to the main gates of OKW at Zossen, south of Berlin. An armed sentry sprang to attention, checked Peter's papers, then the inner red and black guardrail swung up and the car sped under the protective canopy of trees towards Army High Command. It was very familiar now, this dirt road, passing among concrete buildings painted in drab camouflage colours to protect them from enemy aircraft, with sentries standing everywhere and the low humps of manned bunkers rising occasionally above the ground.

Peter paid scant attention to his surroundings, his mind on the meeting ahead, convinced it had to do with the Balkans and Greece — Germany's vulnerable southern flank. Taking advantage of Hitler's preoccupation in the west, Stalin had not been idle. In June 1940, Soviet troops had occupied the Rumanian provinces of Bessarabia and Northern Bukovina. Now, although Rumania had joined the Tripartite Pact in November, Stalin had his eye on the rest of the country, especially the rich Ploesti oilfields.

Torn internally by the allegiances of their inhabitants, the Balkans had always been a seething hotbed of potential revolution and, therefore, a danger to the Reich. Diplomatic negotiations were in hand to bring Bulgaria and Yugoslavia into the Axis, but, in the meantime, the British had allied themselves with Greece, where they were waging a winning war against Mussolini's troops, just as they had been in North Africa, until Rommel had been sent out to give support. A very real danger existed that the British might actually gain a stronghold on the European mainland and use the Balkans for an attack against the Axis.

The car pulled to a halt outside the Command building. The driver jumped out to open the door for Peter, saluted, then drove away to park under protective netting. Again as he entered the building, Peter's pass was scrutinized, then he took the lift down three floors into the bowels of the earth, where the meeting was to be held.

When all the officers were gathered, General Halder rose to his feet. 'Gentlemen, I cannot stress sufficiently the confidentiality of the operation upon which I am about to brief you. If our preparations become known to anybody, there could be extremely grave political and military repercussions.' He paused significantly, then continued, 'It is code-named Operation Barbarossa. Its purpose is to crush Soviet Russia in a quick campaign before the end of the war against England.'

There was a sharp intake of breath. They had foreseen the possibility of a campaign in the Balkans — but they had not anticipated an invasion of the Soviet Union! Peter felt a surge of satisfaction. Communism was inimical to everything in which he personally believed. It sought to undermine the very foundations of his heritage: the entire capitalist system and the feudal rights of the Junkers. The triumph of Germany over the Soviet Union would rid the world of the greatest evil it had ever known.

He felt no compunction about breaking the Nazi-Soviet Pact. It had been made to prevent a war on two fronts — now, thanks to their victories in the west, there was no danger of that. And, once Russia was conquered, Britain would have no choice but to surrender.

The General surveyed them from behind his steel-rimmed spectacles. 'Now the western campaigns — with the exception of Britain — are over, we can start moving units towards the East. Our Military Attaché in Moscow will tell the Russians that we are replacing older men by younger ones — a plausible explanation.'

After explaining the Führer's plan of campaign, he told them that preparations were to be completed by 15 May and that the whole campaign was to be completed before the autumn rains set in.

Peter's mind raced as he contemplated the exhilarating prospect. With an unbroken series of victories behind them, he was supremely confident of another swift conquest. Not only would Germany secure the Balkans, she would regain the Polish territories ceded to Russia, as well as the whole, vast Russian hinterland. Russia's valuable mineral and industrial resources would be appropriated. The Wehrmacht would destroy the Red Army and take Moscow. Where now the hammer and sickle hung over the Kremlin, the German flag would fly in the wind!

Finally, Halder detailed the specific tasks of those present. Peter would be assigned to Field Marshal von Bock's Army Group Centre, his job once again, as in Poland, establishing communications networks, supplies and ammunition stores.

It was only after Peter returned to his office and looked at a map of Russia that he began to fully comprehend the sheer, audacious immensity of Operation Barbarossa. As the crow flew, it was a thousand miles from Berlin to Moscow. Even if the troops started from the German-Soviet demarcation line, it was still seven hundred miles. And what lay behind the Soviet frontier?

Poland, having formerly been German territory, had been an easy matter. Records showed the gauge of railway tracks, the location of the principal military depots, airfields, telephone exchanges and so on. But their files were empty of similar details on Russia.

Since acquiring such information was the province of the Abwehr, Peter made an appointment to see Admiral Canaris. Only as he entered the Admiral's modest office on the Tirpitz Ufer, with its threadbare carpet, iron bedstead in the corner and portrait of Franco on the wall, did he realize this was their first meeting since Castle Podsiadli, over a year ago.

Canaris greeted him cordially enough, enquiring after Ilse and Christa, congratulating him on his promotion. Peter reciprocated, then said, 'I'm in need of basic information on the Soviet Union. Wondered if your department could help?'

'The Soviet Union?'

Uncertain whether the Abwehr was privy to Operation Barbarossa or not, Peter explained that he was involved in planning a precautionary exercise, in case Russia should change her attitude towards Germany.

'Yes, of course,' Canaris replied smoothly, but there was a strange expression on his face. It might have been suppressed excitement. It could have been distaste.

After that, events moved swiftly. At the beginning of March, Bulgaria joined the Axis and German troops entered Sofia. Gradually, nearly three-quarters of a million German soldiers amassed along the Rumanian border with the Ukraine.

On 11 March, the US Congress passed the Lend-Lease Bill which authorized President Roosevelt to lease or lend military equipment to any nation, 'whose defence the President deems vital to the defence of the United States'. In practical terms, it meant that once deliveries were made to England, she would no longer be dependent upon home production and could continue in the war for a very long time indeed. The completion of Operation Barbarossa became all the more urgent.

The very next day — almost as if the British were aware of the highly secret plans being drawn up and chose to mock them — the drone of approaching enemy bombers reached Berlin. Sirens wailed. Flak guns thundered. Their respite over, the people of Berlin again went underground.

The vast transfer of troops to North Africa was completed and, on 24 March, Rommel opened his offensive in the Western Desert, immediately capturing El Agheila from the Allies. The following day, Hitler's negotiations with Yugoslavia culminated in ministers from that country signing the Tripartite agreement in Vienna. The southern flank now strengthened, everything seemed set to launch Operation Barbarossa.

Two days later, staggering news reached them from Belgrade. In a military putsch led by the Air Force and the Army, the Yugoslav Prime Minister and Foreign Minister had been arrested and an anti-Nazi government installed. Prince-Regent Paul had been forced to retire and his seventeen-year-old son Peter had been proclaimed King.

Hitler immediately summoned his top generals to the Chancellery. General Halder returned angrily to Zossen and called a meeting of the officers working on Operation Barbarossa. 'The Führer is understandably furious about the putsch, which has dramatically altered the political situation in the Balkans. Yugoslavia now has to be considered as an enemy and therefore must be crushed as speedily as possible. General Jodl is already planning the invasion and Reich Marshal Göring is preparing the Luftwaffe attack, with specific orders from the Führer to destroy Belgrade. The operation has the codename Punishment.'

The officers glanced at each other and shrugged. It should prove a simple matter. A country in the throes of a *coup d'état* should be quickly beaten and they knew for a fact that the Yugoslav Army was not mobilized. Jodl had merely to divert the troops already gathered in neighbouring Rumania, while Göring's Luftwaffe could operate from Hungarian airbases.

'In view of this new development,' Halder continued, 'the Führer has decided to postpone Operation Barbarossa for up to four weeks. Instead of commencing on 15 May as we have been planning, the invasion of Russia will now take place in the middle of June.'

A victory in Yugoslavia would destroy any possible ideas of putsches by Serbian dissidents in any other Balkan countries, Peter reflected, as Halder dismissed them. As for Operation Barbarossa, a month would make little difference to its success.

At dawn on Sunday, 6 April, Yugoslavia suffered its first experience of Blitzkrieg. Wave after wave of Stukas screamed through the air dropping their bombs on unsuspecting and undefended Belgrade. Fifteen divisions, including five panzer divisions, surged over the borders of Bulgaria, Hungary and Germany itself. Simultaneously, General List's Twelfth Army entered Greece.

Although Peter played no immediate part in Operation Punishment, he monitored its progress with great satisfaction, knowing that within a matter of days the armies of both countries must capitulate and the German military position in the south would be secured for all time.

News of the Luftwaffe's successes in Yugoslavia and Greece spread speedily round the Aviation Ministry. Belgrade had no anti-aircraft guns. Its air force, even if it had been prepared, was no match for Stukas. Flying five hundred sorties in a single day, German bombers had already virtually razed Belgrade to the ground. Huge fires were raging throughout the capital, destroying many municipal buildings, including hospitals and the Royal Palace. The Government had fled. The whereabouts of King Peter was not known. An estimated seventeen thousand people had been killed, most of them civilians strafed as they left their burning homes for safety in the country.

While his colleagues celebrated, Sepp staggered blindly from his office. He scarcely noticed the sentries salute as he showed them his pass. Outside in the cool spring evening air, he lit a cigarette with shaking fingers.

'Operation Punishment,' he told Luise bitterly, when he got home. 'The whole purpose of the exercise is implicit in its name. With their anti-Nazi putsch, the Yugoslavs cocked a snook at Hitler. In revenge, Hitler is using the Luftwaffe to annihilate them and their country. What kind of behaviour is that?'

Silently, Luise poured him a drink. He downed it in one gulp. 'This country is run by a madman,' he said slowly, 'a megalomaniac, who will end up by destroying us all.'

For three days and nights, German planes remorselessly bombarded Belgrade and Sepp's depression deepened. The old nightmares returned. He was awakened by his own screams. Drenched in perspiration, all he could do was to smoke and wait for morning to come.

On the third night, sirens heralded the return of the RAF. Automatically, when she heard them, Luise hurried down to the cellar with Lili and Sheltie. Suddenly, she realized Sepp was not with them. Asking a neighbour to look after Lili, she rushed back up to the apartment, calling worriedly, 'Sepp, where are you?'

He was standing in the dark, staring out of the open window into a night echoing with the thunder of flak guns. The sky was lit up by the weaving criss-cross pattern of searchlights through which could be seen the sinister black shapes of enemy bombers, flying in remarkably low formation. 'Possibly eighty planes,' he murmured. 'Against Belgrade, we used eight hundred…'

One bomber detached itself from the others and dived earthwards. The British pilot swooped up out of his dive and soared up to join the others. Beneath him there was a burst of flame. Within minutes, there were other flares of light, then sparks and tongues of fire leaped up into the night, like a giant fireworks display. Luise clutched Sepp's arm.

Sepp turned. 'Luischen, what are you doing up here? Why aren't you in the cellar?' There was a dull edge to his voice.

She did not reply, but leaned her head against his shoulder, knowing without being told that by watching the bombardment of Berlin, he felt he was somehow assuaging the guilt for Belgrade. And where Sepp was, there she must be too.

For an interminable time, they stood together, watching the British bombers wreak their vengeance over Berlin and a glare of orange light illuminate the city's horizon. At dawn, when the last bombers had gone and the all-clear had sounded, the telephone jangled, the very normality of its sound unreal after the night's experiences.

'Luise, it's Vicki. Are you all right?' Viktoria's voice was strong and calm.

'Yes. Vicki, are you? We saw the bombs falling…'

'We were very lucky. Some of the glass in the Palm Garden Room roof is broken, but apart from that we're unharmed. However, whole buildings at the other end of Unter den Linden are on fire. And apparently the State Opera House has been burned to the ground.'

Tears of reaction rose to Luise's eyes. 'Vicki, it was so frightening. I felt so helpless. And Sepp kept saying…'

Viktoria did not ask what they had been doing watching the bombs when they should have been in the cellar. Instead, she said, 'Is Sepp all right?'

He was still standing immobile at the window, his shoulders hunched, a cigarette cupped in his hand. 'I think so,' Luise whispered.

'Go and make some coffee,' Viktoria instructed, gently but firmly. 'I'll come and see you during the morning.'

'Thank you.'

They exchanged a few more words, then said their goodbyes. Luise rubbed her hand across her eyes, went into the kitchen to put on the kettle, then down to the cellar to collect Lili and Sheltie. When she returned, Sepp was slumped in a chair, clutching a tumbler of brandy. In his address to the Reichstag on 4 May, Hitler had never been more venomous towards Churchill. 'He is the most bloodthirsty and amateurish strategist in history... For over five years this man has been chasing around Europe like a madman in search of something that he could set on fire... His abnormal state of mind can only be explained as symptomatic either of a paralytic disease or of a drunkard's ravings...'

Six days later, an extraordinary event occurred: Rudolf Hess fled to England. Hess was one of Hitler's closest friends and confidants, a founder member of the Nazi Party, deputy Party leader. Rumours became rife. Did this sudden flight signify ruptures among the Party hierarchy? Or had Hess flown with Hitler's tacit approval to try and effect a peace agreement with England?

The Propaganda Ministry was forced to issue a press release to clarify the matter. 'It seemed that Party Comrade Hess lived in a state of hallucination, as a result of which he felt he could bring about an understanding between England and Germany... This, however, will have no effect on the continuance of the war, which has been forced on the German people.'

Under the headline HESS IS MAD!, a German newspaper told its readers that Hess had become a 'deluded, deranged and muddled idealist, ridden with hallucinations traceable to World War injuries'.

The few remaining American correspondents in the hotel enjoyed the situation to the full. Slapping the paper down on the bar counter at the Quadriga and ignoring the hidden microphones, Mortimer's friend Chuck Harris announced joyously, 'The other day Hitler was accusing Churchill of having an abnormal mind, but now he's finally been forced to admit that Germany is also ruled by madmen!'

Around him, people smiled weakly. Not for the first time, Viktoria wondered where Mortimer was, whether he and Stefan were together and how they regarded Hess's flight.

By 14 June, all preparations for Operation Barbarossa were complete. Seventeen thousand trainloads of German troops, nearly three and a half thousand tanks, over three hundred thousand motor vehicles and two thousand aircraft had been moved to the fifteen-hundred-mile-long front, stretching from the Baltic to the Black Sea.

For the last few weeks, reconnaissance planes had been penetrating deep behind the Russian frontier, bringing back detailed information on Russian air bases, ammunition stores and troop movements. There were occasional border skirmishes, but it was clear the Russians were not prepared for a full-scale German attack.

In Berlin, Peter was among the senior officers to attend the all-day conference convened by Hitler at the Chancellery. As always on the eve of a campaign, the Führer was in fiery mood. Upon this occasion, however, his generals needed no justification for the imminent attack and felt no misgivings when Hitler told them, 'This war will be such that it cannot be conducted in a knightly fashion. This struggle is one of ideologies and racial differences, and will have to be conducted with unprecedented, unmerciful and unrelenting harshness.'

Hitler went on to speak about the treatment of Russian prisoners of war and, in particular, Soviet commissars. After explaining that General Keitel would issue exact directives on procedures, he stated, 'The commissars are the bearers of ideologies directly opposed to National Socialism. Therefore the commissars will be liquidated.'

Liquidated. There was a sharp intake of breath and a brief image of a schoolhouse in Poland flitted through Peter's mind.

Hitler scanned the room, then continued, 'You, too, will have to rid yourselves of obsolete ideologies. I would remind you that the Soviet Union has not signed the Articles of the Hague Convention and therefore has no rights under them. My orders will be executed without contradiction. German soldiers who contravene international law while carrying out their duties will be excused.'

For the next half-hour, Hitler spelled out what was going to happen following the invasion. Reichsführer Himmler had been entrusted with the special tasks that would arise from the struggle between the two opposing political systems. In the meantime, it would be the duty of the occupying forces, including the Army, to carry out unprecedented terror by whatever brutal means they thought fit to eradicate all inclination to resist amongst the Russian population.

Peter pushed Poland to the back of his mind. Stalin's generals would not fight with noble, humane conduct. Stalin's political leaders would impose their own vile standards. Therefore, Hitler was right. The only way to rid the world of communism was to exercise the same terror as the Russians themselves, even if it meant contravening the rules of international warfare, even if it meant officers of the Wehrmacht had to bloody their hands.

He thought of the atrocities that had been enacted in Russia under Stalin's rule, of the millions who had been killed or had disappeared during the purges. There must be many Russians who had grown weary of Stalin's excesses and would see the Germans as liberators. Prisoners of war might seize the opportunity to join the Germany Army. Perhaps the whole Russian people would rise up against their Bolshevik leaders, as in 1917 they had overthrown the Tsar.

The following day, he kissed Ilse and Christa goodbye and set off by train for the new General Headquarters near Rastenburg in East Prussia, from which Hitler would command the campaign. Set underground, deep in the forest, it was known as the Wolf's Lair .

Once again, Berlin was permeated with that familiar feeling of tension which had preceded all previous major campaigns. On 21 June, a massive armed guard was mounted in the foyer and outside the Hotel Quadriga, as the occupants of the fourth floor were sealed off from the world. With a feeling of great misgiving, Viktoria wondered which country was now about to come under attack.

Sepp and Luise dined at the hotel that evening. Although Luise exuded an almost brittle cheerfulness, nothing she said could conceal the fact that Sepp was very depressed. At the end of the meal, he lifted his brandy glass with a trembling hand and asked, 'You know what's going to happen next, of course?' His voice was not so much slurred as filled with an infinite tiredness.

Although they were seated at a 'safe' table, Viktoria looked round anxiously.

'It's supposed to be top secret, but you can't keep this sort of operation quiet, not something the size of Barbarossa. In the end, they had to tell me, even though I'm not part of it.' Sepp's eyes held a hint of his old mocking laughter. 'I was never much of a scholar, but some dates were drummed into me at school which I've never forgotten. Do you know that on 22 June 1812, Napoleon crossed the River Neman on his way to Moscow? But then, Napoleon didn't have the same advantages as Hitler, did he? He didn't have Stukas and panzers to wage Blitzkrieg.'

Viktoria stared at him aghast. 'You mean that tomorrow we are going to invade Russia?'

'Yes.' The laughter had gone. Only the bitterness remained. He drained his glass. 'Think I'll have another brandy.'

'Sepp, are you sure?' Luise asked anxiously.

'That I should have another brandy? Oh, yes. That it will transport me to the realms of blissful oblivion? Unfortunately, no. It is one of life's little ironies that the more drunk one wishes to get, the more sober one becomes.'

Viktoria glanced at Benno. His face was white. 'Russia...' he whispered incredulously. 'We're going to invade Russia...'

Later, when Luise and Sepp had returned home and Viktoria and Benno were secure in the privacy of their own apartment, she said, 'I hate everything about the Soviet Union. But, Benno, can we win?'

'I hope so. For God's sake, I hope so...'

The following morning, a 'Special Bulletin' announced that, at half past three that morning, Russian troops had crossed the border into German territory and attacked German soldiers.

The Soviet Union, it was reported, had practised sabotage, terrorism and espionage against Germany. It had constantly sought to undermine all efforts to set up a stable order in Germany. It had conspired with England for an attack against German troops in the Balkans and, by concentrating all its available forces on the long front from the Baltic to the Black Sea, it had continually menaced the Reich. Such a situation could be tolerated no longer. The Führer had therefore ordered the German Armed Forces to oppose this threat with all the means at their disposal.

Accounts were already coming in from German reporters at the front. The first Russian bridges had been captured intact. Russian garrisons had already been seized. Thousands of Russian planes had been destroyed. The first prisoners had been taken. It was confidently predicted that the war would be over within a matter of weeks.

In the throes of his second-year examinations, Vasili Meyer had little time to follow the progress of the imperialist war. When the first air-raid shelters were built that June, blackout precautions installed and anti-aircraft guns erected, he assumed they were simply a precautionary measure. The rest of Europe was at war. It was only natural that the Soviet Union should also be defended.

It therefore came as a great shock when, at noon on 22 June, Foreign Commissar Molotov spoke to the citizens of the Soviet Union, his words broadcast through loudspeakers on every street corner and city square. 'Today at four o'clock in the morning, making no demands of the Soviet Union and with no declaration of war, German troops attacked our country, crossed our frontier in several places and bombed Zhitomir, Kiev, Sebastopol, Kaunas and others of our towns.'

Aghast, Vasili left his books and stood at the open window, as Molotov's faltering voice continued to echo over Moscow, describing the events leading up to the invasion and denying Hitler's allegations of non-observance of the Soviet-German Pact by the Soviet Union. 'The whole responsibility for this act must fall on the Nazi rulers.'

What Molotov said next was infinitely reassuring to Vasili. 'This war has not been inflicted upon us by the German people, or by the

German workers, peasants and intellectuals, of whose suffering we are fully aware, but by Germany's bloodthirsty rulers.'

Mikhail burst excitedly into the room. 'Vasili, have you heard the news?'

He nodded, stacking his books neatly on the table. 'Let's find out what is happening.'

In the city, pandemonium reigned. Long queues had already formed outside shops, women with huge shopping baskets jostling each other to stock up with bread, potatoes, flour and other essentials. Moscovites had long memories. In Russia, war meant hunger. At the tobacconist, there was another long queue. Cigarettes were being bought by the dozen packets.

'Vasili, do you think the Germans will reach Moscow? They have the advantage over us. They are prepared. We are not.'

'No,' Vasili replied confidently. 'The German armies have dissipated their strength fighting England. Our Red Army is many times stronger. You saw our tanks and planes at the May Day Parade. In a few days, we shall beat the Nazi hordes back through Poland to the Odra River.'

'And England?' Mikhail asked. 'Do you think she will now make peace with Germany in order to fight us? After all, Hess went to England. And there was Munich…'

The answer came in a radio broadcast from Churchill that very evening, which Vasili and Mikhail heard on the radio in the main students' hall. In marked contrast to Molotov's stuttering, guttural tone, came the confident, rumbling voice of the man who had, for nearly two years, been leading England's single-handed fight against the Nazis. 'No one has been a more consistent opponent of communism than I have in the last twenty-five years,' he admitted. 'I will unsay no word that I have spoken about it.'

But, he went on, 'I see the Russian soldiers standing on the threshold of their native land… I see them guarding their homes where their mothers and wives pray — ah, yes, for there are times when all pray — for the safety of their loved ones… I see the ten thousand villages of Russia where the means of existence is wrung so hardly from the soil, but where there are still primordial joys, where maidens laugh and children play. I see advancing on all this in hideous onslaught the Nazi war machine… I see the dull, drilled, docile, brutish masses of the Hun soldiery plodding on like a swarm of crawling locusts. I see the German bombers and fighters in the sky, still smarting from many a British whipping, delighted to find what they believe is an easier and safer prey…'

Then Churchill promised the people of the Soviet Union that he would never do a deal with Hitler and that Britain would support Russia both morally and with materials in her war. Finally, he said, 'Hitler wishes to destroy the Russian power because he hopes that if he succeeds in this, he will be able to bring back the main strength of his Army and Air Force from the East and hurl it upon this island…'

When the broadcast ended, the students looked at each other in stunned relief, scarcely able to believe that England should choose to ally herself with the Soviet Union.

Although Vasili had been studying English for many years, he had never been to England and he had no English friends. Politically, he was opposed to everything the British Isles stood for — capitalism, monarchism, imperialism. Yet Churchill's speech demonstrated that it was possible for men of quite different beliefs to reach out towards each other in the common cause of freedom.

To Peter, following in the rear of the Army's fighting force, the initial days of Operation Barbarossa seemed like the Polish campaign again. Above all, the Germans had the tactical advantage of surprise. Within four days, panzer divisions had crossed the River Dvina and the Luftwaffe was bombing Leningrad. On 28 June, Field Marshal von Bock's Army Group Centre captured Minsk. On 1 July, Field Marshal von Leeb's Army Group North took Riga. In the south, Field Marshal von Rundstedt's Army Group was advancing towards the Dnieper River and Kiev, capital of the Ukraine.

Field headquarters were set up at Borisov, north-east of Minsk, and Peter commenced the lugubrious process of organizing supplies, ammunition, reserves, mail and communications. Then he began to realize the full implications of the inadequate information they held on Russia.

The German Army was by no means fully motorized and relied largely upon horses to transport stores and equipment. Russian roads were extremely primitive, for the most part tracks awash with mud in the seemingly interminable and torrential rain. Even fully tracked vehicles like tanks were forced to keep to the few arterial roads. Rail transport was the obvious solution, but it transpired that Russian railways were of a different gauge to their own, so special engineering units had to be detailed to change the rails.

Supplies and spares were therefore lagging days behind the main body of the Army. The further into Russia they penetrated, the worse the situation became.

On 3 July, twelve days after the outbreak of war, Stalin addressed the Russian people. 'Comrades, citizens, brothers and sisters, fighters of our Army and Navy! I am speaking to you, my friends!' He spoke slowly, with a thick Georgian accent, describing the progress of the war. Despite heroic defence by the Red Army, the Nazi invasion continued, although 'the best German divisions and air force units have already been smashed and found their graves on the field of battle.' Yet still, 'A serious threat hangs over our country.'

He drew a parallel with the great patriotic war of 1812, reminding the people that the armies of Napoleon and Wilhelm II had been defeated. 'This war has been inflicted upon us, and our country has entered into a life-and-death struggle against its most wicked and perfidious enemy, German Fascism... The enemy is cruel and merciless. He aims at grabbing our land, our wheat and oil. He wants to restore the power of the landowners, re-establish Tsarism, and destroy the national culture of the people of the Soviet Union ... and turn them into the slaves of German princes and barons.'

As Vasili listened, he suddenly saw again the tenement blocks of Wedding and the Mercedes belonging to Baron Heinrich von Kraus making its way through the gates of Kraus Chemie. As if it were yesterday, he heard his mother saying, 'History is on the side of freedom and freedom will be with you as long as you fight for it. And we shall fight to the end. We are German workers! We shall never be enslaved!'

Stalin had been responsible for Olga's death and yet she would have approved his sentiments today. 'Our people should be fearless in their struggle and should selflessly fight our patriotic war of liberation against the Fascist enslavers... The Red Army and Navy and the whole Soviet people must fight for every inch of Soviet soil, fight to the last drop of blood for our towns and villages...

'Whenever units of the Red Army are forced to retreat, all railway rolling-stock must be driven away. The enemy must not be left a single engine, or a single railway truck, and not a pound of bread or a pint of oil... All valuable property, whether grain, fuel or non-ferrous metals, which cannot be evacuated, must be destroyed.

'In the occupied territories, partisan units must be formed... There must be diversionist groups for fighting enemy units, for fighting the partisan war everywhere, for blowing up and destroying roads and bridges and telephone and telegraph wires; for setting fire to forests, enemy stores and road convoys. In the occupied areas intolerable conditions must be created for the enemy and his accomplices, who must be persecuted and destroyed at every step...'

Finally, after announcing the formation of a Home Guard to support the Red Army, he ended, 'All the strength of the people must be used to smash the enemy. Onward, to victory!'

It was a speech that moved Vasili to the very depths of his soul. This was a new image of Stalin: no longer a man to be feared as he had been during the purges, or to be repeated, parrot-fashion, in class; but a leader, a man of courage and indomitable will, a man to follow to the very ends of the earth.

The war very quickly made itself felt. Posters were plastered on every wall: showing Red soldiers ramming bayonets down the throats of Hitler-faced rats, with the slogan, 'Crush the fascist vermin'; showing Russian tanks crushing giant crabs with Hitler moustaches. Despite Stalin's assurances that this was an all-people war, including that of the German people enslaved by their ringleaders, Vasili took care never to speak German.

All leave was cancelled for the duration of the war and all Soviet men between the age of sixteen and sixty who were not in the military were compelled to take part in civil defence groups. A curfew was imposed and anyone out after midnight needed a special pass. Strict censorship was introduced. All privately owned radio sets had to be handed over to the militia, so that, apart from newspapers, the sole means of learning the news was from public loudspeakers.

Even so, it was clear that the Germans were advancing ever more rapidly towards Moscow. By 16 July, German troops had reached Smolensk, a mere two hundred miles west of the capital. Within two weeks, there were drastic food shortages and on 18 July rationing was introduced. The first women and children were evacuated. Dozens of searchlights and three circles of anti-aircraft guns were erected round the city. Special trucks ran along the tramlines distributing heaps of sand to extinguish incendiary bombs. The people were told that air-raid warnings would be given if German planes were seen leaving Smolensk.

Then came the welcome news that the Red Army had succeeded in bringing the German advance to a halt outside Smolensk. An atmosphere of near gaiety pervaded Moscow. Although the news from Leningrad and the Ukraine continued to be bad, there was a feeling that the tide was about to turn.

By 16 July, Army Group Centre held three hundred thousand Russian soldiers encircled at Smolensk. After twenty-five days at war, hundreds of thousands of Russian soldiers had been captured, thousands of enemy planes and tanks destroyed or appropriated. German troops had advanced four hundred and fifty miles into Russia. Moscow — the ultimate goal — lay a mere two hundred miles away.

Moscow was not only the capital, it was the nerve centre of enemy resistance, of arms production and, even more importantly, the centre of the Russian transportation and communications system. Once Army Group Centre captured Moscow, the entire Russian war machine would be immobilized.

Between Smolensk and Moscow there were no river barriers, no major garrisons and, because of the speed of the German advance, the city must be inadequately protected from air attack. Even if the weight of bombs their planes could carry was reduced by their fuel loads, the Luftwaffe must still be able to inflict considerable damage. Then the panzers could roll in.

On the evening of 21 July, Vasili was a short way from the students' home when the air-raid sirens started. He hesitated for a moment, staring up at the sky, then, as a distant staccato clatter of anti-aircraft gunfire commenced, he followed the crowd scuttling fearfully into the nearby Dsershinskaya underground station.

For a long time, nothing happened. The atmosphere grew hot and stifling. Children started to cry. Convinced it was a false alarm, several people tried to leave, only to be forced back again by civil defence wardens. Then, suddenly, from their refuge deep in the bowels of the earth, they heard the muffled thump of an explosion that sent vibrations even to where Vasili was standing.

A woman screamed. A girl burst into hysterical tears, clawing at Vasili's jacket. 'We're all going to die! The Germans will kill us all!' He put his arm round her shoulder, trying to calm her. But his mind was trying to cope with the incomprehensible. German bombs were falling on Moscow.

Dreadful though it had sounded, little damage was caused by the raid. So effective were Moscow's defences that very few planes had actually succeeded in getting through. The citadel held.

Far from seeing the Germans as liberators, the Russians regarded them as enemies whom they were prepared to fight to the last ditch. Even encircled as they were at Smolensk, they stood their ground with a ferocious tenacity. Russian losses might be high, but so too were German casualties. A massive field hospital was set up at Borisov and endless Red Cross convoys returned every day to Germany.

Furthermore, the Russians seemed to have a limitless supply of fighter planes, tanks and troops, which were of far superior quality to that which the Germans had been led to believe. Because of a lack of suitable airfields, German fighter bases were too far back to supply suitable overhead cover for the swiftly advancing ground troops and the bombers.

The Battle of Smolensk lasted three weeks, by the end of which time Army Group Centre had taken captive over three hundred thousand Russian soldiers, three thousand armoured vehicles and three thousand pieces of artillery. Bloodstained and weary, but confident of victory, the German troops prepared themselves for the final, decisive onslaught on Moscow.

But Hitler had other ideas. From the Wolf's Lair, he issued a directive stating categorically: 'The most important objective to attain before the onset of winter is not the capture of Moscow, but the conquest of the Crimea, the Donets coal and industrial basin, and the cutting-off of Russian oil supplies from the Caucasus. In the north, it is the locking-up of Leningrad and the union with the Finns.'

The decision caused anger among his field commanders. Telephone wires hummed. General Guderian was so furious that he flew to Rastenburg to put his case directly to the Führer. To no avail. Guderian's panzer forces and several infantry divisions were ordered south towards Kiev.

Without its tanks and armour, Army Group Centre was helpless. A mere two hundred miles from Moscow, the massive body of men could do nothing but wait, strung out along the Desna River, until Guderian returned from Kiev.

At Borisov, the Führer's directive caused less consternation. It meant that the German position in the occupied territory could be consolidated; that there was time for refitting and re-grouping; that essential repairs could be effected.

In August, Peter realized it also meant something more.

'Herr General, Herr General!' A soldier burst through the door of Peter's office, his face red and sweaty, his collar askew and his jacket undone.

Peter looked at him in cold disapproval. 'Sergeant, what do you mean by rushing unannounced into my office in such a manner? Do your jacket up, man. Put your collar straight.'

The sergeant recollected himself, gave a poor salute and fumbled with his clothes. 'Herr General, something terrible's happening. You must come at once.'

Peter stood up. 'Sergeant, whatever has happened, surely you have been long enough in the Army to know you should report first to your senior regimental officer?'

There was a desperate look in the sergeant's eyes. 'He's gone to Smolensk, sir. Please, sir. You must do something, sir.' For a moment, Peter thought he was going to burst into tears. 'It's the airfield, sir. They're doing the most terrible things.'

Slowly, Peter nodded. 'My driver is in the mess. Tell him to bring my car.'

They were driven to a small airbase that had been devastated early in the campaign. Now, its perimeter was ringed by soldiers. A procession of military trucks was making its way towards the ramshackle administration block. His car followed them, past a sentry onto the concourse. The driver pulled to a halt and Peter got out.

An extraordinary scene was being enacted before him. SS men were pushing civilians out of the lorries, shoving them into a line behind others already queuing to enter the airfield buildings. They were ordinary-looking people, neatly, if simply dressed. Many were carrying shabby suitcases or brown paper parcels, as if they were going on a journey. Some carried coats, as though they expected to be away for some time. Many wore the yellow Star of David on their arm.

An SS officer approached Peter and saluted. 'Heil Hitler, Herr General.'

'What is happening to these people?'

'Resettlement, Herr General.'

Peter reached in his pocket for his cigarette case, not offering it to the SS officer. He lit a cigarette, then walked towards the offices. It was warm in the August sunshine, still and breathless. From somewhere came a muted banging — it could have been echoes from a distant battle.

Peter marched past the shuffling line into a large room, where several SS officers were seated behind desks, filling in forms with personal details of the people. In the next room, more SS men, armed and accompanied by guard dogs, relieved them of their valuables — watches, jewellery, handbags and money — issuing them with receipts and explaining that their belongings would be returned to them once they landed at their destination. They were then directed to the other end of the runway.

Peter followed them. It was a long walk, past stark, skeletal trees and derelict hangars, to a distant outhouse, well out of sound and sight of the main block. There, more SS men urged them in at gunpoint. Upon seeing Peter, one of them detached himself from the group. 'Heil Hitler, Herr General! Come to see the fun?' He led him round to the other side of the shed. 'It is a very satisfactory exercise. Jews dug the pit earlier this week…'

Peter stopped stock still in his tracks. The people emerging from this side of the outhouse were stark naked. Urged on by whips and with dogs at their heels, they were hustled down towards a vast pit, around which stood more SS men. When they reached the edge, they were kicked to their knees. There was a burst of gunfire and their bodies fell on to the hundreds of others already lying there. As if they were at a fairground shooting booth, the SS men laughed and joked among themselves. One unbuttoned his flies and urinated on the pile of corpses.

For a moment, Peter thought he was going to faint. His companion explained, 'They think they're going to be flown to safety. Once they get out here, they know differently. Look at them! They're just like animals. They haven't even got the intelligence to be afraid!'

Beyond the pit, lining this far perimeter of the airfield were more men, not SS, but Army soldiers, their guns at the ready, prepared to shoot anyone who tried to escape. Their faces were pale and drawn. None of them looked at Peter. None of them looked at the pit.

The Russians were pushed past him, terror in their eyes. One woman held a baby to her breast. An old man talked quietly to his grandson, who was trying to fight back his tears. A couple, possibly the same age as Ilse and himself, passed him hand in hand with a girl of Christa's age. Peter watched them all go, naked and defenceless, to their death. It came so quickly they could scarcely have been aware of it happening.

So this was the special task entrusted to Himmler. This was what Hitler had meant by carrying out unprecedented terror to eradicate all resistance among the Russian population. And Peter had believed him to be right, that the only way to rid the world of communism was to exercise the same brutality as the Russians themselves, even if it meant contravening the rules of international warfare, even if it meant officers of the Wehrmacht had to bloody their hands.

For five minutes, he stood there. Five minutes, in which perhaps fifty people died. After those five minutes, he walked away, back past the endless procession, back past the black, skeletal trees, back to his waiting car. He carried with him the knowledge of hell. And he knew he would bear that hell with him wherever he went for the rest of his life.

He could not let the matter rest. After thinking through his argument carefully, he requested an interview with Field Marshal von Bock, described what he had seen and demanded that something be done to stop the atrocities.

The Field Marshal stared coldly at him. 'General, you must be aware that it is a soldier's duty to carry out his orders without question. The directives concerning the Soviet commissars came from the Führer himself. They are to be obeyed.'

Peter took a deep breath. 'Those people were not Soviet commissars, sir. They were ordinary civilians, many of them Jews. Although SS men were doing the killing, soldiers of the German Army were also involved. In view of this, I wish formally to protest against the Führer's orders.'

'General von Biederstein, I find it impossible to believe that you do not understand the implication of your words. But I warn you that, should you ever repeat them, you will face dire consequences.'

'Herr Field Marshal, I am not concerned for myself, but for the honour of the German Army.'

For a moment, Bock hesitated, a flicker of doubt crossing his face and Peter wondered if he might not, after all, succeed. Then he said, 'You speak of honour, but apparently you are prepared to break your own word of honour. General Count von Biederstein, remember that you swore an oath of obedience to the Führer. Now, leave my sight, before I change my mind and arrest you for criticizing his orders.'

Peter saluted, then left the Field Marshal's office and went to his own quarters. For a long time, he stood at the window, staring out across the devastated countryside. Suddenly he remembered Admiral Canaris at Castle Podsiadli. *So long as you realize that, one day, when the dreadful truth emerges, the world will hold the Army responsible for these atrocious deeds.*

During the weeks that followed, reports reached Peter's ears that the massacre of Jews at Borisov airport was not an isolated incident. Perhaps if the advance on Moscow had recommenced, he would have paid less attention to such stories, relegating them to the back of his mind. As it was, the battle for Kiev continued with no sight of a swift victory and Army Group Centre was impotent to move. And Peter had too much time to think about the horror he had witnessed and been powerless to prevent. War against the Soviet Union had taken on a very different aspect.

At the end of August, Reichsführer Himmler paid his first visit to Schlachtenhausen concentration camp. After a cursory tour of inspection, he told Otto, 'I have a confidential matter to discuss with you, Oberführer. Let us go to your office.'

After Otto had issued instructions that they were not to be disturbed, Himmler said, 'The Führer has given the order for the final solution of the Jewish question. It means the complete extermination of all Jews in Europe. The execution of this very grave order has been placed on my shoulders. We, as the SS, must see that it is carried out.'

For a long time, Himmler spoke, while Otto listened attentively. He explained the role of the SS Einsatzgruppen, who had followed the Army everywhere into battle and the problems encountered in killing vast numbers of Jews in towns, villages or in the open countryside, even with the use of mobile gas chambers. Far more effective would be to send them to special camps for liquidation. 'Schlachtenhausen is ideal for this task. Its situation means that our activities can be effectively camouflaged. And there is ample room for expansion.'

'And the means of extermination?' Otto began to describe the problems he had with the mass graves.

Himmler interrupted him. 'Experts will come and see you to discuss the technical details. In the meantime, you can start clearing the space for new buildings, well away from the labour camp. The death camp should be an entirely separate entity.'

'When do you expect it to be operational, Herr Reichsführer?'

Himmler's pale eyes stared at him bleakly. 'By next spring at the very latest.'

Following Himmler's visit, a succession of officials from Berlin came to Schlachtenhausen. As work commenced on clearing the site, architects and builders arrived to discuss plans. Specifications were drawn up so that tenders could be received for the necessary construction materials and equipment. Most important of all so far as Otto was concerned, huge crematoria were to be constructed. The SS expert on this subject gave a ghoulish smile. 'You may be interested to learn that human ashes make excellent fertilizer, Herr Commandant.'

'Really? My wife is a keen gardener. She's always complaining about the poor quality of the soil.'

Although Anna never entered the prison and was not informed of the purpose of the new buildings, she could not help but be aware of the activity and came up with an improvement of her own. Since the birth of little Adolf, she had become rather sentimental about Schlachtenhausen and felt the first impression prisoners received of it reflected badly upon her. 'Can't we make the railway station and the camp entrance more attractive, Otti?' she pleaded.

Otto opened his mouth to say no, then reconsidered. Why not? The more welcoming the approach to the death chambers, the less suspicious new trainloads would be and, therefore, less likely to panic.

So the station was painted white and hung with baskets of fuchsias and petunias. Lawn was laid along the approach to the camp, surrounded by borders of roses, marigolds and petunias. Silver birch trees gracefully shaded the area, concealing the ugly barracks behind.

Light music played over loudspeakers, tunes from Viennese operettas, waltzes from the Blue Danube.

Otto learned that people in the town were considerably reassured about what went on in the camp. German prestige rose to new heights.

At the beginning of September, Baron Heinrich received a telephone call from Himmler, advising him of a visit from Reinhard Heydrich and expressing the hope that Kraus Industries would be able to assist him with his requirements.

Heydrich's problem was certainly an interesting one. As the Baron was aware, SS Einsatzgruppen followed the Army into all occupied territories, their task being to crush the incipient Jewish-Bolshevik revolution. In Poland, their task had been difficult enough. In Russia, where there were an estimated eight million Jews, it was proving almost impossible. Such Jews as were fit for work were sent to labour camps. Many, however, were quite simply too old, too young or too sick. In the camps, they died a lingering death, demoralizing and spreading disease among the other inmates in the process.

What was needed was a quick, humane method of putting these creatures out of their misery. Since Kraus Chemie had been producing poison gases for various purposes since the beginning of the last war, Reichsführer Himmler had suggested Heydrich ask the Baron's advice.

The Baron was delighted to be of service and explained that, in his experience, hydrogen cyanide was the most efficient method of inducing a swift, painless death. Kraus Chemie had long been manufacturing it for sale as a strong commercial disinfectant. To increase production would be no problem. Then he asked, 'And what about disposing of the bodies, Herr Obergruppenführer?'

'Crematoria are currently under construction at the major camps and specialist companies are offering tenders for furnaces. Since there is some distance between the death chambers and the crematoria, however, I wondered if your concern would be interested in supplying narrow-gauge railways for transporting the corpses?'

For a company that had founded its fortune in the railway age, it was no problem. Since Kraus Steel had a factory at Schlachtenhausen, it was a very simple request to accede to. 'If you send me the necessary information, I shall process the orders personally.' The Baron glanced knowingly at Heydrich. 'In view of the delicacy of the operation, I assume you would prefer it to be kept as confidential as possible.'

Not a muscle twitched in Heydrich's face. 'I'm sure I can rely on your discretion, Herr Baron.'

Baron Heinrich suffered no qualms over this transaction. Business was business. If the SS did not buy from Kraus, they would buy from another company.

As the Russian campaign continued, the theory of an international Jewish-Bolshevik conspiracy was aired more forcefully than ever before. With a feeling of unease, Viktoria read newspaper reports claiming that in the East the German soldier was confronted by the Jew in his most repugnant and fearful form. But the enemy was not to be found only in Russia. He was active within the Reich itself: the German Jew, untiring in his efforts to undermine the home front.

There was nothing new in the anti-Semitism but there seemed to be an added vitriol in the words. For the first time in a long while, Viktoria found herself thinking of Professor Ascher and wondering where he was.

At the beginning of September, a new law required all Jews in Germany to wear the yellow Star of David on their left breast with the word JEW in black letters. Photographs in newspapers and magazines showed Jewish families wearing their new badge and explained: 'The marked ones. The German people has finally drawn a line between itself and the Jews. These rabble-raising swindlers who have tried again and again, under the mask of sanctimoniousness and harmlessness, to meddle with the German people, now carry the badge — the Jewish star — that separates them from all decent human beings. For years, they have ruled Germany and sucked her dry. Now they have the clearly marked position they deserve, as foreign parasites amongst a healthy people.'

Yet, in the select area surrounding Unter den Linden, the yellow star was seldom seen and Viktoria could only assume that most Jews — including Professor Ascher — had left the city for safety elsewhere. She had no way of knowing that her old friend was still living in the Hackescher Markt.

For the Berlin Jews who remained it was the beginning of a new terror. Sara Levi, small and thin, her face lined beyond her years, but still beautiful with her long dark hair and huge brown eyes, asked Bethel Ascher, 'Herr Professor, how can we survive such hatred? My father fought in the last war — he was always proud to be a German. Now he is spat upon. Yesterday, the greengrocer refused to accept Mother's ration stamps. He said vegetables were in short supply and were needed by Germans. And, at Kraus Chemie...'

The Professor opened a small cupboard and extracted a paper bag. 'I was more fortunate than your Mama. I was able to buy some apples. These are for you.'

Sara gazed at the apples in awe, then rubbed one of them against her cheek. It was small, green and badly bruised, but nevertheless it seemed to retain the scent of the orchard where it had once hung. 'Thank you, Professor, you are very kind.'

She knew there had only been three apples. And he knew she would not eat hers, but give it to someone else, even more in need than she was. The Jews of Berlin were a tightly-knit community, very much like a family. In that, lay their only hope of survival.

Professor Ascher pointed to his yellow star. 'Wear it with pride, my child. It is a finer mark to bear than the swastika.'

Throughout August, Vasili felt as if a net were closing in upon him. Although many students were accepted into the civil defence, his and Mikhail's applications were refused. Sometimes, he thought he heard fellow students muttering about spies and *agents-provocateurs*. There were rumours of German émigrés being arrested by the NKVD and that thousands of Volga Germans had been sent to Siberia.

The blow fell early in September, when Vasili was ordered to report immediately to the local military headquarters. The waiting room was full of loudly indignant people — mostly, he realized with a sinking heart, German émigrés, speaking German. They told him they were being exiled to Karaganda in Kazakhskaya, thousands of miles to the south-east.

Ignoring them, Vasili took his seat in a corner. When his turn finally came to be interviewed by the military official, he naturally spoke Russian, impressing upon him his sense of identity with the Soviet Union, pleading to be allowed to remain in Moscow.

The officer was not an unkind man, but he had his orders. 'The great Stalin cannot afford to take any risks,' he explained. 'It's for your own safety as much as anything that we have to send you away. I am sure you are a loyal subject, but a lot of these people are unreliable foreigners.'

'But my studies…'

The officer looked from Vasili to his identity card. 'If you remain in Moscow, you will be arrested. My suggestion, comrade, is that you go with the others to Karaganda. When the war is over, you will be able to return. You will report back here in two hours' time, with your luggage.'

When Vasili returned to his room, there was no sign of Mikhail. He packed his meagre luggage, put on his worn, goatskin coat and went back to the military post. Along with the other émigrés, he was pushed into a lorry, which trundled through the streets of Moscow to an outlying marshalling yard. There, under armed supervision, they were herded not into a passenger train, but cattle trucks. The doors were barred from the outside and the only light was through slats in the roof. The Germans shouted and banged on the walls.

Despondently, Vasili sat down on his suitcase. Under similar circumstances, his mother had left Moscow four years earlier, never to be seen again. Eventually, the train clanked on its way. Around him, some of his fellow travellers gave way to despairing tears. Only pride stopped Vasili from joining them.

Gradually, they adapted to their circumstances. The train stopped frequently at small hamlets, where they were fed and allowed to stretch their legs, and it was on these occasions that Vasili realized the dreadful poverty that existed outside Moscow. Homeless people, dressed in rags, lay on the streets or crowded the train, pleading to be allowed to travel with them. There was no incentive to escape. Contrary to all appearances, the German émigrés were still among the privileged.

The journey lasted sixteen days, during which they traversed the vast Russian hinterland, first to the east then to the south, where the sun shone warm on the plains. Eventually, the train reached their final destination and, dirty, weary and with aching limbs, they stumbled out, dragging their luggage behind them.

Karaganda was unprepossessing, to say the least, and it could have been in another world from Moscow or Berlin. But, Vasili reflected, as he followed the others to the drab building that was to be his home for the indefinite future, at least he was still alive.

At the end of September, Kiev fell in what Hitler described as 'the greatest battle in the world'. Triumphantly, he told the German people, 'The enemy in the east has been struck down and will never rise again.' He ordered Army Group North to capture Leningrad and Army Group South to clear the Black Sea, seize Rostov and push forward to Stalingrad. He also ordered the drive on Moscow to recommence, crying, 'Encircle them, beat and destroy them!'

On 2 October, Army Group Centre set off along the road Napoleon had once followed. Special news bulletins told of victorious battles at Briansk, Vyazma and Orel. Within two weeks, Army Group Centre held over half a million Russian troops encircled and its advance spearheads were within forty miles of Moscow. The Soviet government and diplomatic corps were reported to have fled the capital, where a state of siege had been declared. Jubilant newspaper articles claimed, 'Stalin's armies have been destroyed. They have disappeared for ever.'

At this momentous news, Viktoria forgot her concern about the Jews. If Stalin's armies had been destroyed, so too was the threat of communism that had hung over Germany for so many years. Olga's dream would never come true. The hammer and sickle would never fly in Berlin.

Peter von Biederstein could have told her differently. Far from being over, the war was only just commencing. That long delay at Smolensk must cost Army Group Centre dear. The Russians would have had a lot of time to bring in reinforcements. Furthermore, autumn had arrived in Russia. The rains were beginning to set in.

Deep in his heart, Peter knew Hitler had made a mistake.

CHAPTER FIFTEEN

Baron Heinrich did not believe the war was over either. In his opinion it looked set to continue for a long time, particularly now American aid in the form of arms, equipment and finance was beginning to enter Russia.

For the most part, the Americans, including Congress, wanted nothing to do with the European war. Only Roosevelt seemed determined to interfere in it. From the very outset, the American President had committed himself personally to the fight against Hitler, carrying formal neutrality to the point of co-belligerency, showing his whole-hearted support first for Britain and now for the Soviet Union with his Lend-Lease Bill and his Atlantic Charter. His Conscription Bill had allowed America to recruit and train a formidable fighting force. Lend-Lease had enabled America to build up her armaments production, her Army, Navy and Air Force. 'The Arsenal of Democracy' was how some people described her.

That autumn, however, there were signs of change. Hitler seemed determined to push Roosevelt's patience to its furthest limits. There were incidents of American ships being attacked, to which Roosevelt retaliated by announcing that the American Navy had been given orders to shoot on sight any Axis vessels entering the American defence zone.

In the newspapers, Stalin and Churchill gave way to Roosevelt as 'Warmonger Number One'. Despite Hitler's public avowals that German ships had been ordered only to shoot on American vessels in self-defence, two more American destroyers were torpedoed and one sunk.

Baron Heinrich was in no doubt that, before very long, Japan would enter the war. The question was: would Japan invade Russia from the east or had she set her sights on South-east Asia? And, if she did either, how would America react?

The American people might be against joining the fray in Europe, but they would feel very differently about the Pacific. A precipitate move by General Tojo could well force America into the war. Judging by Hitler's present mood concerning Roosevelt, this could in turn lead to Germany declaring war on America. If that happened, the Baron was sure all German assets in America would be frozen or seized.

In setting up his American operations, the Baron had been careful to have a lawyer of American nationality, but of German extraction, on his board — a second cousin by the name of John Bewilogua. At the end of October, in a very long letter to his lawyer in Switzerland, he issued instructions for him to fly to America and transfer all his interests to Bewilogua. In a separate, secret document, John Bewilogua would agree to accrue the Baron's share of the profits in a separate account until the war was over.

Having assured his ongoing financial security in America, Baron Heinrich returned to the problems Kraus Industries was encountering in Germany. These were manifold and less easy to resolve. The war in Russia was taking a greater toll than anyone was prepared to admit, not only in men, but in vital equipment — tanks, planes, ships, arms and explosives.

One memorandum after another landed on the Baron's desk from distraught Kraus managers. The Aviation Ministry seemed unable to decide whether it needed parts for fighter or bomber planes. As a result, conflicting orders resulted in constant rearrangement of production schedules, with a corresponding loss of output. Army High Command issued instructions that priority was to be given to truck construction, then changed its mind and demanded more tanks. Kraus Steel was finding it almost impossible to cope. In Essen, there was confusion over whether flak guns or naval cannon should take precedence.

The Baron took his problem to Dr Todt, the Minister of Armaments and Munitions, who nodded wearily. 'Herr Baron, what you are describing is symptomatic of present-day Germany. Every activity meets with opposition. Everyone with whom one has to deal has his rivals and his opponents — not because they want to be opponents, but because their different tasks and relationships force them to take different points of view. Perhaps if we were younger, we could see our way through the tangled mess. As it is, it worries me stiff.'

The Baron grunted impatiently. Todt's answer was symptomatic of the present-day Germany. The only people who seemed capable of making decisions were himself and the Führer, and he was growing less certain that the Führer's decisions were always right.

Baron Heinrich was not the only one to be concerned about the future. Benno, too, was growing extremely apprehensive. As winter approached, there were tell-tale signs that the war was not going as well as it seemed. In the newspapers, there was an increasing number of little black crosses. Bomb-damaged buildings were neglected, as the men who had been working on them were sent to the front, never to return.

The first real food shortages became apparent. It had been a short, wet summer resulting in a poor harvest. Immediately, rations of meat, fruit and vegetables were reduced, the best supplies going to the troops. There was a shortage of cigarettes and, even worse, of alcoholic drinks.

Hops and grapes mouldered on fields and terraces. Even if the crop had been good, there were no men to harvest it. With the help of Polish and Slav slave labourers, the women did their best, but unmarried girls had now been drafted into factories and mothers had their hands full with the children they were raising for the Führer.

For many, the situation was disastrous. French wines and spirits were available, but extremely expensive. Cafés and bars watered down their beer, in order to keep their clientele. Chefs served eighty gramme portions of meat against hundred gramme ration stamps. Soon even these portions were reduced. Winter set in early and the sodden earth froze hard. For the first time in history, there were no potatoes available in the whole of Berlin.

The Hotel Quadriga and Café Jochum were more fortunate than most. There were still nearly a million bottles of wine in the Quadriga's cellars, the value of which rose daily. Because it housed a division of the Abwehr and was a recognized rendezvous for military officers, diplomats and politicians, the hotel enjoyed priority status with the Reich Food Estate, enabling it to support Café Jochum. While many hotels, bars and café-restaurants faced ruin, their business increased.

It was by no means a cause for complacency. On the contrary, Benno could clearly remember a similar situation arising in 1917, when the last war was into its third year. Now, he began to do the same thing as he had then — to stock up for the future. Besides ordering from his usual wholesalers, he used one of his father's contacts, the Dutchman, Kok van der Jong , whose wide-ranging brief took him all over Europe. Albeit at great cost, for he was buying into the black market and had to pay a commission to Kok and to Kraus Industries, Benno obtained goods virtually unavailable to the ordinary consumer.

Gradually, the cellars under the hotel and Café Jochum began to fill. Benno was careful to buy not only food, but other necessities — candles, soap and textiles. Some of these, including a supply of petrol, he took to Heiligensee.

'Aren't you being rather alarmist?' Viktoria asked.

'I don't know,' Benno replied soberly. 'But, whatever happens, I intend that we shall survive.'

'I'm sorry, sir, we're stuck again.' The driver pulled the collar of his jacket up round his neck and got out of the car.

Peter wound down the window and sleet beat into his face. Ahead of them, a long line of Army vehicles were sunk up to their axles in mud, their drivers, like his own, up to their knees in slime, struggling to free them. This time, he feared, the attempt would prove beyond them. Tanks would have to be sent back to move them, tanks vitally needed on the front, that could ill be spared for releasing supplies and provisions lorries from the mud.

He pulled his greatcoat around him to protect him from the bitter weather, watching the mud sliding back as soon as his driver shovelled it away from the wheels, noting the man's blue fingers and chattering teeth, as he worked in his thin, summer uniform. So convinced had Hitler been that he would have conquered Russia by now, winter uniforms had not even been issued.

Army operations had virtually ground to a halt. Frequently aircraft had to be diverted from the front line, to drop ropes and chains to free vehicles. Despite all their efforts, supplies often still failed to reach the troops. Not only were men in danger of freezing to death, but of starvation.

Despite all Hitler's bombastic vaunts, Leningrad, Sebastopol and Moscow all held strong. Unlike the German troops, Red Army soldiers and airmen were equipped for winter. Furthermore, they were fighting a defensive war to protect holy Mother Russia, a sacred battle in which they preferred death to surrender. Above all, Peter was beginning to think his subordinates were right when they whispered amongst each other that the Russians had two great generals on their side: General Mud and General Winter.

With a superhuman effort, Peter's driver and some other men succeeded in lifting the car clear of the mud and getting some sodden pieces of sacking under its wheels. Revving the engine furiously, the driver urged the vehicle forward. Peter wound up the window.

A few yards down the road, they were stuck again. The sleet turned to snow.

The reports that poured into Sepp's office convinced him that he was witnessing the steady dissolution of the Luftwaffe. Germany had entered the Russian campaign with nearly three thousand aircraft. Within the first month, eight hundred planes had been lost. Now there were a scant thousand serviceable aircraft on the Eastern Front.

Ignoring the lessons they should have learned from the Battle for Britain, the Fat Man and Milch had pinned all their hopes on strategic bombing. Therefore the Luftwaffe possessed no long-distance bombing formations, making it impossible for German planes to attack bases far behind the Russian lines. With their own and American planes, Russia had a seemingly limitless supply of aircraft and fliers.

Morale within the Luftwaffe was reaching an all-time low. Air crews were tired, depressed and suffering badly from the cold. Many had had no leave since the beginning of the campaign. They were watching their comrades die like flies and were living in primitive billets, with broken window-panes and often no heating at all.

The weather was their worst enemy. During the rains, planes sank in the mud. Once the snows started, there were fewer casualties on landing, but problems of a new kind. Despite special heaters, aircraft engines could not cope with the bitter cold. Warming up procedures had to start at two in the morning for planes to be ready for a dawn take-off. Confident of a short, victorious war, no provision had been made to train men to fly in the dangerous conditions of the Russian winter, when low cloud and blizzards made flying very hazardous.

It was no longer considered an honour to be sent to the Eastern Front. For the first time, men ventured to question why they were fighting the war against the Soviet Union. Suffering from nervous exhaustion and frostbite, wounded airmen pleaded to be sent anywhere rather than be returned to Russia.

On 17 November, Sepp's old friend, Ernst Udet, died. Publicly, it was announced that he had been killed while testing a new warplane and he was given a magnificent State funeral, attended by the entire Nazi hierarchy, including Hitler. Sepp knew differently. Udet had been ill. So strained had his relations become with Milch that, like Sepp, he had not been allowed near a plane for a long time.

At the funeral, Sepp saw Göring for the first time in months. 'A sad loss,' the Fat Man murmured, tragic-faced.

Sepp stared at him angrily. 'Udet didn't die in an accident, did he? He killed himself. He committed suicide, because he couldn't take any more.'

'Sepp, old friend, control yourself. We don't want stories like that to get around. Bad for public morale — and for our boys at the front.' Göring lowered his voice. 'But yes, you are right. He had become very unstable and, apparently, preferred to take his own life rather than face up to his responsibilities.'

They had reached Göring's car. A bitter wind cut through them, but Sepp did not heed it. 'Ernst Udet was my friend. Between you, you and Milch murdered him, as surely as you have sent thousands of airmen to their deaths.'

Göring gave him an icy look. 'I hope you will retract that accusation.'

'No, Hermann. You killed Ernst Udet.'

Göring got into his car. 'I shall not forget this moment, Oberst Nowak. Neither shall I forgive it.'

After Udet's death, Sepp's disillusionment turned into despair. Not bothering to conceal his satisfaction, Field Marshal Milch took over Udet's job as well as his own. He did not miss an opportunity to blacken Udet's memory or to vilify Sepp. Friendless except for his immediate family, Sepp felt that everything to which he had given his life had been broken and defiled.

In Russia, the snows set in. Temperatures dropped to below zero and kept on falling. Outside Moscow, Army Group Centre fought on in deepening snowdrifts, in blizzards that froze the very marrow of the bone, that drove through inadequate uniforms and gnawed at the stomachs of soldiers without enough to eat.

Desperately needed supplies still did not arrive. Tank and truck engines would not start and, if not properly warmed up, stopped for ever. Railway lines were blown up by partisan bands surging out of the forest armed with hand grenades. The Luftwaffe dropped ropes and chains, but pitifully few provisions and no fuel. Although Göring claimed to be giving aerial support, he seemed to have no understanding of the real plight of the Army.

Sometimes, their only food was what they could steal. Waving their guns, bands of starving soldiers burst into Russian villages where small groups of peasants huddled together, horribly near starvation themselves. On occasions, they were lucky and found a hen or a pig the villagers had hidden. More often than not, there was little more than a few mouldy potatoes.

Peter's last hope faded that the Russians would see the Germans as liberators. Incapable of feeding and clothing itself, Army Group Centre had no choice but to leave its prisoners of war on the battlefield, meagrely clad and with nothing to eat. Hundreds of thousands died. And, on top of this, dreadful stories circulated of massacres of Jews and Russians by SS Einsatzgruppen. Mobile gas chambers were said to have been brought into Russia, in which Jews were being systematically exterminated.

Thousands of German soldiers perished too. Many were suffering from frostbite so extreme, they could only drag themselves along with difficulty. For the first time in his life, Peter saw what he had only read about before: men huddling for warmth in the snow and dying with a smile on their faces.

In the south, the Russians recaptured Rostov and Field Marshal von Rundstedt's Army Group was forced into headlong retreat fifty miles back to the Mius River: the first time any Nazi army had suffered such a reversal. Telephone wires hummed with stories of Hitler's fury and Rundstedt's subsequent resignation.

Despite the dreadful conditions under which they were fighting, the consensus of opinion at Army Group Centre was that the Führer was right. The German Army had fought hard to gain its new territory. It should not retreat at the first sign of danger.

On 2 December, a reconnaissance battalion reached a suburb of Moscow and saw the spires of the Kremlin in the distance before it was driven out by Russian tanks. In a two-hundred-mile semi-circular front, the advance spearheads of Army Group Centre surrounded the Soviet capital. The temperature fell to thirty degrees below zero.

At the beginning of December, the remaining American correspondents applied for and received travel permits to leave Germany. Mortimer's friend, Chuck Harris, was one of the last to go. Somehow, while Chuck had remained, Viktoria had felt a lingering contact with Mortimer and Stefan. 'Why must you go?' she asked, sadly.

'There's no point in staying any longer. In case you haven't realized, America is Enemy Number One. The Foreign and Propaganda Ministries treat us like dirt. The Gestapo watches our every move.' Chuck paused, then added in a low voice, 'And from what I've heard, it won't be long before we find ourselves in the war.'

'Against Germany?'

'It seems to be the Japanese stirring up trouble this time.'

Viktoria held out her hand. 'I wish you a safe journey.'

A page boy picked up his case and carried it out to the waiting car. Chuck gave a thin smile. '*Auf Wiedersehen*, Frau Viktoria.'

'*Auf Wiedersehen*, Herr Harris.' She couldn't help feeling that, like so many farewells she had made in recent years, this one was not 'Until we meet again', but 'Goodbye'.

A few days later, on 11 December, it was announced on the radio that following severe provocation by the United States, Japan had declared war on America. Although Germany had always strictly observed the rules of international law in her dealings with the United States, the American Government had nevertheless continued in overt acts of war against Germany. The Reich government had therefore broken off all diplomatic relations with the United States. As from today, the two countries were at war.

When she and Benno were getting ready for bed, Viktoria asked, 'What will happen now?'

Benno put two pillows over the telephone and sat down heavily on the side of the bed. 'Needless to say, Father still listens to the BBC. When I saw him this evening, he told me that the Japanese not only declared war on America, but made the first attack, by bombing Pearl Harbor — an American base in Hawaii.' He shook his head. 'I don't see how we can hope to win against America.'

Viktoria stared at him in horror. 'You mean that we're not just telling Japan that we support her, but we could actually find ourselves fighting the Americans?'

'Vicki, I don't know. Nobody knows. I hope it will remain a war in the Pacific, but if you remember the last war, America sent troops into Europe. If the United States and England can gain control of the Atlantic, there's nothing to stop them doing so again.'

With trembling fingers, Viktoria reached for her cigarettes. It was all too much to bear. First England and now America. First Stefan and now Mortimer.

Benno put his arm round her shoulder. 'Darling, I'm sorry. I know how you feel.'

She leaned back against him, suddenly very grateful for his presence. He did not know the full extent of her sorrow and she could not tell him. But at least he was here and he no more liked what was happening than she did.

In Russia, Peter paid little heed to the news that America had entered the war. The Red Army was not destroyed. It was hardly marked. On 6 December, General Zhukov, a Russian General of whose existence General Staff had hardly been aware, launched a massive counter-offensive. One hundred divisions of infantry, tanks, artillery and airborne troops, fresh, battle-trained but not battle-scarred, equipped to fight in deep snow at temperatures of minus forty degrees, appeared, as if out of nowhere, to push the Germans back from Moscow.

During the days that followed, the soldiers of Army Group Centre were pushed to the very limit of their endurance. Everything was against them: the sheer strength of the Russian offensive, the weather and their own lack of training in organizing a retreat. None of them, not even their generals, had experienced a retreat before. They fell back before the Red Armies in panic and disarray, only to find themselves confronted with devastated villages and burned out garrisons, destroyed by their own men during their advance.

Zhukov employed tactics he had learned from the Germans. In white camouflage uniforms, his soldiers sped through the white countryside, encircling large pockets of German troops. The only chance of escape was to retreat further, leaving hundreds of their men dying from frostbite, starvation and dysentery, their tanks frostbound and immobile, their horses frozen corpses.

Suddenly, men began to remember the fate of Napoleon's Great Army in the Russian winter of 1812, along this very same road.

Field Marshal von Bock was the first to succumb to the strain. The man who had so recently informed Peter, 'You speak of honour, but apparently, you are prepared to break your word of honour' — developed such severe stomach cramps that Hitler relieved him of his command and replaced him with Field Marshal von Kluge.

Field Marshal von Brauchitsch, rumoured to have suffered a heart-attack a month ago, was sent to inspect the disintegrating front and returned to General Headquarters a gibbering wreck. Two days later, he handed in his resignation. Hitler did not replace him. Instead, he himself took over Brauchitsch's post as Commander in Chief of the Army. His first directive was to forbid any further withdrawals.

Perhaps, when issued from the security of the Wolf's Lair, this was a rational order, but to field officers seeing their troops decimated, it was nothing short of madness. In many instances, it was also impossible to obey.

Christmas, which they had once hoped to celebrate in Moscow, turned into a nightmare. On Christmas Day, General Guderian was dismissed for retreating from Moscow without Hitler's permission. General Hoepner was the next casualty. General von Sponeck followed him. Great generals, every one, they were stripped of their rank and sent home in disgrace.

Until Russia, it had never occurred to Peter to question the rightfulness of any order received from a superior officer, let alone the Supreme Commander. Now, for the third time since the beginning of the Eastern Campaign, he experienced grave misgivings about Hitler's judgement.

From his position of supreme power, the Führer was ignoring the courage of his generals, riding roughshod over their expertise and experience. He refused to see that he was in no position to make decisions regarding the Eastern Front, but that the bitter cold and the Red Army were making them for him. By ordering the Army to stand firm, he was consigning them all to certain death.

They were no longer counting captured tanks and prisoners of war, but their own dreadful losses. It was impossible to calculate how many soldiers had been killed, wounded, taken captive or died of frostbite, but it must have amounted to hundreds of thousands.

Among those who remained, an atmosphere of despair set in. Field Marshal von Kluge was in constant telephone communication with General Halder at the Wolf's Lair, insisting, begging, pleading that he be allowed to withdraw. On 8 January, Hitler reluctantly agreed. The retreat began.

At last, Peter thought about America. Everyone assumed that she would be totally preoccupied with the Japanese war in the Pacific. But what if she crossed the Atlantic and, using England as a base, attacked them on the Western Front? With a growing sense of dismay, Peter acknowledged to himself the possibility that Germany might lose the war.

From that day on, nothing could ever be the same in his life. He had lost the blind faith that had sustained him for so long. He had begun to think — not as a member of a group — but as an individual.

On the afternoon of 12 January 1942, Sepp received a memorandum from Field Marshal Milch, instructing him to report immediately to fighter command at Kharkov. 'Morale is flagging on the Eastern Front. Perhaps you, as a hero of the last war, can pass on the fruits of your experience. Since aircraft are in short supply, you should fly there. A replacement 109 has been placed at your disposal.'

Sepp crumpled it up and threw it in the waste bin. Milch's sarcasm was not lost on him. He recognized that this was Milch's excuse for getting rid of him. When he requested an interview with Milch, he was informed that the Field Marshal was attending Reich Marshal Göring's birthday celebrations at Karin Hall.

Sepp left the Aviation Ministry and went home to pack his bags.

Baron Heinrich von Kraus was among the prominent guests attending Reich Marshal Hermann Göring's forty-ninth birthday. In honour of the auspicious occasion, he had commissioned an Italian craftsman to create a model of the Fokker D VII biplane which Göring had flown as Commander of the Richthofen Squadron at the end of the last war. With a wingspan of two feet, it had movable controls and an electrically driven propellor. All metal parts were made from gold and silver.

Costly though it was, it did not look out of place on the birthday table set up in the big library at Karin Hall. Surrounding it were valuable paintings and sculptures, Fabergé eggs, gold bars, expensive cigars, hunting pistols and cases of vintage cognacs and champagnes.

As usual, dinner failed to live up to the magnificent surroundings. Served by manservants in spotless white uniforms, the portions of food were small, the quality poor. Everybody excused this by explaining that Göring liked to live up to his maxim of 'Guns before butter'. The truth was that, unless dining at the expense of others, the Fat Man was rather mean.

The food was of no importance to the Baron. What mattered to him was the company, the opportunity to renew acquaintance with the most influential men in Germany. He was seated next to Professor Albert Speer, Hitler's architect and Norbert's hero. A young man in his mid-thirties, he proved an interesting conversationalist, neither sycophantic in his attitude to the Party leaders, nor under any illusions as to the progress of the war.

When Baron Heinrich mentioned the problems Kraus Industries was encountering because of lack of centralization between the various ministries and services, he nodded sympathetically. 'Dr Todt and I have discussed this, too.' He glanced towards Göring at the head of the table, then said in a low voice, 'Of course, the worst mistake was to put the Reich Marshal in charge of the Four-Year Plan. He has no understanding of economics.' Baron Heinrich decided he liked Speer.

At the end of the meal, the Minister of Economics made a birthday speech, obsequiously outlining Göring's great achievements, praising his many talents and qualities. Finally, he proposed a toast to: 'The Reich Marshal, one of Germany's greatest men!' The company, including Baron Heinrich, rose to its feet. 'To the Reich Marshal!'

The Baron drank the toast gladly. As a result of helping Göring to power, he was one of the wealthiest men in the world.

Early the following morning, Sepp stroked Sheltie, kissed Lili goodbye and took Luise in his arms. 'Take care of yourself, my dearest. If things get rough while I'm away, I suggest you go to the Quadriga.'

'Don't worry, Sepp. We'll be waiting for you here.'

He looked into her fearless green eyes and felt his heart constrict with love. 'Dear Luischen, I'm sorry to have been so unbearable over the last few months. It was wrong of me to take it out on you. You do understand, don't you?'

'I understand. And I love you.'

'I love you, too, Luischen. It's just that sometimes love isn't enough. There are other things in a man's life, other devils that drive him…'

She cupped his face in her hands. 'Take care, Sepp. And no matter what happens, remember that Lili, Sheltie and I need you and believe in you.'

He kissed her on the lips. 'You're a very valiant person, Luischen.'

A car klaxon hooted in the street. There was a ring on the doorbell. Tiredly, Sepp picked up his bag, walked out of the flat in Lützow, got into the car and was driven to Rangsdorf airfield on the start of his journey to Kharkov.

At Army Group Centre's headquarters at Smolensk, Peter made two new friends — Major-General Henning von Tresckow and his ADC, Lieutenant Fabian von Schlabrendorff. Nine years younger than Peter, Tresckow was a Staff officer and of aristocratic Pomeranian stock. Schlabrendorff, only thirty-four, was a lawyer by profession, and married to a cousin of Tresckow.

That January, they discovered that they had more than background in common. The conclusions Peter had reached so recently, Tresckow and Schlabrendorff had come to long before. Once they realized that Peter's faith in Hitler was wavering, they were at great pains to identify to him all the other aspects of National Socialism that had eroded the Army and the country.

Peter did not need much convincing. Now that his eyes had been opened, he saw very clearly how Hitler had manipulated the Army. First he had bought their loyalty by sacrificing the SA, then he had introduced conscription and rearmament, and, finally, he had led them from one bloodless conquest to another, followed by two years of breathtaking victory at war.

In that unprecedented moment in German history on 19 July 1940, he had made his final coup by creating twelve new field marshals and umpteen generals. None of them had seen at this time that their ranks had been belittled by this act. They had seen only the stripes, the medals and the prestige. For fear of losing these accoutrements of power, they had swallowed the bitter pill Hitler had handed out next — subservience to the SS.

Now the worst thing of all was happening. Hitler was leading Germany to defeat, for victory was impossible against the combined strength of Russia, America and the British Commonwealth. Something must be done, and swiftly, to save Germany from another ignominious defeat, the terms of which would be far harsher than those of Versailles in 1919.

'But what can be done?' Peter asked.

Henning von Tresckow raised his eyebrows expressively. 'Until now, we believed it would be sufficient if we could arrest Hitler, but it is too late now for that. Our only solution is to kill him.'

'Kill the Führer?' Peter echoed hollowly.

'It is the only way,' Schlabrendorff stated. 'If Hitler goes, the whole rotten system will tumble like a pack of cards. The Wehrmacht is still stronger than the SS. We have colleagues in Berlin who are ready to take over the administration...'

'What you are suggesting is revolution,' Peter stuttered. 'It could lead to civil war while we are already in the throes of a world war. It could lead only to the most terrible chaos and destruction.'

'Nothing like the chaos and destruction that will ensue if Hitler is allowed to remain in control,' Tresckow said bluntly. 'When Hitler is dead, the war can be brought to a swift end on terms beneficial to Germany. We shall still be a major power — and we shall have earned the respect of our enemies by overthrowing a regime that is inimical to every humane and honourable man.'

Peter shook his head. 'I cannot be party to the assassination of Hitler. Apart from anything else, I swore an oath of allegiance to him and an oath is a sacred pledge.'

'An oath is also a two-way agreement,' Schlabrendorff pointed out. 'When one party fails to honour his word, the other party is freed from his obligation. Has it never occurred to you that Hitler is rather in the habit of breaking his side of any agreement? Time without number, he has made pacts with foreign powers, only to violate them later. He promised that the Army would be the sole bearer of arms, yet now he has effectively placed us under the control of the SS. In our opinion, you owe no allegiance to the Führer.'

Such thoughts were alien to Peter's nature. He could not change overnight. No matter how much they tried to persuade him that, while Hitler stayed alive, millions of innocent people would continue to go to their death, Peter remained obdurate. He agreed that the war should be ended, but he would not be party to the murder of Hitler.

Sepp flew into Kharkov, the fourth commanding officer the airmen there had seen in as many weeks, the previous three all having been killed in action. They looked at him from lack-lustre eyes, none of them bothering to stand or salute. 'God, look what they've sent us now,' one muttered. 'A bleeding grandfather!'

'In another bloody Messerschmitt,' another groaned, a young boy of no more than twenty, adolescent pimples spotting his face. 'Can't they even send us some Focke-Wulfs? The 109 is rubbish.'

'With the FW-190 and a competent commanding officer we might stand a chance,' a third agreed. 'With him and the 109, forget it.'

For a moment, Sepp hesitated, knowing he should call them to order, force them to stand and salute him, then call them out to stand by their planes while he inspected them, followed by a full examination of uniforms, spares, fuel, maintenance facilities and so on. But what was the point? There were almost certainly fewer spares here than there had been in France at the end of the Battle for Britain. If only half the men were present, it was because the rest were asleep after flying non-stop relays for twenty-four hours or more.

'Well, Uncle Sepp,' the pimply youth called mockingly. 'What miracles can you perform?'

'He was called off combat duties years ago,' a voice from the back scoffed.

Sepp stared at the young faces, lined beyond their years. This was what had happened to the Luftwaffe — the finest air force in the world. These were the tattered remnants of the pilots he had helped train — demoralized, disillusioned or dead, because of the cupidity of vainglorious men. 'Perhaps you, as a hero of the last war, can pass on the fruits of your experience,' Milch had written sarcastically.

Without saying a word, Sepp picked up his flying helmet from the table and stomped out of the room towards the aircraft dispersal area. It was a beautiful day — a cloudless blue sky above fresh powder snow. A flying day. The 109 he had flown in on was still standing in the U-shaped bay formed from banked snow. 'Prepare her for take-off!' he barked to the flight sergeant.

'But, sir, it's not…'

Sepp glared at him. 'Prepare her for take-off,' he repeated coldly. Some of the airmen had followed him from the hut and were standing in a desultory group. He pulled on his flying jacket, allowed himself to be helped into a parachute, tugged his helmet over his ears, then clambered into the cockpit of the much-maligned 109. He gave a signal to the ground crew to stand clear, then fired the engine. Clouds of blue smoke issued from the stub exhausts and, as he waited for the engine to warm up, Sepp felt a sudden calm descend on him. He was away from the claustrophobic atmosphere in the hut, away from the men. There was just his aeroplane around him and the clear blue sky above.

He checked instruments, flaps and rudder, then taxied to the end of the snow-covered runway. Foot on brakes, he opened the throttle fully, released the brakes and roared down the white, open stretch of ground, weaving slightly to see and maintain a straight line. When he reached flying speed, he pulled back the stick, felt the rear wheel lift, retracted the undercarriage and climbed rapidly away from the airfield.

On such a perfect day, we should be attacking the Russians, not just sitting around waiting to regroup. No wonder the men down there were demoralized. No wonder they viewed the arrival of a 'grandfather' with such unconcealed dismay. He pulled his hip flask from his pocket and, with practised ease, unscrewed the cap with his teeth. As the altimeter climbed over the 20,000 feet marking, he kicked the rudder bar and banked towards the airfield.

Even from a height of nearly four miles, he could see the black shapes of his men. 'Grandfather, eh?' he muttered. He pushed the control column forward until he was in a near vertical dive. The magnificent Daimler-Benz engine screamed in a rising crescendo as the airspeed indicator flashed from 300 to 350 to 375 miles per hour.

Bf 109s lose their wings, do they? The Spitfire can turn on a pfennig. All the old criticisms of the Messerschmitt raced furiously through Sepp's mind as, at the last moment, he pulled back the stick and flashed over the panicked airmen at only a few feet above the ground.

With his engine still on full throttle, he pulled back the control column to gain height for his next stunt. Then he banked back, tightened his safety straps, inverted the plane, dived, and flew straight and level, upside-down, towards the airfield.

All the old skills were still there. The fuel injected engine never missed a beat. The controls were heavy, but he was strong enough to handle them — and the disorientation. As he flew over the assembled airmen, he executed a perfect flick-quarter roll, changing attitude by ninety degrees — then another and another and another, until he was flying inverted again, whilst still maintaining altitude and direction.

This was what it had been like in the old days, in the early years of the first war, then later in America and Kenya. What fun he had had, when being a flier was all about flying and not bureaucracy and politics. Well, maybe one day he would do it again. Then he remembered the war, the war that Germany was losing, and the old weariness flooded over him. There would be no more tomorrows…

He slammed the throttle lever wide open in order to climb and execute that most difficult of aerobatic manoeuvres — the backward loop. As the engine emitted its familiar exciting sounds, he felt the increasing pressure of the safety belts across his shoulders and thighs, as centrifugal force attempted to throw him out of the aircraft. He fought the controls, while the unnatural attitude of the 109 threatened both his and the plane's existence. As they climbed, a violent shuddering developed in the airframe.

He eased back the control column fractionally. 'Steady, Uncle, this isn't a Fokker biplane. Not enough height and much more speed,' he muttered to himself.

At the top of the loop, he throttled back in textbook style when, suddenly, the engine coughed once, then twice, then again. Alarmed, he executed a half roll. The dancing needles of his instruments corrected themselves and, to his horror, he saw that the fuel gauge read 'empty' and the red warning light was glowing. Assuming that the aircraft had been refuelled after his arrival, it was the only thing he hadn't checked. For a few seconds, the engine ran smoothly, then cut out completely. He rocked the plane from side to side, but no more fuel reached the pumps. He was rapidly losing height.

A distant voice from the past said, *Uncle, I've run out of fuel*, and Sepp saw the body of Andreas Müller, tangled in its parachute, being dragged out of the sea. His chances of making a safe 'dead stick' landing on the Russian snow were as remote as his former wingman's over the English Channel.

There was no sound save the rushing of the wind. Sepp reached for his flask and took another gulp of vodka. What had he said, all those years ago, of Manfred von Richthofen, the Red Battle Flier? 'He died a man. If I go, that's the way I want it, to die in my plane, the only life I know.'

The controls made odd clanking noises. Sepp no longer had any sense of self-preservation, but a lifetime's training prevailed and, before the engine could stall, he put the plane into a steeper dive. The glare of the sun changed to a blinding glare of Russian snow.

He was tired, very tired. He had failed. He had failed his country, his friends and his family. As he raised his flask to his lips for one last sip, the Messerschmitt hit the cruel winter at 250mph and Sepp Nowak passed into oblivion.

Luise received the telegram telling her that Sepp had been killed and part of her stopped living. It was as simple and immediate as that. By returning to her, Sepp had given her a reason to live. Now he was dead, the vital spirit in her died too. As she had been before, so she became again: a living ghost.

Her mother and Viktoria visited Luise every day. At first, they tried to persuade her to come back to the Quadriga, but she refused. 'Thank you, but I told Sepp we'd stay here. It's our home.' When

Ricarda offered to move in with her for a while, she insisted, 'Mama, I'll be all right. I have Lili and Sheltie. And it's not as if I'm the only one whose husband has been killed.'

As soon as they learned the news, Ilse and Christa came to see her. 'Luise, dear, we are so sorry and Peter will be very sad when he hears,' Ilse said. 'If there's anything at all we can do, you know you have only to ask.'

Luise looked at her from lack-lustre eyes. 'Thank you. You are very kind. Everyone is so kind.'

'Perhaps that's because everybody has someone at the front, a husband, father, son or brother,' Ilse replied quietly.

Lili appeared in the doorway, a forlorn little figure in a green dress. When she saw Christa, her eyes brightened and she came across the room and stood beside her. 'Christa, will you play with me?'

Christa's heart went out to her. She sensed the grief in Luise that went too deep for words or tears and knew she could do nothing to help her. But she could do something for Lili. At four, the little girl was too young to understand the meaning of death. Her father had gone away before, but he had always returned. She was certain he must this time, too. So, when her morning's work at the Foreign Ministry was done, Christa played with her, read to her and attempted to take the place of the Papa she had lost.

Luise was grateful. Lili had her life ahead of her and it was better that she spent it among the living rather than the dead, because that was who her parents were — the dead.

A memorial service was held at the church in Schmargendorf where Luise and Sepp had been married. A surprising number of people attended it, not only family, friends and neighbours from Lützow, but many of Sepp's colleagues from the Aviation Ministry. Field Marshal Milch was not present, although he sent a wreath. Reich Marshal Göring sent a personal letter of condolence, describing Sepp as, 'an old and dear comrade, one of the few who shared my memories of the Red Battle Flier and the wind in the struts, in the days when flying was an adventure.' Baron Heinrich gave an address, recalling Sepp's heroism in the first war, praising his courage and patriotism.

The service over, they had tea at the Quadriga, then Luise and Sheltie returned to Lützow, leaving Lili with Christa for the night. The stove had gone out and it was cold in the flat. Still wearing the long brown coat with fur trimmings round its hem, collar and cuffs, that she had worn to church, Luise stood in darkness at the window from which she and Sepp had watched the British bombers nine months earlier. It wasn't possible that Sepp was dead. Any minute now, he must walk into the room...

She wandered around the apartment, touching familiar objects, his clothes hanging in the wardrobe, his hairbrush on the dressing table, his razor in the bathroom, a book where he had left it beside the bed. Viktoria said she should give them to a war charity for men at the front, but she could not do it.

To give away Sepp's belongings would be to lose that familiar masculine odour of tobacco smoke still clinging to his jacket, the dent in his pillow, a few strands of hair in a comb, dregs of cognac in a bottle — so little, but all that she had left of him.

Somehow, death had already blurred his features and his personality in a way absence never had. When she tried to remember how he had looked and what he had said the morning he left for Kharkov, there was only a blank. On the dresser was a photograph of him standing beside his old biplane, *Luise*. Holding a cigarette in his hand, he was grinning, his eyes slightly tilted.

It was not how he had looked in recent months, but it had been a good likeness at the time. Luise picked it up and pressed it to her lips. 'Oh, Sepp, I love you so much.' Tears streamed down her cheeks and splashed onto the glass.

Sheltie sat miserably at her feet, gazing at her from tragic brown eyes, her plumed tail between her legs. Luise was no more aware of her than she was that she was weeping.

Within days of attending the memorial service for Sepp, Baron Heinrich was present at another funeral, this time in the mosaic hall at the Chancellery — that of Dr Todt, the Minister of Armaments, killed in an air accident near the Führer's headquarters in East Prussia.

As he stood with bowed head, ostensibly listening to the tributes, the Baron was actually studying the faces around him. Dr Todt had been a nice fellow, but far too soft for his job. Who would succeed him? Göring? Judging by his sulky expression, it would appear not. Milch? He would seem a logical choice, but he was already over-extended with his responsibilities to the Luftwaffe.

When the formalities were over, Professor Speer took him to one side. 'I thought you might like to know, Herr Baron, that the Führer has asked me to take over Dr Todt's office.'

Without blinking an eyelid, the Baron said, 'My congratulations. You can be assured of my support.'

As he got into his car to be driven back to Kraus Haus, he congratulated himself on his good fortune at having sat next to Speer at Göring's birthday party.

Towards the end of March, the snows began to melt and the bloody battlefields of Russia turned into a sea of mud. For the first time, there was a lull in the fighting. Like two great beasts, the Russian and German armies turned inwards upon themselves to lick their wounds and recoup their strength for the next offensive, the decisive battles that must settle for all time the fate of Moscow, Leningrad and Stalingrad, the Donets industrial area, the wheat-fields of Kuban and the oilfields of the Caucasus.

As trains began to roll again and roads opened up, vitally needed supplies and provisions started to get through. It was also possible for men to get out. Peter was among the first ordered to report back to Berlin.

Tresckow came to wish him a good journey and also to request that he use his visit to renew old acquaintances. 'You may be surprised, Biederstein, how many are on our side.' He named men in Berlin, who had long been conspiring to overthrow Hitler. 'Beck, Oster, Hassell, Canaris... General Halder, too, has helped us in the past. They all know that nobody has ever succeeded in defeating and conquering Russia.'

But Peter was less surprised than Tresckow imagined. A series of incidents filtered through his mind and slotted into a pattern. General

Beck and Colonel Oster riding through the Tiergarten at the time of the Fritsch affair and the circumstances of Beck's resignation. Ambassador von Hassell's recall from Rome. Admiral Canaris's expression when Peter had asked for information on the Soviet Union. General Halder's doubts before the invasion of Poland. 'I will talk to them,' he promised.

Two days later, he was home, in the almost unreal situation of wartime Berlin, catching up with the mundane problems of rationing and fuel shortages, learning that there had been no air-raids since November, hearing about the terrible effect Sepp's death was having on Luise.

It was this last problem that exercised Ilse and Christa most. Christa was concerned about Lili. 'Luise seems to have lost all interest in her, since Sepp died. Lili spends more time here than she does at home. If it weren't for me, nobody would even think about taking her out for walks or reading to her.'

'That isn't quite true,' Ilse said, gently. 'Frau Jochum does a lot for her, too. But Luise worries me, Peter. Nobody can get through to her. It's as if she's living in some other world. She's made her house into a kind of shrine to Sepp, almost as if she believes he'll come home one day. I wondered, perhaps, if you went to see her... After all, you know what it's like in Russia.'

Sepp and Luise had always seemed to Peter like children caught up in an adult world. Nevertheless Sepp had been a war hero, wearer of the *Pour le Mérite* and the Knight's Cross. And he had died in Russia... 'I'll see how much time I've got,' he prevaricated.

Next day, he reported to Zossen, where he found General Halder in grim mood. Staring at a report in front of him, he said, 'There have been over a million casualties — that's nearly a third of our entire force. Of a total of one hundred and sixty-two combat divisions, only eight are fit for action. We have sixteen armoured divisions and they have only a hundred and forty serviceable tanks between them. So far as the Luftwaffe is concerned, its plight is even worse.'

'What will happen now, Herr General?'

'The Führer is determined to continue the war,' Halder said tiredly. 'However, he is making some concessions. He recognizes that we cannot destroy the entire Red Army in a single campaign, so this summer our forces will be concentrated in the south. The oil-fields of the Caucasus are Russia's lifeblood. Without oil, Stalin cannot continue the war. If we capture Stalingrad and block the route from the Caucasus to the Caspian Sea, the Soviet Union will be forced to surrender. And we shall have obtained oil vital to our own needs.'

When Halder had finished, Peter recounted his own experiences in Russia. Finally, he mentioned Tresckow and Schlabrendorff.

Halder looked at him uncomfortably. 'Biederstein, I should prefer you not to say any more. What you do about these things is for you alone to decide. I will admit that I was opposed to Hitler's plans to start a war. I believed it was too soon and, for that matter, I still think it was premature. However, by declaring war on us, England left us with no choice. We had to fight in order to defend the Fatherland.'

He took a deep breath. 'Let me remind you of one other thing, Biederstein. Once at war, a soldier has a clear duty to perform, one that frequently will entitle or even expect him to do many things inconceivable in peacetime, such as those you have described to me. An officer also has another, higher duty: towards the man who recreated and made strong again the German Wehrmacht. Do not forget that you swore an oath of allegiance.'

'That is my dilemma, Herr General,' Peter replied softly.

Halder shook his head. 'There is no dilemma. To break your oath would be an act of treason and there is no such word as treason in the dictionary of the German soldier.'

Peter nodded slowly, suddenly reminded of the time General Beck had told him, *Mutiny is a word which does not exist in the vocabulary of a German soldier.* Yet now General Beck was apparently a leading member of the Berlin resistance.

After seeing Halder, Peter telephoned Beck and made an appointment to see him at his home. To begin with, the conversation was awkward as Beck found it hard to believe Peter's change of heart, but after Peter had explained his reasons, he soon opened up, clearly pleased to find someone with whom he could discuss the vast organizational problems with which he was confronted.

The greatest of these was the risk of discovery by the Gestapo and only slightly less difficult was the dissention between the various resistance groups as to the form the *coup d'état* should take. 'I disagree with Tresckow about killing Hitler,' Beck said. 'I believe it is sufficient to arrest him, but how the arrest is to be staged, I don't know. None of us here ever come into contact with Hitler. The arrest has to be staged by the military.'

Neither did he seem sure what would happen after that. He still lacked any firm commitment from any field commanders, like Rommel, Manstein, Paulus and Guderian. When he and his fellow conspirators succeeded in winning over a general to their cause, it was only to find him suddenly dismissed or moved to another command.

Beck told him that they had the support of General Olbricht, head of the Supply Section of the Reserve Army, responsible for the disposition of new and reserve troops. Peter knew Olbricht well. Six years older than himself, he was a good friend and capable officer. Beck explained that Olbricht had been using his position to infiltrate men known to be loyal to their cause into strategic field commands. Once Hitler was removed from power, he believed Olbricht's senior officer, General Fromm, would be converted to their cause and the Reserve Army could stage the take-over of Berlin.

To Peter's mind, it was all far too nebulous. Filled with deep misgivings, he visited Colonel Oster at the Abwehr offices on the Tirpitz Ufer. 'Canaris is on our side,' Oster assured Peter, 'but he is under great pressure from Himmler and Heydrich, who are trying to discredit the Abwehr and have it absorbed into the SS. In the meantime, certain of our friends have been trying to negotiate with the British and Americans to ensure an honourable peace settlement for Germany, when we succeed in getting rid of Emil.'

'It is too late for that,' Peter said grimly.

Oster gave him a fixed stare from behind his monocle. 'We made it possible for Emil to come to power. Whatever the consequences, it is our duty to free Germany and the world from this plague.'

During the second week of his leave, Peter succumbed to Ilse's pleading and visited Luise. Her face was gaunt when she opened the apartment door to him late in the afternoon. She was wearing a long brown coat with fur trimmings and Sheltie followed close on her heels. 'Oh, it's you,' she said, abruptly.

The flat struck chill and, when she led him into the kitchen, he saw a bucket piled high with briquettes of what now passed for coal in the city, but the stove was unlit. 'Would you like me to light the fire for you?'

'No, it's all right. I'm not cold,' she replied, drawing her coat closer round her. Then, still standing, she asked, 'Well, what do you want?'

Talking to her was going to be no easy task. Peter pulled his cigarette case from his pocket. 'Would you like a cigarette?'

'No, thank you.'

'Ilse and Christa are worried about you. Ilse asked me to come to see you, in case I could help you in any way.'

'You help me? God, I wouldn't come to you for help...'

'Luise, I know it's hard, but, believe me, in a few months' time, you'll feel differently...'

Green eyes glittered at him from across the table. 'Peter von Biederstein, how the hell do you know how I'm going to feel in a few months' time? You've never lost anyone in your whole damned life!'

He took a deep breath. 'I do understand, Luise.'

'No, Peter, you don't understand. You can't possibly understand.' Her knuckles were white, as she tightened her grasp on the back of the kitchen chair against which she was leaning. 'I loved Sepp. I loved him more than anyone in the world. And now he's dead. He was a good man — a simple man, maybe, but a good man, Peter. He loved flying. He loved Germany. And he loved me. And now he's dead. And I tell you,' her voice was reaching a high pitch, 'with Sepp, a part of all of us died. We all helped to kill him and we all died with him!'

'Luise! Stop it!' His voice cut harshly through her hysteria. 'Sepp was my friend,' he said more softly. 'I was fond of him, as I am of you. All I want to do now is help you, if I can.'

'I don't need your help. I'd rather go to Hitler than to you. Dear God in heaven, if you can't even look after your own family, how do you think you're going to do anything for anybody else?'

'I wasn't aware that my family was suffering,' he said stiffly.

Tears were glistening in her eyes. She brushed at them with the back of her hand and slumped down on the chair. 'You're not aware of anything, are you? You really haven't the slightest notion of what goes on outside your cosy little world. Oh, Peter, go away, for God's sake. I can't stand this any longer.'

Peter pulled out a chair and sat down. 'No, Luise, I'm not going until you tell me what you meant by that statement about my family. Has something happened while I've been away?'

For a long time Luise stared at him in the twilight, then, tiredly, she reached across to the gold case lying on the table and extracted a cigarette. 'Yes, I suppose it did start when you went away, but not to this war — the one before.'

'The last war? What the devil are you talking about?'

Her eyes sized him up, then, finally, she took a long drag on her cigarette and leaned back. 'It's strange. This is the first and probably the last time you and I will ever talk alone. You were always Viktoria's friend. You never liked me.'

'That's not fair. You were very young...'

'Not so young that I didn't know what was going on — that Vicki was in love with you and you were not in love with Vicki.'

'Luise, that was a very long time ago. Perhaps I flirted a little with Viktoria, but she was a pretty girl and I was a gay young blade. We lieutenants had to sow our wild oats...'

'Yes,' Luise said heavily, 'that's what I'm talking about.'

Peter stubbed out his cigarette and lit another one, trying to see what she was getting at, trying to remember back twenty-eight years to the beginning of another war. He had already met Ilse then, but had left her in Danzig when his regiment had been posted to Karlshorst. To fill in the time, he had walked out with Viktoria, taken her dancing. They had even gone to her parents' cottage at Heiligensee one afternoon for a bit of rough and tumble. That had been a couple of days before war broke out...

'Vicki was in love with you,' Luise repeated. 'Did you never wonder why she married Benno?'

Peter shrugged. 'Benno's a nice enough chap and he was always fond of her.'

Luise ground out her cigarette angrily. 'Benno's the Archangel Gabriel compared to you. Well, if you can't see for yourself, I'll spell it out to you! You left Viktoria in July. In September, she married Benno in a great hurry. The following April, she had Stefan. From July to April is nine months — exactly the period to conceive and bear a child, Peter von Biederstein.'

Peter closed his eyes, then hid his face in his hands. 'Oh, dear God, Stefan is my son...' And then came the even worse realization. 'That means he is Christa's half-brother. Luise, is that why he ran away to England?'

'Yes, Vicki had to tell him.'

For a long time, there was silence in the room. Finally, Peter asked, 'Why have you told me? Why only now? Why didn't you tell me before? Or, for that matter, why tell me at all?'

'Because I cannot bear the thought that everything should be in vain.' Luise spoke slowly now, as if all emotion had been drained out of her. 'It's too late for Viktoria, Peter, just as it's too late for Sepp and me. You can't go back on the past. But you can do something for the future. You owe the children something — both of them.'

'But, Stefan...'

'Stefan was twice the man you will ever be, Peter. While you were currying favour with the Führer, collecting gold stripes and decorations, he was using his contacts in England to try to stop Germany going to war. In your eyes, that made him a traitor, but to me it makes him a hero. If there had been more Stefans and fewer of your kind, Sepp would still be alive...'

Suddenly, the memory of that August of 1939 flooded back. In the excitement of later events, Peter had forgotten Stefan's involvement in Beck's and Oster's efforts to avoid war and, at the time, it had never occurred to him that he might find himself joining the resistance. He murmured, 'Stefan, my son...'

'No,' Luise said. 'Thank God, Stefan was never your son.'

Very slowly, like an old man, Peter walked round to where she was sitting, took her gently by the shoulders and turned her body, so that her head lay against his chest. He could find no words to express what he was feeling, so he just stood there, feeling very humble, very sad and very, very alone.

From another room, a voice called, 'Mama.'

'That's Lili,' Luise said huskily. 'I must go and see her.'

'Luise! Just one thing.'

'What?'

'Promise me you will never tell Ilse and Christa.'

She pulled away from him and stood up. With quiet dignity, she said, 'They are my friends. Unlike you, I do not hurt my friends.' She left the kitchen, Sheltie trailing along behind her.

Peter let himself out into the evening, but it was a long time before he returned home. Unseeingly, he walked through the streets of Berlin. Luise was right. He could do nothing about the past, but he could do something for the future, for Christa and Stefan. Christa, the daughter whom he had unwittingly hurt so badly, and Stefan, the son whose existence he could acknowledge to nobody, whom he had once branded a traitor and who was now a stranger in an enemy land.

What Stefan had started, he would finish. Tresckow and Oster were right. Hitler was the root of all their evil. If Hitler were killed, the whole rotten Nazi edifice would crumble like a house of cards. He would make his son proud of him. *Stefan, my son...*

He stopped and looked around, not altogether surprised to find himself in the Bayerische Strasse outside Oster's apartment. He took a deep breath and rang the bell. Getrud Oster opened the door. 'Why, General Count von Biederstein! Please come in.'

'I must talk to Hans.'

She asked no questions but led him into Oster's study, closing the door quietly on them. Before the Colonel could utter a word, Peter said, 'Hans, something has happened to make me change my mind. Hitler must be killed. And there is only one person who can do it. The assassin must be an officer permitted regular access to the Chancellery, Obersalzberg or Rastenburg — an officer who can get past his formidable, armed, SS bodyguard — an officer with impeccable credentials in whom Hitler has implicit trust...'

Hans Oster removed his monocle from his eye and asked, 'And you know an officer who is in, or could work himself into that position?'

Very slowly, Peter nodded. 'Yes — myself. I must curry Hitler's favour and then, when the moment is right, I must kill him.'

A few days later, he returned to Russia.

CHAPTER SIXTEEN

Sara Levi's parents died that winter, officially from pneumonia, in fact the victims of a bitter winter spent in a freezing room with too little to eat — and from broken hearts. Perhaps they were among the fortunate ones. Old Jews were a liability in the Third Reich. If they had not died, then they might have been transported to Poland.

The authorities called it resettlement. But Bethel Ascher knew — because so many German Jews went away and were never heard of again — that they were being consigned to death. Rumours had reached Berlin of death camps set up alongside labour camps like Schlachtenhausen and Auschwitz, where Jews were being taken to be slaughtered like animals in specially constructed gas chambers. It was said the programme was masterminded by SS Obergruppenführer Heydrich. Thanks to Heydrich and Himmler, a Jew in Germany no longer even had the right to live.

Towards the end of May 1942, a fresh disaster struck. That Wednesday morning as always, Bethel was up early, waiting for the sound of Sara's steps in the passage, so that he could prepare her meagre breakfast. She worked a twelve-hour nightshift at Kraus Chemie and, since April, Jews had been forbidden to use public transport, so she had to walk the two miles to and from the factory, a tiring and often dangerous journey.

As soon as he heard her, he boiled the kettle and spooned a little barley coffee into a cup and put a slice of stale black bread, thinly spread with fat, on her plate. The door opened and she staggered in. There was an ugly swelling on the side of her face and her eyes were red. Bethel seized her hands and led her to a chair. 'Sara, my dear, what has happened?'

It was a while before she could speak, but then she had a dreadful story to tell. 'For some time, one of the foremen has been eyeing me lecherously. Naturally, I have avoided him whenever possible, but last night, when I arrived, he had been drinking. He managed to force me into a storeroom and there, he tried to molest me.' She closed her eyes, shuddering at the memory. 'Herr Professor, I was so frightened, but I struggled and succeeded in scratching at his eyes. He — he hit me.' She indicated her cheek.

A cold fury welled up in Bethel, but he controlled it. 'Did he…?'

'No, he wanted a submissive woman, not a raging animal. He threw me back against the wall — and then, he sacked me… Because of the curfew I could not come home, so I spent the night in the toilets… Professor, I have no job any more. Oh, what am I going to do?'

Bethel took her in his arms, rocking her like a child. She was so thin, he could feel her bones. 'Don't worry, you'll get another job. In the meantime, you must rest and recover your strength.'

He coaxed her to eat her breakfast and, when she had finished, laid her on his own bed, sitting beside her until she slept. Then he went out in the hope of buying some little delicacy to cheer her up and, while he was queueing patiently in the bakery, he heard one woman say to another, 'Did you hear the news about Heydrich? Apparently some Czech fanatics have tried to assassinate him. He's very ill in a Prague hospital.'

The Professor's first thought was, *I hope he dies a terrible death.* But on reflection, this was the very worst that could happen. If Heydrich died, thousands of Jews would be killed in revenge. The suffering of the Jewish people would not lessen, it would grow worse.

He left the baker's shop without buying anything and hurried homewards. Two streets away, he saw them: security policemen, pushing Jews into waiting vans. So the reprisals had already commenced. This time, he was certain, few would be spared, certainly not an old professor and a young, unemployed woman. If Sara were to live, he must take her away from here, quickly, before the security police reached their block.

He ran home as fast as his tottering legs would permit, to find her staring out of the window. Wasting no time in explanation, he took her coat from the hook and thrust her bag into her hand. 'Are all your papers there? Now, follow me.'

It took them all afternoon, avoiding main streets and hiding in doorways, to reach Wilmersdorf and it was dark when they arrived at Klara Scheer's apartment.

The Pastor's wife was little changed. Her cheeks were still plump if less rosy than before. She hustled them wordlessly into her flat and, finger to lips, went ahead of them into the kitchen and turned on the radio. After the Professor had introduced Sara, she explained, 'We must talk quietly. I have new neighbours, who are very curious about everyone.'

She made some ersatz tea and the Professor told her what had happened. Klara looked grave. 'In recent months, the Gestapo have stepped up their observation on me. A listening device has been put in my telephone, my post is intercepted and many of my contacts have been arrested. However, I still have friends out at Velten, if you can get that far.'

Velten was at least thirty miles away, but the Professor answered confidently, 'I am sure we can.'

'Tonight you will sleep here. And before that you will eat. I don't have much, but you are welcome to it.'

To Bethel and Sara, it was a veritable feast: black bread and thick slices of cold sausage — even some mustard. While they ate, Klara told them that Bernhard was still in Dachau and, so far as she was aware, in reasonable health. Finally, she said, 'You should leave early, so we had best go to bed now. Bethel, you can sleep on the settee. Sara, you can share my bed.'

The first thing Klara did when she awoke next morning was to unpick their yellow stars and press the material so the stitches did not show. Then she roused the two travellers, made some barley coffee and packed the remains of the bread and sausage for them to take with them. She tied a headscarf round Sara's dark hair and gave Bethel one of Bernhard's hats. Making sure they knew the address of her friends in Velten, she kissed them both goodbye. 'God bless you both — you will always be remembered in my prayers.'

So, while Wilmersdorf still slept, Bethel Ascher and Sara Levi set out on their journey, fugitives in the city of their birth.

Although she did not look it, Ricarda would be seventy-five that year. Her thick white hair, dressed in an elegant chignon, framed her face gently, enhancing her rounded cheeks, beady green eyes and a chin that had grown more obstinate with the years. But there were new lines across her forehead and around her eyes and mouth which were not solely a result of age.

So much had changed so quickly and these changes saddened her grievously. First there had been Stefan. Privately, Ricarda wondered if she had been partly to blame for his decision to go to England. She had encouraged Mortimer Allen to talk about Oxford and urged Stefan to study there, with no idea that it would lead to his ultimate defection. Since the microphones had been installed in the hotel, nobody — not even Viktoria — mentioned Stefan's name, but Ricarda knew he was constantly in Viktoria's thoughts, as he was always in her own prayers.

Ricarda did not only pray for her grandson. She often wondered what had happened to that brave pastor from Schmargendorf and his wife Klara, as well as dear Professor Ascher. On the few occasions she saw Jews on the streets, she looked in case one of them was the Professor.

But most worrying of all was Luise. They had always been so different, her two daughters. Viktoria, dogged, determined and sometimes rather ruthless, was very like Karl. She saw life as a challenge and did not allow even the greatest adversities to set her back for long. It was as if, at some time in her life, Viktoria had built a wall round her heart to protect it from pain. As a result, she was a survivor. Even when the end came, she would go out fighting — just the same as her father.

Luise was the opposite. While Viktoria took arms against a sea of troubles, Luise suffered the slings and arrows of outrageous fortune. She had no protecting wall to shield her from the knocks of life — and there had been so many of them. With the death of Sepp, the last and greatest love of her life, she had become utterly defenceless.

Ricarda did what she could. She visited or telephoned Luise every day and made sure that she continued to mix with other people. She encouraged Christa to play with Lili, in the hope that young blood would turn Luise's thoughts outward, to the future. She pleaded with her to come and live at the hotel. She even proposed that Luise take over the management of Café Jochum again, promising that she would use her influence over Benno to make sure the café was run Luise's way. To no avail. Luise merely said, 'Café Jochum ceased to be my Café Jochum a long time ago. Nothing can bring the past back again.'

In desperation, Ricarda suggested Luise, Lili and Sheltie spend the summer with her at Heiligensee. To her surprise, Luise agreed, although her words gave Ricarda scant consolation. 'Sepp will be able to find us at Heiligensee.'

Relieved finally to have stirred her into motion, Ricarda galvanized everybody else into action. While a maid was packing her clothes, she ordered Benno to have the hotel Opel loaded with stores. Disregarding petrol shortages, she instructed Viktoria, 'You go ahead and tell the Webers that we're coming.'

Viktoria agreed with alacrity, delighted at the idea of spending a few hours at Heiligensee all by herself. 'I'll send the car straight back for you and Luise,' she promised.

Although he winced inwardly at the flagrant wastage of valuable petrol coupons, Benno smiled admiringly at his mother-in-law. 'I think the Führer could use you at the front.'

Ricarda shot him a piercing glance. 'Sometimes I do think I could make a better job of this war than he is.'

The chauffeur carried the supplies into the cottage and returned to Berlin. Viktoria did not go along to see the Webers, but stood on the verandah, gazing down the garden towards the lake. It was a beautiful early summer day, the time of year when Heiligensee came into its own, the trees verdant, the water sparkling silver, the air perfumed with pine resin, honeysuckle and roses. The war seemed a long way away.

Suddenly, she stiffened, her eyes catching a movement from the boathouse. For a moment, she thought it was a bird or an animal, then she realized it was somebody in the boathouse itself. She hesitated, wondering what to do. One heard stories about enemy deserters and foreign labourers, desperate in their attempts to escape captivity, so it might be as well to be armed. She took a stout walking stick from its stand and set off purposefully across the lawn.

There was no sound, except for the cawing of rooks overhead. Outside the boathouse, she held her stick threateningly at shoulder height. 'Whoever you are, come out!' There was no reply.

Had she imagined that fleeting motion across the window? Maybe it had been only the reflection of a bird in the glass. 'If you come out now, I promise I won't do you any harm, whoever you are.'

Very slowly, the door opened and a woman's face peered round it, past Viktoria towards the house. She was quite young, with big brown eyes. She whispered, 'Are you alone?'

Viktoria recognized fear when she saw it. She let her stick fall. 'Yes, I'm all alone.'

With a submissive gesture, the young woman stood aside, letting the door swing open, so that Viktoria could see into the gloomy depths of the boathouse. On the staging, a makeshift bed had been made from tarpaulins and rugs from the motor yacht and, on this, an old man was lying. 'He's not well,' the woman whispered.

Viktoria walked past her. The old man was dreadfully thin, folds of flesh hanging loosely from his cheeks. His closed eyes were sunk deep into their sockets, an unhealthy sheen of perspiration beaded his upper lip and his body trembled. 'We must fetch a doctor.'

'No!' The woman grasped hold of her. '*Gnädige Frau*, please understand, we are Jews. No Aryan doctor is allowed to treat us. All he will do is report us to the Gestapo and then…'

The man opened his eyes, so dark as to appear almost black. Startled, Viktoria knelt beside him and laid her cool hand on his forehead. 'Don't worry,' she murmured, 'I shan't give you away. But who are you? I'm certain we've met somewhere before.'

He raised himself on one elbow. 'I am Bethel Ascher.'

Viktoria could not conceal her shock. 'Professor Ascher? But, Herr Professor, what has happened? What are you doing here?'

Seized by a coughing fit, he sank back.

Viktoria turned to the woman. 'We must get him up to the house. Are you strong enough to help me carry him?'

'He is not very heavy. For such a big man…'

They made a seat of their hands and carried him across the lawn, into the cottage and up to Viktoria's bedroom. Viktoria piled the pillows high behind his head, laid a quilt over him, then fetched some aspirin from the medicine cabinet in the bathroom. 'Herr Professor, can you swallow these?'

The upheaval had exhausted him and it was with great difficulty that he took the tablets. Then he lay back, eyes closed, deathly pale against the white linen, a grotesque effigy of his former self.

Viktoria beckoned to the woman and led her down to the kitchen. The stove was ready for lighting and a bucket of briquettes stood beside it. She lit it, filled a kettle with water and put it on the hob, then said, 'I am Viktoria Jochum-Kraus. I have known the Professor since I was a little girl. I shall do everything I can to help him. But why are you hiding in my boathouse? And who are you?'

The woman sank down in a chair. 'I am Sara Levi. I, too, am a friend of the Professor.' In a dull voice, she described the events leading up to Heydrich's death, their flight to Wilmersdorf and their journey as far as Heiligensee, when the Professor had collapsed. 'Your cottage appeared deserted, so we took refuge in the boathouse. I didn't know what else to do.'

Viktoria listened to her with undisguised horror. The kettle boiled and with slightly shaking fingers, she spooned tealeaves into a teapot and poured hot water over them. It did not seem possible that Sara Levi was describing life in Berlin.

'Is that real tea?' Sara Levi asked, incredulously.

Viktoria suddenly felt embarrassed. At the Quadriga they complained about rationing and the deteriorating quality of food. Yet in the same city, there were people who had not eaten for two days, who had forgotten how it was to drink real tea. She found a tin of biscuits and broke the seal. 'Have some of these. When my mother and sister arrive, I'll make some lunch.'

'Your mother and sister? Frau Jochum-Kraus, if anyone knows we are here, it will be extremely dangerous for you as well as for us. It's better that we leave.'

'My dear child...' But Viktoria understood. Helmuth, the chauffeur, was a staunch Party member. If he saw the girl, he would feel compelled to tell someone. Even the Webers, loyal though they were, would tattle in the village. 'Bring your tea upstairs. You'll be safe there for the moment at least.'

Five minutes later, the car arrived. Sheltie and Lili jumped out and rushed straight down to the water's edge. Luise wandered into the kitchen and sat down, while Ricarda supervised the chauffeur unloading their luggage. 'Shall I take the cases upstairs?' he asked.

'No, thank you, Helmuth,' Viktoria said sharply. 'We'll manage. And tell Herr Benno I'll make my own way home this evening.'

With a sigh of relief, she watched the car disappear back up the drive, then she told her mother and Luise what had happened.

For the first time since Sepp's death, emotion showed in Luise's face, not self-pity but sympathy for someone else. 'Poor Professor Ascher... They must stay here as long as they want.'

Ricarda took a deep breath. 'What a dreadful story. I had no idea such terrible things were going on. Of course, Luise is right, they must stay here as our guests.'

'It's going to be difficult,' Viktoria warned.

Ricarda was an eminently practical person. 'I'll see Fritzi and Hilde after lunch to tell them we're here and don't need them until tomorrow. That will give us a bit of time. And it might be best to say nothing to Lili, Luise, in case she lets something drop.'

Luise shook her head. 'What sort of world are we living in?'

They all had a clearer idea of that after talking to Professor Ascher and Sara. The Professor told his story unemotionally, including the atrocities being performed in the occupied territories by SS Einsatzgruppen and the Army, and the death camps in Poland.

At the mention of Schlachtenhausen, Viktoria stared at him, aghast. 'No, I can't believe that. Benno's father has a factory there. Not even the Baron would permit anything that dreadful.'

Professor Ascher laid a thin, blue-veined hand on hers. 'The Commandant of Schlachtenhausen camp is Otto Tobisch...'

A shiver ran up Viktoria's spine. There were no depths to which Otto would not sink. And if there was money to be made from killing Jews, Baron Heinrich was not a man to turn away a profit.

'Herr Professor, Fräulein Levi, we should like you to stay here as long as you want,' Ricarda said, 'but we must be careful.'

'You could live in the cellar,' Luise suggested hesitantly. 'At least you'd be safe — and we could make it comfortable for you. Benno has fitted it out with oil lamps and blankets. You could have books and a radio.'

'With books and a radio, I should think I were in heaven,' Professor Ascher assured her.

That evening, as Viktoria returned on the S-Bahn to the Quadriga, she wondered whether to tell Benno everything that had occurred. In the end, she decided against it. There was nothing he could do and the fewer people who knew the whereabouts of the Professor and Sara Levi the better.

At Schlachtenhausen, Otto Tobisch rose early, dressed and went into the nursery. Adolf was nearly two now, with blond hair and blue eyes, just like his father. Surprisingly gently, Otto lifted him out of his cot. 'Hello, young man, and how are you today?'

Adolf gurgled sleepily, 'Hello, Papa.'

It was a never-ending source of wonder to Otto that he had sired this child. Anna, who had never been very important to him, had faded into complete insignificance since his birth. After nearly fifty years, Otto had found a purpose in life. The war, the camp, the eternal battle against communists and Jews — they had become a personal mission in his determination to make a new world for his son.

He put the child back in bed and strode out into the fine early May morning. He collected Wolf from his kennel and set off towards the new buildings set amidst the forest, in which would be carried out what was known in SS circles as the 'Final Solution of the Jewish Problem'. Today, the first trainload of Jews would arrive and he would discover whether the system was efficient.

He started his inspection at the railway station, newly painted white with Anna's hanging baskets filled with spring flowers. Guards sprang to attention, 'Heil Hitler, Herr Commandant!' They showed him buckets of water waiting for the prisoners when they arrived, thirsty after their long journey. A man turned on a gramophone and 'Tales from the Vienna Woods' echoed across the platform.

'Good. Come, Wolf!' They set off up the long path towards the gas chambers, a pretty walk between striped lawns and herbaceous borders where, even now, prisoners were hard at work, weeding and trimming edges, closely watched by black-uniformed guards. The newcomers would not suspect that, concealed behind the shrubs, were vents through which camp orderlies would tip deadly cyanide crystals.

A sign on the building ahead read RECEPTION. Otto entered and more officers sprang to their feet and saluted. Their routine had been often rehearsed, but Otto wanted no mistakes, so he went through it again. 'You are clear that, unless a prisoner is unusually young and fit, all are to be sent to the gas chambers? They are to be informed that they are being taken for showers and disinfection.'

'Yes, Herr Commandant.'

Otto continued into the next room, where the Jews would be stripped of all their possessions. No matter how poor, they always had something, even if it was only a wedding ring. A large strong-room had been constructed to store the valuables until a security van came to take them away for deposit in the Reichsbank. Another large warehouse had been built for their clothes and other belongings, which would later be distributed among the SS or the labour camp inmates.

Next, Otto went down into the shower rooms, situated underneath the gardens, big enough to hold two hundred people each. Although the vents were open, the air smelt of disinfectant. The shower heads were real. The concrete walls gleamed with water where they had recently been hosed down.

There had been ample opportunity for experimentation although not in such large numbers as could be expected from now on. The cyanide crystals worked quickly, killing the Jews within twenty minutes, half an hour at the outside. It was a much more effective method of mass killing than shooting.

For the next stage, Jews themselves were employed. Wearing gas masks and rubber boots, they dragged the corpses from the room and piled them into elevators which transported them back up to ground level, where more prisoners went through their body orifices for hidden jewels and extracted the gold fillings from their teeth. The bath houses were hosed down and made ready for the next contingent. A narrow gauge railway took the remains to the crematoria east of the camp, where they would be burned.

Otto glanced at his watch. There was no time now for inspecting the crematoria. If possible, he liked to have breakfast with Adolf. After issuing last-minute instructions to his men, he returned to his quarters. Roughly an hour to dispose of two hundred Jews. That meant they ought to be able to kill nearly five thousand a day. Himmler should be pleased.

To Baron Heinrich's relief, Hitler took the Ministry of Armaments out of the jurisdiction of Göring's Four-Year Plan and made it Professor Speer's sole responsibility. Speer was proving an extremely able Minister, with none of Hitler's restlessness or Göring's instability. He had a shrewd mind and was determined to increase armaments production. There were to be no more sudden shifts of programme. Contracts were to be guaranteed. He called his plan 'industrial self-responsibility' and it suited Kraus Industries down to the ground.

Speer was also responsible for securing the future of the munitions industry in another way. Despite their depleted numbers, British bombers had continued their attacks on the Ruhr throughout the winter. Although anti-aircraft defences in the Ruhr were denser and more powerful than any others in Germany, except those of the capital, Speer recognized the vulnerability of the area. He gave orders that such production facilities as could not be taken away from the area should be moved into specially built, reinforced, underground workshops. It was an exercise the Baron had already commenced. Now it was being paid for by the State.

Speer also formed a State Armaments Council, upon which the Baron was invited to sit, with one proviso. Politely, Speer explained he had made a new ruling that any departmental head over the age of fifty-five must have a deputy who was no older than forty. The same must apply to the Council.

The Baron accepted his point. After all, he was nearly eighty-four. To a youngster like Speer, that must seem positively archaic. No older than forty. That ruled out Ernst, who was fifty-six. So the Baron nominated Werner, who had just reached twenty-five and, exempted from military service because he was working in the munitions industry, was making a very successful job of running the Silesian works.

It was a small matter, but it sparked off larger issues in the Baron's mind. A long time ago, the best legal brains in Germany had worked out a complicated trust whereby the assets of Kraus Industries remained within the family and yet were subject to minimum amounts of death duties and inheritance tax, at the same time allowing total power to remain in Baron Heinrich's hands.

At present, the Baron held sixty per cent of Kraus shares and Ernst, Benno, Werner and Norbert the remaining forty per cent. Perhaps it was time to transfer some of his holding. Not that he had any intention of dying, but the British might have the audacity to bomb Kraus Haus or Grunewald, killing him in the process, and it would be very annoying to know that his heirs would have to pay tax on their inheritance, whereas if he made the transfer now in a gift deed, there could be very advantageous tax concessions.

The Baron summoned Dr Duschek to Kraus Haus and told him to transfer eighty per cent of his shareholding to his two grandsons, Werner and Norbert. 'You realize that will give them a larger holding in the company than Herr Ernst?' the lawyer pointed out.

'Just do what I instruct you,' Baron Heinrich said coldly.

Although Ernst was a shareholder, he was allowed no access to confidential papers or any part in policy decisions, neither had he any idea what went on in Berlin, Kraushaven, Silesia, Schlachtenhausen or other Kraus companies. Other than management responsibility for all Kraus works in the Ruhr, Ernst held no authority.

A couple of days later, however, the Baron forgot all about the gift deed. In a radio broadcast, Churchill warned that Britain would retaliate if poison gas were used on the Russian front. Unable to resist an opportunity to boast, the Baron gloated to Benno, 'Little does he know we're already using it!'

Benno narrowed his eyes. Disagreement with his father over the production of poison gas at Kraus Chemie during the last war had been a major contributing factor to his leaving the company. 'We're using poison gas on the Russian front?'

The Baron realized he had said too much. 'Not on the front, boy. However, if Churchill pushes his luck, he'll find it being used in England. We're building up enough stocks to poison half of England. And we're developing another even more lethal type that will penetrate the filters of all known gas masks.'

Benno turned away, so that his father should not see the loathing in his eyes.

On Saturday, 30 May, the Führer made a special announcement from his headquarters at the Wolf's Lair near Rastenburg. In strident tones, he proclaimed that the great battle round Kharkov had ended and that German and Axis forces had transformed their defence against a strong enemy into a proud victory of annihilation. Triumphantly, he added that the Luftwaffe had driven the enemy from the air.

From the security of his underground office at Essen, Ernst listened to the broadcast and wondered if the war were over. Next morning he learned that, far from being driven from the air, a thousand British bombers had attacked Cologne during the night, devastating an estimated third of the city. All night long a blazing inferno had raged and continued to rage, in which hundreds of civilians had been killed, thousands injured and made homeless.

Ernst clutched his chest. How could the Führer say that the enemy was driven from the air, when they could send a thousand bombers over Germany?

On Monday night, not long after Ernst had gone to bed, the air-raid sirens began to wail and, above them, could be heard the drone of bombers. Then came the staccato bark of anti-aircraft guns. He pulled on his dressing gown and padded across the dark room. It was an overcast night, but in the beams of the searchlights he could see the silhouettes of RAF planes, hundreds and hundreds of them, like a swarm of locusts.

Mesmerized by the spectacle, he watched the valley beneath him light up as the first aircraft dropped green phosphorous flares, like Christmas trees hung with glittering baubles, casting an eerie light over the familiar landscape. Incendiaries fell next, brilliant, sparkling, plummeting through the roofs of houses, offices and factories, setting fire to wooden furniture, curtains and carpets, the flames leaping from building to building, high into the sky. The next wave of planes dropped high explosive bombs that landed with such crashing detonations, they sent tremors all the way to the Fortress.

The door to the adjoining bedroom burst open and, an almost ghostly apparition in her white nightgown, Trudi billowed into his room. 'They're bombing Essen! They'll kill us all.'

Strangely calm, he said, 'Trudi, go down to the cellar. I'll join you soon.'

But he could not force himself away. On and on, the bombers came, wave after wave after wave of them, as the flak guns fired impotently against them. Occasionally, a plane was hit, bursting into flames, spinning down into the blazing furnace that was Essen, setting off a new explosion. The noise was deafening now and the Fortress seemed to be shaking to its very foundations.

Ernst did not know how long he stood there, but suddenly, the last plane had gone, leaving the whole town in flames. He pulled on his clothes and went downstairs. There would be little he could do about it, but he had to see the damage for himself.

He drove along the winding road, down the hillside, through the first suburbs, where the sky was lit like the first flush of dawn. People were gathering on the streets, pale and frightened. Fire engines rushed past him. He continued until a policeman signalled him to stop, angry at first, respectful when he saw who it was. 'You can't get through, Herr Kraus.'

Ernst tried another route and suddenly found the sky lit up as in broad daylight, whole streets ablaze, against which a few fire engines were waging a losing battle. Eventually, he reached one of the Kraus warehouses, from which dense smoke issued in a stifling black cloud. Men were already at the pumps, trying to extinguish the fire. Ernst parked the car at a distance and got out, shielding his face from the heat, his ears echoing with the din of falling masonry, breaking glass and the roar of the conflagration, his nose filled with the stench of burning rubber.

A grim-faced security man hurried up to him. 'Heil Hitler, Herr Kraus. This building seems to be the worst hit. It's the rubber that's causing the problem.'

'Have many been injured?'

'So far as I can tell, only Poles, probably a hundred of them. We sent everyone else underground when the sirens started.'

Ernst nodded. A hundred Poles were nothing. Stepping over hoses, picking his way over broken glass and piles of rubble, he stumbled towards the other buildings. Miraculously, the office block still stood, although scarcely a pane of glass remained. The lift had stopped, so he had to walk down the stairs to the vast machine rooms and gunshops deep in the bowels of the earth.

It was like entering another world. Apparently regardless of the fact that a thousand enemy bombers had tried to raze Essen to the ground, the heavy equipment continued to function, the labourers went on working, producing the guns with which Germany would win the war.

But after tonight, how many of those guns, so desperately needed in Russia, would have to be employed in anti-aircraft defence? If the British thousand-bomber raids continued, Germany would be fighting that two-front war she had tried to avoid. And one front line would be right here, in Germany herself.

A couple of days later, he received a copy letter from Dr Duschek informing him of the new shareholdings. Ernst stared at it in horror. In the belief that, when the Baron retired, he would take over the running of Kraus Industries, he had put up with his father's bullying, allowed himself to be sent to America and, on his return, relegated to Essen. Now he was further than ever from total power. Indeed, it was beginning to look as if he would never achieve his ambition to become the second 'Steel King'.

The sour taste of bile rose to his mouth. He reached for the latest pills Dr Dietrich had prescribed and placed two under his tongue.

They did nothing to ease the pain in his chest. He picked up the telephone and demanded that Dr Dietrich be called immediately.

The doctor entered his office with a long face. 'A bomb landed in the slave labour camp last night, Herr Direktor. Thousands of Poles are seriously wounded.'

'Damn the Poles!' Ernst snarled. 'Give me some decent pills.'

The arrival of Professor Ascher and Sara Levi marked a turning point in Luise's life. Putting her own sorrows behind her, she devoted all her energies to their well-being. Food was a major problem, for it was not easy to feed two extra people out of the meagre rations allocated for two adult women and a child, and without arousing the suspicion of Lili and the Webers. Fortunately, none of them were big eaters and they managed to get by.

Despite his underground existence, Professor Ascher's health slowly began to improve, but he was seventy-six and years of hardship had taken their toll. Sara was more resilient. After a few days, her cheeks began to fill out and her eyes to lose their haunted look.

Then, in the middle of June, disaster struck. Lili and Sheltie were in the garden, Luise and Ricarda were lingering over breakfast when Hilde Weber arrived. 'Blockwart Toll is on his way,' she announced importantly. 'He has to check the air-raid precautions again, although, in my opinion, he just wants to nose in everybody's cellars and see what stores they've got hidden away.'

Luise and Ricarda stared at each other in horror, then Luise rushed from the room. 'What's the matter with her?' Hilde asked.

Ricarda smiled weakly. 'She's in a funny mood today.'

Down in the cellar, Luise was telling the Professor and Sara, 'The Blockwart is on his way. Run to the boathouse, quickly, while I tidy up here.' Having done her best to make the cellar look like a conventional, unused air-raid shelter again, she returned upstairs and hurried to the verandah. There was no sign of the Professor and Sara. The boathouse door was firmly shut. She heard the sound of Blockwart Toll's voice and the cellar door opening.

She joined Ricarda and Hilde in the hall. After what seemed an eternity, the Blockwart returned. 'Got it nice and cosy down there, haven't you? A real home from home. Well, let's hope you never need it.' He made his way towards the back door, followed by the three women. 'Personally, I don't believe all this nonsense about thousand-bomber raids. The British haven't got that many planes left. Here, what's the matter with that dog?'

Luise felt a sinking sensation in the pit of her stomach. She looked down towards the boathouse, where Sheltie was barking furiously at the closed door, watched from a safe distance by Lili. 'It's only Sheltie,' she said, as casually as possible. 'Sheltie, Lili, come here!' Lili ran across the lawn to them, but Sheltie stayed put.

'I'd better go and have a look. Can't be too careful, you know. There are a lot of strangers around these days.' Blockwart Toll strode out into the garden and marched purposefully towards the boathouse. He wrenched open the door and peered into its gloomy depths. Luise darted forward and Ricarda seized hold of her arm. Toll shouted up the garden, 'Frau Jochum, telephone the police. You've got two Jews hiding here. Come on, you good-for-nothing scum, out of there.'

Hilde was already on the phone. 'Heil Hitler, is that the police? This is the Jochum house. The Blockwart has just found two Jews in our boathouse. Yes, yes, I'll tell him that. Heil Hitler.' She called out, 'Herr Blockwart, a police car is on its way.'

Lili stood close beside her mother. 'What are Jews?' she asked.

'Jews are wicked people capable of anything,' Hilde told her knowledgeably. 'They murder people in their beds, you know.'

Lili watched Bethel and Sara being dragged up the garden by Blockwart Toll with Sheltie barking joyfully at their heels and murmured, 'They don't look dangerous to me. They look rather sad.'

Luise wrenched herself free from Ricarda's restraining hand. 'Where are you taking them?'

The Blockwart smiled unpleasantly. 'Where they won't trouble you again, Frau Nowak. The SS will see to that.'

Neither the Professor nor Sara looked at them as they were marched round to the drive. A few minutes later, a police car arrived.

A policeman came in and asked them a few questions, which Hilde answered officiously. No, they had never seen these people before and if they had they would have reported them. The policeman nodded. People in the public eye, like the Jochums, were not the kind to help Jews. Satisfied, he and his colleague left, Bethel and Sara in the back of the car, Blockwart Toll following behind on his bicycle, anxious to miss out on none of the glory.

Ricarda took Luise's arm and led her up to her room, where she sat down beside her on the bed.

Luise gazed straight ahead. 'Mama, we should have been able to do something to stop them.'

'Darling, there was nothing we could do.' As she spoke, Ricarda wondered how many other people, all over Germany, were reassuring each other in the same way, hoping thus to absolve themselves from guilt.

'All the same, we've sent them to their death.'

After that Ricarda had the feeling that she was consorting with a ghost. Viktoria spent several days with them, but she could not get through to Luise either. Only when she pleaded with her sister to think of Lili did she get any spark of reaction and then Luise said, 'You're right. It isn't good for Lili to be alone. When you return to Berlin, maybe you could ask Christa if she'd like to come and stay with us? Lili is very fond of Christa.'

'But Christa has a job,' Viktoria pointed out gently.

Luise looked at her blankly. 'Well, I'm sure she'd rather be with Lili than working in some silly office.'

As it turned out, she was right. Christa had become a secretary at the Foreign Office to help her get over Stefan, but that was three years ago and the routine nature of her work had long since begun to pall on her. When Viktoria passed on Luise's message, she said simply, 'I love Lili. Of course I'll go and help look after her.'

So Christa came to Heiligensee to keep Lili company and Ricarda watched helplessly, while Luise's mind turned ever more inward.

Bethel and Sara were put into a crowded, squalid transit camp outside Berlin with thousands of other Jews of all nationalities. A week after their arrival, the guards marched them and hundreds of others to a railway station and pushed them at gunpoint onto a train, the air loud with screams, as wives were parted from husbands, mothers from children. Some tried to scramble free and were bludgeoned to death by the guards. It was sheer luck that Sara managed to stay with Bethel.

The guards slammed shut the doors. They were in pitch blackness, probably a hundred people crammed into a truck in which formerly thirty cattle had travelled. 'Sara, my little one, are you there?'

'Yes, Professor, I am here.' Her hand found his.

Around them, people continued to cry, hammering on the walls, shouting, 'Let us out! Let us out!'

The train started on its way, lurching and clanking. Its cargo jolted and swayed, only kept on its feet by the sheer mass of humanity propping each other up. Gradually, Sara's eyes began to acclimatize to the darkness. She and the Professor were quite near the doors, above which were narrow slats through which she could see the sky. People jostled to make more space for themselves and get nearer these precious vents.

Already the atmosphere in the confined space was growing stuffy from the smell of a hundred unwashed bodies. A babble of panic-stricken voices broke out in a host of tongues. 'Where are we going?' 'What will happen to us?' 'Is there any water?' 'How do we eat?' A child's voice wailed, 'I want to go to the toilet.' A baby cried.

At the other end of the truck, a man began trying to organize some order. Slowly, as the journey went on and the sky through the slats darkened, he succeeded in getting people to move within the truck, so that the very young, sick and the old, including the Professor, were seated against walls, while the others had a little more room to move arms and legs.

The child wailed again, 'I want to go to the toilet.' There was only the floor for a latrine.

Somehow, the night passed. The floor became a squelching mess. The air became hotter and more fetid. Those who could not sit, slept as best they could, standing up, leaning against each other, moving restlessly to ease tired muscles. Still the train continued its slow journey and through the slats a new day dawned.

During the night an old lady died. They said a prayer for her, then, as they moved her body, so that someone else could have her place at the wall, they realized that dead bodies took up more space than live ones.

Sara's stomach churned and she thought she was going to vomit. Somebody did, and a new stench was added to the others. Sara lifted her face towards the vents so that the cool air touched her cheeks and she could see the light. *The train can't go on for ever*, she told herself. *Somewhere it must reach its journey's end and we shall be allowed out.*

A host of distorted images flickered through Bethel's mind — of pine-scented Dahlem, the university, his children and grandchildren, two men and a boy walking through the Tiergarten. Once, he had had such brave dreams of keeping alive the Jews of Germany. Now there was just this stinking cattle truck and the basic human functions of excrement, vomit and death.

Time lost all meaning. Sometimes, the train stopped, but they were not let out. As the temperature rose, thirst became the greatest problem. When they heard SS guards laughing and talking outside, they beat feebly on the doors, croaking, 'Water, water.' If the men heard them, they paid no attention.

Nobody was standing any more. They all lay weakly, closely packed together, amidst their own filth. One by one, they began to die. On the fourth night of their journey, Bethel Ascher died. Quietly, with just the faintest sigh, his spirit passed from his body, out of the noisome truck and into eternity. It was hours before Sara noticed he had ceased breathing.

Next day, the train halted and the doors were opened. Fresh air and daylight flooded into the truck. Music was being played, something by Strauss. SS guards with dogs shouted, 'Everybody out!' Prisoners in striped canvas suits offered them buckets of water, urging them, 'Drink, quickly.' Sara stumbled to her feet and almost fell onto the platform. Shielding her eyes from the light, she took some water gratefully.

More prisoners hurried along with carts and started unloading the dead bodies from the train. Two of them threw the Professor onto a pile of corpses. She limped towards them. 'Where are you taking him?'

A stick descended on her shoulder and a guard said, 'Get moving. Over there with the others.'

From a loudspeaker, a voice said, 'Welcome to Schlachtenhausen resettlement camp. For your own safety, do as the guards ask. We wish you a pleasant stay here.'

Around her, people were muttering, 'It looks all right. See, there are flowers. And a garden.'

In a long, shambling line, they filed between newly mown lawns towards the reception block. More prisoners in striped suits were weeding the beds. In the distance were factory buildings, from which came the sound of voices and machinery. In the other direction, tall chimneys billowed forth smoke. Perhaps the Professor was wrong. Perhaps Schlachtenhausen was just a labour camp. The sun beat down and Sara felt faint.

SS officers walked down the line, occasionally picking people out, mainly men, and ordering them to stand to one side. Eventually, they were moved off under guard towards another part of the camp.

The queue moved slowly forward. It was a long time before Sara reached the reception desk. Waves of dizziness swept over her as she answered the SS officer's questions and she had to hold herself up against the desk. When he had finished, she was taken through to another room, ordered to undress and follow the others into the shower room.

Never had she done anything more willingly. Her skin, hair and clothes were thick with ordure. She shed her rags and staggered down the stairs and along a passage into a room labelled BATHS and filled with some two hundred people. Almost immediately, the doors shut behind her.

No water came out of the shower heads. Instead, strange crystals floated down from vents in the ceiling which were then slammed shut. 'Gas!' somebody screamed. 'They're gassing us!'

A stampede ensued as everyone tried to reach the doors. Crushed by the sheer weight of their bodies, Sara sank to the ground, her head knocking against the concrete wall. People trampled over her, then, as the gas reached them, they fell unconscious on top of her.

Half an hour later, Sara Levi's dead body was thrown into a truck on a narrow gauge railway and taken to the crematorium to join that of Bethel Ascher and hundreds of other Jews.

After the fall of Kharkov, Peter achieved his first ambition, when he was transferred from the front to Hitler's headquarters at Rastenburg, but it was scant cause for optimism. Firstly, there was the very real problem of getting close enough to Hitler to kill him. Not even Peter had anticipated the strength of the SS bodyguard that separated the Führer from all but his most trusted advisers. Secondly, the success of the *coup d'état* depended upon convincing other officers that Hitler was leading the country towards defeat and, that summer of 1942, it would have been hard to convince anybody that Germany was about to lose the war.

Indeed, there were moments when Peter was tempted to doubt his own judgement. In Africa, Rommel scored one magnificent victory after another. At the end of June, his Afrika Corps had reached El Alamein, a mere sixty-five miles from Alexandria and the Nile delta. Between them, Germany and Italy now held most of the Mediterranean. In the west, although most troops had been withdrawn for the Russian offensive, the German position held strong all the way from the Arctic Circle to Brest in France.

In Russia, Hitler was ignoring Moscow. Army Group North continued its long siege of Leningrad and Field Marshal von Manstein's Eleventh Army began the siege of Sebastopol. But the main offensive was in the south. Throughout June, Field Marshal Paulus's Sixth Army steadily drove the Russians east from Kharkov. At the end of the month, Operation Blue commenced, a hundred divisions of German, Italian, Rumanian, Hungarian and Slovak troops, determined to reach the valuable oil-fields of Grozny. In mid-July, the Russians were in full retreat, leaving not only the Caucasus virtually unprotected, but Stalingrad too.

To be closer to the action, Hitler and his entourage, including Peter, moved to Field Headquarters at Vinnitsa in the Ukraine and it was then that Hitler's indecisiveness and megalomania again made themselves felt.

First he stuck to the oil-fields as his main objective. Ten days later, he changed his mind and ordered simultaneous operations against both the Caucasus and Stalingrad. Furious arguments ensued as General Halder, Field Marshal von Bock and other field commanders tried to persuade him that they lacked the strength to carry out two powerful offensives in two different directions, with the result that Bock was dismissed. Hitler believed that the Red Army was finished and nobody could convince him otherwise.

To begin with, it appeared Hitler was right, although he had not reckoned on Stalin's scorched earth policy. On 8 August, Field Marshal von List's Army Group A reached the Maikop oil-fields — to find them destroyed. By the 25th, they were at Mozduk, only fifty miles from Grozny, but desperately short of fuel and ammunition.

In the meantime, General Paulus's Sixth Army and the Fourth Panzer Army had commenced the siege of Stalingrad. However, although the Luftwaffe inflicted tremendous damage from the air, setting fire to vast areas of the city, Hitler's indecision had given the Russians a chance to recover their strength. A month ago, the Germans might have found the city undefended. Now, like Leningrad in the north, it was determined not to surrender.

In the Caucasus, Army Group A could go no further. When List repeated his demands for fuel, ammunition and troops to be diverted from Stalingrad, Hitler dismissed him.

In Stalingrad, the war developed into savage hand-to-hand fighting and bloody street battles, with the Russians determined not to yield a foot. Casualties on both sides took on fearful proportions, but still Hitler sent one fresh division after another into the inferno. Because the Russians sent no reinforcements, he persisted in his belief that the Red Army was finished.

Yet this was not true. Military intelligence reports showed that Stalin had over a million fresh troops north of Stalingrad and another half million in the Caucasus. When General Halder pointed this out to Hitler, the result was inevitable: Halder was dismissed.

Halder's dismissal, coming so soon after that of Bock and List, and all the more so because he dared to speak the truth, caused great consternation. Peter began to feel more hopeful. The greater the dissatisfaction among Hitler's remaining generals, the more likelihood there was of the *coup d'état* succeeding.

But he still had to win Hitler's confidence, so he said nothing in Halder's defence and accepted the appointment of the new Chief of General Staff, a nonentity called General Zeitzler, with apparent equanimity. As a result, he was invited to dine with Hitler and other senior officers. The moment was approaching.

Throughout October, while the rains set in, the siege of Stalingrad continued. Peter's plans now hinged on General Paulus. The Sixth Army needed constant reinforcements, which were provided from the already weak flanks. When Paulus saw that Hitler was demanding the impossible of him, he would turn against him and, at that moment, Peter would strike. But to Peter's utter dismay, Paulus confidently predicted that he would complete the capture of Stalingrad by 10 November.

Certain that victory was on the horizon, and that in the unlikely event of the Russians launching a winter offensive it would be on the Northern Front, Hitler took his heads of staff back to the Wolf's Lair in East Prussia, leaving Peter von Biederstein at Field Headquarters at Vinnitsa in the Ukraine. At the very moment it was most vital for them to be together, they were separated by over five hundred miles.

In November the reverses began. In Africa, after bitter fighting at El Alamein, the British drove Rommel's troops remorselessly back all the way to Tobruk. At Vinnitsa, it was whispered that Rommel had been given no reserves, no tanks, no fuel, no men. 'Just like us…'

In Russia, the ground froze hard and the snows set in, the same fearsome blizzards that Peter remembered from a year ago at Smolensk. And at dawn on 19 November, in the driving snow and bitter wind, Zhukov's armies launched their offensive against Paulus's Sixth Army. All day long, Field Headquarters at Vinnitsa were inundated with terrifying reports, which were promptly telephoned through to Rastenburg. Armoured troops had smashed through the Don flank and the weak southern flank. South of the city, other forces were attacking the Fourth Panzer Army. Their objective was obvious: either the Germans must retreat or be surrounded. Bock, List and Halder's worst fears had been justified.

Once again, Hitler would not listen to reason and ordered Paulus to stand fast, promising that, if he were encircled, he and his troops would be supplied from the air until they could be relieved. Peter could not believe his ears. There were twenty-two divisions involved, who would need at least seven hundred tons of supplies a day. Even if the Luftwaffe possessed sufficient transport planes to carry the supplies, the Russians had ground and air supremacy, as well as the weather on their side.

Within four days, the Sixth Army was surrounded, radio its only form of communication with the outside world. Two days later, the airlift began.

That same day, Vinnitsa was informed that Field Marshal von Manstein had been recalled from the Leningrad front and was being sent to head a new formation, Army Group Don, with the task of pushing through the Stalingrad ring from the south-west to relieve the Sixth Army. Peter was ordered to report to Manstein's new headquarters at Kotelnikovo, ninety miles from the Stalingrad pocket.

Under normal circumstances he would have flown, but all available planes were involved in the airlift, so at dawn the next morning he set off by car on the long journey. The temperature was well below zero when they left, but gradually rose. An easterly wind sprang up and it began to snow again.

As they got into the bleak open countryside, the wind increased and the snow swirled round them in a turbulent maelstrom, reducing visibility to about twenty yards. Soon, they were driving through a veritable blizzard. God, he hated Russia!

He pushed back the seat, stretched out his legs under the dashboard and closed his eyes, wondering whether Manstein would succeed in relieving Paulus and how long Paulus could hold out if

Manstein did not get through. Why the devil hadn't he disobeyed Hitler's orders and retreated while he had the chance?

When the huge army truck trundled round the corner, its headlights full on and its horn blaring, there was only one thing for Peter's driver to do. He slammed his foot on the brakes and steered the car into a snowbank. In doing so, he ignored the glassy layer of ice below the snow on the road surface.

Peter felt the car skid, turning in a half circle, so that its boot protruded across the lorry's path. He saw the lorry driver swerve to avoid them and heard the massive vehicle crash into them with a mighty thump, followed by the splintering of shattered glass. His driver's head was thrown forward through the windscreen and his chest was impaled on the steering column. Peter tried to reach across and lift the man, but his own legs were trapped under the dashboard.

Soldiers jumped out of the lorry, tried to open the driver's door, then rushed to the passenger side. Snow swirled into the car, settling like a blanket on Peter's lap. There was a strong smell of petrol. A man got into the back of the car and pulled the driver's unconscious body off the steering wheel. His face was a crimson mask of blood. Peter felt his wrist. There was no pulse.

The smell of petrol was growing stronger. Peter tried to free his trapped legs and was aware of a curious sensation. Although they were still there, he could not feel them. 'Move the seat,' a soldier suggested.

'It won't go back any further.'

'Slice the air cushion.'

The soldier's knife slashed into his seat. Peter sank down and his legs were released. Strong hands dragged him out of the car into the snow, causing a violent, jarring pain through his upper body, but in his legs there was still no feeling at all. They picked him up to carry him clear. They were just in time. With a crashing detonation and blaze of orange flame, the car exploded. A wave of darkness flooded over Peter and he sank into unconsciousness.

Peter was taken to hospital in Kiev, where there were few drugs, no morphine and inadequate heating, all supplies having gone to the southern armies. The surgeon tried to save Peter's leg, but there was nothing he could do. It had to be amputated. 'Be thankful I could save one,' he said gruffly. 'There have been many men for whom I couldn't even do that.'

Racked with pain and a sense of failure, Peter asked dully, 'What use am I, a general with only one leg?'

'A general with one leg is better than no general at all. At least they'll send you back to Berlin, which is more than they'd do if you were a private.'

While Peter was in Kiev, news came through that, although Manstein's armies had got almost as far as Stalingrad, the Russians were now beating them back to Kotelnikovo. On 28 December, Hitler ordered Army Group A to withdraw from the exposed salient in the Caucasus. The following day, Kotelnikovo was captured by the Russians. Paulus and his men remained beleaguered in the Stalingrad pocket.

In North Africa, the Allied Eighth Army continued to advance, pushing Rommel back from El Agheila, back from Sirte.

At the beginning of January 1943, Peter was considered fit enough to make the long train journey from Kiev to Berlin. Nine months earlier, he had left with brave dreams of killing Hitler. He returned a broken man, leaving behind the tattered remnants of a once great army.

Peter was given a private room at the Charité Hospital and placed under the care of one of Germany's most brilliant surgeons, Professor Ferdinand Sauerbruch. Ilse found him lying in bed, a cage over his legs to keep the bedclothes free, and staring at the ceiling. His face was gaunt, almost whiter than the pillow. She bent down and kissed him. 'Peter, my dear. Thank God you're back home again.' Gently, she laid a hand on his and asked, 'Do your legs hurt a lot?'

He turned his head. 'Leg. I've only got one now.' It was not said with bitterness or even resignation. Just a statement of fact.

'Something can be done about that. At least you're alive.'

'Yes, that's more than the driver of my car. He was killed.'

'My dear, that wasn't your fault.'

'No. Maybe he was the lucky one.'

Ilse changed the subject. Brightly, she said, 'Christa sends you her love. You know she doesn't work at the Foreign Ministry any more.'

'She's all right?'

'Yes, we're all well. We've been very lucky in Berlin, as you probably know. No air raids for over a year now. Some Russian planes came over in August, but they didn't get very far. Life has returned almost to normal.' Silly chatter, but better than talk of death.

She stayed for another half an hour until a nurse came to tend to his dressings, then she made her way to Professor Sauerbruch's office. The surgeon motioned her to a chair and smiled tiredly. 'First of all, let me reassure you that the surgeon at Kiev did an excellent job. I've read his report, from which it is evident that there was no chance of saving your husband's left leg. So far as the right leg is concerned, it was badly crushed, but it will soon function quite normally again.'

'Presumably you'll be able to fit an artificial limb?'

Professor Sauerbruch cast her a shrewd glance. He saw a woman in her mid-forties in an expensive fur coat, with fading blonde hair and huge, china-blue eyes, which looked steadily into his. A practical, realistic person, he decided, and not one to give up easily. 'Once the stump is healed, there is no reason why we shouldn't fit a false leg and teach him to walk again. But first, Countess von Biederstein, he has to want to walk.' His words hung on the air.

'You mean, his injuries aren't just physical?'

The surgeon shook his head. 'He's been under terrible strain and now it's telling on him. I've seen it many times before.'

Ilse stood up shakily. 'Thank you, Professor Sauerbruch. I know you will do everything in your power to make him better. So shall I.'

Christa spent less time with Luise and Lili after her father's return, but she still managed to see them every day. For one thing, she didn't want to disappoint Lili. For another, she hoped that news of Peter's troubles might stir Luise out of her own apathy. She hoped in vain. If Luise saw any connection between her state and Peter's, she was not prepared to admit it.

Shortly after Christa and Lili had left Luise's apartment to go for a walk one morning, Viktoria arrived. She bustled around for a few moments, then asked, 'Is there any more news on Peter?'

Luise opened the packet of cigarettes her sister had brought with her. 'Peter von Biederstein,' she said querulously. 'He's all anyone talks about. I never liked him and I can't feel sorry for him now.'

'Luise, darling, it's not like you to be uncharitable…'

'He's never been particularly charitable.' With trembling fingers, she lit a cigarette. 'Anyway, at least I have had the satisfaction of telling him what I think of him and the way he treated you.'

'Luise, what do you mean?'

Luise shrugged. 'Last March, he came here pontificating about Sepp. I couldn't stand it. I decided it was about time he recognized his responsibilities…'

For a moment, Viktoria's heart seemed to stop beating. 'What did you tell him, Luise?'

'I told him Stefan is his son…'

Although she was very upset that Luise had given away her secret, Viktoria could not blame her. Sepp's death had unhinged Luise's mind. 'Well,' she said, 'I don't suppose it matters much any more.'

But it did matter, and when she left Luise's flat, she went straight to the Charité.

It was as if Peter had been expecting her. Before she had a chance to say anything, he asked, 'Why didn't you tell me about Stefan?'

Shocked by his appearance, she sat down beside his bed. 'Peter, it was a long time ago. Don't let's reopen old wounds.'

'Can you forgive me?'

This was a very different man from the Peter she had known in the past. All the arrogance was gone and, in its place, was a new humility. She could no longer feel bitterness — only pity. 'There is nothing to forgive. You gave me my son,' she said, softly.

Peter's eyes glazed over. 'Vicki, I hope that, one day, I can make up for the harm I've done you.'

Moved, she leaned over and kissed him on the forehead, then quietly left the room.

For a long time after she had gone, Peter lay thinking about the wrongs he had done and the people he had failed. He had thought to compensate by killing Hitler — and even in this he had not succeeded.

That afternoon, he told Ilse everything that had happened, only omitting all reference to Stefan. To his surprise, when he stated his intention to kill Hitler, she expressed neither shock nor horror, but said quietly, 'I have implicit trust in you. If you believe this to be your duty, you must carry it through.'

'I failed. Hitler is still alive. Now it's too late.'

'No, it is not too late.'

He looked down at the cage covering his legs. 'What can I do with only one leg?'

'First, you must learn to walk again.'

He knew that she was right, but still he looked for an excuse. 'There are many who would say that I am betraying my country.'

Her clear blue eyes gazed steadfastly into his. 'If what you say is true, it is Hitler who is the traitor.'

'If we are discovered, we shall be in great danger.'

'So long as the war continues, we are in even greater danger.'

When Professor Sauerbruch entered the room later, he found them sitting hand in hand. After studying the charts at the end of the bed, he asked, 'How do you feel today, Herr General?'

Peter struggled to sit upright. 'Professor Sauerbruch, can you really make me walk again?'

The surgeon glanced at Ilse, then nodded. 'It will take time, but you will walk again.'

He began that very afternoon. First, he had to learn how to get about on crutches. It was a painful and demoralizing process, for he had to develop a new sense of balance and many times he fell. Every bone in his body cried out in anguish and the amputated leg seemed to hurt more than the whole one. But by the end of the week he could swing himself across the ward without any help.

The following day, Professor Sauerbruch decided the stump had healed sufficiently for him to try out his new leg. The ungainly apparatus was strapped on and, supported by two nurses, Peter took his first real step. An excruciating pain shot through him and he screamed aloud. While the nurses clucked sympathetically, the surgeon calmly explained, 'The scar is new. The nerve-ends are sensitive.'

Peter wiped the sweat from his forehead and took a deep breath. 'Damn it all,' he muttered through clenched teeth, 'I will walk again. I will. I will.'

For the two lookouts on the rooftop of the Quadriga, the night of Saturday, 16 January 1943, seemed no different than any of the preceding thirteen months. The blinds of their shelter down, the door closed, one was immersed in a book, the other in a game of solitaire. Suddenly, the book reader said, 'Isn't that a plane?'

'Yes,' his colleague replied absently, 'the Luftwaffe.'

'Still beats me how they see to fly at night.' He frowned. 'Funny, sounds as if it's coming this way.'

At that moment, a siren wailed. By the time the look-outs had pressed the alarm, the bombers were already over the city centre. Gradually the sky was lit up by searchlights and a ragged splutter of anti-aircraft fire cut through the night air. Crouched behind their barricade of sandbags, the two men stared in fascination as the sky was lit up by flares of eerie green light.

On the first floor, Viktoria gazed out at the panorama. 'They're almost beautiful. They look like parachutes or Christmas trees.'

'They're marker bombs,' Benno muttered, pulling his trousers over his pyjama bottoms. 'For God's sake, Vicki, don't just stand there. Get your mother and go down to the cellar.'

The cellar had a sad, neglected look after long disuse, but soon the familiar procedures were being re-enacted. The hall porter took a roll-call and waiters prepared coffee. Guests grumbled among themselves. 'How did the bombers get all this way without anybody noticing?' 'They were overhead before the sirens went.' 'Beats me how the British have so many planes left.'

In Lützow, Luise sat at the window watching the bombs, while Lili hid her face in Sheltie's coat under a table. The dog whimpered and Lili cried, but Luise didn't hear them.

Eventually, the all-clear sounded and the inhabitants of the Hotel Quadriga made their way back upstairs. During the morning, the Baron phoned Benno. 'They were after the industrial area. Daimler-Benz was badly hit, but they didn't get anywhere near Kraus Village. Their marker bombs are nowhere near as good as ours. Most of their bombs were wasted in the suburbs.'

'Do you know how many of their planes we got?'

'One,' the Baron replied acidly.

Christa arrived at Luise's apartment to find Luise staring out of the window and Lili in floods of tears. 'I was so frightened. The bombs made such big bangs and the sky was on fire.'

'Weren't you in the cellar?'

Lili gazed at her from huge, terrified green eyes. 'Mama wouldn't go down. Sheltie and I hid beneath the table.'

Christa was twenty-two, old enough to know she had to do something. If Luise wanted to kill herself, that was one thing, but she should not be allowed to risk the child's life. She put her arms round Lili. 'Would you like to come home with me?'

'Yes, please.'

Christa walked across the room. 'Frau Nowak, I'm taking Lili back with me. Will you come, too? It would be safer for you than staying here.'

Luise looked at her blankly. 'Christa, it's you. Yes, I think you're right. Lili will be happier with you. But I'll stay here with Sheltie. This is our home.'

Christa packed some clothes for Lili and took her home to Schmargendorf, then she rang Frau Jochum at the Quadriga to tell her what she had done.

In their turn, Ricarda and Viktoria both tried to persuade Luise to leave the flat, but she refused, repeating, 'This is our home.'

'It's all right as a temporary measure, but it isn't fair to expect Ilse to look after Lili for long,' Ricarda said to Viktoria that evening. 'She's got problems enough with Peter.'

Viktoria agreed, but decided it best to temporize. 'Why don't we leave her there for the time being and see what happens? There may be no more raids, in which case Lili can go back to Luise.'

That night, however, the RAF returned and the people of Berlin reconciled themselves to the fact that their respite was over. Gaping bomb craters appeared where once houses had stood. A pall of smoke and dust hung over whole areas of the city. Cellars that had been emptied of blankets and provisions were hastily replenished. The cellar restaurant of the Hotel Quadriga began to fill with customers.

Again, the night was filled with the wailing of sirens and the criss-cross arcs of searchlights. They filled Luise with a nervous restlessness. Dressed in her long brown coat, she wandered through the cold flat, Sheltie trailing miserably at her heels. From the distance, came the heavy throb of the bombers, then she saw the planes themselves, their bombs dropping through the sky like little sticks. The first explosions rent the air, sending the china clattering in the kitchen and Sepp's photograph tumbling from the mantlepiece.

Sheltie howled and dived under the table. Luise picked up Sepp's picture and held it to her breast. 'It won't be long, my darling. I'll soon be with you again.' Suddenly, she felt oddly calm.

There was a shriek as a bomb fell into a nearby building, a series of grinding thuds as the roof fell in and the walls collapsed. The vibrations shook Luise's building to its very foundations. She heard the clamour of a fire engine. Somewhere, people were screaming. Still the bombs rained down and buildings groaned, toppled and occasionally burst into flames.

She did not hear the bomb that hit her apartment block until it was upon her. It crashed through the roof, exploding upon impact, shattering the windows, throwing furniture high in the air. Huge chunks of plaster fell to the ground. The walls trembled, then, as the roof caved in, lurched in towards her. Sheltie whimpered, dragging herself across the carpet towards Luise.

A massive hole had appeared to one side of the flat, from which billowed clouds of choking dust. Almost reluctantly, the floors tipped towards it, then, suddenly, they gave way. The building swayed and sagged, then fell in upon itself, burying Luise and Sheltie under a mountain of broken masonry.

Early next morning, Viktoria went to Lützow, worried when she could not get through to Luise by telephone. As soon as she saw men from the Rescue Service digging through the debris, she knew what had happened. 'Where are the people who lived here?' she asked. 'My sister's apartment was on the top floor. Her name is Nowak.'

The man wiped a dirty hand across a tired face. 'We rescued the ones in the cellar, but someone said there were a woman and a dog up there. We're trying to find them now.'

He rejoined his colleagues, moving huge chunks of brickwork, lifting heavy beams, pushing aside pieces of furniture, peering down into unexpected holes, calling, 'Is anyone there? Can you hear me?'

Viktoria could not stand the inactivity. If Luise was still alive, she had to find her. If she was dead, she had to know. She stepped across the rubble and started to help the men. 'Here, lady,' one of them said, 'you're not going to do your clothes any good. We'll find her if she's here.'

'To hell with my clothes. I must find my sister.'

'Well, be careful. Sometimes we find unexploded bombs. Other times, the ground sinks in.'

It was heavy, back-breaking work. Gritty dust got under her fingernails and into her hair and eyes. Sometimes she moved one piece of brick, only to start a minor avalanche. Hanging over the whole site was the acrid smell of explosives. From time to time, they would all pause and into the silence a man would call, 'Is anyone there?'

They were joined by former residents, looking for personal belongings. Occasionally, there were shouts of joy that set Viktoria's heart pounding, only to learn someone had found a treasured photograph album or an item of clothing. It was noon before they succeeded in getting through to what had been the entrance hall.

At that moment, Benno arrived, hurrying towards Viktoria across the debris. 'Vicki, I had no idea what had happened or I'd have come earlier. I just assumed you were with Luise.' He put his arm round her. 'They can't find her?'

Tears welled in her eyes and she leaned her head against his shoulder. 'Benno, we should have made her come to the hotel.'

'Darling, you did all you could. Luise insisted on staying.'

'Why didn't she go down to the cellar with the others?'

There was a shout from inside the building. A voice called, 'We've found the dog.'

An hour later, they disinterred Luise's body, recognizable only by her auburn hair and her fur-trimmed coat. They placed it on a stretcher, covered it and carried it away to a waiting van. 'I'm afraid we'll have to ask you to complete a few formalities,' the Rescue Service man said. 'Details about the deceased and so on.'

'I'll deal with those,' Benno said, gruffly. 'Give us a few moments.' He took Viktoria in his arms.

For a long time, she just stood, her face buried in his chest, trying to come to terms with the fact that Luise was dead. Then she lifted her face. 'I loved her so much. And I never showed it. She needed me — and I did nothing for her. Even Christa did more. She looked after Lili. If it had been left to me, Lili would have died too.'

'You kept in touch with her every day. She knew you cared.'

'But I never told her. And now it's too late. Luise is dead. Oh, Benno…'

He caressed her hair with his lips. 'Darling, Luise understood. She loved you. It isn't necessary to tell someone that you love them for love to exist.'

She looked up at him with sudden hope. 'Do you mean that?'

There was a dreadful sadness in his eyes. 'It has to be true. Otherwise there would be no sense in anything.'

'Excuse me, sir…'

Gently, Benno let Viktoria go. 'The car's over there. Wait for me. I shan't be long.'

They buried Luise in Schmargendorf churchyard after a simple and sparsely attended ceremony — Ricarda, Viktoria and Benno, Ilse and Christa, and a few employees of the hotel and Café Jochum.

Ricarda set the tone for all who were present. Erect and dignified, she did not weep for the daughter she had loved. She knew that true grief was passionless and could only be expressed in a silence as deep as death itself. Inspired by her mother's example, Viktoria also appeared calm, although inwardly she was racked with pain. On so many occasions, she had almost got close to her sister only for something to come between them. Now, the finality of death separated them for ever.

They both threw a handful of earth into the grave and the Pastor intoned '…earth to earth, ashes to ashes…'

Lili burst into tears. She was only five and she could not bear the thought that this wooden box in the ground contained her mother's body. She did not understand what had happened to Sheltie.

Christa put her arms protectively round her and whispered, 'Lili, don't be frightened. I'm still here. I'll take care of you.'

Lili looked up at her from huge green eyes. 'But who'll take care of Mama and Sheltie?'

'They've gone to heaven to join your Papa. They'll be happy there.' It was strange, but she could almost hear Luise's voice saying, 'Thank you, Christa. She'll be safe with you.'

Back at the hotel, the discussion soon centred around Lili's future. 'It's been very kind of you to look after her, Ilse, but now she must come and live with Benno and me,' Viktoria said, with a firmness she did not truly feel.

'She's no trouble, is she, Mama? Oh, Aunt Viktoria, let her stay with us,' Christa pleaded, pulling Lili closer to her.

'I want to stay with Christa,' Lili said, putting her arms round Christa's neck.

It was a difficult situation. Ricarda understood that Viktoria and Benno had more than enough to do in the hotel, while Ilse had sufficient worries with a crippled husband. On the other hand, she was an old lady, with nothing but time on her hands and she loved this little granddaughter, who so much resembled herself and Luise. 'Why don't we compromise?' she suggested. 'I propose that Lili lives with me and Christa comes to see her every day. Then we can all share her.'

Lili looked from Ricarda to Christa and gave a wan smile. 'I'd like that.'

CHAPTER SEVENTEEN

Because of air-raid casualties, the Charité needed every spare bed and Peter was sent home. He had become quite expert on crutches, although it would be a long time before he would be able to walk properly on his artificial leg. Each day, however, he made a little more progress and the stump hardened as it grew used to the pressure. He could even laugh at himself, saying that he walked like a toy tin soldier.

When, on Saturday 30 January 1943, Hitler's tenth anniversary, the sirens sounded and the British made their first daylight raid, he was able to make his way down into the cellar unassisted.

Because of the air raid, Göring was an hour late making his broadcast speech to the Reichstag. When he did, it was to speak of Stalingrad. 'A thousand years hence Germans will speak of this battle with reverence and awe, and will remember that in spite of everything, Germany's ultimate victory was decided there... In years to come it will be said of the heroic battle on the Volga: When you come to Germany, say that you have seen us lying at Stalingrad, as our honour and our leaders ordained that we should, for the greater glory of Germany.'

Yes, Peter thought bitterly, *as our leaders ordained that we should...* When would the German people realize that their leaders had led them into an unmitigated defeat?

The following day, Paulus was created a field marshal and over a hundred of the officers with him in Stalingrad promoted. It was meant to appear that they were being rewarded for victory. Peter knew otherwise. Hitler was gambling on the fact that no field marshal in German history had ever surrendered.

Then the lies ran out. Just three days later, a 'Special Bulletin' was heralded by a solemn roll of drums, followed by the second movement of Beethoven's *Fifth Symphony*. The newscaster announced, 'The Battle of Stalingrad has ended. True to their oath to fight to the last breath, the Sixth Army, under the exemplary leadership of Field

Marshal Paulus, has been overcome by the superiority of the enemy and by the unfavourable circumstances confronting our forces... They fought shoulder to shoulder to the last bullet. They died so that Germany could live.' Three days of national mourning were announced.

There were several visitors to the Biederstein home after that. The first was Hans Oster, who told Peter wryly that he had been promoted to Major-General. 'I'm thankful it's not field marshal. No one seems to hold that post for very long!'

He was bitterly angry about Stalingrad. 'My youngest son is there. A boy, sacrificed on the altar of one man's lust for power.'

'I'm sorry.'

'If he dies, I shall hold Hitler personally responsible for his death as I shall for the wanton slaughter of the whole army.' He took his monocle from his eye and cleaned it. 'Peter, the Gestapo are getting suspicious of some of us in the Abwehr. Last August, an underground communist network was uncovered. In November, one of our associates, Schmidhuber, was arrested. We fear he may have implicated Dohnanyi and maybe even Canaris and myself. You may not be aware of this, but I was responsible for warning the Allies in advance of a number of early campaigns — Norway, Holland, Operation Sea Lion...'

Suddenly, Peter understood a lot of things.

Oster continued, 'On top of that, Heydrich's successor, Kaltenbrunner, has it in for Canaris. He wants the Gestapo to take over responsibility for the Abwehr. The net is closing in. We must act quickly.'

Peter's next visitor was General Beck. He had changed so much since the summer that Peter scarcely recognized him. He was very thin and his face had a yellowish hue. 'Sauerbruch looking after you?' he asked. When Peter nodded, he said, 'He keeps trying to get me in for tests. Thinks I may have cancer of the stomach.' He grimaced. 'Why does one's body let one down, just when one most needs one's strength? But that's a question you must have asked yourself, Biederstein.'

'Sauerbruch is a good man. You should let him do his tests. Perhaps he can cure you.'

'Or kill me...' Beck gave a hollow laugh. 'Dear God, the future of Germany depends on us: Oster, worried about his son and in imminent danger of arrest; Tresckow, far away in Russia; you, with only one leg; and myself, an old man sick with cancer. Behind us, we have a few intellectuals, socialists, clergymen and former diplomats. What chance do we stand of success?'

Peter's third visitor was Henning von Tresckow on a brief visit from the Russian front. 'I'm here to report to High Command, but I'm using the opportunity to forge a stronger link between Berlin and our centre in the east.'

Peter looked down at his leg. 'I feel so damned impotent, Tresckow. Just when I was working myself into a position of trust with Hitler, I was immobilized. I shall never kill him now.'

'Perhaps there is a more important task for you, Biederstein,' Tresckow said slowly. 'Others of us at Army Group Centre are working on ways to assassinate Hitler. It is here, in Berlin, that our organization is weak. Beck is gravely ill. Oster and his colleagues at the Abwehr are in danger. Only the military remains above suspicion. As soon as you are well enough, you must get transferred to the General Staff at Reserve Army Headquarters and prepare to take charge of the *coup d'état*.'

'Me?' Peter echoed faintly.

'You are the only one with the necessary experience and strength of character, now that Beck is ill. Your name will command loyalty from both officers and men.'

Peter could feel the almost physical weight of the burden of responsibility Tresckow was laying on his shoulders, but instinctively he knew his friend was right. He took a deep breath. 'I have worried about the lack of leadership, but I haven't seen myself in the role of leader, only as an instrument in getting rid of Hitler. Tresckow, I have never sought power for its own sake. You can be assured that if I gain it, I shall not abuse it.'

Tresckow nodded. 'I know. The von Biedersteins are an honourable family.'

After that, Peter wasted no more time. He might be crippled, but that did not affect his ability to work from behind a desk. He had the contacts to enable him to obtain a posting to the staff of General Fromm, Commander-in-Chief of the Reserve Army, at the former War Ministry in the Bendlerstrasse. What was more, there was a desperate need for officers of his calibre.

On Monday, 8 February, a car drove up outside the Biederstein house in Schmargendorf to take him to his new office, working with Colonel-General Friedrich Olbricht, an old friend and early member of the resistance, in charge of the Supply Section of the Reserve Army.

He found Olbricht in a despondent mood. Six years older than Peter, he had recently lost a son at the front. 'You are lucky only to have a daughter, Biederstein,' he said.

Peter gave a thin smile and changed the subject. 'Oster and Tresckow have told you I am on your side?'

Olbricht nodded. 'God knows we are few enough and, the longer the war continues, the fewer we become.'

Peter had not come this far to give in to defeatism. He threw himself into his work, using his every free moment to renew old acquaintances and muster up support in Berlin for the resistance movement. He was in a unique situation. He was a respected officer of the old school. His work required him to maintain contact with the Abwehr and the field commanders. He knew the strengths and positions of all the different armies. To a certain extent he could manipulate the detailing of troops and supplies.

Before long, he recognized an opportunity to keep in touch with other members of the resistance without drawing attention to them or himself. Every day, Christa went to see Lili at the Quadriga. A routine was established, whereby Peter's driver dropped Peter off at the War Ministry, then continued with Christa to the hotel. Frequently, in the evening, Peter met her there, first stopping off in the bar for a drink with friends or associates, like General Oster, Dr Dohnanyi, or fellow officers on leave from the front.

Never obtrusive, always there when needed, very little escaped Hasso Annuschek's notice. From snippets of conversation he had overheard, he had a very shrewd idea of General Oster and Dr Dohnanyi's feelings about the Nazis and when they entered the bar, he was careful always to guide them to a table well away from the Gestapo's hidden listening devices.

When General von Biederstein began joining them, Hasso felt a moment's apprehension, but a chance word or two soon satisfied him that the Count was on what Hasso called 'their side'. He had no idea what the men were planning, but he was prepared to help anyone who was against the Nazis. After all, Hasso was one of the few remaining socialists in Berlin.

So far as the SS guards were concerned, they had no reason to suspect a general with only one leg — a hero from the Russian front.

Inevitably, as a result of Christa's frequent visits to the hotel, the two families were brought closer together, but it developed into an easier relationship than either Viktoria or Benno would have envisaged. Peter treated Viktoria with the polite familiarity of an old friend, who had more important things on his mind than a long past love affair, never referring to her visit to the Charité or to Stefan.

Gradually, Viktoria felt easier in his presence. His former arrogance gone, he revealed himself as a man with human doubts and failings. Sometimes, she caught him exchanging a quick word with Hasso, calling the barman by his first name, something he would never have dreamed of doing in the past. And he was particularly gentle with Lili, showing her unexpected kindness and buying her little presents.

Benno, too, slowly found himself growing used to his cousin's presence. Once he had seen him as a threat to his marriage, but now he could only feel pity and a certain admiration for his courage.

In the meantime, the war came ever nearer to home. The air raids increased in intensity, robbing them of their sleep, inflicting ever greater casualties, making more and more people homeless. In North Africa, Montgomery's Eighth Army captured Tripoli and Rommel's troops were pushed back into Tunisia. Thousands more German soldiers were killed, wounded or taken prisoner.

Throughout the country, the mood of the people changed. On 16 February, students staged an anti-Nazi demonstration in Munich. It was quelled by the police and SS, but not before sympathy rebellions had broken out in Frankfurt, Mannheim, Stuttgart, Vienna and the Ruhr. The very fact that the revolt was so widespread meant it could not be concealed from public knowledge.

Two days later, as the leaders of the Munich Revolt were being condemned to death in the People's Court, Dr Goebbels addressed a huge crowd in the Berlin Sportpalast. In an eloquent speech, charged with emotion, he urged the need for total war. He stressed the necessity to mobilize the nation's economy as well as the military, explaining that longer hours must be worked, more stringent economies and greater personal sacrifices made. Only thus could Germany protect herself from the danger that threatened from the east. Only thus could Europe be saved from the communist terror.

An immediate consequence of this speech was that all luxury restaurants and expensive places of entertainment were ordered to close. Anxiously, Viktoria and Benno waited to learn how this would affect them. They were fortunate. Café Jochum did not come into the luxury category and the authorities were persuaded that an hotel de luxe could not function without a restaurant.

However, even with Benno's extensive network of contacts, the food shortages he had foreseen were making themselves felt. Throughout Europe, production was totally geared towards the war. In the occupied territories, land workers had been recruited into the armed forces. The meals Maître Mazzoni now concocted bore no resemblance to the exquisite dishes for which he was fabled.

The following Monday, a distraught Monika telephoned Viktoria from Fürstenmark. 'I've just had a letter saying that Hans has been taken prisoner of war.'

'Oh, Monika darling, how dreadful!' Helplessly, Viktoria tried to find adequate words to convey her sympathy, but all she could think was, *At least he isn't dead.*

'I don't know where he is, or anything,' Monika wailed. 'All the letter says is that he was taken prisoner. I'm sure he was in Africa. Do you think he's still in Africa? Or do the British take their prisoners somewhere else?'

Viktoria had no idea. 'I'm sure he'll be all right. I'm sure the British treat their prisoners well — not like the Russians. When the war is over, he'll be sent home.'

Monika burst into hysterical sobs. 'Mama, I'm frightened. Can I come to Berlin?'

'If you really want to, darling, of course you can. But don't you think you'd be wiser to stay at Fürstenmark? We're in constant danger of air raids here. The children are much safer in the country.' For a moment, Viktoria wondered whether she should go to Fürstenmark, but what good would that do? It wouldn't bring Hans back. Then she had an idea. 'Why don't you go and stay with Hans's parents for a while? I'm sure Frau König would be pleased to have her grandchildren to look after.'

'Yes, I could do, I suppose.' After another ten minutes, Monika had calmed down and decided to do just that. With a sigh of relief, Viktoria replaced the receiver. But a feeling of uneasiness remained. It was almost as if Hans was symbolic of the entire German Army being taken into captivity.

Five nights later, the RAF staged a massive raid on Essen. The Baron arrived in Benno's office the next day in ill humour, informing Benno sourly, 'Our factories took the brunt of it. The worst damage we've suffered anywhere so far. Most of our stores totally destroyed and some of our underground shops badly hit. I'm meeting Speer in a quarter of an hour. Going to tell him the defences around the Ruhr have got to be increased. Of course, I know what he'll say. The more flak guns and guncrews used in the Ruhr, the fewer there are for the Eastern Front. But I can't help that.'

In a sudden moment of sympathy, Benno wondered how it must feel to be very old and see one's life's work in danger of being bombed out of existence.

Then the Baron brightened. 'Speer and I went to Peenemünde the other day to inspect the work our research boys have been doing. Conventional warfare will soon be a thing of the past, boy. You must have heard of the new "secret weapons" we're building? Well, they're becoming reality. We have built a rocket missile — a remote-controlled, flying bomb. This is the weapon that will decide the war.

The Führer has just signed an order for mass production. They'll flatten England to the ground.'

Benno's feeling of sympathy was fast fading. 'And in the meantime, we don't have enough tanks, planes and guns for Manstein in Russia or Rommel in Africa,' he observed drily.

'Before long, tanks, planes and guns will be outdated. These new rockets mean we have grazed the frontiers of space. Work we are doing on the cyclotron could lead to the development of the most powerful weapon of all — the atom bomb.'

'An atom bomb?' Benno repeated in horror.

The Baron shrugged. 'The Americans are developing one and I've got a feeling they may get there first. We were wrong to let the Jewish scientists go. Physicists like Einstein and Ascher would be invaluable to us now, but the Führer wouldn't listen to reason. Always hated the Jews. Extraordinary to let one's personal prejudices influence one to the detriment of one's own country.'

'Will either side have built an atom bomb before the war ends?'

'If they do, it will be the end of the war.'

'Or the end of the world…'

First there had been his father's talk of poison gas, now it was other secret weapons. Certain aspects of this war troubled Benno to the depth of his being. He helped his father heave himself out of his chair and accompanied him to the door of the hotel, where Gottlieb Linke was waiting in the Baron's Mercedes. 'Do you think Germany can still win the war, Father?'

The eyes the Baron turned on him had lost none of their old cunning. 'The Kaiser lost Germany in the last war, boy, and the Führer will probably lose this one. So long as Kraus makes a profit, it doesn't worry me.'

'Does patriotism mean nothing to you?'

'Patriotism?' the Baron snorted. 'More evil deeds are carried out in the name of patriotism than any other principle, except perhaps religion.' With that, he lumbered across to his limousine.

Benno turned to find Peter standing beside him, a strange expression on his face, as he watched the Baron drive away. 'Has it ever occurred to you, Benno, that men like him are the only ones to profit from a war — whoever wins or loses?'

Suddenly, Benno had to ask Peter the same question he had just asked his father. 'Do you believe we can win the war?'

'No,' Peter replied definitely. 'Stalingrad and El Alamein were the turning point.'

'Doesn't Hitler realize that?'

'Hitler will never admit defeat. He will go on fighting until there is not a single house standing or a single person left alive in this country.' There was no doubting his bitterness.

Benno looked at him in surprise, wondering if he might have misjudged his cousin, if they might not have more in common than he had ever imagined. 'When I joined the Party, I did not know I was helping to lead Germany into disaster,' he said slowly.

Softly, Peter replied, 'You aren't the only one. I believed I was doing the right thing when I swore my oath of allegiance.'

The time was right. All they needed was the opportunity and this was suddenly presented to them when Hitler announced his intention to visit Army Group Centre at Smolensk on 13 March. Oster told Peter excitedly that Tresckow and Schlabrendorff were in possession of a bomb, which they would conceal in Hitler's plane while he was at lunch, timed to explode while the aircraft was on its return journey to Rastenburg.

General Beck, having finally been operated on for cancer, was far too ill to participate and certainly to take over the leadership, and this role naturally devolved onto Peter's shoulders. For the first time, he found himself confronted with the very real problems of organizing a *coup d'état*, of gambling on the loyalties of officers and men, of having to work furtively so as not to alert the suspicions of the Gestapo.

In the process, he also encountered another obstacle — his own superior officer, General Fromm. A beefy man, older than Peter, Fromm was a typical example of a career officer, who had managed to survive thus far without incurring Hitler's wrath. Like many other generals, he knew of Peter's and Olbricht's plans, but neither supported nor opposed them. Tacitly, he gave Peter to understand that if the coup succeeded, he would be on their side. If it failed, there was no doubt that he would be the first to deny all knowledge of the plot and to denounce them as traitors.

When Peter described his problems to Oster, the Abwehr man smiled confidently. 'Once Emil is dead, Fromm and the other generals will rally to our cause. They know they cannot win this war.'

Peter wished he could feel so certain.

Saturday, 13 March 1943, was the most anxious day in Peter's life. He ordered his driver to take him early to the War Ministry, where he and Olbricht went over all their arrangements several times. Units of the Reserve Army in and around Berlin were all on alert, supposedly in readiness for an exercise. In practice, their targets were the Chancellery and the Ministries, as well as holding their own garrisons. Once the news was telephoned through from Rastenburg of the Führer's death, radio messages would be sent to all field commanders announcing that the *coup d'état* had taken place and the new military regime was in control.

As the hours passed, Peter grew increasingly aware of the weakness of these arrangements. They were assuming that General Fromm would be on their side; that the Reserve Army would obey their orders; that the field commanders would welcome the news of Hitler's death; that the SS would not turn against the Army; that none of the other Party leaders would assume control on Hitler's death. Peter realized that, although they had discussed in general terms areas of responsibility for the members of the new military regime, there was no fixed programme, no declaration to read to the people.

Slowly, very slowly, the afternoon passed and no telephone call came from Rastenburg. The tension mounted. 'It must mean that the bomb's gone off,' Olbricht said finally.

At that moment, the telephone rang. It was Tresckow. 'Call off the operation,' he said. 'The aircraft has landed safely.'

White-faced, Peter sank back in his chair, not knowing whether to feel relief or disappointment. 'Perhaps it is for the best,' he said eventually. 'We are still far from ready.'

Olbricht nodded soberly. 'The worst thing that could happen would be a failed putsch.'

It was Monday before they learned what had happened, when Fabian von Schlabrendorff arrived in Berlin. Peter met him in the Quadriga bar. The young man was bitterly disappointed. 'The bomb failed to go off. The fuse-timing was faulty. I've brought the fuse here to show General Oster and Dr Dohnanyi.'

'There will be other opportunities,' Peter assured him.

'But not as good. The advantage of these particular bombs is that they are silent,' Schlabrendorff explained. 'Their disadvantage is the ten-minute detonating device. Unless we can smuggle another one into a plane or a train, it means whoever is staging the attack has to stay with the bomb until the very last moment. That means a suicide mission.'

Before the week was out, a second opportunity presented itself. The following Sunday was Heroes' Memorial Day when Hitler was attending a ceremony and exhibition of captured Russian war materiel at the Armoury in Berlin. Colonel Baron von Gersdorff bravely volunteered to go with a bomb in his pocket and be blown up with Hitler.

There was no time to improve their arrangements. Once again the Reserves were placed on alert. Once again, all they could do was hope and pray. On Sunday, Peter and Olbricht were both on duty at the Bendlerstrasse, listening to the live broadcast from the Armoury. First there was a performance of Bruckner's *Seventh Symphony*, Then Hitler gave a short speech. The palms of Peter's hands were damp. The radio reporter announced that the Führer and his entourage were entering the museum. A few minutes later, he said, in obvious surprise, that the Führer had left again.

Olbricht looked at his watch and shook his head. 'Gersdorff's detonator needed ten minutes. There was no time for it to have been activated. Another attempt failed!'

In his heart of hearts, Peter could not feel regret. When he saw Oster the following day, he said, 'The exercise has been useful if only to show up the enormity of the undertaking we are proposing. Above all else, it's shown up our weaknesses — both of our organization and the assassination itself. It is not enough to kill Hitler. Next time, we must think of taking out the entire Party hierarchy — so that the country is left like a headless chicken — so that the Armed Forces and the people have no choice but to accept our regime. And we have a lot of work to do before we are that ready.'

Oster looked at him sombrely. 'We don't have that much time. Any minute now, the Gestapo will strike…'

Nobody paid much attention to the two Gestapo officers who marched peremptorily through the foyer of the Hotel Quadriga in the late morning of Monday, 5 April, flashed their passes at the guard on the lift to the fourth floor and disappeared. When more Gestapo men appeared half an hour later, Herr Brandt brought their presence to Benno's attention. 'Something strange seems to be happening on the fourth floor. There must be twenty Gestapo men up there now.'

'But those are the Abwehr offices.' Puzzled, Benno followed the General Manager into the foyer.

After a while, the lift descended, bearing several Gestapo officers carrying large bags bulging with papers, which they carried through the foyer and into the waiting cars. After more trips, throughout which armed guards stood watch over the vehicles, they drove away.

Benno was not altogether surprised to receive a visit, late that afternoon, from two more uniformed visitors. They introduced themselves as Dr Roeder, a legal officer from the Judge Advocate's department, and SS-Untersturmführer Sonderegger of the Gestapo.

Dr Roeder started pleasantly enough, by apologizing for any inconvenience caused to the hotel. Then he said, 'Herr Kraus, I am in charge of an investigation, the nature of which I cannot reveal, beyond the fact that it concerns a conspiracy against the State.'

Benno's heart lurched. The first time it had been Stefan, the second time Mortimer Allen. Who was it on this occasion?

Roeder's eyes narrowed. 'I believe your son was a colleague of General Oster?'

He nodded, suddenly remembering Oster's comment about the Gestapo and the Abwehr being rival Intelligence services.

'Did your son ever mention any of Oster's contacts? Did he ever talk about Dr Dohnanyi, Pastor Bonhoeffer, Dr Goerdeler, Herr Hassell, General Beck…?'

Was Roeder really trying to tell him that these men — pillars of Berlin society — were part of a conspiracy against the State? 'The names you mention are all familiar to me, but not because of Stefan. He never talked about his work. Dr Dohnanyi often visits the Abwehr offices on the fourth floor. As for the others...'

'Your cousin, General Count von Biederstein, has been noticed in the Quadriga bar, particularly in the company of General Oster and Dr Dohnanyi.'

Benno looked at him in genuine perplexity. 'My cousin is on the Staff of the Reserve Army. I imagine his work often brings him into contact with the Abwehr. General Oster is certainly an old friend of the family...'

Roeder stood up. 'I recommend that he is more selective in his choice of friends in future. Dohnanyi has been arrested. Oster has been suspended from duty pending the outcome of our investigations.'

Benno tried to conceal his shock. Hesitantly, he asked, 'May I ask if this affects the Abwehr offices on the fourth floor?'

Dr Roeder gave a thin smile. 'Accommodation is at a premium in this city, Herr Kraus. I assume the Abwehr will remain.'

Untersturmführer Sonderegger spoke for the first time. 'However, the security guard on your hotel will be increased.'

Benno saw them to the door, then stood looking down Unter den Linden towards the Brandenburg Gate. At that moment, Peter's car drew up. The driver got out, went round to open the passenger door and handed Peter his crutches.

Benno hurried down the steps. God knew, he owed his cousin nothing, but in all conscience he could not allow him to go unaware of the danger in which he stood. 'Peter, I think you should know what has happened today. I have just had a visit from a Dr Roeder...'

Peter paled as he listened to Benno's news. 'So Oster was right,' he murmured.

'And the other names Dr Roeder mentioned? They are not Abwehr personnel...'

Peter shook his head. 'Benno, don't ask questions. The less you know the safer you will be.' Composing his features, he swung through the foyer and into the bar, as if nothing untoward had occurred.

Benno watched him go, positive suddenly that Peter, too, was part of the conspiracy.

During the next few days, Peter learned that Dohnanyi and Pastor Bonhoeffer had been arrested, while a Gestapo guard was keeping watch over General Beck in hospital. Then he heard that the Gestapo had apparently found some incriminating papers in Dohnanyi's office. Canaris was doing his best to defend Dohnanyi, but in doing so was placing himself in grave danger. Although Oster hadn't actually been arrested, he was *hors de combat*. Hassell, Goerdeler and others of their associates were under close surveillance.

During April, the Abwehr offices on the Tirpitz Ufer were bombed. Admiral Canaris and his staff moved to OKW headquarters at Zossen, except for the few who remained on the fourth floor of the Hotel Quadriga. In both places, their every move was watched either by Hitler's generals or the Gestapo.

Tresckow and Schlabrendorff on the Russian front and Peter von Biederstein and Friedrich Olbricht continued to work unsuspected. Apart from a few intellectuals and socialists, who were powerless to do much, the *coup d'état* now rested in their hands.

At the beginning of May, Peter appeared at the hotel for the first time without crutches, walking on his artificial leg with only a stick for support. To celebrate his recovery, he and Ilse invited Ricarda, Viktoria and Benno to dine in the cellar restaurant, while Christa looked after Lili.

They were just finishing their meal when a man approached their table. 'Herr Kraus, I wonder if you can spare me a few moments?' It was the Dutchman, Kok van der Jong.

'Of course. Is the matter private or will you join us here?'

Van der Jong looked doubtfully at Peter and Ilse and Benno hurried to introduce them. 'My cousins, General Count and Countess von Biederstein. Herr van der Jong.'

Still the Dutchman seemed ill-at-ease. 'It's all right,' Benno said quietly. 'There are no hidden microphones at this table.'

A waiter brought another chair and van der Jong sank into it. Benno poured him a glass of wine. The Dutchman took a large gulp then said, 'Herr Kraus, things are happening of which you should be aware. Since Speer's policy of industrial decentralization, I have been travelling extensively. I have just been in Cracow at the new Kraus chemical factory. The train was two hours late leaving Cracow and when we set off there was no heat or light.'

With trembling fingers, he lit a cigarette. 'I was alone in my compartment. Since there was no blackout danger, I lifted the blind to let in the moonlight, even though the window would not close properly and there was a fearful draught. About six this morning, the train drew into Schlachtenhausen and, although it was not a scheduled halt, it stopped.

'There was a freight train in the station, parked in a siding — I assumed it was delivering supplies to the labour camp or the Kraus factory. Then I saw the trucks contained people. Still I thought little of it. All Kraus factories employ slave labour from the East. We were still waiting when SS guards opened the truck doors and let them out. Every one of them wore a yellow Star of David.'

Around them was a steady hum of conversation. At a nearby table, a group of SS officers were having some kind of celebration. The pianist was playing a miscellany of folk songs. Waiters hurried in and out of the kitchen with loaded trays.

'It is two years since I visited Schlachtenhausen,' the Dutchman continued. 'In the meantime, it has grown considerably. The Kraus factory is situated on one side of the camp. On the other side, there were huge new buildings with tall chimneys, belching smoke.'

He drained his glass. 'I have seen buildings like those before, but under very different circumstances. I have smelt that nauseating stench before, but never so strongly. A few moments later, the guard came to my compartment and angrily ordered me to lower the blind, threatening to arrest me for disobeying railway regulations. There was nothing I could do. I lowered the blind, showed him my Party card and travel warrant and he agreed to forget the matter.'

Peter clenched his glass so tightly that it broke. 'I did not know it had gone this far...'

Ricarda's face was pale. 'What were those buildings?'

Kok van der Jong ground out his cigarette. 'Crematoria. The smell from the chimneys was that of burning human flesh. Then I understood why the chemical factory in Cracow was manufacturing such vast amounts of hydrogen cyanide. I had heard rumours of extermination camps in Poland. Now I know they are true. The Jews I saw were going to their death.'

'Next door to a Kraus factory,' Benno exclaimed in horror. 'Is my father aware of this?' He heard the Baron saying, *More evil deeds are done in the name of patriotism than any other principle...*

'Herr Kraus, your father knows everything that goes on within his organization.' Kok van der Jong stood up. 'There is a train for Amsterdam at midnight. If it leaves on time, I can be home tomorrow. Then I shall resign from Kraus.' He scanned their shocked faces. 'I thank God I am not a German. One day, you are all going to have to pay a heavy price for what is happening in Poland. Now you know about it, for God's sake try to stop the madness before it is too late.'

For a long time after he had gone, they sat in silence. A waiter cleared away Peter's broken glass and Benno ordered cognac. Eventually, Viktoria said shakily, 'So Professor Ascher was right.' She related what he had said about the final solution of the Jewish problem.

'Why didn't you tell me this before?' Benno demanded.

'Benno, there was nothing you could have done.'

Peter drained his brandy glass. 'I think the time has come for us to be honest with each other. We all supported Hitler to begin with. Now, for different reasons, we have become disillusioned. If we still had any doubts, what we have heard tonight should have convinced us that Herr van der Jong is right: the madness must be stopped before it is too late.'

Outside the air-raid sirens began to wail. The piano music grew louder. The SS officers at the neighbouring table burst into drunken song. Someone shouted for more wine.

Peter said, 'I am one of a group of people who has decided that the only way to stop the madness is to strike at the very root of the evil. We are going to stage a *coup d'état.*'

An SS man clambered on to the table and began to dance to the frenzied applause of his colleagues.

Still stunned by the revelation of his father's role in what sounded fearfully like a mass extermination programme, Benno felt little surprise at learning that his earlier suspicions were correct and that his cousin was part of a resistance movement.

'You are part of a conspiracy to overthrow Hitler?' Viktoria whispered.

'Not just overthrow him — but kill him.'

'It is the only way,' Ilse said quietly. 'When Hitler is dead, a military regime, with Peter as its leader, will take control of the country. Then a democratic government will be elected, which will negotiate an honourable peace with the Allies.'

With trembling fingers, Viktoria reached for a cigarette. Her voice scarcely audible, she murmured, 'All those years ago, Stefi tried...'

Peter leaned forward to light her cigarette, gazing at her intensely across the flickering flame of his lighter. 'For a long time I have had misgivings about Hitler, but it was Luise who finally made me decide that this was the only thing to do. She reminded me of how Stefan had tried to prevent a war and how I had branded him a traitor. She showed me that it was my duty to complete what he had started, not only for the sake of my country but for our children, for Lili and for Christa and Stefan...'

In the moment of quiet that followed, it seemed to Benno that his heart stopped beating. To Ilse or Ricarda, Peter's words must sound as if he had been fired by the idealistic aspirations of his daughter's former suitor. But from the urgent tone of Peter's voice and the fixed, almost painful intensity in his eyes as he looked at Viktoria, Benno was convinced that somehow — presumably from Luise — he had learned the truth and knew that Stefan was his son. But suddenly it did not matter. The past was unimportant compared to the evils they were facing today.

Benno took a deep breath and held out his hand to his cousin, his old rival and his wife's former lover. 'If you believe this is the only solution, I want you to know I am on your side. If there is any way I can help you, I will.'

Peter turned away from Viktoria and took Benno's outstretched hand, unmistakable compassion in his eyes. 'Thank you, Benno.'

'So will I,' Ricarda murmured.

'And I,' Viktoria said.

When they were in bed, Benno took Viktoria in his arms and kissed her very tenderly. 'I love you. Whatever happens, I want you to know that I have always loved you and always tried to do what was best for you. I'm sorry I have made mistakes along the way.'

Viktoria buried her head in his shoulder. 'It doesn't matter. Nothing matters compared to the dreadful things that are going on in the world.' But she could not help wondering what Stefan would say if he knew how much he had misjudged his real father.

After that, she and Benno seemed to grow closer. Apart from anything else, Benno could no longer do without her help in the hotel. Ricarda took Lili and Christa to Heiligensee for the summer, leaving Benno and Viktoria together at the Quadriga, every room of which was occupied, as air raids made more people homeless or robbed them of their offices. To Herr Brandt's disgust, most of their office personnel were now women, while many of the kitchen staff and chambermaids were Poles and Ukrainians.

Gradually, Viktoria took over most of Benno's paperwork, while Benno had his hands more than full with the hotel's finances and the administration. In a way, it was like the early days of their marriage.

Baron Heinrich had told Benno that whether or not Germany won the war, Kraus would not lose. That spring, he became less certain. For the first time in his life, he was being overtaken by events beyond his control. One was his own health. He began having dizzy spells and headaches. They were of short duration, but none the less debilitating, making his mind go blank for several hours afterwards. He told nobody about them, for he knew they would insist he sought medical advice and he had no faith in doctors.

In the meantime, reports poured in to his bunker office beneath Kraus Haus on the Behrenstrasse of the gradual destruction of his empire. His factories in western Europe were suffering most, from constant bombing raids. Since Kok van der Jong had gone, there was nobody the Baron could trust to visit these works. He had to rely on the word of local managers, who, although German, lacked intrinsic loyalty to Kraus.

Kraushaven and the former van der Jong shipyard in Rotterdam had been so severely damaged as to render them useless. In any event, German U-boats were suddenly proving no match against the integrated air and surface escorts accompanying Allied convoys in the Atlantic.

So far, the Kraus works in Silesia and Poland were unscathed and it was to these areas that the Baron had moved much of the production from Berlin and the Ruhr. However, the Russian Air Force was inflicting great damage on troop concentrations, railways and air bases in German-held Russian territories. It was no great distance from the Ukraine to Cracow, even less from Cracow to Breslau.

By far the worst area to suffer was the Ruhr. At the end of April, Ernst reported the fifty-fifth raid on Essen since the outbreak of war. The town was virtually devastated and at one time or another, all the Kraus factories had been hit. Ancillary works in Bochum, Dortmund, Wuppertal and Duisberg had been badly damaged. Ernst had moved many of his facilities out to Kassel, Hamm and Paderborn, fifty miles or more into the country. Grudgingly, the Baron had to admit that the boy was coping well under great difficulties.

Very early in the morning of 17 May, the telephone rang at the Baron's villa, rousing Gottlieb Linke from a sound, dreamless sleep. 'Can't even get a night's rest on bomb-free nights,' he grumbled to Martha, as he staggered out of bed and pulled on his dressing gown. 'The old boy's got a phone in his bedroom. Why doesn't he answer it?' The telephone continued its strident clamour. 'All right, all right, I'm coming.'

The nearest phone was on the upstairs landing. Gottlieb lifted the receiver. 'Heil Hitler! Residence of Baron Heinrich von Kraus zu Essen. Linke speaking.'

'This is Professor Speer. Tell the Herr Baron that there has been a disaster. The RAF have bombed our hydroelectric plants in the Ruhr. The Möhne Dam has been shattered. We don't know yet about the other dams. I am flying down to inspect the damage. There is room on my plane if he wishes to accompany me.'

Gottlieb was suddenly wide awake. 'Yes, Herr Professor. One moment, please.'

He hurried along the corridor, knocked on the Baron's door and entered the room. Baron Heinrich was sitting up in bed, reaching out towards the telephone on the bedside table, a vacant expression on his face. 'Herr Baron! It's Professor Speer. The English have bombed the Ruhr dams!'

The Baron's mouth worked, but only unintelligible sounds emerged.

Gottlieb stared at his employer in horror. 'Herr Baron, what's the matter?'

Baron Heinrich slumped back against the pillows.

Gottlieb pressed the bell that rang in his and Martha's room, then hurried back to the telephone. 'Professor Speer, I am sorry but the Baron is indisposed. He won't be able to come with you. May I suggest you liaise with Herr Ernst in Essen?'

'Yes, of course.'

Martha was standing beside the Baron's bed when he returned to the room. 'He's had some kind of fit. We must call a doctor.'

'And Herr Benno,' Gottlieb said decisively.

Dr Blattner and Benno arrived simultaneously. While the doctor took the Baron's pulse and blood pressure and listened to his heart, Benno and the Linkes looked on anxiously. The Baron's eyes were open and he was still making pathetic attempts to talk. 'Don't worry,' the doctor assured him. 'You've been lucky this time. You'll soon be right as rain.'

On the landing, out of the Baron's earshot, he told Benno, 'He's had a slight stroke, a warning that if he doesn't take things easier, something worse could happen.'

'Shouldn't he go to hospital?'

'I don't think that's necessary. If it occurs again, we could take him in for tests, but all they will show up is a hardening of the arteries and other effects of old age. However, having said that, he must rest for several weeks.'

Gottlieb suddenly remembered Professor Speer's message and told them about the disaster in the Ruhr.

'Good God!' Benno rushed to the telephone, but the operator informed him that all lines to Essen were out of order.

Benno returned to the Quadriga, more worried about Ernst than his father. He spent the day trying to discover what had happened in the Ruhr and, most essentially, whether Ernst was all right, but if anybody knew anything, they were not prepared to tell him.

He was about to give up for the evening and go to bed, when Ernst rang. 'Our phones have just been reconnected.'

'Ernst, are you all right?'

'I'm exhausted,' Ernst replied simply. 'I have never seen anything like this in my life and I hope I never do again. They wrecked the Möhne and hit the Eder Dam. Thousands of homes, bridges and factories have been swept away in the floods. The electric plant is totally destroyed. Fortunately, they didn't breach the Sorpe Valley Dam. As it is, the damage will take months to repair.'

'I'm afraid I have more bad news. Father has had a minor stroke. The doctor says he will soon recover, but he won't be able to work for several weeks.'

'Oh God... I can't leave Essen,' Ernst said slowly. Benno could imagine his frustration at having control so near his grasp and yet not being able to reach it. 'I'll have to send Werner.'

By the time Werner arrived from Silesia, two days later, the Baron was much better. He still had difficulty using his hands and his speech was slurred, but his brain was remarkably agile.

When Werner explained the damage in the Ruhr, he stuttered, 'Used only nineteen planes? W-W-Werner, those nineteen planes nearly achieved what none of the thousand bomber raids have done.' He gasped for breath. 'If they'd got the Sorpe Dam, they could have brought the entire armaments industry to a halt.' His head waggled grotesquely. 'So the British have changed their tactics. As well as attacking specific targets, they are beginning to attack our nerve-centres: our power supplies and com-communications. Now the future begins to look extremely black.'

If it looked bleak for Germany and Kraus Industries, it looked bright for Werner. Confined to the villa, the Baron relied on him to bring all important papers and orders to his attention and, in many cases, to deal with them. Werner took full advantage of this opportunity to become initiated into the secrets of the vast Kraus empire, as well as ingratiating himself with his grandfather.

After they received the results of Wendel's test flights in the new Me-262 jet fighter, for which Kraus Aviation had provided electrical components, Werner said, 'If priority were given to its production, we could win the air war. Why does the Führer still insist that tanks are more important?'

Baron Heinrich listened approvingly. As he had always suspected, the boy was bright. 'Tanks are needed for the war in Russia and that's a holy cause with H-H-Hitler, although he will never win it.' Although the Baron's speech was almost recovered, the occasional stammer still occurred.

'Then why does he continue?'

'Because he will never admit to making a wrong decision.'

A couple of days later, when Admiral Dönitz suspended all U-boat operations against Atlantic convoys, Werner commented, 'We're playing right into the enemy's hands. Not only are we allowing supplies through to England, but we're giving them every opportunity to bring in troops and equipment from America to launch an invasion. Why is there such a delay in the new U-boat programme?'

'Power has gone to the F-F-Führer's head, boy. He won't listen to advice. The worse things get, the more c-c-convinced he becomes that everyone else is incompetent and that he alone can lead the country to victory. What we have to do is work out how we can turn his mistakes to our advantage.'

Werner smiled. The implications of the word 'we' were not lost on him.

Even when the Baron was fully recovered, he kept Werner in Berlin, appointing the former General Manager, Helmuth Stegmann, as Chief Executive of his Silesian operations. The slight stroke had been a lesson that, despite his belief in his own immortality, time was starting to run out.

Werner had been in Berlin a month when the Baron received a demand for gift tax on the shares he had transferred to his two grandsons. 'The timing is excellent,' he grunted. 'The tax is due on a current valuation of the property. Since so many of our assets have been destroyed, the shares have a paper value of only a quarter of their worth when I transferred them a year ago.'

Werner looked at him thoughtfully. 'I understand that you are only talking about paper values, Grandfather. But the air raids must be putting some smaller firms totally out of business. When a similar thing happened in the 1920s, you managed to acquire a large number of bankrupt companies very cheaply, didn't you?'

'But they still had premises, equipment and labour, boy. Now, we're talking about bomb-sites.'

'No, Grandfather, we're talking about land. Take Essen, for instance. Whatever happens, the resources of the Ruhr mean that it will always be an industrial centre. If you buy bomb-sites now, we could own most of Essen by the time the war is over.'

The Baron's eyes narrowed. Werner was indeed a chip off the old block. 'We'll set up a new company. The land can be purchased from the income accumulating to you and Norbert in the trust. That way, it will cost me nothing and nobody will know they are selling to Kraus. You work out the details with Duschek, boy.'

On 5 July, the Kursk offensive began, which Hitler declared would decide the war, claiming that the new Tiger tanks would smash the Russian defences. A week later, the Russians launched a massive counter-offensive and Hitler was forced to order the German troops to withdraw. Again, Baron Heinrich was proved right.

In the meantime, Allied troops had invaded Sicily, their first step towards the Italian mainland. On 25 July, a contact of the Baron at the Foreign Ministry confidentially informed him that there had been a palace revolution in Italy, as a result of which Mussolini had been forced to resign. King Victor Emmanuel had appointed Field Marshal Badoglio as the new Prime Minister. 'So much for Italy,' the Baron said to Werner. 'It won't be long before Badoglio gives in to the Allies. The Italians always were cowards.'

He didn't have much time to think about Italy, however, for that night the RAF staged a devastating raid on Hamburg. Within hours, the city was engulfed in a horrific fire storm. Explosive bombs had disrupted the city's water supplies, so that the fire brigades were unable to fight the massive conflagrations that spread from building to building and were still raging three days later. Over a period of a week, the British bombed the city by night and the Americans by day. Tens of thousands died or were injured. Factories, warehouses, wharves and ships were burned to ashes.

That same week there was another fearsome attack on the industrial sector of Essen, starting more raging fires, on aircraft works at Kassel and vital machine tools factories in Remscheid.

By then, Landgut AG had been formed. Its manager was Eberhard Hecker, a lawyer by training, invalided out of the Army. Not even Hecker knew the shareholders of Landgut AG — he had no idea he was working for Kraus. He was interviewed and selected by Dr Erwin Duschek, at Duschek & Duschek's offices on the third floor of Haus Jochum, above Café Jochum on the Kurfürstendamm. His offices were a suite in the same building. The flames in Essen and Hamburg had hardly been extinguished before Eberhard Hecker was there, proffering tempting cash to people who had just seen their world destroyed.

At the end of August, it was Berlin's turn again to be bombed. Within a few days of each other, there were three massive night raids. Even in the deep safety of the Quadriga's cellars, they could hear the thunderous detonations and feel the earth-shaking vibrations, that jarred furniture and rocked Benno's carefully stored bottles of wine on their wooden racks. The lights flickered and died, so that they were left in the dark with their fear, until a maintenance man activated the emergency generator and dim illumination was restored.

In the mornings, they returned to a sadly changed city, as, one by one, familiar landmarks were destroyed. A pall of smoke and dust hung over the entire city. No sooner had one set of fires been extinguished, than the RAF returned to start more. No sooner was one stretch of road cleared of rubble, than more buildings were blown up and the work had to recommence.

On Friday, 3 September, another evacuation programme was announced and a million women and children were moved out of the city into the country. Ricarda telephoned from Heiligensee to say she had decided to stay there with Christa and Lili. Not long afterwards, the sirens began to wail and everyone hurried down to the cellar.

As the RAF commenced yet another lethal bombardment of Berlin, Maître Mazzoni asked permission for a few words with Viktoria. His swarthy face was pale. 'I don't know what to do, Signora Viktoria. I heard on the radio this evening that Allied troops have landed at Reggio di Calabria in South Italy. Soon they will be fighting their way up the Italian mainland. The Italian people are tired. Thousands of our soldiers have been killed. Our cities are being bombed.' A loud explosion somewhere on Unter den Linden set the cellar walls trembling and Mazzoni shuddered.

'You believe the Italian King and the new Prime Minister may negotiate a peace with the Allies?' Viktoria asked gently.

Mazzoni nodded. 'If they do, it will mean that Germany and Italy are enemies. I believe in the Führer — but I am still an Italian. I am nearly sixty, Signora Viktoria. I don't like to let you and Signor Benno down, but perhaps…'

'You would like to go home? I understand, Herr Maître. If I were in your position, I should probably do the same thing.'

'I am not abandoning the fascist cause, Signora Viktoria…'

'Family ties are stronger than politics.'

He smiled gratefully. 'I think I should go very soon.'

'Yes, of course.'

Benno nodded tiredly, when Viktoria told him what had happened. 'I suppose, after twenty-five years, we owe Mazzoni something. We'll just have to find another chef. In the meantime, we'll cope somehow.'

Mazzoni left the following morning. A few days later, Badaglio agreed an armistice with the Allies. German troops immediately seized all strategic points and occupied two-thirds of Italy, but the fact remained that Germany's ally had deserted her. 'Rats leaving a sinking ship,' Benno remarked cynically.

That weekend, Norbert suddenly arrived, amazingly bright and breezy. 'I've done the best I can with the West Wall and helped patch up the Ruhr dams. Now I've been given my most challenging assignment yet!' He put his arm round Viktoria and grinned. 'Aunt Vicki, we're going to build you a blast wall!'

'A blast wall?' she echoed blankly.

'It means that if a bomb lands in the street, the hotel's facade and maybe even the ground-floor windows will be safe. Of course, there's nothing we can do to stop a bomb landing on the roof.'

'But why should anyone want to protect the Quadriga?'

'You're lucky. You're housing a military department on the fourth floor, aren't you?'

'I'm glad the military has some uses,' Benno said grimly.

Norbert enjoyed being back in Berlin. The Baron and Werner tried to persuade him to stay with them, but he could imagine nothing worse than a week in their company and accepted with alacrity his aunt and uncle's invitation to live at the Quadriga, particularly since he had set eyes on Reinhild Pacher, one of the hotel receptionists.

A pretty brunette, Reinhild had lost both her parents in an air raid early in the war and lived in at the Quadriga ever since. On his first evening, Norbert invited her to the cinema.

They saw *The Great Love*, a film portraying the brave suffering endured by women whose men were at the front. Soon Reinhild was in tears and Norbert comforting her. When the film ended, he took her to Café Jochum where the Kraus name conjured up two bottles of champagne. By the time they arrived back at the hotel and Norbert escorted her up the main staircase in full view of the night porter, Reinhild felt as though she were floating on a cloud.

In his room, Norbert produced another bottle of champagne and Reinhild giggled. 'Herr Kraus, do you realize I've never drunk champagne before?'

He picked her up and placed her on the bed, sitting beside her, tracing her lips with his finger. 'My name is Norbert, treasure. So long as we are together, we shall drink nothing but champagne.' He kissed her and she responded enthusiastically. 'However, there is a condition.' Norbert's smile made his rather plain features appear handsome. 'Champagne tastes much better without any clothes on.'

Reinhild looked doubtful. 'Herr... I mean, Norbert...'

'Reinhild, my treasure, who knows where I shall be this time next week? Life is so uncertain...'

The Great Love still fresh in her mind, Reinhild felt tears brim to her eyes. His hand fondled her breast and she felt a surge of longing.

'You're so beautiful,' Norbert murmured. 'Has anybody told you that you have a perfect figure?' Reinhild drew closer to him and sighed. 'If it wouldn't be unfair to you, I could easily fall in love with you.' His fingers crept up her thighs.

A Kraus, heir to one of the world's largest fortunes, in love with her? Reinhild whispered, 'I think I am already falling in love.'

Expertly, he undressed her, covering her full breasts, her rounded stomach, her wide hips and firm thighs with little kisses, until she was writhing on the bed beside him. Then he took off his own clothes.

The champagne was warm by the time they drank it.

They were fortunate. No British bombers disturbed that night or any night that followed. Neither, as Reinhild had secretly feared, did anybody attempt to stop their love affair. Her colleagues were too tired, busy or indifferent to interfere. Viktoria and Benno could not help seeing the languishing glances Reinhild threw Norbert whenever she saw him or heard his name mentioned. But they took the view that there was a war on and Norbert and Reinhild were entitled to what little happiness they could find while they had the chance.

While Norbert was in Berlin, Werner told him about Landgut AG. 'Grandfather's amazing, isn't he?' Norbert commented to Viktoria and Benno. 'He never misses a trick. What's more, not even the Manager, Eberhard Hecker, knows he's working for Kraus. And I bet you didn't know the company's office is next to Dr Duschek's, above Café Jochum! Well, I'm not complaining. Judging by the number of bomb-sites there are, we should make a fortune after the war.'

At the end of a week, the blast wall was completed, a monstrous barrier twenty-five feet high, fortified with sandbags, with steel doors let into it to allow access to the hotel. It did nothing to improve the hotel's beauty, but nobody cared. Survival was all that mattered those days.

After a last passionate night of love, Norbert kissed Reinhild goodbye and, promising to write to her, left for his next assignment, back on the Atlantic Wall in France.

In mid-October, a newcomer joined General Fromm's staff at the War Ministry — Colonel Count Claus von Stauffenberg. In his mid-thirties and once a strikingly handsome man, Stauffenberg, like Peter, had seen service in Russia, where he had also met Tresckow and Schlabrendorff. He, too, had been appalled by the atrocities, the wanton sacrifice of Germany's finest soldiers and, above all, the carnage of Stalingrad.

However, he was only a junior officer and, powerless to do anything, he had requested and obtained a transfer to North Africa. In April, when his car had driven into a minefield, he had been severely injured and returned to Germany.

As he had for Peter, Professor Sauerbruch had done all he could for Claus von Stauffenberg. He could not give him back the sight of his left eye, his right hand or the two fingers he had lost from his left hand, but he had stopped him from going completely blind and restored mobility to a badly damaged leg. By mid-summer, Stauffenberg had taught himself to write again. In October, he was posted to the Reserve Army.

From the moment he met him, Peter liked Stauffenberg. Young, intelligent and practical, he brought fresh blood and new vitality to the resistance movement, forming a bridge between the older and younger generations, the socialists and the conservatives, uniting their different factions in a common cause. In a rare moment of sentiment,

Peter could imagine that Stefan might have been like Stauffenberg, had he brought the boy up as his own son.

By that time, there were few key military personnel who believed Germany could win the war. Allied troops had a firm hold on the Italian mainland. Soviet troops were steadily beating the Germans back towards Poland. Admiral Dönitz had resumed U-boat attacks against Atlantic convoys, but the convoys were still getting through. Air-raids continued on German cities, ports and industrial areas. Although, like General Fromm, most of the generals still refused to commit themselves overtly to the anti-Hitler conspiracy, Peter and his colleagues in Berlin grew increasingly convinced that, once Hitler was dead, they would support the putsch.

The assassination again became the prime concern and Hitler its prime target. If they could take other Party leaders with him, all well and good. If not, at least they would have rid the country of its principal evil. In November, two more brave men undertook suicide missions, but neither succeeded in getting anywhere near the Führer.

Peter said nothing of all this to anybody, for he knew that, if anything went wrong, there would be fearful repercussions and the less his family and friends knew, the safer they would be. He no longer went to the Hotel Quadriga, except on official engagements. When the RAF commenced a massive bombardment of Berlin in mid-November and Christa asked if she could stay at Heiligensee with Ricarda and Lili, he agreed with alacrity and tried to persuade Ilse to join her. But Ilse merely smiled. 'You are my husband. I shall never desert you, certainly not at the time of greatest danger.'

That November, the face of Berlin changed. The air raids of the past seemed trifling compared to the onslaught now loosed upon them and there was no doubt in anyone's mind that the Allies were not going to be content until every building in the capital was razed to the ground.

Night after night, week after week, the bombardment continued. All day and all night, a pall of soot, smoke, ash and dust lay over the city, reaching high into the sky. The air was acrid with the smell of explosives and escaping gas. Fires raged for days on end. Roads were strewn with rubble. Yawning craters, where houses had once stood, were filled with blackened masonry, twisted beams and pillars.

The Kaiser Wilhelm Memorial Church was a black ruin. The beautiful cupola on the St Hedwig Cathedral was shattered, its seven-metres-high cross crashing to the ground and shattering into myriad pieces. The new trees that lined the central promenade of Unter den Linden were twisted and bent.

Kraus Village was badly damaged. All production of explosives and other highly inflammable chemicals had already been moved to less vulnerable sites, but still fires raged through warehouses and factories.

A very heavy bomb scored a direct hit on Kraus Haus, wrecking it and the buildings to either side. When Werner arrived on the scene the next morning, the fire brigade was still battling to put out the conflagration. It was evening before he could get into the basement and ensure that the fireproof vaults beneath the bank, where money, gold and documents were stored, were still intact. He and the Baron were among the lucky ones — at least they could work from the villa at Grunewald.

Others were less fortunate. Most of the fine houses around the zoo and in the diplomatic quarter surrounding the Tiergarten were utterly destroyed. Ministry buildings and office blocks erupted in flames. The Hotel Bristol and the Kaiserhof were reduced to piles of rubble.

Their homes and offices blown up or burned down, everyone who could not go to the country came to the Quadriga. It had its share of broken windows, the Palm Garden Room was shattered and slates were missing from the roof, but, so far at least, Norbert's blast wall had served its purpose. The hotel was still standing.

Gone were all considerations of luxury and service. All people wanted were four walls, a roof and a telephone. Four-roomed suites were divided into separate bedrooms, with communal bathrooms and total strangers sharing a room. More often than not, the night was spent in the cellar anyway.

Then, just before Christmas, as Viktoria was helping Herr Fromm and Reinhild Pacher check out the early morning departures, a waiter from Café Jochum rushed into the foyer. Gasping for breath, he

could hardly speak. 'Frau Viktoria. I ran all the way. Café Jochum —
Café Jochum…'

'Oh, no!' Viktoria clutched her throat. 'Oh no, not Café Jochum…'

Nobody around her took any notice. To them, Café Jochum was
just another building that had been bombed. They did not realize
that, to her, Café Jochum was a living entity, almost a part of herself.

She took a deep breath and forced herself to be calm. 'Stay here,'
she told the waiter. 'I'll go and find Herr Benno.'

Ten minutes later, they were standing on the Kurfürstendamm,
staring at the concrete shell which was all that remained of one of
Berlin's best-known and most controversial pieces of architecture. Its
concrete walls still stood but every pane of glass was shattered,
including the huge picture windows, which formed three sides of the
café itself.

They were joined by more waiters, kitchen staff and tenants from
the offices. The office workers were sent home and soon only the
Café Jochum contingent, Dr Duschek and Eberhard Hecker
remained. They all picked a precarious passage across the rubble and
broken glass and entered the building. The carpets squelched
underfoot and in many places the ceiling had come down, contorting
the chrome and leather furnishings into s range shapes.

Dr Duschek studied the staircase nervously. 'I must see if I can
rescue any papers from my office.'

'Let me go first,' Hecker said.

Benno watched them set off, then made his own way towards the
kitchen. When he came back, he said, 'It's hopeless. The whole place
is running with water. Presumably, the bomb burst the water tank as
well as puncturing the mains. I'm glad Luise didn't live to see it. It
would have broken her heart.'

Viktoria remembered the café's spectacular opening nearly twenty
years ago. In her mind's eye, she saw Luise standing at the doorway,
her bobbed auburn hair surrounding her heart-shaped face like a
halo, her green eyes shining with laughter as she greeted her guests.
'No,' she said, dully, 'Café Jochum ceased to be Café Jochum a long
time ago. Perhaps this is the best thing to happen to it.'

Benno put his arm round her. 'One day, we'll make it into the Café Jochum it was. In the meantime, I think our best course is to move everything we can into the cellar. After the war, when we rebuild the café, we'll sort it out.'

She nodded. After the war... What would be left after the war?

Freeing the cellar door took a while, but once it was open, they discovered the basement to be dry. There were some oil lamps down there which Benno had stored, along with tins of food, against an emergency. He lit one, looked around, then turned to the staff. 'Start with the furniture. But, for heaven's sake, be careful. The structure of the building has been weakened. We don't want to be buried alive.'

The waiters and kitchen staff rolled up their sleeves and set to work. Benno and Viktoria returned to the main entrance. Dr Duschek and Eberhard Hecker came downstairs.

Hecker turned to Benno. 'I am manager of Landgut AG — a real estate company. Herr Kraus, I know it's a little soon to ask this, but would you consider selling this site?'

Viktoria gazed at him open-mouthed, then burst into peals of hysterical laughter, which echoed eerily round the ruined building. 'Sell Café Jochum to Landgut?' she gasped, tears pouring down her face.

Eberhard Hecker looked at her in alarm. Benno hurriedly led her across to the foot of the stairs. Dr Duschek cleared his throat. 'Herr Hecker, that was rather tactless under the circumstances.'

'I don't see why,' Hecker said indignantly. 'As a Kraus, he should understand that I was making a business proposition.'

Dr Duschek took him by the elbow. 'Herr Hecker, let me give you a couple of words of advice. Firstly, never try to buy anything that belongs to a Kraus. Secondly, Café Jochum is more than just a café or even a building to Frau Jochum-Kraus. There has been a Café Jochum in Berlin for sixty years, even longer than there has been an Hotel Quadriga. To offer to buy this site is like trying to buy her soul.'

Gradually, Viktoria's hysteria subsided. She leaned her head against Benno's shoulder. 'Oh, Benno, I don't know how much more of this I can stand.'

'Let me take you home,' he said, gently.

The bombing of Café Jochum solved one problem at least. The café's staff, including the chef, were moved to the Hotel Quadriga, where they were desperately needed to cope with around a thousand guests crowded into an hotel designed to house two hundred and fifty.

It took three days to salvage everything possible from Café Jochum and store it in the cellar. Then Benno locked, barred and padlocked the door to keep the contents safe from intruders and vandals. 'We shall rebuild it,' he promised Viktoria again.

On the morning of 24 December, leaving Herr Brandt in charge of the hotel, they drove to Heiligensee, collecting Peter and Ilse en route. It was a slow and depressing drive through streets lined with ruined houses and strewn with rubble.

At the cottage, however, a happier mood prevailed. Fritzi Weber had dug up a small tree and Lili's first words were, 'Aunt Vicki, have you brought the decorations with you?'

Viktoria kissed her, this small replica of Luise. 'Yes, of course I have, darling.'

As they had for so many years now, she and Benno hung the tree with glass balls, carved wooden ornaments, tinsel and lametta, stacked their small gifts around its base and lit the candles. Then, holding hands, they stood round the tree in a circle: Ricarda, Viktoria, Benno and Lili, Peter, Ilse and Christa. They sang the old Christmas hymns: *O Tannenbaum, O Tannenbaum...* and *Stille Nacht, Heilige Nacht...*

The log fire crackled as flakes of snow came down the chimney. It was to Viktoria as if the spirits of many Christmases past had come to join them, as if the room thronged with ghosts, both of the living and the dead.

Under the stringencies of total war, dancing was forbidden, so there was no New Year's Eve Ball to welcome in 1944, but they held what Benno laughingly called a gala dinner in the cellar. The tables were laid in long rows, like an army canteen, with people packed closely together down each side. Silver service was out of the question, so plates of very basic food were prepared in the kitchen and handed out from trays. But the waiters themselves still managed to present an elegant aspect and the wine flowed freely.

Despite the fact that there wasn't a person in the room who had not lost a member of their family in the war and quite a number who had lost very much more, everyone entered into the spirit of the occasion. Such officers as were present wore full dress uniform. The ladies were adorned in their best ballgowns. Those who had lost their clothes in air raids either borrowed from friends or improvised.

For the first time in the hotel's history, off-duty staff were allowed to join in a social event, as a reward for all their hard work. Norbert seized the opportunity to invite Reinhild Pacher. 'Who's that wench?' the Baron asked Benno.

Benno bit back a smile. 'She's a clerk in our reception. An attractive girl, don't you agree?'

'I don't give a hoot what she looks like. I'm not having my grandson consorting with a common clerk.' However, he forbore from saying anything to Norbert.

At midnight, they lifted their glasses and the cellar resounded to calls of *Prost Neu Jahr!*

'There's no need for fireworks this year!' Norbert laughed. 'No doubt the RAF will be providing those!'

But that night, the RAF left them in peace.

CHAPTER EIGHTEEN

Throughout January, the air battle over Berlin continued. More and more factories were hit, more and more companies put out of business. In the centre and in the industrial areas, Berlin presented a black and spectral cityscape, the Chancellery, the Propaganda Ministry and the Hotel Quadriga among the few buildings to remain relatively unscathed. Few were the houses which had not suffered damage of some kind. Those to fare best were in suburban areas: the Biederstein villa, the Kraus mansion and the Jochum cottage were still intact.

Not content with the damage the British were inflicting at night, the Americans added their strength, to launch devastating attacks on the city by day. People struggled up from a cramped, sleepless night underground only to be forced back down when the sirens started wailing again. The city groaned under a yoke of tiredness.

The snows fell. For hundreds of thousands who had lost their homes, who huddled fearfully in ramshackle huts or cellars, who had to fetch their water from standpipes and eat in communal kitchens, was added the bitter discomfort of a freezing Berlin winter. As the bombs rained down, the toll of the dead and homeless rose, and the people's morale worsened. There must be many, Peter thought, who longed for the war to end but were too frightened — or too indoctrinated — to say so. When their coup succeeded and Hitler was dead, the people of Berlin would be on their side.

By concentrating their major offensive on Berlin, the Allies were giving the rest of the country a certain breathing space. Industry had recovered itself to a great extent. Production of vital parts and equipment had been restored, enabling the great war machine to be re-equipped. But, to those in the know, it was an illusory recovery.

Only in Italy were things going in Germany's favour, where Kesselring was putting up a staunch resistance. Elsewhere, things looked grim. In the fear that the Allies might try to stage an invasion across the Channel, Rommel had been transferred to France. The

Russians were sweeping closer to the pre-war Polish frontier. They recaptured Kiev. They recaptured Novgorod. They relieved Leningrad, surrounded and bombarded by the Germans since September 1941.

Despite this, there were still many blindly fanatical Nazi supporters, holding key positions in the Gestapo, the SS and the Army, who believed the war could still be won and, for Peter, these men — the enemy within — were even more dangerous than the enemy without.

At the end of January, Admiral Canaris came to Peter's house. His eyes were red-rimmed with fatigue. 'More arrests have taken place, among them Dr Kiep and Count Helmuth von Moltke, accused of anti-Nazi activities. One of my agents in Turkey is apparently also implicated. He has been ordered to return to Germany, since when he's disappeared. I suspect he's defected to the British.'

'On top of this, I have been ordered to compile a report on the situation in Russia. Needless to say, it will not tell Hitler what he wants to hear. He wants victories. I have no victories to report.'

Peter nodded, knowing only too well the fate of officers who dared to tell the truth. 'It was kind of you to come and see me, Canaris.' He hesitated for a moment, then asked a question which had long been plaguing him. 'You know what we are planning — Beck, Olbricht, Stauffenberg, Goerdeler, Hassell, myself and the rest. You have never tried to stop us. Indeed, you have frequently helped us. Yet are you really on our side?'

Canaris did not answer the question. 'Biederstein, be warned. Himmler, too, knows about the *coup d'état*. He even knows that Beck and Goerdeler are involved.'

'Himmler knows? Dear God! Then why doesn't he stop us?'

'Himmler has a devious political cunning. He wants power. He enjoys intrigue.'

Perhaps that was the answer to his question. As Himmler used his subordinates in the SS and the Gestapo to manipulate events, so, too, did Canaris. To them, Peter was merely a tool in a web of intrigue.

Canaris glanced at his watch. 'I must go now. No doubt, the British will be paying us another visit tonight. It was estimated they were dropping bombs at the rate of seventy-five per minute last week. And

Hitler still believes he can win the war!' He held out his hand. '*Auf Wiedersehen*, Biederstein. Good luck.'

'*Auf Wiedersehen*, Canaris.'

For a long time after Canaris had disappeared into the dark night and the sound of his car engine had died away, Peter sat pondering what he had learned. He had asked Canaris whose side he was on and received a typically enigmatic reply. But what about Himmler? *He wants power*. Could it be that, if the coup succeeded, they would find Himmler on their side? It was possible.

But if the coup failed, Himmler would grant them no mercy.

Peter flexed his false leg. As always when he was under stress, the stump was aching badly. 'No, damn it all,' he muttered to himself. 'Let there be an end to political machinations. I — as a soldier — have a responsibility to save the German nation from destruction. I have set myself a course and I shall not deviate from it.'

On 18 February, an army of Gestapo officers swept into the Hotel Quadriga and up to the fourth floor. The Abwehr personnel who worked there were marched away under armed guard. All day long, SS men with trolleys went up and down in the lift, removing filing cabinets, desks and safes into waiting vans.

In her office, Viktoria tried to concentrate on her work, but all the time, she was wondering fearfully what this new raid meant. Did it just concern the Abwehr or did it have wider-reaching implications? Did it mean that Peter was in danger? And what about themselves and the Quadriga? Every so often, Benno came in, glanced at her worriedly, shook his head and went away again. She knew the same thoughts were running through his mind.

It was late evening, when the Gestapo officer in charge of the operation marched peremptorily into her office, followed by Benno. 'The Führer has ordered that the Abwehr be incorporated into a unified Intelligence Service under SS-Reichsführer Himmler. Admiral Canaris has been dismissed. All Abwehr personnel who have been working here have been transferred to Zossen.'

Sorry though she was for Canaris, Viktoria's immediate reaction was relief. It was an internal matter between the Abwehr and the SS.

What was more, at a time when the hotel desperately needed every available inch of space, the fourth floor had been liberated.

The Sturmbannführer's next words put paid to that hope. 'As from today, the Gestapo is taking over the Abwehr accommodation.'

After he had gone, they sat in silence. Not just a guard inside and outside the hotel, not only microphones in every room, but Gestapo offices within the building itself. The Hotel Quadriga was no longer their home, but their prison.

For Benno, it was the final straw. When Viktoria turned to look at him, his face was drained of colour and his skin seemed to have sagged. He was only fifty-four, but suddenly he appeared an old man. He shook his head in bewilderment and, very slowly, said, 'I never thought the day would come when the SS would take over our hotel.'

That night, as they lay in bed, he took Viktoria in his arms and held her tightly, as though his life depended upon her. 'Vicki, I'm sorry, I've let you down.'

She brushed her lips against his cheek, suddenly more sorry for him than she was for herself. 'Of course you haven't let me down.' He might have given his support to Hitler in the early days, but he was not to blame for this latest disaster. 'Benno, it will be all right,' she murmured, as if he were a child. 'It will be all right, darling, I promise.'

They had a bombless night and Benno seemed better in the morning. But from then on, Viktoria found herself taking over more and more of his workload. As if they knew what had happened without being told, guests and staff came to her with their problems. Increasingly, she found herself not telling Benno things, but making decisions on her own and Benno seemed content to let her cope as best she could.

At long last, Viktoria had got her own way and was again running the Hotel Quadriga. The irony was that, except in name, the Quadriga was no longer her hotel.

On 20 April, Hitler's birthday, Dr Goebbels organized banners to be hung across the streets and from crumbling walls, reading, 'Our walls have broken but not our hearts.' The banners did not tell the truth. Berlin was a city of broken hearts.

At the Bendlerstrasse, plans for the take-over of power were as perfect as they could ever hope to have them. To Peter's relief, General Beck had sufficiently recovered from his illness to play an active role again in the *coup d'état* and it had been decided that he should be the new Head of State while Carl Goerdeler should be Chancellor. Field Marshal von Witzleben would take over as Commander in Chief of the Wehrmacht, with Peter his new Chief of General Staff.

They had the Chief of Police and other key military personnel on their side, as well as most of the junior officers on Peter's and Olbricht's staffs. On the Western Front, Field Marshal Rommel and General von Stülpnagel had been converted to their cause. On the Eastern Front, Tresckow was confident that Field Marshal Kluge would support them when the coup succeeded.

Furthermore, they had the perfect vehicle through which to act. Known as Operation Valkyrie, it was an emergency measure devised by Admiral Canaris just before his dismissal and approved by Hitler himself, that empowered the Reserve Army to proclaim a state of emergency and call out adequate troops to maintain internal security, should the millions of slave and war labourers in Germany threaten any kind of uprising. Operation Valkyrie therefore offered the perfect cover under which Peter and his colleagues could plan their take-over.

All that remained was for someone to get close enough to the Führer to kill him and such a possibility was becoming increasingly remote. On one or two occasions, officers succeeded in getting into the same room, but were never allowed past his formidable SS bodyguard. Hitler knew he was in danger and was taking no risks.

Meanwhile, time was inexorably running out. On all fronts, the enemy was drawing closer and there were rumours of an imminent cross-Channel invasion. On 9 May, the Russians recaptured Sebastopol and on the 13th the last Axis troops were forced out of Crimea. On 11 May, the Italian Gustav Line was attacked. On 16 May, Kesselring ordered the evacuation of the Cassino garrison. On 4 June, the Allied Fifth Army entered Rome.

On 6 June, the event occurred which they had all feared. The weather was bad, the English Channel extremely rough, but despite the conditions, British and American forces landed on the beaches of Normandy, taking the German Seventh Army totally by surprise. They brought with them artificial harbours and articulated steel roadways, so that tanks, guns and equipment could be landed. Within hours they had breached the Atlantic Wall and were onto the French mainland.

Soon it was clear even to those far away from the action in Berlin that the Allies had air, sea and land superiority. The Germans held the long bridgehead encircled, but the initiative had been taken from them. It could only be a matter of time before the Allies broke through the cordon.

The situation was urgent as never before. The coup had to take place as soon as possible. The war must be brought to an end before any more blood was spilled and, even more importantly, before the Russians invaded from the East. Possibly then the Allies would join forces with Germany in a war against the Soviet Union.

Suddenly, not all Peter's colleagues agreed with him. Some argued that it might be better to let the war take its course. They knew the end was near, but the German people did not. The first 'secret weapons' had been launched against England — V-1 flying bombs, which Goebbels claimed would wipe London off the face of the earth. The resistance could well find itself in the situation of the socialists at the end of the last war, accused of giving Germany the 'stab in the back' that had hastened her defeat. Instead of being greeted as liberators, they could find themselves held responsible for a catastrophe.

But Peter was adamant. 'It is our duty to prove to the world and to future generations that honour and chivalry still exist in the heart of the German soldier; and that we of the German resistance movement are prepared to risk our lives to rid our country of this evil.' They knew he was right.

On 15 June, Viktoria celebrated her fiftieth birthday and the Hotel Quadriga its golden jubilee. Realizing that it could easily turn into a day of sadness rather than celebration, Benno suggested they spent it at Heiligensee with Ricarda and Christa and Lili.

By using all his influence and at vast expense, he succeeded in obtaining some of Viktoria's favourite foods, which the kitchen staff packed into a hamper. From the cellar he brought up some bottles of vintage champagne, and finally, from the safe where he had concealed it for so long, he brought out a small box containing Viktoria's birthday present: a gold choker which Kok van der Jong had obtained for him in Paris back in the summer of 1940.

It was a beautiful summer's day. Fritzi put deckchairs beside the lake and Hilde, with squeals of delight at the unexpected delicacies, served the picnic. 'Fresh crayfish, Herr Benno, where did you find them? And wild strawberries!'

Viktoria stared across the lake. 'It's strange. I never thought I would spend my fiftieth birthday like this. I suppose it sounds stupid, but somehow, I feel I am letting the Quadriga down.'

When the meal was over, Christa and Lili glanced at Ricarda then ran up to the house, returning with some packages. 'Happy Birthday, Aunt Viktoria.' Lili pushed a rolled-up paper into her hands. 'I painted it specially for you.'

It was a crude six-year-old's picture of a building labelled THE HOTEL QUADRIGA. Viktoria smiled. 'Thank you, Lili. I shall treasure it.' Christa had crocheted her a shawl and Ricarda had made an elaborately embroidered blouse.

Finally, Benno reached in his pocket and pulled out his present. Viktoria opened the box and gasped when she saw the thick gold choker, glittering with massive diamonds. Then she frowned. 'But, Benno, when shall I ever wear it?'

He smiled tiredly. 'When I bought it, I had no idea Berlin would be in ruins when I gave it to you. But the war can't last for ever, darling.'

'It's beautiful. Please put it on, Aunt Vicki,' Christa pleaded.

Viktoria looked ruefully at her simple cotton dress. 'It will look silly.'

Ricarda pursed her lips and, noticing the gesture, Viktoria undid the clasp and fastened the choker round her neck. Then she leaned across and kissed Benno. 'Thank you, darling. I didn't mean to sound ungracious. It's just that…'

'I understand. So much has changed…'

After that, while Benno dozed in his deckchair and Lili made daisy chains, Viktoria, Ricarda and Christa talked quietly together. For the most part, their conversation was on general topics: the lessons Ricarda and Christa were giving Lili, so that she would be ready for school in the autumn; Ricarda's vegetable and herb garden; air raids, and Karl's foresight in having the cellar so well built.

Towards the end of the afternoon, Christa asked, 'Aunt Vicki, do you often see my parents?'

'Not since Christmas. Since the Gestapo moved in, the Quadriga isn't a very inviting place. But surely you hear from them?'

'Oh, yes, Mama often rings me.' She frowned. 'I don't know why, but I don't think they want me to come home.'

'Only because of the air raids.'

'I think it's more than just air raids. From the odd things Mama has let drop, I think Papa is in some kind of danger.'

Benno opened a sleepy eyelid. 'Don't forget your father's a soldier, Christa, and there's a war on.'

'Yes, I suppose that's it.' But she still looked uneasy.

Suddenly, fortune seemed to smile on the resistance movement. At the end of June, Stauffenberg was promoted to Chief of Staff to General Fromm. On 14 July, Hitler moved his headquarters from Berchtesgaden to Rastenburg to be nearer the encroaching Russian front and summoned Stauffenberg to report on matters relating to the Reserve Army.

The great moment had arrived. At dawn the next morning, the young colonel and his ADC, Lieutenant von Haeften, flew to the Wolf's Lair to carry out his mission.

It was a nerve-wracking morning. There was no doubt in anyone's mind that Stauffenberg would succeed. With only one eye and one arm, he would be above suspicion and would easily get past Hitler's bodyguard. His appointment with the Führer was for 1300 hours. As soon as possible, he would withdraw from the meeting, leaving behind his briefcase and, in it, the bomb which would kill the Führer.

At 11 o'clock, General Olbricht ordered his Chief of Staff, Colonel Mertz, to issue the Valkyrie password to the Berlin troops to march to their prearranged stations outside vital ministries, government offices and Army Headquarters and for panzers to move in on Berlin from Krampnitz.

The proclamations were all ready to be handed to the press and radio. From Rastenburg, Stauffenberg telephoned a coded message that he was about to plant the bomb. At the Bendlerstrasse, nobody dared breathe. For all of them, it was the culmination of years of scheming and plotting. For Peter, it was even more. He was about to prove, not only to Germany and the world — but also to Stefan, his son — that the German soldier was still capable of courageous and noble deeds.

A few moments later, Stauffenberg rang again. Hitler had broken off his appointment. The operation must be cancelled.

In the Bendlerstrasse, there was disappointment and near panic. Olbricht recalled the troops, but not before their strange behaviour had come to the attention of General Fromm and Field Marshal Keitel. Only with difficulty did he succeed in persuading his superior officers that it had been a practice exercise for Operation Valkyrie.

Ilse was still up when Peter arrived home. He took her in his arms. 'It didn't work. If we are lucky, we have just one more chance.'

In France, Rommel was badly injured when a low-flying plane strafed his car. Next day, Goerdeler received a message from a friend at Police Headquarters that an order had been issued for his own arrest.

Their last chance came just two days later, when Stauffenberg was again summoned to the Wolf's Lair. At dawn on 20 July 1944, with the bomb in his briefcase, he and Haeften left Berlin on their second attempt to kill Hitler.

Nobody in the Bendlerstrasse felt the same confidence on this occasion as they had five days earlier. They feared the same thing would happen again: whether from intuition or because of other, more pressing business, Hitler would not see Stauffenberg.

They must be prepared for Stauffenberg to succeed, but in case he did not, they must appear to behave normally. Beck did not dare alert attention to himself by coming to the War Ministry. While Peter remained in his office, Olbricht went out to lunch. He had just returned when Peter's telephone rang. His adjutant said, 'General Fellgiebel to speak to you, sir.'

Peter could hear his own heart pounding. Fellgiebel was OKW Chief of Signals, one of their allies on Hitler's staff at Rastenburg. His job was to cut all telephone and teleprinter communications from the Wolf's Lair once the bomb went off. 'Put him through.'

Fellgiebel spoke in a terse whisper. 'There has been a bad explosion, but the Führer is still alive.' The phone went dead.

Slowly, Peter put down the receiver and stared at Olbricht. 'The bomb exploded, but Hitler has not been killed.'

From the corridor was heard the muffled sound of steel-capped shoes on marble floors, an indistinct mumble of voices. Through the open window came the noise of traffic and news-vendors calling the afternoon newspaper edition. Inside Peter's office, there was silence.

Finally, Olbricht asked, 'And Stauffenberg?'

'Fellgiebel didn't say.'

Peter stared out of the window at the heavy July sky. What was going on at Rastenburg? Had Fellgiebel done his job and immobilized all communications from Rastenburg, or had he simply panicked at the last moment? Had he actually seen Hitler to know he was still alive?

There was only one way to find out. Peter picked up his phone and, telling his adjutant that he had been cut off during his conversation with General Fellgiebel, asked to be reconnected. A few moments later, his aide rang back and said he was unable to get through. The young officer, like many others at the Ministry, knew something was in the air, but had no idea of the details. Peter told him to keep trying and put down the phone.

He turned to Olbricht. 'I believe Hitler is dead. There can be no other explanation.' He glanced at his watch. 'It will be at least four before Stauffenberg gets back. We mustn't waste that time.'

Olbricht shook his head worriedly. 'And if Hitler isn't dead?'

'We still have time to seize control of Berlin. If we can't telephone Rastenburg, nobody else can either. If we say Hitler is dead, they'll have to believe us. We must issue the password to the troops.'

'Remember what happened last time... We must wait until Stauffenberg returns, until we hear from his own lips that his bomb killed Hitler. Biederstein, we cannot afford to make another mistake.'

'Olbricht, we cannot afford to wait. The mere fact that there has been an explosion at Rastenburg justifies putting Valkyrie into operation.'

'We can do nothing without Beck and Witzleben,' Olbricht stated decisively. He stood up. 'I'm going back to my own office. As soon as we hear from Stauffenberg, we'll act.'

After he had gone, Peter's hand hovered over the telephone, but he could not bring himself to pick it up and issue the decisive order. Deep inside him, something said that Fellgiebel had told the truth and Hitler was not dead. He began pacing the room impatiently, cursing himself for his lack of courage, yet very aware that to act prematurely could be the end of all their hopes and plans.

Eventually, at a quarter to four, the internal telephone rang. Peter grabbed it and Olbricht said, 'Stauffenberg's just telephoned from Rangsdorf airfield. He claims his bomb killed Hitler.'

After that they wasted no more time in setting Valkyrie into operation. In a series of terse telephone calls, Peter spoke to the commandants of garrisons inside and outside Berlin, then ordered the guards at the War Ministry to use force against any SS units which might try to get in. While Olbricht went to tell General Fromm what was happening, Peter got in touch with Field Marshal von Witzleben and General Beck, requesting their immediate presence to take over their new posts. Then he went along the corridor to Olbricht's office.

Olbricht returned looking stunned. 'Fromm telephoned Field Marshal Keitel. Somehow Keitel knows about the explosion. He even knows Stauffenberg planted the bomb.' He paused. 'Fellgiebel was right. Hitler is still alive.'

The blood drained from Peter's face. 'What can have gone wrong?'

At that moment, General Beck arrived, followed very shortly by Stauffenberg himself. Briefly, he described how he had succeeded in leaving his briefcase on the conference room floor next to Hitler and made his escape from the Wolf's Lair in time to see the massive explosion. 'It is impossible for Hitler to have survived the blast. He *must* be dead!'

It was a nightmarish situation. Keitel might be bluffing, but equally, since Stauffenberg had not actually witnessed Hitler's death, the Führer could still be alive.

Stauffenberg was suffering from no such apprehensions. Furious that they had wasted four valuable hours while they waited for his return, he put a call through to General von Stülpnagel's headquarters in Paris, confirming that the coup was taking place, then marched into Fromm's office, followed by Olbricht and Peter. When Fromm repeated Keitel's words, Stauffenberg declared, 'Keitel's lying as usual, sir. I myself set off the bomb. Nobody in that room can still be alive. I saw Hitler's body being carried out.'

'In view of this,' Olbricht interrupted, 'we have sent out the code signal for Operation Valkyrie.'

The bull-necked General leaped out of his chair. 'This is rank insubordination! You must cancel the alert immediately!'

'Hitler is dead,' Stauffenberg stated angrily.

Fromm glared at him. 'Count von Stauffenberg, your attempt has failed. You have no alternative but to shoot yourself.'

Suddenly, Peter realized what they should have been doing while they were waiting for Stauffenberg. This ridiculous argument should have taken place hours ago, not now, when time was so valuable. 'General, this is our last opportunity to save Germany. Whether or not the Führer is dead, we have the opportunity to seize power.'

'So you, too, are part of this *coup d'état*, Biederstein? Well, not for much longer. I am formally placing all three of you under arrest.'

'No, General,' Olbricht said, 'it is we who are arresting you.' Fromm moved, it could have been for his gun, and Olbricht jumped towards him, his hands reaching for Fromm's throat. For a moment, Peter gazed in shocked amazement at the two officers wrestling, then he drew his own pistol. Clearly, his voice rang through the room. 'Fromm, hands up or I'll shoot!'

Gasping for breath, Olbricht let go of Fromm and, digging his gun in the General's ribs, Peter marched him into the adjoining room and locked the door. Then he went back to his own office and telephoned the headquarters of the Battalion Grossdeutschland, ordering them to mount guard on the War Ministry. After that, people were only allowed in or out with a special pass.

By now, the tanks should be rolling in towards the city centre and key government buildings should have been seized. From time to time, Peter glanced out of the window, but everything appeared curiously normal.

At half-past six, his aide knocked on the door to tell him there had been a brief announcement on the radio that an attempt had been made on Hitler's life which the Führer had survived. After that, the telephone did not stop ringing as officers from all over Europe demanded to know what was happening. Frantically, Peter and Stauffenberg took their calls, assuring them that the news announcement was false: Hitler was dead.

Towards eight, Field Marshal von Witzleben arrived. He listened to Stauffenberg, Olbricht and Beck's explanations, then said coldly, 'So far as I can gather, no troops have occupied the city. There are no tanks on the streets. It's clear the attempt has misfired.' With a last, withering look, he marched out of the building.

For a long time after that, Peter stood at the window gazing into the dark. It had been a hot, sultry day and the evening was oppressively humid, as if a thunderstorm were brewing. There was no shooting, no troops storming the streets. Whatever was happening out there, it was not revolution. Something, somewhere, had gone terribly wrong. And, even as he looked down into the Bendlerstrasse, he saw soldiers withdrawing from the War Ministry and marching away up the road.

His reflections were interrupted by junior officers from his own staff, including his own adjutant, bursting into his office brandishing submachine-guns. 'Your revolution has failed, General! Now, you're going to obey our orders. Join the others in General Fromm's office.'

Even if he could have reached for his revolver in time, Peter could not have taken on half a dozen armed men. Besides, he knew they were right. Stauffenberg had not killed Hitler. Somebody had given the order to cancel Operation Valkyrie. Their troops had not taken over Berlin. The revolution had failed.

His false leg aching badly, Peter limped to Fromm's office, where his colleagues were waiting. Blood was pouring from Stauffenberg's good arm, where he appeared to have been shot. The others were unhurt, but pale and drawn.

Fromm appeared in the doorway, a revolver in his hand, his red face shining with self-righteous satisfaction. 'Now I am going to treat you as you treated me. Put down your weapons. You are under arrest.'

Peter complied, gazing at him bleakly. Right to the bitter end, Fromm had prevaricated, waiting to see who won before deciding whose side he was on. Hitler had won.

Beck started to plead with Fromm, then, when the General cut him short, picked up his revolver and held it to his own head. Peter looked away, feeling both pity and repugnance. A shot echoed through the silent room. Peter forced himself to look. Beck was lying across the desk, blood streaming down the side of his face, but he was still alive. And, somehow, Beck's unsuccessful suicide attempt seemed symbolic of the whole failed coup.

Fromm turned to the others. 'If you gentlemen have any letters to write, I'll give you a few more moments.' He had no need to say more. They were condemned men. Olbricht and another officer asked for paper and pens, but Peter shook his head. He knew no words to express his feelings. Fromm left the room and, while the two men scribbled hasty notes, the rest of them stood in silence, trying to come to terms with their fate.

Images flickered through Peter's mind: of Fürstenmark, of a young girl at Heiligensee, of Stefan, of Ilse and Christa with eyes bluer-than-blue… Was it possible that he would never see any of them again? Was this really the end?

Fromm returned. 'I have called a session of a court-martial in the name of the Führer and that court-martial has pronounced death sentences on General Biederstein, General Olbricht, Colonel Stauffenberg, Colonel Mertz and Lieutenant Haeften. Well, gentlemen, are you ready? I must ask you to hurry.'

They were pushed down the staircase at gunpoint into a dark courtyard and lined up against a wall in the slit beam of the hooded headlights of a car. No ropes bound their hands. No blindfold covered their eyes.

'Load!' The familiar click of rifle bolts, but now it was Peter who faced them. 'Aim!' Peter closed his eyes. *Dear God,* he prayed, *let it not all have been in vain. Please take care of Ilse and...* 'Fire!' There was a volley of gunfire. Peter was dead when his body slumped to the ground.

Never had Ilse known time pass so slowly as it did that Thursday evening. After the radio announcement that an attempt had been made on Hitler's life, she walked restlessly round the darkening house, never out of earshot of the wireless and the telephone.

It was not until one o'clock in the morning that the music stopped and, after a blare of military music, Hitler's harsh voice poured into the room. 'My German comrades! I speak to you today, firstly in order that you should hear my voice and know that I am unhurt and well, and secondly, that you should know of a crime unparalleled in German history.

'A small clique of ambitious, irresponsible and, at the same time, senseless and stupid officers had concocted a plot to eliminate me and, with me, the staff of the High Command of the Wehrmacht.

'The bomb planted by Colonel Count Stauffenberg exploded two metres to the right of me. It seriously wounded a number of my true and loyal collaborators, one of whom has died. I myself am entirely unhurt, aside from some very minor scratches, bruises and burns. I regard this as a confirmation of the task imposed upon me by Providence...

'The circle of these usurpers is very small and has nothing in common with the spirit of the German Wehrmacht and, above all, none with the German people. It is a gang of criminals, who will be destroyed without mercy…'

When the Führer had finished speaking, first Göring and then Dönitz gave short speeches, then an official announced that the ringleaders of the plot had either committed suicide or been shot by the Army. Across the ether rang the name, 'General Count Peter von Biederstein…'

There followed another fanfare of military music, but Ilse did not hear it. She stood at the window, staring blindly into the night sky, empty for once of enemy bombers. Peter was dead…

At four o'clock, there was a screech of tyres in the street, followed by a heavy pounding on the door. 'Open up in the name of the Gestapo!'

What Peter could endure, so too could she. Ilse steeled herself, then walked into the hall and opened the door. Four SS men stood there. 'Ilse Biederstein? You are under arrest.'

This was the tyranny to which Peter had tried to put an end. Bleakly, she said, 'Yes, of course.'

One spat derisively. 'What does it feel like to be the widow of a dead traitor? Come on, lady, get moving!'

Her head held high, Ilse walked out of the house and ahead of them down the path towards the waiting van.

When the broadcast ended, Benno walked heavily across the room and switched off the radio. Viktoria stared at him wildly. 'Peter's dead? But he can't be! Not Peter…' Tears welled in her eyes.

He could almost read her thoughts: Peter, her former lover, had tried to change the course of history, while Benno, apart from admitting he had made a mistake, had done nothing. He said, 'I'm sorry. You and Peter were once very close. I do understand.'

She looked up at him in anguish. 'No, you don't understand. I know the reason why Peter tried to kill Hitler. It was for Stefi…'

He knew exactly what she was going to say and he did not want to hear. He could not bear to be told now that Stefan was not his son, but the son of a martyr. It was too late. He seized her by the shoulders. 'Vicki, stop it, please. Don't say anything more.'

'But…'

'Vicki, if Hitler knows the identity of the ringleaders, there are going to be the most dreadful repercussions. He is going to want his revenge. The terror we have experienced so far is going to be nothing compared to what lies ahead.'

'You mean that we…?'

Benno shook his head. 'I don't think so. But Ilse, certainly, and possibly even Christa could be in great danger.' He gave a deep sigh. 'There is nothing we can do tonight, but tomorrow I will go to Schmargendorf. If Ilse is still there, I'll take her to Heiligensee.'

They went to bed, but it was a long time before they slept and then very fitfully. Viktoria's tired mind was trying to grapple with the strange relationship that had existed between her and Peter. Benno, more realistically, was wondering what horrors were already taking place in the dark night and thinking about the day ahead.

When dawn broke, Benno got up and set off on his journey through the ruined city. As soon as he reached the Biederstein house and saw an SS officer standing in the doorway, he knew what had happened to Ilse. He pressed his foot down on the accelerator and continued on down the road towards Heiligensee.

It seemed an interminable journey, but finally he arrived at the cottage. Ricarda, in a wide-brimmed gardening hat, was dead-heading roses. Lili was sitting on the jetty, her bare feet dangling in the water. The very normality of the scene was reassuring and somehow unreal. The car skidded to a halt on the gravel and Benno got out. 'Uncle Benno!' Lili's voice rang joyfully across the garden.

Ricarda hurried over to him. 'Benno, what's happened?'

'Where's Christa?' he asked, anxiously.

Christa came round the side of the house. 'I'm here.'

Benno let out a slow breath of relief.

The young woman gave him a searching look. 'Something's happened to Papa, hasn't it?'

Benno put his arm round her. 'Yes, Christa, I'm afraid it has. Your father is dead.'

Her blue eyes did not waver.

'Your father was one of a group of men who had decided that the only way to save Germany from destruction was to stage a *coup d'état*. Yesterday a Count von Stauffenberg planted a bomb in Hitler's bunker at Rastenburg. The bomb exploded, but it did not kill the Führer. In the early hours of this morning, there was an announcement that your father was among the ringleaders who had been shot.'

Christa nodded slowly. 'I knew he was planning something. Some of the people who came to the house — General Oster, General von Tresckow, General Beck…' She buried her face in her hands. 'Oh, Papa…'

Helplessly, Benno held her to him, stroking her blonde hair and eventually, she asked. 'And Mama? Where is she?'

'I've just been to Schmargendorf. There's an SS guard on the house. I fear your mother has been arrested.'

'But why?' Christa asked in anguish. 'She can have done nothing wrong.'

Very gently, Benno replied, 'The Gestapo is going to want to know who else was involved in the conspiracy.'

'Yes, I see.' She looked up, her bluer-than-blue eyes full of despair. 'She must be so frightened and so lonely, knowing Papa is dead, not knowing what is going to happen to her. Uncle Benno, can you find out where she is? I must see her.'

'Now I know you are all right, I shall do everything I can.' He took her hand. 'Christa, you are going to hear some dreadful things said about your parents. You will be told that your father was a traitor and that your mother is a criminal. But I want you to know that your father was a patriot, a greater man than most who have ever lived, and your mother is a very brave woman.'

Tears welled in her eyes. 'I know. Excuse me. I need to be alone — to try to come to terms…'

'Yes, of course.'

She stepped onto the lawn and Lili ran towards her.

Benno called out, 'Lili, come here a moment.'

But Christa held out her hand to Lili and, together, they walked down towards the lake.

Quietly, Ricarda said, 'Lili can probably help her more than either of us.' She turned to Benno. 'How are you going to set about finding Ilse?'

'I am sure Dr Duschek will do all he can.'

Ricarda nodded. She could safely leave things in Benno's hands, while she took care of Christa and Lili.

Benno drove to Dr Duschek's home in Wannsee where the lawyer had set up office since the bombing of Café Jochum. As soon as Dr Duschek learned the reason for his visit, he led him into the garden. 'The telephone,' he explained.

'You, too?'

'I've been under suspicion ever since I defended Pastor Scheer.' He gave a thin smile. 'However, I'm still in practice.'

When Benno finished telling him about Peter and Ilse, he said worriedly, 'I see times ahead that are going to pale all other purges into insignificance. Already it appears that it wasn't just a tiny clique of officers involved, but generals posted as far away as Paris and the Russian front. Anyone who intervenes may be apprehended himself as a conspirator.'

'I'm sure the Countess von Biederstein played no active role.'

'And I'm sure she'll never be brought to trial. They'll get what information they can from her, then she'll just disappear.'

'Do you think the Gestapo will come after Christa?'

'I shouldn't have thought so. They'll be more intent on finding the real culprits than taking revenge on dead men's children. Well, give me a little time. I can't promise to work a miracle, but I'll see what I can do.'

'Thank you, Dr Duschek. Needless to say, I will meet any expenses you incur.'

'It will be reward enough if I can see justice done. God in heaven! That bomb was two metres away from Hitler. Why the devil didn't it kill him?'

It was the middle of August before Dr Duschek rang Benno to request a consultation about his will. Again, they talked in the garden.

The lawyer's face was very grave. 'First, let me put your mind at rest. Countess von Biederstein is in Ravensbrück concentration camp.'

'Is she all right?'

Dr Duschek spread his hands expressively. 'It's a good sign. She was in the Prinz-Albrecht-Strasse, but the prison has become so overcrowded that some of the less important prisoners have been moved to concentration camps.'

'Is there any possibility that she can receive visitors?'

'It's highly unlikely, but I'll do my best.' The lawyer paused, took off his spectacles and rubbed a tired hand across his eyes. 'I have a colleague in the Judge Advocate's department, whom I have persuaded to help me. Not that he needed much persuasion, so appalled is he by Hitler's vindictiveness. Already thousands have been arrested — many of them prominent public figures, like General Oster and Admiral Canaris, General Halder, Ambassador von Hassell, Dr Goerdeler, Dr Schacht, even General Fromm, who conducted the court-martial under which Count von Biederstein was sentenced to death.'

'If General Fromm had no part in the conspiracy…?'

'Himmler is now in charge of the Reserve Army,' Dr Duschek observed drily.

Benno remembered other names Christa had mentioned. 'And General von Tresckow? General Beck?'

'Beck tried to commit suicide. When he failed, he was shot. Tresckow died on the Russian front.' Dr Duschek offered Benno a cigarette. 'Perhaps they and your cousin were among the fortunate ones. The first trial took place last week in the People's Court under Judge Freisler. Needless to say, it was a travesty of justice. Eight men were tried, including Field Marshal von Witzleben. Afterwards, they were taken back to Plötzensee Prison, forced to strip to the waist and hanged from meathooks.'

'From meathooks?' Benno fought back a rising nausea.

'And the trial and the hangings were filmed for the Führer's entertainment.'

Benno knew no words to express his horror. Silently, he shook Dr Duschek's hand and made his way to Heiligensee.

Christa took the news very calmly, but she knew as well as Benno that there was scant likelihood of her ever seeing her mother again. People never came out of concentration camps. From that day on, although she outwardly appeared unchanged, there was a dull heaviness in her soul. First she had lost Stefan and now her parents. All she had left was Lili.

As that summer of 1944 drew towards its close, there were unmistakable signs that the war would be fought out to the bitter end and that the end could not be far off. From the west and from the east, the enemy swept across Europe towards Germany and nothing Dr Goebbels' wizards in the Propaganda Ministry conjured up could conceal the brutal facts. On 25 August, Free French and American troops entered Paris. That same week, the Russians seized the Rumanian Ploesti oil-fields and Rumania declared war on Germany. On 3 September, Brussels fell to the British, the next day Antwerp. On 11 September, the first American troops crossed the German border north of Trier.

The final measures for total war were put into operation. Theatres, cabarets and variétés were closed on 1 September until further notice. Leave for civilian workers and soldiers was stopped. In his new capacity as head of the Reserve Army, Reichsführer-SS Himmler declared, 'What we are now waging is a sacred war of the people.' He announced the formation of a *Volkssturm* — a People's Army — into which boys between fifteen and eighteen and men between fifty and sixty were conscripted.

For the Hotel Quadriga, it was bad news indeed. Benno was exempted on the grounds that he was needed to look after an hotel now housing over a thousand people, but the few remaining page boys were called up, so too were Fritz Brandt, Hubert Fromm, Philip Krosyk and Hasso Annuschek — all in their late fifties — as well as other older male personnel.

As Hasso shook Benno's hand, he said dolefully, 'For all Dr Goebbels tells us about his wonder weapons — his V-1 flying bombs and his V-2 rockets — I don't believe they're having any effect. I think the *Volkssturm* is the only real secret weapon left to Germany. In which case, heaven help us all…'

Benno had a dreadful feeling he was right and, filled with great misgiving, watched his old colleagues leave. A motley crew, in ill-fitting uniforms, many unarmed, they and their new comrades marched out-of-step down the ruins of Unter den Linden towards the West. Himmler might tell them they must fight like werewolves but they were old men and children — no match for the armies of Montgomery and Eisenhower.

After they had gone, Viktoria took over Herr Brandt's work and Reinhild Pacher was promoted to Reception Manager. But it was unthinkable to have women in charge of the restaurant and the bar. A middle-aged waiter with only one arm was given Philip Krosyk's job, while Arno Halbe, now in his late seventies, came out of retirement to take charge of the bar. A number of elderly men were engaged to take on the duties of page boys, commis and maintenance men. Most of them suffered from ill-health and were physically not very strong, but they were better than nothing.

Benno was in no doubt as to what he must do. Viktoria should carry on running the hotel, while he quietly organized their future. The cottage stood in far less danger than the hotel, so that was where he should store their valuables.

During the next few weeks, he made several trips to Heiligensee, usually by S-Bahn for there was no petrol now for private motoring. He jemmied up a flagstone in the cellar floor and dug a hole deep enough for a small strongbox in which he placed Ricarda's and Viktoria's jewels, including the ruby set from her fortieth birthday and the gold choker from her fiftieth. He also put in it the deeds to the hotel and Café Jochum, a duplicate set of keys, his will and his Kraus share certificates.

Like Benno, Ricarda could also remember the end of the last war. As far as rations allowed, she stocked up on flour, salt, soap, ersatz tea and coffee. Due to her careful attention, the vegetable plot reaped a fine harvest and she had a good store of potatoes, as well as seed potatoes for new planting. She preserved fruit in airtight jars against the winter ahead. Herbs, onions, mushrooms were dried and hung in the cellar, along with smoked sausages and hams.

In October, the bread ration was reduced to seven ounces a week, but this worried Ricarda less than others, for she was able to supplement it with homemade bread, biscuits and potato cakes. In any case, Lili ate like a bird, Christa had never been a big eater and, as she grew older, Ricarda's own appetite had diminished. With the tins that Benno had bought through Kok van der Jong at the beginning of the war, she was certain her small family could survive for a long time.

If the situation was disastrous for the Hotel Quadriga, it was catastrophic for Kraus Industries. Despite the massive devastation to their factories throughout the country, the wheels of industry had never ceased to turn. Now, however, Kraus had lost its works in France and Belgium and the enemy was preparing to invade the Ruhr. At this precise moment, when the need for arms, tanks and ammunition had never been more desperate, half the manpower was taken away and not replaced. Foreign slave labour, starved and riddled with disease, was all that was left to mill the steel and make explosives, to work the Silesian mines and to man the gunshops of Essen.

In September, Baron Heinrich began his private preparations for his own and Kraus Industries' survival in the case of Germany's defeat. Although he had had no repetition of the slight stroke that had incapacitated him over a year ago, he complained to Dr Blattner of pains in the chest, dizziness and loss of memory.

The next stage was slightly more delicate, because it meant taking Werner into his confidence, but when he explained his reasons, the boy understood. Soon after that, reports appeared in the papers that Baron Heinrich von Kraus zu Essen was suffering from failing health and that, although he still retained control of the company, its total executive management was passing into the hands of his son, Ernst.

That autumn, Ernst's spirits were reaching their lowest ebb. The industrial basin of the Ruhr, that once great hub of German industry, was reduced to a rubble of blackened ruins. Deep underground, its heart still beat, but its coal mines had caved in and its steel mills were silent. The Allied armies were ranged on its doorstep. They only had to cross the Rhine and they would be in Essen.

Then, two apparent miracles occurred. The first was that the tempestuous land advance of the Allies suddenly halted. Nobody knew what had happened, but it seemed probable that they were intimidated by unexpectedly strong German resistance and had run out of supplies and equipment. Hope surged in Ernst's heart that Germany might be able to launch an offensive that would send the Allies hurtling back to the Channel.

The second miracle was the news that Baron Heinrich had changed his mind about who should take over the reins of Kraus Industries. Presumably realizing that Werner was too young and inexperienced, he had finally decided upon Ernst as his heir apparent.

Almost as miraculously, the aches and pains that had troubled Ernst for so long disappeared. The RAF continued its bombardment of the Ruhr. By day and night, they dropped thousands of tons of explosives and incendiaries, that razed the labour camps, the few remaining houses and factories to the ground, that blew up railway lines and caused massive fires in the vast slagheaps that dominated the landscape.

Ernst did not care. It had taken a long time, but, at last, he could consider himself the 'Steel King'.

The previous year, Peter and Ilse had spent Christmas at Heiligensee. Now Peter was dead and Ilse was in Ravensbrück. At least, Dr Duschek told Benno she was still there, but there was no certainty. Thousands had disappeared as a result of the July Plot. Nobody knew whether any were dead or alive.

Fritzi Weber had been called into the *Volkssturm*, so there was no Christmas tree. Benno sawed a branch from a fir tree and put it in a pot. In a break with tradition, Christa and Lili helped him decorate it, while Ricarda and Viktoria busied themselves in the kitchen.

'The sixth Christmas of the war,' Viktoria sighed. 'Mama, will it never end?'

Ricarda looked at her sharply. It was Viktoria's first visit since the summer and there was a marked change in her. Her thick blonde hair had turned very grey, her face was drawn and there were bags under her eyes. 'It can't be long now, darling. However much Hitler claims that our armies are pushing the British and Americans back in the Ardennes, it can only be a temporary respite.'

'Why don't we just surrender before any more damage is done? We drove here through street after street of ruins. It made me realize how lucky we are — and wonder how long it will be before the Quadriga is hit. Norbert's blast wall can't protect us for ever.'

'Why don't you come and live here with us, darling?'

'No. I have a responsibility to my staff and my guests. The Quadriga is home to a thousand people, who have nowhere else to go. I can't let them down.'

Lili came into the kitchen. 'Grandmama, Aunt Vicki, the tree is ready.'

They followed her into the living room, momentarily transformed into a magic place. A fire crackled in the hearth and the flames of tiny candles danced on the twigs of the tree. They stood in a circle round it, Ricarda, Lili, Christa, Benno and Viktoria, and sang the old Christmas songs: *Stille Nacht, Heilige Nacht... O Tannenbaum, O Tannenbaum...* Then Ricarda's clear soprano rang out in English: Oh little town of Bethlehem, how still we see thee lie...

There was no New Year's Eve Dinner that year. On 1 January 1945, the RAF made their first appearance of the new year in the skies over Berlin. Personnel, guests and SS huddled close together in the cellar of the Hotel Quadriga, social differences and fears forgotten, as the devastation of their city continued.

That winter, trainload after trainload of Jews, Slavs, Gypsies, Bolsheviks and other political dissidents continued to arrive at Schlachtenhausen concentration camp from the Polish ghettos, as well as from camps in the West, from Bergen-Belsen, Nordhausen, Dachau, Grubenmünde and Ravensbrück. On Christmas Day, the gas chambers killed five thousand. On New Year's Day, they gassed five thousand five hundred, setting a new record, a fact Oberführer Otto Tobisch noted in the camp's records.

It was about the only thing of which he could feel proud, because every other aspect of the camp's management was going very wrong, something he scarcely admitted to himself, let alone to SS Headquarters in Berlin. From having been an efficient camp, Schlachtenhausen had deteriorated into a ghastly charnel-house, where living skeletons drew their last breath among the corpses of the dead.

His problems were manifold. All but the most essential guards had been taken away to join SS-Waffen divisions at the front and he was now reliant upon Jews and Ukrainians, none of whom could be trusted, to run the camp.

More prisoners arrived than the camp could cope with. None were fit enough to be sent to the Kraus steel factory, where the labourers were already dying like flies, so they were kept in huge compounds until their turn came for the gas chamber. Many died before they got there and the Jewish trusties dragged their bodies to the vast pile waiting to be burned.

The bodies represented the camp's worst problem. Nobody in Himmler's offices had realized how much longer it took to burn a human being than to kill it. The crematoria simply could not cope. In the summer the mountains of stinking corpses had been crawling with flies and maggots. At least in the winter they were frozen stiff and the threat of disease less dire. But it was still omnipresent and this frightened Otto, not so much for himself as for little Adolf.

Adolf was four now, a strangely withdrawn child, who still wet his bed and found difficulty in talking. Anna kept pleading to be allowed to take him back to Traunsee, convinced that the Alpine air would suit him better than the marshy Polish forests, but Otto refused to let them go. Despite the typhoid, diphtheria, cholera, dysentery and tuberculosis that plagued the camp, it was Otto's duty to remain at Schlachtenhausen. Adolf was the only thing he had ever loved. Therefore, Adolf stayed too.

But, as the marshes and rivers froze and deep snow covered the mounds of putrefying corpses, the fear grew in Otto that it might not be long before all of them would be forced to leave Schlachtenhausen. He was no military strategist, but experience told him that there was something unnatural about the stillness of the Eastern Front.

Winter was the natural element of the Russians: the season in which they had staged their greatest victories of the war over the Germans: Moscow, Stalingrad, Leningrad. Right along the Vistula River, they were waiting. Waiting for what? Waiting for the German armies to be annihilated in the Ardennes? Waiting to launch a simultaneous attack with the Allies on both the Eastern and Western Fronts? Of one thing he was certain: the silence boded no good.

On 14 January, his worst fears were confirmed. The news came through by telephone from an agitated Berlin official, speaking in staccato sentences. 'Zhukov's armies have captured Warsaw. Konev's troops are advancing towards Cracow. Oberführer, you must leave Schlachtenhausen. Waffen-SS troops and regular army soldiers are coming to its defence, but we cannot risk losing our records. You must bring them to Berlin immediately.'

'The prisoners?'

'Must all be disposed of.' It was an order that showed how divorced Berlin was from reality.

'For God's sake, don't send any more. Our resources are already stretched to the utmost.'

The official in Berlin gave a sharp intake of breath. Then he said, 'Your comment has been noted, Oberführer. However, the Bolsheviks must find none of their Jewish comrades alive if they should overrun the camp.'

'Yes, sir.' Otto put down the phone and moved to the window. In the distance, he could hear the sound of gunfire. In two or three days, the Red Army would reach Schlachtenhausen. Unlike the official in Berlin, he understood the perversity of the Russian mind. The prisoners who were still alive would be no use to them. But the Bolsheviks would make dreadful propaganda from a mountain of corpses.

He pressed the bell on his desk and his adjutant knocked and appeared in the doorway. Otto barked his own sharp orders. 'Prepare for withdrawal from the camp. No more prisoners are to be gassed until all corpses have been destroyed. Each administrative officer is to sort through his records and burn all but the most essential documents.'

The man's face remained expressionless. He saluted. 'Yes, Herr Commandant.'

After he had gone, Otto went down to the strong-room beneath the administration block. Taking a key from the bunch on his belt, he unlocked the door and entered the vault where the gold and precious gems which were taken from the Jews were stored. Carefully, he went through the boxes, selecting small, unidentifiable items, which could be sold in any country in the world, and stuffed them into a leather pouch.

Otto had not reached the age of fifty-one without acquiring a very strong sense of self-preservation. Berlin had got the wind up, but he had not. Whatever happened in the future, the jewels were his insurance policy for survival.

At four the next morning, Otto loaded the black Mercedes with as many of their personal belongings as he could cram in, then bundled Anna and Adolf into the front seat and Wolf into the back. He drove out through the gates marked *Arbeit macht frei*, and headed south-west towards Ratibor. Despite the blizzard conditions, the road beside the Oder was fairly clear. Soon they were in Moravia, travelling in the direction of Vienna.

Anna held Adolf on her lap. 'Are you happy, Dolfi?' she crooned. 'We're going home. We're going home.'

The boy just sucked his thumb. Otto peered through the windscreen, working out in his mind what he would do when he reached Traunsee.

At Schlachtenhausen, Otto's deputy assumed control of the camp, urging prisoners to greater and greater efforts to dispose of frozen bodies into crematoria furnaces. Black smoke belched into the leaden grey sky. The sound of Russian gunfire grew nearer.

CHAPTER NINETEEN

On 19 January 1945, Cracow fell. Next day, the Russians captured Schlachtenhausen concentration camp. A few days later, Helmuth Stegmann, who had taken over Werner's job in charge of all Silesian operations, telephoned Baron Heinrich in a panic. 'Herr Baron, I think you should know of the dreadful stories that are circulating about Schlachtenhausen. The camp Commandant apparently left before the Russians arrived, but his deputy was still there and has been taken prisoner. Under torture he has confessed to horrendous crimes. There is to be a trial. People are saying he will be hanged. Our steel-works was situated next door. What if…?'

In a frail voice, the Baron said, 'I am a sick man, Stegmann. The doctor thinks I may have only a few more weeks to live. But if it makes you feel better, what went on at Schlachtenhausen had nothing to do with Kraus. We merely set up a factory to SS specifications.'

'The Russians have found great pits filled with bones and piles of frozen corpses.' The Baron could almost hear Stegmann's teeth chattering. 'Already they are saying over a million people have been killed there. Herr Baron, I swear I knew nothing of it…'

'Pull yourself together, Stegmann. You have more important things to worry about than Russian propaganda.'

'You think it's just propaganda?' Stegmann asked, hopefully.

'It's in the Russian interests to discredit the Reich.'

'Yes,' Stegmann said, doubtfully. 'I suppose it is.'

There was no stopping the mighty Russian advance. The Red Army surged over the borders of East Prussia, seizing Tilsit and Tannenberg. In a massive operation, the evacuation of East Prussia commenced. The Russians broke through to the Gulf of Danzig. They captured Memel.

As the Red Army advanced, so stories of the atrocities its soldiers were committing sped before them: gruesome accounts of German grandmothers being raped, of six-year-old girls being assaulted, of whole villages being burned to the ground, of theft, looting, of the hatred of the Russian people for the entire German nation.

Russian planes dropped pamphlets in German — *Not only divisions and armies are advancing on Berlin. All the trenches, graves and ravines filled with the corpses of the innocents are advancing on Berlin, all the cabbages of Schlachtenhausen and all the trees of Glacow on which the Germans hanged so many unhappy people. The boots and shoes and the babies' slippers of those murdered and gassed at Schlachtenhausen are marching on Berlin. The dead are knocking on the doors of the Joachimsthaler Strasse, of the Kaiserallee, of Unter den Linden and all the other accursed streets of that cursed city…*

On 30 January, the twelfth anniversary of his seizure of power, Hitler spoke to the people. 'However grave the crisis may be at the moment, it will, despite everything, finally be mastered by our unalterable will, by our readiness for sacrifice and our abilities. German workers, work! German soldiers, fight! German women, be as fanatical as ever! No nation can do more.'

The following day, Russian troops crossed the Polish border into the province of Brandenburg. The impossible had happened. Russian soldiers had set foot on the soil of the Fatherland. Baron Heinrich picked up the private phone that connected him to Werner's office. 'We are leaving for Austria.'

There was nothing clandestine about the Baron's departure. On his instructions, Werner sent letters to everyone in authority explaining that ill-health was forcing the Baron to retire to his castle in the country. Benno and Viktoria came to see him the day before he left. They found him in bed, wrapped in a quilted dressing-gown, a tragic expression on his face. 'I shall say goodbye to you, dear children, because I doubt that we shall meet again.'

Viktoria did not believe it. She was convinced the Baron was scuttling to safety, but not to die. She kissed his purple cheek. 'Have a good journey to Austria and I'm sure you'll feel better soon.'

Benno took him more seriously and found in this moment of parting that he was almost sad to see the old man go. 'Goodbye, Father. Try not to worry about business. Ernst will look after everything.'

The Baron's eyes glinted evilly behind his spectacles. 'Yes, I'm relying on him.'

When Trudi heard that the Baron and Werner had gone to Castle Waldesruh, she pleaded to be allowed to join them. Ernst gladly gave his permission. The train journey would probably take a long time, but once she was away from the industrial areas into Bavaria, she should be safe enough, and in Austria she would certainly be better off than in the Ruhr.

Kraus Industries had almost ground to a standstill. They were running out of chemicals, electrical components, engines, fuel and coal, and there were long delays in obtaining steel from Silesia. When Ernst looked out from his hillside citadel, the dark sky was illuminated by tongues of flame, licking through the cloud of black smoke that hung over the valley. To a stranger it must appear that the Ruhr was in the final throes of death.

Ernst knew that was not so. There were still rich seams of coal to be mined. When the war was over, iron ore would again flood in from Lorraine. Ruhr steel would once more be forged. The Baron had finally relinquished responsibility in word if not in title. In years to come, when the Ruhr was great again, it would be Ernst who would receive all the credit.

The Saturday after the Baron and Werner left for Innsbruck, one of the worst air-raids yet took place on Berlin, its target Tempelhof airport and the nearby railway station and goods-yards. When the all-clear eventually sounded and Viktoria and Benno emerged from the Quadriga's cellar, the horizon was livid orange with flame, the sky black with smoke.

Some fires were still burning when Norbert unexpectedly arrived at the hotel. Even his usual high spirits had deserted him. 'Hitler still expects miracles. The next item on the agenda is the fortification of Berlin. A ruined city is supposed to stave off the Red Army hordes.'

For the first time, Viktoria realized the full implications of losing the war. It was not going to be like the last time, when a number of gentlemen sat in a railway carriage and signed an armistice. No, this time, the conquering armies were going to pour into Germany. They were not going to rip Germany apart on paper, but physically tear her, limb from limb. In a hollow voice, she asked, 'Do you really believe the Russians will reach Berlin?'

'It can only be a matter of time. They only have to cross the Oder, just as the British and Americans have to cross the Rhine.'

Because he came from outside the city, Viktoria somehow felt Norbert must know more than they did. 'Do you think the British and Americans will get here first?' It was irrational, but somehow she imagined Stefan and Mortimer might be with those advancing armies…

Norbert was more prosaic. 'I hope so. I know who I'd rather be taken prisoner by, if I have to be taken prisoner. Well, let's hope it doesn't come to that.' He suddenly smiled. 'Incidentally, I gather Grandfather's done a bunk. He obviously wasn't prepared to hang around to find out who arrived first.'

'He's a sick old man, Norbert,' Benno said gravely.

Norbert shook his head. 'He's a ruthless old man. Well, now I'm here, I intend to make the most of my stay. Will you allow Fräulein Pacher to take the evening off?'

'Of course,' Viktoria replied. 'But everywhere is closed. What will you do?'

He grinned. 'I'm sure we'll find some way to amuse ourselves.'

But Viktoria lacked his youthful resilience. Throughout the war, they had heard endless reports of Russian atrocities and the fearful way the Red Army treated its prisoners-of-war. When they were alone in the apartment that evening, she suddenly put her arms round Benno, burying her head in his chest. 'Benno, the Russians won't reach Berlin, will they?'

Torn between wanting to comfort her and telling the truth, Benno could only say, 'I hope not. Dear God, I hope not.'

The Germans in the eastern provinces fled through Lower Silesia towards the safety of the west. They travelled on horseback, in old cars, on bicycles or on foot, pushing their belongings in handcarts and wheelbarrows.

The Russians crossed the Oder and their great tanks rolled along the road towards Breslau.

Helmuth Stegmann knew fear greater than any he had ever known. The Baron and young Herr Werner had gone to Austria. Herr Ernst was in Essen, faced with the imminent invasion of the Allies into the Ruhr. None of them would help him when the Russians arrived and charged him with crimes at Schlachtenhausen. He bundled his wife, children and parents-in-law into an old van and joined the refugees pouring out of Breslau towards Saxony.

He left behind him the results of twenty years' hard work: a well-furnished house with a pretty garden, pictures on the walls and even a refrigerator. He left what he had considered a good job with a secure future. He left his office, staff, his papers and his savings. None of these were worth anything compared to being alive.

It was about a hundred and fifty miles to Dresden, but it took them a week to reach the city, so dense was the traffic on the road. When they arrived, every hotel and guesthouse was full, so they parked in a side street and for the eighth night in succession, prepared to sleep in the van.

At that moment, the sirens began to wail. They tumbled out of the van, looking wildly around for the nearest air-raid shelter. The streets filled with people, running about in pandemonium. From the distance came the irregular drone of bombers. Women screamed. Children cried. Nobody seemed sure what to do. It was the first time Dresden had been bombed.

They were still in the open street when the parachute flares descended, lighting up the sky with an eerie light. Next the bombs themselves began to fall, hundreds and hundreds of black shapes that looked rather like hock bottles, clattering down on roofs and pavements. Then these harmless-looking little containers burst into flames, licked up curtains and woodwork, set fire to doors and floors, ignited oil and petrol. Some landed on the van, which exploded. The house behind them caught alight.

Still the planes droned overhead and still the bombs fell, thousands and thousands of them now, black, fire-bearing pellets that darkened the sky and fed the flames of Dresden. And, suddenly, the whole city centre caught light and became a raging inferno.

In blind panic, the Stegmanns surged along with the crowd. The road ahead of them was blocked by tumbling masonry and blazing buildings. There was a mighty wind, like that of a tornado, which licked the flames high into the sky. Sparks and pieces of burning timber flew through the air, singeing hair, eyebrows and clothes. Glass shattered. Still the bombs rained down.

The air was filled with the stench of burning human flesh. The sheer noise of the conflagration was unbearable. The heat was intolerable. To all sides, they were surrounded by the fire, which was remorselessly sucking them towards it. The children were the first to go, drawn shrieking into the furnace. Then the fire reached out for Helmuth and his wife, leaping up their clothes, enveloping them in a mantle of flames and, within seconds, burning their living bodies to ashes.

Fires raged in Dresden for eight nights, in which it was estimated that nearly seventy thousand people died. Still the Russians continued to advance. Those who had not perished in Dresden fled towards the sanctuary of Berlin.

There was little shelter in Berlin for the refugees who survived the fire storms of Dresden. Their only refuge was under bridges, in parks, in underground and railway stations. Guided by huge fires started by American incendiary bombs, the British continued to flay the hub of Berlin's transport and communications systems — airports, canals and railways. Thousands who had survived one furnace died in another, homeless, nameless and unidentified.

After Hans's capture, Monika had stayed at the parsonage with her parents-in-law. Night after night, she and the Königs listened to the news and wondered what they should do. Russian armies entered Upper Pomerania and slowly fought their way through to the Baltic. On 9 March, they reached the Oder at Stettin. Monika was panic-stricken, begging the Königs to leave for Berlin. 'They'll kill us all if they reach Fürstenmark. If you won't leave, let me and the children go. The Quadriga is still all right. We'll be safe there.'

'No, Monika, you'll be much safer here,' Pastor König told her firmly. 'The Russians aren't interested in Fürstenmark. It's Berlin they want.' He was one of the few men left. All the others had been conscripted into the *Volkssturm*.

'And, by the sound of it, not much of Berlin is standing. Be sensible, Monika dear.' Gerda König paused. Not even she now believed that they were going to win the war. 'And when the war is over, Hans will know where to find us.'

Hans seemed like a figment of her imagination these days, but Monika realized the sense in what the Königs were saying. 'All right,' she agreed. That night, after she had tucked Heini and Senta up in bed, she stood for a while at the window, looking towards the castle. For seven hundred years it had symbolized Teutonic might. She could not believe it would ever fall. It was inviolable. And so was Germany. It must be. Surely?

As the Russians overran Silesia, production in all Kraus mines and factories ceased. There was no coal, fuel or raw materials for the Ruhr.

On 7 March, the US First Army poured across the Ludendorff Bridge at Remagen and established their first bridgehead on the eastern bank of the Rhine. Three nights later, three and a half thousand tons of bombs rained down on Essen and fierce fires raged through what was left of the marshalling-yards and factories.

From the Fortress, Ernst looked down over the town and recognized that it was futile to continue battling against insuperable odds. Better to preserve their equipment and such raw materials as remained for the future. There was no foretelling what might happen in Silesia. Having gained it, the Russians might prove very difficult to remove, in which case a new war could start — one in which Germany, America and England were allied against their mutual enemy — the Soviet Union. In that case, Kraus armaments would again be needed.

Next morning, Ernst gave orders for all production to halt. The huge machines were immobilized. The staff were dismissed. The doors to the vast underground gunshops and factories were locked, sealed and barred. Ernst returned to the Fortress to wait.

On 22 March, the Americans crossed the Rhine at Mainz. Next day, the British crossed it at Wesel. From the Fortress, Ernst could hear the sound of enemy artillery and the answering fire of Field Marshal Model's Army Group B.

Day after day, the fighting continued, as the Americans encircled the Ruhr and slowly began to penetrate its defences. Finally, on 9 April, when Ernst looked out from the Fortress, two American jeeps were wending their way up the winding road. He turned to his butler, immaculate in black frock coat and white gloves. 'We're about to have visitors, Magnus.'

'Yes, Herr Ernst.'

'Take your time finding me, Magnus. It's taken them so many years to get here, it will do them no harm to wait a few minutes.'

'I understand, Herr Kraus.'

From his study, Ernst heard the banging on the door and the American voice, demanding, 'I wanna see the owner of this house.'

'*Ich verstehe leider kein Englisch,*' Magnus replied.

'Der Direktor of this goddamned house.'

'*Jawohl. Warten Sie einen Moment.*'

Ernst heard his footsteps echo slowly down the marble hall and eventually start to mount the carved oak staircase. Together, they waited in the study — one minute, two minutes, five minutes. Then Ernst turned to his butler and, for the first time in the entire forty years that the man had served his family, shook his hand. 'Thank you, Magnus.'

There were ten Americans, all armed with submachine-guns, but it was upon the military police lieutenant who was starting to make his way down the hall that Ernst's attention was focused. Pointing his gun at Ernst, he demanded, 'You this son of a bitch Kraus?' At that moment, Ernst knew something was going very wrong. It was not just the gun and the tone of the man's voice, but something far, far worse. The lieutenant was black.

'My name is Ernst Kraus.'

'Yeah, one of the bastards who started this goddamned war. Well, now you're finding out who's ending it.' A soldier moved forward and handed him a pair of handcuffs, which the lieutenant snapped over Ernst's wrists.

Ernst stared at him in bewilderment. 'What are you doing?'

'You're under arrest, Kraus.'

'But why?'

'You're head of Kraus Industries. That's charge enough for the moment. No doubt we'll be able to find a few more by the time we've finished with you.' He jabbed his gun in Ernst's elegant waistcoat. 'Now, get moving!'

'Where are you taking me?'

'To prison. Though if I had my own way, I'd shoot you and have done with it. Now, move your arse.'

'But I have never done anything against America. I worked in New York for four years, running an American company…'

The gun clicked ominously. 'Shut up, Kraus.'

Ernst was shoved into one of the armed jeeps and driven off down the hill towards the ruins of Essen. 'You see that?' The lieutenant waved his gun. 'Those chimneys will never smoke again, Kraus. You may be president of a solitary prison cell, but you'll never run a business again. Your days are over. You're finished — kaput.'

Ernst hardly heard him. He was trying to come to terms with the bitter realization that his father had sold him out. 'You've made a dreadful mistake. It isn't me you want — it's my father, Baron Heinrich von Kraus.'

'Your father?' the lieutenant scoffed. 'Come off it. You lived in the Fortress. You ran the gunshops of Essen. You're the "Steel King"!'

Life in the ruins of Berlin continued with a sense of unreal, almost insane normality. Such shops as had not been bombed were still open. The underground railway and the S-Bahn ran a spasmodic service, where cave-ins allowed. Postmen delivered letters, policemen directed traffic through rubble-strewn streets, garbage was collected and the telephone still worked. Even part of the zoo remained open. And, all the time, endless processions of refugees from the east dragged themselves wearily towards the west.

Under the supervision of Norbert and his colleagues from the Todt Organization, trenches were dug around the city. The Tiergarten became an impregnable stronghold. Batteries of anti-aircraft guns were ranged on the roofs of the bunkers where Hitler and his staff had their headquarters. Cannon defended the canals that surrounded it.

The Hotel Quadriga was one of the last places to have an unfailing water and electricity supply. On its upper floors, Polish chambermaids attempted to keep the rooms clean, while in its restaurants and bars, elderly waiters dressed in frock coats and white gloves continued to wait on tables, pushing their serving trolleys between crowded, jostling tables, offering meagre portions of food from huge silver platters to their undiscerning clientèle.

Because of its proximity to the Tiergarten and the remaining ministries, the hotel also became part of the defences. The only light to penetrate the windows overlooking Unter den Linden came through narrow observation slits between walls of sandbags. Both Benno and Viktoria were appalled.

'The Russians are going to assume we are a military establishment,' Benno told Norbert. 'Do you mean to say we have survived British and American air raids just to be blown to smithereens by the Red Army?'

'Orders are orders,' Norbert replied. 'You have the Gestapo here. They have to be protected. Personally, I would advise you go to Heiligensee before the Russians get here.'

'Is Hitler really still here in Berlin?' Viktoria asked. Norbert nodded. 'Then it's the only commendable thing he's ever done. If he's staying, so shall we, Norbert.'

Her nephew looked troubled. 'You could be in great danger. I certainly intend to get out as soon as things look serious.'

Viktoria jutted her chin out obstinately. 'You can do what you like, Norbert. But this is *my* hotel. I shan't desert it.'

On Monday 16 April, they heard that the Russians had launched their attack against the German armies ranged along the west bank of the Oder. In frantic haste, the Gestapo moved out of the Hotel

Quadriga. Overflowing files, record books, stacks of papers tied with string, dossiers, registers and ledgers were thrown in confusion into waiting vans and driven away through the Brandenburg Gate.

In their wake, Norbert appeared, suitcases in each hand, Reinhild Pacher at his side. 'If the Gestapo has gone, it's time for us to leave too.'

'Where will you go? To Innsbruck?' Benno asked.

'We're going to Reinhild's grandparents in Lübeck.' Norbert gave his lopsided smile. 'Then we're going to get married.'

Viktoria looked from one to the other of them, thinking again how amazingly resilient youth was. Germany was collapsing, but Norbert and Reinhild still found time for love. She took their hands in hers. 'Congratulations and good luck. I hope you'll be very happy.'

She and Benno stood on the pavement, watching them walk down Unter den Linden. 'Are you sure you won't change your mind and go to Heiligensee while there's still time?' Benno asked.

'No. You go if you want. But I'm staying here.'

His lips touched her hair. 'All right, we'll see it through, the two of us, right to the bitter end.'

The air-raid sirens wailed and a distant drone of bombers came, not from the west, but from the east. Benno took Viktoria's arm and they joined the mass of people, scurrying to safety in the cellar.

Russian tanks thundered over the cobblestoned streets of Fürstenmark, scattering chickens and geese into ditches and hedgerows. At the parsonage, Pastor König sent Gerda, Monika and the children down to the cellar, then locked the doors and shuttered the windows. Not a sound came from the village.

After the tanks came armoured trucks full of troops. They, too, clattered through the village. Finally, as evening drew in, came a procession of cars. They halted in the square outside the church, then drove through the archway into the castle courtyard.

Shortly after this, there was a hammering on the parsonage door. Pastor König muttered a quick prayer and undid the bolts. Two armed soldiers awaited him outside. They seized him by the arm and marched him peremptorily to the castle.

Gerhardt Bishof and the few remaining maids were already huddled together under an armed guard in the galleried dining hall, when Pastor König arrived. They gazed at him in terror and the Pastor tried to smile with an assurance he did not feel.

An officer marched into the room, followed by some aides. He spoke for a few moments in Russian, then one of the aides translated into guttural German. 'The Red Army is in command of this village. This castle is our headquarters. Who is the owner?'

'Count von Biederstein is dead,' Pastor König replied.

The officer stared coldly at him and asked a question. The aide translated. 'What is your position?'

'I am the Pastor.'

'You are put in charge of the villagers. These are the regulations.' He read from a sheet of paper. 'All members of the Nazi Party must register to us. All food supplies must be handed over to the Red Army. All guns, ammunition, radio sets, vehicles, horses and petrol must be handed over. A curfew will operate from sundown to sunrise. Nobody may leave the village without authorization. Is that clear?'

'Yes, sir.'

'That is all.'

Pastor König stumbled across the courtyard to his home. It could all be far worse. At least the few of them who remained were to be left alive. But Fürstenmark castle, the seat of the von Biedersteins for seven centuries, taken over by Bolsheviks? It was a dreadful thought…

Next day, the Russian cars left Fürstenmark, leaving a guard at the castle. Pastor König commenced his soul-destroying task of handing over their possessions to the Russian victors. On his instructions, Monika set fire to her signed photograph of the Führer.

For three months, Otto Tobisch led a quiet existence on the farm that had belonged to Anna's parents in the mountains above the Traunsee in the Austrian Salzkammergut. He had buried the valuables he had brought with him from Schlachtenhausen in a waterproof bag deep beneath a cattle byre. He had put away his SS uniform and let it be known among the villagers that he had come from the Russian front.

In the middle of April, there was a sudden influx from Berlin into the peaceful Salzkammergut. Suddenly, the streets of the local towns thronged with officials from the Foreign Ministry, the Gestapo and the SS. Rumours reached him of a new SS headquarters set up in Bad Aussee, with SS-Obergruppenführer Kaltenbrunner in command.

No longer worried about being charged with deserting his post, Otto went to Bad Aussee. He did not succeed in seeing Kaltenbrunner, but he did meet with several old comrades at a lakeside inn. All told the same story. The Russians had captured Vienna and had surrounded Berlin. The Americans would soon reach the Danube. Himmler had fled nobody knew where.

'There is to be no last stand against the enemy?' Otto asked.

'We have no arms…'

So, it had come that far. The masters of Germany were being forced to run away like frightened rabbits.

Otto returned to Traunsee and prepared to lead a rural existence for a while longer. When the next war began against the Soviet Union, his services would be required again.

The inhabitants of the Hotel Quadriga stayed in the cellar for most of that week, as Russian bombers attempted to finish off the job started by the British and Americans, making sortie after sortie against Berlin. Whenever the all-clear sounded, Benno hurried through the hotel to ascertain the damage. Each time, his face grew longer. There were huge holes in the roof. The ballroom and the kitchens were badly damaged. But still the hotel did not suffer a direct hit. And on Saturday, 21 April, the air raids ceased.

A *Volkssturm* company arrived at the Quadriga, among them Hasso Annuschek, a captain now. His face was tired and drawn, as he commented drily, 'I never thought that I would one day be responsible for the defence of the Hotel Quadriga.' He looked grimly at the weapon in his hand. 'And with what? This is a panzerfaust, one of the most deadly anti-tank guns ever invented. But it fires only one shot. Herr Benno, Frau Viktoria, our city is defended by old men and young boys armed with panzerfausts.'

He brought their first news from the outside world. 'The Russians have formed a ring round the city. The main body of their troops seem to be concentrated on the southern suburbs, but they'll come in from all sides.' He paused, then added, 'They seem to have brought in fresh troops from the East, ferocious units of Mongol soldiers… We don't stand a chance.'

When the Kaiser had opened the Hotel Quadriga in 1894, he had inspected the vast wine cellars and asked Karl Jochum, 'Are you expecting a siege?' Just over fifty years later, the siege was taking place, but when it ended, there was little likelihood that the Germans would be the victors. Far more likely was it that the Russians would commandeer the canned food and the half-million bottles of wine stored there.

At dinner that night, Benno clapped his hands for silence. 'Ladies and gentlemen, from now on all meals will be provided free of charge.' There was a feeble round of applause. 'Furthermore, you are invited to choose from our extensive wine list and enjoy as much wine as you can drink with the compliments of the Hotel Quadriga.' A ripple of laughter and a cheer went up from the guests and staff.

Rather than let his wine fall into the hands of the Red Army, Benno preferred to give it away.

The air raids stopped and a new sound was heard at Heiligensee. It started as a low whistle, then it wailed, sending shivers up the spine, and finally it exploded with a piercing shriek. The first artillery shell burst upon the suburbs.

Ricarda unlocked the cabinet where her father's old hunting rifle was kept. It was a long time since she had used a gun, but she thought she still remembered how. She opened the breech, loaded the ammunition and stared down the firing sight. It would make scant impression on a tank, but it would kill a Russian soldier if he got too close. She bundled the two girls back down into the cellar, locked the door and waited for war to come to Heiligensee.

However, off the main road, secluded in a bay of the lake, the cottage was well away from the main path of the Russian tanks as they raced in towards Tegel, their goal Hitler's bunker in the heart of the city.

That night, when Ricarda looked out, the sky south of Heiligensee was red with flames. *Dear God*, she prayed. *It doesn't matter about the Quadriga. But please spare Vicki and Benno.*

Each day brought the battle nearer to the Quadriga. The sound of mortar bombs and shells grew steadily louder. The red rim of fire that marked the progress of the Russian armies edged closer. Terrified civilians, their houses burned or demolished, their exits from the city barred, made their way to the centre and sought refuge in the hotel.

Each brought with them descriptions of the horrors being inflicted by the Red Army on their city and the courage of the Berliners who were defending it. The Russians had overrun the city's outer defences. Now they were held back only by temporary roadblocks: overturned trams, buses and lorries, rubble from bombsites, furniture from ruined houses. Yet still the Berliners and the *Volkssturm* were fighting back. From rooftops, windows, ruins, railway and underground stations, old men, women and children were doing their utmost to repel the hated Russian armies.

They could not hope to win. Every day, the circle grew closer. Street by street, block by block, Berlin was being forced to surrender. Weissensee fell. The garrison town of Potsdam was seized. Dahlem, Spandau, Rathenow, Neukölln and Tempelhof were overrun. Tanks and heavy artillery blasted at the shells of buildings. Flamethrowers fired houses which had, until then, escaped enemy bombs. Grenades were lobbed. Bayonets stabbed into the hearts of dying men. The streets of Berlin ran thick with blood.

Most of the hospitals had been bombed, so many of the wounded were brought to the Quadriga, among them an army medical officer, an elderly man called Dr Urban Thurn, who was fortunately only suffering from a superficial wound. Having seen to his own injury, he organized the hotel into a makeshift hospital. Viktoria immediately offered her services as his assistant. 'I'm afraid I don't know much about first-aid, but if you'll tell me what to do, I'll do what I can.'

'That's all any of us can do,' the doctor replied wearily.

The most seriously injured were taken to the cellar. The others were put in the Jubilee Room, the restaurant and the bar. Hasso Annuschek put down his panzerfaust to help Benno organize the massive influx, supervising food and sleeping accommodation and making sure the hotel remained as clean as possible. This in itself was an almost impossible task. They still had water from the Artesian well, but the city's sewers had been severely damaged. Soon the stink of blocked drains and human excreta mingled with the putrid smell of gangrenous wounds.

No difference was made any longer between staff, guests or *Volkssturm*. Everyone who was fit enough helped with preparing cauldrons of soup, washing, comforting and nursing the injured. They ripped up sheets to make bandages. Legs were pulled off chairs and tables to make splints for broken limbs.

There were no drugs or antiseptics, so bottles of spirits were brought up from the cellar to anaesthetize pain. Salt and bicarbonate of soda were used to clean wounds. Pans of water were boiled on the kitchen ranges and kept warm on spirit stoves once used for flambés.

Emergency operations were performed on trestle tables in the ladies' salon. A table napkin knotted at the nape of her neck, Viktoria fought back her nausea, as she followed Urban Thurn's instructions, holding down screaming men as he made incisions, wiping damp towels over brows and lighting cigarettes for men with no hands to hold them.

Still they poured into the hotel: men with blood seeping through makeshift bandages, men with limbs sticking out at crazy angles, men with no eyes, no ears, no legs, their faces burned, their heads half blown off, their entrails spilling out. The cellar was full. There were no more beds or mattresses, so they laid them in rows on the blue Savonnerie carpet in the foyer.

Many could not be saved and when they died, there was nowhere to bury them. So the Palm Garden Room was turned into a mortuary, the corpses piled on the parquet floor beneath the dark tarpaulins that stretched across steel girders where once a glass roof had been. A reek of death added to the other smells permeating the hotel.

By dusk on Friday, 27 April, the Russians had reached the Landwehr Canal in the south and the River Spree to the north. Waiters painted huge red crosses on white tablecloths and hung them on the outside walls of the hotel, so that when the invaders arrived they should realize it was not a military stronghold, but a field hospital.

That night, the din of the guns was stilled, but not the screams, sighs and feverish mutterings of the hundreds of mutilated men in the Hotel Quadriga. Neither did the sudden silence abate the fears of those who tended them. They recognized it as a lull before a storm.

Next morning at dawn, the final, decisive battle commenced. For two days and nights, the city resounded to the barrage of Russian artillery and Katyusha rockets, and the returning fire from SS battalions posted along the canal and river banks, in ministries, museums and palaces, under bridges and on fortified islands, defending Hitler's bunker.

On the evening of Monday, 30 April, the first Russian tanks rumbled down Unter den Linden towards the Brandenburg Gate. Scalpel in hand, Dr Thurn glanced at Viktoria from red-rimmed eyes. She wiped a bloody wrist across her forehead and went out into the foyer, where Benno was already gazing apprehensively at the entrance.

The steel doors in the blast wall burst open and wild-eyed Soviet soldiers appeared in the entrance, brandishing submachine-guns. For a moment, they stopped in surprise at the sight of the bodies covering the floor, then one loosed off a volley into the air, bringing stuccowork crashing down from the ceiling.

Benno walked towards them, hands above his head. 'Don't shoot! This is a hospital.'

More soldiers surged through the open door, Mongols waving carbines and bayonets. Uttering blood-curdling yells, they stormed past Benno towards Viktoria. Terror-stricken, remembering all the horrific stories she had heard of Russian soldiers raping German women, she shrank back against the wall, but they charged past her, trampling over the wounded men, up the staircase.

There the *Volkssturm* was waiting, Panzerfausts in hand, their bullets tearing into the Russians, sending them reeling back into the foyer. Those who had not been hit loosed off a cannonade of bullets. Old men and boys tumbled down the stairs, pouring with blood and screaming. The Mongols raced on towards the upper floors.

Another wave poured through the blast wall, firing submachine-guns. All over the foyer, people were writhing and crying in agony. Viktoria screamed, hands to her ears, as before her the foyer turned blood red. With ghoulish howls, the Mongols broke into the operating theatre, burst into the restaurant and the Jubilee Room and surged down the staircase towards the cellar.

Benno tore after them. He remembered the Russian word for stop. '*Stoi! Stoi!* There's nothing down there.'

An officer with a row of medals on his chest appeared in the main entrance, stood for a moment surveying the chaotic scene, then barked a sharp order and the shooting stopped.

The officer's voice was inaudible in the basement, where Benno was still ineffectually shouting, '*Stoi! Stoi!*' The bloodlust was coursing strong through the Mongols' veins. They had one simple purpose — revenge against the Germans. At last, they were in the Devil's City and, before they left, they were going to make sure that not a brick was standing.

Some found the doors to the wine cellar and blasted the locks. There came the sound of shattered glass and hair-raising laughter. They smashed the tops off bottles and tipped the wine down their throats. Others discovered the doors leading into the service area to the workshops, central heating boilers and fuel store. Benno heard the noise of splintering wood and more gunfire.

At the top of his voice, he bellowed, '*Stoi! Stoi!*' They paid no attention to him. He rushed back to where the injured lay. 'Get out of here! They'll blow the whole place sky-high.' Frantically, he started helping the men off the pallets, urging them upstairs. 'Quickly, quickly. For God's sake, hurry.'

In the foyer, the noise could be dimly heard above the thunder of the tanks and mortar fire outside on Unter den Linden and the cries of the men inside. Crippled men dragged themselves up the cellar steps. Suddenly, from the bowels of the earth, came a deafening explosion. 'Benno!' Viktoria screamed and hurled herself across the foyer.

Hasso Annuschek and the Russian officer were there before her. While Hasso seized hold of her arms, the officer pushed against the stream of men coming up the stairs. A gust of smoke blew into their faces. Viktoria struggled to free herself. 'Benno! Benno!'

There was another explosion even louder than before and clouds of dense black smoke billowed up the stairwell. 'The oil tanks,' Hasso gasped. 'Oh, you dear God!'

Viktoria beat her hands against his chest. 'Let me go! I must find Benno! Benno! Benno!'

The explosion had thrown Benno to the ground. He picked himself up and peered through the black smoke. Apart from the Mongols pillaging the wine, there were only about twenty men left in the cellar. Choking in the acrid fumes, he lifted one of them and lurched towards the cellar stairs. A Russian officer suddenly appeared, snatched the body Benno was carrying and took it upstairs. Benno staggered back to fetch another wounded man.

The officer staggered to the top of the stairs and dumped his burden on the floor. 'Out! Out! Fire!' he shouted in German.

At that moment, a third explosion rent the air, making the whole building shudder. There was a huge whoosh as the entire service area caught fire. The blast blew out the dividing walls and lifted Benno from his feet, throwing him to the far side of the room, where he lay stunned.

In the foyer, there was a stampede towards the road. Clouds of smoke and tongues of flame billowed up the lift shafts. Sparks caught light to tapestries and carpets. With a mighty crash, the kitchen floor subsided and, unrestricted now, the flames leaped high towards the sky.

In the wine vaults, the Mongols loosed their submachine-guns indiscriminately, setting fire to the dry straw and paper protecting

Benno's precious racks of wine. Fanned by the wind created by the boiler room fire, the flames licked round the wine spilled from broken bottles. Glass cracked. The wine ignited.

Benno opened his eyes to find himself in the centre of a scorching, raging inferno, loud with the screams of sick men and terrified Mongol soldiers. Once again, he dragged himself to his feet and looked for the staircase. Above him, the ceiling rumbled.

Viktoria wrenched herself free of Hasso and started down the cellar steps, screaming, 'Benno! Benno!' But where the cellar had been was now a white-hot furnace. She could see nobody. Flames leaped out and set fire to her skirt.

In the cellar, Benno covered his face with a damp towel, closed his eyes and ran towards where the exit had once been. Within seconds, his suit was ablaze, his skin scorching and an excruciating pain searing through him. He convulsed into a heap on the floor and the fire consumed him. Then the ceiling fell in and buried him.

Hasso grabbed Viktoria before she fell, extinguished the flames before they took hold, lifted her up and carried her towards the street. The fire had reached the whole of the ground floor now. Pandemonium reigned, as the Russian officer and Dr Thurn attempted to organize a mass evacuation.

Hasso had no care for them. His sole thought was to save Viktoria's life. He made the street, only to find they were in the centre of another battlefield. The nearby underground station had been transformed into an armoured fort. From behind a barricade of sandbags, German SS men and *Volkssturm* were launching a vicious assault on the tanks lumbering towards the Brandenburg Gate and the Wilhelmstrasse. The air was thick with dust and flying debris.

He crossed the avenue to the central promenade and set Viktoria on her feet, his arms round her shoulders to steady her. Her face was black, her hair and clothes singed. She was weeping hysterically, shrieking Benno's name.

People were still pouring out of the hotel through the steel doors in the blast wall. Flames were licking out of windows on all floors. Figures of soldiers could be seen silhouetted against them. Some jumped to the ground. Others toppled backwards into the conflagration. The fire reached the gaping holes in the roof, hurling blackened beams high into the air as from an erupting volcano.

Now the fire was master of the Hotel Quadriga. It rampaged through restaurants, private banqueting rooms, bars and kitchens. It roared through the Jubilee Room and devoured the pile of corpses in the Palm Garden Room. Its giant fingers seared along the Savonnerie carpets and into the once luxurious suites and apartments on the upper floors, eating into the satin sheets, feather mattresses and quilts, smelting the iron bedsteads with their brass prancing horses. The dry timber floorboards cracked under the scorching heat and the huge marble bath tubs plummeted down into the cellars.

For a while, the blackened joists of the roof withstood the flames, then they crashed downwards. Lacking support, the walls caved in. Finally, the long portico and balustraded balcony teetered and fell into the seething furnace with a roar of thunder. The fire tossed its trophies high into the orange sky in glorious celebration of its strength. With ghastly groans and shrieks of anguish, the Hotel Quadriga collapsed inwards upon the body of Benno Kraus, buried deep in the rubble of its subterranean caverns.

'Benno! Benno!' Viktoria screamed.

But no more people emerged from the hotel's portals which were once so imposing and Hasso knew there was no hope for Herr Benno.

So intense was the heat, so dangerous the flying timbers and masonry that the street battle had stopped, the tanks compelled either to retreat or take another route, the Germans forced back down into the station for shelter. The entrance to the subway was undefended. Hasso seized his opportunity. Propelling Viktoria across the rubble, he lifted her over the sandbags and leaped over them after her. Shouting '*Volkssturm!*' so as not to be mistaken for the enemy, he pushed her down the stairs and onto the platform, crowded with homeless civilians and wounded soldiers.

A number of people were making their way up the railway track and Hasso jumped down after them, turning to lift Viktoria down. If they could reach the Stettiner Station, hopefully they would be able to find their way under cover of darkness to his sister Rosa's house in Wedding.

On and on down the long black tunnel they stumbled, their way lit by flickering torches held by people ahead. Often their passage was blocked with rubble. Sometimes, the night sky was visible through holes in the subway roof and the din of the ongoing battle could be heard. Occasionally, a rat scuttled across their path, its eyes glowing eerily in the dark. Viktoria was unconscious of all these things. She saw only the Mongols, the Quadriga on fire and Benno, somewhere down in the cellar.

It was just after the Friedrichstrasse station, where the underground passed beneath the River Spree, that they met an unforeseen obstacle in the form of a steel bulkhead designed to seal the tunnel in the case of a flood. This massive barrier was shut. Their route to the Stettiner Station was barred. People were wrenching at it with steel rails, trying to prise it open, but Hasso had no time for such futile endeavours.

There was only one thing for it. They had to go above ground and find some other way across the river. Seizing Viktoria's hand, he dragged her back down the tunnel, through the ruins of the station, and out in the open. Hasso was a Berliner. He knew the city like the palm of his hand. And he was certain all the main arterial bridges would be heavily defended either by German or Russian tanks. However, there was a faint chance that the Schlütersteg, a narrow pedestrian bridge, might have been ignored.

He was right. Quickly he cut through the barbed wire blocking it with the wire cutters on his Army knife and whispered to Viktoria, 'Run! Run as quickly as you can!' To his relief, they got across without a shot being fired, scrambled down the iron staircase and arrived safely on the stone quay of the Schiffbauerdamm. Now, all that remained was to find his way through the mountains of rubble to Wedding, praying they would not run into any Russian soldiers.

It was a nightmare journey. The moon gave only an intermittent light. Sometimes, the horizon was lit up by searchlights, reflecting the low pall of yellowish smoke which hung over the city. Periodically, the silence was broken by a burst of artillery fire. From the shadows came the whisper of voices. Often, they stumbled over dead bodies.

Keeping under the cover of walls, avoiding all open spaces, they passed the Charité hospital, echoing to the drunken whoops of Russian soldiers, passed the Natural History Museum and turned into what had once been the Chaussee-Strasse. Ahead of them loomed the former barracks of the Fusilier Guards, in more recent times a *Volkssturm* stronghold, now undoubtedly in Russian hands. Hasso delved right into the freight yards north of the Stettiner Station. In the light of a burning hut, he glanced at his watch. It was just gone two.

Viktoria sank down on the ground and Hasso looked at her worriedly. Her clothes were torn, her face streaked with dust, her eyes red and sore. Should they rest for a while, or was it better to keep on towards Wedding in the relative security of darkness? Instinct told him to press on. The night air was damp and travelling in daylight would be even more dangerous than at night. He helped her to her feet. 'It's not far now,' he assured her.

She just gazed at him blankly.

Familiar though Hasso was with the city, he no longer recognized anything in the dark ruins that loomed ahead of him, so he decided to follow the tangled remains of the railway line. At least that was leading him north and, after another hour or so of very heavy going, they reached the Grenzstrasse road bridge.

From then on, the terrain was easier. Although the streets through which they passed had been devastated by bombs, they evinced no signs of a ground battle like the one that had flattened the city centre. Incredible though it seemed, whole tenement blocks in Wedding were still standing. From the broken frames of some windows, red flags fluttered, bearing the hammer and sickle.

The first streaks of dawn showed in the eastern sky when they reached the Max-Strasse. For a moment, his heart lurched, as stark walls reared above him. Surely they could not have come so far and in vain? He dived through a doorway and into a dingy hall. Ahead of him, firm and solid, he saw the entrance to the cellar. He hammered on the door. 'Rosa! Rosa! It's Hasso!'

The door opened and a face peered out. 'Hasso, thank God…'

He pushed Viktoria through the door, then followed her. Lit by a single candle, the cellar stank to high heaven and, as his eyes gradually became accustomed to the darkness, he saw it was crammed with people. In a low voice, he quickly explained to Rosa what had happened and together they helped Viktoria to a mattress in a corner of the room. Rosa made her some ersatz coffee on a small spirit stove. 'Drink this, and you'll feel better.'

Hasso put his arm round Viktoria's shoulder. 'Now you will be all right,' he promised.

Viktoria stared at him mutely. How could she ever be all right again? Her life was over. It had ended with the Quadriga and Benno's death.

Sick with worry, Ricarda sat in the cellar knitting, while Christa and Lili did a jigsaw puzzle. The radio was on low, tuned into a Hamburg station, broadcasting a recording of Bruckner's *Seventh Symphony*.

From the day the Russian tanks had sped past Heiligensee, Ricarda had not let the two girls out of her sight. The nearby Tegel forest resounded to the thunder of gunfire. Heiligensee was a backwater of no immediate importance to them, but once the Russians had seized Berlin's strategic strongholds, they would work their way out to secure the suburbs and then the real danger would begin.

Every afternoon they walked quickly down to the lake and back for a breath of fresh air. The rest of the day was spent indoors behind shuttered windows and locked doors, most of the time near the radio in the cellar.

There had been no news from the Quadriga. When Ricarda had tried to telephone, she had been unable to get through. After the 24th, there had been no newspapers. Electricity and gas supplies were spasmodic. Incredibly, the radio still worked, but there were no broadcasts from Berlin. If it had not been for the pall of smoke and the red rim of fire that hung over it, together with the distant roar of guns, they might almost have believed the city had ceased to exist.

Suddenly, the music was interrupted and an announcer said, '*Achtung! Achtung!* The German Broadcasting Company has a serious, important message for the German people.' There were three solemn rolls of military drums.

Christa and Lili let their pieces of jigsaw fall.

'It is reported from the Führer's headquarters that our Führer, fighting to the last breath against Bolshevism, fell for Germany this afternoon in his operational headquarters in the Reich Chancellery. On 30 April, the Führer appointed Grand Admiral Dönitz his successor. The Grand Admiral and successor of the Führer now speaks to the German people.'

Admiral Dönitz's voice was grave. 'German men and women, soldiers of the armed forces. Our Führer, Adolf Hitler, has fallen. In the deepest sorrow and respect the German people bow...'

'Hitler is dead...' Christa breathed.

'Is the war over?' Lili asked.

Ricarda held her finger to her lips. Dönitz continued: 'It is my task to save Germany from destruction by the advancing Bolshevist enemy. For this aim alone the military struggle continues...'

Ricarda shook her head. 'Hitler is dead, but the terror he created goes on...'

The following afternoon the radio reported that Berlin had surrendered to the Red Army. 'Thank God,' Ricarda whispered. 'If Berlin has surrendered, so must the rest of Germany. Soon we shall have peace.'

Peace... The word echoed in Christa's mind. She tiptoed upstairs, through the living room onto the verandah. The distant sounds of gunfire had stopped. An eerie quiet hung over the city, a silence palpable as the cloud of dust and smoke. Stefan and her parents' dreams had come true — but it was too late. Peace could not bring the dead back to life.

There was a whirring of wings overhead and a brace of wild duck skimmed to a halt on the still lake covered with floating pieces of debris. The brilliant colours of the drake mallard's feathers gleamed against the silver water. Placidly, his mate paddled beside him.

Lost in her thoughts, Christa walked across the grass towards the fallen oak tree by the shore. From some nearby shrubs a blackbird sounded a shrill alarm call. So familiar a noise was it that Christa paid no heed. Too late did she realize her danger. From the bushes, a man appeared, short and swarthy, dressed in a dull brown uniform, with a red star on his cap and a submachine-gun slung on his back. A childish smile creased his face. He beckoned to her.

For a moment, she stood, chill with fear, then she turned and started to run towards the house.

It was too late. Another soldier blocked her way, leering at her with stained teeth. The first man seized hold of her wrist '*Uri, Uri, Uri,*' he said, pointing at her watch. It had been a present from her father, but Christa did not care, provided it would get rid of these horrid men. She undid the gold bracelet and handed it to him. His slanting eyes gleamed and he put it on his own arm. To her amazement she saw he already wore about a dozen.

The other soldier grabbed hold of her blouse. '*Kumm Frau.*'

'Let me go!' She tried to wrench away his hand. It was the wrong thing to do. Roughly, he pushed her to the ground. Christa opened her mouth to scream, hoping that Ricarda would hear her, but the watch soldier's hand came down over her mouth. '*Frau. Frau.*' His comrade started to unbutton his trousers. Terrified, Christa bit sharply into the palm of the hand. It was quickly removed, then came back to hit her hard across the face. She tasted blood.

The soldier's trousers were around his knees and he held his erect penis in his hand, proudly showing it to her. 'No!' Terrified, she tried to struggle to her knees, but she was no match for the two of them. The watch soldier knocked her back onto the ground, then snatched at the material of her blouse and tore it from her shoulders. The other one wrenched her legs apart and pulled down her knickers. She kicked out, but to no avail.

He lowered himself on to her and she beat at his chest with her hands, writhing along the ground trying to escape. But there was neither escape nor any hope of rescue. The watch soldier ripped off her brassiere and clawed at her breasts, while his friend forced himself brutally into her, uttering guttural animal cries. A pain shot through her, as if her body were being split in half.

Again and again he hammered into her, finally collapsing onto her stomach. Moisture trickled down her thighs. It could have been semen or blood. The watch soldier pushed him away, picked up her limp body and turned it over. His trousers were already round his ankles.

'No, oh no,' Christa whimpered, pressing her legs together.

'*Gut Frau.*' The one who had just raped her held her so that her bottom stuck up in the air. The watch soldier gave a crude laugh. She tensed herself. He sank his penis into her and she screamed at an agony she had not thought possible. The world spun around her and she buried her face in the earth. When he had finished, she lay limply, wishing she were dead.

The soldier pulled up his trousers and looked down at her immobile body, then kicked it. She did not move. He said something unintelligible then they both walked away, laughing.

Slowly, Christa lifted her head. Once, a long time ago in another life, Stefan had made love to her here, in this very place that the Russians had now defiled. Her vision was blurred. She could not see the soldiers, but she could see the lake. Painfully, she crawled towards it. Water. Cool water to cleanse herself of the blood and their foul bodies. Water to wash away the shame...

She reached the water's edge. Past the scum and detritus she crept, and the water splashed around her knees and hands, washing away the blood that flowed down her legs, swirling around her in crimson eddies. Suddenly there came a small bank. Christa tumbled. The water covered her completely, lapping comfortingly over her hot, tear-stained face.

Ricarda did not at first notice Christa's absence. Only when she turned off the radio and Lili asked, 'Where's Christa?' did she realize the young woman was no longer in the cellar. She picked up the old hunting rifle and started to mount the stairs.

At that moment, she heard footsteps overhead, not those of Christa, but heavy boots, thumping over floorboards. Then came shouts and harsh laughter as furniture was moved about. The sound of breaking glass. Signalling to Lili to be quiet, Ricarda freed the safety catch on the rifle.

For some reason, however, the intruders made no attempt to open the cellar door. There was further unintelligible conversation, more guttural laughter, then, after what seemed an eternity, the boots clumped away. She let out her breath and, very quietly, opened the door and peered out into the hall. Holding the rifle in front of her, she edged into the living room.

The door onto the verandah stood open and through it Ricarda saw two uniformed men waving bottles in their hands, breaking through the hedge into the neighbouring property. So their uninvited guests had been Russians.

'Grandmama, where's Christa?'

'Lili, go back down into the cellar.'

'I'm frightened on my own.'

It was probably better for Lili to stay with her. Together, they searched the house, but there was no sign of Christa. With a sense of foreboding, they went into the garden.

Lili saw her first, lying face down in the lake, her torn clothes and her golden hair spread out around her amidst the flotsam and jetsam of the war. 'Christachen! Christachen!'

Ricarda waded into the lake and dragged her back to the beach. Christa's eyes were closed and her face had turned a purplish-blue. Her body was scratched and torn and quite still. Ricarda felt her pulse. There was no sign of life.

Lili sank down beside her, touching her face. 'Christachen, please be all right.'

'Lili, run up to the house and telephone Dr Geisler.'

While she was gone, Ricarda tried to effect artificial respiration. By the state of Christa's clothes and body she knew the Russian soldiers had raped her. While she and Lili had waited for the soldiers to go and searched the house, Christa could have been lying in the water for twenty minutes. Lili ran back down the lawn. 'The telephone isn't working. Shall I go and fetch Dr Geisler?'

But Ricarda could not risk letting her out on her own. At the end of an hour, she knew there was no hope of resuscitating Christa. Her eyes did not move. Her heart did not beat. 'Lili, darling, I'm sorry. Christa is dead.'

Tears poured down Lili's face. 'It's not possible. Christa's my friend. She can't be dead.'

There was nothing to do but cover her with a tarpaulin from the boathouse and leave her by the shore. Grief-stricken, Ricarda put her arm round Lili and took her back to the cottage.

For two days Viktoria was incarcerated in the cellar in Wedding, which grew increasingly claustrophobic. The only lavatory was a bucket behind a makeshift screen, which somebody scurried up to empty in the gutter when it was full. The air was foul. There was very little to eat. The women took it in turns to fetch water from a standpipe, but they did not allow Viktoria out.

Again and again, as she lay on a thin mattress, Viktoria relived in her mind that last hour in the Quadriga, wondering if she could have done more to save Benno. If she had not been so terrified for her own safety, could she have prevented him from following the Mongols into the cellar? Could she have gone down after him and dragged him to safety? If Hasso had not stopped her, she might have pulled him free of the flames and he would be here with her now.

Oh, Benno, Benno, you were so courageous. For all my brave words, I did nothing, but you died trying to save a cellar full of wounded men, while I stood by, screaming and terrified.

To avoid thinking, she tried to lose herself in sleep. But sleep, when it came, was no palliative, introducing new demons. She saw Norbert and Reinhild leaving for Lübeck and heard Benno ask, 'Are you sure you won't change your mind and go to Heiligensee?' And when she had refused, his voice replied, 'All right, we'll see it through, the two of us, right to the bitter end.'

And they had, right to the bitter end — and Benno was dead. *Oh, Benno, Benno, I never treated you as you deserved. From the very beginning, I deceived you and told you lies. I let you think Stefan was your son and, when he left, even then I could not bring myself to tell you the truth. I blamed you for supporting the Nazis and taking away my hotel and when you did not heed me, I turned to Mortimer.*

Benno, Benno, please forgive me. I would give anything, anything, to have you back with me again, so that I can tell you how sorry I am. I seem to have done everything wrong in my life. I pinned all my hopes and dreams on Stefan and, finally, hurt him so much that he left me.

But no matter what I did to you, you never stopped loving me, Benno. You were not only my husband, but my best friend, and now you're gone and it is too late for me to tell you that I love you.

The tears streamed down her face and she said aloud, 'Oh Benno, I love you. I love you so much…'

The women in the cellar glanced at each other in the dim light, helplessly sympathizing with her anguish. Hasso crouched beside her, 'Hush, Frau Viktoria, it's all right…'

She shook her head. 'Hasso, it's all my fault. If I had not been so selfish and obstinate, Benno would still be alive and we would both be together at Heiligensee. I killed Benno, Hasso. I killed him — and he was the only man who ever really loved me…'

Late on the afternoon of the second day, the guns fell silent and loudspeaker vans made their way through the ruins, bellowing out the message that Berlin had surrendered. Viktoria turned to Hasso. 'Tomorrow I shall go to Heiligensee. I must go home…'

Hasso knew it was useless to argue. He understood her need to be with her mother, the only person left to her, the only one who could heal the pain in her heart. 'All right,' he said gruffly. 'I'm sure Rosa can find you some old clothes.'

The following morning, at first light, Viktoria pulled on an old pair of slacks, a patched jacket, some walking shoes and a woollen headscarf to conceal her hair. Rosa rubbed dirt into her face to make her look as unattractive as possible. Viktoria tugged an amethyst ring from her finger and handed it to her. 'Please accept this for looking after me.'

Rosa started to protest, but Viktoria was adamant. If it had not been for them she would have perished. Reluctantly, Rosa took the ring and Viktoria set off on her journey to Heiligensee.

The city was shrouded in dust and ash. A stench of explosives, soot, sewers and decomposing human flesh assailed her nostrils. She moved stealthily, stopping at the sound of voices, clambering over piles of fallen masonry, ducking under beams, skirting massive bomb craters and burnt out vehicles, stumbling over corpses and severed limbs. And, for the first time, it occurred to her that the cottage might have been hit, that her mother might have been killed, that even in Heiligensee, there might be no refuge.

As the day wore on, more people appeared on the streets, not just Russian soldiers openly revelling in their victory, but German women fetching water and searching for personal belongings among the debris of their homes.

There were no names to any streets, no numbers on any houses, no houses to bear any numbers. Just long rows of ruins. Frequently she feared she had utterly lost her way, but each time the shell of a once familiar landmark confirmed that she was heading in the right direction. The remains of Kraus Chemie. A devastated area that had once been the Schillerpark.

By nightfall, she reached Tegel. The restaurant, where she had once had lunch with Mortimer, echoed to the music of Russian songs and the sound of an accordion. The doors opened and two soldiers reeled out, arms around each other's necks, brandishing bottles, singing at the top of their voices.

She spent the night huddled under a wall. Too cold, too hungry and too frightened to sleep, she concentrated her thoughts, not on the past or the present, but on the future. Tomorrow she would reach Heiligensee and Ricarda would look after her. And, one day, Stefan would return...

At dawn, she tiredly resumed her journey and found herself no longer alone, but part of a solid stream of refugees fleeing towards the west, pushing their meagre belongings in handcarts or carrying them in bundles on their backs. In the Tegel forest they found the remains of burnt-out German tanks, the ground littered with the bodies of German soldiers. From the distance, sporadic gunfire could still be heard, as last stalwart bands of men continued to resist the Soviet enemy.

Viktoria left the main road and continued her solitary journey towards Heiligensee. Night was drawing in when she reached the top of the drive. The cottage was in total darkness, all the shutters closed, but it was still standing. Tears of relief rose to her eyes. Everything would be all right. She was home.

She knocked frantically on the door. 'Mama! It's me. It's Viktoria!'

Slowly, the bolts were drawn back and Ricarda stood in the doorway, a candle in her hand, smaller, frailer and older than Viktoria remembered. 'Vicki, darling!' She stared anxiously beyond her into the dark. 'Surely you haven't come alone? Where's Benno?'

She opened her mouth to say, 'Benno's dead', but the words died on her lips. Lili appeared at Ricarda's side. The little girl was thin, her skin almost transparent, her green eyes enormous in her pale face. 'Aunt Vicki, Christa's dead. Some Russian soldiers came and Christa — Christa drowned…'

'We tried to save her, but it was too late,' Ricarda said. 'Vicki, she's still lying beside the lake. We have to bury her.'

'Aunt Vicki, you will stay with us, won't you?'

So, the cold fingers of war had reached out even to Heiligensee and inflicted tragedy. She stepped into the kitchen, closing the door behind her. 'Yes,' she said, 'I shall stay. There's nowhere else for me to go.'

She was too tired to eat, so Ricarda made some weak tea from her precious store and while Viktoria drank it, she took Lili down to the cellar to bed. When she returned, she asked, 'Vicki, where's Benno?'

Ricarda listened with growing horror as Viktoria described what had happened and, when she had finished, took her in her arms. She knew no adequate words to express her sympathy or describe her own sorrow. She had always loved Benno and felt his death as strongly as if he had been her own son.

For a long time, they stood locked in a silent embrace, each lost in their own dreadful memories, tears pouring down their cheeks, then Ricarda silently took Viktoria's arm and led her down into the cellar.

Viktoria slept for sixteen hours. When she woke, she found that her mother had managed to make enough hot water for her to have a bath. She took off the filthy trousers, jacket and headscarf and, for the first time in days, looked at herself in a mirror. To her horror, her hair had turned snow white.

CHAPTER TWENTY

The next few days passed in an exhausted daze. There was no electricity, so they could not listen to the radio. The telephone remained dead. Nobody came near the cottage. When they crept to the top of the drive, it was to see Russian cars and lorries roaring along the road into the village. They decided that the best thing to do was to bury Christa in the garden. They dug a deep pit and when it was finished, fetched her body and lowered it gently into it. 'This may not be hallowed ground, but it was her home for a long time,' Ricarda said. 'I'm sure God will understand.'

Viktoria thought of Benno lying beneath the Quadriga. 'What is Germany but a vast burial ground?' she asked, bitterly. 'As for God, He deserted us long ago.'

Lili began to cry and Ricarda handed her a trowel and a clump of forget-me-nots. 'Let's plant these in the middle of the grave, Lili, in memory of everyone we've lost.' They were very blue against the bare earth, as blue as Christa's eyes.

The following afternoon, a limousine with the hammer and sickle waving from its bonnet, followed by two jeeps, proceeded up the drive. Ricarda, Viktoria and Lili looked at each other fearfully. Armed soldiers jumped out of the jeeps. A chauffeur in Russian Army uniform got out of the limousine and opened the rear door for his passenger, a middle-aged officer, who stood for a moment looking around him, then walked up to the cottage door and knocked.

'I'll go,' Viktoria said. While Ricarda and Lili hovered behind her, she opened the front door and stared defiantly at the officer.

A tall, square-built man, with light brown hair, grey eyes and high Slavic cheekbones, he marched past her into the hall, followed by two soldiers. In guttural German, he said, 'This house is being taken over by the Red Army.'

She stared at him aghast. 'You can't do that! We have nowhere else to go. Our hotel on Unter den Linden was destroyed by Russian soldiers. My husband was killed…'

He glanced from her to Ricarda and Lili. 'How many people live here?'

'Three of us.'

'You are permitted to retain one room.'

'But that's ridiculous! You have no right…'

His expression hardened. 'What is your name?'

'Viktoria Jochum-Kraus.'

'Frau Jochum-Kraus, I have every right. Yesterday, Field Marshal Keitel formally surrendered to Marshal Zhukov. The war is over.'

So at last it had happened. The war was over. But there was no joy in the knowledge. Viktoria bit her lip to stop it trembling.

Ricarda stepped forward. 'Last week, a young woman who was living here was raped by Russian soldiers. She died. What guarantee do we have of safety?'

The officer actually looked slightly embarrassed. 'War is war and soldiers are soldiers. However, some of our men did get out of control. They have been reprimanded. You have my word that you will not be molested while I am in this house.'

'Thank you,' Ricarda replied, quietly. 'May we know your name?'

'I am Colonel Ivan Glazkhov.'

He gave them twenty-four hours to move into the former nursery in the stable block. When he had gone, Viktoria sank down in a chair. 'So the war is over… Dear God, perhaps it would have been better that we had all been killed than to live under the Russians…'

'Not all Russians can be bad. Colonel Glazkhov seemed a gentleman.'

'No,' Viktoria said vehemently. 'He's a communist.'

'That,' Ricarda remarked wisely, 'is rather like saying all Germans are Nazis. People should be judged by their behaviour, not by their politics.'

That evening, they moved into their new quarters, taking with them pots, pans, provisions and a spirit stove for cooking. The room was very cramped, but at least, as Ricarda pointed out, they had running water and a roof over their heads, which was more than most Berliners had.

On a separate trip they levered up the flagstone in the cellar and took their jewellery from the strongbox where Benno had placed it, although they left the box itself buried as the safest repository for their documents. 'Even if the Russians find them, they won't be interested in papers,' Ricarda said. Before they went to sleep that night, she took a needle and thread and made a strong belt into which she sewed their valuables. She gave it to Viktoria and said, 'Wear it next to your skin and never take it off.'

Next day, Colonel Glazkhov and his staff moved in. Two sentries were posted at the top of the drive, two more beside the front door. The Colonel took over their living room as his office and it was there he informed them of the first order issued by General Berzarin, the Russian Commander in Berlin.

'All arms, ammunition, wireless sets, cameras, cars and petrol must be handed over to the Soviet authorities. All banks have been closed and all accounts frozen. A curfew has been imposed. You may not leave the house between ten at night and eight in the morning. If you have food supplies exceeding five days' consumption, you must declare them. A rationing system is being introduced.'

He paused and studied the paper on the table in front of him. 'Ration cards will only be distributed to those who register for work. Old people and women with young children will receive lower-category rations. The three of you will be included in that category.'

Viktoria narrowed her eyes. 'Even in a classless society, some people are more equal than others,' she said acidly.

The Colonel frowned. 'Frau Jochum-Kraus, Berlin is in ruins. The streets have to be cleared. Bridges must be rebuilt. Those who do such heavy work need more calories than those who don't.'

'The Red Army caused half the devastation…'

Ricarda put a restraining hand on her knee. 'Vicki, dear…'

'Frau Jochum-Kraus, if you wish to clear rubble, you may,' Colonel Glazkhov said stiffly. 'I believed I was doing you a favour.' He stood up. 'That is all. You can return to your quarters.'

Their radio, the cans of food in the cellar, the last of their petrol and Ricarda's father's old hunting rifle were handed over to the Russians.

During the days that followed, there was a constant coming and going of Russian Army vehicles and personnel, but none of Colonel Glazkhov's men intruded the privacy of the Jochum room. Nobody questioned Ricarda when she made her first trip to the village. She found that the general store was open, although it contained a meagre stock of goods. She also called in on Hilde Weber, who threw her arms round her in relief that she was alive, exclaiming in dismay when she heard that Benno and Christa were dead, and crying out in horror when she learned Russians had commandeered the cottage.

The attitude of the Russians to Ricarda and Viktoria was strictly formal when they met. Lili, however, brought out a soft spot in them and soon they were giving her small gifts of sweets and toys.

Viktoria was angry. 'Lili, you shouldn't accept their presents.'

'Vicki, they are a long way from home,' Ricarda said. 'Probably most of them have children of their own, whom they miss.'

'Let them go back to their families. We don't want them here.'

Shortly after this episode, the Colonel's adjutant stopped Ricarda on her way to the village. 'Colonel Glazkhov wishes you to know that you are free to use the garden whenever you like. He is worried about the child being indoors all the time.'

'That is very kind. Please thank the Colonel,' Ricarda replied.

Viktoria was furious. 'Permission to walk in our own garden! Well, you can do what you like, but I am staying indoors.'

So she remained in the nursery, while Ricarda worked and Lili helped her, weeding the neglected vegetable beds and sowing a new season's crop from the seeds Ricarda had dried the previous year. Although she was used to gardening, Ricarda tired easily these days. Her old bones seemed to creak when she bent over and there was a constant ache in her back. After all, she was seventy-seven and, although she had suffered fewer hardships than most Berliners, the war had taken its toll, added to which there had been the final shocks of Christa and Benno's deaths.

Ricarda was still working one evening in mid-May when Colonel Glazkhov appeared beside her. 'Your garden does you credit, Frau Jochum.'

Ricarda leaned on her fork, staring out across the lake, orange in the rays of the dying sun.

'We have a *dacha* outside Moscow. My wife is probably there now, with our two children.'

'How old are your children, Colonel?'

'Dimitri is thirteen. Tanya is nine. Would you like to see a photograph?' He reached in his pocket and pulled out a wallet. 'See, here they are at the *dacha* with my wife, Irina.'

Ricarda studied the picture. 'A handsome family, Colonel.'

'Thank you.' He replaced the photograph. 'Your granddaughter is also a pretty child. But a sad one. Her parents are dead?'

'Her father was in the Luftwaffe. He died in Russia. Her mother, my daughter Luise, was killed in an air raid.'

'Frau Jochum-Kraus has no children?'

'She has two: a daughter in the country and a son in England.'

'A prisoner-of-war?'

'No. Stefan left Germany before war broke out. He — he disagreed with Hitler's policies.'

Colonel Glazkhov lit a cigarette. 'For nearly four years we have been fighting the Germans on the soil of Mother Russia. Before we reached the German border, we heard of Majdanek and Auschwitz. I personally saw the camp at Schlachtenhausen. I came to Germany hating all Germans. But, somehow, now I am here, I cannot feel the same…'

She gave a tired smile. 'I have no doubt that dreadful crimes have been committed on the battlefields and in the concentration camps. I do not try to excuse them, but dreadful crimes have also been committed against the German people: fire storms in our cities, in which thousands of innocent civilians have died; this last battle in Berlin…'

Colonel Glazkhov nodded. 'Frau Jochum, would you do me the honour of dining with me this evening?'

Ricarda looked at him thoughtfully. *People should be judged by their behaviour, not by their politics.* 'Thank you, Colonel. I shall be pleased to accept.'

As she had expected, Viktoria was shocked. 'You're having dinner with Glazkhov? Mama, I don't understand you!'

Ricarda looked sadly at her drawn face and white hair and kept her silence.

The dining room looked as it had in the olden days. The table was laid with a white lace cloth. The silver candlesticks and cutlery had been polished. The Colonel kissed her hand when she entered the room and helped her to her chair. In a slim silver vase beside her place setting was a single red rose. Ricarda was touched. She had not expected such gallantry.

'We are not all brutes in the Red Army,' Colonel Glazkhov commented, correctly interpreting her expression.

'You speak excellent German, Colonel,' Ricarda said, as they began their meal.

'We are not all uneducated louts. I am a diplomat's son.'

'And I a diplomat's daughter.'

'Tell me about your family, Frau Jochum.'

So Ricarda told him about her father, about Karl building the Hotel Quadriga and the birth of her two daughters, the war, the Spartacist Revolution and Karl's death. An orderly brought in roast pork, fresh vegetables and a bottle of wine. 'After my husband died, Viktoria and Benno took over the running of the Quadriga.'

'Until we Russians burned it down... Her husband was killed in the fire?'

'The hotel had become a kind of field hospital. Benno was trying to rescue wounded men from the basement.'

Colonel Glazkhov replenished her wine glass. 'And Lili's mother?'

Ricarda smiled fondly. 'Luise was very different from Viktoria. She created the Café Jochum on the Kurfürstendamm, very celebrated in its time, until Hitler came to power. Then the artists, musicians and writers fled...'

'Café Jochum still stands?'

'It was bombed in November 1943. I haven't seen it since, because I came out here that summer with Lili and Christa.'

'Christa? Is that the young woman who was raped?'

'Yes. Lili and I found her in the lake. Her father was Count Peter von Biederstein. He was killed on 20 July for his part in the plot against Hitler. Her mother was arrested and sent to Ravensbrück. We've never heard any more of her.'

'I start to understand Viktoria's bitterness…'

'May I ask you a question now, Colonel? What does the future hold for Germany?'

'It's a matter that the political leaders of the Three Powers are still discussing. In February, there was a conference at Yalta, attended by Stalin, Churchill and Roosevelt, at which it was decided to divide Germany into three zones, controlled by a central commission in Berlin.'

'And Berlin is to be in the Russian zone?'

Colonel Glazkhov shrugged. 'At the time, it was to be divided among the Allies. But the Americans and British failed to get here. The Red Army alone captured Berlin in a battle costing us thousands of men. General Berzarin is rightly of the opinion that the arrival of the British and Americans will only cause confusion.'

Ricarda laid down her knife and fork. 'And the people of Berlin are to have no say in their own future?'

'General Berzarin is already in the process of appointing a City Council composed of anti-fascist Germans.'

'How can you know which of us are anti-fascist?'

'Communists and social democrats who spent the war in concentration camps can safely be assumed to be anti-fascist,' Colonel Glazkhov said drily. 'Then there are the German communists who came to Moscow, men like Walter Ulbricht, Wilhelm Pieck and Basilius Meyer. Ulbricht and Meyer returned to Berlin at the beginning of the month and are working closely with General Berzarin on the civil administration.'

'Basilius Meyer…?'

'You know him?'

Ricarda shook her head slowly. 'No, I don't know the boy, but I knew his mother. Olga Meyer was my husband's niece.'

Two weeks passed, two weeks during which a semblance of normality returned. An intermittent electricity supply was resumed. There was a newspaper, produced by the Russian authorities. Lili's face gained colour and her thin frame began to fill out thanks to the generosity of the Russian soldiers. Lili was seven, too young to understand fully what had happened and young enough to find relief from unhappiness in the novelty of a new way of life.

Viktoria, however, was still in a state of shock. She remained listlessly indoors, all the more despondent since she had learned of Basili's presence in Berlin. So Olga's son had returned to make his father's dream come true. But her own son was not here to meet him. There was no knowing where Stefan was, no knowing if he were dead or alive. Her life stretched emptily ahead of her, bleak and without hope.

Ricarda was deeply perturbed about her and desperately wished there were something she could do to give her a new purpose in life, but she could think of nothing.

Then, once again, Colonel Glazkhov found Ricarda in her vegetable garden. 'If the weather holds, you will have a fine crop of peas, Frau Jochum.'

'There is something very satisfying about growing a crop from one's own seeds, Herr Colonel.'

'As satisfying as rebuilding a once great café?'

The hoe fell from her hands. 'Rebuilding…?'

'Even Red Army officers need to entertain their comrades, but at present there is no restaurant in Berlin worthy of them. A couple of disreputable cabarets have reopened on the Kurfürstendamm.' He grimaced. 'They are little better than brothels. In view of your connections with Basilius Meyer, the authorities would be willing to grant you a licence to re-open your business.'

'You mean Café Jochum…?'

He nodded. 'If you are interested. It is going to require a lot of work. The ground is covered with rubble. Somehow, you are going to have to acquire furniture, crockery, food and staff.'

This was the opportunity for which Ricarda had been waiting. 'After the building was destroyed, my son-in-law managed to salvage quite a lot of furniture and utensils. There may even be supplies in the cellars, provided we can get into the cellar...'

'One of my men will drive you and Frau Jochum-Kraus to the Kurfürstendamm tomorrow and collect you again in the evening. You can let me have your decision then.'

Viktoria greeted her news apathetically. 'I don't want to run a café for Russian officers. What's the point?'

It was the reaction Ricarda had been expecting. 'At least come and look,' she insisted.

Next morning, they left Lili with Hilde Weber and a jeep took them into Berlin. It was Ricarda's first sight of the city for two years and it shocked her to the marrow. Because of the damage to bridges and tunnels, they had to take a circuitous route. There were no buses or taxis on the streets. The only vehicles were driven — like their own — by Russian soldiers. One or two bedraggled horses pulled carts. Other people rode bicycles. 'And you made this journey on foot?' Ricarda asked Viktoria incredulously.

'Somehow. What else could I do?'

The closer they got to the centre, the worse the devastation became. Everywhere they looked, women were clearing rubble, dressed in old trousers, heavy boots and socks, bandanas round their hair. In the ruins of every building, makeshift dwellings had been constructed from planks, piles of bricks and tarpaulins. Smoke spiralled up from improvised chimneys. Grey clothes hung from washing lines.

Ricarda scarcely recognized the Kurfürstendamm, let alone Café Jochum, when Viktoria told the soldier to stop and let them out. What had once been a broad avenue was now a narrow track strewn with boulders. Above it, lurched the blackened shell of Café Jochum. Twisted steel girders hung suspended in mid-air. Remains of the staircase were contorted against stark, windowless, concrete walls gaping up towards the sky — a monument to total war.

The two women stood in silence, then Ricarda picked her way across the scree towards the place where the cellar entrance had once been. Desultorily, Viktoria followed her. A lot more damage had been done since Benno had locked and barred the doors, saying, 'After the war, when we rebuild the café, we'll sort it out.'

Ricarda turned to her daughter. 'If Benno were still alive, he would re-open the café. That is why he stored everything so carefully. He did everything he could to safeguard your future. Why else do you think he brought the strongbox to Heiligensee? It was in order that, if the worst should happen, you could start again.'

Viktoria gazed blindly at the women clearing the road, a company of Russian soldiers marching past, a clump of valerian struggling for a roothold among the rubble. 'But even if we get through to the cellar, how are we to run a café? Berlin is starving. We shall need food and staff… And where are we to live while we work? Your Colonel is hardly going to place a jeep at our disposal every day. It took me two days to walk from Wedding.'

'We'll do the same as everyone else. We'll build a shelter. I'm sure Colonel Glazkhov will allow us to bring tarpaulins from Heiligensee. Look, there are two walls and even a bit of ceiling over there.'

'Are you serious?'

Ricarda took both Viktoria's hands in hers. 'Vicki, darling, I'm an old lady, but I should like to see Café Jochum reopened before I die. And, for so long as I am able, I am going to help you make it possible.'

A new fear struck Viktoria. 'Mama, please don't talk about dying. I can't bear it. You'll live for ever…'

Ricarda gave a grim little smile. 'I hope not, but I certainly intend to go on for a while longer. We Jochum women are very tough, you know.' Then she rolled her sleeves. 'Well, now we're here, let's start working…' She clambered towards the back of the site, her forehead creased in concentration. 'The cellar entrance was near the service entrance for deliveries. It shouldn't take us all that long.' She rolled a lump of brickwork down the sloping pile into what had been the kitchen.

Viktoria had no alternative but to follow suit.

It was back-breaking work, for the stones were heavy and the two women were both weak, but, one after another, they managed to lift or roll them away from where the cellar door had been. Dust got in their throats and eyes, their fingernails broke, their muscles ached, but still they battled on.

At six when their jeep arrived, they had been at work for eight hours. Wearily, they stood back to see what they had achieved, but for all their efforts, the site looked little different from earlier in the day.

When they arrived back at the cottage, Ricarda washed, lay down on her bed and fell instantly asleep. It was left to Viktoria to tell Colonel Glazkhov of their decision and request permission to take tarpaulins and provisions to the Kurfürstendamm.

He looked at her with cold disdain. 'Tarpaulins and other essentials, yes. Food, no. The city is running out of supplies.'

'What are we to live on?'

'Rations, Frau Jochum-Kraus, the same as everyone else.'

What Ricarda saw in him, Viktoria did not know. She nodded equally coldly and left the room.

After asking Hilde Weber if Lili could stay with her while they worked on Café Jochum, she went down to the boathouse and sorted out tarpaulins and camping equipment to take with them. Finally, she took the key to the cellar of Café Jochum and hung it on a cord round her neck. So angry was she at the Colonel's rudeness, she had forgotten her doubts. She would rebuild Café Jochum if only to spite him.

In the morning, a Russian soldier dropped them off on the Kurfürstendamm, watching while they unloaded their belongings. Then he uncovered a storage space in the back of the jeep to reveal tins of food and a box of cigarettes. He pointed to Viktoria's watch.

'All those?' she asked.

He grinned.

She handed him her watch. It was a high price for food that had probably come from their own cellar, but it was better than starvation. And cigarettes were becoming an almost unheard-of luxury. They carried them across to their new home and started to erect a shelter. It was late evening before they finished.

Armed with buckets, they went to the nearest standpipe and joined the queue of women patiently waiting. 'Haven't seen you here before,' one commented to Ricarda. She was a big, blowzy woman with a weathered face and calloused hands.

'My daughter and I own that site over there.' Ricarda's genteel accent contrasted strongly to the rough dialect of her neighbour.

'What was that?'

'Café Jochum.'

The woman laughed good-humouredly. 'My old man always used to say it looked like a bleeding battleship. Still, there's been a Café Jochum in Berlin for as long as I can remember…' She studied Ricarda with concern. 'It's none of my business, of course, but you don't want to kill yourself. We call ourselves the rubble women of Berlin, but we're used to hard work, whereas a fine lady like yourself…'

'Being a fine lady isn't going to be much help in this new Berlin of ours,' Ricarda commented drily.

'They say the sewage is leaking into the drinking water system,' another said. 'Better boil it before you drink it, dear.'

'Two children near me have gone down with typhoid already,' someone else added. 'Not that the Russians care…'

It was consoling to feel they were not alone, but part of the vast army of women who were rebuilding Berlin. They returned to their shelter and ate an unappetizing meal of tinned pickled cabbage. In the distance they could hear the sound of Russian music. Closer to, rats scuffled through the ruins.

They slept badly, awoke early and rejoined the queue of women at the standpipe in what was to be the pattern of their lives for days to come. Gradually, they discovered a rhythm to their work. It was exhausting and often dangerous. Everywhere among the rubble lay shards of glass. Some blocks of concrete were so heavy, it took all their combined strength to move them. They might move a beam only to find they had dislodged a pile of stones that threatened to submerge them. But slowly, they cleared a path from the roadway into what had been the main hall of the café.

In two weeks, they had reached the kitchen. Although she said nothing to Viktoria, the hard work and poor rations were taking their toll on Ricarda. The rubble woman had been right: nothing in her life had prepared her for such long hours of heavy labour. Often she felt a stabbing pain in her chest and had to stop to regain her breath.

But that day, an event occurred which convinced her that her efforts were not in vain. Suddenly the streets were full of flags — not just the hammer and sickle, but the Union Jack, the Stars and Stripes and the Tricolour. What the papers called a 'great inter-Allied ceremony' was taking place at Wannsee, in which the military leaders of Russia, Britain, America and France were discussing the future of Germany. For the first time, Allied soldiers had set foot in Berlin.

The following day, while Ricarda was fetching water, Viktoria received a visitor. A young man in his mid-twenties, he arrived in a chauffeur-driven car and wore a well-fitting civilian suit. He picked his way fastidiously towards her and asked, 'Frau Jochum-Kraus?'

Viktoria stood poised over the piece of iron she was using as a crowbar, studying him sceptically.

'I am Basili Meyer. We are related, I believe.'

Ever since Ricarda had told her of her conversation with Colonel Glazkhov, Viktoria had been waiting for this visit. She levered her crowbar under a lump of concrete. 'Unfortunately, yes.'

Basili looked at her coldly. 'You once helped my mother, so I have now come to warn you.'

'Olga is dead?'

'She died in 1937. But I survived. After a brief period in Karaganda, I studied at the Comintern School in Ufa. Then I worked for the Free Germany Committee. Now I have returned to Berlin, as a member of the Administrative Committee of Berlin, to see my parents' dreams realized.'

Viktoria snorted angrily. 'Why don't you get to the point?'

'You are intending to re-open your café. Frau Kraus, remember that licences can be withdrawn. Colonel Glazkhov reported that your family was strongly anti-fascist, that your son left Germany on account of Hitler's policies and that another of your relations was involved in the July Plot. But I know better. Your husband was the son of Baron von Kraus.'

'My husband is dead.'

Basilius flicked a speck of dust from his jacket. 'Yes, he died in the Hotel Quadriga. A fitting burial ground. My mother used to tell me that the Quadriga epitomized the very worst in imperialist, capitalist society.'

'Herr Meyer, what do you want from me?'

'I want nothing from you. I have merely come to warn you that your days are over, that, so long as the communists rule in Berlin, the Hotel Quadriga will never stand again.'

'The communists will not rule alone.'

Basili shrugged. 'Where are the Americans and British?' With that, he turned on his heels and returned to his waiting limousine.

Viktoria stared after him in dismay. Did this mean that all their hard work was in vain? Would they open their café only to find it closed again? Did Basili Meyer have that kind of power? Or was he bluffing? Was he seeking some kind of personal revenge on behalf of his parents, or were his reasons for coming to see her purely politically motivated?

The car drove away, the hammer and sickle flying from its bonnet, Basili Meyer sitting regally in the back, and, at the same moment, Ricarda appeared in the distance, stooped under the weight of a bucket of water. The contrast between the two figures was so stark that Viktoria was temporarily stunned. By what right did Basili Meyer drive round in a limousine while her mother worked like a navvy?

Then she turned towards Ricarda to help her with the bucket and, as she went, she decided to say nothing to her of Basili's visit. But, in her own mind, she determined that, whatever Basili said or did, she would re-open Café Jochum. This little communist pipsqueak had thought to frighten her. Instead, he had given her the best possible motive for continuing what she had started.

From then on, she woke every morning with the thought, 'Will it be today that the British and Americans arrive?'

But the days passed and it became ever more clear that the Russians were going to make it as difficult as possible for the other three powers to reach Berlin. They had captured the city. By fair means or foul, they were determined to retain sole control.

Russian troops occupied the east of Austria, American troops the west. General Eisenhower declared, 'We shall obliterate Nazism and German militarism.' A witch hunt commenced for members of the Nazi Party and officers from the Wehrmacht and the SS.

Early in June, the American Military Police arrived at the farm above Traunsee. Anna panted up to the meadow, where Otto was cutting the first hay crop. 'Otti, Otti, Americans are asking for you.'

Otto put his scythe over his shoulder and lumbered down to the farm, Wolf at his side. Frequently, he had toyed with the idea of trying to escape into Italy as several of his comrades had done, but that meant leaving Adolf behind. In any case, he did not believe he was in real danger. Even if he were arrested, the Americans were unlikely to know who he was, for it was highly improbable that the Russians were liaising with their American allies. They would have a hard job to prove that he had been in charge of a concentration camp.

Wolf growled menacingly when he saw the two Military Policemen and Otto caught hold of his chain collar, eyeing his visitors coldly. '*Ja?*'

'Do you speak English?' one Military Policeman asked.

'*Nein.*'

In laboured German, the Military Policeman said, 'Show us your identity card.'

Otto pulled it out of his pocket.

'You were in the Army?'

There was no point in pretending he had seen no service. 'I was on the Russian front.'

'Nazi Party member?'

Otto looked suitably shocked. 'I was just a soldier.'

They conferred together in English. Then one whipped out a pair of handcuffs. 'Come with us, while we check your story.'

Wolf strained under his collar. 'It's all right, Wolf,' Otto said. He turned to Anna. 'Finish the hay crop. I shan't be gone long.'

Tears trickled down her fat, red cheeks. 'Otti, why…?'

'God knows. Just make sure you don't let Dolfi out of your sight.'

They took Otto to the former SS prison camp at Bad Ischl. For a moment, as he entered the gates, Otto knew a very real moment of fear. Were the Americans going to treat their prisoners as he had treated his? But immediately he saw the prisoners milling round the compound, he knew this was no death camp.

Before he had been there a week, he had met many old comrades, including Franz Stangl, one-time Commandant of Treblinka and Sobibor camps. 'They've no idea who we are,' Stangl reassured him. 'And their security is very lax. Don't worry, we'll soon get out.'

Apart from missing Adolf, it was almost like being home.

Every day, to Baron Heinrich's disgust, Trudi covered him with a blanket and wheeled him into the grounds of Castle Waldesruh. In the middle of May, he had suffered another stroke, worse than the previous one exactly two years earlier, for it had paralysed his right side. His face was lopsided and he could not write. A nurse had to attend to all his personal needs and his only way of getting around was by wheelchair.

Castle Waldesruh occupied a tranquil spot high in the Tyrolean Alps, south of Innsbruck. Above it, cattle grazed in pastures blue with gentians, their bells clanking gently as they moved, guarded by a young cowherd. Its garden commanded a panoramic view of the valley and the main road leading to the Brenner Pass.

It was from this vantage point, at the beginning of June, that the Baron saw two jeeps of the American Military Police start up the pitted track leading to the castle. Snow Whites they called them, on account of their white helmets. He lifted his bell and jangled it furiously. Gottlieb Linke materialized beside him. With his left hand, the Baron pointed to the approaching vehicles. Linke smiled. 'I shall inform Herr Werner.'

Werner greeted them at the door. 'Good day, gentlemen. How can I help you?'

'We're looking for Baron Heinrich von Kraus.'

'My grandfather is a sick man. Can I help you? I am Werner Kraus.'

They consulted a list. 'No, it's the old man we're after. Got a warrant for his arrest.'

'Arrest? What for?'

'He's one of the heads of the German munitions industry. Our records say he escaped here from Berlin last January.'

'I think there must be a mistake, gentlemen. My grandfather and I came here in the winter because his doctor advised total rest. He is eighty-six years old and has not worked for a long time.'

'Germany seems to be full of sick old men who know nothing about nothing. Let's have a look at him.'

They found Baron Heinrich in his wheelchair, his head lolled back against a cushion, his paralysed hand resting limply on a blanket. Trudi was sitting beside him, knitting. 'How long's he been like this?' one policeman demanded.

'He had his first stroke in May 1943, the second one a couple of weeks ago. The doctor doesn't give him long to live.'

The Americans conferred among themselves for a few moments. Then they turned to Werner. 'So who's been running Kraus Industries?'

'My father, Ernst Kraus, from our office in Essen.'

'I think we've already got him. Well, I don't imagine you're thinking of going anywhere?'

Werner shook his head tragically. 'No, sir.'

'We'll have to report back about the Baron. In the meantime, we'll leave him here.'

When the jeeps had disappeared back down the track, the Baron sat up. 'I told you it would work, boy.'

Werner nodded. He also knew that when the witch hunt was over and Kraus Industries started to function again, it would be with him at the head.

'Frau Jochum?' a voice called, and Ricarda stood up, easing her aching back, thankful for an opportunity to regain her breath. A woman made her way along the path they had cleared almost to the cellar door, her thin face wreathed in smiles, showing several gaps where her teeth were missing. Ricarda struggled to place her. The voice was familiar, but the face…

'Ach, Frau Jochum, you don't recognize me. I am Klara Scheer.'

Ricarda forgot her aches and pains. 'Frau Scheer! Oh, my dear, how pleased I am to see you.'

'Somebody told me you were working here, so I came to tell you my wonderful news! Frau Jochum, my husband is alive!' She pulled a letter from her pocket. 'It is dated 5 May, but the Red Cross have only just been able to deliver it. Bernhard was rescued in the Tyrol by the Americans. Soon, he will be coming home!'

'Vicki!' Ricarda called. 'Pastor Scheer has been found by the Americans. He's coming home.'

Viktoria rushed across to them. 'How wonderful for you, Frau Scheer. I'm so pleased.' She paused for a moment. 'It's like a miracle, isn't it? In the midst of all the badness, something good like this occurs and one can start to feel hope.'

'Perhaps your Stefan will also return, Frau Jochum-Kraus. Germany is going to need men like him and my Bernhard.'

Viktoria smiled a little sadly. 'Frau Scheer, I have no idea whether Stefan is even alive.'

'If my Bernhard can survive eight years in concentration camps, I am sure your Stefan has managed to survive in England.'

Yes, Viktoria thought grimly, *and if Basilius Meyer can return, so can Stefan…*

'I think we should celebrate,' Ricarda said. 'I shall make us some coffee.' She went across to their shelter and lit the stove, sinking thankfully down onto the boulder that served as a seat.

Perhaps this news of Frau Scheer's meant that an end was in sight. If people were returning from the concentration camps, the British, French and Americans must also soon arrive in Berlin. Maybe Stefan would come back and Viktoria would no longer be alone. Then she could consider her task well done and return to the cottage to live out the last days of her life in peace and quiet.

On 2 July, Viktoria and Ricarda broke through to the cellar door of Café Jochum. With trembling fingers, Viktoria reached for the key she wore round her neck. The lock must be rusty after so long. Having got this far, was it possible they wouldn't be able to enter? With grinding noises, the key slowly turned. The door opened. She switched on her torch, then, linking her arm through her mother's, started to descend into the musty atmosphere.

They were not alone. In the beam of her torch, bright eyes gleamed and black shapes scurried into dark corners. The whole cellar was alive with the scamper of feet. One of the animals shot past her, up the stairs and through the doorway: it was a rat the size of a small dog. Involuntarily, Viktoria screamed.

Ricarda clutched her hand to her heart and sagged against the wall. Viktoria laughed shakily. 'It's all right. It was only a rat, Mama.'

'Yes, of course. How silly of me.'

The cellar grew quiet. Viktoria went on down the stairs, along the passage and into the first of the basement rooms, where such furniture had been stored as they had managed to salvage after the air raid. Rats had gnawed at some of the leather seats, but apart from the chrome being tarnished, it seemed to be in good condition.

In the next room, she found lamps, candles and candlesticks, tablecloths, cutlery, condiment sets and other restaurant fittings, neatly stacked in piles, some even in boxes. Viktoria shook her head in bemused admiration. Dear Benno, so meticulous... She put a candle in a stick and lit it.

The third room contained kitchen equipment: pots, pans, kettles, coffee filter machines, baking dishes, tureens, piles of plates, cups and saucers. Considering the damage the café had received, it was truly miraculous that so much had been rescued from the ruins.

Finally, she came to the food store. Shortly after the onset of the war, Benno had divided his reserves between the Quadriga, Heiligensee and Café Jochum. There were racks of wine — nowhere near as much as there had been at the Quadriga, but still a plentiful supply. He had bought no perishables, only canned foods, tins of flour, bottled preserves, large airtight jars of coffee beans. Coffee beans! Little had he known what a luxury these would be in postwar Berlin!

Candle in hand, she went into the passage. 'There's even real coffee.'

There was no reply. Anxiously, she hurried back to the stairs, to find her mother sitting on a step. 'Mama, what's wrong?'

Ricarda gave a wan smile. 'I think it's probably a reaction. I suddenly felt strange. Don't worry. I'll be all right in a minute.'

'I'll get you some water.' Viktoria ran up the stairs two at a time, returning with a billy-can of water and a cup.

Ricarda sipped the water. After a few moments, she said, 'There, I'm feeling better already. You see, it was nothing. Did you say there is some real coffee, dear?'

Viktoria looked at her worriedly. 'Would you like some?'

Ricarda nodded. 'It would seem a fitting way to celebrate the new Café Jochum.'

Viktoria fetched their spirit stove and set a kettle to boil. Then she pulled out two chairs and a table, spread it with a cloth, cups and saucers, and placed the candle in the middle. Taking Ricarda's arm, she helped her into a chair. In the 'kitchen', she opened a jar of coffee beans and found a coffee mill. As she turned the handle, a delicious aroma of freshly-ground coffee flooded the room. She put the grounds in a fine sieve and poured hot water over them into a jug, which she then ceremoniously carried into the 'restaurant'. 'I'm afraid it's going to taste a bit gritty and we have no cream or sugar,' she laughed, 'but it's still coffee!'

Ricarda reached out for her cup, but her hand was trembling so much, she could not pick it up. 'Oh dear, this is very stupid of me. What can be the matter? I can't see properly. And I have a pain in my chest.'

Seeking to reassure herself as much as her mother, Viktoria said, 'You're overtired. I shouldn't have let you work so hard.'

'Vicki, hold the cup to my lips. I want to taste your coffee.'

715

Tears welled in Viktoria's eyes, as she crouched beside her, holding the cup so that Ricarda could drink. 'I'll get a doctor.'

Her mother turned and kissed her. In a voice that was scarcely more than a whisper, she murmured, 'Vicki, I hope the café is a success. Your father and Benno would be so proud...' Then she keeled over into Viktoria's arms.

'Mama!' Viktoria picked her up and laid her on the floor, loosening her clothing, kissing her frantically. 'Mama, Mama, oh, please be all right. Oh, Mama, please, please, please...'

But Ricarda's green eyes stared sightlessly at her. When Viktoria put her ear to her chest, there was no heartbeat.

'Mama...!' Her cry echoed through the cellars of Café Jochum. She threw herself onto the lifeless body, clasping it to her, tears streaming down her face. 'Oh, Mama, I love you so much...'

If Ricarda heard her, it was from another world.

One of the rubble women fetched a retired doctor, who confirmed that Ricarda was dead, almost certainly from a heart attack. He also helped her with the registration formalities for the Soviet authorities, but there was nothing he could do about a funeral.

The Russians cared nothing about the death of one old German woman and, anyway, in a city where death had become a way of life, there were no coffins. To stop the spread of disease, all corpses were being incinerated in huge communal pyres.

Viktoria managed to borrow a bicycle to return to Heiligensee and plead with Colonel Glazkhov. 'Herr Colonel, my mother has died. Please, please, can you use your influence so that she can be buried at Heiligensee?'

Colonel Glazkhov shook his head impatiently. 'Thousands of valiant Russian soldiers perished in the battle for Berlin. None of them had proper burials. Be thankful that your mother died on her own native soil. Even if she were still alive, there would be nothing more that I could do for her. One war may have ended, but another still continues: the sacred war of the people against capitalism. In that cause, the individual must be sacrificed for the common good.'

It was the same old communist cant. She had been right all the time: communists, whether they were Basili Meyer or Colonel Glazkhov, should be judged not as people, but by their politics. 'Thank God not everybody thinks like you,' she said, and she walked out of the cottage, got back on her bicycle and returned to the ruins of Berlin.

There was no grave, not even a proper funeral ceremony for Ricarda Jochum. In a scene dreadfully reminiscent of the Middle Ages, a horse-drawn cart carried her body away to be burned.

When she was gone, Viktoria remained at Café Jochum, totally and utterly alone for the first time in her life. She curled up in a corner of the cellar, too numb, too bereft, too full of grief to weep. Night fell upon Berlin. The curfew sounded. Eventually, she fell asleep. She awoke to hear her mother's voice saying, '*Vicki, I hope the café is a success. Your father and Benno would be so proud…*'

She knew then what she had to do. Slowly, she stood up and made her way to the top of the cellar steps. Dawn was breaking over the city, a pink flush suffusing the sky above the silent, black ruins. Viktoria clenched her fist. 'Mama, I promise you shall not have died in vain. I'll open Café Jochum. After that, I'll rebuild the Quadriga. From now on, nothing else matters, except that Papa, you and Benno should know that I have not let you down, that I love you…'

It seemed to her that the spirits of her dead crowded around, infusing her with their strength, and she knew that however lonely she might feel, she would never be alone again.

In a seemingly endless procession, Russian tanks, lorries and soldiers made their way towards the eastern part of the city, and in their wake came the first American tanks, lorries and soldiers. A few days later, the first British troops arrived. What was more, it was clear that now they were here, they were here for good.

That afternoon, Viktoria made her way to Wedding, where Hasso, Rosa and their neighbours were clearing the rubble. They greeted her with joy and listened to her story with dismay. Finally, Hasso asked quietly, 'Are you looking for a barman?'

'The pay is bad, the conditions are terrible…'

'For over sixty years, there has been a Café Jochum in Berlin…'

It was a sentence she was to hear many times in the next few days. In no time at all, Hasso succeeded in locating various old waiters from the Hotel Quadriga. He found an ancient chef and several young women desperate for work. Soon, an atmosphere of optimistic activity permeated the cellar, as Hasso reorganized its underground rooms into a café, a kitchen, a storeroom and two dormitories.

However, even as the transformation took place, Viktoria wondered if, ironically, the café might have even less of a future now than under the Russians. Although the people of Berlin had welcomed the Americans and British with open arms, their feelings were not reciprocated, at least not by the military authorities. The British were cold and stand-offish. The Americans treated them like dirt, leaving them in no doubt that they considered them the scum of the earth. Their soldiers were ordered not to talk to a German, except to issue a command.

To make matters worse, the Americans flaunted their affluence. The United States had not been touched by the war and could afford to fly in planeloads of supplies. While Berliners starved, the Americans lived in the lap of luxury.

'Why should they come to Café Jochum?' Viktoria asked Hasso helplessly. 'And if they do, what can we offer them?'

'The Americans are only human,' Hasso replied confidently. 'Their generals may order them not to fraternize with the enemy, but the soldiers are a long way from home. The war is over. They want wine, women and song. We've got the wine. There's no shortage of women. As for the song, somewhere in this city there must be a violinist or an accordionist willing to play for his supper. You wait and see.'

'What do we feed them on?' Bread, flour, milk, eggs, vegetables were unheard-of luxuries in a city where people queued all day for miserable rations.

Hasso pulled her amethyst ring from his pocket. 'This will do for a beginning. We'll trade it on the black market.'

Viktoria thought of the belt she wore under her clothes. If Hasso were right, they could buy all the food they wanted.

In the middle of July, the Conference of Berlin took place in the Cecilienhof at Potsdam, attended by the heads of the Three Powers: Truman, Churchill and Stalin, their foreign ministers and whole retinues of aides. Churchill drove through Berlin to visit the Reichstag and Hitler's bunker beneath the Chancellery, returning to Potsdam via the Kurfürstendamm.

A small crowd gathered to watch him pass, some of whom had even managed to obtain Union Jacks. They lined the kerb, waving and cheering. Dressed in rags, her white hair concealed under a bandana, Viktoria stood with them and, for the first time, set eyes on the man who had once been considered Germany's greatest enemy and was now, in his unconcealed hatred of the Soviet Union, Germany's greatest friend.

He was unmistakable, a cigar clamped in his square, tenacious jaw. He half-raised his hand, a sceptical expression on his face. Possibly he was thinking how these same people had once crowded the streets to cheer the Kaiser and, in more recent times, to scream their adulation of the Führer. Who could blame him if he viewed their apparently sudden change of allegiance with mistrust?

But to Viktoria, he represented hope in a very tangible form. He was a link with England — with Mortimer, and, above all, with Stefan.

Ten days later, while the Potsdam Conference continued, Churchill returned to England, where a General Election was being held. To the undisguised delight of the Russians, the Labour Party won a massive majority and Churchill resigned, to be replaced by the socialist Clement Atlee as Prime Minister.

Viktoria felt an almost personal sadness, as well as dread. 'This man Atlee will never stand up to Stalin,' she told Hasso.

'And Truman is more concerned about the war with Japan than Berlin,' Hasso added morosely.

The Berlin Conference ended on 1 August and the German people were officially informed of their fate. Germany was to be divided into four zones, occupied by each of the Four Powers: America, Britain, France and Russia. Supreme authority would be held by the Allied Control Council, whose headquarters would be in Berlin. All territories east of the Oder and Neisse rivers were to be ceded to Poland. Fürstenmark, in Lower Pomerania, would be in the Soviet zone, the Ruhr in the British. Once again, Germany would be expected to make massive reparations payments.

Although it was situated in the middle of the eastern zone, controlled by the Soviet Union, Berlin too was being divided into four sectors, ruled over by the Four Powers. Heiligensee and Wedding would be in the French sector: the ruins of the Hotel Quadriga in the Russian sector: and the Kurfürstendamm and Café Jochum in the British sector.

'God help us all. Versailles was generosity itself compared to this!' Hasso muttered, reading the terms of the Potsdam Treaty in the newspaper. Then he threw it down on the floor. 'No, not even God is going to help us now. The only help we're going to get is what we give ourselves. Frau Viktoria, let's prepare for the ceremonial opening of Café Jochum.'

CHAPTER TWENTY-ONE

On the afternoon of Saturday 18 August 1945, an American jeep drew to a halt beside the Brandenburg Gate. The driver turned to his passengers, an American journalist and a young man in the uniform of a British Army captain. 'This where you two guys want to be?'

The journalist stared up at the battered statue of the Quadriga. 'Thanks, buddy. This will suit us fine.'

The two men got out and the jeep drove off. Ahead of them, in the central promenade of Unter den Linden was a massive poster of Stalin, reading: HITLERS COME AND HITLERS GO, BUT THE GERMAN PEOPLE AND THE GERMAN STATE GO ON. STALIN. Beside it, two German women were bartering their jewellery for food from a small group of Russian soldiers.

The two men walked up the derelict avenue, looking around them in dismay. 'Hitler once said this city would be unrecognizable in ten years' time,' the journalist commented, drily. 'How right he was!'

His companion said nothing. He was too intent on trying to come to terms with the devastation, with trying to understand how anyone had lived through this holocaust. Suddenly, he stopped in front of a pile of blackened rubble. 'The Hotel Quadriga was there.'

An urchin emerged from the ruins, a boy of about ten, his clothes hanging in rags from his thin frame. '*Schokolade, schokolade*,' he pleaded.

The journalist reached in his pocket for a candy bar. 'Here you are, kid.' The child grabbed it. 'What happened to this place?' the journalist asked in German.

'The Russians burned it down.'

'And the owners? What happened to them?'

But the boy was already running away.

The Captain rubbed his hand over his eyes. 'Let's go.'

They walked back through the Pariser Platz into the Tiergarten to the Victory Column, still standing amidst the smashed marble figures of Germany's heroes in what had once been affectionately known by

Berliners as Sweetmakers' Alley. The journalist shook his head ruefully. 'Twelve years ago, I stood here with a man and a boy, plotting the downfall of Hitler. Little did we know then what lay ahead…'

They walked past the remains of the zoo towards the Kurfürstendamm. As much for something to say as anything else, the journalist asked, 'Do you really think you're going to have much joy identifying former Nazis?'

A shadow flickered over his colleague's face. 'I'm one of the men best qualified to do the job. After all, there aren't many men still alive who worked with Colonel Oster and were as close to Count Peter von Biederstein as I was. The Germans were always very efficient about keeping records. Amazingly, a lot of them have survived, even from the concentration camps. Your people have found a lot in the Salzkammergut, where the Foreign Ministry and SS went in the last days of the war. Between us, American and British Counter-Intelligence will run them to earth and bring them to trial.'

'I know one or two I'd like to get my hands on. I wonder what happened to Otto Tobisch, for instance.'

'We'll find him.'

The journalist nodded. 'Something about this operation worries me. Of course, the criminals must be brought to justice, but I can't help wondering if, in doing so, we aren't letting another enemy escape.'

'You mean the Russians?'

'Yes. You've heard Olga Meyer's son is in Berlin? Churchill was right and Eisenhower was wrong. We shouldn't have stopped at the Elbe. We should have kept right on and beaten the Russians back…' They turned into the Kurfürstendamm. 'Well, what's done is done, but I can't pretend to be happy about it.'

The Captain put his hand on his colleague's arm. 'Look!' he exclaimed, incredulously.

For the first time since he had entered Germany, two weeks earlier, the American smiled. 'I'll wait here.' He watched the Captain pick his way along a path between piles of rubble, a fine young man, with waving brown hair and serious brown eyes, who had celebrated his thirtieth birthday in April that year.

He had known him for over twelve years, during which time his young friend had gone through university, suffered the effects of a disastrous love affair and run away from home at the outbreak of war. The journalist remembered how he had secured his release from an internment camp on the Isle of Man and eventually obtained him a job with British Military Intelligence. Now he had finally come to Germany with the purpose of helping to eradicate Nazism and establishing a democracy. A man with a fascinating past and an even more interesting future.

Slowly, the Captain descended the cellar steps and entered a room thick with cigarette smoke, full of GIs and British soldiers. In the corner, a man was playing a violin, badly in need of tuning. Three ancient waiters, dressed in tattered frock coats and grey-white gloves, balanced trays high above their heads.

A white-haired woman emerged from the back of the room, her face devoid of make-up, her body pathetically thin. She stopped for a moment to survey the scene, her mouth set in a firm line, her jaw jutting obstinately, then she made her way through the crowd towards the entrance.

Seeing the young Captain standing in the shadows, she said, in English, 'Welcome to Café Jochum.'

Stefan's smile lit up his face, as he stretched out his hands to her. 'Mama, I'm home.'

Outside, Mortimer Sydney Allen lit a cigarette and grinned admiringly at the hand-painted sign that read:

CAFÉ JOCHUM — FIVE O'CLOCK TEA IS NOW BEING SERVED.

But then, he had always known Viktoria to be a truly remarkable woman.

A NOTE TO THE READER

Viktoria is a historical romance set in Berlin between 1933 and 1945, and describes the mixed fortunes of a German family, their friends and enemies, during six years of peace and six years of war.

A prologue, *The Hotel Quadriga*, published last year, set the background to this novel, portraying the period from the unification of Germany in 1871 to Adolf Hitler's appointment as German Chancellor in January 1933. Whilst I hope that a spirit of curiosity will lead some people to read both books, *Viktoria* is a story in itself and can be enjoyed independently from *The Hotel Quadriga*.

The Hotel Quadriga itself has never existed except in my imagination, but I extend a debt of gratitude to the Hotel Adlon as the inspiration behind the creation of this establishment. Café Jochum is an amalgam of several café-restaurants in Berlin. Kraus Industries is a fictional company, although there have been other similar commercial empires in Germany. Grubenmünde and Schlachtenhausen concentration camps existed, if under different names.

The Jochum, Kraus, von Biederstein and other principal families and characters in this novel are imaginary. However, in telling a story set in an historical context, real personages are mentioned and quoted. Every effort has been made to ensure that these factual references are correct and the informed reader will be able to differentiate between those who existed in real life and those who lived only on paper.

Viktoria will be published in 1989, half a century after the outbreak of the Second World War. Yet, even now, the period the work covers is still a source of great fascination to many and one of acute sensitivity to the German nation. My adopted German grandmother, Hanny Rudolph, once told me, 'I stood on the streets and cheered for Hitler, never dreaming he was going to do such terrible things.'

To live in Nazi Germany was not necessarily to be a Nazi. To be a Nazi Party member was not necessarily to be party to Nazi terror.

To those who wonder why Hanny Rudolph — and millions of others of her generation — did not do more to prevent the atrocities committed under the Nazi regime, I commend *Viktoria*.

Jenny Glanfield
Summer 2023

Sapere Books is an exciting new publisher of brilliant fiction and popular history.

To find out more about our latest releases and our monthly bargain books visit our website:
saperebooks.com

Printed in Great Britain
by Amazon

29277783R00403